THE DROWNED REA

RISE OF THE RED HARBINGER

KHALID UDDIN

Can't Put it Down
BOOKS

An Imprint of Open Door Publications

Rise of the Red Harbinger
Book One of
The Drowned Realm

By Khalid Uddin
ISBN 978-0-9972024-7-2

Cover Design by Eric Labacz labaczdesign.com
Map Design by Kaira Marquez
Map formatted for print by Raymond Mohamed

Published by
Can't Put It Down Books
An Imprint of
Open Door Publications
2113 Stackhouse Dr.
Yardley, PA 19067
www.OpenDoorPublications.com

For Jen, Hannah, Emme, and Ava
Who perpetually challenge me, support me, and bring out the best in me,
even when I doubt in my ability to keep going. You are the reasons I am
able to be a dreamer and set ridiculous goals.
I love you.

TABLE OF CONTENTS

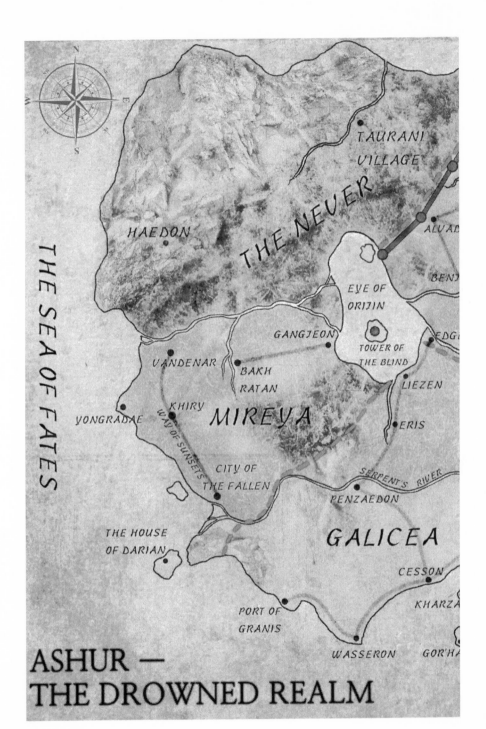

ASHUR —
THE DROWNED REALM

MARKOS
PYRRHA
ROALDON
CONSTANIZA
FERA
TAIJU
SAPHRIA
RIVERHAVEN
DARLING HARBOR
THE SEA OF FATES
ADON
MARADON
LINCHESTER
CERYSIA
NJAM
SHIPSBANE
GEBORO
MAGNON ON
SANAI
SANAI RIVER
KILLINGTON
GANSISHOOR
AGRALUN
VEIDENA
RYLAN
LAKE OF BA-VAAN
RAYAN
SHIVAANA
VISHADAH
MARAMAROSA
ZAABIIL
ZEBULON
HAANZU
SUNDARI
WALDE
FANGH-HAAN
ITARSE
WOLF'S PAW
TONGAM
DAMASZUR
XUYEN
KRANAGH
HEJARO
HAD
QARBETA
JENAA-KU
JAYA

PROLOGUE

"How long do you plan to follow me? Anywhere we go, people will know us." Darian breathed heavily, as if he'd done the galloping and not his horse. "Anywhere you attack me, people will know what you did, and they will hate you for it. And what will you do then? Kill the rest of the world? We are brothers, Jahmash. Brothers. You have already killed Lionel and Abram. Be done with it now. Do you think you will find peace if you kill me as well?"

Jahmash stared at the tall, slender man coldly. "No. I will not." His indignant eyes glared directly into Darian's, which gazed back, unwavering.

"Then why are we here?"

Jahmash's mouth contorted as he spit the words out. "I will find peace after I have killed you and all of your wives and children. And if it takes me decades to find them all, then I will kill your children's children as well. I will find peace when every last person you love is dead. If it means that I must murder the whole world, then so be it. We saved the whole world, Darian. And for what? Gideon died in the process! Damn the Orijin, Gideon was just a boy! And look at how they treat me! They would have you rule the world while I stand behind you like a dog! Women throw themselves at you, and the one – the only one that I love – you have to steal her from me, too. You have a dozen and that is not enough!"

"For the last time, Jahmash. There is nothing between me and Jaya. I am married to her sister, for the love of Orijin."

Jahmash clenched his fist. "As if that would stop you. Your lust knows no bounds, Darian. Don't you dare speak of brotherhood. You bask in the adoration of the world and believe every last word of the praise they heap upon your shoulders. If you could turn those words into a crown, you would. But you are no king."

"Come now, Jahmash. You know as well as I do that I would never have accepted the offer to become king. The last thing this world needs is one man making the decisions for all humanity. If I were to become king, the Orijin would likely have to select five new Harbingers to save the world from me. Mankind is good now. I am content to leave it at that. Go back to your wife. Have children. Let yourself grow old. I have no intentions of staying immortal. Let us become old men together while our children grow up inseparably." Darian labored in his breathing and looked tired. Too tired for any reason to be justified. "It is not too late, old friend. We can still have what we once did, believe me. I am wil-"

"Shut up. What are you doing? What scheme are you hatching? I know you are lying to me! And why, by the cursed Rings, are you laboring so? You rode all this way on a horse and yet you look more tired than your beast! Why are you trying to stall?" As he looked around at the horizon, Jahmash knew it was too late. Water approached from all directions as Darian dropped to his knees, heaving. Jahmash realized his mistake too late. His anger at Darian had clouded his ability to see what the Harbinger was truly doing. He spat and then growled at the man he once called a brother. "You filthy coward. You led me all the way out here to drown me. Do you expect me to beg you to stop? Do you really think I am going to cry and whine for you to spare me?"

Darian looked up and glared at him through sweat-glazed hair, "I expect nothing, brother. I did not bring you here to kill you. I do not have it in me to do such a thing. Perhaps that is your problem, you think too little of the people who love you. I brought you here to trap you." The water drew closer – towering waves seemingly intent on crashing down on Jahmash. "You will live out your days on an island, cut off from humanity. I will provide you with," Darian paused to cough, then spit out blood. He planted his fist into the ground for support. "There will be enough food to survive, if you care to."

The waves continued to glide closer and Jahmash could no longer see anything else on the horizon. He bit his lip so hard that blood poured down his chin. He hated the other man, yet respected his actions. "And the world thinks I am its villain. Yet you would be so diabolical."

Darian looked up at him once more, blood dripping from his own mouth. "I brought you here to save you. And the only way to do that is to commit the greatest sacrifice that I can. No matter what you do, I will always call you brother. I will see you again in the Rings, Harbinger." Darian smiled at him, then outstretched his arms high above his head. The giant waves drew closer and Darian finally slammed both fists into the dirt. All around them, the waves came crashing down with a thunderous roar. Jahmash refused to cower, despite his paralyzing fear of the seas. He looked back at Darian, who had collapsed to the ground. He stalked towards the man with murder in his heart.

***

Jahmash awoke as the sun flickered through fluttering leaves, directly onto his face. Just as on most mornings, his neck ached from sleeping so awkwardly. He'd slept in the same patch of grass and dirt for over a thousand years. Trees and shrubs had come and gone. The ground rose and fell, then rose again and fell again. But the one patch of the ground had conformed to his body.

He'd traveled far enough inland that the ocean's waters could not reach him from any direction, even during storms. Jahmash had found that out the hard way more than once. Rain, he could handle. But the notion of the violent ocean grasping for him was enough to cause panic.

On every clear day since Darian had stranded him over a millennium ago, Jahmash would stand on the shore and stare out, wondering how far away the rest of the world was. He looked out at the cloudless horizon, feeling nostalgic. "Sometimes I wish you had just killed me, Darian." He sighed and shook his fist. "But then, how would I kill your descendants and followers if you had done so?" He talked to Darian quite often, almost on a daily basis. In fact, Jahmash had buried the man right next to where he slept. "And by now, you surely have thousands of descendants. I would bet you are a legend in our motherland. I wonder what they know of me, on the other hand." On many a night, he talked to Darian until he fell asleep. He imagined the man's responses, which were usually self-righteous and condescending, but they made for good conversation.

Jahmash looked down at the sandy shore as water crept up and then pulled back, as if trying to entice him into a dance. Lifeless birds had littered the beach up until yesterday, in various stages of decay. He had grown careless and lazy. Perhaps even hopeless. But there was nothing else to try. Sooner or later, he would find the right grip and he would be able to maintain it. Earlier that morning, he cleared the carcasses and vowed to restart the attempts. He sat and waited while tearing into a ginger melon.

Birds fluttered here and there in the sky and Jahmash ripped open a few more melons and tossed them several feet away from where he sat. A few meals would be worth the sacrifice if this actually worked. Sure enough, half a dozen gulls swooped down and scuffled with one another over the fruit. He'd deduced that the birds fancied ginger melons most out of what fruits the island had to offer.

Jahmash focused on one bird. He cleared his mind and gazed at the one he'd selected. Within a few seconds, the young bird turned away from the others and walked towards him. "Good. Good. Right, come here, my friend." The gull waddled along without fear and stood before him. Jahmash smiled and extended his hand, holding another ginger melon. The bird's head flitted back and forth, looking at him and then at the free meal. Jahmash concentrated a little harder and the bird pecked at the fruit. It ate out of his hand until the entire melon disappeared, except for the purple rind. Jahmash let it fall to the ground and then stroked the bird's head. The satiated creature allowed itself to be petted without flinching. "Just relax, my friend. If this works, you can come back and have ginger melons until you grow old and fat." Jahmash had gotten this far only twice before. He focused all of his attention on the bird and maintained a gentle grip on its mind. The struggle arose because the birds' minds were not complex like people's minds. If he wanted to control it for an extended period of time, he had to focus on its instincts.

Confident that the bird had eaten its fill and that he could sustain control, Jahmash willed it to fly away. Silver-streaked gulls were known for flying high and fast. Their eyesight allowed them to scan the ground and water for food from high altitudes. These assets would come in handy for finding boats and ships. Jahmash hoped that the bird's speed would get it far enough away to find a vessel before needing to eat or rest.

After over three hours of soaring in one direction, Jahmash spotted a ship below through the bird's eyes. Its vision made him mildly nauseous, but he pushed it down and focused on gliding carefully towards the ship. The men aboard were not soldiers, as he'd hoped, but what seemed like pirates. Scraggly and unsuccessful ones at that.

He identified the helmsman and wheel and set down right in front of the man. The man flinched backwards noticeably as Jahmash had the bird perch atop the sizeable wheel and look the man directly in the eyes.

Jahmash gripped the bird's mind just a hair more tightly. The only way his plan would work would be through something drastic and unbelievable. Luckily, other ship hands were nearby, along with the helmsman. Still staring directly at the man who directed the ship, Jahmash opened the bird's beak. He pushed the words out gently, so they would not simply sound like squawks. "If you follow me, I can make you all richer than you have ever dreamed."

The helmsman was visibly taken aback at the notion of the talking bird for several moments, then came to his senses. He looked around at the other men, none of whom flinched. "What sort of magic is this? We should slice your head off right now! And eat you!"

Jahmash closed his eyes and focused harder. "I am a messenger of the Harbinger, Jahmash. Follow me to him and he will bestow you with a mission and a wondrous bounty. Refuse me and I will rip out each of your eyes before any of you can even draw a weapon." Jahmash turned the bird's head from one man to another, just for added effect. It hadn't been necessary, as they'd all paled at the mention of Jahmash's name. "What will it be, friends? Riches? Or blindness?"

The helmsman glared at the bird another moment. "Fine. You win. But only because we're starving. And if you're lying...bird...we are going to eat you." The man flashed a blade in the waist of his breeches. "Show us the way."

Jahmash had the bird flutter to the starboard deck and perch on a plank. "That way. East." The helmsman turned the wheel to the left and the ship set its new course. Jahmash smiled a smile he hadn't managed in over fifteen hundred years. For the first time since Darian's death, he looked forward to the future. He spoke softly to himself, back on his island where no one else could hear, "They are all going to die, Darian. And all of their deaths will be your fault. I hope, by the Orijin, that you are watching me from the Three Rings."

CHAPTER ONE
THE NIGHT OF FIRE AND WATER

From **The Book of Orijin, Verse Three**
Every man must burn at a given juncture of his existence.
The righteous man burns within for justice and for peace.
The indecisive man burns his potential out of fear to act.
The wicked man burns in Opprobrium to rid the evil from his soul.

RAIN INTRUDED UPON the mountain village of Haedon, tucked away in the northwestern corner of Ashur, the Drowned Realm. This rain had no business there and had not been seen by the Haedonians in years; it was an ocean falling from the sky. In another town, any other town, this would be an omen to stay in and pray for sun and tranquility. But then, Joakwin Kontez was not scheduled for execution in any other town. The entire village filled Haedon Square, growing angrier and more belligerent by the second. Even the frail, sickly, and old held their ground against the deluge. Every person, to a man, refused to retreat until they knew for sure that Kontez's life ended tonight.

Hundreds occupied the square and its outer alleyways: men and women, young and old, packed in shoulder to shoulder and surrounded by the two-story wooden buildings in which they worked during the day. They were indifferent to the rain that soaked their robes and cloaks. Visibility was minimal, but it would suffice. Metal lanterns surrounded the perimeter of the hanging platform. There was nothing else to see in Haedon. And nothing else to care about. It only mattered that Kontez be raised into the noose, then dropped. Every voice pleaded for a gruesome, torturous death to come to Joakwin Kontez, the kneeling man on the lonely wooden platform before them. Every voice except one.

A cloaked figure stood among the crowd. Silent. Vigilant. His jaw and face clenched tightly; he resembled more a sculpture than a man. He knew any recognition of his face would mean that his life would end tonight as well. Although only seventeen years of age, Baltaszar Kontez felt like the only sane person in Haedon this night. While the world prayed for his father's death, he pleaded for common sense and rational thought. Yet, futility gnawed at the back of his mind.

Be brave. There is no other way. Orijin, my God, please protect him.
Oran Von, the Chancellor of Haedon, walked gingerly up the wooden

steps to the left of the platform, cane in hand, his knees creaking as loudly as the wood. Titus, Von's bodyguard and the anointed executioner, escorted him onto the stage. Titus needed only to stand over Von to shield him from the downpour, as he easily doubled any Haedonian in height and weight. In his hooded grey robe, Von, once a tall man, hobbled to the middle of the platform where Joakwin knelt. It wasn't the rain that made him so slow. The man was a walking corpse; most wondered how he managed to still rule. His deep booming voice, the only one in Haedon capable of drowning out this rain, was the only part of him that didn't reflect his age.

Von limped to face his people, coughing and hocking. "Joakwin Kontez, you have been formally charged by the people of Haedon for the practice of black magic." He stopped to cough. "The sabotaging of shops and goods with the intention of attracting more business to your farm, for the malicious destruction of your fellow townspeople's homes, and for murder."

Clearing his throat, he continued, "You are a disgusting excuse of a man, and it has been determined that you shall hang until dead. Have you any final words?" Von gazed upon him as a cat would look upon a lame mouse, toying with it before the kill. "I'm sorry; you'll have to speak up Master Kontez. You do understand that the sack over your head, along with this cursed rain, drowns out your voice?" He waited, stroking the long white beard that hung to his knees. "Nothing to say? Very well, let us carry on."

Baltaszar struggled to keep from shaking, to stifle screams, to stand idly while a village cheered and watched his father die. The deluge flooded through his hood to the point that it clung to him, each drop another second of time pounding against his head. The rain soaked his short, jet black hair, washed his unshaven face, and caused his feet to squish in his boots. Baltaszar was too focused on his father to let any of it affect him. He yearned for an escape plan. For any possible way to rid his father of this torment. To get his father's head out of the thick, black, opaque sack, normally used to haul small animals back up the mountain after a hunt. His father was probably drowning in that thing. To attempt a rescue would be futile. It would only mean that Baltaszar would be kneeling up there with his father, which was the reason for the cloak in the first place. Baltaszar readjusted his cowl and wiped the cascade from his eyes with a soaked sleeve.

The rain helped. Nobody would take the time to look under the hood to see who it was. Baltaszar had gone deep into the forest with his twin brother, Bo'az, when they'd learned that their father had been fated to hang. The entire town of Haedon assumed they had run away weeks before anyway, so Baltaszar only had to make sure he didn't draw attention to himself. Every step he took would have to be calculated and precise in order to keep his cover. No looking into people's eyes, no conversations, no incriminating movements. He could not bring himself to celebrate like the other villagers, but he knew he must blend in. He needed to be here. While Bo'az remained hidden as always, Baltaszar understood that the world he knew would end tonight. It was a reality he hadn't fully accepted until a moment ago.

Baltaszar knew his father would not want him to risk his life in some foolish attempt at bravery. Guilt already began to haunt him for doing nothing. One day he would avenge this.

Stay strong. Stay brave. This is what he would ask of you.

"Hang him! Hang the bloody fiend! Let him hear the song!" screamed Fallar Bain. Bain most likely was the first villager to arrive, considering he was the first to accuse Joakwin of committing these crimes years ago. "Kill that bastard! End his bloody life! Put an end to the fires!"

"Patience, my friend, let us all savor this moment, as it marks an end to our suffering and dismay! And most importantly, an end to the fires!" Von was milking this for all he could. Baltaszar realized that Von was making this his legacy. In the decades Von had governed Haedon, there had never been a major conflict, only minor squabbles.

However, concern had formed about Von's age. People worried that, should Von die, there would be no successor who shared his views and methods. Conversely, others grew irritated from rumors of Von hoarding their taxes. In time, no evidence confirmed these claims, but Von never provided any proof to dispel the rumors. Claims became more and more frequent so that, if not for Von's personal soldiers, he likely would have been attacked.

The execution of Joakwin Kontez would earn Von the undying fame and popularity he sought. Haedon would remember Oran Von as the man who drove out the dark magic, who didn't blink at the thought of using one man's death, or life, as an example to hundreds of others. Von turned to Titus, the monumental man standing at the back of the newly-built hanging platform, who inspected the beams to ensure their sturdiness. "Titus, let us begin with the ceremony!"

The crowd's screams reached new levels. If the executioner didn't do his job soon, the villagers would storm the platform and assume the duties themselves. Emotions burned through Baltaszar's veins, adrenaline filled his body, urging him to move farther back. Yet his mind told him differently. His father was now standing, but not of his own accord. Titus pulled the sack from his father's shaggy head, and fastened the noose around his neck. Titus shoved him over to stand on the trap door, which would open beneath his feet in a few moments. The villagers screamed their approval through the rain. They yearned to see Joakwin Kontez's death. Yearned to see him suffer and struggle. They waved hands and fists in the air, fired curses and insults like arrows. The Haedonians ached to see the agony in Joakwin's face during his last moments. Even though the rain limited their sight, Baltaszar knew the exaggerations would be limitless on the morrow. People would contrive stories about how Joakwin cried and pleaded for mercy. Yet, Joakwin stood tall, proud, the look of a martyr in his eyes.

Oran Von limped down the stairs, looking like a wounded bird with his long hooked nose, so distinctive that Baltaszar could recognize Von by that alone. Another of Von's soldiers escorted him now, as Titus gripped the lever that would release the door beneath Joakwin. Knowing Von, he likely wanted to be far away enough from Joakwin to not have to see Joakwin's eyes as he hanged. Baltaszar knew Von didn't wholeheartedly believe that his father was responsible for all the fires, destruction of homes and crops, injuries, and especially the murder. He couldn't. Baltaszar remembered Von coming to visit often when he and Bo'az were small. He remembered Von's friendly, candid conversations with his father. But the visits became less frequent and eventually stopped. Baltaszar assumed it was a ploy to distance himself from Joakwin once the accusations began.

Titus violently threw the lever down. The floor dropped beneath Joakwin; the rope constricted around his neck. Baltaszar's anger roared inside him. His father flailed wildly, resembling more a puppet on a string than a man. Eyes bulged from their sockets. Hands scratched furiously at the murderous rope as he continued to sway before the applause. Baltaszar held his own breath, anticipating success in his father's attempt to break free. More anger. Hatred. Even in the rain, he clearly saw the blue in his father's twitching, spasming face. His father's arms slowed, barely lifting, and ultimately dropped. They twitched with a hint of life left in him; his eyes had completely forced themselves from his face.

Emotions shattered in Baltaszar like broken glass, cutting and stabbing his mind as he wrestled to push them into darkness, nothingness, oblivion.

His father, a tattered and bedraggled figure, writhed for a few more breaths of air. Joakwin squirmed and convulsed in mid-air, desperately gripping the smallest grains of life. His mouth gaped, searching for air, but the rain intruded instead, only drawing out the process of dying.

And then the stones flew. Mostly of a small and medium size. Like a volley of arrows, the crowd thrust them upon Joakwin, most pelting his limp body while a few strays managed to bloody his face.

Baltaszar clenched his eyes tightly shut to fight back the impending tears because he could not run. In the hours leading up to this moment, he'd tried to prepare himself for it. Yet, as he stood there, hiding in plain sight among the entire town, Baltaszar understood that the man who raised him had lost his life in the most dishonorable way. White-hot anger and hatred coursed through his veins, overpowering the sadness and helplessness that had resided there previously.

As his father swayed from the pendulous rope, the life draining from him, a fire ignited beneath the platform, quickly spreading to, and engulfing Titus, who shrilled like a eunuch as the flames charred his clothes and skin. The hulking brute, normally deliberate in his movements, flailed wildly as the mysterious fire burned through his breeches and leather vest and boots, searing his flesh. The crowd gaped and gasped, first unsure whether to believe its eyes, then too frozen from fright and amazement to help Titus.

The blaze roared, moving to the rope from which Joakwin dangled, and then to Joakwin's head and body. As the breath drained from Joakwin's lungs, the rope broke, sending his flaming body crashing to the ground, seemingly giving him new life as his blackened arms and legs violently rolled and flailed.

Although the crowd had not expected this turn of events, it cheered and whooped more loudly as the fire encompassed Joakwin in a smoky shroud.

You cannot sit here and take this. You need to help him. You need to stop the fire.

What? No. I must be strong. They'll give me a fate worse than his if I interfere.

You shall regret this for the rest of your life if you do not interfere.

I have more to live for than to die right now. I can right this. I can atone for this.

How? You are a coward. How can this be made right? You cannot bring him back after tonight. You can make this easier for him right now.

What is this madness? Get out of my head!

You are a coward.

Joakwin Kontez was not completely dead; he lay on the ground screeching like a madman in front of the entire village, his flesh burnt and seared. His incredible stench grew tendrils, spreading through the square. He was yelling something, but Baltaszar could not understand the words. It was drowned out by the raucous cheering of the townspeople and the unending downpour.

Baltaszar watched as the fire engulfed the villagers nearest the platform and realized it would be wise to retreat. Villagers began to run amok, darting and dashing like horses terrified of a predator. Baltaszar turned and fled, tears finally streaming from his eyes. He could not fathom how a fire could ignite and rage so violently during such a torrential rain.

As Baltaszar fled, the fire completely conquered the square. He was sure it would eventually burn down the surrounding buildings, and he didn't care. It could burn the whole damn town for all it mattered, especially Oran Von. The man had conveniently disappeared before the onset of chaos.

His father was dead. Hanged. Then scorched. As an entire town watched and celebrated. *Why did we even stay in this cursed town for so long? Why didn't we just leave when they accused father of these crimes?*

Baltaszar ran southeast as fast as he could, toward the outer parts of the town, through the farms and into the forest. He wouldn't be noticed if he could escape that way. But too many people filled the streets for that to work. He snuck down muddy roads and alleys, past houses and shops, many belonging to people who had turned on his father.

He came upon Fallar Bain's house and produce shop, resplendent and pretentious at three stories high. Baltaszar vividly remembered the spectacle that had occurred at Bain's store over six years ago, when it was a humble shop, no bigger than a shack. Bain, the little bald man who was as wide as he was tall, never wore a smile. He'd sold fruits and vegetables that he grew in the garden behind his house. Baltaszar and Bo'az had gone there with their father shortly after sunrise to get the best selection of apples, Baltaszar's favorite. His father and Bo'az browsed other baskets of fruits and vegetables while Baltaszar inspected the apples. Although he hadn't tasted many varieties, his favorite were reddish-yellow apples, because of the sweet-tart taste.

Baltaszar had felt Bain staring at him from behind the counter. Watching his hands and movements, watching his face and eyes especially. Baltaszar had a vertical black scar intersecting his left eye from the time he was a small child, the result of a house fire that had also killed his mother, though he'd been too young to have any memory of it. Throughout his life, Baltaszar had grown accustomed to others' tendencies to stare at his face. Bain was no different. However, Bain's intense gaze caused more discomfort than others', as there seemed to be an essence of hatred behind it. Regardless, Baltaszar had gone about his business, loading his own basket with apples. As Bain's ogling continued, a fire sparked from one of the baskets. Before Bain or anyone else could react, the fire spread to other baskets and shortly engulfed the entire shop. Baltaszar, along with his father, brother, and Bain, managed to escape with no injuries, but Bain's shop was completely destroyed. In the aftermath, Bain had appealed to Oran Von and accused Baltaszar's father of burning down his shop and home. Because nobody could testify that Joakwin didn't cause the fire, Von decried that Joakwin was responsible for rebuilding Fallar Bain's house and shop, in whatever manner Bain wished for it to be rebuilt. That manner just happened to be an excessively large three story house, with the new, larger shop on the bottom level.

Baltaszar added Bain to his list for revenge, after Oran Von. Down the road, past Bain's house, a crowd had gathered outside the school on the left. The brick school spanned a length of four blocks, and had all of its outside torches burning. It would be futile to stay on this road, as Baltaszar would find little to keep him from being seen.

He turned right at the road behind Bain's house, staying close to the dark wooden fences. Mud caked his boots, breeches, and cloak, causing him to lift his knee to his chest every time he took a step. Luckily, because of the rain, it simply looked as if he was walking carefully to avoid slipping and falling, rather than sneaking by.

Keeping himself cloaked and clinging to the fences on his right, Baltaszar realized that the third house on the left side of the road belonged to Harold Joben and his wife, Carys. About two years ago, the couple had invited Baltaszar, Bo'az, and their father for dinner after a meeting at the Town Hall at the end of the street. They had wanted to betroth their daughter, Lea, to Bo'az, and as a result, they would always find reasons to talk to Joakwin. Baltaszar had wondered why they liked Bo'az and not him, but he figured the black scar on his face had probably turned them toward his brother. Bo'az had reciprocated the interest in Lea, two years his younger, but always grew nervous around her and never spoke.

The Jobens had served a feast including four game hens, rosemary roasted potatoes, sweet yams, onion soup, stewed beef with carrots and peppers, bread, and fruit pies. Carys was known as the best cook throughout Haedon, and she loved to live up to that reputation. She was a pleasant enough woman, always polite and smiling, and her love of talking encompassed everything from the correct way to butcher various animals to the intricacies of religion and the Orijin, their god.

How she ended up with Harold, Baltaszar could never understand. Carys had amassed hoards of money from her talent and had plenty of suitors, even as a girl. While she maintained a slender frame and soft, beautiful features, Harold was physical evidence of his wife's cooking prowess, and his protruding gut expanded every year. Over the years, he had more and more difficulty standing while teaching at the school. He grew so fat that even his chairs were replaced every few months.

At dinner, Bo'az had constantly looked down at his plate while Carys and Lea tried relentlessly to prod him into conversation. It had annoyed Baltaszar how timid Bo'az acted. Mid-meal, Harold, bits of food stuck to the sides of his mouth and soup dripping from his chin, shot up from his chair yelling, "Smoke! Smoke! There's smoke coming from the kitchen!"

Sure enough, when they'd looked toward the kitchen, black smoke billowed through the doorway. The men had rushed to extinguish the fire. They had raced from the kitchen to the well behind the house, carrying bucket after bucket of water. After over an hour of drenching the kitchen and stamping out flames, the men had prevailed over the fire. However, all that remained of Carys' beloved and famous kitchen was a small piece of burnt wooden counter top and a few piles of ash. Even the walls had been partially burned down.

At the time, Harold and Carys had considered the whole event a terrible accident, but in the months that followed, Fallar Bain paid daily visits to them, repeatedly imparting his beliefs of Joakwin's involvement with black magic. Ultimately, Bain managed to convince Harold Joben. Oran Von had been skeptical of any foul play, especially considering Joakwin had been sitting and eating with them and would have no motive. However, Bain and Harold Joben managed to rally the townspeople behind them, all supporting the decision for Joakwin to be either confined to his farm or exiled from Haedon. The town's support came easily. Bain had simply appealed to them, explaining that Joakwin desired Carys for himself and, if he could not have her, would burn down her kitchen to deprive her of her livelihood. Once the masses demanded justice, with no opposition, Oran Von had to appeal to them or it would have cost his own head.

He had at least given Joakwin the reasonable punishment of being confined to his own farm. Von also restricted Baltaszar and Bo'az to curfews, they would only be allowed to leave the farm to run necessary errands, such as trading. The Haedonians were wary that the twins might also know the dangerous magic their father practiced, and therefore, kept Baltaszar and Bo'az under close watch whenever they were in public.

Bo'az took things with difficulty, constantly wandering off to sit under a tree for hours. He'd felt embarrassed about their situation, especially because he'd missed his chance with Lea Joben. Often, Baltaszar ended up running his father's errands alone, because Bo'az had run off and couldn't be found.

The street rematerialized in front of Baltaszar. He could not keep having these flashbacks if he wanted to reach the forest safely, and he didn't have much farther to go. Baltaszar passed the Joben house, then the next house, and turned the corner again. On his right, the enormous Town Hall building towered above. As a child, it had been modestly sized, but Oran Von ordered expansions to it every year. These days, the building was as long as half the town. During town meetings, even if everyone in town showed up, they'd still only fill up about three quarters of the building. Baltaszar realized how little he would miss Haedon and Oran Von's need for pointless structures. With his father dead, and his closest friend having left Haedon over a year ago, there remained no soul in this town who would treat him kindly.

Baltaszar passed one last row of houses and reached a clearing by the forest's outskirts. Looking down the muddy road to his left, he could faintly discern a score of people running in his direction. Judging by the distance and severity of the rain, they wouldn't see him from where they were. Baltaszar sighed, separated from the fence, and sprinted toward the trees and shrubs that waited ahead. The last house he ran past belonged to Dirk and Mila Samson. The occurrences on an autumn night in that house, over a year after the Jobens' kitchen incident, affected his father more than anything Fallar Bain had done. His father had never told Baltaszar what happened. Baltaszar saw the agony and regret straining his father's eyes and face for months after, although he never brought up the situation. Many people started calling his father a murderer after that, so it became easy to assume what happened.

From then on, his father wore a melancholy countenance every day. He'd never revealed the whole story to Baltaszar or Bo'az, but Baltaszar knew it had all revolved around the Samsons' four-year-old daughter dying. He'd just assumed that his father had been accused of it. Once Von dubbed Joakwin a murderer at the execution, his assumptions only seemed truer.

Baltaszar shook his head. He had to focus. Aside from the falling rain, the trees had cast too many shadows for him to be seen now, and no one would dare step foot into the forest.

He ran through rows and rows of trees, past all the trail markers that he and his brother had set to find their way back and forth to the camp, deeper into the thick forest. They had agreed to camp as deeply as possible, as an attempt to keep the townspeople from investigating their campfire. Most people in Haedon were too afraid to walk more than a few feet into the forest, as they'd all believed childhood tales about monsters and demons. They called it "The Never" for more than one reason. They believed that anyone who went in never came back out. They also swore to never go in, believing the forest never ended. Baltaszar had stopped concerning himself with such nonsense when he was about five. There were more important things to spend his time worrying about than scary stories. Besides, he and Bo'az had been hiding in the forest for weeks, and they hadn't been spooked by a single thing. Aside from the swaying of the trees overhead and the occasional animals running around, things had been very quiet.

Baltaszar turned to check how far out of sight he was. The clearing was half a mile behind him and barely visible. Satisfied, Baltaszar turned back around, stepped gingerly, and collapsed to the ground.

The events of the night had drained his body of the strength to do anything except cry. Baltaszar lay, for what seemed like hours, where he'd fallen. His face trembled while warm tears and rain gushed down his face and mixed into the mud he lay in. He felt no desire to get up and had no idea what to do with himself from this point on. Baltaszar had no real memory of his mother; his father was all he knew. And now the man was gone.

Hours later, Baltaszar realized he hadn't even gotten to his camp yet. And that the rain had stopped. Arising, wiping the mud and tears from his eyes and face, he noticed two small red dots in the distant underbrush. He blinked to clear his vision and they were gone. Perhaps it was just the light.

A thought boomed in his skull like a kick from a horse. As far as he knew, his father's body still lay in Haedon Square, mangled and burned. If left there, it would only be desecrated once people saw it still lying on the ground. And Von was the type of man to leave it there to be vandalized.

Looking at the sky, Baltaszar realized he still had nearly two hours before the sun would begin its ascent. Baltaszar ran back to the edge of the forest. By now, everyone in Haedon would be sleeping. With the rain having stopped and darkness still prevailing, his mission could prove easy. The biggest difficulties lay in getting his father's body out of the wide open square, then carrying it through the mud back to the forest.

Baltaszar sprinted to the outskirts of Haedon, stopping only to relieve the ache in his lungs and sides. The houses that lined the perimeter were dark and quiet. If he walked toward the school now, Baltaszar knew he could get to the square undetected. By now, the lanterns and torches would be out and there would be fewer houses for him to pass.

It took him nearly half of an hour to cover the remaining distance to

Haedon Square, a distance that he could walk in a few minutes, given normal conditions. As he walked out into the wide open square, Baltaszar's eyes groped through the darkness to find any evidence of his father's body. Plumes of smoke danced from each of the buildings on the south and east side of the square. The moonlight shed some light into the giant courtyard. Searching across the square, he noticed a lump lying on the ground in front of the hanging platform. It was the only mass on the ground of the courtyard. When he'd fled earlier, bodies had littered the square amidst the chaos. Only one mass remained.

However, what he saw was too large to be his father; it was almost big enough to be two people. And then he saw movement. Baltaszar froze, unsure of what he was seeing. Before worrying about the rational choice, he ran toward his father's body. Despite the mud, he kept his footing and dashed faster and faster ahead.

Something or someone arose beside his father's body. *Another person.* Baltaszar clumsily slid to a halt in the mud and found himself staring up into the eyes of a stranger. The man's chest met the level of Baltaszar's face; he stood taller than Titus the executioner, who until now was the largest man Baltaszar had ever seen.

I have to...No. Don't think. Just act. Lunging, he butted his head hard into the man's ribs and attempted to wrap his arms around the massive tree trunk-sized body. The man pulled him off with one hand and threw him to the ground next to his father's corpse. Baltaszar landed on his back with a thud and, for once, felt grateful that the rain had left the ground so soft.

"I am not here to fight you," the towering man whispered to him. "Stay calm. The last thing either of us needs is for attention to be drawn to us."

The man wore a long dark cloak, similar to the one Baltaszar himself had donned, except that it had no hood. "Then why in the name of Orijin are you standing over my father's body?" Baltaszar managed to keep his voice low, despite the anger that drove it.

"You speak of Orijin. Good. Then you know religion. I was simply checking to ensure there remained nothing of value on him; nothing that someone else could find that would lead to you or anything else."

"What? I don't understand."

"We have never met," the man said. "But I have known of you for some time. Your father and I worked for the same people."

"Nonsense. My father has been a farmer his whole life. I'm warning you now, I have a weapon. I don't know who you are, but if you leave now, I will not attack. I give you my word." *Don't let him see your fear.* He hadn't realized it, but he'd gotten up and was standing and facing the other man.

"Boy, your threats mean nothing. If I wanted, I could kill you. Save your breath and your energy. Where you're going, you'll need it all."

"Where I'm going?"

"I would assume, considering you have the Descendants' Mark, you would be going to The House."

"You're not making any bloody sense." Thought fragments pulled Baltaszar's mind in every direction.

The man shook his head, "There is much you have to learn. Let us move behind the platform. We risk too much by talking out in the open." Behind the burnt and blackened hangman's platform, they sat beside each other, leaning against the wooden posts. "It seems you do not understand the significance of what is on your face," the man said. "That line on your face represents an honor bestowed upon generations of Descendants."

"It's a damned scar from being burnt as a child. My house burned down and the fire killed my mother. It's not some stupid line."

"I imagine that's what Joakwin told you. He lied. The only reason you live in Haedon is because he was trying to protect you. He assumed that if he tucked you away in the middle of the Never, he could raise you as a normal child and you would never question anything."

"This doesn't make any sense. What makes you think I believe anything you have to say? My father has just been hanged in front of my whole bloody village, and you think that I will believe you just because I found you here in the middle of the night? I'm not some little child who's going to hang at your every word just because you've come with these bloody stories about my father."

"Then let me tell you more. If I cannot manage to convince you with what I know, then you are a fool."

"Look, I don't know what you want here, but I'm not going to sit here and listen to you. I have to leave before they kill me as well. I only came to bring his body back with me. My only concern now is finding out why my father was falsely accused of black magic, and then getting some type of justice on those responsible for this."

"Think about it, boy. That scar, as you call it, is a perfectly straight line down your face. How is it that you would only be burnt on that little piece of your face? Are you really that much of a fool?"

Baltaszar was losing his grasp on what to believe. "Fine, and supposing you're right. I'm supposed to just believe you? If I hadn't come back to get my father we would never have met, and you wouldn't have been able to tell me anything. If I had stayed in hiding, what would you have done?"

"Trust me, Baltaszar Kontez, I would have found you." Baltaszar's eyes widened. "Yes, I know your name. You'd be surprised about how many people outside this forest actually do. I was given this mission because of my abilities to find people. I am the best tracker in the world. After searching your father's body I was coming to find you next."

"Y...you could have just asked someone in the town. They would've told you my name along with my father's and my..."

The man cut him off, "There's a voice inside your head that does not seem like your own."

"Wh…" How could he know this?

"You do not know when exactly it got there or how, but it speaks to you as if it knows you, like an old friend. It tells you the things you do not want to hear, but perhaps need to hear from time to time."

Baltaszar now stared at him, his mouth agape. He had never mentioned that to anyone, not even his family. *He's right; I don't even know when it started talking to me. Was it tonight? But even then, it felt familiar, like I'd known it before.* "How…"

"Perhaps now you believe. In fact, there are people in this world who can actually help you with that, help you find the source, or even get rid of it for you, if you desire." Baltaszar was hooked. There was no possible way that anyone could know about the voice in his head. Yet now, this man before him revealed knowledge of it and that there was a possible cure. "Baltaszar, I understand that Joakwin was executed on false accusations. Yet, his death was necessary, perhaps the only thing that could have set you free. This world is much larger than your little hidden town. There are people in this world you need to meet. People who can set your life in the right direction."

"And what direction is that?"

"Did your father never teach you of the original Harbingers? The messengers of the Orijin?"

Baltaszar struggled to understand what connection any of this could have to God, but then, he barely had any idea about anything he'd been told during this conversation. "We learned of the Orijin as children, and my father instilled in us a devotion to Him throughout our lives. But he never spoke of any messengers."

"Pity. Look above us, candles are being lit in the windows. I do not have the time to say everything on the matter of your father, your past, or the mark on your face. There are others in the world who can help you. If you really want answers about your father, you must go to the House of Darian. The Headmaster there is a man named Marlowe. If there is anyone in this world who knows about your father and your past, it is he. And if, after speaking to him, you still have doubts, there are others there who are quite capable of helping you. Now we must part ways."

"That's it? You have not finished explaining things to me! Why did you bloody come here if you would only give me half of a story and then leave?"

"I am a regular man. You are a Descendant. You have a manifestation, use it to help you. People on this side of Ashur will welcome you."

"Every time you say something, you put more questions in my head. Manifestation? I am not asking. I am telling you. You have to stay here and explain. Or let me go with you."

"My only priority was to find you and make sure you would find the House of Darian. Not to bring you with me. To come with me would mean almost sure suffering and death for you. Trust me. There is no time to argue any longer. You will have to begin your journey without me, but I trust you will have success. The mark on your face will grant you certain privileges once you leave this forest." The statuesque man arose. "Your days as a witless farm boy are over, Baltaszar. Whatever you had planned for your life before meeting me, it cannot be. Our entire world will be at war soon; it is time you removed the veil from your eyes."

"I hadn't really planned anything. And now, I'm even less sure, as you've given me piss for a story, with barely much of an explanation. It seems my only choice is to leave this place; I will not be welcomed back." More lights shone through the windows, and voices could be heard above.

"Travel southeast. The only name I can really give you is Marlowe, the Headmaster of the House of Darian, but most people will not recognize that name. Mention Darian or the House of Darian and people will guide you in the right direction, especially with the Descendants' Mark on your face. Just over a day's ride southeast of your camp in the forest is the city of Vandenar. Once you are out of the forest, it is about an hour's ride. Make that your first stop. The people there are generally helpful and respectful toward those of you who have the Mark. Use it to your advantage, but do not overstep your boundaries."

"Help me pick up my father's body; I need to bring him with me."

"Leave him. If you remember anything of your father's teachings, you know that his body is now just an empty shell. To carry the body would slow you down. To give it a proper burial would set you back at least a day. There is no time to waste. War and death threaten this world, Baltaszar. It is very important for you to reach that House. Promise me you will go there."

Baltaszar shrugged and deeply exhaled, then nodded. "I will. My word is my bond." He stood and clapped the mud from his hands. "What is your name?"

"Slade."

"Slade. Thank you. I hope our paths cross again. You have much more to explain."

"If you reach your destination you will not need my explanation. Good luck, Baltaszar." With that, Slade walked toward the buildings surrounding the square and disappeared into an alley toward the north of Haedon. As more and more lights appeared through the windows surrounding the Square, Baltaszar ducked and scampered across it to the narrow roads leading back to the forest. Once again, he sprinted through the mud, sliding and slipping. Guilt poked at the back of his mind about leaving his father's body behind, but he knew Slade was right.

Shortly, he returned to the camp he and Bo'az had set up. Bo'az was gone, but Baltaszar thought nothing of it. He was probably hunting. Finding the flint and some small branches, he started a small fire and sat down against a thick tree. It was only after he lit the fire that he realized the camp itself was completely dry. It must not have rained this far into the forest.

Baltaszar was exhausted, the night had felt eternal, but he was not ready to sleep. Too many thoughts traversed his mind for him to be at peace. He twisted his mouth and rubbed his beard as he contemplated; it had become a habit as of late. Since they'd begun to hide, he and Bo'az hadn't shaved.

Thoughts of his father flooded his head first. Baltaszar knew how simple-minded the people of Haedon were, so it was only fitting that his father would be charged with practicing magic. Baltaszar never understood the vendetta toward his father. He had raised Baltaszar and Bo'az to be respectful, humble, and to stay out of trouble and out of other people's business. The Haedonians' contempt contradicted everything for which his father stood.

His father had never paid any attention to magic. Baltaszar couldn't remember his father mentioning it even once in his life.

Fires were connected to the Kontez family for as long as he could remember. According to his father, when Baltaszar and Bo'az were small boys, a great fire had burned down their first home, killed Baltaszar's mother, and left a black scar down the left side of Baltaszar's face, a straight black vertical line running down his forehead, intersecting his left eye, and ending just below his cheek.

Bo'az had gotten through the fire unscathed. Baltaszar had always been curious as to why his eye had not been affected by the fire, and why the scar hadn't felt any different than his unaffected skin. He'd never had the courage to ask his father about it, for fear that it might remind his father too much of his mother's death. According to Slade though, none of it was true.

Baltaszar had felt scars before. And burns. But none had ever felt like the one on his face. The more he considered Slade's words, the more they seemed to make sense.

Baltaszar wanted revenge. He wasn't sure who had made the accusations against his father besides Fallar Bain. But Oran Von was the one who sentenced him. One day, when he was ready, ready to make another man suffer, Baltaszar would avenge his father's death.

I needed to see all of that. It was the only way I'd be able to avenge his death. As much as the memory will haunt me, it'll drive me to get back at them. I know it.

You will not do a thing and you know it. You will pretend for now that you are angry and vengeful, but you will get over it and then move on with your life. You and your little craven brother.

Shut up! Stay out of my head! I'm so tired of having to listen to you!

I am part of your mind, fool. But if you ever decide to be a man and avenge your father, I shall talk less.

Talk less now! The last thing I need is an argument with you.

Then stop arguing.

Please, I'm begging you. Let me be, at least for now. Until I can rest.

Very well. Expect my return.

The voice finally stopped. Still, questions littered Baltaszar's mind. *How did that fire start tonight? The fire started from the ground, and nobody was close enough to have started it, even Fallar Bain. I was near enough to the front of the crowd that I would have seen if anyone had thrown a torch. And how did it grow so wild in a downpour like that?*

He needed answers. And nobody could give them to him any time soon. Worse yet, if Slade was right. *Who is…was…my father? Better yet, who was my mother?*

Baltaszar knew he would need to leave the forest to find his answers. He wasn't sure how long he would have to search or where this "House of Darian" was, but he would gain nothing by remaining in the forest. He and Bo'az hadn't really discussed what they would do after their father's death, but this seemed like the best course of action. Without his father or the farm, there was nothing in Haedon for Baltaszar and no reason to stay. His best friend had disappeared over two years ago without a word to anyone. And then there was her. Yasaman. He thought they would have eventually gotten married, but she'd shunned and avoided him since his father had been charged. Yasaman suddenly became busy all the time. She would pretend to sleep when Baltaszar snuck to her window in the middle of the night. She'd hardly spoken to him since his father's confinement, but Baltaszar didn't blame her. Her father didn't know of their relationship and she was deathly afraid of telling him, given the status of Baltaszar's father in Haedon. She told him as much. And that as long as her father was around, they couldn't have a real future.

Still, it left a canyon in his gut that he couldn't fill. He'd hoped that eventually he'd be able to come back for her; that maybe the situation would ease. But he knew better. It was another change in his life that he had no control over and would have to accept, just like with his father.

He wished Slade could have stayed to guide him. Bo'az wasn't the type to be a leader or mentor. He was immature and paranoid about everything. The voice in Baltaszar's head didn't stray too far from the truth. Chances were that Bo'az wouldn't be willing to do anything about their father. Baltaszar looked up and saw his brother nearing the camp.

"Where were you?"

"I couldn't sleep; I've been walking around for the past few hours. Just trying to clear my head." Bo'az's eyes were red and bloodshot, his face pallid from tears.

"You should have come; it was important to be there."

"For what? To watch him die? You really think he would've wanted us to see that?" Bo'az dropped down next to the fire, rubbing his hands together. He had looked as tired as Baltaszar felt. Baltaszar guessed that he must not have gotten any sleep at all.

"He was our father. It would have made it easier for him."

"And what about for us? He was going to die no matter what. We couldn't change that, and if we'd tried to, we would have died along with him. Going there would only have put our lives more at risk! We only have each other now, Tasz. We have to do whatever it takes to stay alive. And we have to be safe while doing it."

"Whatever it takes? Be safe? What does that mean? That you're just going to stay in the forest for the rest of your life?" Anger grew within him again.

"I don't know, maybe for a while. It's not safe for us in Haedon and we can't trust anyone. We should stay here for at least a couple months before heading back into the town. Maybe then we can sneak back to the farm and hide out there for a little while."

Coward. You're driven by fear and nothing else. "Go back there? What, by the light of Orijin, would we do that for? No matter how long we wait, we'll never be welcome. Anyone who sees us will either kill us or find someone else who'll kill us. And the farm? The farm will be destroyed by tomorrow, if it hasn't been already." Baltaszar stood and walked to look Bo'az directly in the eyes. "We can't go back and we can't stay here. We have to leave the mountains and forest and go somewhere else. Somewhere new. Our lives are going to be completely different now; we can't expect to be able to do the same things as before."

"You're saying to leave everything we know? Everything we've known our whole lives? For what? You're even going to leave her behind? You're an ass to do that, this isn't her fault."

"She hasn't wanted to speak to me or see me since all this started. I'm not leaving her behind because she's made it clear that she's not mine to leave. We have to start over now, whether you like it or not." Baltaszar hung his head, unsure of whom he was trying to convince. "I'm going to rest today, make up for all the sleep I've lost in the past few weeks. Tomorrow we're gone; staying here is not an option. Like you said, we need to stick together and look out for each other."

"I...I can't. Tasz, we've never been outside of Haedon. We don't know what the world is like. What if the stories are true and there's nothing but forest out there? Maybe there's a reason that father never took us anywhere else. Maybe it's too dangerous out there for two seventeen year olds who don't know anything but farming."

"Bo, if we go back into Haedon we'll be killed. But if we go in the other direction, there's a chance things could be better. I'd rather go where at least we have a chance of surviving." Baltaszar returned to the tree and sat down, then took a deep breath. "Look, I spoke to someone when I went back for father's body. There's a town southeast, not far out of the forest. That's where I'm going once I wake up."

"Spoke to someone? A town? What are you talking about? There's nothing out there, Tasz. At least not for us."

"I'm going to sleep now. You should too. When I wake up later, I'll wake you and we'll pack. It'll be better to leave at night, less chance we'll be seen."

Bo'az continued to plead, "Why do you need to get away so bad? What's so wrong with waiting a little while? And if you swear that everyone in Haedon hates us, why would you trust someone with advice about where to go?"

Baltaszar had hoped he wouldn't have to explain the whole story, but realized it was only fair to tell him. Maybe it would convince Bo'az to leave now, too. "The man was at our father's body, searching for us. He knows who we are and he's not from Haedon. He spoke of things that he shouldn't have known about, things about us. And he said we have to find a 'House of Darian,' that the name Darian would guide us. We have to find Darian."

"So you want to leave to find something you've never heard of, just because a random stranger told you a story?"

"It's something. I can't explain why, but I know he's right. He even told me that this thing on my face isn't a scar, it's a special mark. Something about me being a descendant of someone."

"So you and I are twins, but you have a mark on your face and I don't. And that means you're a descendant of someone but I am not? You're a bloody stupid bastard, Tasz. I'm not going. You can go without me. When you wake up, let me sleep, I'm staying here." Bo'az stretched out, turned away, and closed his eyes. It was clear now he would not give in. He'd always been stubborn as a goat.

Baltaszar decided that when he woke up, he would gather both of their clothes, food, and supplies. Once he was finished, he would wake Bo'az up and threaten to leave with everything, unless he agreed to come along. He gave in to his eyelids, which had been fighting to close for hours now. As he submitted to sleep, he prayed that his dreams would be kind to him. He'd been afraid of what might plague his mind once he drifted off.

***

Baltaszar heard a deafening roar in the forest and began to run. He could not tell whether he was running toward or away from something, but he felt compelled to run. Around him, the blackness conquered his vision. The trees and shrubs clawed, scratched, and ripped the skin from his arms and legs.

Red lights floated in the distance, menacing and welcoming at the same time. Despite his unending flight through the forest, the lights neither grew closer nor diminished. Racing through the jungle, Baltaszar collided into trees, tripped over roots and rocks, and suffered cuts to his limbs, until finally an enormous root caught his foot and sent him hurtling down a slope of dirt and stones. He lay on the ground; face up, his body tangled with the forest floor, his eyes fighting off cloudiness.

Once his eyes triumphed, the dark red spots grew larger until the forest disappeared and he could see nothing but red. The color filled the air. Made it cloudy. Then invaded his eyes, nose, mouth, lungs. The redness burned him from the inside out. Blood oozed from him, black with char. The deafening roar erupted again, louder and louder until it seemed as it was right in front of him. So close that he wasn't sure if the roar came from him.

Baltaszar awoke in a panic, drenched in sweat, unsure of his surroundings. The multi-colored sky approached dusk, darkness not far off. The dream made no sense, but he remained content to let it stay that way, for now.

Baltaszar arose from the ground, ready to pack the sparse clothes, food, and supplies he and Bo'az had remaining. He turned to Bo'az, only to see that his brother was no longer there. All of his belongings remained, yet Bo'az was nowhere in sight. Baltaszar packed both of their things and waited for Bo'az to return.

Baltaszar organized his pack: clothes at the bottom, then supplies, and then food at the top. He did the same for Bo'az. His only weapon was the curved blade he'd taken from the farm. But it would be enough to scare away anyone trying to steal from them. He hooked the blade to his belt.

Baltaszar sat back under the tree, awaiting Bo'az's return, and wondering whether any logic existed in anything Bo'az had said. He waited for more than an hour, nothing on his mind except that the sun was more courageous than he, because at least it was moving. He realized the longer he waited, the more likely he would be to continue stalling and put off leaving.

Baltaszar stood up once more, slung the packs around his back, patted the wooden knife handle with his right hand, and realized he was doing the bravest thing he'd ever done in his life. He started walking away from Haedon.

CHAPTER 2
VISITORS

From *The Book of Orijin,* **Verse Forty-four**
O Mankind, We have made you weak and flawed so that you
may strive to be better. Our judgment is not of your faults,
but of your intentions and attempts to overcome your faults.

AS HIS EYES SLOWLY cracked open, Bo'az inspected the area as quietly as he could. He'd slept on his side, using his pack as a pillow, hoping that when he awoke, Baltaszar would still be asleep. Bo'az craned his still stiff neck over his left shoulder to check on his brother. Sure enough, Baltaszar still lay under the tree, fast asleep.

Bo'az had had no plans to join his brother on a foolish quest. He knew Baltaszar would be fine without him. Baltaszar had always managed to be just fine, whatever the situation. Instead, Bo'az would go back to the farm on the eastern outskirts of the town. He could get there in the dark without being noticed. He knew that Baltaszar had a point about others wanting to destroy it, but he couldn't just assume that it had happened already. Baltaszar had seemed so determined to put the past seventeen years behind him, but Bo'az couldn't let go of things so easily. After all, that was their house; they'd had so many memories there that Bo'az couldn't just move on without going back at least one last time.

If the house was destroyed, he would have to figure out another plan. Perhaps he would stay in the forest for a while longer. But if the house was still standing, he would be able to go back in and save some of their things. His father's tools were still there, along with clothes, food, real beds, and water. *Oh how I miss clean water. I haven't bathed in weeks.* He had no problem staying out in the forest if it meant survival, but it made no sense if there was a chance of staying in a house. Baltaszar was too caught up with that adventure of his to even consider the possibility.

He's so ready to leave. Why? Surely there are some of Father's things at the house that are worth saving. Everyone thinks I'm the coward, yet I'm the one going back to the house. And how could he be willing to leave her? Yasaman is the most beautiful girl I've ever seen, and she was willing to stay with him. How could he have messed that up? Even I would have done everything possible to make her happy. It should have been me she fell in love with. Fool.

Bo'az realized he would have to leave his things at the camp in order to get away without waking Baltaszar. He knew he was too clumsy to try and gather everything without Baltaszar waking up. He'd hoped Baltaszar wouldn't take any of his clothes or food, but he had to take the chance if he wanted to get back to the farm. If he was still there when his brother woke, they would only end up fighting and arguing again, and neither of them would get anywhere. If Baltaszar wanted to go farther into the forest and wander around, Bo'az wouldn't stop him.

Evening had set in, and the sky continued to darken. Before setting off, Bo'az grabbed his black hooded cloak out of his pack and pulled it over his head. It was just like Baltaszar's, a full length woolen cloak with pockets at the waist, in the sleeves, and lining the insides; thick enough for the cool mountain nights.

As Bo'az walked through the forest toward Haedon, he remembered how they'd made the cloaks once Oran Van confined their father to the property. Even though he and his brother were still allowed to leave their farm, they preferred to draw as little attention to themselves as possible. Most townspeople glared at them, cursed, or were even brave enough to throw rocks, apples, bread, or any other handy projectiles at them.

In truth, Bo'az had used his cloak often to sneak away from his brother and father as well. Often, he felt the need to be alone and think about what the future held for them.

After the incident with the Samson girl, Bo'az had a feeling that the three of them would be in for a lot of change. His father, on too many occasions, would sit staring off into nothing. Then, once he'd snapped out of his daze, he'd forget what he'd been doing. His father just seemed sad all the time, as if he'd been holding in more problems and emotions than a human body could contain.

Baltaszar, on the other hand, rarely showed any emotion. Bo'az could never really tell whether their father's conviction and house arrest bothered him, or if he was just holding it all in. Baltaszar never talked about any of it unless Bo'az brought it up first.

Bo'az had always supposed that Baltaszar talked to Yasaman about his thoughts. They'd been together since just after Carys Joben's kitchen burned down. Baltaszar would go off to see her nearly every day, sometimes not returning until nearly sunrise. Supposedly, her father hadn't approved of Baltaszar, but Baltaszar always managed to sneak into her bedroom once her parents fell asleep. It only made sense that Baltaszar would have confided everything in her, which made it stranger still when she stopped talking to him. But that was just another thing that Baltaszar never talked about. *I would've made it work, even if her father didn't approve.*

Bo'az wished he and Baltaszar had talked more, especially with everything they'd been through in the past few years. After the incident at the Joben home, he'd obviously lost his chance to be with Lea Joben. It also ruined the chance to marry any woman in Haedon. *Why wasn't Yasaman afraid to be with Baltaszar? Maybe she was, and that was why she left him. Or maybe he just did something stupid to anger her.* Despite all those hours he'd run off to think about things by himself, Bo'az still had no idea about what to do now. His home seemed like a good start.

As he walked on in the dark, Bo'az could see the forest beginning to thin out. He could decipher faint torches outside people's homes at the edge of the woods. It was early enough that people might be awake, so he'd have to be careful walking to the farm. Stepping out from the trees, Bo'az turned right and headed to the eastern edge of Haedon. He would walk the perimeter of Elmer Guff's farm to get to his own, which didn't figure to be a problem considering that Guff was too old to be out at this time. He was probably asleep. Guff was a quiet, meek man who kept to himself. Age had been getting the best of him the past few years, but he refused to give up the farm to move to any of his children's houses. Three of his sons and two grandsons would come over every morning to take care of the farm animals and any chores that needed to be done.

Bo'az stayed along the high wooden fence around the farm to make himself less visible, careful with every footstep not to wake the sheep and horses that slept in the stables and pens. No one would be walking this way, as it was the outermost part of the town, but there was no need to take any chances. He turned left at the southeastern corner on the shorter side of the farm, where two giant oaks stood side by side to mark the edge of Haedon. There were farms to his left, forest and mountains to his right, mud beneath his feet, and silence everywhere. After close to another quarter mile of grass and mud, Bo'az could finally see the edges of his own farm.

Bo'az hadn't realized it had rained so badly last night. It soaked everything. The path had turned to a thick layer of mud. Every time he took a step, his feet were sucked into the ground and he would have to pull them out, resulting in a loud 'pop' and splash. From the fence, Bo'az could see the horse stables he'd tended for so many years. The fence consisted of three horizontal wooden beams in each segment, supported by thick wooden posts driven deep into the ground, and tall enough so that no horse could jump over it. This also made it easy to climb over or through. As Bo'az climbed the beams and flung himself over, a thought struck him. The only good thing about the accusations against his father was that everyone was afraid of the Kontez family. That was most likely the only reason people didn't sneak on the farm to terrorize them and cause trouble.

He could see in the distance that the house still stood, and it seemed intact from what he could tell. Bo'az hesitated. *I wanted so badly to come back here. So why am I so afraid to go in? Orijin, I beg you, please don't let there be anyone in the house.* He ran as fast as the mud would allow. The splashing and sloshing awoke the few remaining horses, but he chanced it that that wouldn't be enough to alarm anyone nearby. Racing faster and faster, he slid to the front of the house, his arms flailing wildly to keep him upright. Bo'az skidded to a halt right in front of the three steps that led up the porch and to the front door.

Bo'az held his breath as he opened the creaky wooden front door. Pitch blackness completely covered the room. He walked cautiously, leading with his left hand. He could navigate the entire house from memory, but that was assuming everything was where it was supposed to be. He had snuck off enough that returning home in the dark had become a habit. The front room was where his father would relax after working all day, on the cushioned wooden rocker he'd made himself, smoking his pipe or reading a book. Or just sitting there.

Bo'az saw it all in his mind as he felt his way through the blackness. He walked toward the doorway at the back of the room, dragging his hand along the sofa on his right. It seemed that the house remained untouched. He opened the door at the back of the room and walked up the stairs. Some of them had been creaky from years of Baltaszar and him running up and down, and he knew which ones to skip. He climbed the stairs cautiously and quietly, yet didn't know why. The same gut feeling also made him refrain from lighting candles or torches. He skipped the top step, the loudest one, and stepped onto the second floor, where their bedrooms were.

Baltaszar's room lay directly in front of him, the door wide open. He glanced at it and thought he heard the slightest whisper from inside. Bo'az stepped into the doorway and darted his eyes around for any human shadows in the light from the windows. *Nothing. Silence. It was most likely the wind.* He left the room and continued toward his own bedroom, next to Baltaszar's.

Bo'az turned the knob and cracked open the door, wary that someone might be waiting or watching. Peering into the room, he ensured he was safe, and walked in. The moonlight's glow through the window helped him see the entire room. *No one. Just silence.* Bo'az walked to the side of his bed and sat at its edge, then removed his cloak and kicked off his boots. It had been so long since he'd felt something so comfortable. Remembering that he'd left his belongings in the forest, he walked to his closet on the other side of the room to find some new clothes to change into.

He buried his head in the closet to find clean pants and shirts and felt something grasp his shoulder. Bo'az sprang violently, crashing into the shelf above him. He doubled over in pain, swaying in a daze. The pain in his head throbbed so that he almost couldn't hear the voice behind him.

"I'm sorry," the voice said softly, "I didn't mean to scare you."

That voice. Familiar. It was so unexpected that he doubted he'd heard correctly. Bo'az slowly straightened himself to see the voice's owner, still in a daze. But before he could lift his head, a hand cupped the nape of his neck and pulled him forward. Soft, moist lips met his and kissed him passionately. *Yasaman. It's Yasaman! And she's kissing me!* A second hand reached around him and pulled his body closer. After what seemed like hours, Bo'az forced himself to pull away, finally realizing that he'd been kissing back, and stared at her. *She's so beautiful.*

A hint of horror tinged her countenance. "Oh my goodness, I'm sorry Bo, I thought you were Tasz!"

What? No, that's not fair. "I am Tasz!" *Wait, what am I saying?*

"Bo'az, I can tell the difference between the two of you. It isn't difficult, considering there's no black scar running down your face."

No. If she doesn't want Bo'az, then I can be Baltaszar. Why is he the only one who gets to be happy? "No. No, really. The scar has been gone for weeks. I don't know how, but it went away." *He's not coming back. He'll never see her again anyway.*

She sat on the bed with a sigh. "How? How does a scar like that just disappear? You've had the thing for as long as I've known you. Something like that doesn't just disappear! Bo, if this is some stupid trick, please stop now. We don't have the time for it, and I'm too tired to argue."

"Trust me, Yas. It's me, Baltaszar. Really. I left Bo back in the forest. He was too afraid of being caught to come back here." *Work. Please work.* "I don't know why or how the scar is gone, but over the past few weeks, it just faded away."

"Fine. But if you're lying, I'll make sure that there's no way to confuse the two of you ever again."

"What do you mean?"

"I mean I'll kill you."

"Oh. Um, sure." *Oh God, what've I done?*

"And where have you and Bo'az been? No one has seen you two in weeks! I thought you both ran off to get as far away from here as possible! I only came here because I'd prayed to Orijin that there was a remote chance you might come back after last night."

"We're staying in the forest south of the village, a couple miles into it so no one will spot us. It wasn't safe for you to come here, though."

"Look, my parents don't know I'm here. By morning though, they'll realize that I'm gone, and I'm sure this is the first place they'll look. I needed to see you," she said. "I felt so horrible pushing you away, but it wasn't my choice. They forced me to do it! They threatened to marry me off to Garrick Mol right away if I didn't!"

Bo'az interjected. "Garrick Mol? The banker? The man is more than twice our age! Is money that important to them?"

"Tasz, I'm sorry! I know we haven't seen each other in so long and we don't have a plan about what we'll do and we'll have to leave Haedon forever, but I couldn't face living the way my parents want me to. I need you."

Bo'az walked over to her and took her hand in his. "Calm down Yas, calm down. We'll figure something out. It'll be fine." *That's something Tasz would've said, I think.*

"Calm down? Calm down? I just gave up my life here for you, Tasz! The first thing my parents are going to do in the morning is have this whole property torn down to find me! If we're still here, you'll be dead and I'll be the slave wife of Garrick Mol! And if we're not here, they'll comb the forest and mountains to find me! And the best you can say is 'calm down?' We need to get out of here and get a head start to make sure we're not found!"

"I'm sorry; I'm sorry, it's just that this is all so sudden…I came here planning to get some clothes and supplies for me and Ba…Bo'az. Let's just take a second and figure out how to get out of here and what we need to take." He sat on the bed next to her.

Yasaman laid back on the bed, her feet resting on Bo'az's lap. "You're right…I've been so wound up lately, it would be best to take a little while to think things through. I assumed you'd want to just get out of Haedon as quickly as me. You've always been just as whimsical as me. I guess so much has changed since your fa…in the past few weeks."

"You don't have to avoid it. I know my father's dead. Nothing will change that now. That's part of the reason why I'm here. I needed to come back and be around all this one last time. It makes it so much more real."

Yasaman looked on the verge of sleep, getting comfortable in his bed, her eyes fighting to stay open. "Were you in the Square last night?" she paused to yawn. "I couldn't bring myself to go, but I had a nervous feeling you might go and try to save him. I heard a fire broke out. Many were hurt and killed. They blamed that on your father as well."

"I didn't go. I couldn't bring myself to do it. And now I feel guilty about hiding in the forest while it happened." She didn't have to know what Baltaszar really did. Bo'az really did feel guilty about not going now, and at least he could let it all out.

"I'm glad you can finally open up to me. For so long, I felt something was wrong with me because you'd never admit that anything bothered you. But maybe everything is different now." She sat up and kissed him again.

Bo'az seized the opportunity and kissed her back more vigorously. This was wrong. She led him closer with one hand until he lay on top of her slender frame. *I…I can't do this. I've got to tell her.* She pulled him closer, more tightly. Bo'az pulled away, "Yasaman, I can't d…"

A thunderous voice boomed from the front of the house. "Baltaszar Kontez! Come out! We saw you enter the house!"

Bo'az froze. Yasaman's eyes popped open, no sign of drowsiness left in them. He put his finger to his lips. Perhaps the men were bluffing. There was no way he would just walk out of the house and give himself up.

The thundering voice continued, "Baltaszar! We mean you no harm! My name is Linas Nasreddine; I have come with my two acquaintances from afar! We were sent here to help you escape and to protect you!"

Linas Nasreddine. That wasn't a name that Bo'az had ever heard before. Ducking out of view from anything outside, he glanced over at Yasaman. Her expression was difficult to decipher, but she shook her head as well, equally confused. Whether he could really trust them, Bo'az wasn't sure. But he knew eventually they would come inside and check for themselves, and if that was the case, things could get violent and careless very quickly in the dark. Bo'az put up a hand toward Yasaman, implying for her to stay put, then cautiously crept out of the room and down the hall to the left. He had to calculate every footstep, as most of the upstairs floor creaked. While he tiptoed to the window facing the front yard, the wooden floor let out a massive groan at his last step before the window. Diving from in front of the window, he knew he'd reacted too late. *Damn it!*

A gravelly voice exposed him, "I saw him up there Linas!"

"Baltaszar!" Linas repeated. "Look out the window, my friend! You have nothing to fear! We have no weapons drawn. We do not look or dress like the people of your village; we are not trying to kill you. The longer you wait the more danger you will face. Again, my name is Linas Nasreddine. I have come to save your life." Linas' voice now seemed pleading.

Why is it always Baltaszar? Why couldn't they be looking for me? Bo'az, huddled beneath the window, arose to see for himself. He scanned the front yard, noticing that only one man stood on the porch, while two others stood as far back as the fence, all in plain sight, not trying to hide. They were larger men than any he'd seen in Haedon. The one closest to the house, Linas Nasreddine, seemed the biggest of the three. All wore long coats with high collars hiding their faces and any armor or weapons they might be carrying beneath.

Realizing he'd been standing with his mouth agape the whole time, Bo'az finally found something to say. "Even if you're not from Haedon, how do I know I can trust you? Do you think I'm stupid enough to believe three strange men who show up on my father's farm in the middle of the night? Give me a reason to believe you. Prove to me that I can trust you."

"We were sent by someone else to find you, Baltaszar. We are simply messengers for a greater man. He had hoped that your father would have educated you about the world long ago, and that you would seek him out. But he has waited long enough. With your father's passing, the time has come for you to understand the world beyond your town."

Could it be? Could there really be a connection between Father and their master? What if Baltaszar was right? "What are you talking about? What is beyond this town?"

"Baltaszar, you are quite a special young man. Our master has known about you for a long, long time. There are things outside of Haedon that depend on you. My master simply wishes to guide you and protect you."

What was that name Baltaszar said? Damn it, what was it? "Who is this master of yours and how does he know about me? Is his name Da...Darian? Is it Darian that you're talking about?"

Linas paused, and then turned to look at one of the men behind him. The man nodded approvingly, and Linas turned back and looked directly up at Bo'az. "Yes my friend. We answer to Darian. At least your father mentioned something to you. Now please, come down. If we really meant harm, we would have just broken into the house and attacked you."

Maybe it should have just been Baltaszar here instead of me. What am I doing? If he had just come with me, this wouldn't be so difficult. And now he's off on his own, trying to find Darian, when these men are willing to take him right to Darian. Fool.

It was too coincidental that so many people were showing up after their father's death, trying to get them out of Haedon. Someone found Baltaszar, and these men had now found him. Going with them seemed wisest, now that Yasaman had intruded upon his house and made it no longer safe.

I guess it's either go with them or wait for her parents to chase us. Stupid girl. Is kissing her really worth the trouble? Bo'az turned and stared down the dark hallway to see her petite silhouette peeking from a doorway on the right. Linas hadn't mentioned anything about her. There was a chance he didn't know she was here. Turning back toward the window, Bo'az leaned out. "I need to pack some clothes, tools, and supplies. Give me a moment and I'll come down." Linas nodded in agreement.

"Did you hear that?" he asked Yasaman.

"Somewhat. I mostly heard your side of the conversation, and tried to make sense of it all. I guess we're leaving, then?" she pulled him close again.

Be natural. Bo'az wrapped her in his arms and kissed her forehead. "Looks like it. They want me, though. I don't think they know you're here."

She pushed him away. "So what, you're going to run away with strange visitors in the middle of the night and leave me here?"

"You know that's not what I mean, Yas." He almost felt he was Tasz at this point, arguing with her. "I'm just saying that when we walk outside, they might be surprised to see you. So don't do anything crazy or stupid."

"Thanks."

Perfect. Now she's mad at me, and she doesn't even know who 'me' is. "Come on, let's just get our things packed and go."

Bo'az returned to his room and put on his black cloak. He went back to the closet and grabbed another pack, randomly threw clothes and another cloak in it, and slung it onto his back. Yasaman waited in the hall after getting her pack from Baltaszar's room. "Why are you taking your brother's clothes instead of your own?"

Great. Questions. "I...uh, I was going to see if we could stop in the forest first to give these to him. Even if he won't come along, he could use these."

"Wait, he's not coming with us?"

"He's not going to want to. Besides, the man out there, Linas, only seems to be looking for me. He said 'Baltaszar,' not 'Bo'az.' And I don't think Bo would come. He's pretty set on doing his own thing. Ever since Lea Joben's kitchen burned down, he's hated it here and hasn't trusted anyone."

"Yeah. I've always felt bad for him about that. He deserved better. Even if he's scared of *everything*, he has a certain charm to him. Who knows, if I hadn't fallen for you so quickly, maybe I might've ended up with your brother." She smirked at him, making it impossible to tell whether there was any truth in what she said. "So then what are these men going to say when we stop to see Bo'az?"

"I don't know; I guess we'll see when we get outside." *My God, girl, can you please stop?* "Any more questions or can we go?"

"You don't have to be an ass. I'm just curious. You're the one who wanted to plan things out. You go out first."

"Wait here a moment." Bo'az dashed down the hallway to his father's room on the right. It was just as dark in there. He headed toward the bed, lifted up the pillow, and found what he was looking for. Bo'az brought the dagger close to his face to examine it, then, satisfied, tucked it into his belt at his right hip and covered it with his muddy black cloak. He returned to Yasaman at the stairs and they descended.

Slowly nearing the front door, Bo'az gripped the dagger's hilt from outside his cloak. "Before we go outside, promise me one thing. Don't mention Bo'az to them. I'll tell them we have to make a stop." Yasaman nodded in agreement. He opened the door, peered through the crack to ensure there was no surprise attack, then pushed it farther open and walked through. The three men now stood together at the bottom of the porch stairs. As he walked forward, Yasaman came out from behind him and revealed her presence.

Linas glared at her, the annoyance evident in his eyes. "Who is this girl? She is not welcome on our journey." He spat on the ground.

"She comes with us."

"Baltaszar, there is much work to do in the days ahead, we cannot bear the burden of any unnecessary people in our camp."

Yasaman's head swiveled back and forth between Bo'az and Linas. Her mouth opened, ready to defend herself. Bo'az interrupted. "She is necessary for my well-being. I know her and trust her with everything, including my life." She glanced at him, then darted her eyes away. Even in the dark, Bo'az knew she was blushing.

"Baltaszar, we do not have time for this. Our master gave us strict orders that we were only to bring you."

"He'll have to bend his rules then. If I'm that important to this Darian fellow, I'm sure he won't mind. If she doesn't go, neither do I."

Linas took a deep breath and closed his eyes for a moment. "As you wish. But our journey is long and dangerous. If the girl slows our progress or hinders us, I make no guarantee about the consequences. I cannot stress enough the importance of delivering you unharmed as quickly as possible."

"Understood." *No guarantees about consequences? What exactly is he trying to say?*

"Baltaszar, these are my two…associates. Gibreel Casteghar and Rhadames Slade." Linas nodded behind him to the other two, extremely tall men. Of what little Bo'az could discern of them despite their coats, Gibreel had a grizzly, chiseled face, like rock, and very nappy shoulder-length hair with a scowl on his face. Rhadames, who was slightly taller, had longer dark curly hair and a beard just as thick to match. Rhadames stroked his beard and glared at Bo'az.

Linas continued, "On the road ahead we will face forest, mountains, water, and desert. Whatever hardships the landscapes forget, the beasts will surely remember. The three of us will save your life on more than one occasion, but be prepared at all times to defend yourself." Rhadames stared quizzically at Bo'az, and then looked down again.

Linas turned to his associates. "Gibreel, Rhadames, get our horses. Bring the girl; I'd like to speak to Baltaszar alone. Hurry. We've wasted enough time in this forsaken town. We must begin our journey back." Linas spit again.

Gibreel and Rhadames rushed to the fence and out the gate, towards the corner where they'd tied the horses. Yasaman followed unwillingly. Linas took Bo'az aside. "We didn't expect there to be others. The girl will have to ride with one of us. There are only four horses. Are the two of you smart enough to come equipped with a blade?"

Yes. "No."

"Of course not. Well here, boy, take a dagger." Linas reached to his belt and handed Bo'az the small blade. Bo'az tucked it into his belt. Linas moved closer to Bo'az, "Now. Why is there no black line on your face? We were told that was how we would find you." Linas stomped up to Bo'az, close enough that Bo'az could smell sweet rum on his breath. He grabbed Bo'az by the scruff on his chin, pulling it forward. He inspected the full surface of Bo'az's face, from his left eye to his cheek, and the black scruffy mess that covered Bo'az's jaw, as if trying to convince himself that what he saw was real. Finally, he let go of Bo'az's jaw, slightly pushing him back. "Where is the mark, boy? Where is the god damn mark?"

Bo'az had been ruminating on what to say when he was finally asked, but still the words struggled to come out. "I…it must…it healed…I don't, I don't know what happened. I…I, over the past few weeks…it, it disappeared. I don't know how, I swear! I…I've had that scar since I was a boy…it…it's just gone." *Orijin, please protect me!*

Linas now glowered at him, anger and desperation filling his voice. "What in the light of Orijin are you talking about? It healed? Disappeared?

Impossible. What is it you thought was on your face?"

"A scar! My father told me there was a fire when I was a boy and my face was burnt, leaving that black scar. It…it must have somehow healed."

Linas continued as Gibreel, Rhadames, and Yasaman returned with the horses. "You have much to learn, boy. Your father was a fool to lie to you, and you were a fool to believe him. If this news were not so grave, I would truly be on the ground laughing. Now how do I know you're even Baltaszar? All we were told was to identify you by the Mark." Linas turned to Rhadames. "Slade, you're better with the history of all this. Can it disappear?"

"Don't know, Linas." Slade walked up and inspected Bo'az's face. "But the boy looks just like Joakwin. No question that's Kontez's boy."

Linas clenched his jaw. "Simple as that? You know for sure this is the one?"

Slade glared at Linas, "Don't question me, Nasreddine. I was chosen for this journey because I knew this boy's father. I tell you he's Joakwin's son." Slade turned to Bo'az and winked. "You have any siblings, boy?"

Bo'az understood the ploy. "No, just me."

"Good. And what is your father's name?"

"Joakwin Kontez."

Slade nodded in approval. "And what of your mother?"

"She died when I was a small boy."

"Satisfied?" Slade glanced at Linas then walked back to the horses.

Linas took Slade's response as confirmation. "Fine. But our master never once in my lifetime mentioned that it could disappear. I know not what this means for you, but it is even more urgent that we return to him. I can only hope that he will have answers."

Dammit. There's no way I can justify asking to go into the forest now. Yas will be angry. Bo'az interjected, "So then what was it on my face?"

"It's complicated Baltaszar. For now, just know that the black mark on your face isn't a…" He turned his head at the oncoming commotion, forgetting to finish his sentence.

Orange lights grew in the distance beyond the fence, licking the air like serpents, as the ground rumbled. The figures of dozens of men on horses appeared on the road leading to the farm. "They must know I'm not at home! We have to go! They'll kill all of you!" yelled Yasaman as she ran to a horse, not waiting for any of the men to help her.

Linas shouted orders, "Mount up! No time to waste!"

Bo'az raced away across the field.

"Stop! Where are you going, boy! If you dare run away now I will gladly bring you back battered and bruised!" threatened Linas.

"I'm going to get my horse! We'll be faster through the forest if there's only one rider on each! Besides, someone has to open the back gate for us to escape through!"

Linas waved them toward the farm's rear gate, which lay a few hundred yards away from the house.

Pangs of guilt flooded Bo'az as he neared the stable. He'd spent most of his childhood with these horses, and now they'd be left behind, likely killed for having been owned by his father. "Iridian, I need you, girl!" His favorite black mare neighed at hearing her name. He saddled Iridian quickly. Bo'az opened all the stable doors, and then mounted Iridian in seconds. *I hope these horses are able to run away without being hurt.* Iridian was not only his favorite, she was the fastest. "Come on girl, I need you to be faster than the wind tonight," he whispered in her ear. As he turned the horse out of the stable, he saw the men reach the farmhouse. They rode with madness in their eyes and death in their scowls.

Bo'az quickly neared the rest of his company at the high wooden gate. Rhadames had already opened it and was remounting his horse. "Ride to the forest!" Bo'az shouted. "They won't follow us in! Not very far anyway!" Bo'az knew how much fear filled the minds and hearts of Haedonians when it came to The Never. They wouldn't dare ride into the forest.

As Bo'az caught up with his companions, they all flowed through the gate and toward the shrubs and bushes that lay across the field to the east. All they had to do was maintain the gap between them and the mob until they reached the trees. "Ride as fast as you can! We're almost there!" He and Linas led, with Rhadames and Yasaman behind.

Gibreel took the rear, constantly checking the riders behind them. "They're gaining! I can't tell if we'll make it!" For the calmness of his voice, he might as well have said the grass was green.

Linas fired back, "Then make sure we make it!" He turned to glance at Gibreel, who nodded. Bo'az, curious, turned back at Gibreel, and spied him nocking an arrow in his bow. Gibreel fired, spearing the front rider and separating him from his horse. The other pursuers temporarily stopped in awe, unable to comprehend that one of their own had been killed. When they resumed their pursuit, they seemed to be riding harder and faster now.

Bo'az knew he was slowing down to watch, but couldn't help himself. Two more riders at the front fell to Gibreel's arrows, tumbling forward as their bodies entangled the horses. Bo'az could hear the snaps of limbs, even as many paces ahead as he was. He turned back around and sped up to Linas. The forest's interior was now in sight. He could see beyond the hem of the shrubbery into the trees and underbrush.

As he turned to direct the others, Bo'az saw the chaos that had unfolded because of Gibreel. A dozen more riders and horses joined the rolling tangle behind them. The others rode on, their mouths agape with savagery. Behind it all, Bo'az saw his house slowly beginning to burn. Flames encircled the house's perimeter and crawled up each side as a black cloud hovered above.

Gibreel snapped at him, "Turn around and ride to the forest, you god damn fool! We have to bring you back alive!"

Bo'az knew he couldn't argue. He dug his heel into Iridian's sides and strode toward the forest. Linas had already reached the covering of the trees, along with Rhadames and Yasaman. Gibreel kept pace with Bo'az as the two of them reached the others. "Keep going!" Bo'az ordered the rest of his company. "They're brave enough to come in to a certain point. We have to ride deep enough into the woods that we can no longer see the clearing," Bo'az and Gibreel turned to check on their pursuers. Only a few left. Most of them had stopped once they realized that Bo'az and the others weren't bluffing about going deeper into the forest. Bo'az noticed about twenty other men on horses pacing back and forth beyond the trees in the fields.

Content that the men would not continue on, Bo'az and Gibreel rode on without looking back. The other three were already thirty or forty paces ahead. Bo'az allowed Gibreel to pass him and slowed his mare to a trot. He took a deep breath, his first chance to let his guard down in what seemed like ages, though even here, he knew he wouldn't be able to completely relax. Joining these three strangers now felt strangely dangerous, although if it hadn't been for them, that mob of men surely would have killed him. And Yasaman. And it wasn't even him they were after. Still, some of their comments left him wondering how much they really wanted to help him…or actually Baltaszar. And that made it even more complicated.

They want Tasz because of the thing on his face. They don't even seem to know that Baltaszar has a brother. If I change my mind and turn back now, they'll know that something is off.

Before going into hiding with his brother, Bo'az had never been this deep into the forest before. He joked that he didn't believe in any of the stories about The Never being haunted, but he'd never actually made it a point to find out for himself. When they were young children he, Baltaszar, and some of the other boys would compete to see who could stay in the woods the longest. Baltaszar was always the one crazy and brave enough to stay the longest. He held the record among their friends for having gone the deepest and staying the longest out of all their friends. Bo'az hoped Yasaman didn't know about that. *The lies are just going to pile up.*

Bo'az commanded Iridian to speed up so he could catch the others. He could hear the horses' hooves clopping against the hard ground, though they echoed all around him. As he turned to look behind him, something violently crashed into Bo'az from the right, knocking him to the ground. He bounced and skidded off dirt, roots, and stone. He felt the blood pouring from the side of his head and ear, the burn already spreading through his head and face. His left arm snapped more than once under the weight of his body, knives of pain shooting back and forth between his hand and shoulder.

"How dare you try to steal my daughter you coward!" *Her father. Isaan Adin.*

Bo'az was too light-headed and dizzy to respond. Sharp knuckles pounded against the back of his head, repeatedly driving his face into the ground. Darkness invaded. He blinked his eyes. Each blunt smash from Isaan's fist made the world fly around even more.

"I'll kill you! How can you call yourself a man and try to steal someone's child?" Numbness invaded Bo'az's arm and crept through his body. Isaan, now hovering over him, hadn't even bothered to turn him over. He punched Bo'az in the head again and again and broke Bo'az's nose against the ground. Finally, Bo'az felt his body being rolled onto his back. His eyes glazed over and rolled about, but he unquestionably saw the surprise in Isaan's eyes when he looked upon Bo'az's face.

That's...right. Fool. No. Black. Line.

The only thought Bo'az could process was the hope that Isaan wouldn't speak his real name aloud for the others to hear. But his hopes dissipated instantly. "You are not..."

A gleam of silver sliced through Isaan's neck in a flash. Blood sprayed across Bo'az's face, mixing with his own. Isaan's head slid from his body and smashed Bo'az's chin. Even if Bo'az had been able to move on his own, Isaan's headless and lifeless body prevented him from getting up.

Darkness clouded his vision and thoughts. He could barely see Yasaman running toward him, the sound of her yelling garbled. She disappeared for a moment. Darkness. He blinked slowly. She crashed to the ground and didn't move. His eyes closed again, too heavy for him to fight back, and the darkness consumed him.

Chapter 3
The Painted One

From *The Book of Orijin*, Verse Twenty-seven
Humility in all that you do shall guide your path to Omneitria.

"JUST DO IT ALREADY, coward!" Marshall Taurean leaned against the wall of a broken-down house, bracing himself for imminent pain. He'd never pulled an arrow shaft from his own body, but having seen others do it countless times, he was sure it was better to remove it slowly. Dozens of splinters stabbed into the flesh of his shoulder. Even if he removed the shaft, there was no guarantee that it would be a clean pull. The arrows were made from a strange wood, used specifically to splinter inside the target's body.

The sun had not fully risen yet, but the longer Marshall waited, the more likely he was to sweat and heat up. The sun had been uncharacteristically overbearing, even for summer. Most days, Marshall was able to manage the heat. But then, most days Marshall did not have blood pouring from his shoulder. The last thing he needed was to black out.

He started to feel light-headed from the pain and blood loss. He was a warrior, and warriors didn't fear pain. If anyone else could see him, they would turn their backs to him in disgrace. But nobody else was around. They were likely all dead.

Marshall reminded himself that he was one of the best warriors of his people. His heavily tattooed head and body were evidence of that. He was courageous and wise. He knew he must remain that way whether or not anyone watched. Marshall's hesitation had not been solely from the pain. His mind found difficulty focusing one on thing at a time, still confused, exhausted, and overwhelmed from what had transpired over the past hour.

Marshall clenched his teeth and broke off the portion of the arrow shaft stemming from the front of his body in one quick, definitive snap. He'd had worse injuries in his life, and he realized that the pain he presently felt was not the issue. Dozens of splinters remained in his shoulder, and would shift every time he moved his arm. There would be no remedy or elixir to heal this. Someone would have to cut open his shoulder and remove them piece by piece. That was assuming he survived this siege.

Marshall still could not fathom how his village had not been prepared for this attack. Most outsiders had no idea where the Taurani village lay, deep in the northern forests of Ashur. A short tower stood at each corner of the village, where lookouts kept watch throughout the night. Even if the lookouts spotted nothing strange, intruders still had to advance through the eastern or western gate of the village. Any type of attack would result in sounding the horn atop the towers, so that those sleeping could prepare. Marshall once again had been unable to sleep, and had heard no horn calling his people to arms. If this was a full-on attack, as it seemed, the gate would have been torn off, allowing for scores to enter the village at once.

The attackers had come nearly an hour ago. They had already advanced past where Marshall sat, most likely assuming they'd killed everything in their way. Marshall knew the stories and the legends, which were the reasons his people dedicated themselves to being warriors. His people descended from Taurean, one of the original three Harbingers, humans chosen by the Orijin to lead mankind and bring it back to righteousness. They had been proclaimed as Harbingers of the Orijin, the creator of man.

But men generally did not understand the ways of Orijin. Their god was not always fair to the righteous and, based on stories and scriptures of old, Orijin provided no guarantee of anything after one met death. He had not provided even the Harbingers with much insight on the afterlife, except that one existed. Taurani assumed, based on the teachings of their priests, that as long as they believed in and prayed to Orijin, they would escape His wrath. There were rumors of a *Book of Orijin* in the cities of Ashur, but Taurani saw even the idea of it as blasphemy.

Men had generally come to fear death because of the unknown. Taurani, however, raised their children to have no fear of death. They took much pride in their ancestry, and revolved their existence around living up to the accomplishments and accolades of Taurean.

After Taurean, Cerys, and Magnus failed, Orijin anointed five new Harbingers many centuries later. These new Harbingers, Darian, Jahmash, Abram, Gideon, and Lionel, managed to instill in mankind the devotion to Orijin once more, but in the aftermath, they resorted to fighting amongst themselves. Jahmash grew mad, betrayed the rest, and was exiled from the rest of mankind; he hadn't been seen or heard from in over two thousand years. Rumors flooded the world that his return was at hand, and that everything bad that occurred in Ashur was because of Jahmash, often called "The Red Harbinger" because of his bloodlust. None claimed to have seen Jahmash, however the Taurani culture and lifestyle were meant to prepare them for his return, as the ultimate honor to Taurean and the Orijin.

Marshall hadn't heard any distinct names in the chaos of the morning. But if this battalion indeed belonged to Jahmash, then these were the days his people had waited for centuries to come.

Marshall understood that many of his people would die today, but the amount of casualties could be controlled. The Taurani were trained to find the enemy's weakness. Marshall would have to find it himself. His right arm was useless, as the arrow had pierced the bones in his shoulder. He tensed once more and pulled the remaining portion of the arrow from his back. He tasted blood in his mouth from having bitten down so strongly, but he gritted his teeth and handled the pain. He ripped his shirt in two pieces to bandage the wound and use as a sling. His arm would still move somewhat, but it was the best he could do.

This army had interloped upon them so quickly that only those Taurani who had been near the armory and watchtowers would have time to find armor and weapons. Even they could not have all fared very well.

Marshall couldn't stop to think about that now. People were dying and he couldn't help that. He had to worry about his own survival if he wanted to save anyone else. His village would receive no help from outside. Most likely, nobody outside the village would even know this was happening.

Close combat was his only chance. The soldiers were poor marksmen else he would be dead by now. But there were still hundreds of them, judging by the deluge of arrows that had flooded the skies. That had been the first wave. After the arrows killed or maimed anyone outside or near windows, the second wave of soldiers stormed the houses.

Marshall lived at the edge of his village, near one of the blacksmith's workshops. Buildings, trees, houses, and everything else had been torn down in the process of killing anyone the soldiers found. Marshall simply got lucky that he couldn't sleep during the night and was outside, behind his home when it came crashing down. His parents and two sisters, however, did not share his luck; nor did anyone in the homes around him. The soldiers never saw him because he got caught in the rubble, but he had already been struck by a stray arrow.

He had dragged himself across the common courtyard that lay behind his house and those that neighbored it. Marshall sat beneath a cluster of broken wooden planks, against the remnant of a wall, nursing his shoulder. What bothered him the most about having been shot was not that he had been injured, but that the arrow had pierced through one of the quotes in Imanol, the ancient tongue of the original Harbingers, that had been tattooed into his skin. It had been his favorite, the motto of Taurean, Cerys, and Magnus, "My life is an instrument for the good of mankind."

It was a custom of his people to cover themselves in tattoos of quotes, symbols, and markings; it was a sign of bravery. The more one was covered, the more one was respected. Marshall's body was covered head to toe by markings and words in Imanol. He had only lived for eighteen years, but aspired to dedicate his life to the benefit of his people.

The norm was to start at the face. Every Taurani wore two stripes down their faces, starting from the hairline and ending just below the chin. Taurani normally received these black tattoos when they were five or six years old.

Marshall was often called 'The Painted One' by friends and family. He was one of the most completely painted Taurani in the village and was revered for his bravery. He would need it now.

Marshall could hear the soldiers advancing, killing every Taurani they came upon. Sleeping villagers would have had little time to arm themselves. Even if any had managed to kill their attackers, this army swarmed their houses like flies to a corpse. Marshall's people were outstanding fighters, skilled with sword, spear, and in hand-to-hand combat, but the numbers were greatly against them. It was not their way to surrender.

There had to have been a traitor, someone in our village to help this happen. There is no way Taurani could have been overrun this easily, even in our sleep.

He needed to find answers. And find others. He listened to the commotion that buzzed beyond the broken down houses. Footsteps trod the dirt road and the unfamiliar language identified them as the attackers. Marshall would have to wait them out. But minutes meant more casualties to his people. He peeked out from beneath the planks that were once the floor of a house and saw the tail end of a battalion of soldiers with swords and spears passing. They paid no attention to the destruction surrounding them; sure that no one had survived their onslaught. As he readied himself for the opportunity to leave his hiding spot, he realized he was still only clad in his undergarments, a result of having left his bed in the middle of the night. He would have to find breeches somewhere. There were no clothes visible in the remains of this house.

Marshall crawled from his refuge toward the road. As he advanced, he crawled over more and more bodies. Of neighbors. Of friends.

At least my family died in the house. I could not bear to look on them.

Some of the invaders lay dead on the ground as well, but not many. The sun had risen higher and he could see plainly the vastness of the destruction. Even if enough of his people had survived, there would be no way to rebuild this place.

He would have to move slowly and stay on the ground. Marshall was well enough to walk, and had bandaged his shoulder securely enough that the blood was no longer flowing, but he could not risk standing. He crawled through heaps of splintered wood, beds, bodies, and other rubbish. He spied tatters that resembled clothes. He slithered to them and examined the pile. A pair of tan breeches slightly too big for him. They would have to do.

Crawling behind the small pile of clothes and wooden furniture shards, Marshall wrestled on the breeches with his one good arm. He wriggled back out and the dirt road became visible ahead. Every road in the village had once been lined with various types of trees, and the one that should have been standing before him now lay lifeless on the ground like so many of his people.

Footsteps. Coming fast.

Marshall flopped on the road, paying no attention to what might be in the vicinity. The footsteps grew louder. Voices. Marshall realized his left arm rested over the exposed innards of a dead body. More discomforting was that he had to keep his eyes open and unmoving as his head faced the oncoming soldiers, despite the cloud of dust, dirt, and rocks that they were kicking up. Marshall could only pray that the soldiers were more focused on where they were going than on the ground.

The soldiers were not as organized as he originally supposed, at least not in their appearance. They maintained no consistency of armor or uniform, and bore no sigil. No flags of any sort. Their skin colors and features bore no similarities to the races of Ashur. If they did fight for Jahmash, they had to have been taken from various nations and walks of life. *But which nations?* They maintained the visages of desperate soldiers. They were here to fight, kill, and destroy. They were savage, bloodthirsty. Marshall did not need to understand their tongue to know that they fought without honor or mercy. He could see them waving severed heads as they ran past. Their boots trampled. Crushed Marshall's right hand. Kicked his head. He exhaled the beginning of a groan, then stifled it immediately. One soldier stopped to find the source and Marshall held his breath. *Keep going. Keep going!* Marshall fixed his stare. The soldier yelled and shook the severed arm he carried, and then marched on.

They must still be destroying the other end of the village.

Marshall waited for several moments after they had all gone by, then looked around and immediately lifted his arm from the body next to him. His arm was covered in someone else's blood and fragments of bone and skin.

A fallen tree lay only a few dozen feet away. Marshall scampered to it and lay down within the thick branches. As excessive as the destruction was, it would actually be a boon, providing ample shelter for hiding. The elder Taurani always preached that the best warriors knew how to use their surroundings as an advantage. An injured or unarmed fighter could defeat an armed fighter in any battle if he knew how to employ his environment.

Resting within the dense brush of the dead tree, Marshall wiped his arm against the bark. It was disrespectful to disturb the dead. The only time it was allowed was when one was preparing the body for its last ceremonies. He felt shame in having those remains on his skin. As he smeared the blood away, Marshall thought he could hear a faint sound in the rubble on the other side of the road.

He poked his head over the trunk of the tree, noticing two giant heaps that had been houses earlier this morning. A figure crawled between them. It slowly grew closer and closer and Marshall could see it was one of his people, covered in Taurani markings, but also covered in blood, ash, hay, house debris, and bodily remains. The person wore leather armor. He must have come from the stable and armory that had once stood at the northern side of their village. As the figure lifted his head Marshall identified him. His cleanly shaved head bore the two customary stripes of Taurani, except his extended all the way to the back of his neck. It was Aric, one of the Tower Guards whose post was at the northeastern tower. He was also the youngest-ever Tower Guard, because of his keen eyesight and fighting ability. He was only a year younger than Marshall, but Tower Guards normally ranged between the ages of twenty-two to twenty-seven, because it was generally agreed that they needed considerable fighting and hunting experience to train their eyes.

Marshall hated him. Aric had taken a fancy to one of his sisters, Esha, and Marshall did not find Aric fit for her. Besides, Esha never shut up about the greatness of Aric and his accomplishments. Marshall was so tired of hearing about the boy being great at this and the best at that.

Marshall cast his thoughts aside. Now was not the time for petty squabbles, yet he found it difficult to let that hatred go. But he needed help and if Aric was uninjured, he could be a great asset. Marshall glimpsed Aric looking toward the tree, but hesitated to signal him. Images of Aric and Esha flooded his mind and disdain coursed through him. *Of all the Taurani to have survived, it had to be him.* Finally, Marshall allowed reason to guide him, and raised a hand over the tree trunk to catch Aric's attention. Being civil would be just as difficult, if not more so, than staying alive. The road had been empty of soldiers for several minutes, although they could be faintly heard at the other end of the village. Aric rose to his feet and, hunching over, ran to the tree. Marshall begrudgingly made room for him and attempted to mask his disappointment. "Aric, what happened?" Marshall grunted as Aric sat beside him, resting against the trunk of the fallen tree.

"I don't know, Marshall. Rufus was on duty atop the tower during the night. I was to relieve him at sunrise. I went to the stable to feed the horses, when I heard him scream like death. I ran out to see what happened and I saw him falling from the top. I wanted to help him but the arrows were never-ending and the tower was on fire. I saw them coming and ran back to the stable. Hundreds of them came from the forest, weapons in hand, destroying everything in sight. It would have been futile to stand and fight."

Aric had always spoken to him as if he assumed they were friends, as if he presumed he was accepted by the whole family. In truth he was, except by Marshall.

Coward. Marshall nodded. *But then again, I did the same thing outside my own house. Perhaps I can put aside our differences for now; then go back to hating you after we get through this.* "I understand, and I would have done the same. In fact, I essentially did the same thing, which is why I am alive." Aric's explanation did not manage to make anything clear though. "Is that all you know?"

Aric paused, confused. "I don't understand what they are doing. It's organized chaos. First they were walking up to our people. Aggressive. Talking in some strange tongue. But for some reason, they grew angry with everyone and ended up killing any Taurani they encountered"

Marshall considered this for a moment and began to understand. *How dimwitted could you be to not see this?* "They want us for something; otherwise they'd just be killing us on sight. My guess is they wanted to reach us first. And if we won't surrender, we have to die. With what you're saying, this is beginning to make some sense. Aric, it is not our custom to surrender, and you're saying that they are not killing us on sight." *Esha would be able to piece this together just as easily as I, how could she love you when she is so much smarter than you?* "Did you hear what they were actually saying?"

"Hardly. The stable was coming down and I was hiding in the hay. And even when I could hear, I could not understand them. It does not seem like they naturally speak our tongue, and when they do, it is broken and marred by their accents." Aric dusted his body off, inspecting for sources of the blood that was now caked on his leather armor and on his body.

Marshall had the beginnings of a plan. "We need to capture one of them. If they know enough of our language to question our people, then that is enough to get answers. And if you and I are both alive, there have to be others who have survived."

"And what do we do if we get our answers?" Aric retorted. "Even if others have survived, it will not be enough to mount an attack on these people. They outnumbered and overwhelmed us, despite our watchtowers and scouts. Surely you do not believe a handful of us can atone for this attack."

"If we can get answers, then we can find an opportunity. Look at our village, Aric. They destroyed almost everything we know in an hour. They knew we were not ready for this. They knew when to strike. They have been scouting us, studying us. Whether we are the only two left or there are one hundred of us, I cannot simply sit idly and live with this."

Marshall could see acceptance in Aric's expression. Aric looked at him directly in the eye. "What of Esha? I have been trying to be honest with myself, considering she is not with you, but my heart holds out for even the slightest ray of hope. Marshall is she..."

Somehow, Marshall hadn't prepared himself to answer this question. He paused for a long moment. "I am the only one of my family who survived, Aric. I heard their voices screaming as the soldiers killed them. I lay on the ground behind my home, an arrow through my shoulder, a coward for not helping them."

"Are you positive, Marshall? Maybe if we go back there and search, maybe there is a chance. Maybe..."

A figure stood before them. Marshall hadn't even seen the man walk toward them. *How did I not see him coming?*

The man glared at them, smirking. Marshall and Aric sat for moments, agape, stunned at his appearance. The man's eyes pierced into them, enveloped by blackness, making it uncomfortable to stare into them for any length of time. His complexion resembled mahogany, with a tinge of grey mixed in. He was lean, but his jaw was square. Strong. His facial features alone evoked discomfort, as his nose resembled a hawk's and his hair, black as pitch, fell in strings and waves just past his ears.

Marshall and Aric hadn't known where the man came from, as he'd made no noise, but Marshall knew the man could have killed them. He was not like the foot soldiers that had stomped past Marshall. This man had an arrogant countenance. He expected others to fear him. He was toying with Marshall and Aric, measuring, calculating. Neither Marshall nor Aric moved an inch. The man had three swords fastened to his back, two diagonal and one vertical, the hilts all gleaming in the sun.

"I will allow you both this one opportunity to surrender yourselves to me and to the services of Jahmash, The Red Harbinger," the stranger said. "If you obey, I will be fair and I will treat you like my own people: a reward for acquiescing without any complication." His smile grew wider. "If you refuse, I will not kill you right away. I will bind you and cut a piece from each of you each day as we travel. You will be healed just enough, so that you can feel and watch yourselves throughout the tedious process of death. You will be broken so far that you will beg for respite and wish you had surrendered. In the end, I shall bring you to Jahmash. He will peel the flesh from your body, one piece every day."

Marshall glanced at Aric, who was unable to gather any words as he sat staring and agape. *At least hide your fear, coward.* "It is not our custom to surrender," Marshall said. "We Taurani do not fear death. Fight us with honor, with swords, man to man. We have not wronged you in any way. What do you want with us? Who are you?" Marshall already knew he might die at some point during this invasion, so this man's ultimatum had not generated any panic within. It was worth taking the chance to challenge him.

The man's expression remained the same. A smirk on his face, his eyes piercing. "I shall give you the satisfaction of knowing who I am. After all, if your intention is to defy me, I am the man who shall usher you to your death. My name is Maqdhuum. Adl Maqdhuum. Though I have many names. I am a general of Jahmash's armies."

Adl Maqdhuum. Imanol for 'master of justice'.

The man called Maqdhuum continued. "Jahmash has not informed me of his intentions for you and your people that we capture. My advice though, would be to surrender. Look at what good it has done for the rest of your people to follow this foolish custom. I am quite familiar with your prowess and skill in fighting, but I will not agree to your lame challenge even though I am the better swordsman. Understand that even in a fair fight, I would strike you down as easily as I would a Blind Man. But I need you alive, not dead."

There is no way out of this. He has three swords. Aric had superficial cuts, bruises, and scrapes, but Marshall could only use one arm. *He could cut us to pieces.* Marshall grasped for thoughts, for something, anything. *Master your surroundings.*

He and Aric had been raised to have no fear of death, with or without any guarantees in the afterlife. But if Maqdhuum was being truthful, they would not experience death for quite a long time. Nothing entered Marshall's mind, except for emptiness and despair. He looked back up at Maqdhuum, who stood with his hand stretched back toward the pommel of one of his swords. Marshall steeled himself. *Orijin, please, there has to be something. Anything. If only they had attacked in the night. We would have been able to hide and buy time. Concentrate. That can't help now. Focus. Focus.*

Marshall closed his eyes tightly as if searching. A sensation came over his body as if his veins and blood were singing. He felt simultaneously invincible and rapturous. Marshall blinked. Then gasped. "What the…" The world went black. The sun could not have set, but it was no longer visible. Nor were any clouds in the sky. Just darkness all around. As if the light of the world had been extinguished. Like day had instantly turned to night. Yet, no stars shone in the sky.

Marshall's head swiveled from point to point, trying to pierce the darkness. Nothing. "Aric, are you there?" Marshall swung his left arm around, hoping to make contact. His hand smacked a tree trunk. *We're in the same place. Where did Aric go?* An arm wrapped around Marshall's neck from behind. Then pulled him straight back over the trunk of the tree. Marshall landed on his back, still completely blind to the world.

"What is this? What have you done, fools?" Maqdhuum barked, equally confused.

He didn't do this.

"Marshall, what's going on? Why does everything look so dim?" Aric's voice remained right at his side.

Dim? "I can't see anything!" All he knew was that the ground was still beneath him as his good hand waved around.

Aric whispered, "I can see, Marshall, I can see you! Everything has taken on a different color, like the whole world is in shades of grey." He pulled on Marshall's arm to rise. Aric's whisper grew quieter, but Marshall felt Aric's breath in his ear. "He can't find us. Keep hold of my arm. I'll lead us away to hide somewhere. Just keep pace with me."

Marshall's hatred was deflating. *Orijin, I see now why you have brought him to me. Forgive me for not understanding.* He grasped Aric's arm and kept next to him. In their wake, Maqdhuum yelled and searched for them.

Marshall ran with Aric, his hand clinging to Aric's upper arm. Marshall was lifting his knees and feet high with every stride. He had already tripped over a few bodies strewn throughout the street. The stench of blood and entrails filled the air, and only thickened as they ran on. The ground softened beneath him. *Dirt, not corpses. Now grass. We're no longer on the road.* Maqdhuum's voice could not be heard. *We're safe!*

Marshall spoke softly into the blackness. "Aric, are they still invading?"

"From what I can tell, they're burning down every house and building," Aric replied. "Strange that the fire does nothing to illuminate in this blackness."

"Where are we now?"

"At the back end of the village. Everything is broken down." Aric led him further into the darkness. "I see some of the soldiers. They're falling over each other. Most are putting down their weapons and sitting now. The darkness has stopped their advances."

Marshall trusted that Aric would stay a considerable distance away from them, even with the darkness. Aric was quite careful.

All the while that Aric led him; Marshall could feel Aric's concern. Aric genuinely cared for him and his survival, and garnered no ill will or feelings of hatred toward Marshall. *Have I been too harsh? He has only tried to help me thus far. I need to put our people and survival before my own feelings.*

Marshall found himself at ease in the dark. At first, he felt unsettled, but the darkness was the only reason they had gotten away from Maqdhuum.

"Wait here, Marshall, I'll be right back. And don't make a sound." He heard Aric flit away before he could even begin to protest. Marshall knelt down, cautiously waved his left arm around, and sat. Marshall wondered what his companion could possibly be doing.

Where has he gone? He heard someone coming near, almost next to him. "Aric, is that you? Aric?" Something thumped to the ground next to him. "Aric, is that you? Are you hurt?"

"I'm fine, Marshall. I was following your advice. The soldiers who attacked us are in a frenzy right now. They have halted their raid because of this blackness that fills the air, and know not what to do with themselves. Maqdhuum has not caught up to them yet. Because of their confusion, I thought it might help to take one soldier hostage and see if we could understand what is going on. Unfortunately, I smacked him too harshly with a broken piece of wood, so I doubt he will awake for some time." Aric's voice had descended and was now at the same level of Marshall.

"I still don't understand how you can see. It doesn't make any sense. Everything all around is blackness."

"I don't know either, Marshall, but it's not worth complaining about. It got us out of a terrible situation. Let us not question it right now. Let us get to safety, then we can worry about it."

"Indeed. But where do we go now? I cannot see or offer any help in making decisions. I shall trust your judgment."

"I am not even sure of my own judgment at this point. What do you think our ancestors were even thinking, settling a village so far into the forest and away from civilization? The closest city to us is Alvadon, where the king resides. But even that is over a day's ride, assuming we can even steal two horses. On foot we'll never make it."

"And you're supposed to be the optimist," Marshall joked.

"It's one thing to be optimistic and another to be realistic. I've hunted that far to the east numerous times. Even if we managed to get to Alvadon, the Cerysian Wall would block our path. They say the soldiers atop that wall do not allow people through, especially not Taurani. The best we can do is head south. If this darkness lasts, there will be nothing to stop an escape. Maqdhuum knows we are alive. Eventually he'll chase, but we can put a huge gap between us and him."

"Aric, we have to help what people are left." Marshall cringed at the notion of leaving his people to die.

"Marshall, you and I both know staying here means death. I know you think I'm a coward, I see it in your face every time you look at me. But this isn't about bravery and cowardice. The two of us alone cannot help everyone..." Aric's voice trailed off for a moment. "Stay quiet and do not move. He's coming this way."

"He can see?"

"Doesn't look like it. He's walking slow, trying to feel his way around."

Marshall sat, staring into emptiness, too nervous to exhale. He dared not move even a finger, just as he had lain in the street earlier. In the quiet, he could hear the man's footsteps scuff against the dirt, then crunch on the burnt grass. *Maqdhuum*. Even the man's name twisted a knot in Marshall's stomach. Marshall shuddered, and then shifted on the ground. Trying to turn, his right hand slipped and Marshall collapsed to the ground, shoulder first. Each shard of wood that impregnated his bones and muscles shifted inside him and ripped through the fibers of muscle. Marshall reached for his shoulder, his mouth wide open, as the scream formed in the base of his throat. Before it reached his mouth, a hand covered it.

"Hold it in. I know it hurts." Aric's hand pressed tightly over Marshall's mouth. Marshall nodded and Aric let go.

As quickly as it had come, the darkness disappeared like it had been sucked away by the sky. Marshall blinked repeatedly, more from disbelief than from the morning sunlight in his eyes. Looking around, he saw Aric agape once again, his face petrified. Marshall turned his head. Maqdhuum stood in their line of sight. All the man had to do was turn his head and they would be seen. They scurried behind a hill of destroyed houses.

Aric barked at him, "Quickly, is your shoulder well enough that you can carry our captive?"

"If I had to, yes." Marshall would suffer through the pain if he had to. Especially if it meant escaping. *But why would Aric make me carry the soldier when he himself hasn't been hurt?*

"Take his body and run to the forest. As fast as you can. You know how to use your surroundings better than I do. I will cover your escape, but you need to get out of here now." Aric was not asking him.

"What are you talking about? Let's go, Aric. We can get to the forest if we stay low. He hasn't seen us yet; if we move now we might have a chance. Don't be a martyr, thinking you have to sacrifice yourself."

"Stop lying to yourself, Marshall, you know this is the only way. You may be older than I am, but I am ordering you to go now. Esha is dead. I have nothing now. Allow me to do at least this much. I couldn't save her, but at least I can save you. Stay low and run south. You can make it!" With that, Aric arose and revealed his presence. There would be no way to convince him now.

Marshall heaved the captured soldier onto his back, hunched over, and ran through the piles of broken houses. Behind him he could hear Aric yelling to Maqdhuum. He tried his best to clear his mind and run without listening. The weight of the soldier proved a greater burden than he anticipated. *How long can I keep this up?*

Marshall ran through piles and piles of destruction and could see no end to it. He was not going to make it out of the village. He knew that now. The soldier's weight deadened his shoulder, and the guilt of leaving Aric behind increased that burden one hundredfold. Something grasped his ankle from the ground, making him stumble. The man on his back crashed down on him, leaving Marshall vulnerable on the ground.

Marshall rolled the soldier's body from his back, but his movement was limited. He could no longer move his right arm or shoulder. Marshall scanned the area around where he landed; trying to discern what had caused his fall. He lay next to an enormous heap that had once been a house. At his feet, a flap opened up from the grass and two eyes peered through the darkness between the flap of grass and the ground. *What is this?* From the darkness in the ground, a hand beckoned and waved Marshall toward it.

A voice whispered, "Marshall...Marshall down here!"

They know my name. He whispered back, as softly as the wind, "Who is that?" Marshall knew it had to be a friend, but he was still cautious.

"It's Myron! I'm with a few others down here beneath the house. Come inside and I'll explain; it is not safe out there!" Myron Taurean, two years Marshall's junior, waved and beckoned furiously for Marshall to follow him.

Aric! If Myron has found refuge, I can go back for him! He does not have to sacrifice himself! "Myron! Aric and I have a prisoner, take him first. He will not rouse for some time. But keep watch on him. If he awakens, do not kill him, we need him for questioning. I have to go back to get Aric. Do you have any weapons down there?" Marshall used all of his strength to shove the soldier over to the open flap of grass with his left arm. Myron, although younger, was nearly a foot taller than Marshall and heftier as well. He pulled in the captive with ease, relayed the orders to the others in the hideout, and then turned back to Marshall.

"We only managed to arm ourselves with swords, nothing else. They are not even our best blades."

"It will have to do. Aric is out there alone fighting the general of this army. I must go back for him. Give me the best blade you have."

Myron slid a blade from beneath the grass toward Marshall. Gingerly hoisting himself to his knees, Marshall grasped the sword and stood up. He would have to fight using his left hand, putting him at a disadvantage. He'd sparred with both hands numerous times, but his skill with his left paled in comparison to his right. It would have to do. Marshall scampered away toward where Aric had run off.

"I'm coming with you. Who knows what you may face out here, and three to one stands a better chance than two to one." Myron had already equipped himself with a new blade and followed Marshall closely.

"You do not have to defend your actions, my friend. Your help will be needed. We can only hope that Aric is still fighting him." They ran, hunched over to hide from the army that still lingered in the distance. The soldiers stormed the remaining homes and buildings, including the southeastern tower and armory.

Marshall saw some of his people fighting back. Perhaps they'd gathered in large groups to counteract the overwhelming numbers of the enemy. The small Taurani uprising averted any focus on Marshall's direction. He and Myron rushed on. Two figures appeared at the edge of the destruction, beyond the collapsed houses. However, one lay on the ground while the other stood over him. Marshall only needed one guess to determine who was standing.

They slowed upon getting close. Maqdhuum stood over Aric, a foot on his chest, but he was speaking to Aric and his sword was not in a ready position. Marshall remembered that Maqdhuum had no plans of killing them, which was why Aric still lived. Aric's sword lay a dozen feet away from him and his arm clutched his side.

Myron jetted toward Maqdhuum and jumped toward his back. He positioned his sword to slice right through the back of Maqdhuum's neck. However, while Myron hung in the air, mid-jump, Maqdhuum spun and slashed at Myron's sword, knocking it away. The momentum of Maqdhuum's blow caused Myron to stumble and trip as he landed, which left him on his hands and knees. Myron's position allowed Maqdhuum to attack again as he stalked toward him. Marshall charged ahead, but was too far away to head off Maqdhuum's attack. Maqdhuum's blade swooped down at Myron, who managed to roll away, but not before Maqdhuum had sliced through the flesh of his calf. Marshall slowed, nearing Maqdhuum cautiously. He would have to be smart and patient, fighting injured and with his left hand.

Maqdhuum turned to face him, the arrogant smile still on his face. Despite being equipped with three swords, the man only fought with one. He knew he was better and he wanted them to know that as well. Behind Maqdhuum, Marshall noticed Aric rising to his feet and running to retrieve his sword. Myron also slowly stood and armed himself, limping noticeably. Patience would be the key.

Marshall knew all three of them would have to work together in this fight, he only hoped that Aric and Myron came to the same realization. They had Maqdhuum surrounded now, each of them in a ready stance, calculating, waiting for the ideal moment to attack. Despite the fact that he was outnumbered, the man remained unfazed. He hadn't even turned to acknowledge the other two, still facing Marshall and staring him in the eyes. *Mother, Father, Esha, Gia. Even if he didn't kill them all himself, he is responsible.* Inspecting Maqdhuum's armor, Marshall realized that all the man wore was a dark leather breastplate, not metal, likely because of the number of scabbards attached to his back. But aside from that, he'd only protected himself with steel vambraces for his forearms and not even gauntlets. *He must be arrogant to ride into battle this way.*

The sun had escalated; the day grew hotter. Marshall now considered that Maqdhuum was perhaps wise to forego full armor, as the day's heat would sap any fully clad knight or soldier of all his energy. "Do not think for a moment that I will not kill you," Maqdhuum said. "We did not come to take all of your people. Those of you too stubborn and strong-willed are not suited to our needs and are better off dead."

Mother, Father, Gia...little innocent Gia, she had reached barely over seven years. He will not kill me today. "Then let our dance begin, craven." Anger fueled his words, but Marshall remained wary about letting it guide his movements. Around him in the distance, he spotted scores of small fires emerging throughout the village. *They are burning everything, making sure no one survives.*

"Craven? You would call me craven, yet three of you fight me at once?"

"You are craven for sacking our village in our sleep. For destroying a people who had committed no disservice to you. For that you are a coward. We fight in numbers because we take nothing for granted."

"Very well then. If I am the coward, then come strike me down. Give me a coward's death, skinshite."

Skinshite. Marshall had reached his threshold, and he noticed Aric and Myron equally as angry. Outsiders did not call Taurani "skinshite" to their faces. At least not in ages. It was an old insult from those who had spurned the Taurani generations ago for their inked skin and for their devotion to

Taurean.

Marshall engaged him now, gauging his own reach as well as Maqdhuum's. Aric and Myron maintained distance. Too many swordsmen in such a tight space would lead them to unintentionally harm each other. Aric wore full leather armor and an iron helmet. Hopefully it would not make him tire quickly.

Marshall studied Maqdhuum's movements, but the man's eyes were still fixated on his own. Marshall swung, aiming for the leg first, but the man quickly deflected the blow and spun his sword for an attack at Marshall's head. Marshall dodged the counterattack, bending backwards. Marshall feigned another attack but provoked no reaction. He tried to signal Myron, who stood behind Maqdhuum to the right, with his eyes. Myron read the signal and gingerly stalked in. His calf was a slab of red flesh hanging from the leg. As Myron neared, Marshall spun his blade, hoping to distract his adversary. Maqdhuum twisted in a flash and sliced at Myron's leather chestplate, cutting it down the middle and leaving Myron with a gash down his chest. Myron grunted loudly, trying his best to be a man, a warrior. All the while, the foe had drawn a second sword from his back and held it ready. Myron had fallen on his back from the blow, but Maqdhuum knew better than to turn away from the other attackers for a killing stroke on the wounded boy.

He is better trained with a blade. Can we really defeat him? Marshall's doubt lasted only a heartbeat. *Mother, Father, Esha, Gia.*

Marshall and Aric positioned themselves on each side of the man. Aric took the lead, applying a storm of strikes and swoops, his blade flashing through the air. Aric swung high and low at a feverish pace, despite his full armor. Sweat poured from his face and neck. His arms slowed. Maqdhuum parried all of Aric's attempts and Marshall knew this would be his opportunity. Maqdhuum and Aric sparred back and forth, steel clanging upon steel. Marshall swooped in and raised his sword for a killing blow. He meant to separate Maqdhuum's head and body. Marshall spun to his right and slashed his blade backhanded at the back of Maqdhuum's neck.

Maqdhuum had seen it coming. *How could he have known?* Marshall witnessed it in such detail, as if it the moment was an hour long. His blade glided through the air for its target. Maqdhuum swooped his blade behind Aric's legs and swept him to the ground. He ducked in the process and turned to drive his other sword through Marshall's unprotected torso. The metal sliced through flesh, then his insides, and then through more flesh as it tore out of Marshall's back. He could not distinguish between the cold of the blade and the cold of life leaving his body. Marshall fell for minutes. Hours. Ages. The shock struck him more than the pain. As his body bounced against the dirt, sending clouds up around him, he prayed for the process to be quick. Marshall made a feeble attempt to pull out the blade as his eyes lolled about and his mouth filled with blood. He was broken. He had failed.

His vision blurred. The last thing Marshall Taurean saw was the craven standing over him, removing the blade from his near lifeless body, a smile on the man's face. *Mother, Father, Eshhhhh...* and then there was nothing.

***

"It seems as if every mound was once on fire, judging by the char and ashes, Maven Savaiyon, but a few still linger." Adria Varela had been brought mainly because of her ability to listen, to hear things that no other men or women could. That was her manifestation. Her gift as a descendant of Darian. She was almost equally adept at noticing the smallest of details. Things that most others tended to miss.

"I would say we missed the battle by not more than a day or two." She took pride in her talents, especially because she stood barely five feet tall and her slight frame made her look no older than twelve years, despite the fact that she'd already reached nineteen. Her eyes sat like twin moons on her face, bright and blue, which only made her look younger. Her nose was thin and meek, and her lips dark rather than bright, which, paired with her olive skin, made her beautiful, at least according to people in Markos. Her hair, dark like Galicean coffee, extended past her shoulders and enhanced her beauty. However, people tended to see a child rather than a beautiful young woman. She had resigned herself to the notion that she would always be perceived as a child. Perhaps in her old age, others would finally be jealous of her.

"Precisely my thinking, Mouse." Maven Savaiyon had given her that nickname two years ago, a few months after meeting her. It was not meant as a slight against her, though, more so because she was small, clever, elusive, and a nuisance to anyone who underestimated her. Maven Savaiyon was very protective of her at the House of Darian, especially around the boys, many of whom had been seen with mysterious bruises after teasing her or bullying her. He continued, "But, I have seen the aftermath of battle with Drahkunov. This is not his work. Do you understand why?"

Adria knew the answer. "Their bodies are dismembered in multiple places. Legs, arms, heads. It is excessive, unnecessary. Drahkunov battles with honor. These dead soldiers would have been left alone. Even their armor has been ripped apart."

"Good." Maven Savaiyon slightly grinned. He stood nearly seven feet tall. His skin was the tone of chestnuts and he fashioned his black hair in the Shivaani style, shaved almost to the skin but not quite so close. They all bore the mark of the Descendants: Adria, Savaiyon, and Lincan, who walked around nearby inspecting the village. The marks on their faces would make them easily identifiable to any survivors.

"Should the Taurani have been able to defeat Drahkunov?" Adria grew curious.

Surveying his surroundings, Savaiyon responded, "Given their beliefs and stubbornness, I doubt they would have. The Taurani pride themselves in their fighting prowess, yet limit themselves because of a stupid misinterpretation of the Orijin. They hide their Descendants' Marks by covering their bodies. They believe that, because Taurean himself stopped using his manifestation, they should not use theirs either. The Taurani never use their manifestations, and most do not even know they have any ability anymore. Imagine. A warrior culture that robs itself of its greatest weapon."

"So they prepared all this time for nothing then."

"Indeed. And it seems Jahmash has a new general. A very deadly one. Drahkunov was likely not sent *because* he had honor. This attack was meant to be embarrassing, it was meant to mock the Taurani. We can only hope that the king is not moved to act rashly by it. He normally does not need an excuse to make hasty decisions. Then again, who knows if he would receive any word of it."

Lincan finally spoke from one of the ashen piles. "There is nothing but death here. Do you hear anything, Adria? If not, let us leave. I dislike the feel of this place." Lincan was the youngest of their search party, at seventeen. He had only come to the House a few months ago, but his understanding of healing was intricate. He was right, though, they were here for a reason. Adria must concentrate if she would hear any hints of life.

"Both of you be silent then. Let me concentrate." She focused her mind on nothing, closing her eyes to focus, ridding herself of emotion. Her manifestation filled her veins with the sweet intoxicating melody. She knew what she was listening for. Life. Breathing. Heartbeats. Sounds boomed in her ears. She had to concentrate on the correct ones. Adria focused past the nearby insects and birds, past the breeze that rustled trees and grass. *The ground. I must search the ground for vibrations.* She sat, letting her ears grasp for any trembles or vibrations. Nothing. Adria reached farther. In two separate directions, she felt two heartbeats, one faint, one strong. "There are two!" Her voice squeaked with excitement. "I felt one heartbeat echo through the ground! It must be coming from under one of these massive piles! The other was the faintest of breath, like a whisper, but the heart is strong."

Savaiyon cut in, "Let us retrieve the one underneath first. He or she may have less time and more injuries if trapped beneath a house. Where did you locate the heartbeat, Mouse?"

"I felt it nearby. I will focus on it. Follow me." Adria enjoyed giving the orders and instructions. She felt a sort of irony commanding others, given the common perception of her.

She walked slowly on, fixated on the echoes and reverberations of the heartbeat. After walking northeast for a few minutes, Adria found her target. "Here. Beneath this pile."

Lincan observed the crumbled and blackened house. "If anyone survives beneath this rubble, they will need to be patient. It will take hours, if not a day, to move all of this away."

"That is why it is important to pay attention to everything, Lincan. While you remove the pile, piece by piece, I will walk into this hole in the ground." Savaiyon pointed to a small crater, exposed by an overturned flap of grass that was surely meant to cover a hiding spot. "You two stay here; I shall see where this leads. You are certain that the survivor lies beneath?" Maven Savaiyon dropped down into the ground.

"I have no doubts," Adria replied. Since they'd arrived in midday, enough light penetrated into the underground retreat that Savaiyon needed no torch. Given this heat, he may not have lit one even in darkness. Adria heard him below, moving around. Things were being thrown about.

Even without using enhanced hearing, Adria heard Maven Savaiyon groaning as he moved things.

A heap of flesh plopped up by the hole in the ground. Maven Savaiyon emerged after. "His legs were crushed beneath a massive wooden beam. If the heat hadn't already driven me to it, I would be sweating now from the weight of the thing. There was a whole room down there; it must have been a hiding place beneath the house. This man is no Taurani. I do not even know where he is from, but he has none of the Taurani markings. Most likely a soldier." The man was unconscious. One leg dangled from tendons and sinews, a chunk of meat missing.

Adria knew Lincan would struggle in fixing the man.

"Lincan. You are not to heal this man to full recovery," Maven Savaiyon ordered. "There were three dead Taurani down there with him, most likely guarding him like a prisoner. Close his wounds but do not mend his bones. That should be enough to ensure his survival until we return to the House."

Lincan gripped his hands to the soldier's legs and closed his eyes. Adria always found Lincan's healing manifestation impressive. The soldier's muscles and tendons reformed. The skin slowly reconnected. Lincan left the shin bones broken, just as Maven Savaiyon had instructed. Once finished, Lincan sat for several minutes to catch his breath and rest. He and Maven Savaiyon then carried the soldier as Adria led them through the burnt grass to find the second survivor.

They came upon the dirt road again and found a single man lying upon the ground. On second look, he was barely a man, of an age with Adria. He wore barely any clothes, which were shredded anyway, and his stomach had been sliced through. Blood caked his body everywhere: his stomach and chest, left hand, mouth, and the ground beneath him. Adria noticed entrails through the sliced abdomen and looked away.

Adria had not seen much of battle or death in her nineteen years, but she knew that people did not live through injuries such as this. "I do not understand why he breathes. He has likely been lying here like this for at least a day. By now, his body should be drained of blood, and his heart and lungs should have stopped. Yet he breathes, and I can discern a heartbeat.

Enlighten me, Maven Savaiyon; I am not clever enough for this riddle."

"I am equally as baffled, Mouse. I have never seen the likes of it. It cannot be a self-healing manifestation. His wounds would be repairing themselves. Lincan, have you any theories?"

Lincan scratched his short black hair loudly, a habit he'd come to be known for when confused. "I have no answers. Perhaps if I have more time to study him in a more apt setting, I might shed some light on the source."

"Wrap his abdomen with what is left of his clothes. Then lift him to his feet and brace him, Lincan. I shall prepare us a bridge back to the House." Maven Savaiyon's manifestation was the ability to travel anywhere by creating 'bridges' in the air. In traveling this way though, he was also limited to traveling to places he'd been before, as he'd had to be able to picture his destination before creating a bridge to it. Adria also loved watching this manifestation.

After wrapping the abdomen tightly, Lincan lifted the tattooed Taurani up by the arms and dragged him while Savaiyon lifted the soldier. "Are we ready then?" Savaiyon's bridge was ready. A rectangle of bright yellow light floating before them, like a doorway to another room.

A hint of a realization pulled at Adria's mind. "Hmm...that's odd."

"What's that?" Lincan looked back at her, puzzled.

She was sure now, having had the time to fully observe. "The Taurani you're carrying, Lincan. He has no shadow."

CHAPTER 4
THE VOICE

From *The Book of Orijin*, Verse Two Hundred Ninety-one
O Chosen Ones,
We have shared Our essence with each of you,
That shall manifest in your bodies and souls in ways special to each of you.
It is with these manifestations that you shall cure the world of the wickedness
of Mankind.

BALTASZAR HAD MEMORIZED the conversation word for word. It was difficult not to. He'd replayed it in his mind several times a day in the past weeks and more often these past few days.

Yasaman had spoken softly, trembling and fighting back tears, "I...I just can't continue to do this." She lay beside him in the narrow bed, clutching his hand to the point of numbness and staring straight up to the ceiling. "I...I can't continue lying to my father. And the longer we keep this going, the more likely it is that he'll find out."

He hadn't seen it coming. Yasaman had loved Baltaszar's company and found ways for them to be together despite her father. More often, it was she who had derived schemes for their clandestine meetings. Baltaszar had grown used to sneaking over to her house in the middle of the night, once her parents had fallen asleep. This made no sense. "I don't understand. I thought you were happy. I thought we were happy. You said this is what you wanted. You said you loved me. You've done so many things to make sure we could see each other. Why is it all of a sudden not worth it?"

"I do love you, but..."

"If you love me, we would not be having this conversation." Baltaszar hadn't been angry, which surprised him, but remembered being confused. Her words had been hammers pounding into his head, and causing an ache that prevented him from thinking clearly.

"I love you, but I love my father as well, Baltaszar. And I cannot do this to him."

"Then why not simply tell him about me? What would be so wrong with that?"

Yasaman turned to face him, streams of tears flooding her pillow. "You know how he feels about your father. If I was sneaking around with any boy, he would lock me in this room for ten years. Imagine what he would do if he found out it was with the son of the man he wants to see dead." Tears had turned her face from a light brown complexion to splotchy red.

The candle on her night stand had almost reached its base, the wax barely visible between the flame and metal holder. Baltaszar had understood that his ability to argue had also waned, along with the light. "He does not have to be happy with it, I know, but is it not worth a chance?" he pleaded. "For all that we have been through, you would actually give up now?"

"Baltaszar, it is what I need to do. I'm not saying it is what I want, but it is what's best. For everyone."

"This is not what is best for me!" He fell just short of shouting at her. Yasaman's parents' bedroom was at the other end of the house, but many things could be heard in the quiet of night.

"I am not saying that this has to be the end, I just..."

"How could it not be? What will make everything different all of a sudden? Your father will always want to choose your husband and he will always hate my father, unless you stand up to him!"

"Maybe if we just hold off until things calm down, until after..."

"After my father dies? Is that what you want to say?" Baltaszar growled. Yasaman's mouth twitched and contorted at his words, displaying more sorrow than her glistening eyes. Baltaszar hadn't been entirely sure if that was what she had wanted to say next, but he knew it was what she meant and anger infiltrated his veins. "If that is what you think will make your father accept me, then there is nothing more for us." As angered and devastated as he was, Baltaszar briefly reconsidered leaving her. Since he'd met Yasaman, he was sure that she would one day be his wife.

Baltaszar could no longer look at her, though. The only thing left was to leave. He still remembered leaving through Yasaman's window that night. He'd left her crying in bed, her blotchy red face buried in her pillows, and Baltaszar did not look back for the duration of his return home.

That was over a month ago. Why is it still so difficult to accept? The slope of the mountain had reduced markedly as the ground grew more and more even. *I have been so lost in my thoughts that I haven't even noticed I'm almost out of the forest. But why does the thought of her still bother me so much? Was it me who was being selfish? Was our relationship so cumbersome for her that that was really the only way out of it?*

Do we not have more important things to consider?

Baltaszar had not heard that voice since he made the decision to leave Haedon. *Stop talking to me.* The mountain was now behind him and the ground no longer rocky. Towering green pine trees still surrounded him, but Baltaszar recognized that the edge of the forest could not be far off.

You have no one left, wouldn't you like some company?

Leave me alone.

Your mother is gone, your father, the girl, and now your brother. All you have is me.

Stop. Get out of my head! He'd already believed he was crazy because of the voice, but what angered Baltaszar even more was that he finally realized it was identical to his own voice.

Why do you dislike me so much? I could be a great help…

"I said TO BLOODY LEAVE ME ALONE!" A few birds cawed and hastily fluttered away. After surveying his surroundings, nothing else seemed disturbed by his outburst. "Please, just leave me alone. I have enough problems without you." Baltaszar stopped walking and tensed, hoping his request was enough to quiet the voice, at least for now. He doubted it would ever leave him for good.

Baltaszar continued walking. He quietly hummed a song, "Bales in the Summer," an old farmer's tune his father had taught him, hoping to stifle any more of the voice's attempts to speak to him. As the gargantuan pines around him slowly thinned, thoughts of Yasaman grew more frequent and heavy. *Why do I keep dwelling on you? I'd rather think of father.*

You continue to dwell on her because she is still alive. There is nothing to do about your father.

Baltaszar sighed, exhaled heavily, and drooped his shoulders. *If you will not listen to my requests to leave me alone, then at least answer one question for me. If you grant me an honest answer, I will at least try to entertain a conversation with you.*

No.

No, what? Do you not agree to the terms?

The terms are agreeable. No, you are not crazy, Baltaszar. Was that not your question?

Then why are you in…

What bothers you so much about me is that my voice is the same as yours. That is why you refuse to accept me.

That is part of it, yes. But I would also like to be able to think to myself without being interrupted, without knowing someone else is listening. You are saying that I am not crazy to have another voice in my head, but it shall drive me insane to know that my thoughts cannot be private.

It is something you will have to grow accustomed to, Baltaszar. I have no intention of leaving you.

But who ARE you?

I am a friend if you will trust in me. A guide if you will follow me. A light if you will open your eyes to me.

But if I am not crazy, then why are you in my head? I do not understand what you are.

To explain what I am at this juncture would be beyond your comprehension. You would be terrified of me and you would cease to

speak to me. It would be beyond the comprehension of most people, to be honest. There are some secrets in this world that people are not ready to accept. You are not ready to hear or see just yet. But I have been in your head longer than you know. Go to the House of Darian first. Once you have read His word and understand your manifestation, then enlightenment will come.

Then why only speak now? And what manifestation?

Because now is when you need guidance. You will learn of your manifestation there, unless it becomes clear before then.

And I should just trust you then? It was YOU who told me to risk my life to save my father. Why give me guidance if you would have me killed as soon as you appear?

Are you certain that you would have died? Do you know this for a fact?

Everyone in Haedon wants me and Bo'az dead. They would have hanged me along with my father if I had tried something. Besides, why would I trust you? That you are in my mind, does not make you trustworthy.

And how did you know it was not YOU who had those thoughts? Are our voices not the same? How is it you can tell the difference between your thoughts and my voice?

Because I know what I believe and who I am. I have lived for eighteen years; I know what it is to create a thought!

You do not know a damned thing, Baltaszar Kontez. Nothing of your mind and nothing of this world. Rhadames Slade tried to guide you, but deep down, you still doubt his words as well.

"I left Haedon! Is that not enough? Curse you; I thought you wanted to help me! Why can you not just be direct with me? Answer a question without some stupid riddle? If you are going to act like this, then let me be!"

Baltaszar jumped at the volume of his own shouts. The voice bothered him. Put him on edge physically and mentally. Snapping back to reality, Baltaszar discerned the sun descending and the sky's pink and purple response to it. He had been walking for longer than he realized, too caught up in a conversation he wasn't even sure was real.

Very well. Do this yourself. It is obvious you would not listen to me anyway.

By the light of Orijin! Thank you!

With that, Baltaszar stopped at a trio of trees that formed a triangle around him. Numerous grey boulders lay stationed around the trees, providing suitable coverage if he refrained from standing. Baltaszar removed his pack and fished out a loaf of bread. It had grown stale and hard, but he did not find any mold upon inspection. He would just have to break off smaller pieces and drink plenty of water. But even the waterskin was nearly empty. Baltaszar inspected what food remained: only a handful of dried beef strips. He would have to make it to the town that Slade had mentioned by the end of the next day if he didn't want to starve. *I'll have to wake up early and take very few breaks.* Baltaszar tensed, expecting a response from the stranger in his head.

The ground beneath him was lush with long grass, and very soft. Baltaszar reclined, propped up on one hand while nibbling on the hard bread. The conversation with the voice made him forget about his thoughts and regrets toward Yasaman, and peaked his insecurity instead.

Baltaszar questioned his decision to leave and fought himself about turning back. Whether it was for Yasaman or his father's corpse, or for Bo'az and the house and farm he'd grown so comfortable with, he could not tell. From the time he had even begun to have memories, it was his father who'd guided Baltaszar in everything: riding horses, growing crops, devotion to the Orijin and religion, fixing and building things around the house, even general education. Baltaszar never had the opportunity to know his mother, and his relationship with Bo'az had become strained since their father's sentencing. Baltaszar understood he no longer really had any family. The more he thought on it, the more he regretted allowing Bo'az to leave. Now more than ever they'd needed to stay together. Perhaps that was just another reason for his desire to turn back.

What am I doing? He had known for weeks that his father would die, but that knowledge did nothing to soften the blow. In truth, if not for Slade, Baltaszar may have turned back with Bo'az. But Slade knew too many things that he shouldn't have known, especially about the voice. It was too new for anyone else to have known. *Slade could have fought me right there in Haedon Square and hurt or killed me. Slade could also have alarmed other people in the town, but he did none of that.* It seemed excessive that a man would make up so much nonsense in the middle of the night, simply to lead Baltaszar astray.

Baltaszar constantly ruminated over the conversation and always came to the same conclusion. Despite his reluctance to admit the voice in his head was right, he had nothing to lose by listening to Slade. If he'd gone back to Haedon, he'd either have been killed or exiled. And as painful as the thought was, Baltaszar had nobody now. No friends or family. No one to worry about him. No one to be concerned if anything happened to him.

So you finally agree.

Shut up.

At times, the same thoughts also guided him down a darker path. In the few days of walking through the forest, Baltaszar had allowed himself to entertain certain possibilities. *What if I just died? What difference would that make to anyone at this point?* He was unsure whether that question was directed to himself or to the voice. Either way, Baltaszar got no answer.

Too often, he would focus so much on the notion that he no longer had anyone, and considered whether there remained anything worthwhile for which to live. *My life. My world. It all seems so complicated now.* Despite all his thinking, Baltaszar could never quite swallow everything that had happened. Had he been able to stay in Haedon and look after the farm, perhaps he would at least have a purpose. But all that remained was the advice of a man he didn't know and with whom he'd spoken for less than an hour. Indeed, there were dozens of questions that he wanted answers to, and to die now would do nothing to justify his father's death.

But in truth, Baltaszar questioned whether he truly had the capacity to undertake the type of journey that Slade asked of him. He had always believed himself to be brave, but he realized more and more that he could scarcely remember many times throughout his life in which he had acted bravely. His father had taught him that killing oneself was against the laws of the Orijin, and a coward's actions at that. *But what has the Orijin truly given me in this life to make it worthwhile? How much worse would it be to defy Him now?*

Unable, or perhaps unwilling, to make a decision on the matter, Baltaszar lay back and closed his eyes. The day's events left him physically, mentally, and emotionally exhausted. As his consciousness melted away into dreams, he came to one conclusion. *If the opportunity presents itself, I'll go through with it. But I won't go out of my way.* The word 'fool' whispered in his head.

***

The following morning, Baltaszar awoke while the sun barely glanced over the tree-littered horizon. He had trained himself to wake just before sunrise when he was fifteen. Back then, he would sneak over to Elmer Guff's farm and steal the best apples, figs, and grapes, and bring them back to his yard before any light interloped the sky.

Baltaszar arose, stretched off the stiffness of sleep, and slung the packs to his shoulders once more. He planned to refrain from eating for as long as his stomach could hold out, and rely only on water. He walked on, surprisingly calm and clear-minded; and best of all, after walking for four hours, the voice had not spoken once.

This was his third day trekking through the forest, and Baltaszar finally stepped out into the world beyond the Never. Beyond the forest lay grassland with trees interspersed here and there. The sun grew warmer the further he walked, but he felt comfort in keeping the black cloak on. Slade had told him that it would be just over an hour's ride to the city of Vandenar once he reached the edge of the forest, but Baltaszar was unfortunately without a horse. That long on horseback meant almost a day on foot.

Thus far, the journey had been relatively easy. The only difficult part had been when the sky had gone pitch black two days before. The darkness had lasted over a quarter of an hour and all Baltaszar could do was set down until the light returned. He admitted to himself that he'd felt some fear, but mostly because any predator could have hunted him down too easily.

Baltaszar could only hope it would not happen again.

Baltaszar walked faster, excited at the prospect of a town, food, and most importantly, a bed. After an hour, the trees had completely thinned out around him and a river appeared on the horizon. *Slade, how could you fail to mention a river? How am I supposed to cross this blasted thing?* In Haedon, Baltaszar had never accompanied the fishermen down the mountain to the shores. This was the first time he'd come so close to a body of water. He stepped to the moistened dirt at the edge of the river and kneeled for a closer inspection. He expected the water to be blue and clear, beautiful as it had been described by the fishermen of Haedon. This water, however, was a cloudy brown, which he guessed was from the dirt at the bottom. It cooled his fingers as he dangled them in, so Baltaszar scooped the water in his hands and drank.

What am I going to do? I can't even swim. And even if I could, how am I supposed to carry all of this across the water? Hope escaped him. How much more was he supposed to do? There was no way to cross the river. Baltaszar already knew that he would not walk along the bank to find a crossing, as there was none in sight and he lacked the physical and mental energy to search for a way.

Thoughts flooded his mind again. *Father. Yasaman. Bo'az. Haedon. Slade. Those bloody dreams.* The thoughts repeated continuously, faster and faster. A rumble formed deep down in his belly and it grew stronger and stronger as it reached his mouth.

"RRRAAAAAAAAAAAAAHHHHHHHHHHHHHHHH!" Baltaszar roared again and again, surrendering to the catharsis until a burning rawness plagued his throat.

He lay back and closed his eyes. *Should I do it? Is this the opportunity presenting itself? Can I actually go through with this?* Hours had passed when Baltaszar arose from the ground; the sun had already begun its descent, and the weight in his mind remained just as overbearing. He was not ready to die yet. And regardless of everything else, Bo'az was hopefully still alive. If not in Haedon, then somewhere else. As long as he had his brother, Baltaszar would continue on.

Tiny objects dotted the water's surface in the distance. *Boats! They must be boats! Yes!* Baltaszar doubted they would see him this far away. He had never even walked in the water, aside from puddles here and there. *Now is not the time to be a coward. I need to cross this damn thing, and I need to cross it now.*

Baltaszar took one tentative step in, the cloudy water immediately soaking his leather boot and filling it. Another step. The water chilled both of his feet more than he would have liked, but it was a minor nuisance. He continued. At first too quickly. He slipped and jerked about to regain balance. After several feet, Baltaszar learned his lesson and slowed his pace, testing every step. The water level rose higher up his body, reaching his waist. His cloak clung to him. His steps became half steps. He waved his arms wildly and shouted. "Hey! Over here! Help me!" again and again. "Help! Over here!"

After yelling and flailing his arms for a few minutes, a nearby boat turned its bow toward him. *They turned! They can see me!* The boat slowly drew nearer. *Well, like I told Bo'az, this could work out good or bad. Hopefully Slade was right and this thing on my face will help.* The small boat continued toward him.

Baltaszar stopped yelling and stood in place. His cloak still clung to his legs. *Why is it tighter than before? I haven't even moved.* Baltaszar reached down to pull the cloak away from his body. He felt for the clinging fabric. *That...that's not my cloak.* Two long teeth stabbed into his hand, slicing through to the bone. Baltaszar pulled his hand out of the water. *A snake? A snake!* The serpent's head still clung to his blood-soaked hand, unable to pull its teeth out. Baltaszar staggered. *Must...think. Must...pull...out.* He snatched the snake by the neck and pulled. It writhed wildly in his hand, whipping its tail against his body. *Too weak.* With his remaining strength, Baltaszar yanked at the snake. Its scaly body burst into flames. The head ripped away from his hand, the fangs still in him. The snake's lifeless body turned to ash and crumbled in his grip.

How? Father? No. I don't...under...stand. The boat was less than a hundred yards away. Baltaszar took one step toward it. His foot, which he could no longer feel, gave out beneath him and Baltaszar crashed face first into the water. By the time he had sunk to the riverbed, Baltaszar could no longer feel the rest of his body.

CHAPTER 5
THE PRINCE

From *The Book of Orijin*, **Verse Ten**

It is in your nature, Mankind, to create,
destroy, pervert, and explore truth.
Know that the only truth is in Our word.

PRINCE GARRISON BRIGHTON HAD SOUGHT truth for the past year of his life. Truth about the Orijin and His followers. About life. About his father, King Edmund, and his father's decrees for the world, especially the decree that required Garrison to travel through Ashur and hunt down Descendants—people marked with black lines down their left eyes. But the truth was that Garrison was one of those same Descendants bearing a black line on his face.

There had been too many things Garrison had seen in his travels that had unsettled him. Finally, over a year ago, he'd decided to learn about the world and its history beyond what his father had told him. Unfortunately, Garrison had found more truth about himself than he cared to know.

One of those unavoidable truths was that Vanna Wynchester, the beautiful girl lying naked in his bed, meant nothing to him.

"Take me with you," the girl pleaded, holding the bed sheet tightly around her body. Her chest pressed through the silk and her silky black disheveled hair did more to arouse Garrison than put him off.

It was easier for Garrison to tell himself that she meant nothing when he wasn't staring at her smooth petite frame. It was also easier *after* he was finished sleeping with her. "You know I cannot. The House of Darian would not welcome you. You are not one of them. One of us." He still lay next to her, but looked away. It was easier to have the conversation this way.

"You assume they will accept you. They know who you are, Garrison. They know your crimes. Do you really believe that you can simply walk up to the House of Darian and they will welcome you with open arms? Of course, Garrison. That sounds incredibly reasonable! They will see you and say, 'Prince Garrison, you and your army have killed scores of Descendants, but we will forgive you for that because you are here now and would like to join us.' How can you be so foolish?"

Now he was angry. He turned to her. "If you speak of my past again, *our* future will be done. I am going. It is final." He sat up at the side of the bed.

"And what would you have me do while you are gone, my love."

Garrison's eyebrows shot up. *My love? That was a new trick.* "Vanna, between the two of us, I cannot be certain that I shall return." That was a lie, but a necessary one. Garrison could not have her know the truth. She would have to move on. If she didn't, all of Cerysia would expect a betrothal between them once he returned. And Garrison could not bear to think of Vanna Wynchester as his future wife and queen.

Although a nice girl, beautiful, and sinfully seductive behind closed doors, Vanna was at best completely shallow. She slept with Garrison because he was a prince, not because he was Garrison. Garrison had enjoyed her as a young man. But he could no longer think like a young man. Now he must think like a prince...a future king. Only those decisions that would prepare him to become a great king to the entire continent of Ashur were the right decisions. Vanna was no longer the right decision.

"Tell me you love me, my Prince. Tell me that you shall marry me as soon as you return. I shall give you all the heirs that you desire. I shall bear you an army of sons." When all other reason failed, Vanna resorted to seduction. Quite often it worked.

No. Not this time. "I will not say nor promise any of that. None if it is true or possible." Garrison arose from the bed and walked to his closet against the stone wall to find undergarments.

A candle crashed into his back, the flame and wick burrowing into his flesh while the hot wax seared down his back, slowly hardening. Garrison had a habit of being too honest with Vanna. Quite often he went unpunished; the burning candle was a first. Although annoying, Vanna still had feelings. Garrison only now realized the difficulty of the situation for her. Not many people knew of her exploits, but those who did were the wrong people. If Garrison cast her off, her prospects would be few.

"I apologize. My words were harsh," Garrison grimaced as burnt, raw flesh stretched while he picked up the candle and blew it out. "Truthfully, Vanna, it is more likely that Donovan will become king. I cannot guarantee that I shall return." *The lies we tell just to achieve truth.*

"Are you suggesting that I am only interested in your title? Or that I marry your brother?" Vanna let the sheet fall and walked over to him, her slender golden-brown body beckoning with every step. "I am not as stupid as you think I am, my Prince," she kissed the red flesh of his back where the candle had burned. "I can make a good wife. A good queen. I would be whatever you require me to be." Her lips had reached his shoulders and neck. "Your partner. Your confidant. Your support. Your *whore*." The last work lingered in Garrison's mind longer than he would have liked. Her hands pressed his chest and slowly slid down his body. *Perhaps I can make this decision when I return.*

Garrison turned around and roughly kissed Vanna's moist lips. He lifted her by her hips and tossed her back onto the bed. "You need to convince me better than that. Remind me of how you would ease my troubles as a queen would for her king." Garrison crawled onto the bed and pulled her close from her waist. With a seductive grin, she straddled him.

***

A loud and impatient knock sounded at the door. Garrison's eyes shot open. *Donovan!* Garrison's guards would have been more considerate. He peered out the tower window. The sun still hung low over the amalgamated orange and purple horizon. Vanna lay next to him, snoring softly. *Even her snoring makes my blood race. Would this be the worst thing to get used to?* Garrison donned a robe from the closet and opened his chamber door.

"You are still planning to do it today?" Donovan, Garrison's younger brother by a year, glared into his eyes. Donovan was a hair taller than Garrison and kept his hair cropped short, as opposed to Garrison's cleanly shaved head. Their skin tone was near identical, the golden-brown hue natural to Cerysians.

"What would have changed my mind?" The moment he heard the knock, Garrison knew that Donovan would make one final attempt to persuade him not to leave Cerysia for the House of Darian.

"There are things that must be said. Brother, hear my words. Heed my advice."

"Not here, Donovan. There are too many ears. Wait downstairs while I get dressed.

Donovan peeked into the large circular room and laughed, amused at the sight of Vanna sleeping on Garrison's bed. "Ah, you have the orphan sleeping here again, do you? I suppose it is easy for a girl to spend her nights with a prince when she has no father or mother to answer to. And even Vanna could not sway you? Surely she does not want you to leave!"

Garrison rolled his eyes at the accuracy of Donovan's jests. "Just go downstairs and wait!" He returned to his room and quietly dressed himself. Vanna snored more loudly now; the last thing he needed was for her to wake and start asking questions. He met Donovan outside at the base of the tower.

"Let us take a ride, Garrison. A final ride if you intend to be your normal, stubborn self." Donovan smiled as they walked toward the stables.

"Fine. The usual place then?" From the time they could barely ride, the two brothers and their best friend, Wendell Ravensdayle, were inseparable. They would take trips daily to The Stones of Gideon, an ancient battlefield, thousands of years old, from the time of the second set of Harbingers.

The Orijin's second wave of Harbingers, meant to rid the world of mankind's corruption and evil, consisted of Gideon, Darian, Lionel, Abram, and Jahmash. According to legend, the Orijin had graced The Five with specific manifestations in order to bring mankind back to justice. Gideon had been graced with the ability to turn anything to indestructible stone. At the time that the Harbingers had developed these manifestations, the world had been at war for decades. A great battle threatened to plunge it into further chaos. No matter which side won, the victor would have continued on until the entire population of the losing side had been decimated.

Gideon, barely Garrison's age at the time, sacrificed himself to protect the innocents left in humanity. Before the battle began, Gideon positioned himself between the two sides and ordered them to stop fighting, to come to peace, and return home. Not a single soldier listened to the decree. As a result, Gideon used every ounce of life he had to turn the entire battlefield, including every soldier present, to stone. The battlefield spanned the size of a small village. The legends said that Gideon had tapped into so much of his power that it consumed him as well, turning him to stone in the middle of the battlefield.

The grey stones had remained the same, perfectly preserved, for as long as Garrison could remember. He'd spent hours and hours studying the remains of the soldiers, Gideon especially. Gideon looked like a young boy, standing there between thousands of soldiers. The Harbinger stood with legs apart and arms raised to the sky. His head was tilted up with his eyes tightly shut and his mouth wide open in agony.

Gideon looked so innocent to Garrison: shaggy haired and lanky with a boyish face. The Harbinger's features shone quite clearly, despite being stone. In fact, all of the stone on the battlefield was incredibly smooth and preserved in minutest details, as if they'd been intricately sculpted.

As a child, Garrison could never fathom why someone so young would give his life to so many people for nothing in return. His father, King Edmund, had never done much to ease Garrison's wonderment. His father insisted firmly that the Stones of Gideon were not comprised of real people turned to stone, but instead a giant sculpture created over centuries. For years, Garrison swayed back and forth about whether he believed his father.

It was easy as a child to believe the stones had been real people once. But growing up, it was also easy to follow his father's teachings that they were no more than sculpture. Garrison decided on his own once King Edmund decided to build the Cerysian Wall. The king's original plan, despite much opposition, was to use the rock from The Stones for the wall. However, once the miners and soldiers began, not a man could chisel away even a scratch from anything. In fact, most men broke their tools trying. King Edmund rationalized it by explaining to everyone that the rock was not the correct type to be used for a wall. That was one of the many factors that prompted Garrison's search for truth in the world.

He and Donovan arrived at the center of The Stones, between the two sides of the battle. They'd always come straight to Gideon. Somehow,

Garrison had always felt comfort in his presence.

As always, they let the horses walk around on their own. The beasts never wandered too far and seemed equally amazed at the surroundings. Donovan broke the silence. "Garrison, if you leave, everything changes. Father will become more obsessed with wiping out the Descendants. He will feel betrayed. No matter what you tell him, he shall only see it one way." Donovan no longer pleaded, but seemed forceful and insistent instead.

"I cannot live for him any longer. I must go. I have lived with this manifestation for over ten years now, Donovan. Most Descendants would be at the House at my age, anyway." Garrison could not back down. "I am doing this so that I can become a better king than he."

"Then wait until one of his enemies finally kills him and have Descendants come here to counsel and instruct you. I agree. He has turned this world to shit. But if you confront him, he will only make it worse."

"And if he lives for another thirty years? What then, Donovan? Am I to continue to waste my life away blindly following his ways? You have seen as much of the world as I have. People are poor. They suffer. They live in hiding and fear the throne. And they are correct in doing so because the throne has done nothing for them in over twenty years. The Descendants are a light in our world of darkness. They give people hope. Whether I become king one day or not, I would rather do some good with the House of Darian as a regular man, than sit here and do nothing as a spoiled prince."

Donovan sighed. He looked down, his countenance reflected defeat. "Your intentions are noble, brother. I truly believe they are. But be honest. What will the House of Darian do to you if you simply show up at their doors? Do you really think they will welcome you with warm smiles? For more than four years you have hunted them and killed them. Yes, you did so for your father, for the King. But that will not matter to them. They will not accept you, Garrison. You are a fool to go there. Up until about a year ago, you were never really a nice person either. You never granted mercy to your prey. You and your soldiers killed them openly and violently."

Garrison cheeks reddened. "What exactly are you saying?"

"Do not be so sensitive or stubborn. You have always been a good brother and friend. But you are the one who sought truth. Perhaps you should accept the truth about yourself as well. I am not judging you, brother. But if you truly believe that you are a good person, or at least that you *were* a good person, in the eyes of Ashurians, then you are mistaken. You killed— massacred—people. And you enjoyed it. Regretting your actions now does not change that. You are...or at least *were* a murderer. I look past it because I am your brother. The rest of the world will not."

Anger flooded Garrison's mind every time his actions were mentioned. He was angry with himself for the things he'd done. "I still must try. Our uncle Roland committed his services to them long ago. Perhaps he has some influence with them." Garrison looked off into the distance for a few moments. Rows and rows of soldiers stood. So much anger in their eyes and faces. *What was the point of all their anger?* Garrison recognized the irony of the situation he was in. Like Gideon, he would have to make sacrifices. He was no Harbinger, but he had the power to change things. He was one of these very soldiers that Gideon was trying to convince. Not so long ago, Garrison looked at his opponents with the same murderous scowls, relishing the chance to kill or inflict suffering.

One day, he would come back to Cerysia and be king. One day the world would be fixed. But in order for that to happen, people would have to be willing to fix it. Just as Gideon had done. "I must go, Donovan. In my absence, I expect you and Wendell to do what is best for Cerysia. Do what you can to slow any plans father has. Father is hearing his subjects' grievances later this morning. That is when I will tell him."

***

The throne room was filled with Cerysians of all classes. Garrison's father, King Edmund, was entertaining his weekly hearing of requests. Most of the day would be spent listening to the problems of his subjects. Usually, the gigantic room, adorned with sculptures and tapestries, maintained a low rumble of numerous conversations. The morning had started that way. However, no one was accustomed to seeing the Prince standing publicly before the King with a request. Especially when that request was to leave the nation in order to pursue something King Edmund strongly opposed.

"You have read a book. You are telling me you have read a book, Garrison, and so you no longer want to be a prince?" King Edmund projected so that every person of every class in the throne room could hear his words.

King Edmund was a grey-bearded, skinny, sinewy man, so much so that the golden crown atop his head had been resized when he became king. He had the tendency to speak to people as if they were invalids when their ideas conflicted with his own. Garrison had seen it happen enough with his own mother. "No father. That is not what I said. I only stated that I wish to pursue an education from The House of Darian."

His father's knuckles grew white around the golden armrest of the gilded throne. "You will address me as 'Your Grace'! Or have you already denounced me as King as well?" Garrison's mother, Queen Valencia, sat in her own throne next to the king, a beautiful sight with her long curly black hair and light golden skin tone. She'd been clenching her jaw since Garrison had announced he wished to leave.

"Forgive me, Your Grace."

"Are you a fool, Garrison?"

Sometimes I do wonder on that, father. "No, Your Grace."

"Then why would I allow you to renounce your duties, especially to form an allegiance to the very people whom I have been trying to exterminate since before you were born?" Garrison had never met a different king, but from the time he was small, his instincts told him that his father did not act as a king should. King Edmund did speak properly and eloquently, but his language was not the issue. It was more *how* he spoke to his subjects, when he even spoke to them.

"I do not wish to renounce my duties, Your Grace, only to take a short leave of them, with your and mother's permission. Donovan would act in my place and I would resume my duties as Prince on my return. Of course, if any emergency were to arise, I would return immediately." Donovan had chosen not to be present for Garrison's plea, as he assumed the outcome would be negative. Garrison searched his father's face for any sign of letting up, of giving in. However, King Edmund constantly frowned or grimaced, no matter his mood. This news, if anything, added genuineness to the scowl.

"And a prince can do that? Simply decide to leave for a holiday and thrust his responsibilities upon others?"

"This is not a holiday, Your Grace."

King Edmund shot up from the throne. "Cursed Stones it is not! You would leave for personal gain, defying me in the process! Defying your people! Your nation!"

"No father...Your Grace. I have seen the truth. The words of Orijin. There is no reason why the House of Darian and the Descendants cannot coexist with this world."

King Edmund sat down again, "I am glad that you sought to discuss this in public, rather than in my chambers. Now all of Cerysia will know of your treason. That mark on your face is as meaningless as your mother's love for me. The Descendants are nothing but criminals and infidels."

"Then you believe the same of me, Your Grace. And what of the occurrence two days ago? The whole world went black in the middle of the day. How would you explain that, if not by some Descendant's manifestation?"

"Is your head only filled with rubbish and dreams? The moon blocked out the sun, foolish boy! An eclipse! Have you not seen one before?"

"You always have some stupid explanation for the miraculous things in this world."

The king surprisingly laughed at this accusation. "Garrison, you explain everything with magic and miracles, yet my explanations are being questioned? Enough!"

"No! Father, you are wrong. You have seen firsthand what I can do. As has your army and your Royal Guard. I have invented weapon after weapon for the army, all because of the manifestation that comes with the black line on my face! Why would the Orijin give me these gifts if he intended for me not to use them. I have been blessed! Let me learn to harness this blessing to its full potential."

"If you leave this place, you will only return as an enemy. Your desires have been noted and I name you a criminal, an enemy to the nation of

Cerysia, and the continent of Ashur. I will not do you the service of putting you in a cell, as we both know you will eventually find a way out. Guards! Kill him!" The entire throne room, full of peasants, city folk, servants, and knights, gasped at the King's words.

Garrison's chest tightened. He barely got the words out. "What? Father, no! I am no criminal!"

"Edmund, no!" the Queen interrupted. "He is our son; you cannot do this!" Queen Valencia rarely spoke a word in public and, in the rare cases in which she did, it was to agree with the King. The room had been deathly silent. Now, maids and servants dropped trays; others in the room cowered behind pillars, froze, or crept toward the doors at the Queen's outburst.

King Edmund's eyes bulged from his face. "Woman, you dare question my decisions? I am King! This criminal is no longer our son!" He stretched out his arm and swung at her, the back of his hand crunching into her cheek and jaw. The blow flung her so violently that she hung limply over the side of her throne. "Maids, take her away and clean her up. The Queen's services are no longer required here." Two maids rushed up the steps and helped the Queen rise from her throne. A red lump covered her cheek while blood flowed from her nose and mouth. The maids covered her face and rushed her from the room.

King Edmund returned his attention to his Royal Guard, ten armored knights who stood behind Garrison, and glowered at them. "I said kill him. Here and now. Let my son, my first-born son, be a lesson to all of Ashur what happens when you disobey a royal decree."

The Royal Guard marched from behind Garrison and surrounded him, their hands ready at their sword hilts. They hesitated in attacking. Many had grown up and trained with Garrison. King Edmund saw their hesitation and issued a new threat, "Guards, kill him or I will have you all killed!"

Garrison wouldn't let them all die on his account. His father's threat was serious, and it would be followed through. "Do as you are commanded! Fight me! You are not to die out of sympathy for me!"

King Edmund would not be outdone by Garrison's orders. "I said, kill him!"

One knight advanced. Garrison encouraged him, "Do not fear me, Broderick, I will not kill you."

His opponent smiled at that. "You taught us everything you know, my lord. We are all hesitant because we do not want to kill you."

"You are wrong," Garrison corrected him. "I taught you well, but I did not teach you everything. A swordsman never teaches all of his tricks." Before the words completely left Garrison's mouth, he reached into his shirtsleeve and flung a dagger at Broderick's face. While Broderick lifted his arms to deflect it, Garrison sprang at the knight, pulling two more daggers from his belt. He stabbed Broderick in both unprotected underarms until the tips of each blade broke through to the metal of Broderick's shoulder plates. The knight doubled over and crumbled to the ground. "I told you I would not kill you."

Three more Royal Guards engaged Garrison. As he turned to face them, others dragged Broderick away. *I could have used his sword. Virgil, Connor, Brandon. I need to disarm one of them...even out the number of blades on each side. Not Brandon. Connor, he is the most passive. I need to draw him away from the other two.*

Garrison drew his sword from its scabbard. His three attackers inched closer. Despite their armor, their expressions were wary. Connor stalked to Garrison's right. To his left, Virgil and Brandon still disagreed about who should attack first. Garrison seized the opportunity. He advanced on Connor, swinging his blade rapidly at Connor's face and torso. Connor parried clumsily under the weight of a full coat of arms.

Garrison stalked closer to Connor. Swinging high, he hacked away at Connor so that the knight had to keep his arm extended in the air. *I will not get away with the same trick twice.* Garrison fingered the handle of another dagger in his belt as he repeatedly swung his sword with one hand. He was only an arm's length away now. Feigning another attack, Garrison raised his sword. As Connor raised his arm to block, Garrison pulled the dagger and stabbed into the opening of the vambrace in Connor's sword hand. Garrison pushed the blade until it ripped through the knight's forearm and hand, and the sword clattered to the ground. If Connor wished to wield a sword ever again, he would have to do so with his left hand.

The knight fell to his knees, clutching his forearm while blood seeped through his gauntlet. Garrison crunched the heel of his boot into Connor's face, sending him sprawling backward into two knights standing at the perimeter of the makeshift fighting ring. He then retrieved Connor's sword and faced his other two attackers. Garrison realized that his fight with Connor had lasted only a few moments. Virgil and Brandon stood in the same place as before. If they were not hesitant before, then they were visibly so now.

"Remember with whom your loyalty resides, knights!" A hint of desperation tinged King Edmund's voice. "And remember who has the power to execute you!"

That last threat drained any remaining respect Garrison had had for his father. In Garrison's eighteen years, and even before, King Edmund had made many controversial decisions, orders, and laws. The one that had caused the most discord throughout Ashur was the decree that turned all Descendants into public enemies.

The law was made before Garrison was born; in fact, it was Edmund's first order upon becoming king. However, Garrison, as Prince and Captain of the Royal Army, had led attacks against Descendants from the time he was fourteen. Quite often, he developed strategies to track down Descendants or expose them from hiding places. The irony in it all was that he was a Descendant himself. Garrison had assumed that was his father's method to ensure that the Descendants would never accept him.

But now Garrison had had enough. In the past year, he'd educated himself on the Orijin, the Harbingers, and the Descendants. A king was supposed to be the voice of the Orijin on Earth. King Edmund was anything but that. Nothing Garrison had read of the Orijin had supported this treatment of the Descendants. If anything, they were to be revered more than anyone else, aside from the king.

Garrison needed justice and knew that the only way to attain it was to accept who he really was. The black line on his face reminded him of it every day. And if it meant he would also be an outcast to his own people, Garrison would make the sacrifice. Given his father's reaction, Garrison found his decision easier to accept. Especially considering the knights' hesitation to attack him.

"They are more my knights than yours. Father." He spit the last word out forcefully. "I trained them. I gave them respect. All you have done is threatened to kill them if they do not kill their Captain."

"It is a promise. Not a threat," King Edmund fired back.

With that, Virgil and Brandon quickly flanked Garrison on both sides. He at least had two swords now. Garrison pivoted his head from side to side. Virgil charged first, holding his sword above his head with both hands. Garrison knew Virgil's plan of attack the moment he moved.

As Virgil reached striking distance, he struck downward for Garrison's unprotected head. Rather than deflect the attack and leave himself open to Brandon, Garrison spun out of the way and positioned himself behind Virgil. *Good, now they are both in front of me.* He sheathed one sword and pulled the last dagger from his belt, wrapping his arm around Virgil's neck. Before Brandon could determine how to help, Garrison ripped the helmet from Virgil's head and slashed his face diagonally from forehead to jaw with the dagger.

Virgil's screams forced Brandon to action, but Garrison pointed the dagger to Virgil's neck. Brandon froze, looking back and forth between Virgil and King Edmund. With Brandon's hesitation, Garrison swept Virgil forward to the ground and smashed the knight's face into the tiled floor.

Horror painted the king's face as he reprimanded the six Royal Guards who had yet to join the fight. "Why do you six stand there while only Sir Brandon fights? Can so many cowards be charged with protecting me?"

Garrison secured the dagger in his belt. Brandon stared at Garrison, his bewildered countenance revealing his reservations about attacking. Garrison gritted his teeth and picked up Virgil's helmet, then hurled it at King Edmund's head. The king dove from his throne, narrowly avoiding the helmet. As King Edmund rose from the floor, all attention shifted to him. With the diversion, Garrison walked briskly toward the main doors of the throne room. Knights, citizens, servants, and peasants all made way for him.

"Garrison. If you leave now I will send the entire army to hunt you down and kill you! Do you hear me?"

Ridiculous. "You would sacrifice your nation's protection to kill one man. This is why you are not fit to be King. They are more my army than yours. What will you do without my ability for invention? My *Descendant's manifestation?*

King Edmund sat back down and exhaled heavily. "You are a traitor to me and to the world. Perhaps ten cowardly knights cannot kill you. But I can gather enough brave soldiers to do the job."

"You mean pay enough soldiers."

Brandon, normally quiet and obedient, removed his helmet and spoke up, sheepishly. "Your Grace, forgive my intrusion on these matters. But while he is a criminal to the nation, he is also your son. Is there perhaps a lesser penalty to instill than death?"

King Edmund mulled Brandon's words for a moment. Garrison expected Brandon to have been beaten down already. This reaction was quite odd.

"Perhaps you are correct, Sir Brandon. Garrison, I will not have you killed here and now. I will give you three hours to flee before I send a battalion after you. That should give you enough time to make for an entertaining chase." The King arose and walked down to Brandon. "Sir Brandon, please kneel." Brandon heeded the King's command. "Lend me your sword. You are a loyal knight. Honorable. Because you have proven to be quite noble and altruistic, I imagine you will have no quarrel with sacrificing yourself for Garrison here and now."

Brandon paled and stared up at King Edmund. But he'd understood too late. The killing blow sliced through Brandon's neck and sent his head rolling across the floor. Blood sprayed everywhere from the headless neck, soaking the King and the few nearby knights. The King sneered as he wiped the crimson from his black and grey beard. "Foolish boy, you ask mercy for a traitor. That makes you a traitor as well."

"You are no king! You are a fool! Ashur is in just as much danger with you as our king as if the Red Harbinger himself were to sit on that throne!" The room collectively gasped at Garrison's words.

"Blasphemer! Leave at once! Or you will be killed here and now!" King Edmund walked toward him.

"Send your army. I shall kill *your* soldiers one by one. Until there is no one left to protect you." Garrison turned, threw open the heavy wooden throne room doors, and left.

He ran north from the palace toward the army barracks at the Cerysian Wall. For nearly ten years now, the wall had separated Cerysia from The Never. But more specifically, King Edmund had wanted to block the Taurani people who lived in the forest. The King had outraged the Taurani by having over a dozen of them killed. The Taurani had been hunting near the border of Cerysia shortly after King Edmund had decreed that all Descendants were to be killed or captured on sight.

Cerysian soldiers had seen the Taurani from lookout posts from afar and assumed they were Descendants, because of the markings on their faces and heads. All the Taurani in the hunting party were shot down with arrows, and then stripped of weapons. Days later, three Taurani leaders appeared in King Edmund's throne room, asking questions and demanding justice. Garrison's father had been lucky then that the Taurani had only brought three. They expected King Edmund to meet their demands. However, they had also mistakenly expected that the King was rational and fair.

King Edmund threatened to kill the Taurani then and there if they did not leave at once. The Taurani, understanding they could not win, left with a promise to get retribution for the wrongs committed against their people. It was on the heels of this encounter that King Edmund ordered three quarters of his forces to the Taurani-Cerysia border to erect the wall.

The Cerysian Wall itself was an impressive feat. It was made of stone, towering higher than anything man had seen before, except for the Tower of the Blind, and was thicker than ten houses side by side. Towers were built into it at four points, and the steps within each tower were the only ways to reach the top of the wall.

Garrison had spent many months orchestrating the construction of the wall. In all, he'd bonded with the Cerysian soldiers for years. They would not kill him as easily as his father thought.

He arrived at the wall and hurried to his workshop within the armory. King Edmund had bestowed many privileges on Garrison; rightfully so considering that Garrison was the prince and the army's commander. One such privilege was the workshop. Garrison, while grateful for the privacy, would have thought his father foolish for not granting the space. King Edmund hated that Garrison was a Descendant, but that distinction gave him the ability of invention. He could essentially create anything that entered his imagination. The process was not always easy, because exotic ideas required exotic ingredients. Many times, Garrison's inventions were not completed because he simply could not find the materials to finish them.

But in the past six years, the Cerysian army had become so formidable because of those inventions that were completed. Garrison had designed scores of weapons to help trap and kill Descendants, including all sorts of crossbows, blades, and traps. Those inventions worked just as well on other enemies of Cerysia and the throne.

I will not be able to take everything. Only what will help me the most. And what will help the House of Darian as well.

He searched the organized workshop for the best inventions to take with him. *Vambrace blades. Yes.* What else? Garrison searched through drawers and countertops. *Climbing claws. Trees are good hiding places. Wrist blades. Poison darts. Poison vials. There is something else. What am*

I forgetting? Garrison looked over the room once more, his mind grasping to remember what else he would need. "The Dust!" He ran to the wooden shelf at the back of the room and unlocked the bottom drawer. It was full of pouches containing various colored powders: red, black, blue, brown, green, and yellow. *All of these powders will be essential. I was smart to keep my secrets. Let them come after me. Perhaps when their bodies are returned to my father, he will see his foolishness.*

Garrison tucked some of the pouches in his waist and put the rest in a pack on a counter, along with the other inventions. Stale bread and dried beef sat next to the pack. Garrison tossed them in.

"Captain!" A voice shouted from the doorway. Garrison turned to see his best friend, Wendell Ravensdayle, also his second in command. "I have heard the news, my lord."

Garrison shut the drawer quickly and fingered a dagger. "Have you come to kill me then, Wendell?"

"Of course I have, Garrison. You know, now that you are a criminal, the army is mine to lead. It would be treason if I did not either kill you or arrest you." Wendell was average looking with the faintest evidence of a beard, but his exceptionally rare blonde hair, coupled with the brownish golden skin tone of Cerysians made girls and women alike dote over him. He was a year older than Garrison, and had been loyal for as long as Garrison could remember. "Seriously though, my lord, what help do you need in fleeing. Ask anything and it shall be done."

"Anything you do for me, Wendell, anything…will result in my father killing you. He beheaded Brandon for asking to be lenient with me. Pretend you never saw me."

"Yes, I heard. Captain, surely you know most of us would follow you before your father." Wendell's words were true. In the time that Garrison had sought truth about the Orijin and Descendants, his soldiers had eased on killing Descendants as well. At least, those who traveled with him did. Garrison had known they only did so because of his beliefs and wishes. When returning home, they would lie and tell the king that they killed any Descendants they'd found.

Because of this loyalty, Garrison refused to let his men die for his actions. If they chose to attack him, that was different. "I know Wendell, but I cannot accept your sacrifice," Garrison rolled his pack. "I appreciate your loyalty, friend, I sincerely do. But you and the others must think of the grander scheme. Jahmash will return in our lifetime. I don't know if the Blind have foreseen it, but I have that feeling. You must now lead this army. There is no one better than you to do that."

Wendell rolled his eyes in annoyance. He was one of the few who could do that to Garrison. "Enough. Garrison, I am speaking to you friend to friend. Not soldier to captain or subject to prince. There are thousands of soldiers who fight only for the coin. Remember that not everyone in your kingdom is wealthy. They will follow the king's orders as long as it means their families are fed."

"I understand, Wendell, but…"

"No you do not. I said thousands, Garrison. Sooner or later they will find you. I know you can defy certain odds with your skill and weapons, but no man can kill or outrun thousands of soldiers by himself. And you know your father will send every last soldier until you are dead. Many people will have no problem betraying you to the king, because of how we used to treat them." Even fewer people could interrupt Garrison while he spoke.

But Garrison knew Wendell was right. "Fine. But no combat. Do what you can to help, but without sacrificing your lives. Set them in a different direction, set traps, whatever. But do not fight them unless you have no other choice. Otherwise you are no better than my father."

"I am insulted you do not think we are smarter than that." Wendell smirked. "We are the leaders of the Cerysian army, Garrison. We control Cerysia. Any soldiers who hunt you will be amazed at how many accidental roadblocks, fallen trees, and flooded roads lie before them. They know you will go to the House of Darian. The King will send them to every possible road and path that leads there. Tell us which way you intend to travel, and we can hopefully steer them in other directions."

"I will follow the Cerysian Wall to the Eye of Orijin, and then sail across. I will have to leave my horse, but at least they will lose my trail." Garrison donned a regular soldier's leather chest plate and vambraces. No need to be recognized in his own armor. He then secured a bow and quiver of arrows to his back.

Wendell nodded in approval. "Good. I have already sent men ahead of you to create a multitude of trails. They will wait for your pursuers to ambush them. I will send more just behind you so that your tracks are not solitary. The King's soldiers will be looking for a single rider and single tracks. The squadron I send will follow you to the water. Hopefully, any other soldiers will assume my squadron is hunting you as well, and will go in a different direction. It is time you left though. We have wasted too much time with this conversation." Wendell turned in the doorway.

"Indeed. Go give your men their orders. I apologize in advance Wendell, but I must set fire to this place. My father will surely send soldiers here to raid my workshop. And I cannot allow them to study my inventions." Garrison hefted the pack onto his back and lifted a torch from the wall.

Garrison walked to the doorway, then turned and scanned over his workshop one last time, regret weighing on his shoulders. He exited quickly to where Wendell awaited outside. "I suppose this is goodbye then, Garrison."

"No. We shall meet again. I will return to resume my duties as Prince, despite what my father may think. Ashur deserves a fair and righteous king. One who accepts all of his people. They will have that in me. When I come back, Ravensdayle, you and I will return Cerysia to a respectable nation. We'll reunite Ashur and give people a reason to love their king." Garrison shook Wendell's hand and clapped him heartily on the shoulder. "Now go. There is work to be done. Have your men meet me at the base of the tower. I will wait there and ride when I see them coming."

Garrison walked the perimeter of the armory, lighting the base of the building all around. Satisfied with the blaze, he walked to the stables and saddled a black destrier with a special saddle he'd created, which had footholds at the front and back of the seat, allowing the rider to securely stand balanced atop the horse if necessary.

He rode to the nearby tower. It was the second post of the wall, coming from the Eye of Orijin, an enormous lake that bordered Cerysia. Sailing across the Eye would not necessarily save Garrison time rather than riding around it. But that was what he counted on. He hoped his pursuers would simply ride along the Eye. Once he was across, Garrison could visit the Tower of the Blind, a home for the blind men and women who received prophecies, for temporary shelter and food, and then head west through Mireya. The people of Mireya were much more welcoming of Descendants. His stalkers would most likely ride along the border of Galicea, directly toward the House of Darian.

Garrison hoped the journey would take no more than six days. But that was assuming no soldiers caught him. Deep down, even a one-day journey felt like too long. Ever since learning the truth about the Orijin, that there was no shame in being a Descendant of Darian, Garrison could hardly wait to reach the House of Darian.

At times he had wished he was never a prince. That title made his decision incredibly more difficult. Garrison had known he could not avoid confronting his father. To do so in private would have allowed the king to react in much more extreme measures than had happened in the throne room. Garrison had expected to be exiled. But not to be hunted like a criminal. He should not have been surprised, though. His only consolation was that subjects and soldiers alike had witnessed the exchange. It would only be a matter of time before his father lost the support and loyalty of Cerysia.

In his eighteen years, despite all the strategy and planning of military strikes, Garrison had never been the type to plot against others. He had witnessed enough of that among the lords of Cerysia. Regardless, he was determined to put the pieces in place so that Cerysia would readily follow him on his return home after the House of Darian.

He didn't know yet if that meant killing his father. He would have to evaluate the circumstances upon his return and decide then. It was the first time since he'd stopped his hunting sprees that Garrison was somewhat relieved that he had experience with killing people. He was sure if it came to it, he would have what it took to kill his own father. Until then, he would embrace who he really was. *Orijin, please just let him already be dead by the time I return.*

Ashur had never had a king who was a Descendant. In fact, Descendants had only started significantly populating the world in the past two centuries, and still their numbers were not more than a few hundred, as far as Garrison knew. And he would be the first to become king. Not for the glory, but for the betterment of mankind.

Garrison had seen much of the world in his few years as commander of the army. The world was broken. Too many people were poor. Nations were constantly at war with each other. Galicea and Fang-Haan had constructed a wall at their border in the aftermath of their war. It was likely the only thing the two nations had agreed upon in the past few decades.

Garrison had not expected the world to be like the stories he'd read as a child, where everyone loved the king and the only evil in the world was done by monsters. But in his experiences in certain nations, people spat at him, not caring that he was a prince. It seemed that the world didn't care about the king anymore. People were mostly poor because of constant taxes, money used to keep the army well trained and fed, as well as to put up a wall to keep Taurani out. If anything, he and his father had been the monsters.

He remembered reading that thousands of years ago, after Darian had drowned the world to defeat Jahmash, the world was in great harmony. The nations loved each other. People accepted each other no matter their race or wealth.

Now, things were different. King Edmund had failed his people. According to many people as old as, or older than, Garrison's father, the world had been a much easier place to live in before Edmund became king over twenty years ago. It hadn't taken long for things to change for the worst.

Garrison sighed as he rode on. It would take time. But his purpose in this world was to return it to what it once was. His manifestation, or ability as a Descendant, was the ability to invent. To create. The House of Darian would give him the ability to create a better world. And to protect it from Jahmash. That was a task with which his father would surely fail.

He was getting closer to the next tower, and closer to the Eye of Orijin. Wendell's men would not be very far off. Garrison glanced at the sky. He'd already used roughly a half of an hour. He knew his father would send soldiers before three hours had passed. If he was lucky, Garrison would have another half hour before the king was able to finish giving the soldiers their orders and then send them out. The king would also likely send soldiers to raid Garrison's workshop in the armory. Regardless, the soldiers would be very close, very soon.

Riders appeared in the distance, the red dyed horse-hair bristles on their helmets peeking over the horizon. Garrison dug his heels into his steed and galloped away. Gales of wind blew into his face, which should have been refreshing, yet sweat still dotted his shaven head.

Garrison rode along the wall, merely a few yards away from it. Wendell would have given any soldiers in the vicinity news of Garrison's flight, and would have had them swear to secrecy as well. *Oh no. The fire! What more obvious sign could I have given them about where I was? What was I thinking? Those soldiers…they could have been…*

As if Garrison's thoughts had signaled for reality to follow, a soldier barked down at him from atop the tower, gesturing wildly. The man's words were near impossible to understand because of the height of the wall, but Garrison gathered the meaning from the urgency of the soldier's voice.

He dug his heels into the horse and sped on. The biggest flaw in Garrison's plan was that he allowed himself no coverage. All he had was open land ahead and the enormous wall on his right. *How did I think I could outrun so many soldiers? Stupid!* He knew better than to waste precious arrows from this position. It would only slow him down to turn and shoot, and it would take even longer to ensure accurate shots. Flight was Garrison's only ally.

On horseback, Garrison could reach the last tower quickly. He only hoped to stay outside the reach of the soldiers' arrows. The tower marked the end of the wall, which was also the shore of the Eye. Something buzzed by his ear and bit into it. Without touching it, Garrison knew an arrow had grazed his earlobe. Luckily, it was just the earlobe and not his whole ear. His attackers were within range after all. He glanced backwards as the horse galloped on. *Just about twenty of them. What happened to Wendell's men? Could they have all been killed? Did they even come?*

More arrows whizzed by, each missing Garrison by inches, a few feet at most. Wendell's soldiers would not have shot so close. The last tower appeared on the horizon. Garrison desperately grabbed the front of the saddle and swung himself sideways on the horse. His legs and left arm wrapped around the beast's torso while he clung to the pommel atop the saddle. He kept his body as close to the horse as he could while it galloped on. *At this pace, I should reach the banks in a few moments.* Arrows continued to fall nearby, but the tactic worked. In his position, the soldiers would have great difficulty finding the proper angle to shoot him.

Garrison gazed ahead. He could not see the tower from this side of the horse. He could see canoes tied up on the shore of the Eye. As thoughts of freedom were about to fill Garrison's mind, the horse shrieked and tumbled to the ground. The fall sent Garrison hurtling through the air and he finally landed several feet away. Luckily, his momentum carried him forward. He felt the burn of scrapes and bruises, but nothing felt broken.

In the distance, the soldiers charged on toward him. He stood his ground, firm and unmoving. As the soldiers neared, Garrison nocked an arrow and aimed at the lead rider. "Stop where you are! I am Garrison Brighton, Prince of Cerysia, Heir to all of Ashur! And Captain of the Royal

Army! *Your* Captain! I order you to cease and dismount!"

The riders slowed until they were only a few feet away. They dismounted at the squadron leader's signal. Garrison followed his every move with the bow and arrow.

"Prince Garrison, we do not want to fight you. But King Edmund has ordered us to bring you back dead or alive. That is our duty. We are soldiers. We swore an oath to the king."

"My father's words mean nothing to me. That same man also promised me three hours to leave the city of Alvadon before he would send out riders after me. Yet here you are, less than an hour later. You swore your fealty to a liar!" The soldier's gaze dropped to his feet at Garrison's words. Garrison continued, "Every man makes his own choices. A king's duty is to ensure that every man has the freedom to choose his own path. A king's word should be the strongest bond there is, yet this one has broken that bond to his own son. A good king does not order soldiers to kill his own son; much less waste the lives of his own army in doing so. This is the king you follow."

"But my lord, King Edmund pays us. We need the coin to live. If we let you go free, he will kill all of us." While the soldier spoke, the rest of the squadron formed a semicircle around Garrison, each with an arrow aimed at him.

"And if you fight me, I will kill all of you. So you choose money over honor. If the coin is your only concern, then the Cerysian Army has already failed. And the world is already lost. Think, you fools. Jahmash is coming! Why throw away your lives now when the world will need you soon!" The soldiers maintained their ready position. Garrison lowered his bow and fingered a black pouch at his belt.

What were the Orijin's words? 'In the face of injustice, violence is necessary. Acceptance is unforgiveable.' It is a waste to kill you all, but it is necessary. "Very well, soldier. I yield." Garrison dropped his bow and arrow to the ground.

As he pulled his waterskin from his belt, three soldiers fell to the ground screaming. Three heavily tattooed figures emerged from behind them, their swords dripping crimson, their leather armor drenched and in tatters. *Taurani? What are they doing here?*

The remaining soldiers turned to face the new threat. The Taurani spun and swooped, slashing a few soldiers down with ease. Garrison could only stand and watch it all unfold. He could not simply allow them to handle his responsibility for him. He yelled to them, "Taurani, fall back and cover your faces! I will finish them!" They looked at him and Garrison nodded reassuringly, holding up the black pouch. *I can only hope they understand.*

Garrison doused the black pouch with water while the Taurani fell to the ground and covered their faces. He threw the pouch to the center of the remaining ten soldiers. It landed on the ground without any of them taking notice. *One. Two. Three. Four. Five.* The pouch exploded in a black mist that engulfed the soldiers. At first they coughed, unable to find clean air. *Good. Coughing means inhaling.* One by one, each soldier fell to his knees, gasping for air. They scratched for their chests, throwing off metal and leather chest plates, ripping away undershirts. As they exposed their chests and torsos, tendrils of black and grey crept through their skin, changing their complexions completely within moments. They gasped desperately, mouths wide open with blood oozing down their chins. As the Black Dust spread further through them, they lay on the ground clawing at the dirt as well as at their chests. Red scratch marks turned into bloody skin. They writhed silently, now unable to produce a sound as the dust corroded their throats and vocal chords. *In a few moments, it should be done.*

Garrison forced himself to watch. It was the second time he'd ever used the Black Dust, and only the first time he used it on multiple people. Obviously, it worked. The soldiers' movements slowed. Blood seeped through their black skin until they were all lifeless red and black masses. He would leave them there for the next squadron to see. Hopefully, someone would bring a body back to his father, and the rest of the army would be dissuaded from pursuit. *How much coin would any man be willing to take at this risk?*

The Taurani finally arose from their crouched positions several feet away. They moved gingerly and hobbled toward Garrison, hands still covering their mouths and noses. As they came closer, their features revealed that they were older. In fact, the woman and two men were all old enough to be Garrison's parents.

The woman spoke first. "Put down your horse, Cerysian prince. It is in agony." Garrison realized his horse still lay off in the distance, shrieking and flailing its broken limbs. An arrow stuck in its rear leg. He picked up his bow and walked over to the horse, patted it on the head, and whispered, "I am sorry my friend. Thank you for your sacrifice." He shot an arrow in its head to bring death as quickly as possible, then retrieved his pack, fastened his specialized saddle to his back, and walked back to the Taurani.

"I am grateful for your help, but why are you here?"

The taller of the two men replied, "Did you see the world black out two days ago?" Garrison nodded. "Our village was destroyed that day. While our whole village slept, we were attacked by an army larger than our whole population."

Garrison was puzzled. "Was that why the world went dark? Did they use some type of magic?"

"We do not know what happened. That was hours after the invasion. In fact, it was the reason why the three of us were able to escape. We were not together at the time, but we each separately ran for the forest in the darkness and eventually found each other wandering around yesterday."

Garrison worriedly looked off toward the wall. "Come, let us take a boat and be off. We cannot afford to be found talking here, especially with the three of you injured. More soldiers will come." They walked to the shore and found a canoe large enough to fit four of them. "Untie the other boats so we cannot be followed." Garrison gave the Taurani unfastened all of the boats and pushed them off, except for one.

They all returned to the canoe and sailed off. The two men had sustained injuries to their arms and chests, which left Garrison and the woman to row. "You're saying your whole village and population are gone? In one day?" Garrison could not fathom how warriors as established at the Taurani could have been wiped out.

The woman spoke up as the men bandaged their wounds. "A day? No, more like a few hours. Somehow, they knew how and when to strike. We were decimated in our sleep. We don't know how they got past the guards and the gates, but we never even had the opportunity to fight back." She shook her head, still in disbelief. "They didn't just kill us, Cerysian, they destroyed everything. They tore down and burnt down every single building. There is nothing left. I cannot imagine how Cerysia did not see the smoke from your *wall*."

She seemed vaguely familiar to Garrison. He had only seen Taurani up close once before. And she knew he was a prince. *My father!* "You. You came to Alvadon once before! To see my father!" Her face was relatively bare for a Taurani, which is why Garrison recognized her. She wore only two markings on her face: two vertical lines starting from her forehead and intersecting each of her eyes down to her chin. However, with her dark blonde hair, it made her look dangerous.

"All three of us came to see your father, in fact."

"So then why did you save me? You have been hoping for revenge for a long time."

The woman gazed into Garrison's eyes with a look his own mother would have given him if he'd said something foolish. "Look at us, Prince. We are tired, beaten, and broken. We have no resources and no friends remaining. Alvadon was the closest place. We were looking for help. From anyone. We had hardly snuck across your border when we saw the soldiers coming upon you. We knew who you were. Your face has barely changed since we saw you last." She stared off into the distance, aloof. "There is no honor in twenty men engaging a prince, or any man, in battle. It was only right to help you."

"Call me Garrison. I am no longer a prince. And thank you for your help. Who are the three of you and where do you plan to go now?" Garrison only now noticed that the two male Taurani were fast asleep.

"My name is Marika. My two companions are Yorik, my brother, and Kavon. We do not know where to go now. Our only thoughts were to escape. I suppose we could travel with you for some time, if that would be acceptable."

"I would welcome the company. Believe me; I need all the friends I can find at this point." Garrison managed a small grin. The woman had a comforting effect. Something inside him told him that everything would work out as long as he had her nearby.

"Where are you traveling? And why was your father's army hunting you down? Only something as grave as treason would warrant that."

Garrison sighed. "I am going to the House of Darian to learn how to use this manifestation better." He pointed to the mark at his left eye. "I will stop at the Tower of the Blind first. They will be hospitable. We can at least rest there for a short time and find some sustenance. My father did not agree with this decision, so he branded me a traitor to Cerysia and is now using his army to kill me."

Marika's eyes shot up at Garrison's words. "You seek the House." She closed her eyes and stopped rowing for a moment. After a few moments, she finally looked at Garrison once more and continued to row. "Garrrison, we cannot follow you into that place. It is not our way. The House of Darian violates Taurani beliefs."

Back to being on my own. "Oh." He paused for a moment, "I understand, Marika. Then when we reach the Tower, we shall part ways there." Garrison let out a deep breath.

"You misunderstand. The three of us will see that you reach the House. But that is where our ties will break."

"Why go through all that trouble. Once we reach land again, you can go off and find new lives for yourselves. Rebuild the Taurani somewhere else."

Tears streamed from the corners of her eyes now. "If your father is hunting you down, you will need our help to make it all the way to the House. You will not survive on your own. I cannot bear the burden of more innocents dying, Garrison. Especially children."

Begrudgingly, he replied through gritted teeth, "I am no child."

"You are of an age with my eldest child, Garrison. I had three. And now all are dead at the hands of savages. Esha and Gia were just girls. Innocent girls. And Marshall. My son Marshall had the potential to be one of the greatest Taurani warriors in the history of our people. All of it was wasted." Marika's face was slick with tears. "You have many years, many possibilities ahead of you, boy. I cannot let it go to waste."

Garrison saw the futility in arguing further. "Very well. Then it is settled.

CHAPTER 6
REVELATIONS

From *The Book of Orijin*, Verse Sixty-One
Righteousness lives in your hearts, as does wickedness, for We have placed them there. We have not created but one of you with absolute righteousness or wickedness.

BO'AZ'S EYES ADJUSTED to the blinding afternoon sunlight as he led Iridian out from the seemingly endless forest. Perhaps another reason for calling it 'The Never' was that nobody had ever gotten out of it. They had trekked through it for three days and, finally on the fourth morning, the forest gave way to new landscape. However, once his eyes accustomed themselves to sunlight, which they hadn't seen clearly in almost a week, Bo'az realized he wasn't really better off. Craggy mountains towered across the horizon, no end to them in sight. The sharp rocks stretched out at every peak, like rows and rows of swords and daggers. Their grey and white complexion offered him no solace, as he realized instantly that climbing through snow and rock would not be an enjoyable experience, especially with the injuries he'd been nursing. His three new "friends" had been kind enough to tend to his broken arm and create a sling from a piece of his cloak, and his nose and head had been stitched up, quite painfully at that. They had no knowledge of medicine, so aside from sharing some of Linas' rum here and there, Bo'az had had to become accustomed to the pain in his arm over the past few days. Bo'az had headaches just about all the time, and they ranged from bad to excruciating.

"Rhadames says they're known as 'The Endless Mountains', I'm sure you can see why," Linas grumbled as he reached Bo'az's side. His long nappy beard stunk of old rum. "As I warned, the path ahead offers no comforts. We've no choice but to go directly through the mountains."

First the Never, now the Endless Mountains. Maybe these places wouldn't seem so bad if people gave them more bearable names. "I suppose that telling you that I hate the snow won't change your mind about the mountains?"

"It has nothing to do with changing my mind or any preference of mine, for that matter. The truth of it is that we have no other way around the mountains. It would take us at least thrice as many days to walk the base of this range, and even then it would only lead to water. Our ship, if it's still there, sits at the other side of this range, and the fastest route is simply to go straight." Linas dismounted from his steed, took a few steps forward, and scanned the view ahead.

"Ship?"

Linas' frustration grew tangible through his narrowing eyes and downturned mouth. "Yes, ship. Will that also be a problem for you, Baltaszar?"

Bo'az still hadn't gotten used to being called that, even after a few days of being called his brother's name. "No problem, it just seems that this journey of ours is excessively difficult. Is that why Darian didn't himself come? Is he too old or sick to be able to travel like this?"

"Our master has his reasons for not coming, but you are correct about the journey itself. It is and will continue to be extremely taxing and unrelenting. The forest was the easy part. I will not make any attempts to describe it more pleasantly than it is. The mountains you see ahead are treacherous and indifferent to travelers, especially when we have to lead our horses through them. It is quite likely that any of us could be seriously injured or killed along the way. And even after all that, we face a very rough sea, followed by the desolation of the desert. Don't even get me started on the beasts."

"And all this is necessary? You still haven't even told me why Darian needs to see me so badly."

"Honestly, for as much as you whine and complain, boy, I can't imagine how he won't be disappointed when he meets you. He sent us to collect you and deliver you to him; that is our job. He will gladly explain everything when we get there. All I can really inform you about is that your father was a liar and you were never meant to be hidden away in the forest. You've grown too sheltered and naïve, perhaps that is why you carry on like a woman so often."

"My father was no liar; he was a good man who did everything he could, after my mother died." Bo'az grew tired of hiding his annoyance. His conversations with Linas got him nowhere and left him just as confused as when they first met, and Linas seemed less than fond of his father. At least Linas actually spoke to him, though. Gibreel made no secret his disdain for Bo'az. Rhadames never really spoke to anyone; he seemed to always be thinking, calculating, or resting his eyes and stroking his thick brown beard.

Yasaman, on the other hand, he knew why she hadn't spoken at all since leaving Haedon. She'd watched Gibreel slice her father's head off in order to save Bo'az's life. Bo'az knew Yasaman didn't get along with her father, but that didn't make it any less painful to see him die so brutally right in front of her. In her attempt to run to her father's lifeless body, Gibreel caught her and threw her to the ground, her screams echoing through the forest. During her fall, she'd hit her head against the ground and lost consciousness, but she awoke with a startling jump a few hours later, with no seemingly serious injuries. At least that was what Linas had told Bo'az. Bo'az himself hadn't awoken for a day after he'd blacked out.

Yasaman hadn't spoken a word since waking, and barely acknowledged that she was in the company of others. While they trod through the forest, Yasaman would normally stay at the rear, just within sight, and always with a look of aloofness, unaware of her surroundings. Yasaman's and Bo'az's three companions had no apparent worries of her falling behind or getting lost. In fact, they had originally expressed their distaste at her accompanying them, so they were only proving that point.

"Your father told you that the mark on your face was a burn for Orijin's sake. I can understand that you'd believe that as a child, but you're a grown man and you still swear by his word. That makes you a fool along with your father. Especially considering it's gone now…do you really believe a burn as big as the mark on your face would magically disappear and leave you without a scar?"

"I don't know what I believe, but regardless, it is gone now, so it's of no consequence."

"It is of more consequence than you could ever dream. For your sake, Baltaszar, you'd better hope it reappears before we reach our destination. Our master will not be pleased if you do not bear the Mark."

"Why? What's so special about a line on my face?"

"Again, that is something my master will explain to you in due time. For now, let us continue on. If I tell you, for all I know you'll either use it against us or try to run off. Which would lead to us having to kill you. And while I might tolerate you, I do not trust you, Baltaszar."

"No. We'll take a break here. Yasaman looks tired and I need to catch my breath before we venture up any mountains, especially if we'll have to walk the whole way." Bo'az realized he could get away with some assertiveness, since there was always the threat of him turning around and abandoning the whole endeavor. Gibreel cursed a few paces behind him.

Linas stared at him flatly. "You're trying to take advantage of us now. I am not stupid. You've realized that our journey must include you, and now you plan to leverage us if we do not humor your silly demands. Very well, we shall concede to your request, but only a short break. We must find a safe location somewhere on the mountain directly ahead of us before dusk. We know of caves not far up. We found shelter in them on our way to finding you. Our survival through the mountains depends on our ability to get to shelter before nightfall. If we stay here, the predators will find us. It's already past midday, so we've only a few hours to cover the base of the mountain and reach the caves. I would prefer to be comfortably in the caves with fires lit well before the sun descends."

Bo'az hadn't expected Linas to acquiesce so easily, but he was beginning to suspect that Linas Nasreddine was not necessarily a completely bad person. Linas had been the one, along with some help from Rhadames, who had stitched him and secured his broken arm, and Linas had taken Yasaman on his horse and led hers until she'd awoken after her fall. "Why is it that you are the only one who is willing to talk to me? I thought you were all sent to find me and bring me back safely."

Linas slowly sat down next to a tree and dug a flask from his pack. "Trust me, if we don't get you back, the three of us shall suffer so much that we'll wish we were dead. I speak to you because you deserve no less. We arrived at your house unannounced and unfamiliar, asking for your trust. You have many questions and I can only answer some of them, but regardless, I understand that you are in a difficult situation. Your townspeople no longer accept you, you've no family, and you barely know me or my companions. Regardless of what I think of you, I realize your dilemma and your curiosities."

"And what exactly do you think of me?"

"Honestly, I think you are too naïve for what my master has planned for you. You've been protected and misguided your whole life and have no idea what the world beyond your village is really like. Tell me, have you ever even left? Even once?"

"No. This is actually the farthest I've been from home." Bo'az's cheeks reddened at the admission.

"That is what I mean, boy. All you've known your whole life is a farm. You've never experienced anything real or even used a weapon, for that matter." As Linas uncorked his flask and gulped a mouthful of rum, he could see the downtrodden expression on Bo'az's face. "Listen, boy, my opinion of you means nothing. I am not here to be your friend. Once I deliver you to my master, our business with one another is done. You will have much bigger responsibilities than to worry about what an old drunk thought of you."

Bo'az realized that Linas was right. There was no sense in caring what Linas or the other two thought, but for some reason, he sought their approval. He needed to be accepted and respected by them. Linas was correct about his other point as well. Bo'az had been sheltered his whole life. Only now did he realize how silly it was that he'd never been anywhere outside of Haedon. At almost eighteen years of age, this was the first time he'd actually been so far away from home. Baltaszar had tried to make him see that, but he'd been too stubborn to understand. He also realized that for as long as he could remember, he'd told himself that he was better off never leaving home or wondering about the rest of the world, if there had even been a bigger world beyond The Never.

When this adventure began, he'd had the thought that this would be an opportunity to begin anew and reinvent himself. At the time, they were words to be excited about, but now he believed them. His twin brother was off in another direction of the world, getting on with his life, and Bo'az now realized that when he saw Baltaszar again, he wanted to be able to say he'd done the same thing. "What about Gibreel and Rhadames? Have they not spoken to me because they think the same thing?"

"Gibreel…his impression is rather harsh. Gibreel began this mission in higher spirits. However, he currently believes that our mission is a waste of time, and not worth the difficulty. He doubts you and your potential. In general, Gibreel has never been known to think positively, if that is any consolation. Rhadames, on the other hand, barely ever speaks to anyone, except when necessary. I've only known him less than a year, but he is on this journey more because of his knowledge of the terrain and experience with animals."

"Animals?" Bo'az sat on the ground near Linas and noticed Yasaman had dismounted and was feeding her horse, stroking its mane. He then curiously scanned the area for Gibreel and Rhadames. He found them on his left, just entering the field of tall grass. The highest green blades reached their black-cloaked shoulders.

"The beasts in this part of the world are particularly dangerous, especially those in the mountains. We encountered a few on our journey coming here. Ultimately, Rhadames was the one who was able to kill them, after many futile attempts from myself and Gibreel. We were actually told that the forest housed extremely dangerous creatures, but apparently those were mere rumors. We have spent days riding through the forest, and barely encountered any life."

"Strange." Bo'az, barely listening to Linas anymore, saw Yasaman sitting at a tree about thirty paces to his right. She had her knees bent with her arms around them, and her head buried. He'd tried numerous times to talk to her in the past few days, but she'd never reciprocated. A few times, he'd rode his horse even with hers, hoping for some type of acknowledgement, but she'd always stared ahead or kept her head down. He understood that, as she'd believed him to be Baltaszar, he had a responsibility to make her feel better, but he also felt strange attempting any type of physical affection. He dared not hug her, but even putting a hand on her shoulder was beyond his capacity. Yet, he knew, regardless of who he was or was not, it was wrong to let the girl feel alone in her circumstances. Suddenly emboldened, he shot up from the ground and walked toward her. If Bo'az was going to change himself, he needed to start now and stop being afraid to act.

Bo'az walked confidently toward Yasaman and crouched in front of her, gently touching the side of her head with his good hand. She did not respond, so he moved his hand to hers and gently pulled it, whispering. "Yasaman, it's me. Please, you can't ignore me forever."

She finally lifted her head, her eyes raw and glossed over with tears, which ironically, caused her face to shine. Her cloak's sleeves had already absorbed pools of tears, and were quickly becoming soaked. She looked him straight in the eyes, but the melancholy in her face remained. Although her crying had been nearly silent, it was still evident in her broken voice as she spoke. "I'm sorry. I know you're trying to help, but there's nothing you can do right now. There's so much going on in my head. We'll talk soon, I promise." Her voice held no hint of thanks or friendliness, merely matter of fact. Yasaman then removed her hand from Bo'az's and got up to check on her horse.

Dejected, Bo'az turned and headed back to Linas. He had hoped to be able to do more for her, but she left him no room to argue the point. Gibreel and Rhadames had returned and were in the middle of planning the next step of the journey. "The high grassland between us and the mountain is rampant with traces of ranza cats." Gibreel, despite his detestable personality, was quite an efficient tracker and land surveyor. "However, they usually sleep during the light hours and hunt at night. I don't know how far they tend to stray from the grass; I've heard they hunt best in packs and prefer to stay hidden as much as possible. So, if we leave right now, we can be across the field and safely up the mountain with time to spare. Better to do it now while there is plenty of sunlight."

"Baltaszar, you heard Gibreel, we must leave now. I suppose you should tell the girl it is time to go." Linas still hadn't really warmed up to Yasaman. At least he, unlike Gibreel, went through the motions of pretending to care. As Bo'az turned in her direction, he realized she had already mounted her horse and was riding toward them, her face like stone.

"Ride as fast as you can and have your weapons drawn. If any of these beasts are nearby and catch our scent, they'll attack. And if they reach us, our horses won't survive," Gibreel warned them.

Linas, still sitting at the tree, nodded to Rhadames, "You and Gibreel pack up our things. Baltaszar, come here. I need to speak to you. Privately."

Gibreel and Rhadames wasted no time in gathering the food and supplies. Bo'az glanced at Yasaman sitting stoically on her horse; he then sat beside Linas once again.

With a tone barely over a whisper, Linas leaned toward Bo'az. "From here on, we do things my way. This whole journey revolves around your well-being. Do you understand?"

Bo'az stared at the ground for a moment, and then looked Linas in the eyes. He matched Linas' tone, "I think so. You mean no messing around. Listen to your command."

"That is only part of it. If anyone is hurt or killed, you follow my orders or theirs." Linas nodded toward his two companions. "Things will get dangerous now and you are the highest priority. Not the girl. I've adhered to your requests thus far. But from now on, if she slows us down, we leave her behind."

Bo'az's eyes widened. "Listen..."

"No. You listen." Linas continued whispering sternly, "I am responsible for you. Not her. If you die, my fate will be worse than death. If she dies, it only makes our journey easier. Protest if you like, but if we must bind your limbs and tie you to a horse, we will."

Bo'az shook his head in disapproval. "There has to be another way."

"I warned you of this when we first met. The girl is a liability. She has impeded us enough already. It cannot happen again. You deny that you are a fool, but look at reason, Baltaszar. Our journey has been easy thus far. Now we face difficult terrain and the threat of being hunted day and night. Chances are she will fare just fine. But if things get complicated, certain decisions will be necessary."

Bo'az pursed his lips. *He's right.* He massaged his temples slowly with his fingertips, ruminating over Linas' words. "Fine. But you will protect her just as closely as you will protect me. I won't let her be sacrificed just so you have a reason to leave her behind."

Linas looked over to Yasaman for a moment then turned back to Bo'az. "Very well. Understand that if I must choose between saving her life or yours, I will choose yours." He stood without waiting for Bo'az's response. "Now mount your horse. They are waiting for us."

"But..."

"We discuss this no further. Accept it. And perhaps pray to the Orijin that no trouble befalls the girl." Linas catapulted onto his horse. Next to him, Rhadames stood, holding the reins of his and Bo'az's horses. With a broken arm, Bo'az could not mount his horse without help.

Rhadames genuinely inquired, "Will you be able to ride on your own, boy? The voyage will be difficult from here."

Bo'az had too much pride to give in to the offer. *They will see me as weak if I don't ride on my own.* "I can manage on my own." Bo'az mounted Iridian as Rhadames shoved him upwards. Rhadames then detailed what the group would do next.

"Listen. Baltaszar, Linas will lead. You and the girl will follow and Gibreel and I will flank you just in case anything follows us. Any sign of trouble, you sprint until you reach where that mountain levels off. That will be the meeting point." Rhadames pointed to the mountain directly across the field of high grass. Up the base of the mountain sat a ledge nearly a hundred feet up. "Your horses will be tired, but spur them on no matter what. There is no time for idling."

"I have a name. It's Yasaman. I would prefer that you would stop calling me 'the girl'." Yasaman glared at all three companions as she led her horse up to Bo'az's. She'd cleaned up her face since Bo'az had gone to talk to her.

Gibreel cut in, spittle flying and catching in his thick beard as he spoke, "Shut up girl. Be grateful that we allowed you to come." He glowered at her, "when you aren't sobbing like baby, you're unappreciative of our hospitality. We did not invite you. Your name does not matter."

"Enough! This is pointless. Let us go!" Bo'az dug his heels into Iridian and the horse galloped into the grass. Linas immediately followed along with Yasaman. As Bo'az rode on, Linas sped past to assume the lead.

"Don't do that again!" Linas barked at him then turned forward again and drew a spear from a holster in the horse's saddle.

Rhadames grunted from behind, "Stay quiet! Not a word!"

Yasaman caught up to Bo'az and rode beside him. They strode onward; the only sounds audible to Bo'az aside from the clopping of hooves were the swishes of the horses against the tall grass and the dull hum of pepperflies in the distance. And then came a growl behind them that drowned everything else out. Bo'az realized the deep guttural sound came from multiple spots behind them. *There's more than one.*

Bo'az turned to Yasaman, her eyes wide. "Don't panic, Yas." *At least not yet. Save the panicking for me.* "They can handle this." Bo'az glanced backward.

Rhadames sat backwards on his horse with arrows drawn and aimed at the grass just over twenty yards behind him. Gibreel had just leapt high from his own horse, his nappy hair flailing while he clutched his sword with both hands, ready to thrust downward into the neck of an oncoming ranza. As the cat jumped at Gibreel, Rhadames speared it in the neck with an arrow and it lunged sideways, exposing the cat's side for Gibreel's killing blow to its ribs.

"We'll be okay. Even if those two don't like us, they've protected us against everything so far."

Rhadames cut in, "Save it, boy. Both of you get to the meeting point now! There are enough ranzas following us to feast on us *and* our horses!"

Bo'az dug his heels into Iridian and the mare galloped faster than even Bo'az had ever witnessed. His eyes darted right to check on Yasaman. She kept pace, her horse galloping along right next to him. *The horses must know.* As he was about to return his focus to what lay ahead, Bo'az espied a hulking black mass running alongside Yasaman's horse on the other side. The beast's back nearly reached the horse's height. *Focus. Think quickly!* Bo'az steered Iridian closer to Yasaman's horse until they were almost touching. "I need you to jump! Don't think, don't ask questions! Just let go of the reins and wrap your arms around my neck!"

But she hadn't listened. "Why? What's wrong?" Yasaman turned to her right and saw the monstrous black cat, grey and white stripes lining its fur, looking straight at her as it unleashed a thunderous roar.

Bo'az hooked his broken left arm through the reigns and leaned over horizontally, wrapping his right arm around her. He yanked her off the horse and onto his own so that she sat facing him. All the while, her horse neighed and shrieked as the ranza tore its entire thigh from its leg. "Don't look at it!

Cover your eyes and just pray that we reach the mountain!" Yasaman buried her face into his chest, her arms wrapped tightly around his torso.

If there was no danger of death, Bo'az would have stopped right there and ran his hand through her long black hair. Despite traveling for nearly a week, she'd still smelled of flowers and sweet berries. Maybe he would have kissed her too. *Stay focused, dummy!* "Hey, um…Yas? I might have spoken too soon. I…sort of need you to keep lookout for me."

Yasaman lifted her head and rolled her eyes at him. "Some hero you are." Her sarcastic smile offset any insecurity that might have stirred up in Bo'az's mind. She rested her chin on his shoulder, "I don't see any other cats coming our way. Three of them are tearing apart my horse. And there are about half a dozen places where the grass has folded over. I hope that means most of the cats are dead. Are we almost out of the grass?"

"Yeah. We're nearly out. I just hope Iridian has the energy to carry us both up to the landing."

She stared back into Bo'az's eyes, "Am I too fat for your horse, Tasz? Should I just walk up the mountain?"

"No! You know that's not what I meant. I was just saying that…" *Great. Now I'm panicking. First she doesn't speak for a week and now she has sarcasm.*

"When did you get so sensitive? I'm only joking with you."

Oh for the love of Orijin, there are more important things to be worrying about, and here I am worrying again that she'll see through me. "I know. I'm sorry. It's just the situation. How is it that you can be so cavalier right now? Your horse was just killed and you barely survived."

"Baltaszar. In the past week, your father was killed. My parents practically disowned me. I ran away from home, and then watched my father die as he tried to kill you. My horse…I think I'm simply finished feeling like a victim. I am tired of crying. I am tired of feeling like I have no control. Even this stupid journey we're on. Maybe we shouldn't have come. Who are these men? For Orijin's sake, look at them! They kill wildcats as big as horses like boys stepping on spiders! What business do we have traveling with them? We should just leave now, while they all have their hands full. Let's just turn around and go back."

"Go back to Haedon? We'll both be killed if we go back now. I don't trust our 'companions' any more than you do, but this isn't the place to be going off on our own. We'll bide our time." They reached the mountain and Iridian carried them up the slope, forcing Bo'az to look up at Yasaman. "Let's give it another day or two. Now that we're out of the Never and the wilderness, the mountains or the sea will provide better chances for us. We just narrowly escaped death; I don't feel like going back through that."

Yasaman looked at him curiously. "Maybe you're right; we could give it a couple days. But we have to find a way to escape before we get on their ship. Once we sail off with them, we won't have a chance."

That's a couple more days to figure out how to tell you I'm Bo'az.

"Hurry up!" Linas' voice echoed from the landing. "We have to set up camp soon before it gets dark! I've already found the caves." Bo'az and Yasaman had nearly reached him. The mountain must have had regular travelers for some time, as Bo'az had only just realized that Iridian was walking along an inclining path. Bo'az hadn't considered that the ride up the mountain had been rather smooth the entire time.

"Where were you? You were supposed to protect us! We were attacked!"

"You seem all right to me. If all we lost was one horse—the girl's horse at that—then I'd say we were quite successful. By the time the ranza reached you, I would have been unable to help you anyway. They are quite adept at going unnoticed." Bo'az and Yasaman had finally reached him. "Follow me. The caves are a little further up the mountain."

Bo'az helped Yasaman dismount then hopped off Iridian. "Wait! Linas! You saw it coming for us?" Linas revealed a smug grin. "You saw it hunting us down and you didn't even warn us? I thought you were supposed to be protecting me!"

Linas waved his hand at Bo'az, "Look. If I had alerted you, you would have both panicked and would both most definitely be dead. I needed to see how you would react, Baltaszar. At least now I know you are not a complete coward. You handled yourself rather well, with a broken arm at that! Gibreel might even be impressed!"

Blood raced through Bo'az's veins. "You bloody jackass! Your idea of a test is playing with our lives? I'll show you just how brave I can be! Just watch yourself!"

Linas laughed heartily, as if he'd been holding it in for some time. "Foolish boy. Why are you so angry? You should be proud! You saved both of your lives! Besides, I was not playing with your life, only hers." He nodded to Yasaman. The blood drained from Bo'az's face as Yasaman's jaw dropped and her eyes squinted in disbelief. "Oh, I apologize, Baltaszar. Did you not mention to your lady that she is expendable on this journey?"

Bo'az's choked out the words, his throat betraying him as it dried up. "You...you. What is...your problem?" Coughs interrupted his retort, "I thought you...I thought you were helping me! You don't need to be so cold. What has Yasaman done that you hate her so much?"

"I do not hate her, boy. I only find her unnecessary for our journey."

Yasaman finally spoke up, "Where is our cave? Tell me that much and I shall be out of your way. I would hate to be your child, you nasty old man."

Linas turned his back to lead them and walked on. "Follow me. It is just at the top of the next landing." Linas stopped for a moment and turned back to Bo'az, his long brown and grey hair covering half of his pale face. "Baltaszar," he sighed, "I am rigid because I have my orders. You constantly and conveniently forget that I was sent to find you and you only. Girl, I have no personal quarrel with you. But I am wary that you will complicate our plans to return with Baltaszar. Our master is a very deliberate and temperamental man. If we fail on this trek, he will not kill us. And that is what worries me, Gibreel, and Rhadames. We are too old and battle-weary to fear death. But he will make us suffer for years if we fail. I have been through too much life to deal with such things." Linas faced them fully once again.

"Look at me. I am old, greyed, scarred. My nose resembles a tree root because it has been broken so many times. I have three daughters not much older than you, girl. Do I want to kill you? Of course not. But I want to see my daughters again. I have not been home in nearly five years because I have been too busy searching the world for Baltaszar. I do not hate you, but I would gladly leave you behind if it means bringing Baltaszar back safely. Without question, I would readily trade your life to see my daughters again." As Linas turned back around, the stream of tears that dangled on his chin splattered loudly against the rocky path. He walked on briskly, not waiting for Bo'az and Yasaman to follow.

They reached another landing after another few hundred yards up. The path became more difficult the higher up they walked, but it was manageable. A series of cave openings grew visible ahead on the left. Linas shouted back to them, "The first cave is for me. Gibreel and Rhadames will share the second. You two take the third. It would be best if you two stayed in the same cave. It will be easier to guard. Gibreel will keep the first watch. Then Rhadames. They will sit outside just in case you prefer not to be disturbed. Build a fire. It will get quite cold up here. We leave at first light. No matter what."

"And what of our horses?"

"That's part of the reason for keeping watch. Our horses are trained to not leave us. Now that you only have one horse between the two of you, it will be rather easy to keep an eye on it during the night. It will only run if we encounter another predator," Linas stated matter-of-factly, "which is not impossible, but easier to handle up here." With that, Linas left his horse on the path and retreated into his cave.

Yasaman looked at Bo'az, "Let's go inside and start a fire, Tasz. I'm so tired of these men. I'd rather we were settled in before the other two return. Light of Orijin, I hope they don't come back. Just let them die out there. They deserve worse!"

"I don't even know what to think anymore, Yas. You saw him. The man was crying and still telling you he would let you die in the same breath." The thoughts buzzing through Bo'az's mind grew tangible and gave him another headache. Linas' words were harsh, but they held a certain honesty that Bo'az could not help respecting. *He has daughters. He has a family. He's a regular man, just like me. Just like my father.* Bo'az wedged a stick between two large stones at the gaping mouth of the pitch black cave. "Can you tie the reins? My arm…" He nodded to his broken left arm. Iridian was a rather obedient horse and would likely rest for a while after her frantic pace across the high grass. "I'm not saying I trust him or anything, don't get me wrong. But I do see some good in him." Though the cave's darkness shadowed much of Yasaman's face, her icy cold glare sent chills through Bo'az. *Am I constantly just saying the wrong thing or is this girl just naturally angry?* "Yasaman, don't give me that look. You know I'm not saying I agree with him." Bo'az hushed his voice, "But we need to find an escape soon. Especially now that you have no horse. They're going to be very impatient."

"What a relief. So you're not going to kill me yourself while we're sleeping?"

I hope that's sarcasm.

"Can you start a fire for us, Tasz? It's getting cold. Or will you need help because of your arm?" Bo'az must have furrowed his brow instinctively, as Yasaman clarified, "No, I mean that seriously. I'm not making fun of you."

Bo'az grew excited at the request. "Of course I can! I'm an expert at this by now!" Since Bo'az had left Haedon, Linas had asked him to build fires for the group every time they needed one. After the first couple of times, Bo'az had managed to spark a flame within seconds, no matter what the environment, even with a broken arm. He had grown quite proud of himself, though Linas and Gibreel always seemed disappointed.

Bo'az removed the pack from his shoulders and left it against the cave wall. He gathered sticks, branches, leaves—anything he could find that would burn—until a huge pile had formed at the center of the cave. Just as with the previous times, he started a flame in mere moments and heat permeated the cave almost immediately. He and Yasaman sat with the fire between them and the cave's opening. The light outside was fading as the sun had already begun its descent.

"I just realized, I don't have any clothes or…well anything really. All of my things were on the horse." She leaned against Bo'az and rested her head on his shoulder.

"You can use my clothes and cloak to stay warm tonight. I'll be fine." Bo'az removed his black woolen cloak and draped it around her.

"Baltaszar?" She whispered the name so innocently and curiously that Bo'az could not help being seduced.

"Hmm?"

"What happened to you? I mean, after that night in my room when you left?"

Oh no. Not more questions. I should just tell her now. "What do you mean?"

"I dunno. I…I guess I'm just surprised at how easily you accepted me back after the things that I said. I waited at your house for almost a day when you came and found me in the closet. And the whole time, I was sure that you would be furious with me. I had it all planned out in my head how I would convince you that we should get back together. But, there's no anger in you. None whatsoever. I just don't understand why you're not holding anything against me."

Bo'az was grateful for the fire. It kept him from having to look her in the face. "It's just…I…well so much has happened since then. So many things have changed. I…I suppose I simply don't have room for anger right now. At least not toward you. All we have here is each other. I'm just thankful to have you back at all." *Please let that suffice. No more questions.*

"What did you do when you left that night? What was going on in your head? I know you were so angry and I don't think I can ever apologize enough for the things I said."

Is this really happening? "Are you still cold? Should I make the fire bigger?"

"I'm fine. But answer the question. I need to know. Please?" She nestled closer and rested her slender hand on his knee.

Oh God. Orijin, get me through this, please. I swear I'll never do anything wrong again for as long as I live. Please just help me get out of this. "That night? Well, um…let me think. That night I…uh…I really just went back home."

"That's it? You blew up at me, stormed out of my window and just walked back home without a second thought about anything? I know your temper, Tasz. Just be honest. It's me."

"Seriously. I went home and went to sleep. My…my father needed me to be up early to milk the cows and sheep. I had no choice."

"You told me that night that Bo was covering for you in the morning. Baltaszar, just tell me the truth. Did you break something? Hurt someone? I just want to know exactly what I did to you. That's all."

Bo'az had been so focused on her words that he'd only just realized that Yasaman's other hand was freely exploring his back and chest. *That's it. I can't do this anymore. I have to tell her. I have to. There's no way I can get away with lying anymore.* "Yasaman, look…there's something…there's something I should tell you. I'm…I'm not…"

"Shhhh," she whispered, intentionally seductive this time. "Look at me, Bo'az. Look into my eyes. I know you're not your brother. I just wanted you to admit it." Bo'az stared her directly in her hazel eyes. They held no anger, no scorn. She pulled his shaggy face closer to hers and kissed him with an open mouth.

Bo'az hesitated for a moment. A thought drowning in the back of his mind told him this was wrong, but it was instantly subdued. Yasaman's tongue entered his mouth and flicked at his own. Bo'az pulled away. "Wait. I…should we be doing this? How can you be willing to do this if you know I'm not Baltaszar? You just said that you still love him and want him back.

And how long have you known?"

"This is what you'd rather do than kiss me? Ask questions?" Yasaman let out a long breath, "I have known since we left Haedon, to be honest. I first suspected when I kissed you in the dark. You don't kiss like him. When Tasz kisses me, there's so much passion behind it, like every time will be the last time he'll ever kiss me. With you, it...it was...different. But then you kept swearing that you were Baltaszar. And it was dark and I was so tired and emotional that I believed you. I mean, what reason would you have to lie?

"But then when we were outside with those three, I realized why you would lie. The way you defended me...insisted that I come with you. Bo'az, you've fancied me for some time, haven't you?"

Bo'az surprisingly felt the tension drain from his body. The lies and secrets were done. He didn't have to pretend anymore. He shrugged, "I have. But please don't think the wrong thing. I wasn't even aware that I felt this way until we kissed in my house. It was then that I realized what I actually felt...what I feel for you. But...but what about Tasz?"

"This isn't about Tasz, Bo'az. It's about the two of us. Where ever Tasz is right now, he's doing fine. He can always handle himself. I realized something while we were trekking up this mountain, though. Bo'az, don't be dense. We both know what Linas was hinting at. They don't want me around. They'll either kill me or leave me behind. I've accepted that."

Yasaman's words stabbed Bo'az between the eyes. "What? No, they won't. I wouldn't let them do that. Linas isn't that evil. I can see it in him. He wouldn't kill you, I know he wouldn't." He shook his head, trying to convince himself just as much as her.

Her tone held no sorrow or regret. "Bo'az, regardless, this is not a journey we'll return from. Please don't argue. I'm tired of thinking and planning and worrying. For one night, let's just forget about the world. We've been so caught up with trying not to die that I can't remember the last time I just...lived. Touch me, Bo'az. Lie with me. Let us have at least one last pleasure before we worry about dying again. I love Baltaszar. And I know you are not Baltaszar and I accept that. Tonight I want you. I want your body against mine. Inside mine. I just need that comfort." She pulled him closer once again and resumed the kiss he'd interrupted.

This time, Bo'az kissed her back. He hoped it was with as much passion as his brother. *Stop thinking about him. Make her happy, give her what she wants. What I want, too. At least if she's right and I die on this journey, I'll die as a man. A man who's been with a woman.*

***

Bo'az opened his eyes slowly, with the hopes that his memories of the night before hadn't betrayed him. He lay on his back and craned his neck. *Yes! I'm naked!* Bo'az threw his arms up in triumph. Next to him, Yasaman lay on her side, facing him and curled up in the cloak he'd given her. The rising sun had thankfully brought some warmth, as the fire had died out in the night and nothing separated Bo'az's bare body from the cool stone ground. Even his broken arm ached less than usual.

He turned on his side and wiped Yasaman's raven-colored hair from her face, then softly caressed her cheek. She squinted then opened her eyes at Bo'az's touch, smiling as she glanced upon him. "Good morning," she quietly grunted.

"Good morning. You look so beautiful." She smiled at his words. *Should I say it?* "I love you." It was a bold move, but Bo'az was confident in his feeling. An incredible energy filled his body, made him excited to live and to think about a grand future, something beyond the next few days.

"WHAT?" Yasaman shot up and widened her eyes so quickly that even the crusts in her eyelids fell away. "What do you mean you love me?" There was no kindness in her voice, no warmth, and certainly no reciprocity.

"No. Please don't be mad. It's just...it's...I mean, after last night. It was so perfect! I thought that you...that we...oh goodness. I'm sorry. I thought that maybe with what we did last night, that maybe you felt something, too."

"Bo'az, what happened last night was physical. It wasn't about feelings. My body needed yours. For comfort and for pleasure. Not for love. I'm sorry; I know how much courage it takes to say those words. But I still love Baltaszar, Bo'az."

"How? How could you do that to both of us? If you love him, then how could you do that with me? And how could you expect me to not feel anything toward you? Especially after you said last night how you knew how I'd felt? I've never been with any girl. I gave in last night, despite my brother, because of these feelings I have for you!"

Yasaman put her hand on Bo'az's face. "It's not that I feel nothing for you, Bo'az. But I'm confused about the situation. I love Baltaszar deeply, but I don't know if I'll ever see him again. I don't even know if I'll live to see the end of this journey."

Bo'az pulled her hand away. "So you seduced me just to have some pleasure before dying? Is that all?"

She glowered, "Don't act so high and mighty. I made my intentions clear! You knew what I wanted last night. There was no deception whatsoever. You could have stopped or refused, but you didn't." Bo'az sighed and quickly looked away. Yasaman continued, "Bo'az, our situation is a difficult one. Even aside from Baltaszar. Who knows what will be in store for us. Maybe I can grow to love you, I don't know. I've only come to know you well in the past few days and I think you are a wonderful person. Our future is too uncertain to quarrel over this. Please don't be angry with me."

Bo'az hadn't expected her to be quite so honest. She had called him on his behavior the night before. Yasaman was right. He could have refused her. But he wanted it so badly. *Perhaps I can give this some time. Perhaps her feelings can grow as strong as mine.* "Can you promise to at least be open to feeling something for me? Be open to considering that we might grow toward having something serious in the future?"

Yasaman took him by the scruffy beard on his chin and turned his face to hers. "I can be open to that." She smiled and kissed his cheek, then stood with the cloak still draped around her. "Come, let us get ready. They will no doubt be calling on us shortly. You should check and see what's happening outside."

With that, Bo'az fastened his breeches and boots, and then stepped outside. Rhadames sat just outside the cave entrance. He turned at the crunching of Bo'az's boots on the gravel of the path. Rhadames smirked at him and softly quipped, "It might be best for you two to be quieter from now on. It's amazing that no beasts found us with the way you both were carrying on. Let me guess, first time you've had knowledge of a girl?"

Bo'az flushed. Was it so obvious? What had he heard? *What if he knows about me?* He nodded in response. "It is not your business what we do in there. Perhaps you should focus on other things, like looking out, rather than listening to us."

Rhadames fired back, "Boy, consider yourselves lucky that Gibreel is a deep sleeper who snores and that Linas was too far to hear you both. Otherwise they may have killed your friend just to shut you up." He stood and towered over Bo'az. "Now get your things so we can go. The other two are already ahead of us."

"What about breakfast? Is there no time to eat? I'm starving!"

"We can eat soon. We are in a bit of danger right now though."

"Now what?" Bo'az could only imagine what they faced next. "Did the ranza cats follow us?"

"I wish it were that easy. Gibreel found silberlow droppings about a quarter mile ahead. And there is only one path to the other side of the mountain."

More strange names. "Silberlow?"

"Mountain cats. If you thought the ranzas were vicious, well, the ranzas stay out of the mountains because of the silberlow." Rhadames glanced ahead then back at Bo'az. "Now go get your things. Silberlow are stronger, leaner, and deadlier than the ranzas, and they can blend in with the colors of the mountain."

As Bo'az turned back into the cave, he shouted, "So then why didn't you wake us if these things are so deadly and nearby?"

"You were safe in the cave! The silberlow hate fire. All you would have to do is restart your fire and the cat would not enter. Unfortunately, it would also wait outside until you finally left."

Bo'az crouched inside the cave and gathered his pack. He found his shirt and put it on. Yasaman stood beside him now, "Are they all ready? It is time to go?"

Bo'az nodded in response then stood and exited with her. "Where is my horse, Rhadames?"

"Linas and Gibreel led it with theirs when they embarked. After Gibreel saw the droppings, we thought the horses would be better targets. So they took three and I have mine." Rhadames started walking, "Come. Follow me. And stay close."

"You took my horse to use as bait?"

Yasaman cut in, "Wait. Droppings? What's going on? She looked back and forth between Bo'az and Rhadames for an answer.

Rhadames explained, "There are mountain cats—silberlow, nearby. Gibreel found their droppings not far ahead. So we must be cautious. And yes Baltaszar. Your horse is a better sacrifice than you are. Or would you rather we sacrificed your precious bedmate here? You know how the others feel about her."

Yasaman blushed and fired back, "Are you implying that you do not want me dead, Rhadames?"

"To be quite honest, I do not care if you live or die. Our journey is difficult either way. You are beneficial because you provide an easy sacrifice for any predators. But you are also a burden because you can potentially slow us down. But do not take any of it personally. I would not go out of my way to kill you." He stroked his thick dark brown beard as he walked and spoke.

They reached Gibreel and Linas after walking a half mile upwards. The mountain had a wide flat clearing with a few short trees and shrubs interspersed, with a few low-topped caves several yards to the left. The two of them held five lit torches in their hands.

Gibreel muttered "Finally," to himself, but loud enough for Bo'az to hear. "Let us go quickly. We will go on foot and carry torches. If any silberlow come upon us, we don't want frightened horses throwing us over the side of the mountain. We must make haste. Their tracks litter this trail." Gibreel handed each of them a torch.

Linas interjected, "Let us go now. No wasting any more time." He turned and walked to the path, leading his horse along. Bo'az and the others turned and followed as Gibreel once again flanked them.

Bo'az glanced constantly over at Yasaman as he walked side by side with her. *Should I say anything else? Should I tell her again how I feel just so she knows? Or maybe I should tell her I'm okay with what she wants to do. That way she won't think this situation is awkward for me.* Bo'az was about to fumble over more words to say to Yasaman when something slammed into him from behind. His body lurched forward as his head whipped back and then something else punched his head forward. His torch dropped and he tumbled to the ground along with Iridian. Rocks and horse's limbs scratched, stabbed, and beat against his defenseless body. Bo'az was twisting and turning too fast to feel the pain of any of the blows.

Bo'az scraped along the rocky path, knocking against horses and people. In the hurtling frenzy, Bo'az caught glimpses of Gibreel and his horse tangled with the rest of the mess. When they finally stopped, deafening growls and the shrieks of a horse drowned out Bo'az's groans as he lay on his stomach. All of the cuts and bruises felt like fire burning through Bo'az's skin and dull aches penetrated his bones. Iridian lay on her side, trapping his already-broken left arm. Thankfully, his arm had gone numb.

"Yas!" He swiveled his neck searching for any glimpse of her. "Where are you? Yasaman, can you hear me?" Chances were slim that she would hear him over the snarls of what was clearly a silberlow ripping apart Gibreel's horse. A few moments later, the growls and snarls of the silberlow turned to shrieks and sounded further away. The same beast then screamed in a deathly agony amid men's shouts. *Who could be rescuing us?*

Iridian rocked back and forth, neighing and trying desperately to stand. The more the horse shook, the more Bo'az worried about his arm.

"We're going to shift your horse, boy. When we do, roll yourself away." Rhadames nodded to Bo'az as he and Linas heaved and removed the weight from Bo'az's arm. The moment the pressure was released, Bo'az rolled his body, thankful for the long awaited freedom. He tried to stand but wobbled on his knees and put his good hand down to stabilize himself. Only then did Bo'az actually look at his body and see the pools of blood caked and stained on his clothes. He shook his head vigorously to clear out the cloudiness and rose again slowly. This time he managed to stand and surveyed his surroundings.

Yasaman lay face down on the ground twenty yards ahead in a disheveled heap. One of her shins was bent forward. *She won't be able to walk like that. They won't let her go on.* Bo'az walked as quickly as he could toward her, though he was still wobbly. Running would only have caused him to fall. He knelt and rolled Yasaman to her side.

"Bo'az, my leg," she croaked, groggily.

"Shh, I know. I know. We'll have to figure something out. Some way for you to walk without them taking much notice." He sat her up.

"There's nothing Bo. There's no way to hide this. I'm…I'm scared. I don't want them to kill me Bo." Tears flowed from the corners her eyes and dripped onto Bo'az's hand as he cupped her face.

"Listen. They will not kill you. I won't let them. We have too much to look forward to now for me to lose you." Bo'az fought back the tear that tried to break free from his eye. He stifled a crack in his voice.

Gibreel limped over. "Go help them with your horse, boy. She's going to have to be put down. You should be the one to do it. Here, take my blade." The man was surprisingly warm. But then again, Gibreel knew animals well. *Maybe he knows how difficult it is. Maybe there's something human in him after all.*

"I have to stay here with Yasaman. I need to help her."

"I will get her to her feet. Go take care of your horse."

"Are you going to help her or kill her? Or are you going to leave her here as bait for more silberlow? I don't trust you." Bo'az had gingerly walked a few feet, but turned and faced Gibreel, inspecting the man's every move.

"Now is not the time for this, boy. Your horse is in agony. Comfort it in its final moments and then kill it. I promise I will not leave the girl here to die or use her as bait. Now go." Gibreel's notorious scowl returned to his chiseled face as he spat on the ground.

Bo'az gazed at Yasaman for a moment and staggered to Rhadames and Linas. Behind him, Yasaman whimpered in pain as Gibreel lifted her and acted as her crutch. Bo'az turned once more, his heart still aching at the thought of Yasaman in so much pain. Realization punched his mind as he turned, seeing Gibreel dragging Yasaman toward the edge of the path. The side of the mountain was completely vertical here, allowing for an easy drop. Rage and madness invaded him as his heart beat through his chest. Summoning all of his body's willpower, Bo'az found the will to run and raced to the pair. His legs still wobbled somewhat, but Bo'az would not give in. He reached Gibreel's back just as the man shoved Yasaman over the side of the mountain. Her scream echoed on and on.

Bo'az realized he was screaming aloud, as well as in his head. Gibreel stood before him, looking over the side of the mountain. With all of his remaining strength, Bo'az shoved the muscular man off the side of the mountain. Gibreel screamed, just as Yasaman had, as he hurtled to the ground so far down below.

"What happened, boy?" Rhadames demanded over Bo'az's shoulder, "What just bloody happened!"

"He...he threw her off the side!" Bo'az's body convulsed as he stepped away from the mountain's edge. "He...he killed her!"

In the distance, Linas shouted a nonchalant order, "Tie him up Rhadames. He will travel the rest of the way bound hand and feet."

Rhadames shouted back, "Understood!" He then turned back to Bo'az and shoved him to the ground. "You had better hope that we don't face anything else on our way home. You may not have liked Gibreel, but he's the one who saved us from being attacked more times than you know."

Bo'az doubled over. The numbness had left his arm and the pain throbbed from fingertip to shoulder. "He killed her, Rhadames. What was I to do? I loved her. I am nothing now. My life is nothing. He deserved to die. He wanted to kill her from the start. She was mine. Mine to love. He had no right!"

"Look boy, I don't know what your name is. But I'm sure your brother, the real Baltaszar, would beg to differ about this girl you love."

Despite his pain and the world beginning to swirl, Bo'az shot Rhadames an icy sneer and then dry heaved. There was nothing in his stomach to vomit except water.

"I told you that you were loud last night. It was not Baltaszar she was moaning for in the night, but it was his name she was saying in her sleep." Rhadames looked around and then lowered his voice. "Obviously I'm not here to kill you, or you'd be dead already. But listen and listen well. Linas is a good man, but if he finds out that you're not Baltaszar, he'll kill you on the spot. That's why I lied to him back at your house when he asked about the line. You look exactly like Baltaszar except there's no black line on your face. Twins, then?"

Bo'az refused to answer.

"Don't be a fool. I met Baltaszar the night before we came to your house and sent him on his way. He had the mark on his face. Yet, the next day, *you* claimed it had already been gone for days."

Bo'az acquiesced, clutching his arm. "Yes. We're twins."

Rhadames nodded, his eyes showing he already knew the answer. "You've kept the lie pretty well so far. Keep it going if you want to stay alive."

Bo'az could feel the rope tightening around his feet. "Can't you just kill Linas and let me on my way? Then you could just tell Darian that we were all killed."

Trust me, boy. If I could, I would let you escape. But I need to keep an eye on you now to ensure that you live. And I still have unfulfilled promises to your father. I cannot afford to die or to be tortured just yet, which is what would happen if I let you go. In the meantime, it would be in your best interest to sleep. And no matter what, do not tell me your name. It's better that I don't know it. And now I'm going to have to put you to sleep."

As Rhadames finished speaking, the cloudiness in Bo'az's mind once again turned to blackness and oblivion as something smashed the back of his skull and knocked him flat on the ground.

CHAPTER 7
A BLIND MAN IN VANDENAR

From *The Book of Orijin*, Verse Forty-Nine
We do not merely judge you by your treatment of those whom you love. Be kind to those whom you do not know. Whom you do not understand. Whom you do not love. This fault has twice been the downfall of Mankind.

THE BLACKNESS REMAINED despite opening his eyes. The only difference was the innumerable pairs of beady red dots. Baltaszar sat up, as if from lying in bed, but could see nothing around him nor beneath him aside from the darkness.

Eyes. They're eyes! The epiphany did not comfort nor disturb him. It was merely an admission to something he realized he'd known all along.

The air grew heavy and hot, as if an invisible fire roared all around him. The eyes simultaneously melted and dripped, forming a red pool that moved toward him. As the thick liquid reached his right hand, Baltaszar screamed from the scorch of heat.

The darkness ripped away and Baltaszar jolted from sleep and sat upright. *These damn dreams again.* He inspected his hand; it was surprisingly very warm but not burnt. And all evidence of the snake bite had disappeared. *How is this possible?*

He heard a knock nearby and, for the first time, realized he lay in a bed in an unfamiliar room. The walls were bare, with the exception of empty candle holders and a mirror and dresser to his left. Before he could respond, the door opened and a young girl peeked inside.

"Is there trouble, Lord Harbinger?"

What did she just call me? "Lord Harbinger?"

She opened the door and stepped into the room. "I apologize, my lord. We do not know yer name but, well, the black line. Obviously ya are a Descendent. So we've taken to callin' ya Lord Harbinger."

At further glance, the girl wasn't really so young, but likely of an age with Baltaszar. She was slightly shorter than he and had a thin frame. Her grey, almond-shaped eyes were more beautiful than any he'd ever seen, even Yasaman's. She'd tied her silky-thin black hair behind her head and wore a simple brownish-grey frock, similar to those that the maids wore in Haedon. The only difference was how low cut it was, revealing the girl's huge bosom.

Baltaszar caught himself staring too long and the girl giggled at his gaze. He cleared his throat, "Baltaszar. My name is Baltaszar. I'm fine, just a bad dream."

"Lord Baltaszar. Just like Darian's best friend. Or so they say. I am Anahi. If ya need anything, anything at all, all ya have to do is ask." She winked at him, "I make it a point ta take care o' all Descendants to the best o' my abilities. Especially ya br...we don't get many o' ya brown-skinned boys this far west."

"I...all right." Baltaszar had too many questions and didn't want to start asking while naked in bed.

Anahi turned to leave the room and gave Baltaszar one last smile. "Weird that Desmond didn't mention anythin' about other Descendants bein' in this area. He just left a few weeks ago." She didn't wait for a response and closed the door behind her.

Baltaszar got up and found his clothes folded in the dresser, washed, dried and smelling of lavender. He pulled them on and left the room. As he'd suspected, he was at an inn. Though it could have been anywhere. He had no idea how long he'd slept or how far he'd traveled. With any hope, he was in the town Slade had told him to find. *Van...Vandenar. Well, let's find out, shall we. Are you still not talking to me?*

He got no response.

Good. Maybe I'll never hear from you again. Baltaszar walked down the hall past other rooms and then down a wooden staircase at the end. The bottom gave way to a large community room where a few people sat eating at tables. He cautiously entered the room but no one even glanced up at him.

"Lord Harbinger!" A hearty voice shouted from his left, "Yer finally awake! That's one heck o' a bite ya took, we were wonderin' how long ye'd be out."

The voice belonged to a middle aged man behind the bar. His almond eyes and yellow skin were similar to Anahi's, though that was the extent of the resemblance. The man had only short grey hair on the sides of his head, which matched the hair sprouting from his ears. He was chubby but not fat, and as soon as Baltaszar saw his smile, he knew the man was the type who was always smiling. "My name is Baltaszar. Baltaszar Kontez. Is this Vandenar? Am I in Vandenar?"

"Baltaszar, huh? Will do, son. Name's Cyrus Baek. Yes, this is Vandenar, well no, this here is my inn, the Happy Elephant, but well, yeah, in Vandenar. Anyway, how ya feelin' son?"

Baltaszar leaned on the bar counter, "I'm better, tha..."

"Go on, sit down boy. Ya don't hafta worry about bein' polite an' so lordly ta me! Go on, sit on the stool; get comfortable!" Cyrus pointed to the high wooden stool next to Baltaszar.

Baltaszar sat and continued, "I'm fine, thank you. Was it you who rescued me?"

"You bet it was. Me an' my fishin' crew. We saw ya from way off, wavin' an' thrashin' about an' once we saw ya go down, we knew exactly what happened. That river is darn full o' them sea serpents. We catch one of 'em for every five fish we get. An' they got so much poison that ya can't even cook 'em. Just gotta throw 'em back! Some reason, they only eat certain fish though, so at least they save some fer us.

"But anyway, like I said we saw ya from far. Only when we actually picked ya up did we realize yer a Descendant. Hopefully ya can forgive us takin' so long. Had we known we woulda tried ta get ya much faster."

Baltaszar looked around at the few other patrons eating and yawned. His mouth watered at the sight of plates with hot food. "It's nothing. You came and saved me and I'm alive and well because of it. Thank you. It doesn't matter who I am or what's on my face. You're a good man."

"Least I could do. Ya look hungry son; let me fix up a plate fer ya."

"I have no coin to pay you. Besides, you've done enough already. I'm sure you could use my room for someone else."

Cyrus chuckled, "Ha! Yer money's no good here, my lord. Any friend o' Desmond is welcome here, no charge. The King can bring his ass here an' I'll tell him the same darn thing! Vandenar an' the Happy Elephant protect our Descendants! Anyway, what was I sayin'? Oh, right. You folk eat an' stay free. Whenever ya want."

What is he talking about? "Desmond? I don't know who Desmond is."

"Oh. Yer new ta the House? Maybe Desmond doesn't know ya too well then. He just left fer the House couple weeks ago, too. Doesn't really know many o' ya. Speakin' o' which, what brings ya all the way up here anyway? Summer's endin' an' ain't much happenin' in Vandenar now. Ya lookin' fer someone in Vandenar? Or were ya lookin' for somethin' in the Never? Is that why you were crossin' the river from up there?"

Baltaszar's eyes shot up. "You know of the House of Darian? Is it far from here? Slade told me to come here and people could direct me to it. I'm not here on business. I'm from Haedon. That's why I came from the Never.

"House is about a few day's ride from here. Just gotta follow the road south. Ya never been there yet? Never heard o' Haedon. How far is that?"

"Haedon is in the mountains. About a three day walk into the Never."

Cyrus chuckled again and whipped the counter with his white hand towel. "In the Never! Haha, boy! All ya gotta say is ya can't tell me yer business. Psshh. I'm used ta Desmond givin' me the secrecy bit. He's my nephew an' he ain't even straight with me. So ya want some food or what?" He poked his head through a door behind the bar, "Ellie! Make me a plate o' eggs an' a steak! I got a hungry Black-line boy out here! Desmond's friend! Make it quick!"

"Thanks again. I am starving. But seriously. It's no joke or trick. My town is in the forest up in the mountains. It's called Haedon. Our chancellor is Oran Von."

"Yep. Now you're definitely lyin', boy. 'Haedon' means 'hidden city' in Imanol, the old tongue. Who in their right mind would call a town 'hidden city' an' then put it in the middle o' all that haunted forest?" Cyrus shook his head at Baltaszar, "I know I look dumb, son, but I still got more wits than hair. What ya drinkin'?"

Baltaszar understood now that it would be pointless to pursue the argument further. "Water."

"Anyway, yer welcome to stay as long as ya need, boy. Friend o' Desmond or not, I know ya boys're always up to somethin' important. I won't get in yer way, just holler if ya need anythin'. 'N if anyone's snoopin' around, I won't tell em' yer here. Have some breakfast then go back an' rest up some more. I'll send Anahi up ta take care o' ya. She's lookin' forward ta seein' ya anyway. Won't shut up about 'the brown-skinned Lord'."

A maid came through the door with Baltaszar's breakfast, three eggs over a giant steaming steak. Baltaszar took the knife and fork and immediately shoveled food into his mouth.

"Eat up boy, we got plenty o' that. Not many travelers now that summer's done, so let me know if ya want more." Cyrus set a mug of water next to Baltaszar's plate.

Baltaszar could only nod; he stuffed his mouth with a new mouthful as soon as he'd swallowed the previous mouthful. The steak was twice the size of any he'd ever had in Haedon. It tasted a bit gamey, compared to steak up in Haedon, but it was still amazingly delicious. After a few minutes, he'd cleaned the plate and would have asked for another, except that he didn't want to impose. The feeling of a full belly made him lethargic and he decided he would heed Cyrus' advice to rest for a while more.

"Anythin' else I can get ya, boy?"

"No thank you, Cyrus. That was incredible. I think I'll go take a nap." Baltaszar returned to his room and lay down. Sleep would come easy with his body still tired and coupled with a full belly. He drifted off for what seemed like hours of thankfully dreamless sleep and woke up to something warm pressing against his body. Baltaszar blinked away the sleep in his eyes to see Anahi nestled against him, her head on his bare chest. "What are you doing, girl?" Baltaszar jolted out of the bed as the well-endowed girl awoke, disoriented. "Are you crazy or something? I didn't tell you to come in here!"

Anahi furrowed her brow, confused and insulted, "I told ya that I would take care o' ya, my lord. Ya didn't refuse, so I assumed ya were fine with some good ol' snugglin'." Her confusion turned to annoyance. "Are ya so dense that ya didn't understand my meanin'? Or were ya so enchanted while starin' at my breasts that ya didn't hear anythin' I said?"

Baltaszar flushed at the accusation. He had no defense against her, he should have known better. "No, you're right. I didn't do anything to turn you away. I suppose, deep down I didn't think you were serious. That maybe you were simply flirting casually."

"So then, do ya want me ta stay or not, Lord Baltaszar?"

"Please don't call me that. It's just Baltaszar. I am no lord. And though I would love for you to stay, I cannot. My heart belongs to another, and I cannot be with another girl knowing that we might still have a future."

"That's quite noble o' ya. Most men forget they're taken the second another girl offers herself ta them."

"Well I suppose I'm not most men. And believe me, it's nothing personal. I'll regret refusing you, but I'd regret accepting your offer even more."

Anahi nodded her head then stepped to him and kissed Baltaszar on the cheek, and pressed her chest to his. "Very well, my lord, perhaps another time when I'm the lesser o' two evils."

I'm such an idiot. "You said that you take care of us Descendants. Do your services extend beyond sneaking up on people while they sleep?"

Anahi cocked an eyebrow at the question. "I suppose it depends on the service ya require."

"Well, the thing is, I know incredibly little about the world beyond my town. I was thinking that you could escort me about Vandenar, show me the city."

She smiled at the request. "I would love ta, Baltaszar."

Baltaszar smiled back at her acceptance. "Will Cyrus be angry at your absence?"

"Cyrus doesn't get angry at anythin'. An' he loves any Descendant who stays here. Besides, this is a slow time o' year. Ya saw the common room; there are hardly any guests fer me ta entertain or rooms fer me ta clean. Let me just change inta normal clothes. Meet me downstairs in a few minutes."

Baltaszar dressed and headed to the common room. Cyrus was sitting at a table chatting with what Baltaszar assumed were some friends. He nodded and smiled to Cyrus as he walked to the door and Cyrus returned the gesture with an ear to ear grin. Baltaszar was unsure of whether he'd simply grown jaded over the past few years in Haedon, but he had difficulty accepting that people could be as generous and genuine as Cyrus seemed to be. *Perhaps the world isn't as dangerous and evil as Bo'az had always thought it to be.*

He'd only had to wait a minute or two before Anahi came downstairs to meet him. She'd changed into a long light blue ruffled skirt that covered her feet and a tight white high-necked blouse that was mostly covered by a thick brown scarf she'd wrapped around herself. Again, Baltaszar stared at her for a moment too long.

"Does this not suit yer tastes, my lord? Or is there a different meanin' in yer stern expression?"

Why do girls always read into every little thing? "No no, don't take it the wrong way. You look beautiful, it's just…you're dressed very modestly."

"Is that such a bad thing? Yer quite confusin', Baltaszar. First ya stare down my shirt an' lead me ta believe ya want me. Then ya refuse me. An' now I'm too modest fer ya?"

Anahi's wittiness elicited a silly grin from Baltaszar. "I wasn't complaining. I guess I just assumed that the way you dressed here was the way you always dressed. And yes, I confuse myself on many occasions. It's nothing personal."

"Silly boy," she said innocently, yet seductively, "if I dressed like that out in public, I would have nearly every man in Vandenar propositionin' me. Even modestly, too many men get too brave fer my likin'."

"So do you only seduce men as part of your job then?"

Anahi rolled her eyes. "Come, let's start walkin'. If we waited here fer yer wits to kick in, we'd never leave." She put her hand in Baltaszar's arm and led him down the wide street.

Baltaszar could not let her comment go undefended. "It's not that I'm a dimwit. I've just been sheltered in my life. There's too much of this world that I don't know about. In fact, until a day or two ago, I had no idea that there really was a world beyond my town up in the mountains."

"Ya know enough ta be true ta the woman ya love. There are thousands o' men more intelligent an' worldly than ya who cannot say the same. But enough o' that. Ask me anything about Vandenar, or life beyond yer forest, an' I'll give ya an answer if I can."

"You don't think it strange that I come from the mountains and forest? Your friend Cyrus didn't believe me."

"It is strange, considering how close Vandenar is to the Never, an' yet not once have we met anyone who's claimed ta come from there. But I myself have never been out o' Vandenar, so it's not my place ta judge. Perhaps Cyrus has better reasons ta doubt ya."

"Fair enough. Tell me about Cyrus."

"What is it ya want ta know?"

"Is he really as nice a man as he seems?"

"Nicer. Cyrus is one o' the biggest reasons why people even visit Vandenar. He doesn't turn anyone away until lit'rally no one fits. He doesn't care about where yer from or anythin'; he'll welcome anyone in without judgin' 'em. He'll feed an' help anyone in need, as ye've seen fer yerself."

"Why? Why would anyone be that kind, even to strangers? And how can he afford to be that nice?"

"The how part is easy. When yer that nice, at least in Vandenar, people tend ta repay their debts. Fer all Cyrus gives ta the people in need, he gets repaid ten-fold. Maybe not always in money, but it could be in goods, clothes, supplies, fixin' up his inn, whatever. The why, well he's always been like that, at least fer as long as I've known him, which is near ten years.

After his wife passed, he just got nicer. The thing is, his whole life now is 'The Happy Elephant'. He doesn't know anythin' else an' he thrives off o' havin' people there all the time. Keeps his mind off the sadness, I suppose."

A pang of sorrow stabbed Baltaszar's insides. "I'm sorry to hear that. People like him don't deserve to feel that kind of sadness in life."

"Believe me; Cyrus had more support than he could ask fer when she died. It wasn't sudden; all o' Vandenar saw it comin' fer months. She was sick, beyond the help o' our nurses. It's because Cyrus is the man he is that we were all there for him ever since. I'm not sayin' I don't feel bad fer him, but some people have it much worse when a loved one dies."

Baltaszar bit his lip hard, "Yeah. Definitely."

Anahi looked like she was about to ask a question, then held it back. "Baltaszar, did ya really just ask me ta walk ya around so we could talk about Cyrus an' depressin' things?"

"Well, no. But…one more question about Cyrus and then that's all, I swear."

"Fine."

Baltaszar glanced over to Anahi as they walked, "Why is it called The Happy Elephant? I've never even seen an elephant except in drawings back home."

"Ha! Ya really have lived a sheltered life, haven't ya." She smiled at Baltaszar as if there was a lot more laughter being kept in than let out. "Vandenar is known for elephants! Haven't ya wondered why the streets are so wide? Every year in the spring an' early summer, we walk 'em through the main road o' Vandenar ta show off the stock ta our residents an' visitors. Elephants are our main source a industry."

"Wait, so what exactly do you use them for?"

"Well, food fer one thing. I'm sure ya know what a cow is. An elephant can provide three or four times as much meat than a cow, an' the meat is just as tasty. Not ta mention the hide is more durable than a cow's leather."

Baltaszar felt an uneasiness within his stomach. "What do you mean, food? People actually eat those things?"

"Did Cyrus give ya any food today? Any meat?"

"Yes, but he gave me a steak."

"Cyrus doesn't serve beef, Baltaszar. I'm sure the steak ya had was much larger than any beef steak ya seen before."

Baltaszar was now torn between acceptance and nausea. He'd never actually seen an elephant before, so he wasn't overly disturbed about the notion of eating elephant meat. Yet, for as long as he could remember, he'd only eaten beef, chicken, mutton, and fish. *I suppose this is the first of many new things I'll have to become accustomed to.* "All right, fine. I'll admit it was likely the best steak I've ever tasted."

"I must say I'm impressed. Dimwit farm boy fresh out into the world an' the thought o' eatin' an elephant didn't disgust ya. Perhaps there's hope fer ya yet. So many foreigners turn their noses at the thought o' elephant. Until they taste it o' course." Anahi squeezed Baltaszar's arm tight, pulling him closer.

"Just because I've been sheltered doesn't mean I'm afraid of new things. So are you going to keep poking fun at me or are you going to give me a tour of Vandenar? What kind of guide belittles her customers?"

"Oh yer payin' me now are ya?"

"Only if you're good!"

"Fine then, I'll give ya a history o' every single buildin' in this city." She walked faster, pulling him along.

They walked on through the streets of Vandenar while Anahi discussed the intricacies of the town and details about the littlest of details. She held conviction in her explanations, passion for her home. Vandenar used wood for buildings and homes, because people worked so hard during the day that brick would only make them sweat more.

There was no one ruler of Vandenar, such as how Oran Von was the Chancellor of Haedon. The people all had the best interest of the town in their minds and hearts, so the elders of Vandenar made the decisions that were in the best interest of the masses. Of course they were overseen by the Lord of Mireya, the nation in which they resided, who then reported to the King. But they all appeased the Lord's tax collectors when they came through, so there was never any trouble. At the heart of it, people didn't come to Vandenar to cause trouble.

***

After over an hour of walking through Vandenar, Baltaszar had grown well accustomed to the habits, customs, and history of the city. *I wish Bo'az had come with me. All that fear and apprehension he had about the world would have been gone by now. I wonder what he's doing now.*

They walked along a side road toward the wide main road at the heart of the city. A few merchants and shop owners sat outside their stores and smiled and waved at Anahi as she and Baltaszar walked by.

"Do you know them all or are they being nice with the hopes of getting to know you?"

Anahi grinned and blushed, "I know them all. Most shop owners in Vandenar are men with families. And the city is too close knit fer men to be havin' affairs. It's usually the outsiders who abandon their morals at the sight o' a pretty girl."

Baltaszar nodded. "So...do you..."

"No, I am not a whore, Baltaszar." Her tone and countenance suggested that she'd taken offense at what Baltaszar had implied. "Just because I offered ta sleep with ya doesn't mean I sleep with every man who comes ta the inn." She walked faster and Baltaszar quickened his pace to keep up.

"Look, maybe that's what I was going to ask, but I didn't mean to offend you. You yourself said plainly when we first met that you 'take care of' the Descendants who come to this town. What was I supposed to think?"

She pursed her lips and rolled her eyes, "You assume too much, farmboy. We hardly get any Descendants this far north. In the past few years, we've had less than five come up this way. An' four o' them were originally from this city. An' before ya ask, I slept with one o' them. I'd fancied him fer a long time. Does your lady back home allow ya ta be so forward when you speak ta her?"

Baltaszar looked down at the road as they walked on, "Well, while she was still speaking to me, she was just as forward as me. So I guess it didn't really matter to her. I guess perhaps I didn't realize that I couldn't speak that way to other girls."

"You really are sheltered an' naïve," Anahi quipped as she shook her head at him.

Baltaszar smiled as he sensed her mood softening, "I wasn't lying."

"Baltaszar Kontez! Come here boy! Come in! I have a prophecy fer ya!" A voice called for Baltaszar from one of the shops along the right side of the road. Baltaszar looked over to the porch from where he heard the voice. An old bald man stood up from his wooden chair and continued to shout, "Baltaszar Kontez!"

Baltaszar looked to Anahi, "Who is that? How does he know my name?"

"Are ya not familiar with the Blind Men? Augurs I think is the proper term."

Baltaszar shook his head, confused.

"They are seers. The Blind Men give prophecies. Not at command, but visions an' prophecies come ta them randomly. Arbitrarily. Actually I think there are Blind Women, too."

Baltaszar eyed her suspiciously. "So why are they called Blind Men?" The man continued to call for him in the background.

"I supposed it is the Orijin's way o' givin' 'em balance in their lives. The legend is that children who are born blind develop this ability in their lives. So while they can't physically see, their minds are gifted with this ability."

Baltaszar looked again at the man, then back at Anahi. "What should I do?"

"Go humor him. The Blind Men are not evil. That he knows yer name is very tellin'. Probably it means he's already seen somethin' about ya. He probably knew ya would even walk by at this moment. Why else would he shout yer name, if he can't even see ya? Go see what he wants. I'll wait here."

Baltaszar looked back at the Blind Man, who still stood and stared directly at Baltaszar, despite his blindness. Chills ran up Baltaszar's body at the unfocused gaze. He walked up the porch stairs to the man. "I am Baltaszar Kontez. What do you want with me?" Upon closer inspection, the main was frail, barely filling out the loose green robe he wore, and liver spots covered his wrinkly, yellow-hued skin. He barely reached Baltaszar's shoulder.

The old man's bright green eyes flitted about in their sockets as he smiled and shook his head. "No need fer hostility, boy. I mean ya no harm."

"Then what do you want?" Baltaszar said, a bit more harshly than he intended.

"I've a prophecy fer ya boy, though I do not remember it from the top o' my weathered head. Come in an' have some tea while I find what I must tell ya. Farco, help me inside." The man motioned to the doorway, where a boy, no older than ten or eleven years, stood with the man's cane. The boy, Farco, helped the Blind Man inside. Farco bore the typical features of everyone else in Vandenar: yellowish skin, almond-shaped eyes, and his black hair was long and shaggy, almost covering his eyes. Baltaszar followed and Farco gestured for him to sit down at a table covered with piles of books. The room smelled musty and the walls were lined with bookshelves, all tightly packed with more thick, dusty books. The young, dark-haired boy helped the old man to a chair on the opposite side of the table, and then left the room to make the tea.

"If you are blind, why do you have so many books? Does the boy read to you?" Baltaszar couldn't imagine how annoying that process would be to have to read all of these books to the old man.

"Open one up an' ya shall have yer answer." The man held his hand out to the piles of books on the table.

Baltaszar took one from the top of a dusty pile and opened it, the leather of the spine cracking a bit. As soon as Baltaszar opened the book, he understood. The pages were filled with patterns of dots and dashes, raised slightly off the page. "Did you create this language yourself?"

At that, the man let roar a hearty laugh. "Me? Ha, oh no dear boy. The 'Patterns' have been around fer ages, most likely since the Tower o' the Blind was built over in that giant lake. What do they call it? Oh yes, the Eye o' Orijin. Ironic that we Blind Men would situate ourselves in the Eye. Ya see, we Blind Men are very studious people and we like ta document everythin', so we needed a way of writin' as well. Most o' us are taught the Patterns from the time we are little."

"How did you know I was outside? How did you know my name?"

"I've seen two prophecies o' ya in my life. I think. Well, I don't quite remember the first one, which is why I'll have ta consult my books. But the second one, well that one only came about a week ago, which was a vision that ye'd walk by when ya did. I've just been keepin' track o' the days. Today is Lionsday, isn't it?" The old man's eyes continued dance around in their sockets. They made Baltaszar uncomfortable when they fell on him.

"Lionsday? What do you mean? What is Lionsday?"

"Did yer parents never teach ya the names fer the days o' the week, boy?"

"Where I'm from, we never bothered to name the days."

"What cave were ya livin' in then? The whole world knows the days o' the week! I wish part o' my vision was ta see how uneducated ya are!"

Farco returned with two cups of steaming tea. They smelled of ginger and honey. He set one down on the table in front of Baltaszar and, after setting down the old man's, took the man's hand to the cup. Baltaszar was still sore from the insult. "Instead of belittling me, teach me."

"Ah, a boy who's willin' ta learn. Good, then. Are ya familiar with the Harbingers o' the Orijin?"

Again these Harbingers? How much of this world and life don't I know? "I am aware that there were Harbingers, but I know nothing of them."

"The original three were Cerys, Magnus, an' Taurean. Centuries later, the Orijin chose five more. They were Abram, Gideon, Lionel, Darian, an' Jahmash." The old man counted on his fingers as he named them, "Eight in total. Jahmash betrayed the rest, which leaves seven Harbingers that the world presently honors. Seven Harbingers, seven days o' the week."

Baltaszar nodded. "Okay, that makes sense. So what are the names of the days then?"

"The week begins with Cersday, after Cerys, because she was a lady. Then ya have Magnaday, Taursday, Abraday, Gidenday, Lionsday, an' Dariday. I assume ya can see the connection ta the original names?"

"Yes, yes. I am not as stupid as you believe. And by the way, you haven't told me your name."

The old man smiled again, "Eh, when yer old like me, ya sometimes forget introductions because ya assume everyone knows who ya are by now. My name is Munn. Munn Keeramm."

Maybe I can finally get some answers. Baltaszar sipped his tea, which tasted even better than it smelled. The honey gave it a nice smooth taste while the ginger added a small kick of spice afterward. "It's a pleasure to meet you, Master Keeramm. I am wondering, do you have some time to educate me? At least a little? You are not the first person in the past few days to talk about these 'Harbingers'. Tell me about them. Please."

Munn waved his hand dismissively. "O' course, my boy, o' course I will teach ya. I'm used ta ya young folk always rushin' off. Farco here is just like that, always in a rush, except with the tea. Very well, then. Farco boy, make a whole pot a tea an' leave it on the table." Farco disappeared into the other room once again. "I have ta warn ya, boy, this will take some time."

"I don't have anywhere to rush off to. Except Anahi is waiting outside."

Munn smiled widely at that, "Good, good, son. That girl has a world of patience. She'll understand, especially fer this. An' then I can tell this right. All right, well, somewhere around a thousand years after the Orijin put people in the world; he grew a bit annoyed at 'em. Ya see, people became bad, lyin', stealin', killin', all kinds o' sinful things. So Orijin, what He did was He chose three people, Cerys, Magnus, an' Taurean, an' blessed 'em with the power ta do some amazin' things. Things regular people couldn't do, an' so the Orijin intended fer people ta look up ta these three.

"Ya see, they were stronger an' smarter an' better than everyone else. Real heroes. Real leaders. Fer years, them three traveled the whole world spreadin' the Orijin's message, convincin' people ta act right."

Baltaszar furrowed his brow. "Where were these three from? Taurean, Cerys, and Magnus? And why did the Orijin choose them specifically?"

Munn nodded in approval, "Good questions, boy, very good. Well, the world was a much different place at that time, much bigger. The nations an' cities we have today weren't the same. Even Ashur, this continent we live on, was much different. Everythin' changed once Darian came along an' drowned the world. But that's a part o' the story that will come much later. Where was I again?"

"Where Cerys, Magnus, and Taurean were from. And why they were chosen."

"Yes, yes. Right. They were from very different parts o' the world, which is part o' why they were chosen. The Orijin chose 'em when they were young, even younger than ya. They weren't educated, couldn't read, weren't wealthy, didn't come from very devout families. An' that was the point! He chose them because they were already humble an' had good hearts. They weren't seekin' power an' didn't have enemies.

"So they each spread the message an' gained followers an' traveled from nation ta nation. City ta city. In fact, they didn't even meet one another 'til their work was done. Accordin' ta the scriptures, they were aware o' an' accepted one another, but the three didn't meet until over ten years after they'd begun spreadin' the word. Magnus an' Cerys married each other eventually, Taurean married someone else, went off inta the forest an' started his own family. Eventually, two o' Taurean's daughters even married Magnus' an' Cerys' boys."

"So what happened to them? They just lived normal lives after that?"

"Sure they did! They still did what they could ta inspire people an' preach an' such, but the world had gotten better under their watch. They grew old an' eventually died peaceful deaths. The problems came again after they died though. The world followed their example fer a few hundred years, but things got worse again, o' course.

"An' that's where the Five came in. The first set o' The Orijin's Harbingers were called 'The Three'. Second Harbingers were 'The Five'. The world got much worse than before. It wasn't just crimes anymore, there were wars goin' on. Stupid wars over borders an' rights ta thrones an' money. The Orijin chose five this time, though ya ask me, mighta been wise ta choose more. Jahmash, Darian, Abram, Gideon, an' Lionel. Orijin chose 'em the same way. Young, humble, good hearts, all from different parts o' the world.

"That was the extent o' the similarities though. For the Five, the Orijin blessed 'em differently. He endowed 'em each with a specific, different ability, stronger an' more outrageous than what the Three could ever even imagine. O' course, to keep em in control, the Orijin also gave them a weakness. I suppose it was a safeguard to keep 'em from abusin' their powers.

"So Abram was the Traveler. Ya see, he could blink in an out, disappear, an' show up somewhere else. Boy, I'm blind an' I tell ya, that would still scare me outta my wits. Just imagine how somethin' like that would affect people a couple thousand years ago." Farco reentered the room with a pot of steaming tea and set it down on the table after filling Baltaszar's and Munn's cups. "Anyway, Abram sought out the other four. The Five traveled the world together, a band o' heroes, although they were all barely men when they first met. I tell ya though, Baltaszar, they brought some kinda order ta this world. But it wasn't without sacrifice.

"I told ya how they each had their weaknesses. Gideon was the youngest, but that boy was somethin'. He was able ta turn things ta stone, but he was so very afraid of death. An' I suppose that's what makes Gideon so much more incredible. He's really the one who set things in motion fer the whole world. That's when everyone got scared. Ya see, there was a great battle brewin'. One a Jahmash's abilities was ta be able ta persuade people ta see things the right way. But Gideon didn't want Jahmash ta interfere with tryin' ta change the minds o' the soldiers on either side o' the battle. The way Gideon saw it was, people should have ta think fer themselves sometimes, or they'd never learn.

"So Gideon told both armies ta stop fightin', ta turn around, go home, an' decide on a peaceful resolution. Course, nobody listened, the boy was barely sixteen. So once both sides had lined up, ready ta fight, Gideon walked right in between 'em, raised his hands ta the sky, an' turned everything ta stone, himself included."

"I don't understand. Why would he do that to himself? Did it wear off after a while?"

Munn continued, "No, no, dear boy. That was part o' the point, ya see. Gideon sacrificed his self so the whole world would understand. So everyone would feel how important it was. It was a very meanin'ful thing, fer him ta die. If he'd a just turned the armies ta stone, people woulda just been afraid. He didn't want that. He wanted them ta see what their choices were doin ta him. Here was a boy o' sixteen, who gave up his life ta fix the world. An' it worked! People saw the stones or got word o' them, an' they realized two things. One, all the fightin' was pointless an' futile, an' two, the Five had humanity's best interest in mind."

Baltaszar sipped his tea and set the cup down. "Wait. You said that was part of the point, to make humanity see his motivation. But what was his other reason for sacrificing himself?"

"Ya see, boy, the thing with these Harbingers, well the Five anyway, was that whatever they used their abilities fer would be permanent once they died. Sure, they could reverse things if they chose, but death made things unchangeable. Gideon sacrificed his self so that the stone battlefield would be an example fer all time."

"You're saying the battlefield is still there? That people can actually go to it? See it? Touch it?"

"Oh sure they can. It's over a week's ride from here, next ta the royal city o' Alvadon in Cerysia. Well, in theory, people can. King Edmund doesn't allow it any longer though; he doesn't much care fer the Harbingers an' what they stand fer. But the whole thing is there, boy. I've met a few people who have seen it an' they say it's an incredible sight."

"Incredible indeed. Tell me more about the others. The rest of the Five. Please."

Munn cautiously reached out for his teacup, then gulped down the contents. "Fill my cup, if ya don't mind. All this storytellin' makes an old man thirsty." Baltaszar refilled the cup and sat back down. "Thank ya, boy. Well, where was I again? Oh, right…the others. Well, ya see, after Gideon's death, the job fer the others got much easier. Sure there were some battles they had ta fight. Some people are stubborn fer the sake o' bein stubborn. But I'd say within three or four years after Gideon died, the Harbingers' work was done. In fact, people loved 'em. Especially Darian an' Lionel. Lionel, ya see, could speak any language. Ya can understand how people would be drawn ta that. We all want ta be understood an' heard. Lionel didn't much care fer recognition though. He preferred ta keep a low profile, an' so he tucked his self away in some quiet corner o' the world.

"The other three, Abram, Jahmash, an' Darian, they stayed close together in what's now the City o' the Fallen. I can't remember what the old name was, but that city has been around since their time. That's why so many people want ta go see it. Anyway, them three were tight as can be. I told ya how the Orijin ensured they each had their weaknesses? Well that's how it all fell apart, ya see.

"Abram was rather quiet. That boy just liked ta be included, remembered. His biggest fear was that he would end up lonely an' be forgotten. But his friendship with Darian an' Jahmash counteracted that anyway. The other two though, I suppose nobody saw it comin. I mean, how could ya? Darian was the most charismatic o' the Harbingers. People loved him; he was a very good speaker an' could befriend anyone. His greatest vice was women though. The books document that he had twelve wives an' even more children, but that's the ones that were known. There could very well have been more."

"So this man that the whole world still adores—he treated women this way? How could humanity accept that?"

"I can understand how you would be confused, Baltaszar. But here's the thing, ya see. Darian wasn't necessarily a rascal. Like I said, these women were his wives, not his mistresses. Legend says that Darian truly loved 'em all, an' never let any o' them want fer anythin'. It's recorded that they all accepted one another an' got along. I suppose that's strange by today's standards, but who are we to judge?

"Where was I now? Oh yes! Now Jahmash, he had two weaknesses. An' if ya ask me, the Orijin gave him a bad deal. Not that I'm defendin' him, though. Jahmash was known ta be very jealous, even o' the people he loved, an' aside o' bathin', he was deathly afraid o' water. Now, that wouldn't be such a bad thing, boy, but, well, Darian's Orijin-blessed ability was controllin water."

"Goodness, I think I can see where this was going. Did Jahmash grow jealous of Darian and his wives?"

"Not quite, dear boy, but ya almost have the right idea." Munn gulped more tea. "Because o' the way Darian was, he got most o' the attention an' glory. Jahmash his self wasn't nasty or anythin', but people were just more drawn ta Darian. An' I suppose that would lead ta lots o' feelins buildin' up inside o' Jahmash. Which is just what happened. Jahmash likely held his jealousy fer a while. Ya see, he married a woman named Jaya, who was the sister o' one o' Darian's wives. Around this time, people around the world were callin' fer Darian ta be their king. I'm not quite sure how that woulda worked, if there was a king o' the whole world already or anythin', but regardless, Darian refused. He didn't want the glory or attention, an' he knew what Jahmash was like. Darian didn't want ta start trouble.

"Even though Darian refused, Jahmash still held a grudge about it...ya know, that Darian was asked an' he wasn't. I think that was the thing that did Jahmash in. That Darian could have so many wives an' children, an' the people still loved him more than Jahmash. Fer one thing, it ruined Jahmash's marriage. Jahmash grew obsessed with provin' that he was better than Darian, over time he spoke out more an' more in public against Darian, an' insulted him. Darian made his attempts ta talk behind closed doors, but Jahmash simply shunned him. He wouldn't even speak ta Darian anymore.

"What blew everythin' ta chaos was that Darian went ta Jaya ta discuss whether there was any way ta resolve the whole mess. Ya see, that's what made Darian better than Jahmash. Despite everythin', Darian still sought a way ta remain friends, ta put it behind them. Regardless o' everythin' Jahmash was sayin an' doin, Darian was willin' ta forgive. Where was I again?"

Baltaszar hung on Munn's every word. "Darian met with Jaya!" He felt like a child again, sitting at home while his father told him and Bo'az stories of warriors and monsters.

"Yes, yes. Darian met with her one day while Jahmash was out huntin'. He knew the toll it was all takin on Jaya, so he went ta talk. Well, boy, it didn't end so well. Jahmash arrived home while Darian was still there. Jahmash threatened Darian ta leave or he would attack him, so Darian left. This only made things worse fer Jahmash."

"Let me guess, he grew jealous, thinking that Jaya was having an affair with Darian?"

"Exactly! Though he didn't accuse Jaya right away. He stewed over it fer days, watchin' her, suspectin' her, waitin' ta see if she would run off. But she loved Jahmash, an' tried constantly ta talk sense inta him. After a week or so, Jahmash finally caved ta his jealousy an' threatened Jaya ta admit an affair with Darian. O' course, she denied it ta no end, but Jahmash would not believe her an' beat her inta a bloody mess. Jahmash left her there in anger. The maids cleaned up Jaya an' brought her ta her sister Sarai's home. Sarai was one o' Darian's wives.

"One thing I have forgotten ta mention, boy, is that Jahmash had the ability ta enter people's minds. But only people who did not have a strong will. People who were mentally weak. He also was very good at persuasion. However, once the Harbingers had brought peace, they had agreed ta live normal lives an' not use any o' these powers any longer, because their work had finished.

"So anyway, the day after Jaya fled, Jahmash hunted down Darian at one o' his wives' houses, I believe it was Zara, but there were so many that it's hard ta be sure. Anyway, where was I? Oh yes, Jahmash confronted Darian about the suspected affair, but Darian denied it as well. Jahmash still had a bit o' sense left, because he didn't fight Darian, but he refused ta believe either Darian or Jaya that there was nothin' between 'em. Jahmash left after threatenin' Darian that he would have revenge fer the slight against him.

"This is when Jahmash broke his pact with the other Harbingers. He found what weak-minded soldiers he could throughout the city an' commanded 'em ta go ta the houses o' each o' Darian's wives an' kill 'em. The soldiers killed every one o' them, except one. I believe it was Katia who lived, because Darian was at her house. Darian snuck away her ta Abram's house an' had Abram whisk her away ta a place where Jahmash couldn't find her. It was ta Lionel's house, far away, that Abram took her, then he returned with Lionel. Darian then had Abram hide all o' his children, who were very young, at Lionel's house as well. Once Darian's remainin' family was safe, he, Abram, an' Lionel schemed ta confront Jahmash.

"Darian wanted ta avoid violence, so he sent Lionel an' Abram ta speak ta Jahmash alone. Darian assumed that if he was not present, perhaps Jahmash might be calmer. Unfortunately, that was not the case. Upon seein' them, Jahmash knew Darian had sent 'em an' stabbed Lionel in the chest. Abram was not so easy ta kill, because he could disappear an' reappear so quickly. But Abram did stand an' fight Jahmash. Both were said ta be excellent swordsmen. In time, Jahmash injured Abram very severely. It is a topic o' controversy whether Jahmash actually killed Abram or not, as no body was found. Many suspect that Abram blinked away before Jahmash could kill him. However, Abram was never seen again, so nobody really knows if he ever died or not."

"What do you mean, 'ever died'? You're implying that he could still be alive?"

"The thing about the Five is that, once they reached a certain age, they stopped agin' all together. It was one o' the blessings from the Orijin. The Five were given the choice of when ta die. So, quite honestly, unless someone else killed 'em, they could choose ta live forever."

Baltaszar's confusion grew into anger. "But then, what would happen if Jahmash never died? That would be horrible for this world! How could the Orijin allow something like that?"

"I apologize that I must bear this news ta ya, boy, but Jahmash did not die. But let me continue my story before I get ta that part. Where was I again?"

"What! How could he not die! Oh, fine. You were saying that Jahmash killed Lionel and Abram may or may not have escaped," Baltaszar said sarcastically.

"Oh, yes. Well, ya see, once Lionel and Abram were out o' Jahmash's way, he went after Darian. But Darian was a smart one, boy. As soon as Darian got word o' what happened ta Lionel an' Abram, he fled the city on horseback, headin' north. Darian rode fer days, possibly weeks, always leavin' subtle clues so that Jahmash would be able ta follow him. An' Jahmash did. Darian rode further an' further north, past the Never, past the Endless Mountains. It is unclear o' whether he rode through them or around them, but it seems more likely it woulda been easier fer him ta go around. Anyway, in those days, miles an' miles o' desert lay beyond the mountains. Darian rode an' rode through to the edge of the desert, then waited until Jahmash caught up ta him. By then, it was likely a fortnight after Jahmash had killed Lionel an' Abram."

Baltaszar broke in, "Allegedly killed Abram."

"Yes. Allegedly indeed. Once he lured Jahmash far enough, Darian broke his own end o' the pact an' flooded the land with water. The details o' this are sketchy at best, as there was no one ta record what happened fer sure. But it was obvious enough what Darian did. He flooded the world an' cut off Jahmash from any human contact. The continent we live on, Ashur, is an island because Darian turned it inta that. Fer centuries, sailors an adventurers set out in search o' other lands, but either failed or never returned. The common belief these days is that Ashur is all that remains o' the world. Though many are skeptical that other lands are out there."

"While all of this is interesting, you're getting off track, Master Keeram. What about Darian and Jahmash?"

"Oh yes, well boy, Darian allowed his self ta be killed once he was satisfied that Jahmash could not return ta civilization. The man truly turned a desert inta an ocean. They say his body eventually washed ashore. An, well, as ya know, boy, Darian's legend has held up through time. Anyone who is even somewhat devout ta the Orijin reveres Darian. An' Abram an' Lionel an' Gideon as well; they are all celebrated."

"One thing doesn't make sense. If nobody has ever seen Jahmash since then, how do we know he isn't dead?"

"Yes, yes, a good question, boy. That goes back ta Silas Vaskol, a Blind Man who died about fifty somethin' years ago. Silas had a vision o' Jahmash livin' on an island with no other land in sight. Jahmash was survivin' off birds an' such, but he was talkin' ta someone about how he would return ta civilization an' get revenge on the descendants o' Darian fer what Darian did ta him."

"What does that mean, descendants of Darian? How is he going to know who Darian's descendants are so many centuries later?"

"Well, that's a debatable question. Most people who believe the prophecy say that Jahmash will simply terrorize everyone. Others believe that Jahmash is only concerned with those o' ya who have the black line on yer faces, since ye've come ta be called 'Descendants'."

"Does anyone know when this is going to happen? Or who the other person in the vision was?"

Munn gulped more tea, "Ahck, it's cold. Farco! Another pot o' tea! There are other prophecies at the Tower that'll answer yer question better than I can. I haven't been there in some time, an' I honestly don't remember things like I used ta. Regardless, most o' Ashur believes Jahmash will be back in the next few generations."

"But how would that happen? If Darian is dead, he can't get rid of the water, right? So how would he come back here?"

"Baltaszar, the man has had centuries upon centuries ta think about that. An' he's a smart man. I have no doubts he'll find a way, if he hasn't already. Farco told me the world went dark fer nearly half an hour a few days ago. That can't be a good sign."

"Yes, that's true. I was still walking in the forest at the time. Everything was black. Like nighttime with no moon. But Jahmash. How can he be stopped?"

Munn closed his eyes. "That is a question better suited fer Zin Marlowe. He is the headmaster at the House o' Darian."

"Very well. Would you happen to know…well, what exactly they do there? At the House of Darian?"

"I have never had much interest in the place. It seems like it attracts a great deal o' trouble. Especially with Edmund, this ass o' a king we have. But I would assume the House helps ya understand yer manifestation an' how ta use it an' control it."

All these new things I don't understand. "Manifestation?"

"Yes, manifestation, boy! Ya got a black line on yer face, don't ya? It means that when ya were a child, ya got a line on yer face which allowed ya ta do somethin' special."

"I've never been able to do anything special. What do you mean by special, anyway?"

"Yer goin' ta have ta talk ta Marlowe about all that. I don't know if everyone gets the line at the same time. But it means ya can do somethin', like manipulate somethin' or create somethin'. Fer instance, Maven Savaiyon is a very well-known Descendant. Supposedly he can create 'bridges' in the thin air so that he can get ta places very quickly. He could go from one side o' Ashur ta the other in a few seconds. Similar ta what Abram could do so long ago, but Abram would just vanish."

"So how do I know what I can do?"

"Most Descendants simply know. Ya see, boy, whatever it is, it's somethin' miraculous. Somethin' a normal person couldn't do. If yer not sure, then just think back on yer life an' try ta remember if there's any miraculous thing that ye've always been around or connected ta."

Baltaszar could remember nothing miraculous in his seventeen years of life. "Nothing comes to mind. Is there someone who can tell me what it is?"

"From what I'm told, ya can't force anyone ta have a certain manifestation. An yer not supposed ta talk ta a child about his manifestation until he discovers it fer his self. Ya see, manifestations…they say these things come out o' some dire need, desperate situation. It would be artificial fer a child ta be told a manifestation. But I am no expert on these matters. I would assume yer goin' ta the House o' Darian anyway. Discuss the matter with Marlowe."

"Very well. Thank you."

Farco returned with a new steaming pot of tea. Munn sipped from a newly full cup. "I suppose yer goin' now then?"

"Well, no sir. The whole reason you invited me in was because of a prophecy. I believe you still have to share that with me."

Munn nodded his head vigorously. "Yes! Yes, o' course, dear boy! A prophecy indeed! Farco, please fetch me the prophecy book fer this boy. It will be on the 'People' shelf under 'K' for Kontez."

CHAPTER 8
A PROPHECY

From *The Book of Orijin*, Verse Seventeen
We know all paths. Though We have blessed you with free will, We have already foreseen the outcomes of all possible decisions.

"IS THAT...IS THAT whole book just prophecies?" Baltaszar gasped incredulously.

Farco plopped the book atop one of the shorter stacks of books on the table, pushing a cloud of dust up into the air, and opened it to a page close to the end of the book. Munn replied, "This is one o' many books. Our system o' filing our prophecies is complicated, and at my age, sometimes even I forget how things oughta be sorted. Luckily, I have Farco here ta keep things in order." The boy smiled genuinely then turned his attention back to the book. Once he found what he was looking for, he grasped Munn's hand and placed it at the middle of the right page.

Munn moved his hand slowly from left to right over the line of dashes and dots. "Oh dear. I fear I may have set ya up fer some grave news, my boy. I apologize in advance fer bein' the one who has ta give ya such a message, but please do understand that I am just a medium. I don't choose the prophecy nor the person. It simply comes ta me."

Baltaszar put his cup down and peered at the book, despite knowing he wouldn't be able to understand it. His eyes narrowed, "What do you mean? The prophecy is something bad? What if I don't want to know it then? Why is it so important for me to know this thing? If you don't tell me, I can leave here and be perfectly happy not knowing about whatever bad thing is going to happen."

"It's important that I tell ya this thing, Baltaszar. Prophecies are set in stone, so it is not as if ya can change it. But emotionally, at least if ya have this news, ya can prepare yerself for the worst."

Baltaszar sighed, twisted his mouth and, after a few moments of deliberating, consented to hear Munn's prophecy. "Fine, tell me this terrible thing."

Munn slid his hand over the writing again, as if to confirm that it said what he thought. "Baltaszar, yer goin' ta kill yer brother."

Baltaszar's eyes bulged. *What?* "What are you talking about? I would never kill my brother! Are you sure this is what you saw? You said yourself that you didn't even remember the vision in your head!"

"I may have forgotten, but I did write it down. We always do. What it says here is that, in a fit o' rage, ya will stab yer brother ta death. Yer exact words in the vision were, 'I am the hand o' justice. An' I cannot forgive ya. Ya will pay fer yer sins an' ya will hear the Song, brother.' An' after that, ya proceed ta stab him."

"No. That cannot be. Although I fight with Bo every now and then, I love him. I could never even imagine harm coming to him, much less kill him. How can you be sure? Did you see his face?"

"When we see prophecies about people, we tend ta assume the point o' view o' a person in the vision. Accordin' ta what I wrote down, I saw things from yer brother's point o' view. I saw ya attack me. I felt the stabbin' an' everythin' went black. Although I didn't actually hear the Song, but, well…that's ta be expected."

"What song are you talking about?"

"The Song o' Orijin. It is an ancient belief from the time o' the Harbingers. It is said that when we die, we hear the most unimaginably beautiful melody. It is believed that it is the Orijin's last gift ta us in the physical world, regardless o' where our souls end up in the afterlife." Baltaszar slowly shook his head. Munn continued, "Do not lie ta yourself, boy. Ya seem like a nice enough young man, perhaps there is good reason for such a thing ta happen.

"Accept it for what it is. As I said, ya cannot change things like this. In the history o' Blind Men, there has not been a prophecy that hasn't come true. This is simply the will o' our creator. The longer ya live in denial o' this truth, the worse it will be fer ya. I know my words may seem cold, but ya are not the first person I have had ta give horrible news. But in my experience, it's better ta resign yerself ta this fate, an' prepare yerself emotionally an' mentally fer what will happen."

Baltaszar hung his head, puffed his cheeks, and stared down at his boots. "I'm sorry, I must go. I don't really know how to handle this right now. Perhaps in time I will see wisdom in your words, but right now, I simply can't grasp how your vision could be true." He stood and pushed in his chair. "It was…a pleasure…I think, to have met you." He looked over to Farco, who stood in the doorway to the other room, "Thank you for the tea, Farco." Before Munn could rise, Baltaszar turned and walked out the door.

He walked back onto the road, looking for Anahi. She had been talking to the shop owners next door and came to Baltaszar upon seeing him exit.

"How was it? Ya were in there fer a while."

Baltaszar turned away and looked down the road. "Not so great." He turned back to her, "Tell me, do these things always come true?"

Anahi frowned. "That bad, hmm? Everyone I know who's been given a prophecy has had it come true. That's how we all knew about Cyrus' wife. Good or bad, these things always end up happenin'." Baltaszar could see the concern in her squinted eyes. "What did he say, Baltaszar?" Baltaszar considered whether he should tell her, and walked on up the street. Anahi caught up, "Talk ta me. Whatever it is, it'll only be worse if ya keep it in. I can help ya deal with it."

He shot her a cold glare. "You barely even know me. How do you plan to help?"

"That's not fair, Baltaszar. I'm not yer enemy here. I know how difficult things can be."

"You know nothing about how difficult my life has been. You have your friendly little city here where everyone loves each other and your welcoming inn with Cyrus to go to everyday. What, in the name of Orijin, do you know about difficult?"

With that, Anahi returned the icy glare he'd given her moments ago. "My parents died when I was barely seven years old. I watched from a fishin' boat as my mother fell over the side an' my father jumped in after her. In all the commotion, the damn sea snakes were on them in seconds. With all the bites they suffered, they likely died before they even had the chance ta drown. I stood there, screamin' an' sobbin' as my older brother held me back. If not fer him, I would have jumped in right after my father an' would have died as well.

"Five years later, my brother went off ta the House o' Darian. He had one o' those lines on his face, just like yers. On his way, not far past the town o' Khiry, one o' the King's squadrons ambushed him an' killed him. Just because o' the line on his face. I have nothin' left. Cyrus took me in because I had nowhere else ta go. He's the closest thing I have ta family anymore. So don't ya dare stand there an' think yer the only person who's ever had trouble in yer life. Be grateful that, whatever this stupid prophecy is, ya have the blessin' o' knowin' about it in advance. At least ya can deal with it, prepare yer mind for it."

Knots were forming in Baltaszar's shoulders and back. "Look, I'm sorry. You're right. Can we just end this? I don't really want to fight right now. Let's just go back to the inn. If you still want to talk to me, I'll welcome it. But I'd rather wait until we have some privacy."

Anahi nodded in agreement. "I'd like that."

***

Just over two hours later, Baltaszar sat in a cushioned wooden chair beside the bed in his room, biting his lip. He leaned forward, head cradled in his hands, waiting for Anahi to come in and trying desperately to clear his mind. *What's happened in the past few months? Everything's become so crazy.*

A knock came at the door and then it opened. "Ya do realize that ya can lock the door from the inside, don't ya? I mean, anybody could just come on in while yer sleepin'. Not that that's a normal thing here, but ya can never completely trust the foreigners.

Baltaszar lifted his head slightly. "I'll keep that in mind."

Anahi still wore the same long skirt and modest blouse she'd worn when they walked the streets of Vandenar. She sat on the bed, legs crossed beneath her. "Still bothered, are ya? I wish I could tell ya it gets better, but I honestly can't if ya don't tell me anything. Baltaszar, I..."

"All right, enough. Look. I'll tell you some things. But not everything." Baltaszar took a deep breath and twisted his mouth to one side, then sat back in the wooden chair and pressed his fingertips together. "We have certain things in common. My mother died when I was young. Our house caught fire and, according to my father, she sacrificed herself to save me and my brother and father. For the past seventeen years, my father has let me believe that this line on my face was some strange scar from the fire. Then, in the past couple of months, my father was given a death sentence for supposedly setting fires throughout our town."

Anahi interjected, "What do ya mean? He actually set fire ta homes an' such?"

"Well, he happened to be around when fires were started in a few homes and a shop. I don't really know how to explain it, to be honest. I think he was blamed because he was the common link. Regardless, the people of Haedon fell in with one person's accusation, and our Chancellor, Oran Von, passed the sentence."

"Well if ya knew anythin' about our King, that kind o' justice is common in Ashur."

"Why?"

"He doesn't like any o' ya Descendants. Has his son's army hunt an' kill ya. Did yer dad have a line on his face?"

"No. Never saw anyone else with it. Like I said, I thought it was a scar up until a few days ago. Don't know anything about the line otherwise."

"O' course ya don't."

Baltaszar smirked at her, then quickly grew solemn. "Anyway. My father was hanged only a few days ago. I left the forest the day after he was hanged. My brother was skeptical about how well we could trust the world beyond The Never, and so he returned to our home. I honestly don't know if he's still there, though. I truly hope he isn't. It's only a matter of time before our home is destroyed."

Anahi shifted so that her legs stretched out in front of her and she leaned back on her arms. "If he's anythin' like you, I'm sure he's just fine."

Baltaszar snickered reflexively. "That's the thing. He's always so afraid of things. Of life. I know that sounds bad to say, and he has tried many times to be bold or daring, but his first instinct is to always choose the option that prevents him from having to try something new. And that's why I worry about him now. He's always had me and our father around to guide him. Look at me, I can hardly even handle the world beyond my town, and Bo'az is worse than me. By the Orijin, I hope nothing has happened to him."

"Ya just have ta pray fer him, then. Ye've mentioned the loss o' yer parents an' yer brother. But what o' this girl that ye've sworn yerself ta? Ya haven't mentioned her."

Baltaszar sighed. *Blast it, why do you need to know?* "I don't...fine, I'll tell you. But only because I brought her up before. I courted her and we had something special for a time. She's the most beautiful girl in all of Haedon. The thing is..."

"Doesn't she have a name? How rude! Ya boys always speak about us girls like we're objects."

"She is no object. It's painful enough to even think of her name, much less say it. But very well. Yasaman. Her name is Yasaman. May I continue?"

Anahi waved her hand dismissively.

"Thank you. As I was saying, her parents never approved of me. In fact, they thought our romance ended much earlier than it did. They wanted her to marry a rich man, so that they could elevate their status in town. I was never sure why that really mattered. Then came the news of my father. They were strong supporters of the decision to hang my father. And once the decree was made that he would definitely die, they would probably have killed her to keep her away from me. Of course, the easiest way to make a boy and girl desire each other even more is to tell them they can no longer see one another. And that's what happened. We grew even more passionate. Talked about marriage. Children. Running away. They all seemed like possibilities for a time. For me, anyway. I think for her, they were fantasies. Ways of temporarily escaping the reality that she would go along with her parents' wishes.

"The last time I saw her, she implied that we could be together once my father was dead, as if that would make everything normal again. I left her in anger. But the more time that goes on, the more I miss her, and the stronger my love grows. I'm constantly torn between continuing on this journey and just turning back to go see her. I mean, what if I could convince her to come with me, you know?"

"Ya mean ta the House o' Darian?"

"Yes. And wherever else I go in my life."

Anahi shot him a doubtful stare. "Baltaszar, I don't think ya fully understand what yer going off ta do. They train ya at the House o' Darian. It's almost like a school an' army trainin' in one. Help ya learn about yer...what do they call it...yer 'manifestation'. They've got no place there fer family or friends or lovers."

"I'm sure there's a chance they could let in outsiders. If I reasoned with..."

"Baltaszar, trust me. Do ya know how badly I wanted ta go off with

Arden, my brother? Don't ya think he would've brought me if he could have?"

"Yeah, that makes sense." *Well, I suppose, at least...that decides about turning back.* "How much do you know about the House of Darian? And what is a...manifestation?"

Anahi shrugged, "I suppose I know a thing or two, seein' as how I knew a couple o' Descendants well. Though Arden didn't know much about the House. All Arden really knew was where ta go. Most who go there don't really discuss what goes on, but I assume it revolves mostly around yer manifestations...the ability ya develop when the line appears on yer face. Arden got the line on his face when he was about six years. They say most Descendants get the line when they're between four an' eight years. When did ya get yers?"

"So Master Keeramm was right? The line develops? To be honest, until a few days ago, I was under the impression that this line was a scar on my face. That's what my father told me my whole life. That I got this black...thing...on my face in a fire. I never had any reason to question it. What abilities are associated with the manifestations? Keeramm implied magic. Can that be true?"

"To be quite honest, Baltaszar, it is inappropriate fer me ta discuss it. Those o' us who do not bear the Mark are not supposed ta discuss yer manifestations with ya. It is seen as disrespectful ta ya Descendants."

"Anahi, does it look like I have been disrespected? I'm the idiot here, trying to understand all of this. Believe me, the last thing I would be in all of this is disrespected! Can't you just tell me generally what they are?"

She moved to the edge of the bed and let her knees bend over the edge. "The only two people in this town I ever knew very well who had the Mark were Arden, who has been dead fer four years, an' Desmond, who just left fer the House o' Darian a few weeks ago. Hopefully he hasn't been killed along the way, too. Truthfully, neither o' them actually shared the nature o' their manifestations with me. I never saw my brother use his, but I suspect Arden's was quite dangerous, because certain people in this city were strangely afraid o' him. And it is rumored that he managed ta kill quite a few o' King Edmund's soldiers before he died. I wouldn't call it magic. More like a blessing from the Orijin. As fer Desmond, he was always a rather private person. Not unfriendly, just private. With the way the King treats 'em, Descendants don't really like ta talk about themselves. At least not ta people without the Mark. I'm sorry Baltaszar, I know that's not much help, but that's all I know."

"That's all right. It will have to be enough."

"So yer really goin'' ta the House, are ya? Yer sure ya don't want ta stay here with me?"

"Trust me, Anahi, it is tempting. But there are a great deal of questions that I need answered. If you were able or willing to give me those answers, perhaps I could stay."

"Well then I apologize fer my ignorance," Anahi smirked. "Baltaszar, if yer goin' ta go down there, ya have ta be careful. The king's soldiers stalk the roads every day. Arden was a good fighter an' even he died. Don't take my words the wrong way, because I'm not askin' fer selfish reasons. But are ya positive that ya have ta go? It's dangerous out there, especially fer someone travelin' alone."

"I have to go. Though I enjoy your company, there's not much for me here. Anahi, I don't even know what my manifestation is. I need to be down there. Instead of persuading me to stay, tell me how to get down there alive. Is there no coverage, like forests, mountains, rivers?"

"There is nothin' but grass fer miles on both sides o' the road. To the west is the sea, which is why they call it the Way o' Sunsets. Travelers can clearly see the sun setting from the road. And in recent years, the Way o' Sunsets has also taken on the meanin' o' death fer Descendants who travel it. There is no hidin'. I would suggest crawlin' through the tall grass, but ya would be Master Keeramm's age by the time ya reached the City o' the Fallen.

"One thing I have heard, though, is that many Descendants can be found in the City o' the Fallen. If ya reach it, ya will have many allies. They say it is the last city before the House o' Darian an' is very accommodatin' and friendly toward Descendants. I know Desmond planned ta stay there a bit before going ta the House. Perhaps ye'll come across him there. He's around the same age as ya, ya might get along."

"So you're saying I should head to this city, which is quite friendly to Descendants, and keep lookout for a man with a line down his face?"

Anahi laughed at that. "I wasn't sayin' just approach everyone who has the Mark. There are certain inns the Descendants stay at down there. Go ta them an' ask around. His skin has the yellow hue like everyone in Vandenar, and he's got crazy black hair that doesn't fall in any sort o' pattern. It's sorta all over the place, an' sticks up a lot."

"I suppose that makes things a bit easier." Baltaszar leaned forward again and looked Anahi squarely in the face. "You know, under different circumstances, I wonder if there could have been something for the two of us. Not that I'm implying that I think anything should happen between us, but…"

"Then why even bring it up, fool boy? Ya 'men', I swear!" Anahi waved her arms about overdramatically, "What do ya think it does fer a girl ta hear, 'I would love ta court ya darlin', but under different circumstances.'"

"Wait, wait. That's not what I said. I definitely did not call you darling," Baltaszar smirked. "Besides, is it not a compliment to hear that a man would be willing to court you?"

Anahi smirked, "You are a dimwit, Baltaszar. Am I some hag that needs yer pity? Or a dirty street beggar with no prospects? Ya sound as if ya would be doin' me a favor ta fall in love with me."

Baltaszar rolled his eyes and threw up his arms, "Oh, Light. Are you really so sensitive? All I meant was that, if I wasn't in love with Yasaman, I think that there could be something between us. It wasn't an insult or pity or a favor. It was just a dimwit farmer's way of stating that there's a connection between us! Goodness, woman, are you all this difficult?"

Baltaszar had his head facing the ceiling, and only too late did he notice Anahi slowly leaning into him. She moved her face next to his, then barely touched her cheek against his and whispered, "Clever boy, ya haven't said anythin' about the prophecy."

He leaned back in his chair and looked her in the eyes. Those beautiful grey eyes. "And I don't plan to," Baltaszar whispered just as softly.

Something loud knocked against the door, hitting it so hard that the door opened nearly a foot. A young man, of an age with Baltaszar but a few inches taller, walked through the open door. He wore a green woolen riding coat and black breeches and boots. His dark brown hair was short and somewhat curly, and his face bore a grin nearly as big as Cyrus'. Most importantly, a vertical black line started at his forehead and intersected his left eye, stopping at the top of his cheek. His skin was lighter than Baltaszar's. "Oh, sorry for knocking so hard, I didn't mean to interrupt. Should I leave?" Before anyone could answer, he continued. "I was so excited when the innkeeper told me there was another Descendant here, I had to come see you right away. I've been traveling throughout Ashur, and I haven't had much chance to meet many like me. Like us, I should say. You know, with all the hiding and being hunted. What's your name?" He looked at Baltaszar the whole time, and had barely glanced at Anahi since intruding upon the room. "I'm Horatio. Horatio Mahd."

Horatio walked up to Baltaszar and stuck out his right hand demonstratively. At the gesture, Anahi sat back on the bed. Baltaszar stood up and grasped Horatio's forearm, allowing Horatio to grasp his as well. He had seen his father give certain people in Haedon the same salutation from time to time. "Baltaszar Kontez."

"Baltaszar! It's great to meet you! I didn't think I would meet anyone until I actually arrived at the House of Darian. This will be great; we can ride down together! When were you planning to leave?"

Baltaszar twisted his mouth to one side. "I hadn't really thought about it. Listen, Horatio. I know you're very excited to meet me, and the feeling is mutual. Well, somewhat. But without any intention of rudeness, you need to slow down a bit. Anahi here, and I, were in the middle of an important conversation, and to be, well, quite honest, you barged in and interrupted." Baltaszar noticed Horatio's wide-eyed abashed countenance and suddenly guilt invaded his mind. "Don't get the wrong idea. I'm not kicking you out or implying that I don't want to get to know you. It's just…"

"No. You are absolutely right. I have a bad habit of forgetting my manners when I get very excited. My father used to reprimand me for that constantly. And for making silly noises at the most random and inappropriate times as well. When I was younger, I just thought it was part of my charm. But well, that doesn't seem to be the case. Did I mention that I also ramble on and on when I get nervous or insecure?"

Baltaszar felt the shroud of awkwardness envelope him more and more as the conversation went on. And Anahi sat behind Horatio, making incredibly silly faces the whole time Horatio talked, which only made things worse. "Ah, no you didn't mention that, but I will definitely make a note of it. If your destination is the House of Darian, though, I'm sure we'll have plenty of time to get acquainted. When are you leaving Vandenar for the House?"

"Tomorrow morning. I want to be there by a week from today and I would really like to visit the City of the Fallen before getting to the House. It's the only big city that I haven't seen yet. Figured I should save it for last."

"I'm planning to go there as well. We can share the whole trip together, how about that?"

Horatio nodded in approval. "Amazing, I can't wait!"

"Uh...great! Well why don't we meet up in the morning then? I have some things to discuss with Anahi," Baltaszar gestured toward Anahi, intending it as an introduction. Anahi smiled as Horatio looked back at her, and Baltaszar continued, "Then I will likely go to sleep. I've had a long day and I'm quite tired. In the morning, we can find each other and set off together." Baltaszar put a hand on Horatio's shoulder and led him toward the door. "How does that sound, friend?"

"That sounds just fine. Again, I'm sorry for intruding and disturbing. It wasn't my intention to be so rude. Have a good night," he patted Baltaszar on the shoulder and waved to Anahi as he exited the room, still grinning from ear to ear.

Baltaszar shut the door and, for the first time, turned the lock. He sat back in his chair again, smiling at Anahi. "So where were we?"

"I know exactly where we were. Ya were not tellin' me about yer prophecy."

Baltaszar nodded, "Yes. That sounds about right. I have no intention of telling you about the prophecy." Anahi opened her mouth to fire an objection. "But before you interrupt me, Anahi, understand my reasoning. This prophecy, according to you, will definitely come true. If that's the case, then I must keep it to myself. What I was told was a terrible thing, something extremely bad and if the wrong people knew, it could be quite incriminating for me. The last thing I need as I learn about this world and try to become a part of it, is people judging me and assuming I'm a horrible person, just for something that hasn't even happened yet."

"But ya can trust me. I only want ta know so I can ease yer burden. Get some o' the weight off yer shoulders."

"I really want to trust you with this. But despite that, I do not trust the world. You said yourself that there are bad people in this world. Those same bad people who could eventually use information like this against me and to their advantage. If there's one thing the ordeal with my father taught me, it's that a man can spend a lifetime building a strong reputation, but all it takes is one word to destroy that reputation."

Anahi sighed and nodded, seemingly giving up on the argument. "So then what are these important matters that ya must discuss with me? Matters so important that ya had to rush yer great friend Horatio out o' the room?"

"Well, it seems I shall be leaving in the morning. Which means that I don't have much time left to talk to you. I need you to at least tell me something about the House of Darian. I know it brings back bad memories and that you don't want to insult me. But I need this, Anahi. I know nothing of this world. Anything you can tell me will help my chances of survival."

Anahi sighed. "Very well...perhaps I should have 'em send up dinner first. That's a lot o' information ta discuss. Hold yer wits fer a moment." She left the room and within a few minutes, returned and sat in the same spot on the bed.

"Where's dinner?"

Anahi pursed her lips. "It takes some time ta make, fool boy. Did ya really think I could just go downstairs an' they would magically know what I was goin' ta ask fer? Have some patience."

Baltaszar mocked her, mouthing her words with a funny face.

"As fer yer questions, ye'll be a bit disappointed, I'm afraid. I have some answers, but not fer everythin'."

"Tell me what you can then. It's fine."

"All right, well...the House o' Darian. From what I know, it's a meetin' place fer all ya Descendants, like I said before. Ya all tend to go down there after a certain age. I don't think they have a requirement, but I suppose everyone has their own family obligations an' such. Most go when they're around my age."

"Exactly how old are you? You never told me."

"This past summer was my sixteenth."

"Well then I suppose at least I won't be too late. The coming winter will be my eighteenth. But why go there? What's there that is so important?"

"Like I also said before, King Edmund is huntin' all o' ya, but yer all protected at the House. I would imagine they also teach ya about them manifestations. But again...we've already been down that road."

"Fine. But what about these bloody manifestations and black lines in the first place? Why do we even get them?"

"I don't know much about that either, Baltaszar. I'm sorry, but look who yer askin'. I work at an inn nowhere near the House an' I've never left this town. I believe it's got a lot to do with the Orijin an' the Harbingers an' all. But I've never been properly educated on those things."

The door opened once more, Baltaszar realizing only now that it wasn't locked. Two new dark-haired, almond-eyed maids walked in with plates of food and folding trays on which to eat. The maids set the trays in front of Baltaszar and Anahi, then set the plates down, steam billowing from each. Both plates bore a steak, smaller than the one Baltaszar had eaten for breakfast, accompanied by a mixture of roasted onions and diced red-skinned potatoes. After setting the plates, one of the maids placed a glass of deep red wine on each tray top and left the room.

Baltaszar salivated and exhaled loudly. "You're not being as helpful as I'd hoped. Maybe I should just go have dinner with Horatio."

"I'm sure he would love that. Go then."

"If I went, I'd take your dinner with me. There's no reason Horatio should miss out on something like this. Anyway, back to the point. What about the Descendants? Any idea what that means? Who are we descending from?"

"Well, that one's simple. Yer descendants o' Darian! That's why ye've got the House o' Darian, fool boy!"

Oh that's right. Keeramm did mention that. "But how? I mean, I have a twin brother, yet I have this line on my face that says I'm a descendant of Darian, but he doesn't. Neither does my father. It doesn't make any sense how I would be related to Darian, but they wouldn't be."

Anahi nodded and smiled. "Well, that's ta do with the manifestations. So many people these days descend from Darian, but not all o' them get the black line or the manifestations. Ya ask me, that's an answer only the Orijin can give…who gets em an' who doesn't. If ya have the black line, yer whole family descends from Darian, or one o' yer parents anyway. It's just that ya were chosen as a child ta bear the Mark. Remember, my brother got the Mark an' I didn't. Same situation. Happy now, fool boy?"

Baltaszar smiled. They'd both forgotten to start eating. He cut into the steak and stuffed a big piece in his mouth. It was seasoned differently than the one he'd eaten for breakfast. This one was a bit spicier with hints of garlic and mustard. He washed it down with a sip of wine, which was dry but very fragrant and tasted of berries, with a touch of spice. It went extremely well with the food.

Anahi eyed him, "Ya like it, I see. I thought ya would. This is my favorite meal."

Baltaszar was about to speak, but his mouth was full again. For the remainder of the meal, he and Anahi sat and glanced back and forth at one another, smiling from time to time. It was an innocent flirtation. Baltaszar knew he wouldn't do anything, and he understood that Anahi respected his feelings for Yasaman enough to not make any advances.

Once they finished eating, Anahi rose from the bed.

"Are you leaving already?" Baltaszar stood in response.

She walked to him, putting one hand on his shoulder and the other in his hand. "We both know that it is best for me ta leave. Ya would be wise ta wake early. You'll be travelin' on the road, out in the open. The king's soldiers are very unpredictable with how they scout, though they don't normally come up this far. Ya should be well on yer journey by late mornin'. At least that way, ye'll have yer wits about ya by the time they're up an' ready. I hope fer yer sake that Horatio is better with fightin' than with manners. At least ya won't be alone though." Anahi pulled his head close and kissed him on the cheek.

"An' do me a favor, Baltaszar. Well two favors. When ya have a chance, go back to…wherever it is yer from an' talk to Yasaman. Figure things out one way or another. Not for my sake, but fer yers. It'll drive ya crazy the longer ya go on without knowin' what the situation is." She looked him straight in the eyes.

"All right, I promise, I will. What else?"

"The second favor is silly, but fer yer own good. When ya find yerself deep in thought, please don't keep makin' those funny faces. I don't mind 'em because I find 'em amusin' an endearin', but no one will take ya seriously when ya puff up yer cheeks like that and stare off inta space. Or when ya twist up yer mouth all crazy. Yer not a very scary Descendant."

Baltaszar chuckled. "You know, I never really realized that I do that until now. Fine, I will make a conscious effort to avoid that. Is that all?"

"One more thing. Be safe. Please. I don't get too attached ta visitors at the Elephant, but yer nice. An' genuine. An' I care. Please just don't let me find out in a few days or weeks that some handsome brown-skinned Descendant was killed on his way ta the House o' Darian, along with his silly friend Horatio, who talked too much."

Baltaszar bit his lip and nodded solemnly at the request.

Anahi hugged him tightly. In an instant, she let go and left the room, glancing back at Baltaszar one more time before closing the door.

One piece of advice. Once you leave, keep a clear mind at all times.

Shut up. Leave me alone.

CHAPTER 9
TOWER OF THE BLIND

From *The Book of Orijin*, Verse One Hundred Thirty-Five
The mind will see what the eye cannot begin to fathom.

TWO ISLANDS SAT within the Eye of Orijin, the giant lake that bordered Cerysia, Galicea, Mireya, and the Never. The Tower of the Blind had been built on the southernmost island, mainly because of its proximity to all of Ashur. The island itself had five docks, located at each of the outermost points of the island. Roads led from each dock straight to the tower at the center of the island. The Tower had been a welcoming place from the time of its inception a few hundred years after Darian's death.

Garrison hated that most people assumed Gideon, one of the Five Harbingers, had built the tower, just because of his ability with stone. It was one of those rumors that would never go away, even amongst educated people. The truth was that the tower had been built by the ancestors of Galiceans. Even modern Galiceans were master builders and craftsman, as evidenced by the wall erected at their border with Fangh-Haan. But the Tower of the Blind was a true marvel, a sight that everyone should see at least once in their lives, just like the Stones of Gideon.

The Tower was so tall that on cloudy days, one could not see the top of it. Its exterior had been created solely of grey, unpainted stone. To this day, people could only speculate how the builders were able to bring the stone to the island.

The entire structure was cylindrical and nearly three hundred feet wide. Garrison supposed it had to be so big in order to house a few hundred Blind Men and their servants. Even now, sitting in the front of the wagon on the road toward the Tower, Garrison had to crane his neck upwards in order to see the top of it, though with the sun having already set, the top was difficult to see. Rows and rows of windows lined the building. As a boy, Garrison had come to the Tower with his mother to visit her uncle, a Blind Man, and he wondered why there would be windows. In truth, for each Blind Man living in the Tower, there lived at least three servants. Servants of the Blind were treated quite well, but they required extreme patience and dedication. Surely the windows were there more for the servants than the Blind, or

Augurs, as they were formally known. But even the Blind Men and Women enjoyed the natural sunlight to anything artificial.

Garrison and his Taurani companions reached the base of the Tower. The road led directly up to the high wooden doors at the entrance. The doors were twice the height of a tall man, made of a cherry-hued wood, and in them the symbol of the Blind was carved. It was a man's, or perhaps a woman's, face with closed eyes, and on the forehead, an open third eye. The face itself was expressionless, with no hair atop the head. Garrison remembered the symbol from the time he was a child. It had always raised the hair on his skin and neck when he saw it or thought of it. The symbol did not elicit fear in him, more a feeling of reverence. Garrison had the deepest respect for anyone who was born with such a severe limitation, yet lived such a scholarly and almost regal life.

Dozens of white-robed servants flocked to Garrison and the Taurani to greet them. Although he hadn't been to the Tower in years, all the servants greeted him by name, but without the title of 'Prince', in various accents. *Could they have gotten word already?* The servants helped each of them from the wagon and hurried the two injured Taurani, Yorik and Kavon, away into the Tower. They then collected Garrison's pack and the rest of the belongings and ushered Garrison and Marika inside.

Although Garrison had never personally known any of the servants, he knew much of their background and history. He supposed that was one of the benefits of being a prince. In his lifetime, Garrison had traveled through most of Ashur and in the past few years, he'd read dozens of books, especially on the history of Ashur.

The servants of the Blind were, on the surface, very humble, friendly, and good-natured. They were genuinely good people; Garrison knew they had to be if they were willing to dedicate their lives in the service of the Blind. However, beneath the surface, the servants were some of the most lethal fighters on the continent. Garrison had never seen any of them fight, but he had read dozens of stories in which a servant had to protect a Blind Man. Once a man or woman accepted the white robe of a Blind servant, they were sent to Fangh-Haan to be trained to fight. Fangh-Haan was the home of the Anonymi.

According to legends, the Anonymi predated the Drowning of the World. They were a clan of warriors who had existed even before the time of Darian and the others of the Five. From generation to generation, the Anonymi passed their knowledge and wisdom of fighting only to accepted members of the clan.

Once the Tower of the Blind had been built, every nation signed a treaty agreeing that the Tower was immune to all wars and battles. No violence could be conducted on its grounds, as the punishment for such offenses was death. Even the throne supported these laws, though Garrison wondered whether his father would make exceptions if they suited his tastes.

As an extra measure to ensure that none were tempted to break these laws, the king at the time, Roald, forged an agreement with the Anonymi that they would train all servants of the Blind, with the condition that the servants would not pass this teaching onto others, and that the Servants would live out the rest of their days at the Tower. The punishment for breaking these agreements was death, as well as an end to the Anonymi training the servants. It was argued by many that the Anonymi were just as dangerous, if not more so, as the Taurani.

Garrison and Marika were led to the main hall, where the servants gestured for them to be seated on a white cushioned bench. More servants came with trays of colorful juices and small plates of pastries balanced atop their heads. Garrison had remembered this detail from his last visit so many years ago. All of the servants of the Blind wore loose, flowing white robes with scores of pockets of all sizes. However, many also wore wide, deep square hats that they used for carrying trays, books, clothing, and all sorts of things. As a child, Garrison had asked an elder servant why she wore such a strange hat, and she had replied, "Dear boy, you try leading around a Blind Man while also carrying his lunch and his books as well!"

The servants did not wait for Garrison and Marika to accept or deny food and drink. They left the trays with them and ran off to tend to other responsibilities. After the flourish, only one servant remained at the bench. "What happened to our things?" Garrison asked. "Have they put them away?"

The servant, a slender boy not much older than Garrison, held his index finger before his lips, and whispered. "We have secured your belongings in your quarters. It is likely that you plan to stay for at least a day. Though may I advise that you wait until your companions' health has been restored for you to depart? I would conjecture that it will be at least two or three days until your companions are capable of leaving."

The young servant's accent was Cerysian. Servants of the Blind hailed from every part of Ashur. Many were relatives of the Augurs, the official title of the Blind, but not always. Garrison imagined it would be interesting to spend a few days in the Tower to hear all of the accents. He lowered his voice to a whisper as well. "Your hospitality is appreciated, but we shall leave in the morning. We are being followed and the longer we wait, the more dangerous it becomes for us." Garrison picked a pastry from the tray.

"It is not my place to argue. If that is what you must do, then it is so. We shall provide you with any needs and supplies necessary for the road ahead."

Garrison finished chewing the pastry, it had been filled with peaches, not his favorite but quite enjoyable considering he hadn't eaten since morning. "Thank you. Why is it that we must whisper? And what is your name?"

"We whisper to maintain the silence of the Tower. Because they cannot see, the Augurs function better when relying on their ears. However, speaking tends to disturb their concentration. Concerning my name, it is forbidden that I tell you."

"Forbidden? Why? And if you are not allowed to speak, then does no one speak at a normal volume in the Tower?"

"As you know, we are trained by the Anonymi. One of the conditions for the Anonymi to agree to train us was that we must adopt their customs and rules. And one of those customs was that we discard our names."

"Is that not difficult with the Blind? How do they know who you are?"

"Oh, the Augurs have their ways. They are quite keen when it comes to minute details. They tend to give us their own names as well, usually based on how they identify us. When each of us completed our training, the Anonymi leaders gave us a new name. But those given names are only used among Anonymi. To answer your other question, speaking is allowed in designated areas. There are numerous common rooms throughout the Tower where conversation is allowed, as well as in the Augur's quarters. It is simply a courtesy to them that we cater to their preferences in the public areas of the Tower. After all, this was built for them, not us."

Garrison nodded his head and looked around. It became very clear to him that the Tower catered to the Blind. The main hall in which they sat was an enormous circle, as were all of the pillars. Garrison imagined the dangers to the Blind being around sharp corners. Furthermore, there were no tapestries or paintings or any designs on the walls. The whole place had a very sterile feel to it. "The hospitality has been impeccable, my friend. But why have we not met any Blind Men or Women yet? Surely some would be willing to greet us?"

The servant nodded. "Yes, I understand your confusion, Master Garrison. You and your companions arrived at the onset of evening, which is when most of the Augurs are sitting down to supper. They are very routine oriented and strongly dislike straying from their timetables, I hope you understand. That being said, some of the servants went to notify one or two Augurs of your arrival, as some do not like to eat until later. However, it is a custom that, when graced with visitors, the Augurs relish the opportunity to greet their guests with a personal prophecy, positive in nature if possible. I imagine that any delay is because the Augurs are searching for a prophecy to share."

Garrison bit into another pastry; this one was filled with raspberries and much tastier than the previous. As many as Garrison had eaten, Marika sat quietly next to him and had already cleared half of the tray. "I have noticed that I have yet to be addressed by the title of 'Prince'; would I be correct to assume that part of your agreement with the Anonymi is that you shed any fealty to nations and leaders?"

"That is an accurate assumption. I hope you do not take any offense to the matter. Before my training nearly five years ago, I held a great deal of reverence for you, as well as for your brother and the Lion Cub. I grew up in Maradon, so we only heard stories of the three of you."

The Lion Cub. Wendell would laugh if he knew people still called him that. Because of Wendell's distinct blonde hair, coupled with his tan skin, he'd been given that nickname as a little boy. Garrison smirked and stifled a laugh. "Thank you. You should be aware, however, that I am no longer the Prince of Ashur, as of this morning." The servant's eyes widened and Garrison continued, "My father has charged me as a criminal and traitor because I wish to be formally trained by the House of Darian. His soldiers are now hunting me down." Garrison noticed the servant stifle a grimace at the mention of the king.

The servant still stood before Garrison, erect, with his hands clasped behind his back. "That is...unfortunate. You have come to the right place for asylum. Now I understand your desire to leave in the morning. A lengthy stay here would not only bring your pursuers closer, but would also allow their numbers to increase. Do they know you are here?"

Garrison slumped against the back of the bench. "They would be foolish to think any differently. We were chased to the Eye and my horse was killed. Although we killed the soldiers who pursued us, anyone who followed them will notice that the boats are gone, as we set the rest of the boats free."

"Yes. You did not leave much room for other possibilities. Have you a plan for the rest of your journey?"

"I barely had time to plan the beginning of my journey. From here, my only two options would be through Galicea or through Mireya. Galicea is overrun with soldiers and by morning, news will have reached that I am a criminal. I have no doubts that there is a price on my head. The only question is whether my father wants to kill me himself."

"I do pray that the Augurs have foreseen your safe arrival to the House, Garrison. Why even consider Galicea when Mireya will provide a faster route to the House of Darian? Not to mention, Mireyans are notoriously protective of Descendants. The town of Gangjeon sits southwest at the banks of the Eye."

Garrison could only smile regretfully at the suggestion. Marika sat quietly next to him, likely regretting the decision to help him. "The problem is, my friend, I am an enemy to both sides of that conflict. Until recent years, I led the king's soldiers to hunt down and kill Descendants. I have not been to Mireya in over two years, but I fear the Mireyans will be just as eager to kill me as my father's soldiers."

The servant cast his eyes to the floor at Garrison's admission. "I see. Perhaps it may still be better to take your chances with the Mireyans."

Marika interrupted, "No. From here, we go directly to the House. The more we prolong this journey, the more we risk being caught. Servant, is there anything that will give cover between here and the House? Mountains, forest, caves?"

"Indeed. To the southwest there is an extensive forest. At the other side of it is the Serpent. Perhaps you can also use that to distance your enemies."

Garrison cut off Marika before she could ask the question, "The Serpent is a river that flows through Galicea. The southernmost part of it is less than a day's ride to the House."

Marika nodded. "Our course is set. However, there is one thing that must be done once we depart." She turned to the servant, "You must send another boat toward the town you mentioned. In the chance that an ambush awaits us, at least that might throw off anyone waiting for us."

"Very well. It will be no trouble for us to provide an additional boat. There may even be one traveling to Gangjeon tomorrow anyway. We can also equip you with horses and food if you would like."

Garrison smiled once more. "That would be quite helpful. Is there any possibility that you have weapons to loan us?"

"I apologize, Garrison. It is not our way to keep weapons in the Tower. We do collect the weapons of any guest, but they are untouched and then returned when guests leave."

"I understand. Then perhaps we could have a look at your storage rooms in the morning?"

The servant's brow furrowed. "That should not be a problem. I shall refrain from questioning your interest in this. I shall meet you at your quarters in the morning and show you the way. Why, what timing. Here comes Augur Harlan now. Hopefully he has glad tidings for you."

"One question before you leave. You made it clear that the Tower does not take sides in the wars and quarrels of the rest of Ashur. Yet, you are helping us against the King of Ashur. I do not understand."

"Garrison, you are not seeing the situation from the correct perspective. I am not taking a side. I am helping to preserve a precious life. Four precious lives, in fact. While the Tower abstains from the conflicts of the outside world, we support the preservation of life above anything else. I shall see you in the morning." The servant scuttled away without waiting for a response.

Another servant slowly approached, leading a Blind Man who must have been Harlan. Garrison stood and Marika followed his actions. Garrison glanced down at the pastry tray, which was now empty, then looked agape at Marika. She understood his countenance immediately and the twin black lines on her face could not hide her reddened cheeks. Marika then smiled, "Do not judge me, dear boy. It has been over a day since I have eaten anything of substance."

Harlan now stood before them in a dark green robe with a white stripe down the center and at the end of each sleeve. He was younger than Garrison realized, but in his head, Garrison pictured all of the Blind to be old. He wasn't sure why, he supposed it was simply because he thought Blind Men and Women were all full of wisdom and experience. Harlan looked about twice Garrison's age, tall and slim with yellowish Mireyan skin, and long hair tied back behind his head. *Perhaps it is good that he cannot see me. Likely he would attack me as well.*

"Sit, sit, my friends. I have heard yer journey has been quite tryin' thus far. No need ta stand on my account."

Garrison and Marika obliged him. "How did you know we were standing?" Garrison felt foolish asking the question, but it slipped before he could think twice about asking.

Harlan smiled at the question, "My escort here informed me that ya had stood up ta greet me. Ya see, despite what everyone says, they're useful sometimes." He patted the servant on the back. "I'd like ta apologize fer keepin' ya waitin'. We were lookin fer a prophecy that might be useful to ya, but couldn't find anythin' about ya, Garrison."

Garrison sighed. "No apology is necessary. Thank you for searching. We only came here for shelter and a short rest. We shall be gone in the morning."

"Ya didn't let me finish, boy. I couldn't find anythin' about ya, but well, when that happens, we like ta give a prophecy anyway. Usually somethin' that at least might interest ya. Now, o' course I can't see yer face, but ya got a line down yer eye, don'tcha?"

"I do."

"An yer headed fer the House o' Darian?"

"Yes."

"Then perhaps this one'll be o' some help. My servants tell me we haven't told anyone this prophecy yet. Apparently it was only seen about a year ago. An' well, it's been some time since any o' ya from the House has been here. Anyway, wait, let me see if I remember this correctly." Harlan paused for a few moments, mouthing words silently to himself. "Oh yes. The Night o' Fire an' Water will mark the beginnin' o' Jahmash's retaliation."

Garrison cocked an eyebrow, "What does that mean? 'The Night of Fire and Water'?"

"Well. I forget." Harlan turned to his servant. "Hey. Did ya bring the volume like I asked ya ta?"

"Of course, sir." The servant reached into his broad hat and retrieved a volume. He flipped through several pages, then placed the book in Harlan's hands. Once Harlan had the book secure in one hand, the servant placed Harlan's right hand at the top of the left page.

"Thank ya. Ya see Garrison, so many o' these servants are unreliable. But this one. He's not sa bad. They all think they know better than we do, since they can see an' we cannot an' all. As if sight means ya got better sense." Harlan must have sensed Garrison's discomfort, or perhaps he heard Garrison tapping his feet. "Ah, boy. I'm just jokin' with ya. We Blind Men have a habit o' poking fun at our blindness an' ribbin all o' ya who can see. Can ya blame us?"

Garrison hesitated for a second. "No, of course not. It is just surprising that you can take it lightly."

"O' course we can. We live with the thing our whole lives. Anyway, let us see what this thing means." Harlan ran his finger slowly over a few lines of raised dots and dashes on the page. "Yes. That makes sense now. Armaan saw this one. A Shivaani fella. Anyway, he saw a night o' severe rain. He described it like someone poured the sea from the sky. It was in the middle o' town, they were all watchin a hangin. Then, right after the man was dropped, the hangin platform caught fire despite the rain. Town was called Haedon. Armaan wrote that he heard a boomin voice loud enough ta drown out the rain, that said 'The era o' Ashur an' Darian's Descendants has come ta an end. The era o' Jahmash begins.' Armaan wrote that nobody around him heard the voice or responded ta it. Usually a sign o' two situations overlappin'."

"This prophecy seems rather shaky. I have traveled through all most of Ashur and have never heard of Haedon. Besides, even the man who saw it said that nobody heard what Jahmash supposedly said."

The Blind Man retorted quickly. "Garrison, yer young. I wouldn't be so bold ta call ya a fool, but travels alone don't educate a man. Just because ya never heard o' anythin' doesn't mean it doesn't exist. If we relied only on our senses an' never thought fer ourselves, we'd all be fools. Look at the Blind. None o' us has ever seen a thing. That mean the world doesn't exist?"

"Well, no. But..."

"O' course it doesn't. What yer also forgettin' is perhaps the world is bigger than Ashur. Anyone who's studied the history o' this world an' the Harbingers knows the world was much bigger before Darian—bless the man—drowned it. What if this Haedon place existed beyond Ashur?"

Garrison breathed deeply. His stubbornness often got the best of him, but Harlan had a point. "Fine. I'll assume that Haedon is a real place. But why would Armaan be the only one who could hear the voice?"

"I can explain that easily. Ya see, when we see these prophecies, some o' the Blind can experience more than one thing at a time. Ya forget, while we see what is real, we aren't in the real world. It isn't the norm, but it's happened enough that a Blind Man or Woman can see one point o' view an' hear another. Even if the two aren't in the same place. I can see yer still havin' some trouble believin' me, boy. Never mind whether ya believe or not. There has yet ta be a prophecy that hasn't come true."

"I still have my doubts. But I will refrain from arguing. Assuming the prophecy is true, how will we know when this is going to happen? Should we not find this Haedon place and have scouts inform us of this night?"

"Garrison, this prophecy is over a year old. Tryin ta find Haedon is a futile task. This may have happened already an' we wouldn't even know it."

"Very well. What do you suggest we do about this then?"

"Yer goin ta the House, aren't ya? Tell them o' this when ya get there. They got some real intelligent folks there, might be able ta do more with this information than we can."

Garrison yawned and acquiesced. He was too tired to argue. "Very well, Augur Harlan. I will deliver this message."

"Thank ya, Garrison. And o' course, yer free ta stay until yer companions are fully healed. We will accommodate yer needs until yer stay has ended."

A curious thought struck Garrison's mind. "That is very generous of you. However, we shall leave in the morning. Your hospitality is greatly appreciated, but we are being chased and time is of the essence. There is something I am wondering about though, if you would not mind explaining it to me?"

"Well, that depends on yer request. I cannot guarantee ya I'll answer. But go ahead, boy. Ask yer question, ya won't offend us regardless."

"Very well. All of you at the Tower have tended to our every need. From the moment we arrived, you asked no questions. Stones of Gideon, you were not even surprised that we were here. And beyond that, you have no issue with us staying here. I am simply surprised that the Tower can be so welcoming, yet it is not overrun by people, especially the poor, looking to take advantage of your hospitality."

Harlan and the servant both smiled at Garrison's words. Harlan then gestured for the attendant to lead him to the bench, where he sat between Garrison and Marika, who looked especially worn down as she fought heavy eyelids and still wore tattered leather armor. "That is not a difficult thing ta explain. I suppose there's a bit o' irony that exists on Augur Island. That's this island in case it wasn't obvious. Ya see, we're a bunch o' blind fools, but well, we have eyes everywhere on this island. We know about everything that happens, especially who's showin' up at our docks, all five o' them.

"O' course, that doesn't mean we're adverse ta visitors. But we have rules in place so people don't take advantage o' us. Anyone who comes ta the Tower is only allowed ta stay fer so long. It's not like we just let ya move in if ya got nowhere ta go. Most o' the poor don't have the means ta get all the way here. An' those who do come, we give 'em a choice. Ya see, if they ain't got many prospects fer a better life, we only let em stay if they agree ta become a servant. An' if ya don't understand my meanin, all servants are sent ta Fangh-Haan fer trainin'. That's not so pleasant a thing."

Garrison understood now. "Do many of them agree to go through with this? It seems like the servants here have a decent life."

"Oh they have very good lives! Aside from dealin with the nonsense an' whims o' us unseein' folk, the servants here do well fer their selves. However, the processes an' preparation ta get here is the difficult part. Many o' the poor are willin ta be trained. I'd say less than half o' them comes back. Tell ya the truth though, I don't think the Anonymi let 'em go if they quit. Too many secrets with them folk. I believe anyone who goes there an' can't finish the trainin ends up bein a servant fer them. Still a better life I suppose."

"I suppose it is. At least there is still dignity in being a servant. I have seen my share of beggars and poor folk. They have so little that even pride is beyond them. Though I cannot fault them for being that way. I imagine that when you have nothing, you will do whatever it takes to better yourself. To just live."

"Indeed ya will boy. Indeed ya will. But let us stop takin up yer time. It's late an' by the sound o' ya an' yer friend's yawnin, ya need some rest." Harlan directed his voice toward the servant, who was still standing a few yards before them. "Hey, boy. Let's get them ta their quarters, huh." Harlan stood and the servant interlocked his own arm with Harlan's, then waved for Garrison and Marika to follow.

They walked toward a doorway in the wall, then turned right and continued up a ramp that seemed to have bordered the circular perimeter of the Tower. Luckily for Garrison, they only walked up to the second floor, which was wholly different from the first. The common area was much smaller, relatively, and the room was surrounded by doors. However, the lack of color and decoration were still consistent with the room Garrison had just left. He supposed that would not change no matter what floor he was on. Although this floor contained several rooms situated around the perimeter, there still existed well over one hundred yards from one side to the other. A few servants still walked about here and there, some leading Blind Men, some not.

The servant and Harlan led Garrison and Marika to two adjacent doors, and the elderly servant spoke for only the second time. "Each of you has your own quarters and you'll find everything you need inside, including anything we carried in for you when you arrived. We left some trays of food as well, mostly fruits, cheeses, and thinly sliced cured meats. Servants will check on you shortly to ensure that you have everything you need. If you would like to bathe before sleeping, please let them know and they will arrange it. There are additional robes and clothing inside that should be of an appropriate size to fit you comfortably. If at any time there is something else you need, simply come out to the common area. Servants patrol every floor, and if you don't see anyone, it will not be long before you do. Is there anything with which I can accommodate either of you at the moment?"

Garrison and Marika simultaneously shook their heads in refusal and Garrison responded, "Nothing at the moment. But please have someone wake me at sunrise. Preferably the same Cerysian servant to whom I spoke before. Thank you."

"Very well. I will arrange it. May your sleep be peaceful."

Garrison could not place the servant's accent, though he was light-skinned. It sounded similar to the way Galicean's spoke, yet different. The servant opened his and Marika's doors then bowed and led Harlan away.

Although Garrison and Marika were alone, Garrison spoke softly to her. "I will wake you in the morning. We will need to be very resourceful about what supplies we take with us. Things that can be useful as weapons as well as defense, protection, and survival. I know we will not have a proper night's sleep, but we still must be alert and ready for anything once we leave here."

"Yes, I know. Do not worry, I know how to function in dire situations. I will see you at sunrise." Marika disappeared into her quarters and shut the door.

Garrison entered his room, which was dimly lit by two candles, one by the bed to his right and the other on a dresser at the opposite end. A large tray of food covered nearly half of the table at the center of the room and as tempting as it was, exhaustion suddenly weighed Garrison so heavily down that he dragged himself over to the bed, kicked off his boots and dropped down like a falling tree trunk. By the time he finished an enormous yawn, his eyelids were so stubborn that they did not reopen until morning.

***

Garrison wondered how long the knocking had been going on as he fought to open his eyes. "Come in," he managed to groan, hoping it was audible enough for the servant.

A dark-skinned Shivaani man entered the room, his large belly evident despite the loose white robe. "Good morning, sir. You requested to be awoken at sunrise." His accent was similar to Garrison's Cerysian style, but less pronounced.

Garrison was still shaking off the sleep. "I did. But you are not the servant I spoke with yesterday. I requested for him to wake me."

"I apologize if you are offended at my presence, sir. The one you speak of is currently aiding a Blind Woman with her breakfast. He will be arriving to your quarters shortly, but he asked me to wake you in his absence."

Garrison felt slightly guilty. He had a habit of speaking too sharply to Shivaani. It was one of the few traits that he had inherited from his father. The King disliked many things, but utterly hated the Shivaani. During the rule of Garrison's great grandfather, King Waylon, Shivaana had still been a part of Cerysia, but threatened a civil war if the King did not lower the taxes of their region. All of the cities from Gansishoor and southward were taxed more by the Throne because they attracted thousands upon thousands of travelers year-round. Shivaani cities were still extremely popular because of their markets, fashion, snake charmers, exotic animal fights, and of course, Daughters of Tahlia, the entrancing dancers in Sundari. Gamblers also flocked to Sundari to bet on all types of rare beasts such as Bhujanga, giant snakes found only in the mountains between Shivaana and Fangh-

Haan, Ranza cats, and extremely rare Vrschiika which were enormous insect like beasts with six legs, giant claws, venomous tails, and skin strong as steel that could change its color according to its surroundings. Garrison had never actually seen one, but enough people, Shivaani and otherwise, had marveled at the sheer viciousness of Vrschiika in the fights that he was unsure of whether he really wanted to.

Supposedly, the Shivaani had massacred the King's army with its ability to command all of these animals. Deep down, Garrison understood that they had been treated unfairly, but he still resented the reality that so many of his countrymen were slaughtered. Garrison looked once again at the servant in his room. None of what had happened in the past was this man's fault. And even if the servant had previously favored one side or the other, he'd given up that allegiance when agreeing to be a Servant of the Blind.

The harsh truth that Garrison had so much difficulty coming to terms with was that he was the biggest hypocrite he'd likely ever know in his life. He could think as lowly as he'd like about his father, but at least his father was consistent in how he mistreated everyone. As for Garrison, in his eighteen years, he had been a follower of someone else's ideals for nearly sixteen of them. It was a painful reality to have to swallow.

Garrison recovered his senses and sat up in bed. "I apologize for sounding so brash. You caught me somewhat by surprise. You have no need for an apology, the offense is mine."

"It is nothing, sir. I understand that certain…prejudices…are difficult to shed. The most difficult part of my servant training was to let go of the same resentments that you feel. And since I've become free of such emotional burdens, my life has become so much brighter. Perhaps you should try to let go as well."

"That is good advice. Perhaps I should."

"Is there anything I might bring you? Would you prefer that I bring you food or would you like to eat in one of the common rooms?"

"I will eat in here while I wait for the other servant to arrive. Would you mind bringing food for two? I will ask Makira to join me."

"Very well, sir. What would you like for me to bring?"

"I am rather partial to ham, eggs, and rice for breakfast, if you have it. Unless it would be an inconvenience?"

The servant looked up confusedly, as if he'd never heard of such a thing before. "I'm sure that could be arranged. Shall I bring the same for Marika?"

"I do not really know what she prefers."

"That is no trouble. I will inquire with her upon leaving here. Do you think it would be appropriate to wake her?"

"Yes, that would be fine. I planned to do that once I awoke anyway. It would be better to ask her preference. Thank you."

As the servant turned to leave, another servant entered the room. It was the Cerysian man Garrison had met the night before. "Good morning, Garrison. I trust your sleep was enjoyable?"

Garrison walked over to the window. The sky was empty of clouds, allowing him to see the sun clearly. It was almost completely over the horizon. "I slept wonderfully. I must have blacked out the moment my head fell into the pillow."

Marika entered the room, but to Garrison's surprise, she wore only a long thick white robe tied at the waist. She sat down at the table in the center and looked over to Garrison, who still stared at her. "What boy? Is it so ridiculous to you that I act as a normal woman? First I am not allowed to eat; now I must wear armor at all times?"

Garrison panicked. "No it is not that. Just...well..."

"Out with it, child. You clearly have your judgments about me. Tell me why you have such issues." The servant sat down at the table, joining Marika's gaze at Garrison.

Why must women always be so difficult? "I was never judging you about anything. I was simply surprised about certain things. About the pastries, I was taken aback because you are rather...small. I did not think you were capable of eating so many." Marika frowned at that. Garrison often caught himself saying the wrong thing to women. On too many occasions back at home, Vanna had become cross with him for the same reason. "I do not mean that in a bad way. But...well the robe. When you wore your armor, you looked deadly. Dangerous. Now, you look so...I do not know...regal? Even with the tattoos on your face, you look so much...softer." Marika pursed her lips and rolled her eyes.

Garrison swore that the servant was holding back a laugh. Whether that was truly the case or not, the servant's countenance changed to solemnity. "Concerning your departure, Garrison, I have some news. After our conversation in the evening, I took the liberty of speaking to some servants who had returned from Gangjeon earlier in the day. They confirmed that a battalion of the King's soldiers are there questioning the townsfolk. They also said there are scores of them, Garrison. Easily over one hundred."

Garrison cut in, "And once they realize we are not hiding there, at least some of them will move on. Likely along the path that we plan to follow. Thank you. We must act quickly. Let us see your supplies instead of sitting here to wait for breakfast."

The servant arose. "Exactly what types of supplies would you like me to show you, Garrison?"

"The kitchen supplies would be best. Will it be inconvenient for us to go there?"

"Not at all. I will bring you and give instructions that you are allowed to take what you need. Simply tell the kitchen servants what you request and they shall deliver it up here to your quarters. I imagine you will need packs with which to carry everything." Garrison nodded in affirmation. "Very well. It shall be done."

Marika stood from the table, holding her robe tightly around her, as if wary of Garrison looking at her. "Perhaps you could also have Kavon and Yorik meet us outside? It would save time to have them down there already."

"Yes, that will be arranged. Would you like to change first, my lady?"

Marika nodded then smirked at Garrison and returned to her chambers.

***

Garrison and the three Taurani had managed to board a small boat on the southwest dock, toward Mireya, in less than half an hour of collecting their supplies. They'd gathered various items at Garrison's request, such as cooking oil and fat, a collection of knives, nearly a dozen broomsticks, which Marika was sharpening at the moment, and chopped up small animal parts. They had three packs and each of them would carry one except Kavon, whose ribs were badly bruised and likely broken. Standing straight, Kavon was more than a hand taller than Garrison, but the pain forced him to hunch, even when sitting.

From the bow of the deck, Garrison could still see the other boat they'd sent to Gangjeon. He was starting to doubt its effectiveness. The servant had told him earlier that a boat had returned from Gangjeon yesterday, leaving Garrison to wonder how often the Tower sent boats there. *What if they think nothing of that boat?* One of the servants on the decoy boat resembled Garrison in build and had a cleanly shaved head. The hope was that, from afar, scouts would mistake the servant for Garrison and wait to ambush him at the docks of Gangjeon.

Garrison was sure the soldiers would not attack from far away, as they would have to be certain of his death and return his body to Alvadon. If all of that went according to plan, Garrison and the Taurani would be far ahead by the time the soldiers realized that they'd been tricked.

It would take hours to reach the shore, but there would be no docks. Garrison and the Taurani would have to ride their horses off of the boat and into shallow water. The servants had specifically chosen four horses that would not get skittish walking through deep water.

"The spears are done," Marika informed him. Garrison had been so lost in thought that he didn't even hear her walk up behind him. "Is there anything else you would suggest we do to prepare?"

Garrison turned and shrugged his shoulders, "Pray. I believe that is all we can do at this point."

Marika smiled at him sympathetically. "As long as Kavon, Yorik, and I are with you, Garrison, we will do everything we can to ensure you reach your people."

Garrison smirked, "Ha. My people. Two days ago, my people were to the north and not hunting me down. Funny how life can change so quickly. How it can be so delicate."

Marika walked up next to Garrison and stared out toward the sea. "You do not have to tell me, child. Only a few days ago, *my* people were all alive. Now there is nothing left."

Garrison turned back toward the sea. "What will you do now? Is there any hope for the Taurani? I do not mean to overstep my boundaries…but, well, I understand that you and Yorik are siblings. But couldn't you and Kavon…well, extend the Taurani legacy?"

Marika laughed heartily. "Ah, thank you for the laugh, Garrison. That was very…genuine of you. I am too old to be birthing children and raising babies. Once we see you safely to the House of Darian, we will sail around Ashur to its eastern shores. Yorik and I believe there may be some hope there to help rebuild the Taurani. And sailing will at least keep us safe, instead of risking conflicts with soldiers. After that, we shall return to our village in the hopes that there are other survivors. But let us focus on the present. Perhaps you are right. The best thing right now is to pray."

Garrison nodded. "I do not mean to offend, but I would prefer to be alone up here until we reach shore. It is not personal; I just have a great deal on my mind."

"Of course, boy. Of course." Marika turned and patted his should as she walked away.

For the next hour and a half, Garrison stood at the bow, and stared straight ahead. His only movement was fingering the pouches of colored dust in the pockets of a brown cloak the servants had given him. Garrison silently asked the Orijin to allow him and the Taurani to all reach the end of their journeys safely. In his head, he repeated the same request continually until the words echoed on beyond his will.

The time for praying had finished. He needed to steel his resolve and become the same cold, stoic warrior he had been so many times when he'd hunted down Descendants with his father's soldiers. It had been more than a year since he'd killed a man, but Garrison remembered vividly the feeling of looking at a man with nothing but hatred. Not caring whether the man was a good man or bad, whether or not the man had a family, or whether the man was ready to die or not. Garrison found it difficult to regain that frame of mind, but he was confident that it would return once he was in the face of adversity. If it didn't he would never make it to the House.

The shores of Mireya appeared in the distance. One of the servants called him from the stern. They were leading the horses from the stern to the center of the deck. Garrison met the servants and the Taurani there and threw a pack over his shoulders. His horse had been saddled with the specialized saddle he'd brought to the tower. Garrison had volunteered to equip his horse with two packs, given Kavon's injuries. One pack held some supplies they had taken from the Tower, and the other contained the inventions Garrison had taken from his workshop before leaving Alvadon. He and the Taurani mounted the horses, though Kavon needed help from two servants. Once they'd all mounted, Marika passed Garrison and Yorik each four spears, made from broomsticks with the ends honed down to points. She kept three for herself.

They'd reached as close to shore as they could and two servants dropped the anchor. A few others brought several long thick wooden planks to portside and stacked them over the boat so they became a ramp from the boat to the water.

"Is that thing going to hold us?"

One of the servants replied with a smile, "Of course it will, Garrison. You each simply must walk down one at a time."

Garrison turned to the others and shrugged. Kavon spoke for the first time since leaving the Tower. "I'll go first. At least if it breaks, I'm hurt anyway." Garrison glanced over at Marika and she nodded in agreement. This was not the time for arguing. He held his palm out, signaling for Kavon to proceed.

Kavon rode his horse toward the plank and the horse gingerly stepped onto the stacked wooden plank. It placed one hoof at a time until it was walking down the long plank and into the water. The wood slightly bowed under the weight, but not as much as Garrison expected. One by one, they ventured down the plank and into the shallow water. Marika went second and Garrison followed as Yorik insisted on taking the rear.

The servants waited until they reached the shore to raise the anchor and turn back. Unlike the sandy shore at the north of the Eye, the southern shore was verdant and littered with rocks. Garrison and the Taurani navigated slowly; the last thing they needed was a horse turning its ankle and becoming lame.

Before their departure, the familiar Cerysian servant—Garrison hated that he had no name—informed them that the forest was a straight ride from the shore, no more than two hours once they reached land.

They swiftly rode on, side by side. Garrison had struggled to decide whether to ride this way or in single file. But none of their pursuers would know that he was with three Taurani, considering they'd killed everyone who'd seen them before sailing to the Tower. Hopefully the number of tracks would divert the King's soldiers.

The four riders continued for over an hour and a half through high grass when a dark outline appeared in the distance. The forest was still a few miles away, but it filled Garrison with encouragement and hope. It wouldn't be very long before he could let his guard down, if only for a few minutes.

Just as Garrison began to entertain thoughts of relaxation, something whistled in the air behind him. Before he could turn around, Yorik yelled out, "Arrows! They're flanking us from the north! Ride faster and stay low!"

Garrison heeded Yorik's advice and leaned forward, hugging the horse's neck as he commanded it to go faster. With any luck, they could reach the forest in a few minutes. Looking to his right, the soldiers were still far off, but advancing quickly. What unnerved Garrison was that there was easily one hundred of them, if not more, all riding in an enormous silver-armored wave ready to crash down on Garrison and his three companions.

Ahead of him, Kavon's horse shrieked as arrows pierced its neck and front leg. Both Kavon and the horse went crashing down after a few clumsy steps. *Why is he holding on? Let go!* "Let go!" Garrison tried to will Kavon into letting go of the reins, but the man clung tightly to them as the horse fell onto its side and crushed Kavon's left leg. Garrison would need no inspection to know that Kavon would never walk again.

He slowed his horse and bounded to Kavon. Yorik joined him immediately and the two lifted Kavon's horse enough for the injured Taurani to pull his leg free.

Fury contorted Garrison's face and mouth. "Why did you hold onto the reins? Why didn't you let go!"

Kavon yelled back at him, "There is no time for reconsidering! The three of you must ride on! Leave me here; I'll only slow you down!"

Yorik cut off Garrison's words before they could escape his throat. "He's right boy. We have to reach the forest now or we'll all die. Taurani understand when it is their time, and today Kavon will hear the Song. Let us go!" Yorik didn't wait for Garrison to argue. The man mounted his horse and raced away with Marika on her horse matching stride.

Garrison considered a plan for a moment. "Quickly, can you sit up until they reach you?" Garrison only now truly realized that the tattooed stripes on the bald man's eyes continued up his scalp and curved into horns at the side of his head. It was an incredibly intimidating sight, especially now with blood scraped across the man's head.

Kavon nodded and sat up leaning against the dead horse. He grimaced and clutched his leg. "What is it you need me to do, Garrison?" A few more arrows thudded into the ground a few yards away. "Hurry!"

Garrison reached into a pocket and pulled out five pouches of yellow powder. He then ripped the waterskin hanging from his neck and handed it to Kavon. "When they are in your throwing range, wet the pouches and throw them into a crowd of riders. Each pouch should be enough to take down a score of men. By the Orijin, I hope you can stay alive long enough."

"I will succeed with your plan. My injuries are not enough to kill me. Yorik knows I will hear the Song because the soldiers will send me to it. Now go!"

Garrison vaunted onto his horse, a tinge of guilt settling into the back of his mind. He spurred his horse to a gallop and shouted "Thank you!" to Kavon. Yorik and Marika had nearly reached the forest. Garrison repeatedly swiveled his head behind him to gauge when the soldiers would reach Kavon. If he judged correctly, he would reach the forest just around the same time. An arrow grazed Garrison's left arm, just below his leather armor, and sliced through the flesh. Luckily for Garrison, the arrow was shot from his right; otherwise it would have likely pierced his horse between the shoulders. He urged the horse on until he reached the cover of the trees.

Garrison brought his horse to a halt behind a tree and dismounted. From behind the trunk, which was wide enough to protect the horse, Garrison peered out in time to see Kavon throw the first yellow pouch in the distance. The soldiers were coming from Kavon's left and Garrison worried that the Taurani might not be able to reach all of them with the pouches.

The first pouch exploded in a flash of yellow light amidst a pack of riders. Garrison smiled. He knew that was only the beginning. The small explosion slammed a few soldiers and their horses to the ground. From the source of the flash came thin streaks of lightning spraying about in dozens of directions, which struck down nearly two dozen more men. They all convulsed at the shock, and though Garrison was too far away to see, he could still see wisps of smoke rising from their burnt bodies.

By the time other riders could react, Kavon had hurled a second pouch and then a third. Two more booms came and flashes of lightning shot out from them. Men and horses collapsed everywhere Garrison could see. Yorik and Marika joined him in watching from behind the tree. They had likely left their horses ahead to rest.

More soldiers advanced, confused and alert. Kavon threw another pouch, causing another score of soldiers to fall. Garrison imagined that Kavon probably enjoyed being able to cause such trouble before he died.

Ten soldiers rode through the sea of dead men and horses. They were too spread apart for Kavon to hit them all with the final pouch, but the man threw it anyway. Even if the pouch could eliminate half of them, Garrison, Marika, and Yorik could defeat the rest.

The pouch's effects worked better than Garrison had hoped, felling eight of the men. Two soldiers rode on. One stopped in front of Kavon, stood over him and shot an arrow through the Taurani's skull. The other soldier had waited for him to catch up and both rode toward Garrison and his companions.

By the time Garrison had turned to Marika and Yorik, they were already armed with spears. When the two soldiers were within twenty paces, the two Taurani strafed from behind the tree and launched their spears. Garrison shuddered at the accuracy as each spear impaled its target through the neck.

Marika and Yorik ran out to retrieve their spears and returned with the soldiers' bows and arrows as well. Yorik smiled, "These will be of good use, no?" Garrison bit his lip and nodded. "You killed over one hundred men today within five minutes and without putting yourself in any danger. Do you have more pouches like that, boy?" Garrison continued to nod. "Good. We'll need them if we're going to have a chance. I won't ask where you got them. I do not think I want to know."

Marika started walking further into the forest. "Come. Garrison, knowing the type of man your father is, it is only a matter of time before more soldiers come to hunt us down." Yorik and Garrison flanked her as they walked on.

Garrison clenched his fist. "No. From here on, we are the hunters. They will come to us, but Stones of Gideon, we will hunt them and kill them all."

Marika and Yorik looked to the eastern sky simultaneously. "Smoke," Yorik said gravely.

Marika studied the sky for a moment longer. "It is beyond the forest. But that is not the smoke of a burning house. Do you see how the wisps are thin and separated?"

Garrison voiced what all three had already known. "Campfires. Soldiers."

CHAPTER 10
GRASPING AT SHADOWS

From *The Book of Orijin,* **Verse Three Hundred Three**
*We have selected Harbingers from the ranks of Mankind because We trust
in your goodness. You must learn to trust in the goodness of your brethren
as well.*

"LOOK AT ZEM down zere. They vill likely be ze best fighters ve
have one day. And zey only just arrived a veek ago! Maybe even better zan
you Taurani. Zen again, I suppose zey'll have to be if ve stand any chance
against Jahmash's armies."

Marshall should have taken offense to that, but the stocky man had no
malice in his voice when he said it. The man had almost said it to himself,
pondering with aloofness.

Marshall had been sitting at the side of the bed for several minutes
while the man stood at the window with his hands clasped behind his back.
He'd introduced himself as 'Gunnar' and hailed from Galicea. Marshall had
been unfamiliar with Galicea, along with Gunnar's accent. It bore no
resemblance to the way Cerysians spoke, which was the dialect that the
Taurani had adopted decades ago. Traditionally, Marshall should have been
fluent in Imanol, the language of Taurean and the people of Taurean's time,
but Marshall had used it less and less growing up and now had little fluency
with it, save a few phrases and words here and there.

Marshall stood with a grimace and walked next to Gunnar at the
window. His stomach muscles ached with every movement. It had taken
several minutes for him to embrace his surroundings. The last thing he'd
remembered was a sword piercing his insides and then everything went
black. He awoke in a bed half of an hour ago and saw Gunnar sitting to his
right. Apparently he had been unconscious for several days.

"You see very well to be watching them. Why do they fight in the
darkness? Is that part of their training?"

Gunnar pursed his lips, "It is because of ze order of Zin Marlowe. He
is ze headmaster of ze House of Darian. It is his belief zat ve should not use
our manifestations or lives for aggression. Marlowe believes ze House
should be peaceful. So of course Descendants who come here are taught

how to use zeir manifestations, but not aggressively."

"That seems rather foolish. Every man should know how to attack."

Gunnar nodded. "Zere are quite a few of us who agree viz you. And zat is vhy fighting is done in ze darkness. Zis type of training is clandestine. To defy ze Headmaster is grounds for excommunication."

"I see. Is it you who trains them? If so, perhaps someone else should teach. That one with the staff. He only looks impressive because his attackers are slow. He has too much time to prepare."

Gunnar shot Marshall a sharp glare. "Desmond is fast. Agile. Zat is vhy ze ozers look slow."

"Put someone in there as fast as him. I guarantee you that Desmond will limp away covered in bruises."

"I see. Zen once you are vell enough, I vill allow you to fight Desmond. And zen Badalao as vell."

"Once I am well enough, I shall be leaving this place. I must return to my village to find other Taurani."

Gunnar turned to him now, "Boy, vhy do you zink you are here?"

"What do you mean?"

"Ve sent a scout team to your village to find survivors. Zere's a reason you're ze only Taurani zat vas brought back."

Marshall sat back down. Memories of his village's destruction came back. He could once again picture the bodies strewn all over the ground, houses decimated into piles of rubbish, smoke and fire all around. "I remember. But I still believe that you are wrong. Perhaps you did not find survivors in the village, but there must be others who likely fled. I still must return there."

"You can take zat up viz Zin Marlowe once you're better. He vill definitely not allow you to leave until you fully recover. But rest easy. Zat boy Lincan healed you. He almost fell over in ze process viz how much vork you needed, but you should be fine in a few days. Until zen, accept ze fact zat you're not going anyvhere."

Marshall nodded. There was no use in arguing. Truthfully, he could use the recovery time, and he would be of no help to his kinsmen in his current state anyway.

Gunnar continued, "Zough I do have a question, boy. Descendants come from all over Ashur. I have seen every Ashurian race come to ze House, even combinations of races, in my fifteen years here. But you are ze first Taurani. Vhy is zat? How is it possible zat no Taurani has ever borne ze Mark of ze Descendant?"

Marshall responded hoarsely, "Taurani do not believe that people can or should create magic. We leave those foolish fantasies to the rest of the world. If you would like to think of yourself as a false Harbinger, that is your folly. We are not so brazen."

The broad-shouldered man laughed heartily. "Look at my face. Eye of

Orijin, look at ze face of everyone in zis place, boy. Including you. Ve all bear ze mark. Ve have all been chosen for something special. Even you had to have done somezing magical or miraculous to have zat line down your left eye. Ve're no Harbingers, I agree. But zat doesn't mean ve're not chosen for somezing special."

What is this fool talking about? "Left eye? Now I know you are mad. My body is almost completely covered in tattoos. There are lines intersecting both of my eyes. That is the Taurani tradition."

Gunnar laughed again. "Are you sure I am ze crazy one? I have been blessed viz ze manifestation of heightened eyesight. Like zat of a hawk. But even a Blind Man could see zat you bear only one mark on your body, ze Descendant's Mark down your left eye. Look at yourself. Look in a mirror."

Marshall pulled up the sleeves of his tunic. Nothing. His arms were bare. "What trickery is this?" The long-haired Cerysian looked at him as if he was crazy. "What did you people do to me?"

"Lincan told us zat it was an effect of ze healing process. You were so close to death zat ze healing was intense. It was probably too difficult for him to make exception to your skin. Now you understand vhy I told you zat ze only mark on you is ze Descendant's Mark."

Marshall refused to accept Gunnar's explanation. His tattoos were too sacred to just be healed away. He would have rather died than lose them. Especially with what had happened to his people. "Is there a mirror in here? Show me a damn mirror! I need to see for myself!"

Gunnar pointed to the other end of the room. "Over zere. Next to ze cabinets."

Marshall walked to the full length mirror on the other side of the room. As he stepped in front of it, he squinted with annoyance and then blinked a few times. "What magic are you people practicing?"

Gunnar's brow furrowed, "Vhat magic do you mean?"

"My reflection! It is not there! I see nothing! What are you trying to do to me?"

Gunnar's voice had grown devoid of patience. "Are you a fool? Truly? Eye of Orijin, look at ze damned zing. Do you not see yourself in it? Who vould…"

Marshall looked again. He could see what was behind him and the reflection of everything else, but Marshall bore no reflection. "NO. I do not see myself in it. Gunnar. Is this more of your cursed magic? More *healing*?" Gunnar stared at him. "Come and see for yourself. Step in front of the mirror."

Marshall stepped aside as Gunnar stood at the mirror. "Hmm. Perhaps zis ordeal has affected your mind more zan your body, Marshall. I zink it's best for you to lie down again. I vill have Marlowe come back viz Lincan to check on you."

"What are you talking about?"

"Marshall, I see myself just fine in ze mirror. I believe zat all this might have caused a great deal of stress on your mind."

Marshall had had enough. He stepped in front of Gunnar before the mirror, and still only Gunnar's reflection appeared.

Gunnar gasped. "Eye of Orijin, vhat is zis?"

Marshall turned to him. "That is what I would like to know. Is this part of Lincan's healing as well?"

"I...zis is very strange. Marshall, listen. Vhen zey found you, Adria noticed zat you didn't have a shadow. In ze time zat you have been viz us, ve have not seen one at all. Ve believed it to be connected to your manifestation, vhatever zat might be. But ze reflection...I cannot explain it."

Only then did Marshall inspect his body and his surroundings. Gunnar was right. No shadow. Panic drowned everything else in his head and then shortened his breath. Marshall stumbled toward the bed but hit the floor head first and once again, everything faded into blackness.

***

When Marshall awoke a few hours later, he found relief that he was in the same room. However, instead of Gunnar sitting beside his bed, a young girl sat in the chair with her chin resting on her elevated knees. Behind her, a pale yellow-skinned boy leaned against the wall with his arms crossed.

The girl spoke first, her face still somewhat hidden behind her knees. "You are fine. You took the news about your reflection and shadow harshly, as would anyone, I suppose." Her voice held a strange familiarity, as if Marshall had heard it before. Her accent was slightly similar to that of Taurani and Cerysian, though her olive skin tone marked her as something starkly different than a Cerysian.

"Your voice. I have heard it before, though I do not know how."

"My name is Adria. I rescued you with Lincan," she pointed behind her, "and Maven Savaiyon. You likely heard me talking while we brought you back here."

The girl intrigued Marshall. She looked like she could be several years younger than he was, but she spoke with a formality that could have been several years older. After glancing at Lincan a few more times, Marshall deduced that he was likely of a similar age as Marshall. The few stubbly pieces of hair on Lincan's chin were laughable, but his eyes gave away his age. Marshall shook off his ponderings. He had questions. "Then you can explain what happened to me?"

"What happened to you as far as..."

"I was stabbed through my core. I felt the steel of the blade slice right through me. I also felt the blood pour out of me. I am no stranger to injury or combat. I should be dead. Gunnar told me that Lincan can heal. And while I do not accept the practices of you 'Descendants', even if you can perform miracles, Lincan, do you regularly bring the dead back to life?"

Adria sternly cut in before Lincan could respond. "We found you because I heard your heartbeat. You would be a fool to not accept our abilities, because the only reason you are here speaking to us is due to the manifestations of me, Lincan, and Savaiyon. I do not expect gratitude, especially now that it is clear that such a thing is beyond you, but I do expect you to recognize and accept a truth when it is clear before your eyes."

Lincan spoke without shifting his demeanor or position, "She's right. Resurrection is beyond my abilities. But you were still breathing when we found you. We don't know how there was any blood left in you. Your clothes, skin, and armor were caked in it, along with the ground beneath you. You only had one wound, yet I've never had to heal anyone so extensively as with you. I nearly passed out from overworking myself. Maybe it has to do with your missing shadow and reflection. Maybe there's a connection between that and you being alive."

Adria's head shot up, "Brilliant! Linc, Savaiyon would be so proud of you! When did you realize that?"

"Hold on, Mouse. I just now thought there might be a connection. That doesn't mean that it's true."

Marshall looked at Adria peculiarly. Lincan had called her 'Mouse' and she hadn't even blinked. "Whether that is true or not, how do we go about testing such a theory? Do you propose we miraculously find my shadow and reflection, and then try to kill me? And to be sure, did he just call you 'Mouse'?"

Adria smiled brightly, "It is a pet name. Only certain people are allowed to call me that, though. Think of it more as a term of endearment. I tend to have a great deal of...conflicts here. Too many of you *men* have an issue with my size. But do not think that you are deserving of calling me that; you have not earned the right." Her smile faded as she spoke those last words.

Marshall nodded, "Understood. But besides that, what would you suggest we do about my dilemma? Now that I am well again, I would like to have a reflection...and a shadow."

Adria answered excitedly, "Is it safe to assume that you never noticed your shadow was missing? Or your reflection?"

"Trust me; I would have remembered not seeing either. I had a shadow before I was attacked."

"Very well. Then perhaps we should return to your village. I mean, it seems like this whole ordeal happened between that invasion and us finding you. However, I am curious of one thing. You bear the Mark. I hope I am not being intrusive, but what is your manifestation?"

Marshall rolled his eyes. "By manifestation, you mean magical power?"

Adria smirked, "If you want to call it a magical power, then fine. But it is widely accepted that what we can do is the Orijin's will manifested through us. Hence, manifestation."

"Give it whatever fancy name you want. It is magic. And I do not have one. Whatever mark is on my face is likely a remnant of a tattoo that did not disappear when Lincan healed me."

"It wouldn't work that way," Lincan insisted.

Adria stood and held a hand up as if to cut Lincan off. "How can you be such a fool, Marshall? Are you so stubborn to refuse logic? The mark on your face is the same exact line that appears on every single man and woman in this place. But only yours is there by accident?" Adria's voice continually got louder. "Tell me; are all Taurani as dense as you? If so, I can see why you were all defeated so easily!"

Marshall jumped out of the bed and closed in on Adria. Lincan stepped closer and clenched a fist, his eyes fixed on Marshall's. Marshall grabbed the chair that Adria had just been using. "Get out! Both of you! Leave me! Now!" He lifted the wooden chair and smashed it against the tiled floor. Lincan and Adria left the room casually, obviously not threatened by Marshall's anger.

Marshall picked up a large piece of the chair and threw it against the wall. He held his hands and arms out before him, inspecting them, then walked to the mirror once more. Once again, he saw right through where his reflection should have been. Marshall punched the mirror, cracking it as shards of glass fell. He then picked up the entire thing and smashed it against the wall. Glass shattered and wood splintered and debris flew all about. As his anger subsided, exhaustion set in. Marshall dropped to his knees. *What...happened? To everything? How can all this be? They must be lying. They must be!*

He sat unmoving for several minutes, lost in repeating thoughts and questions. The opening door pried his attention. Gunnar stepped in and immediately walked over to bring Marshall to his feet. "Let's go boy. It's time you spoke to Marlowe." Marshall followed him out of the room, tiptoeing to avoid glass fragments that littered the floor.

Gunnar led him down a long, wide corridor that opened to a common room. The walls and mood of the entire place felt very gloomy to Marshall. Aside from torches on the grey stone walls, the only color in any room was the blood red of the rugs in the common room. "This does not look like the happiest of places, eh Gunnar." Gunnar grunted. They traversed two more similar rooms when Marshall saw two men speaking by an open doorway. Both bore the golden brown skin and features of Cerysians. Gunnar continued toward them.

The two Cerysians turned their attention as Marshall and Gunnar neared. The taller of the two clasped the other's shoulder, bowed his head, and then walked away. The shorter Cerysian man shifted his attention to Gunnar and Marshall. "Ah, Gunnar! Is this the Taurani?"

"Ja, and he is a feisty vun. I zought it vise for him to see you now ozervise he might have destroyed all of ze recovery room."

"Yes, I see. Very well. You may leave us then, Gunnar. Thank you for your discretion." Gunnar bowed slightly toward the man and left. "Come boy, come in. It is Marshall, correct?" Marshall nodded. "Splendid. My name is Zin Marlowe. Come, let us sit in my office. There is much for us to discuss, and I think it is best if we have our privacy." Marlowe gestured for Marshall to enter the room then signaled for a hulking man inside to leave. "Blastevahn, please leave us." The brute, who also had a black line down his left eye, walked out and shut the door behind him.

The office was as bare as the rest of the building, aside from a desk with a few wooden chairs surrounding it and two long couches. Marlowe led Marshall to the desk and sat behind it. Marshall studied him for a moment. "Gunnar said you are the Headmaster here. I assumed you would be...older. You look like you could be my older brother."

The man paused and then smiled. "Does that bother you? That a man so young would lead so many?"

"Bother? No. Not if you are a good leader. But it is rare that someone as young as you can handle the responsibility."

Marlowe looked to be contemplating Marshall's words. "Marshall, I am known to be a very direct man. Some would say honest and others would say rude. And some here would likely have worse words to describe me. At times, I am sure they are all true. The point I am trying to make here is that I will always say what needs to be said. People will not always like it, but it is not my way to sweeten words for the sake of one's feelings. I tell you this because you will not like what I have to say to you. You will also not agree with it, at least not right away. But that does not mean I am wrong. Do you understand?"

Marshall stopped short of rolling his eyes. "Go on. Since I awoke here, your people have made it clear how wrong and stupid I am."

"Wrong, yes. But not stupid...more like foolish. First, to address your view on leadership, you should never assume a leader is unfit simply based on his age. In my time, I have seen boys half your age better at leading than men twice your age. Leadership comes from necessity, not age. A good leader knows what his people need and will do anything he can to get it for them. You are a man—barely—who I am sure has yet to leave his village. You know nothing of leadership. You know that the Taurani are...*were* feared throughout Ashur because that is what your elders have engrained in your mind since you were a boy. You look at others as if they should kneel before you simply because of the reputation of your people. But you Marshall, you yourself have done nothing in your life except train for the possibility of danger. You do not have the right to judge leadership because you yourself are not fit to lead. You would do well to remember that, especially if you wish to continue the bloodline of your people. You understand that because of recent events, the responsibility now falls on you to lead?" Marlowe's unwavering stare fixated on Marshall's eyes the entire time he spoke. His eyes pierced more than his words.

Marshall nodded reluctantly. "I had a feeling the burden was mine. Though I had not quite gotten to addressing it. I would like to first return to my village. And I seem to have an issue with my reflection and shadow."

"Everything will be addressed in time. What I was getting to was that even I am not what I may seem. I am much older than you think and I have my manifestation to thank for that. You undoubtedly have noticed that everyone here bears a line down their left eye? Are you so stubborn to think that is a strange coincidence or that we put them there ourselves? You need not respond; we both know the answers to those questions. But answer this instead. What is your manifestation, Marshall?"

Marshall's eyes widened, "For the love of Taurean. This question again?"

"You heard me correctly, boy. You bear the same mark as the rest of us. What is it that you can do? Or do you not know just yet? I would not be surprised, given how blind you Taurani tend to be. I have only ever met one Taurani who embraced his manifestation, and even he turned out to be a fool. But answer me boy. What can you do? It is nothing to be ashamed of here."

"Taurani do not practice magic. We are warriors. The Orijin blessed Taurean and his partners with the ability to perform miracles. And then the Five after them. Those of you who would practice your spells and charms only defy the Orijin."

Marlowe's voice rose. "Taurani do not practice magic because your people cling to outdated beliefs. Boy, do you know why your people cover your bodies with markings and tattoos? It is not some warrior code or tradition. It was done centuries ago to hide the fact that you all bear the Mark. You are all direct descendants of Taurean. So was Darian. One of Darian's wives was also a descendant of Taurean and that is where you all came from. The rest of us who are not Taurani descend from the children of his other wives. Marshall, we are all descendants of Darian, and thus descendants of Taurean. It is not dark magic that we practice; it is the blessing of the Orijin."

Marshall's anger surfaced through the redness of his face, and he then slammed his fist down on the desk. "And who told you such lies? Is this the nonsense that you feed your followers here so that you can control and manipulate them?"

"You are not angry because I have offended you. You are angry because you know there is a chance that I am right. I know the difference. Regardless, I can prove my words. A few centuries ago, one of the first to bear the Mark was a man named Arild Hammersland. Hammersland had the unique manifestation with which he could communicate with the Orijin; however he made it clear that this communication was on the Orijin's terms.

Hammersland himself could not choose when such dialogue would happen." Marlowe continued his intent gaze at Marshall, "At the Orijin's request, Hammersland wrote a book that detailed guidelines for life, descriptions of the Three Rings, and even mentioned the Descendants of Darian—those of us who would bear this mark." Marlowe pointed to his eye. "He entitled it *The Book of Orijin*. We have dozens of copies of it here. It is something that all Descendants must read within one year of being here. Now that you are with us, you will be required to read it as well.

"Marshall, I do not blame you for being skeptical. In fact, I understand truly and completely why you would be. Everything the House of Darian stands for is contrary to your entire way of life. It should not be something you readily accept. But I do expect you to have an open mind about this place. We are concerned only with helping you, which is why we brought you here in the first place. It was not something that we had to do."

Marshall shook his head and bit his lip. Marlowe had a point; they had nursed him back to health without being obligated to do so. *But what if they only did that for leverage so that I might become one of their followers?* "So then restoring my health…am I supposed to have an obligation to you now?"

"Obligation? Truthfully, everyone here feels an obligation to be here before they even meet us. There are few places in Ashur anymore where Descendants are safe. Especially for you now. This has been the way for decades, thanks to King Edmund. And you have no people to whom you can return."

"You do not know that for sure."

"Marshall, we sent a team out to your village to find survivors. If there were others, we would have brought them back with you. Adria and Savaiyon are very good at what they do."

"I want to see for myself. I want to go back."

"And you will. We have no quarrel with that. You can see for yourself the desolation of your village. But truthfully, Marshall, if I am right about your people, then what do you have to lose by staying here? At least here you have a chance to follow a new path. If you are the last of the Taurani, then there is nothing left for you out in the world."

Marlowe had cornered him and they both knew it. For all his stubbornness, Marshall could not deny that point. If the Taurani had been vanquished, then there was nothing left for him outside the House of Darian. But that did not mean that he had bought into their ideologies. Their way of thinking was still vastly different than his own. "I still do not share your beliefs. If you are correct about my people, then there is nothing for me inside or outside of this place."

Marlowe breathed deeply. "Marshall. Let us compromise. You are not obligated to me or anyone here, though I hear you could be more polite. Perhaps we can make an agreement, however. If I am right about your people, then you return to the House of Darian. While here, we will give you as much time as you need to accept our way of life. During that time, you will read *The Book of Orijin*. After you have completed it, if you still refute our ideology, then you are free to leave. No arguments. No questions. Agreed?"

Marshall leaned forward, clasped his hands, and rested his chin on them for several moments with his eyes closed. *My people would ostracize me for agreeing to this. But my people may not even be alive any longer.* He looked at Marlowe once more, "If I still disagree with you, no one will stop me from leaving? No one will come after me the moment I step out?"

Marlowe looked Marshall in the eyes once more. "If you choose to leave, no one will touch you. My word is my bond."

Marshall sighed, "I cannot do this. To even have this conversation with you brings shame to my people and my way of life."

"You *have* no people."

Marshall's eyes shot up. "Forget it, forget your stupid deal. For someone who seeks compromise, you lack the skills to make me trust you."

Marlowe stood and leaned forward across the desk and growled, "Forget compromise, boy. I have made my offer and you have refused it. There is no more choice. You will stay here, whether you like it or not. You belong to me now. If you try to fight or escape, I will have my Mavens destroy you. And then what will be left of your people?"

Marshall smiled and stood to meet Marlowe's eyes. "Do you think you are the first man to threaten me? Do you think I am afraid to die?"

"Your arrogance means nothing to me and it betrays you. Tell me, boy, if you die, what chance is left for your people? The Taurani will end with your stubbornness and pride. And we will destroy all evidence that you ever existed. You would be stupid if you were not afraid to die."

Marlowe had cornered him too easily once more. Marshall had no argument left. Until he could know for sure whether any Taurani still lived, he would have to obey. He reluctantly nodded, "Very well. I will do your bidding. But if I am to be your prisoner, and am to agree not to fight or cause you any problems, you must allow me to see my village one last time. If my people are truly dead, then I must carry out the rituals for my family. Grant me this one request and I will cause you no problems."

Marlowe nodded with a smirk, "It is done. You will depart tomorrow morning. You will arrive moments later. Maven Savaiyon will transport you there. I will also send Badalao, Desmond, and Maven Gunnar with you. You will realize immediately the benefit of a manifestation. And if you attempt anything foolish, you will regret it instantly. Do not think we will allow you to escape."

"Understood."

"No. You are a Descendant in the House of Darian now. The only words I will accept from you are 'My word is my bond'."

"What?"

"Say it. Without those words, we have no agreement."

Marshall rolled his eyes. "My word is my bond. Look, although I do not agree with your magic, I would like for the girl to join us. Adria."

"And why is that?"

"If she was able to find me, then perhaps she can find others. It is worth the chance."

Marlowe nodded. "I will ask the Mavens if she is available. There are always missions and errands going on."

"Mavens. What are these Mavens?"

"Maven is a title one earns here after achieving a certain excellence in the control of their manifestation, along with a rigorous regiment of study and training. Think of the Mavens as your superiors, your guides, your teachers. They will also report to me about your behavior and progression."

"As long as your people do not give me trouble, my behavior shall be of no issue. Do I have your permission to leave, Master Marlowe?"

Marlowe walked around the desk and waved for Marshall to walk with him to the door. Before opening it, Marlowe turned to face him. "Of course your behavior will be of no issue." Marlowe squeezed Marshall's tender shoulder then punched him in the stomach. Marshall doubled over and grimaced. He refused to give Marlowe the satisfaction of making a sound. If his stomach and shoulder hadn't been injured, Marlowe's strike wouldn't have hurt him. He took a few deep breaths then stood erect once more. Marshall said no words, only smiled and then left the room.

***

"We shall leave as soon as all the rest are prepared." Maven Savaiyon towered over Marshall and Gunnar to the point that Marshall felt awkward sitting down.

"And when will that be?" Ever since his meeting with Marlowe on the previous day, Marshall had been anxious to be outside the walls of the House of Darian.

"Have patience. They should be ready soon. All were awoken at sunrise, just as you were. They shall be here shortly."

"Who exactly are we waiting for?" Marshall refrained from asking about Adria directly. Just then, the door opened and two boys walked in, of an age with Marshall. The first bore a yellowish complexion with black choppy hair and almond shaped eyes. The second was a few inches taller and olive-skinned, similar to Adria's, and light brown hair tied back into three rods that protruded from the back of his head. Marshall stifled a chuckle. "Ah, I suppose we were waiting for your hair to be ready?" The boy scowled instantly at Marshall.

Gunnar, standing next to Savaiyon, spoke up. "Marshall, zis is Desmond and Badalao. Near inseparable, zey are."

Marshall made no attempt to rise. "Inseparable? Ohhh, I see." Marshall smiled. If he would be forced to stay at the House of Darian, he would make the most of it and push as many boundaries as possible. "Yes, we had our own 'Desmond and Badalao' back in my village. Fabian and Alden. They were more discreet about it than you two, however. Of course, the only reason I even knew they had a romance was because Alden was my cousin."

Desmond and Badalao looked at one another quizzically, and then fired glares at Marshall. Desmond stepped forward and dug a finger into Marshall's chest. "What did ya just say? Just cuz yer a Taurani an' Marlowe is givin ya special treatment, don't think fer a second I won't lay another beatin' on ya. Worse than the one ya came here with. Lincan told me ya cheated death when they found ya. I'd really like ta see if ya can cheat it again."

Marshall didn't bother with a clever retort. He grabbed Desmond's wrist and used the momentum to slam him face-first into the floor. As soon as he'd stood up again, Badalao wrapped an arm around Marshall's neck, choking him. Marshall ran backward into the wall as Savaiyon and Gunnar bolted out of the way. Badalao's grip loosened just slightly and Marshall forced his head from the clutch then folded Badalao's arm behind his back in one swift movement. Marshall tugged Badalao's arm higher, then whipped Badalao around and slammed his face against the wall. Marshall let go and Badalao fell to his knees. "There. Now when you two kiss each other, you can taste each other's blood." As the words left his mouth, something snatched Marshall and held him in the air. He struggled to break free and then looked around him. No one in the room was even close enough to touch him.

Desmond, the yellow-skinned boy, stared at him and finally spoke. "Ya forgot where ya were, didn't ya? Sure, yer a good fighter. With yer hands. Bet ya don't even know how ta use yer manifestation, do ya."

Marshall continued to struggle as he hovered a few feet above the floor. "Put me down and fight me fairly, coward."

"What's unfair? I've got a mark an' I see one on yer face, too. Looks perfectly fair ta me. I could kill ya right now without even liftin' a finger."

Savaiyon cut in, "Put him down, Desmond. Marlowe would not condone this and neither do I. Marshall is one of us now." He looked up at Marshall, "Even if he does not believe it yet."

The door opened once more and Adria walked in. Marshall's cheeks warmed as she looked up at him. "What are you fools doing? I could hear you all from down the hall. I thought you were destroying the room! Put him down! Zin Marlowe was not far behind me! No doubt he is coming to see for himself."

Savaiyon echoed her order. "Release him, Desmond. If Marlowe is coming, we should depart now."

Desmond wiped blood from his face, "Fine." As he wiped his hand on his pants, Desmond looked Marshall in the eye. Marshall floated horizontally now, facing the floor. He slowly descended until he hovered nearly three feet above it, and fell suddenly with a thud. Desmond continued, "Doesn' feel so good, does it."

Marshall stood and straightened out his clothes. He turned to Adria and smiled. "Hi."

"Save it. Why did you even request that I come with you? I saved you the first time. If there were other survivors, I would have known."

Before Marshall could respond, Desmond chimed in with a chuckle, "He asked fer ya ta come?" Marshall reddened as Desmond continued, "Look at him, Mouse. He's blushin'! He doesn' need yer help! He fancies ya." Desmond's chest convulsed as he laughed heartily and wiped his nose with his sleeve.

Badalao cut in, also wiping his nose clean, "Maven Savaiyon, before you make that gateway…should we not arm ourselves before we go? It is one thing to assume there are no survivors, but it would be foolish to assume the attackers are gone."

Savaiyon responded, "You're correct. We'll go to the armory first." Savaiyon turned again. A tiny speck of light appeared in the air a few feet in front of Savaiyon. In seconds, the speck expanded into a bright yellow square wide enough for three people to walk through side-by-side and high enough for Savaiyon, who was easily a foot taller than Marshall, to walk through without ducking. Marshall stared for a moment and realized his mouth was hanging open.

Savaiyon, Adria, and Badalao walked through instantly. Gunnar and Desmond looked at him and laughed. Desmond then patted him on the shoulder, which was still sore, and said, "Yer mouth is about as big as that gateway now. If a gateway surprises ya that much, then yer jaw'll be hurtin' by the end o' today." Gunnar walked into the bright yellow light and Desmond and Marshall followed.

They appeared in a large stone room that smelled of oil and mustiness. Weapons of all sorts lined the racks on the walls, including swords, axes, maces, and spears. Marshall nudged Gunnar, "I thought you said that Marlowe doesn't approve of violence and fighting."

"He doesn't know about zis room."

Marshall chuckled at the response as he armed himself with a sword and two daggers. One of his personal rules was to aways have a knife. Taking too many big weapons would only burden him and slow him down.

***

Marshall stepped out of another gateway onto familiar ground. Savaiyon had brought them just outside of Marshall's village. The sight did little to comfort his already queasy stomach. He couldn't fathom how Savaiyon would travel this way regularly. Perhaps the effects diminished after getting used to the gateways. The yellow gateway shrunk after they'd all stepped through.

The stink of char and burnt flesh struck his nose, bringing back the memory of all the burning houses the day his village was attacked. Marshall covered his nose and mouth and advanced toward the village. Adria walked with him as the others followed. "Do you even have a plan, or are you just going to lead us through without telling us anything?"

"Why do you have so much anger and aggression toward me?"

Adria rolled her eyes, "For one, I think you are very arrogant and too stubborn for your own good. You think you are better than us, despite knowing nothing about us. Along with that, you and your people deny your similarities to us despite the proof being on your face. Such foolishness resulted in all this," she waved her hand at the village. "And lastly, you demanded to come back here after being told more than once that there is nothing remaining here but death. I saved your life once, and even if you were grateful for that, I would still find it pointless to put six of our lives in danger." Her tone held less anger than Marshall had expected. If anything, it was more logical.

Marshall stopped and turned to the whole company, "Look, there are three things I want to accomplish here, and then we can leave. I would first like to be sure of whether there are any survivors. Once that has been determined, I would like to give my family members their proper funeral and I will need your help with that. And somehow we need to find my shadow, if that can even be done. As soon as that is finished, we can leave." He didn't wait for a response as he turned and continued walking. Since being attacked, Marshall had yet to face the fate of his family. He was not wholeheartedly convinced of their deaths despite what he'd told Aric. It was the obvious assumption to make, but Marshall needed to see for himself.

When Adria spoke again, annoyance clearly filled her tone, "So it is that easy to you? We will simply determine if there are survivors, tend to your family, and then leave?"

"What is your problem?"

"My problem? My problem is that a day ago, you denounced the House of Darian's way of thinking. The belief system of everyone with whom you now travel. And now you have the nerve to ask us for help? Tell me, rockhead, how do you plan to find out if there are survivors? Will you stop at every single body and examine it for signs of life? Because without our manifestations, which you do not accept, that is exactly what you will be doing."

Marshall reddened and stopped just before the edge of the village. She was right. It had eluded him that he was essentially using them to carry out his wishes. A tinge of guilt hung in the back of his mind. Marshall's anger at Marlowe had clouded his judgment toward the others. "Fine. You are right and I apologize for using you like this. But if you people were not forcing me to be your prisoner, then perhaps I would not have to resort to this. So do not put the blame solely on me."

Desmond spoke up, "None o' us are forcin' ya ta stay. Truth is, yer forcin' us ta follow yer wishes." Badalao and Gunnar nodded in agreement. Savaiyon merely stared at Marshall, as if studying him.

That makes no sense. "Of course I am forcing this upon you, but that was my agreement with Marlowe. If he and you are going to force me to stay with you and be open-minded to your way of life, then I would be allowed to come back here."

Desmond and Badalao both chuckled, confusing Marshall even more. Badalao then responded, "Marlowe is a fool. Why do you think we spar in secret? Marlowe refuses to believe Jahmash will return in this lifetime, or any lifetime in the near future, so he has barred us from developing any fighting and combat skills. Marlowe believes we should spend our days solely in study and that we should know as little of violence as possible. He tells us that because the King and much of the world hate us so, we should be meek. Tell me, Marshall, did you respect every Taurani and believe that each and every one was a good person?"

Marshall could see Badalao's point. He responded begrudgingly, "No."

Badalao continued, as if already knowing the response before it left Marshall's lips. "Then why do you assume that all Descendants are bad people? The five of us who accompany you now, we are nothing like Marlowe. If you stay with us, you will quickly see that the House is divided. Broken. But even those who side with Marlowe are becoming the minority. I have been there half a year and that was obvious very early. People barely see Marlowe anymore. He hides in his office or his quarters all day and makes others do everything for him. You ask me, he could rot in Opprobrium…"

Savaiyon cut in before Badalao could continue. "That is enough. It is one thing to dislike the man. But do not get carried away, Lao. Like it or not, Marlowe is still our headmaster. Focus. You have the facts from Marshall. He is obviously unable to gauge the situation correctly, given his lack of experience with manifestations. What is the plan, Lao?"

Marshall assumed Savaiyon's comments regarding him were merely logic and not meant as a jab, so he took no offense. Savaiyon was right, anyway. They understood their manifestations better than Marshall, so it would be foolish for him to lead.

Badalao thought for a moment and then spoke. "You will be our scout, Maven Savaiyon. You can go ahead and then keep us updated on whether there is any danger. Maven Gunnar and Mouse, you two will work together to search for survivors, given that you are our eyes and ears. Literally. Desmond, Marshall and I will break off and go to Marshall's family. I will bond Marshall to make the process work better."

Marshall perked up. "You will what?"

Before Marshall could react, Badalao was before him with his hand on Marshall's head. In a split second, Marshall felt a small tug in his mind, like someone popping a cork from a bottle. The tug continued for a moment and suddenly Marshall felt as if his mind had expanded. As if it had opened up and was larger than he'd previously known. Badalao released his hand and smiled. "There. It is done."

"What have you done to my mind?"

"I created a connection to my own. It means that I can enter your mind, read your thoughts, and see things through your eyes. Trust me, it is a useful tool. It is what makes Desmond and me such a lethal duo."

"Lethal. Sure. And now I will have you in my head whenever you want? That seems hardly fair."

"You do not yet understand the nature of manifestations, which is expected. Using such power takes energy, just as sparring, fighting, or any physical exertion. Instead, you are exercising your brain. Furthermore, my manifestation only works in the daylight."

"Oh, wonderful. So you can only invade my mind during the daytime. I find that much more comforting."

Badalao playfully punched Marshall's shoulder and exhaled a laugh through his nose. "Mouse is right. You are a fool. Think of how great of an advantage this would be in battle." Badalao shook his head in frustration. "Forget it, we can argue about this another time. Let us go, I would rather not spend all day here. It stinks. You all know your responsibilities? Maven Savaiyon? Mouse?"

Savaiyon nodded. Adria spoke up, "I will look for the shadow while Gunnar and I search for survivors. I have a hunch about where it is anyway. If you need to find us, we will finish where we found Marshall the last time." Savaiyon stepped through a gateway. Adria and Gunnar walked into the village down the main path.

Desmond walked on, not waiting for Badalao or Marshall to follow. "Show us ta where yer family would be."

Marshall turned and walked in stride with his two companions. Badalao broke the silence as they walked. "So you really know nothing of manifestations? Surely you have one if you bear the Descendant's Mark."

Marshall sighed in frustration. At some point he knew he would have to address the manifestation topic. In truth, his biggest fear was that he would be wrong. If his companions were right, it would shake the foundations of the whole Taurani way of life. "It is true. I know nothing of manifestations. I never have. No Taurani has ever mentioned the notion to me. I have no magical power. I have never seen any of my people practice magic either. We have always believed that that privilege died with the Harbingers."

Badalao shook his head in disagreement. "Like I said, I cannot accept that. You bear the Mark. The only reason you, or anyone, would have it on their face is if they'd developed a manifestation. I can believe that you do not know what it is. But I refuse to believe that you do not have one."

"And how would I know?" Marshall actually appreciated the

conversation. It was the lesser of evils compared to acknowledging all the destruction around him.

Desmond cut in, "When ya were younger, say between six an' eight or so, ya woulda felt it through yer body. Manifestations appear fer the first time when those o' us who have great faith in the Orijin are in a desperate situation an' genuinely ask Him fer a solution. We recognize somethin' is happenin' because we feel the harmony coursin' through our veins. It's like there's a melody in yer blood an' ya feel more powerful than ya ever have before. That sound familiar?"

Marshall furrowed his brow. He'd experienced that very thing, but he found difficulty placing exactly when it happened. "I do remember something like that. Vaguely when I was so young but definitely more recently. I...I think that happened the day we were attacked. Aric and I were confronted by their general and we had no way out. I remember closing my eyes and focusing so hard. Praying to the Orijin...and then...the world went...black."

Desmond blinked and then stared at him. "That. Was?" He pointed at Marshall.

"What do you mean?" Marshall felt uneasy at the way Desmond and Badalao stared at him.

Badalao answered, "If that was you who did that, you put the whole world in darkness for a quarter of an hour. There was confusion everywhere. Some thought it was a Descendant, others Jahmash, and others the Orijin himself."

"The whole world?" Marshall searched for reasons for the explanation to be irrational. For it not to make sense. But it pieced together too well for his liking. "Light of Orijin, if this is true, then...then what do I do now? I cannot be here! I am a traitor to my whole people!"

Badalao brought Marshall back to reality with a squeeze of Marshall's tender right shoulder. Marshall jumped at the pain, but Badalao didn't notice. He kept his hand on Marshall's shoulder as he spoke. "You are no traitor. This is what I meant before. How is it your fault? You prayed to the Orijin and he blessed you with a miraculous ability. How much more of a sign do you need? And look around fool. It sounds harsh, but sooner or later you will have to accept the reality before you. You are one of us now. Of course you tried to fight us, but we forgive you." Desmond huffed at the last part of Badalao's words, though Badalao was smiling. "We'll get payback for that anyway."

I cannot wait to see Gunnar again. He has such an incredible body. Marshall shook his head. *Did I just think that? Where did that come from?* Marshall looked around, his cheeks burning. Beside him, Badalao and Desmond guffawed loudly. Badalao finally composed himself to speak again, "See what I mean? Do not think about attacking us again. You do not want to mess with someone who can see into your mind."

Marshall pressed his lips together tightly, but could not stifle the laugh. He was more relieved than angry, knowing that the thought hadn't been his own.

The levity only briefly distracted him. Marshall's conundrum was more complicated than the others made it seem. They kept telling him everything that was happening was moot because his people were dead. *That is like saying you can abandon everything you believe in once your family dies.* They had finally reached what was left of his home. He would deal with his manifestation issue another time. "There," Marshall pointed to a pile of burnt rubble. "My family is in there." A lump formed in his throat as he said the words. "How…how do we get them out?"

Desmond stood next to him. "I'll handle it." Desmond clenched his jaw and stared at the blackened pile that used to be Marshall's home. Marshall watched as broken pieces of wood hovered and moved away from the pile. He stepped closer as the pile eventually shrunk, searching for any signs of his family. Badalao did the same from the opposite side of the pile. As Desmond cleared the debris, Marshall found the bodies of his two sisters and dragged them to the grass. *Esha. Gia. Oh Orijin. Why?* As he set them down, he noticed Badalao dragging a larger body out from the debris. *Father.* All three bodies were blackened. Marshall choked on a combination of ash and sorrow.

"Only my mother's body remains in there, Desmond."

He watched as Desmond cleared the rest of the pile slowly. Pieces of the destroyed and charred house were moved carefully so that Marshall could inspect everything to find his mother's body. After a few minutes, nothing remained where the house had fallen. Panic dotted Marshall's mind. "Where is she? We must have missed her. Her body must still be in the pile. We have to search again!" Badalao had dragged Marshall's father's body next to the two girls.

Desmond walked to him and stared at the ground. "She's not in there, Marshall. I searched everythin' as I was movin' it. If I had seen her body, I woulda said so."

Badalao cut in, "Maybe this is a good sign, Marshall. What if she managed to escape? That would be the only explanation for her not being here, right? She likely survived and escaped."

Marshall shook his head vigorously, hoping it would clear his thoughts. "I…I hope so. Where is Adria? She would be able to tell me for sure, would she not? If my mother was still alive?"

Desmond nodded, "Yeah, she could tell ya. If yer mum's alive an' nearby, Mouse would know."

"Then let us get her. Once we know for sure, we can come back here and bury my family." They walked on in silence for another few minutes until they saw Adria and Gunnar standing at a clearing. "There. That is where I fell fighting Maqdhuum."

Badalao asked, "Maqdhuum?"

"The leader of the army that attacked us. He said his name was Adl Maqdhuum. It means 'master of justice' in Imanol, the Old Tongue. Three of us fought him. I saw him cut down Myron. I would assume the same thing happened to Aric after Maqdhuum defeated me."

They were several yards away when they saw Adria and Gunnar searching the ground. Adria yelled to Marshall. "This is where you fought, is it not?"

Marshall looked around at the area and ran to where she and Gunnar stood. Marshall studied the area, analyzing and trying to remember his fight with Maqdhuum. "You are right; this is where I fell." He walked around the area, thinking. "Did you find anything?"

"Nothing. We searched what we could, but we're looking for a shadow, not a person. I have no clue how you would find it."

"Summon your manifestation! Maybe you can control it with that." Badalao yelled from behind. "It is probably something you control with your manifestation, considering you can bring the darkness and all." Adria and Gunnar looked at Marshall incredulously.

"And how do I do that?" Marshall couldn't believe he was entertaining the suggestion, but it bothered him that he had no shadow. He felt incomplete.

Badalao continued, "Clear your mind and focus. Drive all thought and emotion away. You will know the feeling. You have felt it before. Your blood and veins will sing with a melody that you will not want to go away."

Marshall followed Badalao's instructions. Sure enough, once he managed to empty his mind, the harmonious feeling flooded his body. He felt more than just human, like he could fight a whole army.

He looked around and waited. "Now what?"

Badalao responded, "Reach out to it with your mind. See if you can somehow connect to it."

Marshall closed his eyes and focused. He thought only about his shadow and about the darkness. He maintained his focus for several moments until he heard Adria gasp. Marshall opened his eyes and saw a black figure on the ground; it looked like it was walking toward him. Marshall stood still and waited another moment until the shadow was at his feet. Once there, the shadow no longer moved. Marshall took a step. Then another. The shadow was part of him once more. Marshall felt some of the tightness in his shoulders release. He let the manifestation go and the melody stopped. "Wow." He blinked his eyes a few times and took a deep breath. "That was…something."

He turned back toward Badalao and Desmond and noticed that Savaiyon had rejoined the group. Badalao smiled and said, "See. We told you it was not so horrible to be one of us." Badalao shifted his gaze to Adria. "Mouse. We could not find Marshall's mother with the rest of his family.

Think you could locate her?"

"If she is nearby, there is a chance. We are in the middle of an enormous forest, so if she is outside of the village, it will be difficult. Too many animals." Adria focused her eyes on the ground and concentrated. Marshall wondered if the feeling was exactly the same for everyone. Summoning the manifestation would make his decision much more complicated. After a few moments, Adria spoke, "I am sorry Marshall. I do not hear any heartbeats in the village. If, by the slim chance you are correct about survivors, they are not here. It would have been wise for them to escape into the forest anyway."

Marshall gritted his teeth. "We have to find her. She is alive and we must rescue her." Marshall studied the area, thinking of a strategy of where his mother might have gone. Only then did he notice Myron's lifeless body several yards away. He looked around again. "Wait. Where is Aric's body?"

Savaiyon responded, "What do you mean?"

"Three of us fought Maqdhuum here. Myron and I both fell. There is no way Aric would have defeated him alone. Aric's body should be here."

Badalao offered encouragement, "Perhaps he escaped as well, like your mother. They could be in the forest somewhere. It has been nearly a week since you were found. Perhaps in that time, any survivors may have gotten far away."

"There is no way Aric..." Marshall's words were cut off by a blood-chilling scream behind him. He turned and saw Gunnar on his knees, clutching his elbow. His arm below that point had been sliced cleanly off and it lay on the ground. A familiar man stood beside him with an ear splitting grin on his face. "Adl Maqdh...." Before Marshall had even finished saying the name, Maqdhuum had Gunnar and Adria clutched with each hand and all three disappeared into nothingness. Marshall blinked, unable to process what he'd just seen.

A bright yellow gateway appeared just before his feet. Savaiyon yelled, "Go! Now!" Marshall had barely moved before Desmond pushed him through the gateway.

CHAPTER 11
BURNING THOUGHTS

From *The Book of Orijin*, Verse Three Hundred Forty
*Our grace is manifested in those of you who are innocent and shine a beacon
of faith in your darkest hour. Even you shall falter at certain junctures, but
you have been given your manifestations for a reason.*

"IT HAPPENED SHORTLY after I reached six years. I think I was
about six." Horatio looked up at the top of the wagon quizzically. "Was it
six? Maybe seven. No wait, definitely six. Ah, I don't remember now.
Anyway, I just remember that I was being beaten by a horde of older kids.
My family didn't have much and we were ridiculed quite often." A heavy
gust of wind slapped against the wagon cover.

"Where did you come from again?" So far, Baltaszar was able to
maintain control of Horatio's tendency to ramble. He decided that this
journey would be infinitely more tolerable if he guided the conversation,
rather than letting the other boy say whatever came to mind. They'd only
left Vandenar a few hours ago and the duration of it had been spent in
conversation. Earlier in the morning, Cyrus thought up a plan to send a
merchant named Varan Ika with a wagon down to Khiry. Baltaszar and
Horatio were to stay in the back and, if the merchant was questioned, they
would hide behind the goods and wares, beneath blankets.

It was the best option, considering they were originally planning to ride
in plain sight. Cyrus and Anahi were both certain that royal soldiers would
be on the road, and would attack them on sight. Merchants regularly traveled
the Way of Sunsets, so they hoped to simply blend in.

All of this meant that Baltaszar was stuck in the back of a wagon with
Horatio, with nothing to do but talk. Horatio continued, "Down south, there
is a group of islands called the Wolf's Paw. I come from Damaszur, a town
on the main island. Most of us there live off of fishing for most of our trade
and sustenance. The thing is, my father left us when I was fairly young,
around the time when I started remembering anything. So my mother had to
play the role of two people to keep us going. My brother and I were teased
daily by just about everyone our age. We heard just about every insult, from
being called bastards to japes about our mother...all kinds of horrible

things."

Baltaszar cut in, "Wait," something sounded a bit off, and Baltaszar had always had a sharp memory for picking up on minute details. "Back in Vandenar, when you came into my room…you mentioned that your father was always getting on your case for talking too much. Or something like that. But you just said he was already gone by the time you could remember anything. That doesn't make sense."

Horatio wrinkled his brow. "I said that? Really? Maybe I meant my mother then. I don't always have the best memory when it comes to things that happened a long time ago. I don't know why I would have said that." Genuine concern and confusion riddled Horatio's face at the realization.

"It's not a big deal, Horatio. I was only confused. Continue your story…you said you were constantly harassed by others."

"Yeah. I usually tried to avoid confrontations, but my brother Leonard had the bigger mouth of the two of us, so you could say we were getting into scraps regularly. One day it was worse than usual. Nearly a dozen kids chased me and my brother to the docks at the edge of our town. They had us cornered so we tried fighting, but they mauled my brother and then pushed him into the water. I jumped in and managed to keep him afloat. But they all followed and surrounded me. I was only six. Or seven. Whatever. I knew that was it though, I was certain I would die there. All I could think to do was pray to the Orijin to help me get out of it somehow. I begged and I pleaded with the Orijin for a way out. Something, anything that could help me escape. After that my mind cleared and I closed my eyes, clinging to Leonard's limp body while treading water. I didn't think about anything. I really don't know how I knew, but it just felt natural."

Baltaszar was deeply interested now. "What did? What felt natural?"

Horatio looked at him after having stared at the wagon's roof the entire time. "I felt a connection to the lightning. Like I could summon it. And that's exactly what I did. I don't know how it happened. I just wanted it and it reacted to my will. I summoned the lightning with my mind and bolts struck every single one of those boys who were chasing me. Some of them died. The rest of the boys were rescued and remained bed-ridden for weeks. I swam back to the docks and carried my brother all the way home. The first thing I did even before tending to my brother was looked at my reflection in the mirror. Sure enough, there was a black line down my left eye."

The winds continued on, pressing the wagon cover against Baltaszar's body. "Did you feel guilty about it? Did you get into any trouble?"

Horatio pursed his lips. "I did feel guilty for a while, but my brother, once he got better, convinced me that we both would have died if I hadn't done what I'd done. And after that day, we were never bothered by anyone again. Enough people, enough *honest* people, were at the docks that day to vouch for the fact that I'd acted in self-defense. Don't get me wrong, I had nightmares about it for years. I even wondered why the Orijin would allow me to kill other kids. But after a while, especially after waves of conversations with my mother, I came to understand that the Orijin has a plan for everything, so maybe I'm just not able to comprehend it. Thankfully, down in the Wolf's Paw, it isn't a crime to be a Descendant." Horatio smiled while saying that last part. "And what about you? When did you get yours?"

"Well that's the strange thing. I don't remember getting it. According to my father, I got the line on my face before six or seven. If I got it when he said I did, then I don't think I would have been old enough to remember."

"That's not even possible."

"That's the story that I was told. And besides, for as long as I can remember, I've had the line on my face. Of course, up until a few days ago, I thought it was a scar. That's what my father told me my whole life."

Horatio chuckled at that. "Seriously? You thought *that* was a scar? I've believed in some stupid things in my life, but nothing as water-brained as that!"

"Yeah, trust me, I'm embarrassed to even tell you that. But seriously though, I never had one of those experiences or epiphanies like you did. Nothing like that ever happened in my life."

Horatio's eyebrows shot up. "I don't believe that either. But fine. Assuming, just for the sake of humoring you, that that's true…what is it you can do? What's your manifestation?"

Baltaszar sighed, "You're going to think I'm even more stupid now." He looked Horatio in the eyes. "I don't know. I don't know what my manifestation is." Baltaszar felt his face grow warm with embarrassment.

"Bunkum." Horatio shook his head.

"Bunkum?"

"Nonsense. How could you not know? You're telling me that you have never been associated with anything miraculous or magical in your life? There's nothing out of the ordinary that you've ever felt yourself doing or creating?"

"The Blind Man asked me the same thing. I've never done anything out of the ordinary. I wish someone could just tell me what my manifestation is, so I could just get on with it."

Horatio leaned forward from the opposite bench as the wind howled outside. "Well then it wouldn't work, fish-brain. You are supposed to develop it yourself. They have tested those types of things in the past. I read about it. When Descendants first started appearing and people realized the patterns and methods of it, they tried fabricating situations to influence manifestations. But none of it ever worked. I supposed that's how you know it's really a blessing from the Orijin."

"So then, how in the name of Orijin am I supposed to know what I can do? My life to this point has been a repetition of hardships and disasters. I'm not one to feel sorry for myself, but I'm being honest, Horatio. There has truly been nothing miraculous about my life."

"You had me fooled on that one, Baltaszar. You don't seem the type to feel bad for yourself. Just based on our conversations in the past day, I've noticed that you tend to focus on the good in everything."

Baltaszar shrugged. "I suppose that's true. But I always feel so...disengaged from things. Distanced from certain realities."

Horatio squinted his eyes. "Explain."

"I don't know. I suppose what I'm saying is that I don't let things affect me. My father was publicly hanged and burned only a few days ago. Just over two months ago, Yasaman, the girl whom I'd hoped to one day marry, made it clear that we had no future together. Then yesterday, a Blind Man gave me an incredibly morbid and disturbing prophecy. And on top of all that, right after my father's death, the same stranger who revealed to me the truth of the line on my face, informed me that my mother did not die in the fire that burnt down my house as a little boy, despite what my father told me. Yet I sit here in the wake of all this and the only emotions I feel are confusion and helplessness. That's what I mean by disengaged." Baltaszar suddenly realized his fists had been clenched so hard that his fingernails had broken the skin of his palm.

"We all handle things differently. What you've been through...it's a great deal for any one person to handle." Horatio's eyes shot up. "You said there has never been anything miraculous in your life. So instead, focus on the opposite. Perhaps look at all of the horrible things that have happened. Are there any connections between all of them?"

Baltaszar looked at Horatio confusedly for a moment then closed his eyes to think. "The only thing I can think of is all of the fires that happened in Haedon throughout my life. But those were tied to my father, not me."

Horatio bit his lip and stared at Baltaszar for several moments, then looked down.

"You don't think? I can...create fire? Oh light of Orijin, I...I can create fire." A wave of nervousness flowed over his skin, causing goose bumps to form on his entire body and every hair to stand. "I should have known this already. I'm so stupid. I killed a bloody snake with it only two days ago." Baltaszar rubbed his temples and closed his eyes.

"Show me."

"What?"

"Show me fire. We'll stop the wagon and get out. I want you to show me."

"You don't believe me?"

"Oh I believe you. I just want to see it." Horatio smiled widely, "Besides, if we end up getting caught by royal soldiers, you'll need to know how to use it." He peeked through the opening at the front and asked the merchant to stop the wagon.

Baltaszar got out and stood at the side of the dirt road as Horatio studied his movements and expressions closely. The intense inspection made Baltaszar uneasy, causing him to pull his hood back onto his head. "Well...what should I do? Is there a trick to this? All of those other times that the fire happened, I had no idea anything different was going on."

Horatio nodded as if coming to some conclusion. "That's likely the problem. If you don't know that you're doing it, it means that you're doing something wrong. The trick is actually to clear your mind of all thought and emotion. That's the only way to truly control it. You have to focus only on the manifestation and nothing else."

"That sounds much harder than you're making it seem."

"Oh it is. Don't feel bad, I haven't gotten a complete grasp of mine yet either. I suppose that's why we all go to the House of Darian, right?"

Another strong gust of wind blew Baltaszar's hood back off. There were no trees in sight to slow the wind down. Baltaszar was glad he'd been able to shave while at Cyrus' inn, otherwise the wind would have made his beard extremely annoying. "What does it feel like? When you're using it I mean. Will I feel any different?"

"Rapturous. Like no emotion or feeling you've ever felt before. The only thing I can compare it to is...like music is flowing through your veins and warming your whole body. And once it goes away, you can't wait for it to come back. Have you ever been with a woman? I mean, intimately?"

Baltaszar answered tentatively. Yasaman was the only one he'd ever been with. "Yes," he said curtly.

Horatio responded, "Oh, well I haven't. But it's supposedly even better than that."

Baltaszar thought for a moment. "That sounds...dangerous. If it's so addictive, why don't people just use their manifestations all the time? That is, assuming they don't manipulate dangerous things like fire or lightning?"

"There are those who have died as a result of constantly needing that power. And it has certainly driven others mad. Manifestations are not an unlimited power. They tap into our body's energy. Just as how running or sparring or any other physical activity makes us tired, using our manifestations has the same effect. And because you have to concentrate and focus, they tire our minds as well. You will find that many people with manifestations eat a great deal just to replenish the energy they've lost. Stop stalling Baltaszar. Are you going to do this or what?"

"Fine, fine. Stop talking then so I can focus." Baltaszar closed his eyes and focused only on the thought of fire. He took a deep breath and stared into the blackness of his mind, then held up his right hand and opened it, palm up. Baltaszar concentrated, wondering in a deep dark corner of his mind how hard he was supposed to strain to make something happen. He focused more specifically on creating a flame in the palm of his hand. A strange warmth crept from his head and moved slowly down his entire body. Horatio had described it entirely accurately. It felt like his veins were singing a glorious melody, filling the rest of his body with ecstasy.

Horatio yelled out, "You did it!"

Heat permeated from his right hand and Baltaszar opened his eyes. A small ball of fire hovered above his hand and for the first time in his life, Baltaszar Kontez confidently believed that his future could be happy, perhaps even meaningful.

Another strong gust of wind came. Baltaszar held his hand in place, unsure of whether the gale would affect it. The wind blew the fireball down onto Baltaszar's hand. For some reason, the shock of the burn was not as great as the shock that he could be hurt by his own fire. However, the agony of burning flesh obliterated all focus and Baltaszar shook his hand violently. The flame had caught the edge of his sleeve and Baltaszar quickly clapped his arm to extinguish it. He slapped and slapped at his hand and sleeve until finally the flame died out and his right hand was a charred mess of red and black.

Despite the pain, Baltaszar was confused as to why Horatio and the merchant hadn't rushed over to help him. He looked up to find an answer and understood why. The top of the wagon cover had caught fire and the other two were pulling it off before it could spread to the wooden frame. *It must have been when I was flailing my arm. I must have thrown the flame somehow.* He ran back to the wagon and did his best to help with one hand. After a few seconds, they'd managed to rip the wagon cover from the frame and threw it onto the dirt road.

"I'm so sorry! I panicked when my hand caught fire!" He clutched his wrist tightly, hoping to stop his burnt hand from bleeding.

Horatio simply stared at Baltaszar's hand while the merchant gazed in agony at the bare wagon.

The merchant was a squat man with a grizzly face and short black hair, which he was rubbing back and forth vigorously. Baltaszar had no idea whether the man had heard his words, so he attempted to console him. "I'll repay you, somehow. I promise!" Another horse-drawn wagon strode by, the merchants craning their necks at the spectacle. "Just give me some time to find the money, sir. I swear by the Orijin I'll fix the wagon for you." A sense of panic and guilt interloped Baltaszar's mind, combined with the roaring of uncomfortable memories. He realized now, this type of thing had happened before.

The merchant finally spoke, reluctantly. "S'all right boy. Yer here as a favor ta Cyrus. An' I owe him more on top o' that. Once I get back ta Vandenar, I'll let him know that we're even. Save yer worries fer the road ahead. That wagon cover was more fer yer protection than my wine. Them King's soldiers are goin' ta have a real easy time o' seein ya now. We'll travel til dusk an' then stop fer the night. Tomorrow, ya both will have ta hide under them covers I got back there when we get closer ta Khiry. Even then, there's a good chance they'll find ya. Understood?"

Horatio cut in, "Why don't we just arrive during the night time. If it's dark, it'll be easier for us to hide.

"People have tried it, boy. Them soldiers don't care fer it much. Merchants an' travelers know not ta go by night because it just makes the soldiers angry. During the day, they'll give the wagons a regular inspection. But durin' the night, they go an' rip everythin' apart since they can't see so well. They don't care if they break yer goods in the process. I got no problems with ya boys, but I'm not willin' ta lose all my wine over ya."

Horatio nodded, but Ika's words had barely made it into Baltaszar's ears. A revelation had formed in his mind as a result of the wagon. *Fallar Bain. Harold and Carys Joben. Lea Joben. The fires were all my fault. I burned down his shop. Carys' kitchen. I did all that. And my father took the fall. He died because of what I could do. Did he know it was me? Was he protecting me?*

You already know the answers to these questions.

But why? Why would he protect me? Why would he give up his life for mine if I was so dangerous? Wouldn't it have been easier to let me die instead?

You know these answers as well.

I'm not asking for answers. I'm angry that he made the choices he did. He should have let me take the responsibility.

Perhaps now you will see that you were meant for a higher purpose and you will understand the folly of wishing to be dead. Consider the fleeting feeling of confidence and fulfillment when you created the fire before. Continue with your journey. You have many questions. They have many answers where you are going.

I will listen to you. This once.

Baltaszar had been so confused that he'd even forgotten his disdain for the voice in his head. But it was right. And Slade had been right about everything thus far. It would be stupid to not go. The worst thing that would happen would be that the House of Darian would have no answers for him. But at least he'd be around Horatio and others like him.

Baltaszar hadn't realized that he was once again sitting in the back of the wagon, across from Horatio, and they were moving again. Even his right hand had been bandaged, although blood had stained it almost entirely red.

"What is it?" Horatio asked, leaning forward and resting his arms on a barrel of wine. "You definitely realized something back there. Something big. Even bigger than being able to create fire. What happened, Baltaszar?"

Baltaszar hesitated. It was a humungous step to trust anyone else at this point. But Horatio was the first person he'd met who was like him. Horatio, with the black line down his left eye, was living proof that there was purpose in Baltaszar's life. They had the same goals, the same destination. This was the ideal situation in which to start trusting other people. "Remember how you asked me if there had been anything miraculous in my life to this point?"

Horatio nodded vigorously, "Yes. Yes, of course I do. And then you couldn't think of anything and I suddenly thought, well 'maybe it wasn't a miraculous thing for him, because these manifestations can have their bad sides as well', and so that's when I asked you…"

"You asked me about the opposite. If there was any connections between negative parts in my life." Baltaszar had to cut the boy off, otherwise Horatio would have kept talking and the conversation would likely turn to some arbitrary topic. "The fire. It…it's caused more trouble in my life than I realized."

"What do you mean?"

"The fires are the reason my father is dead. Everyone in Haedon blamed him for them and he took the fall instead of letting me answer for it. I should have died for everything that happened, but instead, he was killed for it. They publicly hanged him, Horatio. And…oh by the Light of Orijin. That was me as well." Tears streamed down Baltaszar's cheeks.

"What? What was you, Baltaszar?"

Baltaszar gulped back the lump in his throat. "As he was being hanged, a fire broke out on the hanging platform. It was pouring that night, Horatio. That fire had no business being there. I caused it. I scorched his body while he was being humiliated before all of Haedon. I still remember it so vividly. He was hanging there then the fire engulfed him. He flailed around like a madman. I only burned my hand and it was an unconceivable agony. How much did he suffer, just because of me?"

Horatio opened his mouth to speak, but hesitated and said, "I'm sorry Baltaszar, I'm terribly sorry. You couldn't have known how to handle it. Nobody had taught you."

Baltaszar had grown tired of talking. He hoped Horatio wasn't offended, but there were too many thoughts weighing him down for Baltaszar to be sociable. He spent the several remaining daylight hours staring off into nowhere in particular. When dusk had arrived, he went through the motions of helping them set up a fire, though he did not use his manifestation. Once Horatio and the merchant had set themselves down in front of it, Baltaszar returned to the wagon and lay down on the floor of the cart. He had no idea how long he tried to fall asleep, but when he finally did, fire and blood filled his dreams.

***

Baltaszar woke up to find that the wagon was already rolling and slightly bouncing along the road. Horatio sat in his usual spot.

"I left out some bread and cheese for you. We thought it best not to wake you, I hope you don't mind. Just seems like you've been through too much in the past week or so. Thought you could use a sound sleep." Horatio smiled uncomfortably at him, likely unsure of whether Baltaszar would be angry.

"Thank you! I'm starving, thanks for saving me food. That was very considerate of you. I feel like it's easier to be asleep; that way I don't have to deal with all of this guilt and regret." Horatio handed him half a loaf of bread and a small block of yellow cheese. Baltaszar didn't worry about manners as he gnashed a chunk of bread from the loaf.

"Baltaszar, I understand why you might feel guilty. But that's a father's responsibility. To protect his children and make sure that they're safe, even if it costs his own well-being. Believe me, if anyone understands that, it's me. I only wish I had a father who was willing to raise me and show me the right way. Maybe I wouldn't have gotten this manifestation, but I would trade lightning for a good father any day."

"Maybe you're right. But honestly, Horatio, you won't change how I feel right now. I'm too angry with myself to think that way. Part of me wants to go back to Haedon and burn it all to ashes."

"You do that and you're no better than the people who killed your father. Let the Orijin determine the proper justice for them. Their souls will spend the rest of eternity in Opprobrium. That's the way I live, Baltaszar. Let justice happen naturally."

Opprobrium. Baltaszar's father had taught him about the Three Rings. The three destinations of the afterlife. Baltaszar had never given it much consideration until now. Being a farmer with a daily routine, there was never much conflict or need for deep reflection on where one's soul would end up.

According to his father, good people went to Omneitria. Bad people went to Opprobrium. And those who did nothing with their lives...who lived off the hard work of others, who did nothing productive, and who feigned devotion to the Orijin while ignoring him...they were destined for Oblivion.

Baltaszar had always loved the symbolism and aesthetic nature of the Three Rings and the fact that their names all began with "O". To him, it was a small piece of evidence that there was a higher power. That life itself wasn't accidental. But that was generally the extent of his devotion to religion. "I'm starting to believe that I am destined for Oblivion anyway. Getting revenge wouldn't change that and at least it would give me satisfaction." Horatio was about to respond, but Baltaszar held a hand up to stop him. "I don't really want to talk about this any further. Can we just sit in silence for a little while?"

Horatio nodded in acquiescence and Baltaszar continued eating. The ride paralleled that of the previous day, as Baltaszar sat in a sort of daze, allowing all sorts of thoughts to fly around in his mind while not focusing on any specific one. The weather was noticeably warmer than that of Haedon, though Haedonian summers were never unbearable. The winds hadn't died down much since the day before, which forced Baltaszar to keep his hood down, much to his chagrin. The hood brought him much comfort.

As the day wore on, traffic on the Way of Sunsets increased. Baltaszar assumed they were getting very close to Khiry, a town that supposedly boasted a great selection of wines and foods from all of Ashur. They had traveled for half a day sitting in silence.

The sun had reached its pinnacle in the hours after noon and not a single cloud dotted the sky. "Find cover now! Behind the barrels an' under the blankets! Lay flat an' do not move!" Varan Ika barked from his seat up front. The soldiers must have been nearer than Baltaszar realized. He and Horatio lay on their backs, on the floor of the cart, the barrels of wine blocking them from anyone looking from the back of the wagon. They covered themselves with a few thick wool sheets. With any luck, the King's inspectors would not suspect anything was beneath the blankets. Only now did Baltaszar realize what a grand and stupid risk they were taking.

Horatio whispered, "Remember what I told you? Clear your mind. Be ready for anything. If they find us, they'll attack. Which means we have to attack first."

"Understood," Baltaszar whispered back. He closed his eyes and tried to focus on just the darkness. The merchant must have been acting overcautiously by warning them, because they'd ridden on for quite a while without anything happening.

The wagon slowed to a halt. Baltaszar heard an imperative voice at the side of the wagon. "Name and destination?"

"My name is Varan Ika. I'm travelin' ta Khiry. Make a run every month or so ta trade my wine. I'm sure ya seen me before. Ya look kind o' familiar. Er..Sir."

"I do not recognize you. Trade it for what?"

The soldier had a strange, formal sounding accent. Baltaszar wondered if it was a common way of speaking.

"Tween me an' you, I trade it fer beef. Don't really fancy the elephant an' that's all they got in Vandenar."

The soldier's tone didn't lighten up, despite Varan trying to be friendly. "You said there is wine in every barrel? All nine of them?"

"All nine sir."

"I am curious. What happened to your wagon cover? This cart is definitely equipped for one and has the proper clasps and hooks to support a cover."

"Ripped before I left town," Varan said with a nervous chuckle. "Didn't have time ta patch it up. Figured the weather's warm enough anyway."

"I see. And what is beneath the blankets?"

"Nothin', sir. Just more blankets an' a couple pillows."

The soldier climbed onto the wagon cart. Baltaszar heard him jostling a few of the barrels, likely listening for liquid. Baltaszar dared not move. The soldier stopped inspecting the barrels and Baltaszar heard the clomping of his boots come nearer.

Baltaszar tried to clear his mind once more but had trouble focusing. Shackles of guilt and remorse clung tightly and he could not shake them off.

The rapturous feeling of his manifestation lay just beyond his grasp and there was nothing he could do to reach it. As Baltaszar grappled with his mind to control his emotions, something blunt boomed into his torso, causing him to grunt loudly. The guard yelled, "Get up! Hold your hands up so I can see them!"

Horatio kicked up into a standing position in one smooth movement. While Baltaszar rolled over to his hands and knees, wheezing and getting his wind back, he heard a sizzle and a crack and something crashed down onto the road. Baltaszar looked up and saw the soldier, in leather armor, lying a few feet away on the ground with wisps of smoke drifting from his lifeless body.

"Get ready Baltaszar. They're all going to come now. I get the feeling I'm going to need your help for what's next."

Baltaszar stood and jumped to the ground. His stomach ached, but the pain was dissipating. He attempted to focus once more and clear his thoughts, but his mind was still plagued with memories of his father and Yasaman and Bo'az. Closing his eyes only made it worse, as images of them flashed around nonstop.

As he gritted his teeth to concentrate harder, a storm of arrows rained down around them and the wagon. Varan Ika had still been sitting in the front as three arrows pierced the thick man through his chest and head. Baltaszar and Horatio simultaneously ran and crouched behind the coverless wagon. "You hurt?"

Horatio sighed, "I'm fine. Our merchant is dead." Arrows continued to pierce the wagon and road, some falling only inches away from them. "The second they let up, we have to attack. Are you ready? Focused?"

Baltaszar reddened. "I don't know what's wrong with me. I can't focus. I can't seem to get that feeling back. There's just too much in my head."

"You have to try. I cannot do this by myself. Look at all of the arrows coming down." Deep red wine seeped down the sides of the wagon as more and more arrows pierced the barrels and flowed onto Baltaszar's shoulders looking like blood. The arrows came to a stop. "Now Baltaszar. Stand and embrace your manifestation." Horatio stood and stepped toward the left side of the wagon to face their attackers. Baltaszar mirrored his actions on the right of the wagon. As soon as Baltaszar stepped to the side of the wagon, an arrow pierced his right thigh. The impact was so strong that it knocked him to the ground, which turned fortuitous as another arrow whizzed by right where his head had been.

Baltaszar hit the ground with his shoulder blades and rolled behind the wagon once again. He sat up and stretched his legs out in front of him, elevating the injured one. His thigh burned deeply as blood quickly flowed from the wound. Baltaszar took the curved knife from his belt and cut a long strip from his cloak. *Now comes the difficult part.* He would only be able to completely remove the arrow if he broke it first. It would have to be cut and the motion of that would hurt even more than the burn in his thigh. Baltaszar wrapped the strip of wool tightly around his thigh above the wound. He breathed deeply then gripped the arrow with one hand and struck the shaft with his blade in one quick motion. The burn flared through his leg from the vibration and he clenched his jaw from the pain. To make matters worse, gripping the arrow with his burnt hand only elevated Baltaszar's pain.

Waiting to pull out the other piece would not do much good. Baltaszar grasped the shaft protruding from the back of his leg and pulled as hard as he could. Droplets of tears formed in the corners of his eyes as the burns in his hand and thigh grew unbearable. Baltaszar relaxed his leg and finally the arrow shaft came out completely. His hand and the ground beneath him were stained crimson. *Focus on the task, not the pain.* Baltaszar thought only of what needed to be done, rather than the excruciating burn in his thigh. He cut more fabric from his cloak and wrapped it tightly around the wound. Once satisfied, he inspected the arrow he'd just pulled out of his leg.

The entire shaft was completely smooth. He was nearly positive that no splinters remained in his leg, which was the only encouraging part of the whole situation. Baltaszar had been so focused on his leg that he'd forgotten about Horatio. *Oh no, what happened to him?* It was only then that Baltaszar realized that blasts of light had been radiating the sky the whole time he'd been tending to his leg.

***

The King's soldiers were almost completely depleted as the road ahead was littered with men in silver armor and helmets with red horse-hair ridges. Horatio had put down nearly two dozen men with the lightning and twice that many had fled as a result. He assumed Baltaszar had been injured, but Horatio needed to focus on the threat first. He and Baltaszar had gotten lucky with these soldiers. They grew arrogant with their numbers and fought out in the open. Likely, the soldiers didn't expect that a boy could control lightning. But Horatio found that to be the oddly marvelous thing about manifestations. It was nearly impossible to imagine just how many different things people could do with them. Something like lightning was violent by nature, so of course it made for a considerable advantage in combat.

But then again, the King's soldiers had been hunting down Descendants for years, so this squadron should have known better than to take anything for granted. Horatio considered that perhaps the soldiers had grown so accustomed to killing and defeating Descendants that they simply expected to defeat any they encountered.

Two soldiers remained roughly fifty yards away. They were searching their dead counterparts for more arrows. Horatio still clung firmly to the focus of his manifestation and the melody flowing through his veins. He cleared his mind and willed two more streaks of lightning upon the two crouching soldiers. One fell but Horatio had narrowly missed the second. The soldier spun and wildly fired an arrow back at Horatio, catching him off-guard. Horatio reacted barely in time, as the arrow grazed the left side of his torso. He clamped his hand to his side and knew instantly he would need someone to bandage him up, but it was still a blessing that the arrow hadn't impaled him. The graze would burn and likely bleed a good deal.

Quickly regaining his focus as well as he could, Horatio summoned down five more bolts of lightning upon the soldier. There was no point in risking a miss with just one bolt. The soldier convulsed and fell over immediately.

Since his first incident when he'd developed his manifestation, this was the first time Horatio had injured or killed anyone with it. He'd expected that his conscience would weigh more heavily for such a thing, but he wasn't bothered at all. His father had taught him that violence was acceptable when fighting for what one believed in or when defending one's life. Horatio shook his head at the thought. *Wait. How could he have taught me that? He was never around.* For years now, Horatio had wrestled with his memories and whether or not to believe them sometimes. His mind had proved to be a strange thing quite often.

He'd spent so many years adjusting to the idea that he'd had no father, yet at times, he could picture in his mind exactly what his father looked like. There had never been a single instance in which his father had returned to Damaszur, or that his mother or anyone else mentioned even seeing his father. Horatio did not remember ever seeing any man he'd even slightly resembled anyway. Yet, there was a specific image in his mind of his father, and even rare times in which a memory, or what Horatio assumed to be a memory, surfaced of his father.

Too often Horatio succumbed to these ponderings and got lost in this maze of thoughts and questions. And when that happened, he would snap back to reality at some point and realize he'd been staring off into nothingness for several minutes, sometimes hours. He shook his head vigorously once more and turned toward the back of the wagon. He clutched his side to temper his open wound.

So many arrows had rained down upon the wooden wagon that every barrel of wine had leaked its contents and the wood and surrounding ground were soaked a deep red. Baltaszar had propped himself up against the back of the cart and was holding his thigh with his left hand while his right hand was tucked firmly under his armpit. Clearly the boy was in a great deal of pain. Judging by the amount of blood soaked into Baltaszar's pants, he'd taken an arrow right through his leg.

"They're all gone," Horatio declared with relief. He walked to Ika's body and ripped off a portion of the man's shirt, then tied it tightly around his torso. It would do for a bandage until they reached Khiry. "Got speared through the leg, huh? Have you tried to walk yet?"

Baltaszar smiled. "I'm so light-headed, I can't tell if I bled too much or if the wine soaked right through my skin. I don't think walking is such a good idea right now. And you can thank me later for getting rid of all the soldiers while you sat back and did nothing."

Horatio let out a hearty laugh. Now that he was paying better attention, he noticed Baltaszar's head was swaying. They would need to get to Khiry quickly. "We'll have to get you on a horse. All of ours have either been bombarded with arrows or have run off from the lightning. But a few of the soldiers' horses are still over there at their camp. You get hit in the hand too, or is that still the burn?"

Baltaszar took a moment to respond. "Burn."

A deep realization erupted through the surface of Horatio's mind. Right here, at this time and place, was the beginning of something much larger than he could fully comprehend. He shook his head at the notion; this wasn't the time to be lost in thought. Horatio knelt down and wrapped Baltaszar's arm over his shoulder, then lifted the boy to a stand. "Lean against the side here. And don't fall. I'll be right back with a horse." Horatio sprinted over to where the soldiers had set up and approached a brown mare that seemed the least skittish of the bunch. He mounted the horse and rode back to Baltaszar, who thankfully still stood. "I'm going to hoist you up. But once you're on the horse, please don't fall off." He couldn't tell if Baltaszar had nodded in response or if the boy's head was just swaying more wildly now.

Horatio was thankful that he was somewhat taller and bigger than Baltaszar, who was lean, rather than skinny, and was a few inches shorter. He hoisted Baltaszar up, holding his injured leg so that Baltaszar could throw his other leg over the horse. Horatio's wound from the graze burned. The moment Baltaszar had settled into the saddle he tilted forward, but managed to steady himself on the horse.

Horatio considered for a moment the best arrangement for both of them to ride the horse. *Oh man, what do I do here? This is going to be awkward whether he's in front of me or behind.* Horatio sighed audibly. *The ride to Khiry is nearly an hour's ride. If people see us, will they think he's injured or will they assume something? What if Baltaszar gets the wrong idea about me? Oh Orijin, why does this have to be so awkward?* "Baltaszar, you still there?" His injured companion slowly nodded his head. "Good. Listen, we have to ride the same horse. You're too injured to ride alone and Khiry is still an hour away. I'm...um...I'm going to have to...sit right behind you on the horse so I can keep you steady and hold the reins. Don't uh, don't think the wrong thing, it's just because...you know...because you're hurt that I..."

Baltaszar cut him off in a hoarse voice, "Horatio, can we just go. I'm going to die on this horse if you keep going on and on about how you're just doing this to save my life." He slumped forward once again.

"Sure, sure." Horatio mounted the horse behind Baltaszar and took the reins. As he looked behind them at the wagon, he realized other merchants had resumed their travels as well, as they littered the road as far back as he could see. *Great, now everyone will see us.* Horatio commanded the mare to a gallop and they were off.

***

Horatio sat at the table in the corner, his back turned to the rest of the room. The Weary Traveler was an inn that was quite friendly to Descendants, but after the altercation he and Baltaszar had had on the Way of Sunsets, Horatio wasn't up for any similar encounters any time soon. Despite having been bandaged up, his side still stung. After the shock of fighting and racing to Khiry, coupled with the drain from summoning the lightning, he was too exhausted for anything except eating and sleeping. In truth, the ride to Khiry hadn't been as bad as Horatio feared. He'd been so determined to get there and keep Baltaszar alive that he barely had time to entertain the foolish thoughts he'd had before.

Now he could relax for a short while. Baltaszar was upstairs being tended to and would likely sleep until midday tomorrow, despite the fact that it was still only early in the evening.

He dug into the roasted half chicken on the plate before him. The inn-keeper, Soren, had insisted on serving it to Horatio, along with a chunk of bread, peppered corn, and a glass of deep red wine. Horatio decided it futile to argue and accepted graciously. The moment Horatio had walked inside the Weary Traveler, Soren, a tall stocky man with a booming voice and the yellow-hued skin typical of Mireyans, had rushed to him and Baltaszar and tended to their every need. It hadn't been a surprise, honestly. Once Horatio saw the inn's name outside, he was sure they'd be welcome here. In his travels through Ashur, he'd learned to look for signs and symbols marking those who were friendly to Descendants, especially in nations and cities that were notorious for being enemies to those with the black line on their faces. From what Horatio had learned, Mireya supported the Descendants rather than the King.

Any inn that welcomed Descendants had a lowercase "l' in its name, and the inn's name was written outside so that the bottom of the "l" extended lower than the rest of the letters, so it resembled the black line of the Descendants. It was how Horatio had known to stay at the Happy Elephant as well.

After Soren had gotten his maids and nurse to attend Baltaszar, he'd set Horatio up with a room and a change of clothes. Horatio had decided to eat before going to his room. He knew that once he went upstairs again, very little would be able to pull him away from a bed. A couple of maids had brought him up briefly to bandage his torso while the rest tended to Baltaszar.

The common room was busy with the murmur and bustle of merchants, travelers, and gamblers. Every town had at least one inn like this. Horatio knew, however, in certain nations, while inns like this were welcoming to Descendants, certain people frequented them just to spy. Soren sat down across from him. Horatio was about to speak but the broad-shouldered man held a hand up to stop him. "Eat boy, eat. An' let me know if ya want more. Got plenty o' food."

Horatio realized that although Khiry was a long way from Vandenar, the accent was still the same. Soren continued as Horatio bit a huge chunk of meat from a chicken leg. "Yer Shivaani friend'll be back ta normal soon. Lost a lot o' blood but he was smart enough ta tie up the wound I guess as soon as it happened. Likely saved his life."

Horatio cocked his eye, "Shivaani?"

"Yeah. The boy ya came in with. Got that brown Shivaani skin from the east."

"He told me he's from Haedon, and not far from Vandenar."

"Impossible. Nobody on this side o' Ashur looks like that. An' I never heard o' Haedon. Maybe he's makin it up. Ya know how ya Descendants are. Always tryin' ta be mysterious an' all. Anyway, he just needs ta rest fer a day or so an' take it easy. Let him rest today an' tomorrow. Ya can explore Khiry if ya want. Let me know if there's anythin'' I can get ya. Doesn't look like either of ya got any coin. Anythin' ya need, horses, food, clothes, just let me know boy." Soren stroked his slicked-back hair."

Horatio swallowed a gulp of wine. "Well wherever he's from, we're both very thankful. But why are you helping us so much? The moment we walked through your door, we were in need and you haven't stopped helping us since. Why?"

Soren's eyes narrowed. "The King, curse his name, sees all o' ya Descendants as abominations. Like yer lower than everyone else or somethin'. Been livin in Khiry my whole life, never seen a single Descendant wanted ta cause trouble. Ya 'Black-liners', as we call ya in Khiry, were always in an' out o' this city until Edmund's soldiers set up camp on the Way o' Sunsets. That's when all the trouble started. Ta hell with the King an' his soldiers. They can all rot in Opprobrium." Horatio listened intently as he wolfed down his food. Soren continued, "There's a war comin', boy. Whole world knows it's only a matter o' time before Jahmash comes back." Horatio nervously looked around at the rest of the crowded room. Soren reassured him, "It's no secret. They all know, too. An' they all think the same way as me. If he does come back in my lifetime, I'll bet the 'Traveler' that ya Black-liners stand a better chance against him than King Edmund does. That's why I take care o' you an' yer folk, boy. We need ya. The world needs ya. It's wrong the way yer all treated. Yer lives are graced by the Orijin his self, yet ya live like ghosts. Yer the Ghosts o' Ashur."

"Are there any others here now? Other Descendants?"

"We haven't had any o' ya in months. Them soldiers out on the 'Way' been deterrin' Descendants fer years now. Even when we do get Black-liners here, they usually come in like ya an' yer friend did. Hurt, dead tired, in need o' medicine an' nurses. Pardon me fer bein forward, but how did ya manage ta get past the soldiers anyway?"

Horatio finished chewing and hesitated another moment, then spoke quietly. "I can control the lightning. They bombarded our wagon with arrows. Killed our merchant and took down Baltaszar before he could attack. I was able to take enough of them quickly from a distance, which caused most of them to run away. Those that stayed were either badly burnt or killed."

Soren nodded. "Ya see what I mean, boy. It took one o' ya ta defeat dozens o' them. What good are they ta the world if they're attackin' our only hope? Anyways, I only sat down here ta check on ya. Make sure ya got everythin' ya needed. Eat 'til yer stuffed. An' like I said, when ya go out inta town, come back an' tell me before ya decide ta buy anything. I'll give ya the money fer whatever ya want."

"Thank you, you're too generous. I'm already stuffed, so I think I'll go check on Baltaszar and then get to sleep. I'll be sure to visit the markets when I wake up in the morning." Horatio arose from the table with Soren and picked his plate up with him.

"Leave it boy, we'll clean it up fer ya."

Horatio nodded in appreciation and walked upstairs.

***

Baltaszar groggily awoke to a pair of young women sitting beside his bed talking quietly. *Another unfamiliar bed.* When he tried to move, they sprang from their chairs and forcibly held him in place. Both women possessed similar features to Anahi, yellowish skin and almond-shaped eyes, though both were older than her. One was slender and not well-endowed as Anahi had been, while the other was plump with a small nose. Both wore frocks similar to the maids in Vandenar, except these were dark blue.

The chubby one spoke first. "Please don't move sir. We've given ya lots o' herbs an' ointments ta help with the pain, but as ya see, we're not nurses. We can only do so much. If ya start movin' around, ye'll certainly start ta hurt again."

Baltaszar could barely remember any of the past day. He remembered leaving Vandenar with Horatio and trying to use his manifestation. He also remembered coming upon soldiers on the way to Khiry and being hit with an arrow. Everything after that was lost to him. "What happened to me?" His words were somewhat broken, likely from not having spoken in a while.

The chubby maid responded, "Yer hand was burnt black an' ya got an arrow through yer thigh. Yer friend brought ya here an' we took ya in. Soren had us tendin ta ya the moment both o' ya walked through the door. 'Twas smart on yer part ya wrapped yer leg. If ya hadn't, well either you'd be dead or usin' a wooden leg the rest o' yer life."

Baltaszar knew he'd been hurt, but felt a certain shock about the direness of what had actually happened. "So I'll be back to normal soon?"

"Ye'll be fine, dear. Just stay in bed a while an' let us care fer ya. Soren will make sure we all cater ta yer every need. Ya can bet on that. In fact, now that yer awake, we'll have the cooks bring ya up some breakfast, though actually it's about time fer lunch. What's yer fancy, dear boy?" The woman had a jolly nature to her, as if she was always seeing the upside to everything.

"Fancy? I...I don't really know. I'm sure I'll enjoy whatever you bring. Wait, you said time for lunch? How long have I been lying here?"

"You an' yer friend showed up early in the evenin' yesterday. Ye've been lyin' here ever since. Sleepin' most o' the time. That boy yer with, the handsome fella, he came in ta check on ya in the night, but yer snorin' made it clear not ta wake ya."

"Oh. Have you both been here with me the whole time?"

"We've been takin' turns, me an' Vera here." She nodded to the slender woman to her right. "My name is Shara, we're sisters. Our other sister Cara has been helpin' as well. Cara's been very anxious ta help, givin' me an' Vera lots o' breaks. She's more yer age, an' most o' ya Shivaani don't come this far west. Usually ya go ta the City o' the Fallen, but don't come up this way. An' most Black-liners don't come here anymore."

"Shivaani? I'm no Shivaani."

Shara chuckled. "Sure ya are, boy. Sure, yer a bit light-skinned, but ya still look just like them brown-skinned folks from Shivaana. Only people in Ashur that look like that."

"I swear. I'm from Haedon, up north past Vandenar."

"It's probably just the herbs messin' with yer head. Or maybe ya lost too much blood. Only thing north o' Vandenar is the Never. An' people don't live in that place. Just monsters"

How many people am I going to have to convince? Baltaszar was too tired to keep arguing. "Fine, fine. Believe what you want. I'll take that breakfast now if you don't mind. You can both leave now. I'll be fine." Vera eyed him skeptically. "Don't worry, I'm not going anywhere. Besides, I wouldn't be able to move fast enough to get far." Satisfied with that, Vera followed Shara out the door to the right of the bed.

Baltaszar sat up and hung his left leg over the side of the bed. Shara was right; now that his blood was flowing, his injured leg had started to throb. He wondered if they had any medicine to help with that. His hand also throbbed and burned now that he'd sat up. Baltaszar wondered what Yasaman would have thought of all this. He imagined her watching him now, and wondered if she'd be worried about him or maybe impressed that he had made it this far. At times Baltaszar wanted to stop thinking about her, but other times he couldn't get himself to stop. Meeting Anahi hadn't made him stop loving Yasaman, but it did make it obvious to Baltaszar that he and Yasaman were no longer together. He wasn't completely sure what he wanted to do, but Anahi was right. At some point, he would have to go back to Haedon and confront her. In the meantime, he would just continue on to the House of Darian.

The door opened and Horatio walked in followed by a girl who looked like a younger and shorter version of Vera. While Vera had been pleasing to the eyes, this younger version was much prettier. She was carrying a tray that held a mug and a slice of some sort of dark brown bread or cake.

"Is that my breakfast?" Baltaszar had never seen anything like it before. Steam billowed from the mug and whatever was in it smelled strong and somewhat nutty.

Horatio sat at the foot of the bed, already smiling. "Cara's sisters came down and said you were awake. She had just finished making this cake for you, so we figured we'd come up together and bring you some food."

Out of the corner of his eye, Baltaszar could feel the girl, Cara, staring at him the whole time Horatio was speaking. Then she spoke up. "Horatio had just come back ta the inn an' I came over while Soren was talkin' ta him. We got ta talkin about ya an' he said ya haven't seen much o' Ashur. So I thought ta make this cake fer ya. It's chocolate. He said ya likely hadn't had it before."

More strange food. First elephant. Now chocolate. At least it smells good. "No I haven't. What is it? Chocolate? And what's in the mug? It smells…interesting." Baltaszar put his good leg back on the bed and took the tray on his lap.

Cara sat next to him on the bed, closer than Baltaszar was comfortable with. "Chocolate…it comes from a bean that's only found in Galicea. It's bitter by itself, but it is wonderful if ya mix it with milk an' sugar. Khiry an' the City o' the Fallen are the only places ya can find it outside Galicea. Same fer the coffee. That's what's in yer mug. Also comes from a bean, but we roast the beans an' grind 'em ta make a drink, an' then mix it with milk an' sugar. This one ya got was roasted with hazelnuts. It's unfortunate fer that wall between Galicea an Fangh-Haan, else yer country might be able ta get it too."

"I can't wait to eat. Wait…my country? This again?"

Horatio cut in, smiling, "I tried to tell her, Baltaszar, but it was, well…difficult for me to explain."

Cara looked confused. "Yes yer country…Shivaana? Yer Shivaani, ain't ya? What else could ya be with that skin color?"

Baltaszar was growing frustrated at these presumptions. "What is it with all of you? I'm not a blasted Shivaani! I come from a town called Haedon, north of Vandenar. I've never been to Shivaana. I don't even know where it is!" Cara stood and moved to sit at the foot of the bed next to Horatio. Baltaszar felt guilty at the outburst. He couldn't tell if he'd angered or offended Cara, or both. "I'm sorry. I didn't mean to offend you. It's just, since leaving Haedon so many people assume I'm from this Shivaana place that I've never even heard of. And the people who do actually ask me where I'm from don't even believe that Haedon is a real place. It's like everyone thinks I'm crazy or a liar or something."

Cara's expression softened. "I can understand that. But ya don't have ta get so angry with me. Yer too cute ta be huffin' an' puffin' an' such. Now eat yer breakfast before everythin' gets cold." Horatio looked at her with a somewhat stern look that Cara understood immediately. "Oh don't start cryin'. What are ya, a baby? Yer a handsome fella too. There, ya happy now?"

Horatio pursed his lips and shook his head. "You're just saying that now to make me feel better."

Cara leaned in closer to Horatio, "O' course I am, dear boy." She kissed him on the cheek and then walked to the door. "Enjoy yer cake an' coffee Baltaszar. An' if ya need anythin' else from me, anythin' at all," she glanced at Horatio then back at Baltaszar, "just let me know." Cara winked at Baltaszar and left the room.

The moment the door shut, Horatio's head swiveled back to Baltaszar. "Before your head swells up, well before both of your heads swell up, she was flirting with me the same way downstairs."

Baltaszar chuckled, "I wasn't going to say a word." He bit into the massive slice of cake. "Wow. This is amazing! What did she say it was called? Chocolate?" He then sipped the coffee to wash it down. "By Orijin, that's even better! Chocolate and coffee. How have I not known about these things my whole life?"

"You were so busy being 'too cute' up in Haedon."

"Just wait until I'm better, 'handsome fella'. I'll push you off your horse."

"Yeah, tough words for a man laid up in bed. Take on some soldiers next time we're in trouble. Then you can talk."

Baltaszar gulped down more coffee and nodded emphatically. "Oh, you're going to bring that up, huh? Lucky for you...I'll save the threats for now. Maybe next time I'll do it on purpose. Then I can have Cara to myself when you're out of the way." Baltaszar couldn't help but laugh at his own threats. "And I'll have all the chocolate and coffee I want."

Horatio pursed his lips, "I don't like the coffee anyway; you can have it all. I did try the chocolate when I was traveling west through Galicea. It is pretty damn good. And who do you think Cara likes better? The one lying in bed because he couldn't defend himself or the one who can take down dozens of soldiers with lightning?"

Baltaszar knew Horatio was joking, but he took some of those words to heart. *He's right, I do have to start learning how to use this damn manifestation.* Baltaszar finished the cake and coffee and set down the tray beside him. "Just wait until I've had enough practice. Then we'll see. Anyway, when are we leaving this city?"

"I'm going to buy some things at the market today. We're out of supplies and Soren, the owner of the inn, has offered to finance whatever we need. I spent all of my coin by the time I got to Vandenar. Figured you didn't have any either. We'll stay tonight and leave tomorrow."

"Why would he do that? Pay for us? Does he think you're handsome too?"

Horatio laughed. "Everyone thinks I'm handsome. They can't help it. Soren is a strong supporter of Descendants and does whatever he can to help any of us. And the truth is we really need some things if we're going to make it to City of the Fallen and the House of Darian."

"I'm not arguing. Do we even have horses?"

"We took one of the soldier's horses. Don't you remember?"

"I don't really remember anything after getting hit." A sense of relief seemed to wash over Horatio's face. Baltaszar grew curious. "What's that look for?"

Horatio's face flushed. "It's...nothing."

"Oh come on, man. Tell me."

"No, it's just...it was sort of awkward having to ride on the horse together because I had to ride sitting right behind you and make sure you didn't fall off."

"Oh. Well. Yeah that's a bit awkward. But still, you only did it because my life was in danger. I'm glad that you did." Baltaszar laughed, "I'm also glad that I don't remember any of it."

Horatio loosened up at that, "Yeah, lucky you."

"Anyway. I want to go with you when you go to the markets."

"No way, you have to stay here and rest up. You need your strength for when we leave tomorrow."

Baltaszar eased his legs over the side of the bed. His right thigh was throbbing and burning from the movement, causing Baltaszar to grimace. It took all of his will power to subdue the winces and groans that moving caused. "Look, you might be right. But the only way my leg is going to get better is if I use it." He stood and put pressure on his left leg to maintain balance. Baltaszar then took a step to see how his right leg would hold up and he quickly had to recover by shifting his weight.

"See what I mean? You can barely walk."

"Shut up. I just got up after lying in bed for a whole day. Let me get used to it. Go work your charm on Cara some more and when you're ready to leave for the markets, come get me. I guarantee that I'll be able to walk."

Horatio rolled his eyes, but listened. "Fine. It's still early enough in the day. You have a few hours to figure out how to walk before we leave for the markets. I'm going back to take a nap." He arose from the foot of the bed and left the room.

Baltaszar was relieved at the solitude. Once Horatio was gone, he sat back on the bed and rubbed his thigh. It throbbed, burned, and ached.

Baltaszar wasn't even really sure why it was so important for him to go with Horatio and Soren. It would have been best for him to stay in bed and rest. He would feel foolish finally arriving at the House of Darian with a severe limp and unable to walk properly, if at all.

But deep down, Baltaszar felt embarrassed. Although Horatio was joking, the truth was that in his first experience in battle, Baltaszar had had absolutely no impact. Now he was being pampered and waited on because of it, even though he hadn't done anything heroic. He was tired of being a victim. He wouldn't survive in Ashur if everyone always had to take care of him.

Baltaszar gingerly got up again and limped considerably while his leg got used to the pressure. He gritted his teeth and let loose a few guttural growls as he hobbled laps around the room. The pain was severe but he could get used to it. In time it would be tolerable. Baltaszar realized now that he didn't need to do this to prove anything to Horatio or Cara or anyone else. He needed to prove to himself that he was strong and resilient.

Baltaszar was fully awake and energized now. He was physically and mentally ready to get used to the pain. It would take a great deal of practice, but he had hours to do so. All he needed was the will power. And perhaps more chocolate cake and coffee. He peered through the door and yelled out for Cara.

CHAPTER 12
HUNTERS

From ***The Book of Orijin*, Verse Thirty-Six**
You shall all endure pain and suffering. Man cannot truly appreciate joy without suffering. But We shall not bestow upon you more pain than you are capable of overcoming.

THE NIGHT HADN'T been as quiet as Garrison would have liked. Insects hummed and buzzed throughout the forest, while owls and bats screeched. Garrison crouched atop a high branch in a tall, leafy tree. Yorik and Marika had done the same in separate trees. Yorik had insisted that he would keep lookout first while Garrison and Marika slept, but Garrison refused to sleep when he knew the arrival of more soldiers was imminent. He doubted that Marika slept either.

The air remained thick and humid despite the sun having set hours ago. Garrison saw it as a boon, considering they didn't dare start a campfire. He had argued with Yorik and Marika about whether to continue on or hide. The Taurani implored him to keep riding, but Garrison knew that the only way they would have a chance against the king's soldiers would be the element of surprise. If the soldiers had caught up to them while on the run, there would be very limited options for the three of them. But waiting in the trees in the dark brought certain advantages. The moonlight penetrated the forest enough to see on the ground, but the trees were too dense for Garrison and the Taurani to be noticed.

Garrison had explained his plan to the two Taurani and they hesitantly acquiesced. They'd ridden throughout the day and there was no concealing that all three were tired, as were their horses. The Taurani agreed that it would be foolish to continue riding while there was a risk of any of them dozing off or losing focus. Hiding in the trees, whoever saw danger first would whistle out to the other two. At least if any of them fell asleep, they wouldn't be exposed. And Garrison had given Yorik and Marika each pouches of Red Dust, which would be the first element of surprise. If anyone was sleeping, the boom of an exploding tree would wake them up.

Garrison groped the pouches in his pockets at the thought. He had given Kavon all of the Yellow Dust. Garrison hadn't regretted it, but the Yellow was his favorite and would surely be useful against soldiers in the dark. Once he reached the House of Darian, he would promptly make more.

He briefly thought of Kavon and regretted losing him. Yorik and Marika had expressed no sadness, or any emotion for that matter, regarding Kavon. Garrison supposed that they'd understood that death was a possibility on this journey. Garrison refused to entertain that notion, however. He was simply too stubborn to accept it as a possible outcome. He shook his head and returned his focus to the ground below.

Garrison felt the warrior in him returning. Although he personally hadn't killed any soldiers earlier in the day, he'd been in the middle of conflict and had kept his head level. It was a reassuring sign that he possessed necessary skills and military focus to reach the House of Darian, no matter what. He'd felt no regret about the soldiers' deaths. In truth, a part of him welcomed the challenge of the chase. The soldiers would all underestimate him, he knew. He'd led so many of them to hunt down and kill Descendants over the past few years and most of the time it had been a relatively easy task, to the point that the soldiers had grown arrogant and pompous. By the time Garrison had become fed up with their conceit, he'd already stopped taking part in the hunts, so he'd seen no point in informing the soldiers that they'd only been so successful because of Donovan's, Wendell's, and his expertise and tactics. Without the three of them developing plans and strategies, most Descendants would have destroyed the battalions quite easily.

Let them come. Let them think they can defeat me. A whistle came in the distance from Garrison's right. *Yorik.* Garrison looked eastward. He couldn't see anything, but the ground softly rumbled. *They are smart to not have torches.* The rumble grew louder and in moments Garrison could see shadows moving from the east. Garrison began to distinguish the sound of barks and yelps from the rumble. *Dammit. Dogs.* Marika had encouraged them to leave the horses a good mile ahead and then walk back. That would likely buy them several minutes of going undetected. Enough time to watch the soldiers' movements and wait until the precise moment to strike.

Despite the thick foliage of the trees, the dogs would eventually sniff out Garrison and the Taurani. But with the horses hopefully far enough away, the dogs would need a few moments to specifically locate Garrison, Marika, and Yorik. It would prevent each of them from acting too quickly. Judging by the rumble of the ground, Garrison estimated that this squadron was about half the size of the one that had attacked them earlier in the day. With any luck, they could dispose of these soldiers without any serious injuries.

Shadows raced across the ground beneath Garrison. For nearly a minute the dogs raced from tree to tree. Another whistle came from the right. Yorik had been spotted. Seconds later, about the same time the barking started at the base of his own tree, Garrison heard a whistle from his left. All three of them had been found. Garrison had instructed Marika and Yorik to wait until soldiers had surrounded their trees. If any of them had acted too hastily, it would only leave them with dead dogs and exposed to the soldiers.

The battalion had separated. Garrison heard shouts from his left while another group of soldiers reached the barking dog at his tree. More soldiers moved on to where another pair of dogs barked at Marika. One soldier spoke up and yelled, "Garrison! Taurani! If you come down now without a fight, we will kill you quickly! If you make this difficult, we shall make all of your deaths slow! Painful!"

Garrison remained still. The key would be to not give away their exact locations in the trees. He'd instructed the Taurani to do the same and to not speak. He and Yorik had both taken the bows and arrows while Marika volunteered to use a spear. She'd felt more confident with her accuracy that way. Garrison pulled a red pouch and a small vial of oil from his pocket. He doused the pouch with the oil and rested it on his thigh. Of all the pouches, the Red took the longest to react, allowing for time to draw the soldiers closer. *One.* Garrison slowly pulled the bow from around his shoulder. *Three.* He then unsheathed an arrow from the quiver on his back. *Six.* He nocked it meticulously and aimed at the soldier closest to the tree. *Eleven.* Garrison had instructed the Taurani that the pouches would explode at a count of twenty-two after dousing them. They were to leave them as near the center of the tree as they could. Each of them had deliberately hidden in a part of the tree where many branches met the trunk. *Twelve.* The group of soldiers still searched the tree for him. They'd all craned their heads upward, leaving their necks exposed. Garrison pulled the bowstring back and fired. The unassuming soldier dropped to the ground as the arrow sliced through his neck and Garrison quickly returned the bow to his shoulder. *Fifteen.* The rest of the soldiers crowded in to discover what happened. *Seventeen.* They quickly readied their own bows and aimed at the tree. *Eighteen.* Garrison set the pouch on the tree, ran along a branch, and jumped as far out as he could. As his feet hit the ground, his right ankle rolled and he grunted loudly. Garrison stumbled and collapsed. His knee burned like streaks of fire were shooting through it. As the soldiers turned to face him, Garrison curled up and covered his head.

The tree exploded in a brilliant flash of red light, hurling several soldiers through the air. Shards of the trunk and branches shot out from the midst of where the remaining soldiers stood. The blast had been so violent that some soldiers were impaled through their armor by shards of wood, while others had been hit directly in the neck or face, dying instantly. Others were simply knocked to the ground. Garrison grinned widely despite the pain in his leg. For those who survived, it would take them several moments to recover. He would have to attack first, but his knee and ankle would not cooperate with standing up.

Garrison heard an explosion in the distance to his right. Another sounded a few moments later to his left. He could only hope that Yorik and Marika were successful. More than a dozen soldiers around him were standing and looking around. Garrison heard another rumble in the distance as he struggled to rise from his hands and knees. *More soldiers coming? Damn it!*

The rumble turned into the beating of hooves; Garrison guessed more than two dozen. He fingered his belt for more dust pouches as the new battalion neared. The soldiers around him yelled and screamed and some even fell to the ground. Garrison looked up to see the new soldiers engaging the others in combat. He shook his head and looked again as more soldiers rode past toward Marika. The new battalion wore the same armor and helmets. The only difference was that the horse-hair ridges of their helmets were colored differently-definitely not the red of the Royal Vermilion Army.

Garrison couldn't make sense of the situation, but he was grateful for the help. Swords clanged all around and Garrison cautiously crawled toward a tree for cover. Soldiers from both sides were falling. Though the red battalion had been bigger, the yellow was gaining the upper hand. Garrison fought the urge to find a weapon and fight. The pain in his leg had become so severe that the urge to clasp his knee controlled him.

The fighting seemed to diminish, as Garrison could hear less and less yelling and screaming. He craned his neck from the side of the tree and realized what had actually occurred. He thought he recognized some of the soldiers in the new battalion. They were part of Wendell's personal battalion. *They really rode all this way down?* The thought filled Garrison with confidence and adrenaline. He used the tree to pull himself up, then braced against the trunk. From the light of burning trees, Garrison realized the new battalion's helmets bore yellowish and brownish ridges.

As Garrison looked up, a helmetless soldier charged toward him, sword in hand. The scowl on the man's scarred faced left no confusion about whether he was friend or foe. Garrison staggered backward away from the tree as the soldier neared. The attacker leapt as he reached the tree, then convulsed violently as a spear impaled his head from the side and slammed him into the tree. The spear had pierced the tree trunk, leaving the limp soldier slumped against it. Garrison looked to his right where, several yards away, Donovan flashed him a toothy grin. Garrison nodded back and dropped to his hands and knees.

The fighting had finished, but very few soldiers remained standing. Garrison judged that Wendell's squadron had originally numbered just over twenty. Even after the exploding trees had killed some soldiers, Wendell would likely have still been outnumbered. Garrison sat back and stretched out his leg.

"Looks as if we came just in time!" Wendell crouched down and sat beside Garrison. Donovan followed with three other soldiers and Yorik.

"Not a chance, Ravensdayle. I had this taken care of." Garrison laughed before even finishing his sentence.

Donovan cut in, "Of course you did, brother. Old Clint hanging from the tree back there is proof that you would have handled everything perfectly."

Garrison turned to his right to see a bloodied Marika returning with two more soldiers. "Marika! Are you hurt?"

Marika retorted quickly, "I have had much worse." She and the two soldiers sat down and joined the arbitrarily arranged circle. Garrison looked around at the others; they were all exhausted. Two of the soldiers had already laid back and were asleep.

"What now, Prince?" asked Wendell.

"Do not call me that. It is no longer my title. Donovan is the sole prince now. Treat him as if he is sole heir to the throne."

Donovan challenged Garrison's assertion. "But once you return from the House of Darian, you would regain your claim to the throne. I would not interfere with that, Garrison."

"I know, Donovan. But the King has renounced my title. Lawfully, you are the sole heir. And that is how you must act and think. I have no idea how long I will be at the House of Darian. You may be in a position to succeed the throne before I even return. That is why you must set it in your mind that you are the future king. If something happens to our father while I am at the House of Darian, and you are required to succeed him, I would not dare ask you to step down at any time after that."

"But…"

"There is no 'but.' That is how it must be. Everyone here is a witness." The others nodded their heads.

Wendell spoke up again. "That is all good and well, but back to my original question. What now? I think it would be best for us to sleep through the night and then leave for the House at dawn."

Garrison shook his head and massaged his aching knee and ankle. "No. You are not going to the House. Especially not you and Donovan. The two of you are too valuable to be risking your lives now. You will travel back to Alvadon and prepare the Royal Vermilion Army. Properly. Our soldiers are too arrogant and have lost sight of how to fight properly and intelligently. Jahmash's return is apparently imminent. You must have our soldiers ready in time."

Donovan looked back at Garrison incredulously. "You cannot be serious, brother. Look at the three of you! You will not reach the House on your own. Who knows how many more soldiers are out there!"

"That is exactly my point. Who knows how many soldiers are still out there? There are ten of us sitting here. Only ten. The two of you are more beneficial back in Alvadon. Jahmash is coming. Soon. The Blind have confirmed it. If we separate, at least our chances of survival are greater. The

Taurani and I will travel southeast to the House. Donovan, you and Wendell will ride back to Alvadon to…"

Wendell cut off Garrison. "With all due respect, Garrison, you are no longer the Prince. We do not really have to listen to you."

"I am not commanding you. I am providing you with common sense. If we all ride to the House and are attacked, the risk is that we all die. At least if the two of you ride back north, you would wear your armor and would be left unharmed. The Taurani and I will take your five soldiers. Surely you see the sense in that, Wendell."

Wendell nodded reluctantly as Donovan spoke up. "But…"

"He is right, Donovan," Wendell cut in, "We must not forget our own responsibilities. Your father will do nothing to ready the armies. If Garrison does not reach the House of Darian, it is even more important for us to be in Alvadon. We must lead the Royal Vermilion Army now."

Donovan shook his head in annoyance as he rose and walked to the tree where Old Clint still hung. Donovan pulled the spear from the tree. As the dead man's body fell to the ground in a heap, Donovan grunted and threw the spear into the dark forest.

Garrison braced himself to stand, but Wendell had beaten him to it. "Stay, Garrison. I will speak to him."

Before Wendell could turn to leave, Donovan had already returned. "I understand why you are doing this. I truly do. I will follow your plan, brother. But that does not mean that I agree with it. And if you die before even reaching the House of Darian, I swear that I shall never forgive you."

Garrison failed to suppress the chuckle, "What would you do? Follow me in death just to show me how angry you are?"

Donovan's clenched jaw softened. "Hmmph. I would! I would search each of the Three Rings and once I find you, I would bloody your face until the Orijin banishes me to Oblivion for eternity."

"Oblivion? Ha! He would send you to Opprobrium for something like that!"

"Oh. I see. So you speak for the Orijin now, brother? Rather overzealous, no?"

Garrison rolled his eyes at Donovan, but it was too dark for his brother to notice. "Forget it. Let us sleep while we have the time. In the morning, your soldiers will ride south with me and the Taurani. You and the Lion will return to Alvadon. Wear the red-plumed helmets. Which reminds me. Why the natural-colored ridges?"

Wendell cut in, "What did you call me?"

Garrison smiled again, "When we were at the Tower of the Blind, one of the servants we met was originally from Maradon. He remembered me and the two of you from when we were younger. Remember how everyone used to call you the 'Lion Cub' back then? You are grown now. Why not call yourself the Lion? Every great general is associated with a powerful symbol. Think about it, Wendell. You could fit all of the helmets to bear blonde ridges. Once my father is out of power anyway. It would be a new army."

Wendell traditionally kept his composure unless on the battle field, but Garrison assumed he'd liked the suggestion, as Wendell emphatically threw his hands up. "Yes! Why did I not think of that! We only used the blonde and brown ridges because we wanted to stand out from the red and we had no time to dye them. But that makes perfect sense!"

Garrison continued, "Good. Finally you agree with me about something. So as I said, we shall separate in the morning. The Taurani and I will also wear the royal armor. If anyone sees us, we will simply look like a small band of trackers. As long as no other soldiers attempt to confront us, it may even make for an easy journey. Though that is wishful thinking. Now let us sleep."

Donovan and Wendell had volunteered to keep the first watch while the rest slept. Garrison laid down where he'd been sitting and tried to clear his mind. His knee and ankle still throbbed, but his weariness proved stronger as he drifted into a deep sleep in barely a few moments.

***

"Aron, Ronan, Lewis! Stay at a pace with Marika. She will stand out if seen by herself." Garrison and his small band had ridden for most of the morning and afternoon, stopping only briefly when absolutely necessary. He'd continued to silently thank the Orijin throughout the day for their horses remaining where they'd left them. The more they rode, the more Garrison's ankle swelled, but he maintained a sense of gratitude that they didn't have to walk.

Marika wore royal armor, just as the rest of them, but even the smallest armor was big for her stature. Because of that, she had foregone the vambraces and wore only the chest and shoulder plates and a helmet. If she rode too fast, her armor flopped about, making it obvious that she was no soldier. Garrison had to continue to remind the soldiers to slow down. He would take the risk of a longer journey if it lessened the chances of being noticed.

On the other hand, Yorik fit in perfectly with the soldiers. He was bigger than all of them save Kale, a massive man from Alvadon, eight years Garrison's senior. Despite his colossal and intimidating frame, Kale was the biggest joker of the group, constantly playing tricks on the others and poking fun at them. He'd already tricked Lewis into rubbing horse dung on his forearm to relieve soreness. And when he wasn't causing trouble, Kale never stopped talking about combat stories and battle strategies. As a result, he and Yorik got along like brothers.

Garrison had split the group into to riding lines. Lewis, Marika, Aron, and Ronan rode in front with a pack horse. Aron and Ronan were twins with hawk-like eyesight; Garrison needed them to keep lookout for any evidence of other soldiers. Clay accompanied him, Yorik, and Kale on the second line. Despite Marika's pace, they rode rather swiftly. As the day wore on, Marika had figured out ways to ride more comfortably and lessen the movement of her armor.

Ahead, Aron raised his hand high, signaling for them to stop. "Do you hear that?"

Garrison listened for a moment. "Hear what?"

Aron continued, "Exactly…"

"…It is too quiet." Ronan finished the sentence. The twins had a habit of doing that. Most people, especially Donovan and Wendell, found it annoying, but Garrison found it oddly humorous.

"No animals around," Garrison deduced. "Soldiers must be near. How many do you think could actually hide here, though?"

This time, Ronan began, "Most likely only a few."

Aron continued. "Scouts. We are nearly out of the forest. The rest of them would…"

"…be waiting for us once we are more exposed."

Garrison signaled for them all to draw in close. "Do you have an idea of their numbers?" Aron and Ronan both swayed their heads negatively. "Then what is our best option? We do not have enough time to hide the horses and take to the trees."

Aron and Ronan looked at one another and nodded before Ronan spoke up again. "The two of us will ride ahead…"

"…and scout their numbers and position."

"Then we can properly strategize the situation." Ronan scratched his patchy beard. It was the only way to tell him and Aron apart.

Garrison nodded and the twins rode off. While they waited, Garrison ordered the others to take inventory of their weapons. On his own person, he carried a sword, two spears, a belt of daggers, a bow and a half quiver of arrows, and his other belt of pouches. Before they'd parted ways with Wendell and Donovan, they raided the bodies of dead soldiers and took everything they could carry.

Garrison inspected his pouches. He'd already used all of the black, yellow, and red. The blue would only be of use if they were near water, which left the green and brown. Each would be easy to camouflage in their current surroundings. If they were greatly outnumbered, the brown would work best, as it caused the ground to break apart. If he could manage to plant all of the pouches, it might cause a massive enough rift to keep a large number of soldiers away. The only problem was that blood was the catalyst that triggered the brown. He would have to find a way to trigger it quickly and easily.

In the hour that the company had taken stock of their weapons, the twins had returned. Aron began with a half-smile, "The news is rather…"

"…fortunate," Ronan continued. "Their numbers are less than twenty.

They must have…"

"…broken off another squadron to cover more ground."

Garrison still wondered how anyone could find their back-and-forth annoying. "You are sure of this? Their supplies fit their numbers?"

Ronan responded, "If there are more,"

Aron continued, "…then they are too far away to be detected. If that is the case, they do not pose…"

"…any immediate threat."

Kale spoke up, "Good. Then the best plan is for the five of us to ride out toward them, Commander Garrison. They will see us and think nothing of it. We can kill them when the time is appropriate. You three will ride directly south toward the Serpent and we will meet you once we are done. Take the pack-horses as well. Cross the river as soon as you can. Do not wait for us, just in case we run into trouble."

Kale must have been spending a great deal of time with Wendell. His plan was sound and Garrison could find no point to argue. "Very well. We shall see you at the river. Yorik, Marika, let us go."

Garrison turned his horse and urged it to a gallop heading south. The sun was still high enough to cross the Serpent with plenty of light. Marika and Yorik caught up to him within a few moments.

They rode on for another two hours in silence. Yorik had tried to make conversation early, but Marika warned that talking would slow them down and draw their focus, and they needed to reach the Serpent as quickly as possible. In the far recesses of his mind, Garrison had questioned briefly the reality of their success. He understood how difficult it would be to reach the House without any casualties, if at all. But he'd repressed those thoughts quickly. He'd had to if he was going to be successful. There could be no second guessing, no being caught off-guard, and no shaky strategies. A part of him thought Marika might even make a good general in the royal army. But he would bring that up another time.

The forest had cleared and led directly to the banks of the river. "We will keep riding along the bank until we can find an appropriate place to cross. It is too far to the other side right now."

Yorik disagreed. "Why waste the time? Let us leave our horses and swim across! None of us will need our horses on the other side."

"And what if there are more soldiers on the other side, Yorik?" Garrison turned in his saddle to look at the Taurani. "Will you outrun them on foot? We do not have the luxury of taking risks just yet. I know you are eager, but Ronan and the others have bought us some time. We will ride for a few more miles. If we find nothing, then we will do as you say. Fair?" Yorik nodded, though his countenance still expressed disagreement. Garrison let it go. As long as the man listened, he didn't care if Yorik had doubts. They were hours away from the House of Darian. Garrison wouldn't dare risk anything now. As he was about to turn forward once again,

Garrison espied a cloud of dust in the far distance behind Yorik. It was too far to confirm whether it was more soldiers rushing to attack, but they had to be ready. "Be ready," he nodded toward the riders. "I cannot tell whether they are our friends or foes, but I doubt it will take long to know for sure."

Garrison and the two Taurani turned to face the riders. As the company drew closer, Garrison counted only four soldiers on horseback. He instantly recognized Kale, towering above the rest. Four riders meant one had been killed, but Garrison could not determine who was missing from so far away. One was even helmetless, but still too far away to recognize.

"One of your friends is missing, boy," Marika pointed out. "The quiet one who hardly speaks."

As the four rode closer, Marika's observation was confirmed. Clay was the one missing. In a few more moments, the four had reached them at the riverbank. Kale spoke first, "We thought you would be further ahead by now, given how much time you had."

Garrison smirked. "The forest extended for longer than we anticipated. We thought it best to keep the cover of trees as long as possible. What happened to Clay?"

"Sword through the neck. There was no saving him. The soldiers were wary of us from the start. Always keeping their eyes on us. They all stood up when they saw us coming, even after we were clearly visible. Aron made up some story about us being the survivors of a battalion that fought you in the forest, but like I said, they were suspicious the whole time. Tense, hands on their weapons. I suspected they might even attack first, so I gave the others a look and we initiated. Three advanced on Clay; he never really had a chance. The rest of us took some minor injuries, but nothing that will slow us down. As you can see, Aron's helmet got bashed in pretty well. He tossed it as we rode and I yelled at the fool for not doing so while he could have stolen another helmet."

Aron quipped, "Do not worry Kale, if I die…"

Ronan continued, "…he will not blame you. Neither will I."

Kale rolled his eyes. "I have often wondered. I rarely hear the two of you talk to each other. How can you even have a conversation if you finish each other's sentences? It would be like one person talking."

Ronan laughed, "If you think our conversations would be complicated,"

"…you should hear our arguments." Aron added with a wide grin.

"Enough. We must go. We will continue to ride for a few miles along the bank. If we cannot find a way to cross by then, we will swim." No one argued with Garrison this time. He took the lead with Aron and the others followed. As they rode, Garrison realized their chances were likely futile. The river was wide and he knew it would not get any narrower as they rode closer to the House of Darian. In his previous travels, he normally led soldiers through Mireya and knew there were no bridges or crossings until the very end of the river, where it flowed out to the sea. It would take over an hour to reach that and there would surely be soldiers there. The crossing point would be too obvious. He took a deep breath and raised his hand as he slowed his horse.

Just as they'd come to a full stop, Aron came crashing into Garrison, which threw Garrison down to the ground. Garrison sat up, pulling his helmet off and rubbing blood and dirt from his eyes. Aron lay still before him with an arrow protruding from his head and blood seeping out. Garrison shook his head. *Kale was right. He is a fool. Stop. There is no time for this.* He stood up. The others had already turned away to defend themselves. His horse had been unharmed, but he decided against remounting. Garrison stepped forward to see a few dozen riders coming their way. More arrows hailed down toward them, but the riders were still far enough off that the arrows couldn't pierce their armor.

Garrison quickly realized how Aron's death could still help them. His companions had begun firing back upon the attackers. Garrison crouched down and hoisted Aron's limp body into a sitting position. He removed his belt of pouches and loosed all of the brown pouches into a pile on the ground. *I apologize, my friend. At least your death will not be wasted.* Garrison pressed a pouch against Aron's head where the blood oozed, and then stood and hurled it toward the attackers. The brown dust only needed a few seconds to react with the blood. Garrison threw it close enough that it could hit the ground before the reaction occurred. In a few moments, the ground rumbled in the distance. The first tremor threw two soldiers to the ground as their horses rollicked then turned and galloped away. A small hole opened in the ground which swallowed another rider and horse. Garrison would need to use the rest of the pouches quickly. Lewis, atop his horse, was the closest. "Lewis, come!" Garrison drew a dagger and deeply sliced open Aron's thigh. Lewis crouched next to him. "These pouches need blood for the reaction and we need to throw them quickly! Use his thigh, then throw them at the ground between us and the riders!"

The boy, barely fifteen years, nodded. "Understood."

Seven pouches remained, but if they could throw them all quickly enough, Garrison knew it could even the numbers between the two sides. He threw another bloodied pouch, killing four more soldiers. His companions fired arrows back but only managed to kill one rider so far. Garrison and Lewis threw two more pouches which landed right next to each other. The ground erupted and swallowed several more soldiers.

The tumult of the tremors caused their own horses to panic. The pack horses had already run off and Ronan and Marika had jumped off their horses to avoid being thrown. Marika threw off her helmet then pulled Garrison's bow and arrows from his back. The soldiers were drawing in very close. Garrison knew his window for the brown dust was narrowing. He threw one more as Lewis stood to make a good throw. As Lewis brought his arm forward, an arrow struck his breastplate and staggered him. The pouch dropped to the ground in front of Lewis, who stood only a few feet before Garrison. *No. Not enough time to get it.* "Everyone get to the ground! Now!" Garrison rolled away. Marika dropped next to him while Kale and Yorik dove from their horses away from Lewis. Ronan had been standing next to Lewis and hesitated for a moment, as if not knowing which way to go.

The ground erupted from beneath Lewis, catapulting him toward the enemy soldiers. Garrison looked up from the ground and saw the soldiers drawing their bows toward Lewis. There would be no saving him.

Ronan was thrown several feet away, somersaulting through the air. He'd landed awkwardly on his head and didn't move. From where Garrison lay, he couldn't tell if Ronan had been knocked out, severely hurt, or killed. He would have to wait to find out. Aron's body, along with the rest of the brown pouches, had been thrown in numerous directions. Yorik and Kale had ridden out toward the soldiers by the time Garrison had remembered about them. He had no idea how they'd reigned in their horses, but he didn't care. His own horse milled about several yards away. Garrison ran to it and mounted it before it could think to run away. He rode out toward the soldiers. About fifteen remained and Yorik and Kale engaged them, while Marika fired more arrows from afar. Garrison readied his first spear and vaulted it toward a group of soldiers, striking one and knocking him from his horse. Without hesitation, Garrison clutched his second spear and hurled it harder than the first. This one struck a man through the neck and tossed him so hard that he knocked another soldier from his horse. He rode closer to engage.

Only then did Garrison realize that Yorik had fallen to the ground in the middle of four soldiers while Kale clashed swords with three more. Kale had killed three already. Garrison glanced back at Marika, who was running toward the soldiers with a sword in her hand. A deathly scream turned Garrison's head toward Kale. The soldiers had taken him down as well. "Marika! To the river!" There was no longer any sense in hand to hand combat. Ten soldiers remained and Garrison only had Marika left. He turned his horse toward Marika. She had been much closer to the river and ran toward it.

It took a few moments before all of the soldiers realized Garrison and Marika still lived. Once the two were noticed, the soldiers climbed their horses and pursued. Marika ran to the edge of the water and Garrison met her there. He looked behind them then turned to Marika, "They have no more arrows! If we swim, we may be safe. They cannot cut us down and swim at the same time!"

Marika shook her head, "Boy, we are too tired. We would drown before making it across."

"Stones of Gideon! Then what do you suggest? We would die if we stayed to fight!"

Marika closed her eyes and clenched her teeth. "You will tell no one of this. And if we ever meet another Taurani, you will never speak of this." Marika closed her fists tightly and lowered her head as if trying desperately to concentrate.

Garrison realized what she was attempting to do. *Impossible. Stones of Gideon, Taurani cannot...*

Loud crackles came from the river and Garrison turned back toward it. It had become a sheet of ice as far as he could see in either direction. Marika dropped to her hands and knees, heaving loudly to catch her breath. The riders were closing in.

Marika looked up at the river, "We must..." as she fell forward, Garrison saw the handle of the knife protruding from the back of her head.

"NO!" The riders were within twenty feet. Garrison commanded his horse to a gallop and rode across the ice. His horse slowed to a nervous trot, but Garrison knew even that was asking a great deal from the steed. Even with horseshoes, there would be no traction on the ice. *They will have the same problem.* Garrison whispered in the horse's ear, "Just be steady, my friend." He glanced back and quickly realized that his pursuers were having difficulty following him, a result of urging their horses impatiently.

He dared to take a longer look behind. The soldiers all held their horses' reins tightly with both hands. Garrison felt his waist to ensure he still had daggers. Still there. *But how do I throw them from here?* He pondered the question for several moments as his horse skittered on. *Wait. The saddle. Of course! Ten against one. The only time I will have any advantage is right now. Might as well take the risk.* Garrison kept one foot in the stirrup and brought his right to the saddle. He placed it in the holster at the front of the saddle then braced his hands so he could bring the other foot up. Once both feet were secure, he crouched sideways atop the horse as it trotted slowly.

The ten soldiers were not far behind, but their horses slid as they ran, preventing them from gaining any ground. Garrison pulled the first dagger and threw. It actually hit a soldier in the face with its handle rather than the blade, but the man was only stunned. He tried once more and struck another soldier in the throat. Garrison knew the hit was more luck than skill, given the bouncing of his horse. *I have no choice.* He aimed the next dagger at the lead horse and struck it in the face. *Forgive me, Orijin.* The horse neighed wildly and bucked its rider from the saddle, then flailed its head crazily and collided with another horse, sending both falling to the ice. *Eight remain.* Garrison had seven daggers left. If only he could be so lucky with the rest.

The next two he threw missed completely and the third struck a horse in the shoulder, but barely impeded the beast. He could not garner much motion for an accurate throw, considering he was crouching, bouncing up and down, and gripping the saddle with his left hand. The next dagger struck another horse in the side of the neck. It panicked and crashed to the ice, crushing its rider beneath it in the process. *May the Orijin bless you, Marika.*

After missing with his remaining daggers, Garrison accepted the desperation of his situation. He removed his helmet and threw it at the feet of the closest horse. As it attempted to sidestep the helmet, the horse slipped on the ice and slid sideways. Garrison swore he heard the snaps of bones in the process. The sliding horse caused another behind it to attempt to jump over it, but when the horse landed, it lost its footing and tossed its rider, then fell to the ice as well. *Five more.*

Garrison reached to his back and threw his swords, one after the other. Only one successfully brought a horse down. He had nothing left to throw. He glanced forward again to see where the horse was going. The other side of the river was not far. Just as Garrison began to think about what to do once reaching the bank, one of the soldiers threw a sword at Garrison, which missed. But it had come close enough that Garrison realized he would go down with the horse if it was struck and he was strapped in to the holsters. He loosened his feet enough to be able to jump out if necessary. As if reading Garrison's mind, another soldier followed suit in throwing his sword. The blade also missed Garrison, but struck his horse in the leg. As soon as Garrison saw the sword strike, he launched himself to the ice. He let his breastplate break his fall and then quickly stood. The bank was no more than a hundred yards away. He pulled off the breastplate and hurled it toward the remaining pursuers.

Garrison turned and ran without waiting to see the result. His pace was surprisingly fast despite the continuous pain in his knee and ankle. He soon reached the bank and, once on firm ground, turned to assess his pursuers. In the distance, four ran toward him, none on their horses, while a fifth hobbled behind. Judging by the distance, Garrison had barely a minute on them. He turned and ran toward the mountain on the horizon, which he gauged at nearly two miles off. That was the entrance to the House of Darian.

The towering peak before him seemed so close. Violence chased him while the mountain sat at peace in solitude before the sea. His feet ached of weariness and rawness, and they kicked up as much dust as the five men behind him. The mountain drew nearer as his pursuers chased. Their yells were the only evidence he had that they were not far behind. Garrison dared not slow himself down by turning his head. He put the sound aside and exerted his remaining energy to his legs. They were all he focused on. His knees throbbed and his muscles twitched and tightened, but to stop now would cost him his life. He only hoped he could gain access to the House. He continued on for several minutes before the mountain finally seemed within reach.

In his previous visits here, a porter guarded the entrance and only those with the Descendants' mark disappeared into the mountain. Unfortunately, he was never one of those who'd disappeared, despite his Mark. His dealings with the House of Darian mostly consisted of dropping off captured Descendants who'd bribed him to be delivered there.

His arms swung crazily as he ran and his mouth hung open, sucking in air and searching for any moisture. The mountain now lay close enough that he could discern the guard standing at the boulder that marked the entrance. Behind him, the soldiers gained ground, but he had kept enough distance that he would survive, assuming the guard granted him entrance.

The guard stared straight at him, armed with a one-handed sword and a bow and quiver on his back. As Garrison ran on, the guard, of a similar build and height, met his eyes but did not alter his countenance or position. He was now about thirty yards away. If the guard had not initiated a fight stance by now, he had no intention of attacking. Garrison let out a yell that tore at his raspy throat, "Let me...brother! ...am be... chased! They will k... me!" Most of his words were truncated by the fire in his throat, and he intended for his yell to project more than it had. But the guard understood, and also saw the pursuers in the distance.

The guard yelled back, reassuring him, "Fear not, Prince Garrison, for I am a decent and somewhat understanding man! Of course I will allow you passage!" Garrison had come upon the guard, thankful that he was not required to say more or plead for admittance. "However, Prince, admittance is allowed only to those accepted by and trusted by the House."

What? With that, the guard thrust a leather-gloved fist into Garrison's temple, collapsing him to his knees. Garrison, floating between awareness and unconsciousness, saw the mountain swirl before him and only heard the world through muffles and echoes. The man dragged him along the ground, only making Garrison dizzier. His presumed savior spoke, but the words broke down into more echoes before reaching his ears.

Still lolling and swaying, Garrison felt the world before him speed up. He raced through darkness without having moved. He swore he still kneeled on the ground, but the ground no longer existed and black space surrounded him, while emptiness raced past him.

In a few more moments, the world slowed back to stillness and its color returned, only now Garrison knelt on the hard stone ground outside a castle. His vision regained enough focus to see a modest castle before him, though he still found difficulty in seeing the details of it. Two men grabbed him by the hands and dragged him, he assumed, inside. The ground cut open Garrison's exposed knees, but the pain from it was miniscule compared to the aches everywhere else on his body.

Although his mind still felt a bit cloudy, Garrison understood that he was safe. After running for a week, he had managed to outlast his father's soldiers. That was who they were now, his father's soldiers, not his own any longer. He would become the very thing his father hated. Garrison was free to live his life as he wanted, and once he healed, he would commit himself fully to the lifestyle of a Descendant and make the world understand that Descendants were not the scourge his father claimed them to be.

The dragging stopped. The two men lifted him to his feet, still supporting him beneath the shoulders. He could only imagine how he looked: filthy, clothes in tatters, stained with blood, dirt, horse guts, and chunks of his own flesh missing. But soon enough, he would be healthy again. A short man stood before him now, dark with his hair closely shaved to his head, in the Shivaani fashion.

The man to his right spoke. "Maven Jelahni, this is Prince Garrison of Cerysia, son of King Edmund. He seeks refuge with the Descendants in the House of Darian."

The Shivaani replied, "I know who he is, though he looks like a simple beggar before me. I have seen him many times, yet he likely has no recollection of me. Tell me boy, is it your intention to fulfill your duties as a Descendant here?"

Garrison still could not project much from his dry, cracked mouth, so he nodded, trying his best to meet the man's eyes despite the knot in the back of his neck.

"Then you are a fool. I know of your crimes against Descendants. All of Ashur knows of your father's decree to eliminate us from the world. And you are the leader of his army." Garrison could only look at him now, hoping the man could see the genuineness in his face, see that he meant no harm. He bent his neck despite the lack of cooperation from his muscles, and saw only anger in eyes of his accuser.

The man to his right spoke once again, "What shall we do with him then, Maven? Would you have us bring him to Zin Marlowe?"

"No. I say kill him. This...prince. Ensure that it is painful and use whatever means you feel is necessary. Zin Marlowe need not know about this. Once he is dead, send for me. I want to see his lifeless head for myself, and then I will send it back to his father."

CHAPTER 13
CITY OF THE FALLEN

From *The Book of Orijin*, Verse Eighty-Nine
We have blessed the ordinary with the power to perform miracles. We have given sight to the blind. Verily, We understand the laws of the world where you cannot.

"LESS THAN A MILE away! And I think we'll be out of the rain before we get there!" Horatio's voice snapped Baltaszar out of his ponderings. The heavy, steady rainfall coupled with the clopping of hooves had sent him into a sort of trance. His leg still ached, but he'd used it enough in the past few days that he'd grown accustomed to the soreness.

They'd left Khiry on the opposite end of the city from where they'd entered. Soren had explained to them that they could ride along the coast almost all the way to the City of the Fallen. It would take nearly twice as long, but there would be no soldiers there. Baltaszar hadn't been sure whether to be annoyed that Cyrus and Anahi hadn't suggested the same. Regardless, he was alive. His hand still stung constantly, but it would heal. He would recover and be back to normal soon.

In the past few hours, they had returned to the Way of Sunsets, because there was no entrance into the City of the Fallen from the coast, as Soren had informed them. Horatio shouted again, "Look Tasz, the sun is shining up ahead!" Baltaszar did not have to strain to see what Horatio was talking about. The darkness of rain clouds was almost at an end. Baltaszar suspected his horse noticed as well, as it quickened its pace.

"Good God." Baltaszar immediately lost his train of thought and cursed the clouds and rain. The intruding sunlight illuminated a wonder Baltaszar could never have imagined. "Who? What. Is. That?" At the edge of the city stood the towering light grey stone statue of a man with his right arm outstretched and his palm open as if welcoming the world to this city.

"Lionel." Horatio finally spoke. "One of the Harbingers of Darian's time. He was the great speaker; everyone loved him."

Baltaszar finally collected his thoughts. The marvelous statue toward which they rode solely provided affirmation that leaving Haedon was the right choice. "Is the world truly this marvelous? That things like this exist?

You're telling me that men created that, Raish?" Over the past couple of days, he had developed the habit of shortening Horatio to 'Raish'. Horatio hadn't seemed to mind.

"Oh, men definitely built this. The Galiceans, they have been master builders and sculptors for centuries. If you look around, in the distance you'll see that there is a statue of each of the others, except Jahmash, facing out from each side of the city. Darian to the north, Abram to the south, and Gideon to the west."

Baltaszar chuckled, "Why didn't you bloody tell me about this earlier? If I had known about such things, we would have gotten here at least two days sooner!"

"Right. You would have rushed away from Cara and her sisters fawning over you? For this?" Horatio nodded toward the statue.

"I likely wouldn't have met them! I wouldn't have allowed myself to get hurt!"

Horatio rolled his eyes, "And then you would have never known of chocolate and coffee. Do you see how everything works out?"

Baltaszar simply shook his head and spurred his horse on. As they reached the base of the statue at the edge of the City of the Fallen, Baltaszar fully grasped the magnitude of the statue's size. One of Lionel's feet was large enough for at least thirty people to sit on with room to spare. The statue was easily a hundred feet tall, maybe even two hundred. Standing directly in front, Baltaszar could barely tilt his head far enough to see the top of the statue. "Such creation and invention. I can't believe I have been missing out on such an incredible world my whole life." Baltaszar gritted his teeth. It was the second time in his life that he'd felt resentment toward his father.

"Come on fool. Believe it or not, there is more to this city than one nice statue." Horatio dismounted and led his horse between the statue's legs into the busy city. Baltaszar dismounted and followed, still enamored by the statue. They followed a wide stone road full of people traveling in all directions. Every so often, Baltaszar would eye a disheveled mass of torn clothing lying in the street or propped against a building.

"Why do they do that?" He shouted to Horatio above the din of the city.

"Why do who do what?"

"Those people. Why do they just lie in the streets like that? Why not just go home and clean up? Are they that lazy and tired?"

"Seriously?" Horatio glanced at him as if he'd just said something incredibly stupid.

"Of course I'm serious."

"They don't have homes, fish-brain! I'm sure they would love to have homes where they could be clean, but they have no money and likely not enough talent to be good at any jobs. You ask me, they should just go to the Tower of the Blind. Word is, the Tower will take in anyone and feed them, as long as they become a servant of the Blind. Maybe that's just too far and demanding, though."

"But look at all these people going by in their horse-drawn carriages, wearing rich clothes and jewelry. You're telling me they couldn't do something for them?"

"The world is not that simple, Tasz. Like it or not, there are homeless in every city of Ashur, som…"

Baltaszar cut him off, "We had none in Haedon."

"Fine. With the exception of your perfect little hidden city, there are homeless in the rest of Ashur. Don't blame the rich for not helping. It starts at the head. King Edmund taxes every country excessively, and for those that he knows are not loyal to him, he taxes them even more. Do you think any of these people can afford to just give away their money? Do you think anyone can afford to hire an extra hand just to be nice? I wish Ashur was all nice statues and pretty girls, Tasz, but there is more ugliness than there is beauty."

Baltaszar shook his head in anger. "Then something needs to change. People cannot just accept…this." He waved his hand at another heap lying in the road. "Someone needs to do something."

Horatio shrugged, "Well, we are going to the House of Darian. If there are people anywhere in this world capable of great things, it's there."

"I suppose we'll find out soon enough. I just don't understand how the whole world can put up with the bad decisions of one man. But fine, that's enough. I'll leave it be for now. Where exactly are we going?"

"We have to find an inn. A specific inn."

"What's the name?"

"Well that's the thing, I don't exactly know. But I will know when I see it."

"And I have the fish-brains?"

"No, you don't understand. There are certain inns that have a secret in their names and signs. That's how Descendants can tell if they are welcome inside."

"We're in the City of the Fallen. I would think we would be welcome anywhere."

Horatio waved his hand in annoyance, "For the most part, yes. But Descendants will still only go to certain places. Places that are familiar to them. That's where we want to be."

"What secrets are we trying to find then? How do we know when we've found it?"

"There will be an 'l' in the middle of the name somewhere. It will extend lower than the rest of the letters, meant to resemble the marks that we bear. You probably didn't notice it with 'The Happy Elephant' or 'The Weary Traveler'."

Baltaszar nodded his head. "Clever. Very clever. All right then, let us search."

"Yes. We'll get to the middle of the intersection first and then evaluate each direction. There are so many streets here; it may take days to find what we're looking for." Horatio nodded, "We'll walk to that statue." He nodded to a life-sized statue of a man at the center of an intersection.

Baltaszar glanced ahead toward the destination, then snapped to attention to make sure his eyes hadn't deceived him. He walked to the statue and studied the face for several moments. *This face. This nose!* "That...I know this man! He's the one who sentenced my father to be hanged!"

"What? Tasz, that's impossible. This is a statue of Vitticus Khou, a former chancellor of this city. He died decades ago. Look, it even has a name plaque on the base."

Baltaszar's eyes narrowed as he clenched his fists. "I don't give a bloody damn what you or that plaque says! That is Oran Von! He may look years younger, but I would never mistake that face. The hooked nose. The chin."

"Seriously, control yourself," Horatio grunted. "Khou was infamous for his support of Descendants. Thousands of people attended his funeral. This all happened before we were even born and still I know about it. Ask any one of these people in the streets and they will tell you the same thing. You are mistaken. It is not the same person."

Baltaszar's face warmed as he gritted his teeth. "You listen to me, wazzock. I'm not stupid. I wouldn't just make up some story based on a fleeting thought. I know this man; I have seen him regularly for the past fourteen years. Does Vitticus Khou have siblings? Children?"

Horatio smirked. "Wazzock?"

Baltaszar snorted, "Wazzock. As in bugger, plonker, berk, twonk, idiot, fool. My father used the word all the time. I picked it up after a while. Answer my question.

"I've heard the word before, but only in Galicea. How would your father have picked that up living in a secluded little mountain town? And no, Khou had no family. This city had an incredibly difficult time finding a worthy replacement as Chancellor."

"People left our town regularly, mostly for hunting. It's not unlikely that there was exposure to the rest of the world. Especially considering that Oran Von was the Chancellor of Haedon. Come on, Raish. Why would he give himself that title if he hadn't used it before? That's more than just a coincidence."

"Who knows, maybe Oran Von was a follower of Khou or a friend. Maybe he used the title as a tribute to Von."

"You know what, forget it. You won't believe me until I actually bring you to Von and you see for yourself. Of course, I will probably kill him shortly after. Or maybe I could just bring you his head."

Horatio flagged down an older man who was walking by. "Excuse me, friend. Might you help us for a moment?"

The short man nodded his head and stopped. "Sure, sure. Vhat can I do for you boys? Directions? Looking for someone?"

Horatio responded, "Do you remember Vitticus Khou? The man this statue honors?"

"Of course, of course. Anyone who has lived more zan zirty years remembers Vitticus. Great, great man, he vas. I vas not living here at ze time, but I came for his funeral, you know! He vas loved by so many people. So many people. Zere are statues of him all over ze city."

Horatio smiled. "Were you able to see his body at the funeral?"

"No, no. Nobody vas allowed. Terrible zing, his death. Terrible, terrible zing. He vas beaten to death by soldiers on ze Vay of Sunsets. It vas said you could not even recognize him, he vas beaten so bad." The man shook his head, as if recounting the whole thing.

Baltaszar's eyes widened. "So, nobody was able to look into his coffin when he died? How old was he when this happened?"

"I vould say near my age. Perhaps between fifty and sixty years. Ja. He had been Chancellor for a very long time. Very long time."

Baltaszar subdued a smile out of politeness, but looked at Horatio and raised his brow. "Thank you, friend. And Khou had no family?"

"It is my pleasure, dear boys. My pleasure. No, Vitticus had no family. Zough I know many vomen vere interested. Vitticus insisted he must spend his time counteracting all ze vorld's attempts to harass ze Descendants. He zought zat he vould be an unfit husband and fahzer. Are you sure zat you vant to be asking me zese questions, fellows? Not zat I mind, not zat I mind. However, you can go to his tomb at ze Chancellor's Chamber, and zey are qvite knowledgeable about Vitticus Khou's whole life."

Horatio nodded. "Perhaps we will take a visit. We were only asking for your help to settle an argument. Thank you. Now, might you give us one more piece of information?" Horatio patted the man's shoulder.

"Ask avay. Vat can I help you viz?"

"Thank you. This is our first time in the city. We are looking for an inn that we might meet more Descendants, perh..."

"Ah. You vant to go to Ze Colored Road. Zat is ze place for you. Incidentally, it is very close to ze Hall of ze Chancellor. Very close. Only a few buildings avay. Unfortunately, zat is on ze ozer end of ze city. But since it is your first time here, you vill likely appreciate ze valk anyvay."

Horatio nodded clasped the man's forearm. "Thank you dearly for your help. Your accent is Galicean, correct?"

"Ja. Ja, I am from Galicea. Ze town of Penzaedon along ze Serpent. Vhy do you ask?"

Horatio smirked, "Have you ever heard the term, 'wazzock'?"

The man laughed heartily. "Ja. Of course I have heard *and* used ze vord. My vife calls me and my son zat all ze time! All ze time! Vhy, do you also zhink I am a vazzock?"

"No, of course not! I was only trying to prove to Baltaszar here that the word came from Galicea. Many thanks again. Is there any way we can repay for your time and help?"

The man continued laughing and waved his hand at the offer. "No, no dear boys. Knowledge is free. And ze laugh you gave me is enough payment. Good luck viz your travels!" He shook Horatio's and Baltaszar's hands vigorously and walked away.

Baltaszar lightly punched Horatio's shoulder. "You see. They never actually saw him die. Whatever it is you think you know, I am positive that Vitticus Khou is now hidden away in my forgotten little mountain town. Even his age matches the story. Oran Von is a hobbled old man who looks like he's nearly one hundred years old."

Horatio shrugged his shoulders. "Looks like you *will* have to show me one of these days. Now let us go find Ze Colored Road, 'vazzock'."

***

Marshall had never been to an inn before, so there was no method of comparison. However, the room in which he, Desmond, and Badalao sat was bigger than most houses in the Taurani village. In fact, the number of people in the room could likely account for a small village.

"Lincan and Vasher will arrive any moment." Badalao said before taking a gulp from his pint glass.

"How do you know that?" Immediately after Marshall asked, Badalao tapped a finger against his head. Marshall felt somewhat silly for not having considered that. "Oh, right. So then have you bonded yourself with everyone at the House of Darian?"

Badalao and Desmond both laughed at the question. "I wish! We haven't been there long enough for that. I still have to warm up to quite a few people. Many do not trust me enough yet. They think the same way as you-that I only intend to spy on them and play mind games. And the girls, well they are another story." As Badalao spoke, two more Descendants joined them at the high-top table. Marshall recognized the slightly yellow-skinned one as Lincan, who had been in his recovery room with Adria. The other must have been Vasher, a brown-skinned boy of a height with Lincan and floppy black hair. Badalao continued as he shook hands with the two newcomers, "Now if I could also do what Vasher does, perhaps that would not be a problem."

Vasher reached across the table and clasped Marshall's forearm. "Marshall. Vasher. Delighted." His accent was virtually the same as Marshall's.

"How did you know my..." Marshall paused before finishing the question. "Oh. Badalao." Marshall shook his head. "What exactly is it that you can do then, Vasher?"

"Let's just say...I can be very persuasive when I want to be."

"What does that even mean? Was that intended to impress me?" The others chuckled at Marshall's challenge.

A hefty woman brought two pints of ale and placed them in front of Vasher and Lincan. Vasher took a drink and then responded with a grin, "Lighten up! We're all friends here. No need to be too serious, especially with everything that's going on. But to answer your question, I have the ability to persuade people through speech. The stronger your mind, the more difficult to persuade."

Marshall bit his lip for a second. "That sounds like a dangerous thing to control. Very easily corrupted."

Vasher shrugged, "Then I suppose it's a good thing I am on your side."

Lincan cut in, "I don't mean to ruin the fun, but can we talk about this situation with Gunnar and Adria? Maven Savaiyon didn't give us much, only that some man kidnapped them simply by vanishing."

Marshall responded first. "Maqdhuum. His name is Adl Maqdhuum."

Vasher took another swig and asked, "How do you know?"

"He led the armies that destroyed my village. Lincan, the way you found me, that was his doing. Three of us fought him with swords. He killed Myron, nearly killed me, and who knows what he did to Aric. He told us his name was Maqdhuum. He also said he was one of Jahmash's generals."

Lincan scratched the side of his head vigorously. "Exactly what happened with Gunnar and Adria?"

Badalao spoke up, "Simple. We were all talking. Marshall had just reconnected with his shadow. Then, bam. Gunnar was on his knees screaming because his forearm had been cut off. Cleanly off—that blade had to have been incredibly sharp—and maybe a second after we looked at them, Maqdhuum sneered at us and all three of them were gone."

Vasher leaned forward, "Lao, did he…"

"No Descendant's Mark. That is the strangest part." Badalao continued, "Since it happened, I keep going back to that one detail. It just doesn't make any sense."

"Perhaps some of the early Descendants didn't have a Mark," Vasher theorized.

Desmond retorted, "We've all read Hammersland's book. He made it clear that every Descendant bore the Mark."

Marshall attempted to contribute, "What if some of them did not have a Mark and simply kept it private that they were Descendants."

Desmond shook his head. "Ya don't understand. Hammersland said that all Descendants bear the Mark because the Orijin told him so. Hammersland didn't make it up his self. The Mark is part o' the privilege an' burden o' bein a Descendant. Lao, tell 'em yer theory."

Vasher and Lincan smirked at one another before simultaneously asking, "What theory?"

Badalao shot Desmond a sideways glance before taking a deep breath. "You all know how I think there are other lands beyond Ashur. I told

Desmond that it is quite possible this man came from somewhere else. Who knows what people from other lands might be capable of?" Vasher rolled his eyes and Badalao held up a hand. "Just humor me for a moment. Darian drowned the world. We know that. But why do we all assume that Ashur was the only piece of land that was saved. Seriously, we all believe that Jahmash is trapped somewhere, right? Why is it impossible for other lands to exist far out in the seas if the Red Harbinger is definitely out there somewhere?"

Vasher responded, "People have been exploring the seas for centuries and have yet to find anything. Do you know how many ships I have seen leave the docks of Sundari for the sake of exploration and never returned? Too many."

Badalao countered, "There are a few cities on the coast of Markos that could say the same. What if that only proves my point? What if even *some* of those ships found places and just never returned?" Vasher did not look convinced. "I am not saying I'm right. As Desmond said, it is only a theory. The man appeared out of nowhere, sliced Gunnar's arm off like it was a block of cheese, and disappeared again in a matter of seconds. He bore no Mark and told Marshall plainly that he is loyal to Jahmash. By the steel of my father's blade, I say the man is not from Ashur. Jahmash is recruiting and I highly doubt that he only looks to Ashur for followers. So if you have a better explanation, then please, Vasher, share. But it will take more than your manifestation to convince me."

Marshall cut in, "Perhaps we can discuss something else? Something that will not lead to quarrels?"

Badalao nodded his head. "Indeed. What did you have in mind, Marshall?"

"I don't actually have a suggestion. I simply meant that it was getting annoying to listen to you two argue. Surely there are better topics."

Desmond spoke up as a girl replaced his empty glass with a full one. "I have somethin'. I hope none o' ya think that this is too soon, considerin' recent events, but we obviously need ta focus heavily on combat. Who knows if we'll even see Gunnar again. An' even if we do, he won't be the same. We need ta organize a group." He looked across the table at Vasher. "Maybe convince people that the threat is real an' that if we don't prepare, we'll all be dead." Vasher, Lincan, and Badalao nodded in agreement. Then, as if rehearsed, they all looked directly at Marshall and smiled.

"What?" *Blood of Taurean, they have got to be joking.* "You cannot be serious. I know nothing of your people or of the House of Darian. Marlowe would likely try to kill me."

Desmond pursed his lips. "Marlowe is everythin' that is wrong with the House. Why do ya think we're even talkin' about this?" Desmond lowered his voice, "The man can rot in Opprobrium. It's like he's settin' the whole House up ta die. All he talks about is bein' peaceful an' lettin' Ashur see that we're harmless. I almost wish that damned Prince woulda gotten around ta killin' him when he was huntin' down Descendants. Marshall, ya saw fer yerself what's happenin' in this world. First yer people, an' then Adria an' Gunnar. We can't waste any more time foolin' ourselves that nothin' is happenin'."

Vasher cut in, "He is right, Marshall. At least Descendants like you and Desmond can use your manifestations in the middle of battle. But what about people like me, Lincan, and Badalao?" Marshall realized Vasher had a point. "Suppose we are in the midst of battle? In a split second, I cannot rely on talking my way out of getting killed. I, no, we, need to know how to fight."

Marshall found himself nodding in agreement to everything Vasher was saying. Lincan joined the recruiting attempt. "You know he's right. And Taurani have a reputation as fighters. Of course, I'm partial to the Anonymi, being from Fangh-Haan, but you'll never find one of them in the House of Darian. That's beside the point. You obviously have the most fighting experience of any of us and I've heard you're a better fighter than some of us here who have been trained." Lincan smiled and nodded at Desmond and Badalao, who both rolled their eyes. "So why not?"

Marshall's brow furrowed. "The Anonymi?"

Lincan explained, "A warrior clan that dates back to the time of the Harbingers. Just as fearsome as you Taurani, but even more secretive. The only clan members that leave Fangh-Haan are those who take up servitude in the Tower of the Blind."

Marshall put a hand to his head. "This is too much information for me to take in all at once. What is the Tower of the Blind?"

"Forget about it for now, I don't feel like explaining. We can teach you all of these things back at the House. Back to my question. Will you train us to fight?"

Marshall took a deep breath. "Well, if I agree to this, then it leaves no doubt that I am one of you."

Badalao smiled, "You were instantly one of us the moment you called me and Desmond faeries."

"Very well. I suppose if any of you go running to Marlowe or try anything stupid on me, then I can still give you the beating of your lives." Marshall laughed as Lincan raised his glass to toast everyone at the table. Marshall raised his own and then gulped down the remaining ale in his glass. Through all their talking, Marshall hadn't noticed a quarrel that had started a few tables away.

***

The moment that Horatio had chosen this particular table, Baltaszar had known it had been a bad idea. The inn had been packed and the two men that previously occupied the table walked away before even finishing their food and drink. But Horatio had insisted on standing at it. The man behind

Horatio, who was a foot taller and likely a foot wider, continually bumped into Horatio's back. Baltaszar assumed it was the ale in Horatio's veins, though it just as easily could have been the lack of a black line on the other man's face that gave Horatio the courage to bump the man right back. *This is why we tried so hard to find this place? Our being Descendants means nothing to that man.*

"Bump me again, lad. Bump into my back vun more time and I'll beat you so bad, ze road outside zis inn vill be colored viz your blood!" Most of the people around them had backed away. It was clear that nobody wanted to stop a fight. The man turned around, though Horatio's back was still to him. He liked being ignored even less than the bumping, as he palmed Horatio's shoulder and spun him around. Horatio simply looked up at the man, but made no indications that he wanted to fight. Baltaszar leapt to his side and stared into the man's eyes. Baltaszar embraced the melody in his veins, which was becoming easier now, and held his good palm out. A small ball of fire hovered above his hand, high enough that the heat would not burn him. The man, clearly drunk now that Baltaszar was closer, turned to him and glowered. "Put zat out, dog. Fight me like men, viz your fists. I have no magical powers. Let zis be a fair fight."

Baltaszar let the flame go. As the man nodded his approval, Baltaszar punched him in the chest. Though visibly older, the man's size compromised nothing in old age. The strike forced him back a step, but didn't faze him. The man lifted Baltaszar up by the front of his shirt and tossed him into a group of spectators, knocking them all down. Fists, knees, elbows, and feet flailed wildly as Baltaszar freed himself from the tangle of limbs and bodies. He looked back toward Horatio, who was also on the ground after being smashed through a wooden table.

The man's friends arose from their table, splitting up to continue their assault on Baltaszar and Horatio. Baltaszar gingerly stood to ready himself for the attack and a wiry man with a thick mustache pounced on him. He had Baltaszar pinned to the ground and cocked his fist. Baltaszar realized at that moment that he'd never been punched in the face before. *Focus, idiot.* The hit never came. In the split-second it had taken Baltaszar to blink, the mustached man had levitated to the ceiling. *What is this?* Baltaszar looked around the room while still on his back. All of the assailants were in the same position, floating in the air and looking dumbfounded. A hand reached down to him and Baltaszar grabbed it, allowing himself to be pulled up. The hand belonged to a light-skinned Descendant with a shaved head. Two more Descendants pulled Horatio from the ground. Five of them now stood before Baltaszar and Horatio. One, whom Baltaszar thought looked peculiarly familiar, like the people he'd met in Vandenar, looked up to the ceiling at the floating men.

"Six against two isn't really a fair fight, Reed. Thought I'd even things up. Ya know better than ta be startin fights with Descendants in this place, don't ya? The new ones are supposed ta feel welcome in here!" The men immediately fell to the ground in a chorus of smashes and grunts. "Let's go, we can talk outside." The boy waved his hand and the other four Descendants followed him. Horatio glanced at Baltaszar. He nodded to Horatio, who turned and followed. As Baltaszar walked through the crowd of people, he tried to mouth 'Sorry' to as many people as he could.

Baltaszar followed the group out onto the road. After walking for several feet, the one who had spoken inside stopped and turned around. The rest formed a sort of scattered circle, allowing everyone to face one another. Baltaszar stuck his hand out, "Thank you for helping us. That sort of thing hasn't happened to us before."

"Desmond. It's Desmond. An' don't worry about it. Reed is a regular there. He likes ta start trouble when he's drunk. Nothin' personal. Next time he sees ya, he probably won't even recognize ya."

That's why he looks familiar. "Desmond? Anahi mentioned your name. She told me to try and find you, that you hadn't left Vandenar long before I had gotten there."

Desmond smiled, "Oh ya know Anahi, do ya?"

Baltaszar felt his face heat up. *Dammit.* "Yes. She…took care of me."

"It's fine. What did ya say yer name was? Even if ya fancy her, there's nothing ta worry about with me. I think o' her more like a sister now anyway."

"Baltaszar. My name is Baltaszar Kontez. This is my friend Horatio."

Desmond pointed to the others as he introduced the others. "Vasher, Lincan, Marshall, an' Badalao. Say…ya can create fire? Never seen anyone be able ta do that before."

"Only realized I *could* do it while traveling down here. That's why we're going to the House of Darian. I need to be able to control it. I almost melted my hand off just showing Horatio what I can do."

Lincan spoke up. "You only just found out about your manifestation?"

"Less than a week ago."

"And you're our age? How is that possible? How long have you had the Mark?" Lincan scratched his head roughly.

Baltaszar shrugged. "From what my father told me, I've had it since I was about three or so. But I was brought up my whole life thinking it was a scar. It wasn't until about a week ago, just before I left my village, that someone told me what it really is." The others bore mixed reactions to Baltaszar's admission. A couple looked at him incredulously while the others unsuccessfully suppressed laughter. "Look, I know how bloody stupid that sounds. I don't need all of you telling me what a fool I am for thinking so."

Lincan retorted with a smile, "I apologize. The thing is…the Mark is something that the whole world knows about. How is it that any town in Shivaana could let you go on thinking that? Were there no other people there with a Mark?"

Baltaszar clenched his teeth tightly. Horatio seemed to know his thoughts and spoke for him. "He's not from Shivaana. He's from a town north of Vandenar, hidden in the Never." Horatio's explanation only brought more confusion to the others' faces.

Desmond tried to clarify. "But yer skin, it's brown. Only people in Ashur with brown skin are Shivaani. An' I think I would know if there was a town in the forest near Vandenar."

Baltaszar's frustration boiled over. "For the love of Orijin! Don't you all think that I would know where I'm from?! Why would I bloody make up a stupid story if I was really from Shivaana? I come from a town hidden in the mountains of the Never! It is called Haedon! I have lived there all my life! There are no people there with marks on their faces! Not everyone there is brown-skinned! They come in all hues from pale to copper! And no, Desmond! You would not know if there was a town in the forest because, as far as I know, I was the first person from Haedon to leave the village for anything besides fishing in the seas nearby! I am so damn tired of having to explain this to everyone!"

Lincan responded sarcastically. "Fine, fine, you're not from Shivaana. It's not like 'Haedon' is on any maps—ever. At least you're not sensitive about where you're from, though."

Baltaszar attempted to stifle the laugh, but it escaped more loudly than he'd hoped. Vasher quipped, "No, that's better. I didn't want to share my country anyway."

Marshall chimed in, "The two of you could pass for brothers though." Baltaszar shook his head, feigning annoyance.

"When are you two riding to the House?" Badalao looked back and forth between Horatio and Baltaszar.

Horatio looked at Baltaszar, then back at Badalao. "We were looking forward to seeing more of the city. It is our first time here. Our plan was to spend to explore today and spend the night. Then take in more of the city tomorrow morning and leave for the House afterwards. When are you all headed back?"

Badalao looked around at the others. "We really only came here to regroup. Certain…events…unfolded this morning and we desperately needed to relax for a bit. But I think I speak for everyone in saying that we have no issues with following your agenda. We do not get to have much fun at the House these days and it would be nice to unwind." The others nodded in agreement, sharing the sentiment.

Desmond asked, "It's goin' ta get dark soon. We should start walkin' if ya want ta see anythin' today. Any idea what ya want ta do first?"

Baltaszar immediately responded, "If you all don't mind some business before the fun, I would like to go to the Hall of the Chancellor first."

Desmond looked at him curiously. "What's there?"

"I need to learn about Vitticus Khou."

CHAPTER 14
AN UNFORTUNATE IDENTITY

From *The Book of Orijin*, **Verse Seventy-Four**
Life is balance. Before Our judgment is cast, you shall answer to Mankind for your sins for a final opportunity to repent before hearing Our Song. There can then be no question that We are unfair or unjust.

LINAS SPIT ON the deck and looked up at Slade. "Rhadames, this idiot has been a disappointment since we found him. No Descendant's Mark, his one courageous moment was killing our other companion, and he has yet to control any fire. I tell you, I am afraid that if we bring this...joke...back we will be tortured. Tell me truly, Rhadames, why we traveled so far and wasted so much of our own time looking for him?"

Rhadames Slade turned from looking off into the sea. "We scoured all of Ashur. I was chosen specifically for the purpose of finding him. It is no mistake. And if," he looked down at Bo'az, "our master is unhappy with what he requested, then you can blame it on me. I will suffer for it. If that is what you are afraid of."

Linas shook his head and spit again. "Enough is enough. We should tell him the truth about who he is going to see. He is tied up; he cannot run. Even still, what would he do, swim to escape? Baltaszar, do you really think you are being brought to see Darian?"

He shrugged his shoulders and instantly regretted it, as his arms both scratched against this mast of the boat. "I never had any reason to believe otherwise. I barely even know who Darian is, aside from his name." Slade looked at him with a frustrated countenance. "What? Look, I get it. You all think I'm stupid and a waste of the effort. You don't have to keep saying it. Just tell me what it is that I don't understand."

Linas stroked his beard; likely his mouth was out of spit. "Near eighteen years old, boy, and nobody bothered to inform you that Darian, your beloved and precious Harbinger, has been dead for thousands of years? Are you so dense? All of Ashur celebrates the man. For Orijin's sake, your whole culture and way of living is based around his death and the events that led up to it. The whole reason Ashur is the way it is, is because the man killed himself flooding the world. And you don't know anything about him? And you think he's alive? Slade, what am I missing here?"

What is he talking about? Father never told us about any of that. Bo'az glanced toward Slade for help, who nodded to affirm what Linas had said. "My father never taught…me…about anything you just said. What are you talking about?"

Linas sighed deeply. "The Orijin and his Harbingers? First the Three, then the Five? The Red Harbinger? Not familiar?" Bo'az felt lost. "You've never heard of Magnus, Cerys, Taurean, Darian, Jahmash, Abram, Gideon, or Lionel? You have no idea who they are?" The way Linas stared at him dumbfounded, Bo'az swore a second head had grown from his neck. "You asked us if we were taking you to Darian! Why would you mention that name, of all names, but know nothing of him? This is frustrating me, Rhadames. I am beginning to wish that Gibreel pushed him off the mountain instead of the girl."

Slade responded tacitly. "Calm yourself, Linas. It will be sorted out once we get there."

Bo'az grew more confused by the moment. "Look, all my father ever taught me about the Orijin was…that there is one and that there are three rings that await us in the afterlife: Omneitria, Oblivion, and Opprobrium, depending on how we live our lives now. None of the extra bunkum that you spoke about. Nobody in my entire village ever mentioned any of it, even once. How do I know that you are not mistaken?"

Linas finally smiled, but it wasn't one that made Bo'az feel at ease. "Because you are going to see Jahmash, fool!"

Bo'az got the feeling that what he was being told was a great deal more profound than he could grasp. He looked back and forth between Linas and Slade, the latter's face bearing and expression of guilt and regret. "And obviously that is a bad thing?"

"Maybe Gibreel was that much more intuitive than I. I wonder if this is what he saw in you from the beginning and I was merely too blind. Or stupid. Baltaszar, if Jahmash wants you, then your life is likely over, one way or another. He would not dare tell peons like me and Slade what he truly wants. But I am sure it involves using you, likely for your manifestation."

"So he needs me for something special. Why is this Jahmash such a bad person?"

Linas shook his head. "Seriously? It angers me that I even have to explain this. Thousands of years ago, Orijin chose five Harbingers to bring order to the world. Mankind had become very corrupt and vain, so these five were charged with the task of fixing things. Once they did set the world right, Jahmash killed three of them. Darian was the only other, and he forced Jahmash to follow him. This sea was never here before then. Darian could control the water, so he flooded the world and stranded Jahmash on an island so that Jahmash could not harm anyone else."

"So now you're talking about magic and a lot of crazy things. And you're saying that this Jahmash has been alive for thousands of years? But I'm the stupid one?"

Linas palmed his head. "You know what, I am finished talking to you. Jahmash can sort out your idiocy when we get to him in a few days."

"A few days?! We've already been sailing for several days! What are both of you even getting out of this that you would hunt me down, lie to me, drag me along this damned journey, and then tell me that you're bringing me to a man who just wants to exploit me?" A sense of desperation formed in the back of Bo'az's mind. "Is your reward so great that you are willing to sacrifice someone else's life? I know, I know, you get to go home to your family. And in the process, you have destroyed all that is left of mine! My parents are dead and I am all that remains." He nervously glanced at Slade. "Your whole nonsense story about your daughters and crying and all that— I don't feel sorry for you, coward. You're compromising my life because you are too afraid to stand up for your own."

Linas opened his mouth to respond, but Slade grasped his shoulder and stopped him. "That is enough. You should be the last person to speak of dishonesty and cowardice, boy. You have whined nonstop since leaving your house and the only times you dared abandon your cowardice were when you were worried about the girl. And where did that even get you and her? Despite your efforts, she is dead now. Before you dare judge us for our actions and sins, accept the reality of your own life. We have done nothing but coddle you this whole time." Bo'az could feel his face redden. He hadn't expected Slade to be so direct and curt. He looked down at the deck to avoid eye contact. Slade continued, "I see. You dislike the truth, yet demand it from us. Perhaps you will reconsider the next time you question another man's motives."

As Slade walked away toward the front of the boat, Linas walked closer to Bo'az. Linas grabbed his torn shirt and lifted him to stand. He loosened Bo'az's manacles and then punched Bo'az in the jaw, knocking him to the ground. Despite the pain, Bo'az had grown used to it over the past few days. Since they'd gotten to the boat, the routine was to stun Bo'az as soon as the manacles were undone. In truth, Bo'az preferred Slade's punches to Linas'. Slade had a tendency to only hit hard enough to knock Bo'az down. Every time Linas hit him, the pain lingered.

Linas secured the manacles once more and lifted Bo'az back to his feet. Bo'az forced himself to walk, despite the daze making him clumsy. If he didn't walk, Linas would drag him the whole way. Linas brought Bo'az below deck to his quarters, which really was only a corner where empty sacks had been laid on the floor for him to sleep. Bo'az knew what came next and almost cringed at the thought. Whenever they brought him down here, they would hit him again, but hard enough to knock him unconscious.

The previous morning, Linas hadn't knocked him out on the first try and Bo'az hadn't been clever enough to lie still. Instead he smugly moved around, thinking he'd gotten the better of Linas. Linas had responded by hitting him a few more times, even harder. Bo'az had thrown up when he awoke later on. He'd learned quickly and did not make the same mistake last night. It was Linas again who had brought him down and after the first strike Bo'az closed his eyes and lay still, clenching his jaw so hard that he was surprised his teeth hadn't cracked.

Bo'az lay still with his eyes closed, expecting Linas' kick or punch to come at any time. By the time Bo'az realized there was no hit coming and opened his eye, Linas was already gone.

***

Bo'az awoke with a startle, not remembering that he had fallen asleep. As he looked around, the long shadows and dim light revealed that the sun was either setting or rising.

He pushed himself up to a sitting position and leaned back against the wall. One thing he was thankful for, and likely the only thing, was that Linas and Slade had always left his hands in front of his body when they manacled him before knocking him out. From the day that he'd killed Gibreel until they reached the boat, Bo'az's hands had been behind his back the entire time. His shoulders and back ached continually, even when his hands were tied in front. His broken arm still hurt incredibly, but luckily for Bo'az, the manacles did not position his forearm awkwardly. In the past few days, Bo'az somehow had gotten very accustomed to pain.

Bo'az jolted again when he looked up and saw Slade sitting on the ground only a few feet away. "Have you come to break me down even more? I thought at least you were on my side after what you told me in the mountains. But you are no better than Linas, are you?"

Slade put up a hand, gesturing for Bo'az to stop talking, and then whispered, "Quiet. Linas has gone to sleep and he assumes you are sleeping as well. I was harsh with you up top because Linas needs to believe that he and I are no different. Well, truthfully, I was also harsh because it was necessary. You have a habit of talking too much and letting your emotions overrule your sensibility. That is something that you need to control."

Bo'az whispered back, "Why did you not tell me the truth about where we're going?"

"Would it have mattered? Would you have known the difference between Jahmash and Darian?" Bo'az reluctantly shook his head. "The night before we found you, I spoke to your brother. He knew nothing of Darian or the other Harbingers. It would have taken too long to explain the whole truth to you. And it was better for your spirits that you didn't know."

"If you are really trying to help me, then why did you agree to bring me to see this man? You said something about owing my father, but from the looks of things, you're just bringing me off to be killed."

"None of this was supposed to happen, Baltaszar."

"Bo'az." Bo'az wasn't sure if Slade had even known his real name.

"Bo'az. You were never supposed to come with us. Neither was your brother. I accompanied Linas and Gibreel because I intended to stall them and throw them off. Neither of them, nor Jahmash, knew of my true intentions. All they know is that I am very good at finding people and that I would be able to track down Baltaszar. I brought Linas and Gibreel through all of Ashur looking for your brother."

"Ashur?"

"Right. If you had ever thought to leave your town, there is a whole continent beyond the forest. It is called Ashur. I brought Linas and Gibreel to every nation in Ashur and nearly every city over the last few years. I knew where your father really lived, so I stayed away for as long as possible. I thought that if I had stalled long enough, Baltaszar would have left for the House of Darian by the time we arrived in Haedon."

"So Tasz was telling me the truth." Slade tilted his head at Bo'az. "Baltaszar. I call him Tasz. He told me he was leaving Haedon to search for some House. He wanted me to go with him. I thought he was crazy for believing some stranger, which it turns out was you, wasn't it?"

"It was. But why did you stay? I came to Haedon at that specific time because I knew your brother had not been in the town in weeks. The plan was for Linas to interrogate the town after I told him of your father's death. By that time, Baltaszar would have had at least a day's head start on us. Linas insisted on starting at your house and I agreed because…well, because I had no idea about you. All this time, I thought it was only Baltaszar."

"What do you mean?"

"The last time I saw your father, your mother was still pregnant with the two of you. Obviously they had no idea they were having twins. They told me then that if they had a girl, she would be named 'Sarai'. If it was a boy: 'Baltaszar'. I had gotten word years ago that they'd had a boy, so I knew Baltaszar existed. But when you walked out of that house and there was no line on your face…I knew you were not Baltaszar. By then, it was too late, though. Gibreel would have killed you quickly if he knew you were Baltaszar's brother, and not actually Baltaszar. The only way to save you was to lie to them."

"Sooner or later, someone will realize I am not Baltaszar. And when that happens, I am going to die. Yasaman was right, there is no way out of any of this. Coming with you three was a death sentence." Bo'az said the words more calmly than he'd expected.

"You should have more faith in me than that. I have kept you alive this long despite some bruises and broken bones. And truthfully, the broken arm had nothing to do with me. Once we arrive at Jahmash's fortress and are brought to him, the best course of action will be to tell him the truth."

"Fortress? I thought the man lived on a small, remote island. How does he have a fortress?"

"The man has been alive for thousands of years and has the exceptional capability of controlling weak-minded people. You should be very wary of that, actually. If you are not strong-willed and if you lose your focus easily, he will be able to look into your mind and make you do things against your will. That is how he has a fortress. He found other men who could build it for him."

Bo'az nodded, though the room had become so dark that he doubted Slade could see him. "Very well. But why tell him the truth? Are I not worth more if he thinks I am Baltaszar?"

"That is the part of my plan with which you will likely not agree." Slade sighed audibly. "The only way to keep you alive is to use you as a bargaining piece. As bait. We have to convince Jahmash that Baltaszar would willingly come to him to save you. If Jahmash believes he can lure Baltaszar by keeping you prisoner, then you will become extremely valuable to him. Although he may kill me and Linas for failing to retrieve your brother."

"Why? Why is Baltaszar so damn important? You are all so afraid of this Jahmash? Why does he need my brother so badly then if he is capable of all these miraculous things? What is so bloody special about Baltaszar?"

"You likely already know and simply do not realize it. Linas told you that Jahmash is deathly afraid of water. As long as this sea separates Jahmash and Ashur, he cannot follow through on any of his threats and cannot carry out revenge. Baltaszar is the one who can eliminate that threat."

"But how?"

"All of those fires that occurred throughout Haedon. All of them were caused by Baltaszar."

Bo'az shook his head, "No. He was in a different room when the Jobens' kitchen caught fire."

Slade snickered, "Baltaszar is a Descendant. He does not need to physically start it. He needs only his mind."

Bo'az grew angry. "Then why did he cause so much trouble? Our father died because he was blamed for them. That goddamned cretin-he did all of it and let our father die for his deeds."

"Keep your voice down. Joakwin did so willingly. Toward the end of his life, your father knew he was a fool to think he could keep Baltaszar hidden. He accepted death because he knew it was the only way to get Baltaszar to leave Haedon. Believe me, I tried to convince your father otherwise a long time ago. I see where you and Baltaszar get your stubbornness from."

Tears formed in Bo'az's eyes and he quickly wiped them away. Anger filled him. Anger at Baltaszar. At his father. At the whole world. He swallowed hard before speaking again. "So what...Baltaszar is supposed to burn away the sea for Jahmash? Is that what he expects my brother to do?"

"Precisely. Jahmash has not told most people of his plan because he wants Baltaszar first. And the only reason I know is because I know what Baltaszar can do. But Jahmash is very powerful. He assumes that once he has Baltaszar, he can control him and force him to eradicate the sea."

"And what if Baltaszar does not come? What if he decides to be selfish or thinks that I am a worthy sacrifice for the rest of the world? If our roles were switched, it would not be such an easy decision for me."

"You need to let go of your resentment. Your anger is based on things that are beyond Baltaszar's control."

"Beyond his control? Why is he so bloody special and not me? We are twins. What magic do I have?"

"That is the way it works sometimes. I have seen other cases where one sibling bears the Mark while the other does not. It depends on the faith of the person. Baltaszar has borne that Mark since you were barely little boys. Normally a person is not eligible for it until around six years. I would imagine his faith is stronger than yours, especially for him to earn his mark so young. Baltaszar is your only hope to survive. You would do well to keep faith in him and hope that he is a better person than you."

Bo'az snorted. "Better? If he never had that damn Mark, I would not be here in the first place."

Slade stood up. "I wonder how he'll react once he finds out that you pretended to be him, and then laid with the girl he loves, just before she died. Perhaps if he had that knowledge, he might not come for you at all. Like I told you before, consider your own sins before you scrutinize anyone else. You have so much anger. Why? Because of what happened to your father? That night that I met Baltaszar, he found me at your father's dead body. He had come back to retrieve it so he could bury Joakwin. Where were you then if you cared so much for your father? Why was Baltaszar alone?" Bo'az mumbled as Slade turned and walked away. Slade turned back, "What was that, boy?"

"Nothing. I was talking to myself." With that, Slade ascended to the boat's deck. *I said 'Rot in Opprobrium,' you stupid prat.*

***

For the next few days, Bo'az barely moved of his own accord, except to eat and relieve himself. When Linas and Slade wanted to move him, they dragged him below deck or up onto the deck. The rest of the world could do what it wanted. He was merely a pawn and had no say in how anything turned out.

Bo'az sat against the wall below deck, resting his head against it with his eyes closed. If his death was inevitable, he would find as much peace as he could.

For the first time in days, Slade sat down near him. "We have arrived, Bo'az. Whatever anger, hatred, or ill will you have toward me, or anyone else, you must let it go now." Slade paused for a response, but Bo'az had had enough of talking. "I imagine they will bring us directly to Jahmash.

Our return will mean only one thing for him, that he now has Baltaszar in his possession. No matter what emotions you feel now, let them go before you are brought to Jahmash. You will need all of your focus, all of your strength, to keep your mind from him. And that still may not be enough. Remember that we are telling him who you really are. It is the only chance of keeping you alive."

Bo'az sniffed a sort of laugh at that. A group of men descended into the room. Before Slade could turn completely, three men forced him onto his back and cuffed his hands behind him. Four more surrounded Bo'az and did the same. Three held him down while the fourth covered Bo'az's head with a sack. He was helped to his feet and then led to the deck of the boat. None of their captors spoke a word to them or even to each other the whole time. Bo'az instantly wished he'd been nicer to Slade during the past few days. They'd descended down a steep ramp and Bo'az assumed they'd left the boat. Shortly after, he was lifted onto what he assumed was a horse, and the rider sat behind him. He could no longer even be sure that Slade was near him. They rode on for several minutes and then stopped to dismount. Bo'az was lifted horizontally and several arms wrapped around his body. He bounced along in their grasp for another few minutes and finally he was allowed to stand again. The sack was removed from his head and Bo'az looked around to see Linas to his left and Slade to his right, standing in a small wooden room.

Four of the men stood against the wall to the right, each with a spear in hand.

"Welcome, friends." A deep voice came from behind them as the door shut. A light copper-skinned man, nearly a foot taller than Bo'az and nearly as tall as Linas and Slade, circled around them and stood a few paces in front of Bo'az. The man smiled at them and eyed all three up and down. He stared at Bo'az the longest. He turned and walked to the opposite wall and sat in a cushioned wooden chair facing them. "Well, is this my Baltaszar? He is certainly more battered and bruised than I was expecting. Master Nasreddine, was this boy a problem during your voyage?" The man, whom Bo'az assumed to be Jahmash, spoke slowly and deliberately to the point that Bo'az almost felt that Jahmash was toying with them. *Focus.*

Linas cleared his throat and spoke solemnly. "He...he was not a problem, Lord Jahmash. Just...quite stubborn. There were many times when he...he needed to be put in his place."

The man's grin grew wider than before. "Ah. Was he not thrilled to be coming to see me?" Bo'az could also sense arrogance in Jahmash's tone, yet it was so subtle that he could not be certain of it.

"My lord, he...he did not know of your existence until a few days ago. The source of his anger was that he was taken against his will. And...and that his lover was killed by Gibreel."

"You dared to bring a companion, Master Kontez. I imagine she proved to be a burden, and that is why Master Casteghar killed her?" Linas nodded. "Where is Gibreel Casteghar, then? Surely he is overjoyed to return so that I may send him on another journey. How that man loves to kill."

Linas cleared his throat again and paused before speaking. "My lord...the boy killed Gibreel. He pushed him off of a mountain." Linas stared intently at the ground."

Jahmash showed no emotion at any of the news. "Killed Gibreel. I suppose his personality did not afford him any favors, but you killed one of my favorite soldiers, Master Kontez. That is your first offense against me."

Bo'az knew he should be afraid of Jahmash, but his mannerisms and even the way he spoke made him seem incredibly harmless. Even likeable. Bo'az could see how a man so charismatic could have a fortress and followers, and why Slade had stressed so much about this meeting. "I apologize for my offense, sir. Gibreel killed the girl I loved. Surely you would have done the same?" Bo'az could feel Slade staring at him. *Have I overstepped my boundaries by explaining myself? Could I have offended him? Light of Orijin, stop talking you fool!*

Jahmash showed no evidence of having taken offense. He remained reclined in his chair and spoke matter-of-factly. "If there is something I might relate with, it is the anger and rage that come with losing a loved one, whether in death or betrayal." He squinted at Bo'az. "Do you have more news to share with me, Master Kontez?"

Bo'az's heart pounded. *Should I have anything else to say? What does he want to know?* Bo'az looked at Slade, hoping for some sort of help. Slade closed his eyes and nodded. *What does that mean? What...oh.* "There...is...something. We...I think you should know. I am...I am not...Baltaszar Kontez."

"What!" Linas turned to Bo'az and looked like he would have strangled him, had his hands not been tied. One of the soldiers used a spear to jab Linas in the back, sending him to his knees.

"Master Nasreddine. This boy is clearly not Baltaszar Kontez. He does not bear the Descendant's Mark."

"Rhadames told me that it was him! Why would I believe otherwise! Rhadames came with us so that he could identify the boy! That was his job!"

"Indeed. It was his job." Jahmash glanced at Slade and back at Linas. "But you were the leader of this expedition. His faults are yours. Master Slade clearly lied to you. And we shall discern the reason for that shortly. There is something more important that I would like to know first. You are not Baltaszar Kontez. We know that. But then, who are you? How have you managed to fool my three collectors?"

Some of the nervousness left Bo'az. His heart calmed slightly. "I am Bo'az Kontez. Baltaszar is my twin brother."

Jahmash rubbed his short dark brown hair then stroked his stubbly beard. His face was angular and sharp, yet powerful. He looked at Slade.

"And Master Slade, were you aware of this when you found him? And when you lied to Master Nasreddine?"

Slade took a deep breath. "I knew he was not Baltaszar right away. I assumed they were twins. This boy looks just like his father. I knew he must be related to Baltaszar."

"I charged you three with this mission over three years ago. Why is it that, in all that time, you could not find Baltaszar Kontez? Why do you have his ordinary brother here instead?"

Linas spoke first. "My lord, I apologize. Clearly if I had known, this would not have happened. I would not have allowed us to return without Baltaszar! Slade even said that he would take the blame!"

"Linas. Come here. Let me show you something." Linas arose and walked toward Jahmash, though he looked to be straining to stand still. "Face your peers. Do you see them?"

"Yes, my lord."

"How? Jahmash's voice maintained a pleasant, yet deliberate tone. "How could you possibly see them? You are so blind that you could not tell the difference between a Descendant and this ordinary boy. Now tell me, do you see them?"

Linas furrowed his brow. "No, my lord."

"Very good, Linas. Very good. You are so blind that you do not see things right in front of you."

"I do not, my lord," Linas said, flatly.

Linas' hands moved to his face, twitching the whole time while Jahmash spoke to him. "And if you are so blind, then you do not need your eyes for anything. Obviously, they betray you." Jahmash had spoken so soothingly that Bo'az would never have guessed what came next. As Jahmash finished speaking, Linas silently dug his fingers into his eyes and pulled them out of his face.

Bo'az shut his eyes tightly and fought the urge to vomit. At first, he had no idea how a man could do that to himself and not scream from the pain. Only then did Bo'az truly understand just how powerful Jahmash was. He opened his eyes, but tried to focus on something besides Linas. Simultaneously, Bo'az and Slade were hit in the chest by small objects. Only when Bo'az looked at his feet did he realize that Linas had thrown an eyeball at each of them. Bo'az gagged and recomposed himself.

Jahmash spoke again. "You are now just as useful as you previously were. Only now, you cannot be deceived by your eyes. Do you understand?"

Linas said plainly, "I understand, my lord."

"Very good." Jahmash grinned widely again and spoke to Linas as if he was encouraging the man. "Perhaps you might even gain the gift of prophecy now, just like those Blind Men."

"If I am lucky, my lord." Linas jolted and fell to the ground screaming. His hands clung to his face and he rocked back and forth. Bo'az assumed that Jahmash had released whatever control he'd taken of Linas' mind. Jahmash raised a hand to his soldiers. Two walked to Linas and carried him out. Bo'az continued to hear Linas' screams for several minutes after he'd left.

Jahmash turned his attention toward Bo'az and Slade once more, speaking just as pleasantly as if nothing out of the ordinary had just occurred. "Gentlemen. Now you may explain to me why we have arrived at this situation. Bo'az, while I am sure you are a charming young man, I am still quite disturbed that you stand before me rather than Baltaszar Kontez. Master Slade, why do you bring me a dog when I clearly asked for a lion?"

Slade stared down at Linas' eye for a few moments before answering. "It was not until we had searched almost all of Ashur that I had heard rumors of Baltaszar Kontez's true whereabouts. His father was not originally from Ashur, so I did not know where they might reside. It turns out that Joakwin Kontez had been hiding in a small forest village; it was so well hidden that the rest of Ashur had never even heard of it."

"You are not answering my question, Master Slade."

"I apologize if my words sound like pretense. I am getting to the point. It had taken me so long to find Kontez's village that by the time we did get there, Baltaszar had left for the House of Darian." A glimmer of anger flashed across Jahmash's face for a split-second, and then it was gone. If Bo'az's eyes had not been focused intently on Jahmash, he would have missed it. "At that point, I thought that if we attempted to capture Baltaszar, it would cost us our lives. According to the rumors, his manifestation is a dangerous one. Surely he would not be traveling to the House of Darian alone. I chose to stop tracking him because I thought there was a strong possibility that he'd found other Descendants. If that was true, we would surely fail in capturing him.

"Believe me Lord Jahmash, I understood clearly that this choice would make you unhappy. But in both scenarios, Baltaszar would have escaped us. I chose the path that kept us alive. Bo'az Kontez stands before you because he is our only bargaining piece. If you hold him prisoner, I can go back to Ashur and convince Baltaszar to come here. Bo'az is all that remains of his family. Baltaszar would assuredly do your bidding."

Jahmash put a hand to his chin. "Your mind is incredibly strong, Master Slade. Too strong for me to invade. But I do not need to look into it to know that you are being truthful with me. Some of my 'eyes' have confirmed that Baltaszar Kontez currently travels to the House. And he does indeed have allies now. Regardless, it bothers me that you took so long to return to me. But your ability to surmise such a contingency plan makes me regret that I put Nasreddine in charge of your mission instead of you. Perhaps the ability to control my soldiers is not the highest priority."

Slade took a deep breath. "Thank you."

"Nonetheless, you have still failed me. I will send you back to Ashur to retrieve my prize. But with a reminder to not fail again." Jahmash nodded to the two remaining soldiers against the wall and touched a finger to his ear. In seconds, one soldier jabbed Slade in the stomach with a spear and knocked the wind out of him. Slade fell to his hands and knees. The other soldier unsheathed a dagger and severed Slade's right ear. Slade croaked, clenching his stomach with one hand and the side of his head with the other. Jahmash stood up and walked to Bo'az and Slade, who was now breathing heavily and grunting. "Master Slade, you did not listen to me. I wanted Baltaszar and you brought me Bo'az. You have one ear remaining. Hear what I ask. I want Baltaszar Kontez. We have finally found out where the House of...*Darian* is hidden. Once Maqdhuum returns, we will amass an army so large that one thousand Descendants could not stop it. You will travel to the House with Drahkunov and Maqdhuum. Their armies will destroy the House of Darian and as many Descendants as they can. You will bring me Baltaszar Kontez. If you fail me this time, you will lose more than your other ear."

CHAPTER 15
THE HOUSE OF DARIAN

From *The Book of Orijin,* **Verse Fifty-Two**
*Use balance in grasping the past. Grasp it tightly enough that you
may learn from it. Grasp it loosely enough that it does not replace
your future.*

AS THEY RODE across the desert plain toward a small range of
mountains, Baltaszar realized that he'd become so lost in his thoughts
that most parts of the ride had become a blur. He'd gained nothing of
use about Vitticus Khou–nothing that could prove Khou and Oran
Von were the same man. But Baltaszar was not deterred. He had a
talent for remembering faces–he could still picture Yasaman's
perfectly–and could plainly see that Khou's and Von's faces were
identical. If he could only find someone who had known his father,
perhaps then he might get answers. If he'd remembered correctly,
Slade had mentioned having known his father. But Baltaszar reasoned
that his chances of seeing Slade again were as arbitrary, if not more
so, as their first meeting.

During the entire ride from the City of the Fallen, Baltaszar's
memories and ponderings had consumed him. He kept searching his
mind for some detail about Von that might connect everything, but he
didn't know enough. Most of the time, thoughts of Yasaman invaded
and then he would think about her until something brought him back
to reality–usually a question or comment from one of the others.
Baltaszar decided he would eventually go back to Haedon to see her.
Once he became comfortable at the House of Darian, he would
request permission to return for a few days. First he would find
Yasaman. He still was unsure of what he would say, but he needed to
know where they stood. After that, he would see Von and demand
answers about his father.

Baltaszar's father was another matter. Anger tugged at his mind every time Baltaszar thought about him. *Why didn't he tell me about any of this? Why did he hide me away?* He hoped that Slade had been right about having questions answered at the House of Darian.

"Dismount at the boulders!" Desmond yelled from ahead. Baltaszar focused on the scenery before him. An enormous craggy mountain dominated the horizon. He brought his horse to a halt and dismounted. Boulders densely littered the sandy ground.

A stout man, slightly taller than Baltaszar, in leather armor emerged from behind the boulders. "Welcome back, lads." The man bore a tan complexion, darker than Desmond but lighter than Baltaszar. "Brought some fresh fish, did you?"

Desmond responded, "Ya know how it is, Kadoog'han. We need all the help we can get. Met them at 'The Colored Road'. Nice fellas. Baltaszar an' Horatio."

The man nodded his head toward Baltaszar and Horatio. "The pleasure is mine, lads. Kadoog'han at your service. Shall we proceed, then?"

Badalao answered him. "Yes. Let us not waste time. I am eager to speak to Maven Savaiyon."

Kadoog'han nodded. "Then let's go." He led them through a path in the boulders and they shortly arrived at an opening in the mountain. The others led their horses off to the side and were tying them to posts jutting from the ground. Kadoog'han nodded for Baltaszar and Horatio to do the same. "The portal is not friendly to horses. Descendants found that out the hard way. Long time ago."

Baltaszar's confusion must have been evident as he walked to a post. Desmond informed him, "When they first created the portal ta the House, they tried ta bring the horses through, also. Horses didn't survive it. They learned quickly not ta bring 'em through. We just tie 'em up out here. Not like anyone else is goin' ta take 'em."

"Portal?" Baltaszar was even more confused.

Desmond smiled. "Ye'll see."

They all walked back to Kadoog'han once the horses were tied. He led them into the cave in the mountain. Once they'd walked about twenty feet in, Kadoog'han stopped and waved them forward. "I will see you soon, lads." He looked at Baltaszar. "Stay calm all the way through." Baltaszar nodded and followed the others as they walked forward. For several moments, blackness surrounded him. It was so strong that he could not see the others. The ground remained firm, although Baltaszar could see only darkness beneath him. Baltaszar realized he was traveling forward quickly, despite the fact that he was not moving his body at all, like the world was racing by him.

The world finally rematerialized around him, except that Baltaszar now stood outside enormous doors. They were open and a giant common room could be seen inside. Baltaszar marveled at the intricacy of the design on the front of the House of Darian. It had the look of a castle. The others all stood beside him, in the same positions as in the cave. Baltaszar looked around at them as they all walked through the doorway and into the main common room. "What...was that?"

Badalao turned to him. "We are now on an island off the coast of Ashur. It is the only way to keep the House of Darian safe from those who would seek to harm us. We use a touch portal to reach the island because, as you can see, it gets us here in mere moments. Before it was created, they would walk through a maze of paths in the mountain and then travel by boats."

"So nobody knows where the House actually is?"

"Except for those of us who have stepped foot here, no one knows that it is on an island. Most people throughout Ashur assume that is it in the mountains or underneath it. Now that you are here, you are sworn to keep that secret safe."

Baltaszar nodded. "Understood."

Desmond led them to the left down a drab corridor. "We need ta find Maven Savaiyon. Likely he's talkin ta Marlowe." The hallway eventually opened to another common room.

To the left, two men stood in a doorway, talking. Their voices lowered slightly once they noticed the group. Baltaszar overheard the smaller man telling the larger one, "I have done all I can for the moment, Roland. He will not be killed unjustly. We shall schedule a hearing when there has been enough time to assemble the facts. If you would like to attest to his character, then by all means, do so. We shall speak more on this later. We have company." He patted the taller man on the shoulder and the latter turned toward the group, nodded solemnly, and walked away. The shorter golden-skinned man faced Baltaszar and the group. "Young masters, is there something with which I might help you?" The man stared at Baltaszar long enough that Baltaszar shifted his gaze to his feet.

Marshall was the first to respond, from the back of their group. "If you please, Zin Marlow, we were hoping for details on what happened to Gunnar and Adria, sir."

The man closed his eyes for a moment. "I see. I have discussed the matter with Maven Savaiyon. The details will stay a private matter for the time being." Baltaszar assumed that the man had normally spoken this curtly. Even Desmond hadn't flinched at the man's rejection. "For the time being, I would urge you all to return to your quarters and relax for a short while. Afterwards, have your fellow Descendants tutor you on the lessons that you all missed. Also, have Maven Villem find quarters for…what is your name, young master?" He pointed to Horatio.

"I am Horatio. Horatio Mahd. It is a pleasure to meet you Zin Marlowe." Horatio stepped forward and thrust his arm toward the man. Marlowe, visibly irked, grasped Horatio's forearm and let it go in one swift movement.

"Horatio. Have Maven Villem find appropriate quarters for Horatio. Horatio, I shall send for you later, so that we may become acquainted. Now you should all be on your way. However…Lincan, is the other half of your room occupied?"

"No, Headmaster. Just me."

Marlowe nodded in approval. "Superb. I must speak with Baltaszar for a short while." The rest of the group looked at Baltaszar in surprise. Even Baltaszar himself was beside himself that Marlowe knew his name, and even more so that Marlowe wanted to speak to him privately. "Once I have finished with him, Lincan, he and you shall share quarters. Wait out here until we have finished speaking." Lincan nodded as the rest of the group walked away.

Baltaszar overheard Desmond and Badalao asking each other how Marlowe could have known about Baltaszar. Marlowe turned to Baltaszar. "Come inside, boy. I hopefully have more answers than you have questions." Baltaszar walked into a very plain room. Marlowe gestured for him to sit in a wooden chair at a desk, while Marlowe sat facing him from across the desk. "You are curious about how I know who you are?" Baltaszar nodded. "I knew your father. You look exactly like him."

"I wanted to…"

Marlowe cut him off, "I can only imagine how many questions you have. Let me speak first. Hopefully what I will have to tell you will answer questions. If you have more, you may ask when I have finished. Is that fair?"

Baltaszar took a deep breath. "Sure." *This conversation is going to go the way he wants it to.*

"I trust that, by your age, you are aware of your manifestation?" Baltaszar nodded. "Fire"

"Interesting. Perhaps Joakwin's actions had some sense in them. You may or may not know, but your father and I worked together for a time. I had always hoped we could maintain our correspondence, but he did not share that sentiment. I know that he hid you away from the world, so I must determine how much you actually know of Ashur. There is much to discuss and I would prefer to not tell you things that you already know. Your father hid you from the world with the hopes that he might save us from Jahmash. Do you know who that is?" Baltaszar nodded in affirmation. "Always the martyr, Joakwin. What was it that changed his mind about sending you here?"

How well did he actually know my father? "Nothing changed his mind. He's dead. And what does hiding me have to do with Jahmash?"

Marlowe looked down at the desk. "I am truly sorry to hear this. He and I did not always agree, but I had a great deal of respect for him. I still do. We shall get to Jahmash later. This conversation will not be as structured as I had planned. Would you mind telling me how your father died?"

Baltaszar took a deep breath. "I would rather not go into details about it. It's mostly my fault. Nobody in our village knew about manifestations. He took the blame for my fires and they hanged him for it. The whole time, I had no idea that I was the cause. I guess he did. I went to retrieve his body later that night and found a man named Slade. He directed me to this place."

Marlowe's eyes grew wide at the mention of Slade. "Rhadames Slade. That is…interesting."

"Why?"

"Three men knew of your father's whereabouts once he took you into hiding. Slade, myself, and Asarei - a man with whom I have cut my ties. I have many resources throughout Ashur. Asarei has not been seen or heard from since your father went into hiding. Neither has Slade, until you mentioned his name."

Baltaszar furrowed his brow. "What does that mean?"

"I cannot be entirely sure. I have not known anything about his involvements or doings for the past sixteen years. But if he has surfaced in Ashur, then it is because something important is happening. So you had never met Slade before your father's death?"

Too many questions were forming in Baltaszar's mind for him to keep track of everything he wanted to ask. "No, I never did. Wait. Wait, stop. You are going too fast. Why did my father go into hiding in the first place? And where was he from? Since I left Haedon, everyone has assumed I am Shivaani. They don't even believe Haedon is a real place."

Marlowe smirked. "Haedon? That was the name of your village? In the mountains?" Baltaszar nodded. "I thought Khou would have been more clever than that. 'Haedon' literally means 'hidden city' in Imanol–the language of people in the time of the Harbingers. He must have assumed nobody in the village would have thought anything of it."

Baltaszar's eyes widened. "So it *was* Khou there? He and Oran Von are the same man?" Baltaszar leaned forward and folded his arms on the desk. "Why did my father go to him? He's the one who killed my father."

Marlowe held up his palm. "Now you are the one going too fast." He gazed intently into Baltaszar's eyes long enough for Baltaszar to feel uncomfortable. "I will trust you with these secrets. But only because I knew your father. If you tell another soul, if you even repeat any of it in your sleep, I will denounce everything you say and have the entire House believe that you are a liar. Understood?"

Baltaszar nodded. "My word is my bond."

Marlowe smirked again. "Did your father teach you that?"

"Yes. From the time we were little. How exactly did you know him? What did you together?"

"That is a conversation for another time. I think if I were to give you a detailed answer to *all* of your questions, we would be sitting here for a few days. 'My word is my bond' is one of our mottos here. It is important for a Descendant in the House of Darian to have an upstanding reputation. You said from the time we were little. Who is 'we'?"

"My twin brother and I. My father taught me and Bo'az to say that when we were quite young."

Marlowe shook his head. "This conversation is turning into a learning experience for both of us, lad. Your father sent me two letters after we had gone our separate ways. In the first, he informed me that your mother was with child. They were still in Galicea at the time, with your mother's brother. The..."

"My mother had a brother? Is he still alive?"

"There are already too many questions. We shall address that later." Baltaszar huffed. "As I was saying, in the second letter, your father informed me that he was leaving for Khou's village in the Never. It was after your mother was taken and the house had burned down, and Joakwin feared that you would become a target once people noticed that you bore the Descendant's Mark as a boy of only three years old."

What? "My mother was killed in that fire, not taken!"

"Oh no, Baltaszar. Your father made that very clear. He detailed the events of that night quite specifically. Your mother was taken. Her captors would have taken you as well and would have killed your father, only the house spontaneously caught fire and blocked their path. Your father was in the room with you. He wrote that he saw the Mark appear on your face the moment the house caught fire. That was how he knew that you had caused the fire. But he never mentioned that there were two of you."

"Likely to protect Bo'az. Why wouldn't he have told me that she was taken? This whole time I thought she was dead." Tears started to form in the corners of Baltaszar's eyes, but he gritted his teeth until the emotion dissipated.

"Think of your father. I am sure you already know."

"Yeah. He knew I would want to leave Haedon to find her."

"More than that, Baltaszar. If he had told you the truth, it would have contradicted all of his efforts to protect you. He would have had to explain too much, and he brought you to Khou's village to avoid exactly that. The people there are not Ashurians. Vitticus Khou started that village to give certain people refuge. Foreigners with no prospects in Ashur and ostracized from their own nations. You would be surprised at how many people in this land, no matter how nice they seem, are quite cold to those of different backgrounds and colors. We as Descendants experience that regularly. You asked why your father would align himself with Khou. That is why. Joakwin was not Ashurian either. I do not like to share this with others because so many have departed in the name of exploration and never returned. But, your father and Rhadames Slade are proof that there are other lands out there beyond the seas. Joakwin and Slade both came from the nation of Semaajj. And the truth is, there are likely scores of other nations out there of which we are not aware.

"Once your mother was taken, your father did not have many places to which he could turn. I could not justify his staying in the House of Darian without the Mark on his face. Khou was his best option."

Baltaszar's eyes narrowed. "Khou was the one who killed him in the end. I highly doubt that he was my father's best choice."

Marlowe looked directly into Baltaszar's eyes once more. "I knew Vitticus Khou while he still governed the City of the Fallen. That was not in his character to act in such a manner. You said before that your father shouldered the blame for fires–which you later realized were of your own doing. If Khou carried out Joakwin's execution, it is because Joakwin forced him to do so."

"How would you know? You had no idea of my father's doings for the past fourteen years. You just said so."

"That might be so, but Vitticus Khou personally determined the fates of criminals in the City of the Fallen for decades. *Decades.* Do you know how many men he had hanged or killed in any manner during that time?" Baltaszar shook his head. "None. Khou was not a killer. Even to murderers. He believed in the good of all men and that anyone could atone for sin. No, Vitticus Khou did not have your father executed because of personal reasons. If you would like to direct your anger to someone, blame your mother's captors. Or even your father. Those are the parties responsible for your father hiding in that village. That is why we ended our correspondence in the first place. I responded to his letter, urging him to bring you here. I never got a response. I am sure that you know just how stubborn your father was. I could not reason with him, so I stopped trying and just let him be. I hoped that at some point, he might see for himself that he was wrong. His death hurts me a great deal more than you realize. For the past seventeen years, I have always held out hope that we might see each other once again. That we might resolve our differences."

Baltaszar snorted out a breath. "Yeah. At least you knew who my father really was. I'm his son and I had to discover all this from someone else. After he died. I don't really want to think about him right now. Tell me about my mother. Might she still be alive?"

Marlowe sighed and paused for a few moments. "One thing I shall never give you, Baltaszar, is false hope. Your mother, Raya, was abducted fourteen years ago. I find it highly improbable that she would still be alive. I believe the only person who might have knowledge of her would be her brother–your uncle. But that will also prove difficult. Hugo Hammersland has not been seen in the Port of Granis, or anywhere in Galicea, since your father left for the Never. Hugo bore the Mark, but never actually came to the House. He had two daughters, near your age, I believe. But we know nothing of that family's whereabouts any longer." Baltaszar squeezed his temples with his fingertips. "I apologize, Baltaszar. I imagine you came here expecting better news. It is truly disappointing about your mother and uncle, especially considering the prestige of their lineage."

Baltaszar looked up and stared at Marlowe. "What do you mean 'prestige'?"

"Well, at least this is something uplifting. Your mother's family directly descends from Arild Hammersland. He was one of the first Descendants to bear the Mark. It is said that the Orijin communicated with him regularly. Arild eventually penned *The Book of Orijin*, directly from the words of the Orijin. I assume that if you are not familiar with Arild Hammersland, then you know nothing of *The Book of Orijin*?" Baltaszar shook his head. "This book is one of the most sacred of our time, especially for Descendants. Anyone who resides here is required to read it and understand its message. You will do the same in your time here."

Baltaszar snickered. "I believe that our definitions of uplifting might differ. I left Haedon because my father died and a stranger told me that the House of Darian was the best option for me. I left behind my brother and a girl I'd hoped to eventually marry. You've just informed me that my mother was kidnapped and that I have no chance of finding her or any of my other family. What difference does my ancestry make if I will never find my ancestors?"

Marlowe held up his palm. "I understand that you are frustrated. I was merely trying to help you see a piece of light in an otherwise dark story."

Baltaszar took a deep breath. "I appreciate your efforts, I truly do. But the truth of it is that the only family I have left is Bo'az. Once I have gotten settled here, I would like to return to Haedon. I need to ensure that my brother is safe and I would also like to sort out a few affairs."

The annoyance in Marlowe's voice was quite clear. "Why is it that you pups come here and then rush to leave? This is your home now. We are your family now. Everyone you meet here is your brother or sister."

Baltaszar now grew annoyed. "I was not asking for your permission. I am telling you that I need to go back for a few days at most. There are people there that I must see. Believe me, I have no intention of staying in that blasted village. Once everything is in order, which should not take very long, then I shall return. You are right; this place will be my home and my family. But for me to fully accept that, I must be able to have closure with what I've left behind."

"Very well. But before you leave, you must be acclimated here. We provide schooling for all Descendants and you will be no exception to that. Your case is different than others here. Most Descendants who come here understand the nature of the House and the history of this world. I will not object to your request, but I ask that you complete your reading and study of *The Book of Orijin* before doing so. It would be appropriate to at least be familiar with your ancestor's contribution to the world."

Baltaszar waited a few moments to consider. *How long is that going to take? I need to get back. What if Bo'az needs me? What if Yas is waiting for me?* "And once I have finished reading *The Book of Orijin*, you will not object to me leaving?"

"I believe that you will come back. You did not have to come here in the first place. It took a great deal of faith for you to make this journey, so I shall reward your faith with faith of my own. Once you have completed your reading, I will grant your request." Marlowe arose from his seat and walked to the door, beckoning Baltaszar to follow.

Baltaszar hesitated to rise. "But…"

"I know you have many questions. We have nothing *but* time to address them. Believe me. However, I do not have the time to discuss it all at once. You will have several opportunities to meet with me. My word is my bond."

Baltaszar stood reluctantly, "Very well."

"Now go with Lincan. The two of you will share quarters. I have a feeling that the two of you shall get on quite well." Lincan sat on a bench across the room from Marlowe's office, leaning back against the wall with his eyes closed. He opened his eyes as Baltaszar and Marlowe walked out of the office. "Lincan, show Baltaszar to your quarters."

By the time Baltaszar and Lincan reached their quarters, the room had already been furnished with an additional bed and cabinets for Baltaszar. Baltaszar hadn't really thought about it until now, but he'd expected the room to be more spacious. "It isn't much, is it?"

Lincan scratched his head. "We don't spend much time in our quarters anyway. Days here tend to be busy. Don't get me wrong, we have plenty of time to relax, but our days are filled with education, work, duties, and every so often we get to go on missions if Marlowe thinks we've earned it." He sat on his bed and leaned against the wall.

Baltaszar sat on his own bed across the narrow room from Lincan and faced his new roommate. "Do you like it here?"

Lincan smirked. "It's better than where I came from."

"Where's that?"

"Fangh-Haan. Southeast. I know you don't know much about geography and all, but my nation doesn't look favorably on Descendants. My parents were lucky that we lived in a fishing town. Once I developed the Mark, I was basically confined to our boat. My parents told people that I fell over and drowned on a fishing trip. They faked my death and hid me just to keep me alive. Once I was old enough to travel, they snuck me out of Xuyen, my home town, and had me sail off to the Wolf's Paw."

"They sent you off and left you to fend for yourself?"

"For a while. They had to put all their affairs in order. And then even when they did arrive, it took them about two extra weeks because they didn't know where to find me. Five islands make up the Wolf's Paw. Luckily I was on the second one that they checked."

"Man. That's rough. At least for me, people just looked at me awkwardly all the time. I never had to think about running away. Then again, I didn't think there was even a rest of the world until about a week ago."

Lincan smiled. "You really thought that? It hurts my head to try and imagine how you could think that way."

Baltaszar shrugged, "I know. It sounds stupid. And I feel stupid knowing that I thought that way, having seen so much now. But my life was pretty simple. And busy. I guess I just never really had the time to give it much thought, you know? The funny thing is, every single person in Haedon acted as if it was the only village that existed and that there was nothing beyond the forest."

Lincan scratched his head roughly. "So they don't want to be found then. They're all there because they want to be away from the rest of the world."

"Well that becomes incredibly obvious when you're on the outside of it all." Baltaszar glanced at the wooden door of their room. "You said that they keep us pretty busy here? Why is it that we've been able to sit and talk like this? Or is this not going to last much longer?"

"We were out on missions – all of us that you met at that inn, The

Colored Road. The other three – Desmond, Badalao, and Marshall – had been in Marshall's village looking for something, but the mission was cut short because Adria and Gunnar were taken. I was already in the City of the Fallen, looking for some items to help with my healing manifestation. I got bored and went to grab a few pints. Ladies tend to be attracted to that place–the type of ladies that love to get a little drunk and crazy, especially with Descendants.

"Anyway, Marlowe gives us a small grace period to relax when we return from missions. That way we don't have to overexert ourselves as soon as we return. I assume since you just arrived here, he's allowing you the same privilege so that you're not overwhelmed. Don't worry; he will have certain expectations of you soon. Enjoy this while it lasts."

Baltaszar nodded, "Got it."

"Do people call you anything? Or do I have to say Baltaszar every time?"

Baltaszar smirked. "Back home they called me 'Tasz'. Well a few people did, anyway."

Lincan contemplated. "Tasz works. Or do you prefer 'Balt'? I could call you Balt from now on."

"Tasz will do just fine. What about you? 'Linc' or 'Can'?"

Lincan glared at Baltaszar with a somewhat suppressed smile. "Linc."

"How long have you been here?"

Lincan scratched his head once more. "Less than a year. Honestly, I should have come earlier. My parents were reluctant to let me go for a while, though. I think they felt guilty for sending me off the first time. Almost like they thought I felt unwanted or unloved by them. I understood why they did everything, though. This world isn't good or bad. It's just full of people who fall in the middle of all that. Sometimes good people have to do bad things. Go against their consciences. But when you think about what options they have, the choice they make isn't really such a bad thing. My parents sent me away because it was my best chance at staying alive. That's all it was." Lincan looked up at Baltaszar. "What about you, Tasz? How did you actually end up coming here?"

Baltaszar sighed deeply and waited a moment to speak. "It's not a story that I feel like retelling every time I meet a new person here. Can you help me with something?"

Lincan nodded, "Of course."

"If people ask, or if I happen to be mentioned in conversation, just tell my story. It'll be easier for me to get acclimated if people know about my situation already. I'm not saying you have to go around telling everyone about me, but…"

"I get it. That's no problem. If you don't want to talk about it right now, I understand."

"I don't mind telling you. The way I see it, we'll be seeing each other every day—you might as well get to know me pretty well. The thing is, my father lied to me about this line for my whole life. I feel stupid that I thought it was a scar for so long, but to be honest, I never had any reason to think otherwise. And it's not like anyone else in that stupid town ever said it was anything different, so how was I supposed to know? Anyway, my father ended up taking the fall for my manifestation, because people accused him of starting all the fires and I guess he didn't want to put me in danger."

"So your village…"

"Haedon."

Lincan looked at him quizzically. "People in Haedon were all opposed to Descendants? But wouldn't they know what was on your face, then?"

"No…the people there," Baltaszar thought about Marlowe swearing him to secrecy, "they just didn't know about any of it. I don't know why, considering how the rest of the world is. But that's the reason my father was executed in the first place. Everyone in town accused him of practicing dark magic. There was no way he would've gotten out of being killed." Baltaszar was unsure of whether he was actually defending Oran Von. "Anyway, my twin brother and I left Haedon the night my father was executed. We ended up going separate ways because my brother didn't trust where I was going. Bo'az has always been somewhat hesitant about tough decisions. He wanted to stay there and go back to our house. He wasn't ready to leave yet. Someone named Slade tracked me down in my village and told me to find my way here. He pointed me in the right direction and what he said made sense, so I listened."

"Someone named Slade? You didn't know this person?"

"He apparently knew my father and knew of me. He knew things about me that no one had any business knowing. Besides, where else did I have to go? Up until that point, my plans in life were to stay in Haedon, get married if any woman would accept this blasted line on my face, have a family, and get old. Before that night, I had no idea there was even a world beyond the Never. If Slade hadn't found me, my options would have been to either survive in the forest or give in to Bo'az and return to our house. There was likely more danger in those choices than following Slade's instructions. Even now, I have no clue if Bo'az is safe. If people knew he'd returned to our house, his life would be in danger. Marlowe told me that I could go back there once I've finished reading *The Book of Orijin*. Have you read it?"

Lincan scratched his head, "I just finished reading it a few weeks ago. It is a very compelling read."

"What is it even about?"

"One of the first Descendants to bear the Mark wrote it. Arild Hammersland. He was able to communicate with the Orijin. So the book is pretty much the lessons that the Orijin imparted on Hammersland. Rules to live by. How to treat people. History. Mistakes of mankind. Things like that. To be honest, for someone like you, who has very little knowledge of the world, I think it would be very interesting and helpful. I think once you complete it, it wouldn't matter that you lived in the middle of the forest for seventeen years." Lincan gave him a toothy grin.

"Yeah, you're probably right. Besides, it turns out that I'm directly related to this Hammersland guy. That was my mother's surname. So I owe it to my ancestry to read it."

Lincan's eyes shot up as he stared at Baltaszar. "You're a descendant of Hammersland and your mother never mentioned it?"

Baltaszar bit his lip and tightly shook his head. "Do not feel bad when I tell you this, because you had no way of knowing. But, my mother died when I was a few years old. Wait, that's not true any longer. I just found out from Marlowe that my mother was abducted when I was a few years old. I have no recollection of her whatsoever."

Lincan looked down, "Wow. I'm sorry Tasz. It's true, I had no way of knowing; but still, you've had a tough go at life so far. I can't imagine how someone goes through all that you have and isn't just angry all the time."

"I have my moments. I'm not really an angry person, though. I just try to focus on the upside of situations.

"Things will be better here. Trust me. I'm not going to pretend like this place doesn't have its flaws, but I think most people who come here come from a more difficult situation, and end up being happier. I haven't been here that long, but I am glad that I came."

Baltaszar nodded. "Thanks. Have you made many friends here?"

"So far, I've become well acquainted with a few of the others that are new here. You met them all already. And there are more that I am friendly with, just not as close. My biggest goal, though, is to get the girls to flock to this room." Lincan arose from his bed and picked up a wooden contraption held together by strings. "It's been difficult so far, but I think this is the key."

Baltaszar's brow furrowed, "What is it?"

"It's a harp," Lincan chuckled. "Girls love men that can play instruments and the harp is a very sensuous one. I've been practicing for a few months now and nearly every day I leave the door open and play. I think I just have to get a little better at it and that will be the difference."

Baltaszar masked his disbelief. "Sure. Just keep practicing." *He's going to do this every day?*

Just as Baltaszar completed his sentence, the door swung open and Horatio stepped in as if the room had belonged to him. "There you fellas are." He walked in and sat at the edge of Baltaszar's bed. "I was supposed to go back over to speak to Zin Marlowe but I wanted to find you first and see where your room was. I'm one floor up, but I'm sure I'll be around here all the time."

Lincan cut off Horatio's next words, "If you are supposed to meet with Marlowe, I would strongly urge you to go do that now. He does not like to wait, especially for novices like us. Marlowe is a very busy man, very private. He spends much of his time alone in his office. You should go there right now."

"I just wanted to say hello…"

"I'm not kicking you out, Horatio. We'll be here when you have finished. Seriously. A meeting with Marlowe is not to be taken lightly, especially on your first day at the House."

Horatio looked to Baltaszar. "I just met with him, Raish. Lincan is right, the man is all business. That's not the man that you want to annoy as soon as you get here. Like Linc said, we are not going anywhere." Baltaszar had tried to sound as genuine and amiable as possible.

Horatio nodded, "That's true. So…I'll stop in after I speak to him." Lincan glanced at Baltaszar and rolled his eyes. Horatio stood and left the room. "See you later."

As soon as the door had completely shut, Lincan huffed and looked wide-eyed at Baltaszar. "That boy…he's got something missing, right? He's a fish-brain."

Baltaszar laughed, "Horatio is a bit goofy, but he's all right. He means well and just gets excited easily. For all I care, he can be as strange as he wants. He saved my life during a standoff with the King's soldiers. So if it wasn't for him, I wouldn't even be here right now. I'm sure you noticed me limping a bit. If Horatio hadn't killed the King's soldiers and gotten me to Khiry, the best scenario for me would've been a lost leg."

"Fine. I'll refrain from judgments, then. If you're willing to vouch for him, then I'll go easy on him."

***

"And that's where the problem lies. I don't want to throw it away, but if it's too hot for me, then how can it be put to good use?" Lincan cradled the glass jar in his palm. He had purchased it as a guilty pleasure in the City of the Fallen on his last trip. It contained a liquid spirit, a condiment made from venom tail peppers, the hottest he'd ever tasted. The effects had been much worse than he'd expected. For Lincan, it had resulted in frequent races to the outhouse the first night, when he'd mixed a few drops in his soup at dinner.

Baltaszar had tasted a drop from the tip of his finger three days before and spent the whole night awake because of constant tearing, drooling, and numerous trips to the outhouse as well. The same had happened to Horatio, Badalao, Marshall, and Desmond at various points of the past week. Lincan had only given the spirit to a few people to try; he didn't want to get in trouble for causing harm to strangers.

Baltaszar, Desmond, Marshall, Badalao, and Horatio all sat around the dark room with him. One flame existed, hovering in the middle of the room as they sat around it. Lincan had to admit, in the past few months, Baltaszar had learned quite well about using his manifestation. For someone who had only found out about it on his way to the House of Darian, Baltaszar was advancing rather well.

Most of the House slept, and they should have all been doing the same in their respective quarters, but many nights had been like this in the past few weeks. Baltaszar, Lincan's roommate, had been at the House just over a month and they'd gotten on quite well, aside from Baltaszar being a little too sarcastic at times. Horatio was in the room just as much, so it felt as though Lincan had a second roommate. Horatio no longer annoyed him, though. He'd frequently proven to be good company. The six of them had bonded well, and most nights went this way, with all of them sitting in Lincan's and Baltaszar's room, letting the conversation go where it may.

Marshall responded to the dilemma. "That thing should just be thrown out and kept out of everyone's hands. Literally." Lincan couldn't tell if Marshall had suppressed a smile, but the rest of them snickered. A week ago, Marshall, while taking spoonful of the spirit on a dare from Desmond, had a droplet splash into his eye. Desmond had washed his eye while Badalao had run off to retrieve a jug of milk and a loaf of bread for Marshall. Marshall's eye was still red. The six of them were the only ones in the entire House that knew why.

Baltaszar spoke excitedly, "Wait, have any of you told others in the House about the spirit? Does anyone else know about it besides us? He looked around to Lincan and the others with a half-grin. They all shook their heads or mumbled a negative response. He looked at Lincan and then at Badalao.

Lincan grinned; he knew what Baltaszar had in mind. "Lao, you have kitchen duty tomorrow, right?"

Desmond stood up demonstratively. He waved a finger at Lincan and Baltaszar, "I know what ya both have in mind...let's do it!

Badalao arose next to Desmond. "I'll be in the kitchen again tomorrow for dinner." He looked knowingly at the rest of them. "We will definitely be serving soup."

"So how do we ensure that this is successful? I would love for as many people to suffer as much as I have." Marshall waved his fist in the air, as if the success of the plan would bring him vengeance.

Baltaszar spoke from his bed, "The jar is small enough to conceal, especially if we walk to the mess hall in a group. Once we get there, we get on line for dinner and distract any witnesses while Linc gives Lao the jar. Lao, you can dump it in quickly, right?" Badalao nodded a confirmation.

"Right, that would ensure that we don't get bad soup–we'll take ours before Lao dumps the jar in. Then we sit down and eat dinner," Lincan chimed in.

"Linc, you can pass Lao the jar at the counter." Desmond waved his hands about to demonstrate. "Me, Tasz, Raish, an' Marshall will stand aroun' ya an' make sure that nobody else is lookin when that happens. We can't get there too early or else people will notice."

Lincan nodded quickly. He was excited about this plan. They rarely had a chance to have fun within the walls of the House, and the risk involved with this idea had him wishing it was the next day already. "All right, we'll arrive at dinner at the same time we always do. There are still scores of people who usually arrive after us. I think everything is set." The others nodded in approval and departed.

In the past few months since they'd all grown close at the House, they'd caused a great deal of mischief. Innocent mischief, however, such as sabotaging out-houses, spreading untrue gossip, hiding to scare unsuspecting passers-by. Only a fortnight ago, a few of the others had shown up in Lincan's bedroom in the middle of the night. They'd worn masks and hoods, but Lincan had known it was them right away. Marshall had been the leader in a plot to tie Lincan up. They had meant to bring him into the forest and leave him there. Tasz had sworn it was only going to be for an hour or so. As a result, Lincan organized a plot to kidnap Marshall in his sleep and leave him in the common room naked. Marshall had slept through the whole thing and didn't wake up until the morning. He'd been a good sport about it, and was unabashed about everyone looking at him.

This plot would be much worse, yet also better than anything they'd done before.

***

Lincan sat down at the round table and quickly suppressed a smile. Marshall, Desmond, Horatio, and Baltaszar set down their trays and sat, trying to look around without seeming obvious. Marshall asked quietly, "Did Lao say how long it would take? Was he able to do it right away?"

Lincan matched Marshall's volume, "He said he's bonded most of the other kitchen workers, so he should have been able to distract their minds and make them focus on other things while he emptied the jar." *Mission complete. Now we wait and see what happens.* The five of them all received Badalao's thought simultaneously, and looked at one another and smiled.

Desmond pointed out, "Good thing sunset still comes late. Else Lao wouldn'ta been able ta tell us anythin'."

Baltaszar responded, "See? Now we sit here and enjoy the proceedings."

They ate their food slowly, agreeing to save their soup until last, just in case anyone noticed they'd finished their soup and hadn't felt any ill effects. A few minutes later, their plan began to take effect. Lincan heard a girl two tables over exclaim to her friends, "Light of Orijin, the soup is so hot! I can't feel my tongue!"

The men at the table next to them huffed and coughed into their handkerchiefs as tears flowed down their cheeks. Another young man their age jogged past them to the counter, interrupting those who were receiving their dinner trays. He spoke directly to Badalao, waving his hands and fanning his mouth. It took all the fortitude that Lincan and the others could muster not to laugh.

Badalao provided them with another update after a few more people approached him. *Luther overheard the complaints. He told me to add more broth and stir the soup some more.* Lincan could practically hear the laughter in Badalao's voice. Luther was the head of the kitchen and a very stubborn man. The kitchen used his recipes and he hated being criticized. If people were complaining about Luther's soup, nothing much would be done about it. Luther was pompous enough that he likely wouldn't even taste the soup to entertain people's complaints. Lincan appreciated the brilliance of their plan.

As more moments passed by, the room was filled with red, tear-filled faces, hands fanning mouths, gasps, and a ridiculous number of requests for water jug refills. Lincan held no ill will toward any of the people in the large room, and he was sure that his co-conspirators felt the same way, but he could not help but feel a guiltless amusement at the events unfolding. The five of them agreed to depart and leave their soup noticeably untouched, as well as to go directly to their respective quarters to avoid any suspicion.

He and Baltaszar barely spoke before going to sleep. If anyone might've been listening, they wanted to avoid incrimination. Lincan fell asleep quite easily, much more so than he'd anticipated. He woke up early the following morning and roughly scratched his head at the first thought – a rather alarming one - that entered his mind. He craned his head to see Baltaszar sitting up on his bed, against the wall, sketching away on a parchment pad that Maven Savaiyon had given him. He whispered imperatively, "Tasz!" Baltaszar glanced up from his sketchbook. "I just realized-what if the liquid spirit caused some sort of reaction? What if we seriously hurt someone?"

Baltaszar bobbed his head around, entertaining the possibility, and then flashed a smug smile. "Even better: if enough people were affected by the venom tail spirit, guess who would likely have to heal them?"

The thought hit Lincan like a punch in the head. He looked sternly at Baltaszar, "Did you do that intentionally?"

Baltaszar whispered back, "No, I swear I didn't even think about it until I now. I honestly didn't really think the spirit would affect people as much as it did. That soup vat is huge. I assumed it would just dilute." A knock at the door alarmed both of them.

The timing had been too perfect. "Come in, "Lincan responded after a moment.

Maven Delilah walked in, the ever-present smile on her face. Lincan's heart sank. Delilah was in charge of the infirmary. "I am truly sorry to disturb you so early, Lincan. I have some good news and bad news, depending on how you look at it." She didn't wait for a response. "The good news is that we have excused you from all of your normal responsibilities for the next two days. At least." She studied his countenance. "The bad news is that there was a large issue with the mess hall last night and we need you immediately in the infirmary. Dozens of people need to be extensively healed."

"Let me have a moment to get dressed." He expected Maven Delilah to leave the room, forgetting that she was a Daughter of Tahlia from Sundari—where the women knew no discomfort or shame about undressing or being naked. She watched him arise and dress without showing the slightest sense of awkwardness. Daughters of Tahlia generally had no interest in men, except for procreation. They chose women for their romantic and marital partners. The thought didn't lessen any of Lincan's embarrassment while changing his clothes. Once Lincan was ready, Maven Delilah turned and walked out of the room, expecting him to follow. As he left, Baltaszar smiled again, staring intently at his parchment pad. Lincan shook a finger at Baltaszar as he walked by and uttered through gritted teeth, "Intentional or not, I am going to get you back!"

Chapter 16
My Word is My Bond

From *The Book of Orijin*, Verse Forty-Eight
We have created you in wondrous varieties and have breathed into you countless differences. Do not confuse Different for Evil, for Evil causes harm. Others are not evil simply because their customs are different from your own.

HE'D RUN SO FAR and for so long that he'd lost sight of the other boys. Every year the trial was different. This year, all they had been told was to run into the forest at sunset. After ten minutes, the scouts would come to find them. If they could last until the darkness of the evening, they would be accepted for soldier training. The gist of it had sounded so simple, yet only a handful of children were accepted every year. Only children who had reached six years could participate. Any child that was not selected could retry each year up until nine years of age. Most importantly, every child had to receive the facial tattoos before six years, regardless of whether they were taking part or not.

Marshall's chest heaved; he had had no inkling as to why becoming a soldier was so important, other than that it would surely make his parents proud. His cousin Alden had refused to take part and Marshall's parents had voiced their disapproval quite openly. Alden had received his facial markings less than a year ago–two black lines straight down his face, each intersecting an eye. Every child received the same tattoo to start. Ever since then, Marshall had wondered why Alden would go through the pain of the tattoos and then forego soldier training. Surely the agony of the ink was worse than anything else they would face.

Marshall slapped his own face vigorously. Alden did not matter at this point. He looked around as he ran–many of the other children had already stopped running in order to find a decent hiding spot. His friend Cason had kept pace and was running several yards to Marshall's left. Cason had stopped at a tree and had begun climbing. They had discussed the strategy as soon as they were informed of the nature of the trial. Marshall targeted a suitable tree with high, dense branches, and climbed as fast and as high as he could. He and Cason had agreed that they should not hide too close to each other, lest one of them give away the other's location.

Marshall perched upon a somewhat-thick branch and waited. He was a rather wiry six year-old boy, but then most of the others in his village were the same way. Most were always active, helping their fathers with various tasks. Marshall stayed completely still, with the exception of his head swiveling back and forth. The scouts would be nearing soon; in fact, they might have already started searching for the boys. Marshall relaxed. Tensing up would be no help. He focused his eyes in the distance ahead, searching for movement. As he waited, he prayed. Staying hidden had become the most important thing in that moment and just as he'd started whispering requests to the Orijin, shadows bobbed and wavered in the distance.

He and Cason wore dull brown breeches and shirts. As the search party neared, doubt bubbled in Marshall's mind. Though his body would blend, his face and head would still be obvious if not hidden. Marshall prayed more desperately. *Orijin, I beg you, please hide me. Please protect me. I will devote my whole life to honoring you if you please do not let them find me.* Marshall repeated the request over and over as he watched half a dozen men split up to search his and Cason's tree. They'd reached his first and looked curiously into the branches, as if confused. Marshall jerked his head behind the branch and dared not move it again. The voices circled the tree, sure they were missing something. As he heard them finally agree that there was no one in it, a prolonged scream came from Cason's tree.

Marshall darted his eyes to it just in time to see his friend, falling upside down, smash into the ground. Marshall froze. The six men ran toward Cason and huddled around the boy's body. They stayed in the same position for what felt like hours, as Marshall clung to his branch, unable to move. The men eventually arose, the largest with Cason hunched limply over his shoulder. Marshall looked away and clenched his jaw. *No. You are not allowed to cry. You are six years old and a Taurani. You have just passed this trial. Crying is for five year olds and failures. Taurani warriors do not cry. Or mourn. Or show weakness.* After several minutes, Marshall pried himself from the branch and climbed down the tree. A single tear streamed down his cheek and dangled from his chin. He wiped it away quickly.

Marshall gasped and contorted in his bed until he was positive of his surroundings. He had been at the House of Darian for a few months, and Cason's death had regularly haunted his dreams ever since Marlowe's defamation of the Taurani.

In truth, Marshall needed to believe that Marlowe was wrong. If his people were anything like what Marlowe had said, then Marshall had no idea how he could live with himself. Since he had begun reading *The Book of Orijin*, Marshall had not discussed it with anyone. During schooling he tended to keep his mouth shut. The book was actually interesting and that annoyed Marshall even more. He wanted to disagree with it, but the book made sense.

He had been able to control the darkness when Maqdhuum was about to kill him and Aric. The more he dreamed about Cason, the more apparent the connection became. He had prayed desperately in that tree for the scouts to not find him. They were mere feet below, with trained eyes, and did not even suspect that he had been hiding there. The only logical explanation would have been that the Orijin had given him that manifestation then.

And if his people had been going through so much trouble to hide their manifestations, then the tattoos and the trials at age six were all fabrication and meaningless. *Even worse, it would mean that Cason's death meant...*

Marshall shut down the notion and sat up. There were other things to focus his attention on. He still wondered about his mother. She had to have popped up somewhere. Unfortunately, the world was too big beyond the Taurani village for Marshall to be able to even guess where that might be. Marlowe would likely be of no help, so he would have to pursue other avenues. The instructors were the most knowledgeable people at the House, but seeing as how he was only under the tutelage of three of them, Marshall had little idea of specifically who might be able to help.

It was Abraday, and he would have to meet with Maven Savaiyon shortly for his "History of Ashur" lesson, with the other new arrivals. The subject matter was interesting, especially to him and Baltaszar, both of whom knew next to nothing of the world. However, Maven Savaiyon constantly changed the days and times of their lessons because he was always needed to travel.

Marshall didn't bother with breakfast. He usually had no appetite after the dreams about Cason, but along with that, he was not in the mood to talk to the others. Instead he pulled on the first shirt and pair of breeches he found and walked downstairs to the first-floor common room where Maven Savaiyon would be waiting for them.

Maven Savaiyon sat on a stool, eyes closed as if pondering something important. Marshall moved as silently as possible, but Savaiyon opened his eyes at Marshall's entrance into the room. The others would not arrive for another half of an hour.

Savaiyon perked up, "For a lesson this early, no one arrives *earlier* because he has nothing else to do. What can I help you with, Marshall?"

Marshall smirked, somewhat abashed that his intentions were so obvious. "I need some information. I do not know who can help me, though. I do not feel comfortable turning to Marlowe, so I thought that the Mavens might be of some help." It had become clear over the past few months that several Mavens did not see eye to eye with Marlowe on numerous issues. Savaiyon did not openly discuss any dislike of or disagreement with Marlowe, but he had been known to admit to his stance in private and discreet discussions. Marshall had never actually had such a discussion with Savaiyon, but he felt confident in confiding in the man.

"Are you so brazen as to make such presumptions that I or other Mavens would oppose decisions made by Zin Marlowe?" Maven Savaiyon stood at least a foot taller than Marshall, but now his head seemed to be at a level with the ceiling.

Marshall composed himself. "This is not presumption based on the gossiping of little children, Maven Savaiyon. There is a growing faction here that opposes what Marlowe stands for. And while this faction practices great discretion and does nothing to make others aware of its existence, it is known within the faction that you are an ally. I understand, Maven Savaiyon. You are an honorable man. You live with dignity and character. It is understood even within the faction that one does not speak openly about your views or attitude toward Marlowe. And that is why I come to you now. I seek your guidance out of respect. Not brazenness." Marshall had managed to look Savaiyon in the eye without wavering.

Savaiyon eased his posture and sat on the stool. "Good."

Marshall had expected, at the least, that he would be reprimanded for speaking too sharply. "Excuse me?"

"You have heard me correctly, lad. It is good that you would explain your meaning, rather than clumsily try to defend against my accusation. It is true, there are those within the House that oppose Zin Marlowe's way of thinking. Does this make them villains? No. Cowards? Not necessarily. Mistaken? Most likely. Most people in this world make decisions based on what they think is best for those that they love and for whom they care. Do you know anything of the man?"

Marshall shook his head, "No. He explained that he is older than he appears. That is all."

"Zin Marlowe hails from Cerysia, a nation that abhors Descendants. He earned his manifestation at seven years and that was the last he saw of his family. Of Cerysia. I do not know how long ago that was, but once he bore the Mark, Marlowe's parents had him brought to the banks of the Eye of Orijin. They did not have the heart to kill him themselves, so they abandoned him. To make a long story short, Marlowe has nothing in this world except for the House of Darian. We are his family.

"He is very open about his disdain for violence and combat. Especially within these walls. Marlowe will do whatever he thinks is necessary to ensure that the House of Darian is not threatened. For him, that means that its residents must be peaceful. It is bad enough that Prince Garrison hunts us while being a Descendant, himself. For Marlowe, it is enough that the House of Darian exists and harbors Descendants, because it gives us the same opportunity that it gave him.

"The man knows much of this world, especially the worst of it, Marshall. It is easy to judge a man based on his appearance. Based on a conversation. Too often, we do not have the patience to learn about a man before we decide whether he is good or evil. Consider my words before you decide what kind of a man Zin Marlowe is."

Marshall meekly uttered, "I understand. But then why would you oppose him in the first place?"

"I disagree with certain decisions that he has made, because they are not in the best interest of the Descendants. There have been numerous signs pointing to Jahmash's return. In my opinion, Zin Marlowe has placed the safety of Descendants from King Edmund as a higher priority than the world's safety from the Red Harbinger. I do not know whether he genuinely does not believe the signs, or if he refuses to believe them out of stubbornness, but Marlowe's aversion to violence and combat will diminish our ability to protect and defend ourselves from Jahmash. I disagree with Marlowe because I believe that the Descendants need to be proactive in learning to fight, with and without our manifestations. Gunnar had taken strides to begin that process. You saw what happened to him. Even if he is alive, and even if we can save him, we can no longer turn to Gunnar to train us." Savaiyon gave him a suggestive glance.

"I cannot give you a definitive answer right now about training others. You are not the first person to make the suggestion, but I have other affairs to handle before I can make that a priority. And that is why I am here in the first place. I would like some help in deducing where my mother might be. When we returned to my village, I found the remains of my family members, all except for my mother. If she was not there, then she likely managed to escape, possibly with other survivors. There are several instructors here, many who have an intricate understanding of Ashur's history, as well as the histories of specific people. Is there a specific person that might help me narrow the possibilities of where Taurani would go in such a situation? Have knowledge of nations and towns that would welcome my people?"

Savaiyon eyed him curiously, "Your people, specifically your parents, never mentioned possible destinations in such an event?"

"Not to sound facetious or haughty, but the Taurani never considered the notion that we might lose a fight. Surrendering and fleeing were never options to us."

Savaiyon stared with an unfocused gaze for a few moments. "Maximillian. Maven Maximillian instructs a course on the histories and cultures of the Taurani and the Anonymi. You should speak to him."

Marshall perked up. "How do I find him?"

"Maximillian is the groundskeeper of the House. Every morning, he is out tending to the lawns and flora for hours. The only issue is that only Marlowe tends to know exactly where he would be working each day. It would be better to seek Maximillian out during meal time in the dining room." Savaiyon continued, as if knowing Marshall's next question. "He is Cerysian: golden tan skin with short, dark hair and a full, graying beard. He is shorter than you. His eyes…they carry a great deal of wisdom. That is the only way I can explain it, but you will know it when you see him."

"Can you not just show him to me during dinner tonight?"

"Unfortunately, I cannot. Every day now, if I do not need to be here, I am out searching Ashur for Gunnar and Adria."

Marshall attempted to subdue the level of his interest. "Have you had any leads? Anything with which to work?"

Savaiyon pursed his lips in futility. "Nothing. I have been searching for several weeks, in every nation. Not a soul has seen anyone bearing their description. You saw the man who took them. He disappeared even faster than I could create a bridge. Someone with that ability could go anywhere. He might even hide in places I have already checked and I would never know. Or worse. They may not even be in Ashur at all."

"What? Is that even possible?"

"If a man has the ability to disappear into thin air and does not have a Descendant's Mark on his face, then I am afraid that anything is now possible."

As Marshall nodded, others walked in. In total, Maven Savaiyon instructed nine of them. The friends he had made all shared the same schedule, as Descendents were required to learn specific subjects in a set order upon arriving at the House of Darian. Marshall had objected at first, but truthfully, the subject matter had been strikingly interesting. Maven Savaiyon instructed them on the general history of Ashur, Maven Villem covered the history of the Orijin, and until Maven Gunnar had disappeared, he had instructed them on *The Book of Orijin*. Once Gunnar had been abducted, Marlowe had informed them that they would simply have to read the book on their own, as the other instructors were too busy to take them on.

The remaining two courses were enjoyable. Maven Savaiyon taught them with a great deal of passion. He had truly been the perfect Maven to teach them of Ashur, because of his travels. Quite often, he would create a bridge and show them places throughout Ashur first-hand. Maven Villem, on the other hand, was a very animated and funny man. He captured their attention and even allowed for a little ribbing from his students every now and then.

The nine of them sat around the common room, on couches, stools, or the floor. The boys always proved chivalrous and reserved the best couch for Elysia, Taran, and Sindha, the three girls in the group. Luckily, the rest of the group was comprised of Lincan, Baltaszar, Desmond, Badalao, and Horatio. They had already bonded quite well, especially during the caper with the venom tail spirit. They found as much fun as they could, despite what seemed like Marlowe's insistence on the opposite.

Maven Savaiyon had started speaking, but Marshall's mind

wandered, mostly to his mother's whereabouts. In random moments of clarity, he noticed Baltaszar drifting in and out of sleep. Lincan would likely catch Baltaszar up on everything throughout the day. Horatio, Desmond, and Lao stifled laughter while Sindha and Taran both stared dreamily at Lao. It was probable that each did not know the other was also staring.

An hour later, Marshall only realized the lesson was over because the others had arisen and were leaving. Thankfully, Maven Savaiyon had not asked him anything. Marshall stood to follow the others when Savaiyon clasped his shoulder. "I understand your pensiveness today, but do not make it a habit. You need this information much more than most of the others do." Savaiyon offered him a warm smile and walked away.

***

The following morning, Marshall walked across the sprawling lawn toward where Maximillian had said he would be. Marshall had approached him during dinner, but their meeting was short. Maximillian simply confirmed who he was, then informed Marshall to meet him here in the morning.

Marshall had always appreciated the beauty of the landscape around the House of Darian, but he had never thought much about who had made it so. Marshall marveled at the thought that Maximillian maintained the grounds by himself. Alone, it must have taken the man weeks to completely prune and tidy everything. Marshall wondered why nobody had been assigned to work with Maximillian. Perhaps Marlowe was punishing the man for something. Marshall would definitely not put it past the headmaster, especially after he had shown his true colors in their first meeting.

Marshall reached Maximillian, who kneeled on the ground, ripping weeds from beneath a shrub and, judging by the soil to his right, his last one for that section. Before Marshall could even greet him, Maximillian nodded to the next section of shrubs several feet away, and gestured for Marshall to join him in working. Marshall did as was asked. "Maximillian…"

"Max. Call me Max. Do you really want to say 'Maximillian' every time you address me?"

"Max is fine. I have no objection."

"Good. I have already discussed you with Zin Marlowe this morning. As of this morning, you are my new assistant on the grounds."

"Assistant?"

"Ever since Adria disappeared, I have been out here by myself. That is over two months now. I do not even know you, but I would rather talk to you than continue talking to myself for hours every morning. I asked Marlowe immediately for a new assistant, but as you can see, he felt no urgency in the matter." Max's voice reminded Marshall of his father's–deep without being threatening. "After our meeting last evening, I approached Zin Marlowe this morning and requested you as my assistant. I must have caught him while a more pressing issue weighed on his mind, as he agreed dismissively with nothing more than a nod and a wave of the hand."

Marshall grabbed a fistful of soil and kneaded it in his hand. Something wriggled and then squished in his hand. "You worked with Adria?" Marshall had meant to ask something else, but forgot what it was.

"Indeed. Best Descendant here, if you ask me. Did you know her? I did not think that you had arrived in time to have known her."

"Barely. She is the one who found me, left for dead in my village. She is the reason why I am here in the first place. Our time here overlapped for a few days, I believe. It was when we returned to my village that she was taken."

"Ah, so you feel responsible then, do you?" Max had moved onto the same segment of shrubs that Marshall was weeding. "Let me tell you something, Marshall. We are Descendants of Darian, the descendant of Taurean, chosen Harbingers of the Orijin. Our God chooses for us what he will, and we have to accept that."

"Well, that is not necessarily the entirety of it. You see, I…"

"I see it now." Max grinned a wide, toothy grin. "You are smitten."

"I had thought I was hiding it well. Is it so obvious?"

"Marshall, you are one of dozens of young men here who are taken by Adria Varela. If Zin Marlowe actually allowed combat, we could arrange competitions for the right to woo her and even then it would not be enough to impress that girl. The trouble for all of you boys is that Adria is tougher than all of you and she knows it. And to make matters worse, every time a boy summons the courage to try impressing her, he thinks he can win her over by some show of dominance or strength. Adria does not care for such things."

"She has said this to you?"

"She does not need to. All one must do is pay attention to her.

She does not need a young man to be her protector or rescuer. She wants someone who will accept her as an equal, who will take her seriously."

Marshall flung a handful of weeds. "You speak as if you know that she will definitely return."

Max rolled his eyes, "I would think that after one conversation with Adria, you would know enough about her to be sure of that as well. Adria is a fighter. A survivor. Whoever has her, it does not matter. Even if tortured, Adria will be too much for her captors to handle. Trust me, boy, she will return. Likely battered, broken, or injured, but she will survive and find a way back to us."

"Your manifestation is what? Foresight? Wisdom? Or blind faith?"

"Remember yourself, Marshall."

Marshall nodded, "I apologize. That was disrespectful."

"Indeed. I am aware that the notion of manifestations is new to you. But the fact remains that you are now in a place where everyone else sees manifestations as a normal part of their lives, and you must conform. I do not know the nature of how yours came about, but Descendants manifest out of necessity. These gifts do not simply arise from nothing. There is always a situation in which faith and desperation are involved. For many Descendants, a manifestation is what saves them from death." Max's face had grown very tense.

"Was that the nature of yours?" Marshall hesitated. "I apologize once more if I am crossing the line in asking."

Max stared to the sky. "My father used to hit my mother. Sometimes it would be so bad that she could not leave the house for weeks. Sometimes it would extend to me and my older sister, if my mother could not satiate him. One night he got angry while he was holding a knife and slashed my mother's arm. He dropped the knife immediately, perhaps realizing that he wasn't far from killing her. But he looked at me and Victoria, my sister, like we would receive the 'apology' he could not give my mother. From the moment he'd gotten the knife, I prayed and prayed for Orijin to help us. When he walked toward us, I felt the desperation and prayed so hard that I cried. That was the first time I felt it. You know what I mean – the melody in your veins, like your blood is drunk with emotion.

"I pushed Victoria behind me and when my father struck me, I simply absorbed the blow and felt no pain. It must have been the Mark appearing on my face that pushed him over, because he punched and punched until he was exhausted and each time he hit me, I felt stronger and stronger. Once he realized punching did not work, he grabbed my throat. I had not even thought of striking him until that moment. It took me a few seconds to muster the courage to throw a punch. When I finally did though, it sent him through the wall on the opposite side of the room. He stayed there for a while. We left him there, fixed my mother up, and went to sleep. It took me a few days to fully realize what it was that I could do. Turns out I can absorb energy and re-channel it. So if you have ever wondered why the plant-life on this island looks so amazing, it is because I can absorb the energy from the sunlight and use it to help everything grow. However, I only do it once a week, as it requires incredible energy."

Marshall ripped another handful of stringy weeds from the ground. "What happened to him? Your father?"

"He returned a few days later with a few of the King's soldiers. I imagine he knew what had happened to me. Why I'd had the ability to strike back at him with such force. It was illegal, and still is, to bear the Mark in Cerysia. Though I hear King Edmund's firstborn does bear it. They were merciful to me. They arrived in the morning and informed my mother that I had until sundown to leave the country. If no sentry witnessed me leaving through any gates, they would hunt me down and kill me. That was the King's justice–side with the monster who forced his son into the desperate situation that called for the Mark in the first place."

"I assume you obeyed, which is why you are here. Is there such a thing as a comfortable life for a Descendant?"

"My mother, sister, and I traveled through Galicea. They went on to the Wolf's Paw and I continued on to come here. Galiceans do not like Cerysians anyway. I imagine nobody truly does anymore. Even those nations that have formed alliances mostly do so because it brings less scrutiny. *This* is our comfortable life, Marshall. Criticize Marlowe if you will, but we want for nothing at the House of Darian. We have luxuries undreamt of to any Descendant out in the rest of Ashur, believe me."

Marshall shook his head, "Does it not seem like a cruel joke, though? If everything that everyone here says and believes is true, along with that book, then how much of a blessing are these manifestations?"

Max stopped weeding to look Marshall in the face. "There is no such thing as a Descendant who has not faced difficulty. Who has not put his or her faith in the Orijin in the direst of moments. You question the worth of a manifestation, but without it, my mother would have endured beatings, bloodier each time, until she was dead. This place is full of people who have faced similar and worse atrocities. You should learn to respect that."

Marshall turned from Max's gaze. "I apologize. Again, I did not mean to offend. Truthfully, I am enjoying what I am learning here. Though it is difficult to come to terms with, at times, because of my way of life before coming here. I just wonder sometimes, what is the point of the Orijin giving us these manifestations if we are to be confined to an island and not accepted by the world?"

"That is where many of us differ from Marlowe, as I am sure you know. Make no mistake, Jahmash is coming. We do not know when, but it is fate. I hope that his return is after Marlowe's leadership has expired, so that at least the Descendants have an opportunity to defend Ashur, but who knows. All that we can really hope is that what manifestations we do have are enough to stop him if the responsibility falls upon our shoulders."

Marshall noticed a certain sadness creep into Max's eyes and tried to abruptly change the subject. "So will I have to fight you for Adria as well?"

Max chuckled. "You will never have to worry about me in that regard." He eyed Marshall tentatively, as if unsure of whether to say more.

Marshall nodded his head. "I understand. Rest easy, I will not tell anyone." He thought of his cousin, Alden, for a moment.

"Quite astute. Thank you."

They continued working for another hour while Max raved about how observant and aware Marshall seemed to be. Once their knees and arms ached, they walked toward the building where Max informed him they would find Desmond and Baltaszar, who would transport the weeds with levitation and then burn them at the beach on the southern shore of the island.

"There is a reason why I came to speak with you this morning, Max. Truthfully, it had nothing to do with tending the grounds."

"It is of no matter; I would have requested you sooner or later. But tell me your reasoning."

Marshall eyed him speculatively. "I would like some council about my people and potential survivors. Maven Savaiyon informed me that you are an expert on the history of the Taurani. My whole village has been destroyed and the chance of survivors is slim. However, I have reason to believe that my mother might have escaped. When I returned, her body was not with the rest of my family in the rubble of my home. I would like to know if you have suggestions or advice about where she may have gone, assuming that she is alive."

Max stopped walking and turned to face Marshall, though Marshall stood nearly a foot taller. "First, you must truly embrace the possibility that your mother is dead. If we go down this road, I can make no promises about her being alive. I can only give you suggestions based on what I think. Understood?" Marshall nodded. "Good. Your mother's whereabouts all depend on her escape. If she escaped toward the west..."

"That is unlikely. We were attacked from the west. If she had fled that way, she would likely have been killed anyway."

"Unfortunately, that makes things difficult. North would only bring her to water. East would bring her to the Cerysian Wall, or whatever King Edmund calls it. That means that her only option would have been south. It would have been quite possible for her to head south, as she would most likely have come to the Eye of Orijin," Max eyed Marshall, "which of course I must explain to you. It is an enormous lake in the middle of Ashur, and also contains an island that is home to the Tower of the Blind. That is inconsequential right now, however, because the Taurani who know of the Tower do not accept it. The problem is that, if your mother reached the Eye, then she would have many options in terms of where to go. She could feasibly be anywhere in the nations of Mireya or Galicea. Doubtful Cerysia"

Marshall hung his head. "At least it is something. It is more than what I had this morning. Thank you."

"It is nothing. The very least I could do. However, you may want to consider another source. Savaiyon would not disclose this to you because he is too honorable. But he, Adria, and Lincan brought back a soldier when they found you. One of the soldiers who attacked your village. They keep him in the dungeon with the other prisoners, as far as I know. I do not venture down there, so I do not know if they have killed him or not."

Marshall tensed. "They have had him there all this time and no one thought to tell me? I expect that Marlowe would not tell me, given his personality, but nobody else thought that this might be something I would want to know? What happened to this place being a brotherhood? A family?"

Max gestured for Marshall to start walking with him again. "Calm yourself. Raising your voice to me will not help you. You must understand that the soldier was not brought here because of anything to do with you personally. They had planned on questioning him. They want to interrogate him to see if they can find anything out about his general, or about Jahmash. The destruction of your village was much bigger than however it affected you, Marshall. I know that sounds heartless, but such events serve as a dire omen to all of Ashur. Go to the dungeon if you like. You will need a different reason to go down there, however. If you tell them you are there for the soldier, they will ask who sent you. If you say my name, then I shall help you no longer. Simply find a different reason to be there."

Simply? They were not far from the back of the House, "Is there another prisoner that I could request? Someone that it might make sense for me to speak to? It would be stupid of me to show up for an arbitrary reason."

"The only one that I know of is the Prince. But you did not hear that from me either. Only Mavens and those with dungeon responsibilities know, and take an oath of secrecy." As they neared the path that led to the western entrance of the House, Marshall eyed Desmond and Baltaszar waiting for him and Max impatiently. They made no attempt to hide the displeasure on their faces. Just as Marshall was about to lighten their mood with a joke, a blur swished past him, so heavy that it knocked him to the ground. Marshall looked up quickly enough to see the blur stop. It was another Descendant, but the boy took another step and dashed several feet away.

He stopped again and faced Marshall from afar, "This is not a place for clumsy people, Marshall. You should watch where you are going. Or perhaps go back to your people. Ah, never mind that." As Marshall stood, the boy dashed toward him head on and knocked him flat on his back. Marshall pounded his fist against the ground. The boy stood over him. As he turned to dash away again, flames appeared around the boy, completely surrounding him. Marshall looked toward Baltaszar, who nodded at him and half-smiled. As Marshall looked back, the boy rose a few feet in the air and turned upside down as if an invisible hand was moving him. *Desmond.* Baltaszar and Desmond walked closer and stood side by side with Marshall.

Desmond put a hand on Marshall's shoulder and turned to the boy. "Fool. Ya mess with him an' ya mess with a bunch o' us. What's the matter, ya can't swoosh away when yer facin' upward?" Desmond was clearly stronger with his manifestation than this boy, and the boy's countenance indicated that same sentiment.

Max stepped forward and gestured for Desmond and Baltaszar to stop. The boy fell to the ground on his back and quickly tried to stand as the fire dissipated. "Reverron! Do not run away!" The boy turned and faced Max, shame shaping his mouth. His complexion marked him as a Cerysian, just like Max. "I know you to be better than this. And smarter than this. Explain yourself."

Reverron looked at Max and then at Marshall. "I am sworn to secrecy. My word is my bond." With that, Reverron turned and, in a few dashes, retreated into the House.

Max eyed the burnt ground where the fire had just been. "I apologize on his behalf, Marshall. Reverron is not normally that way. Arrogant yes. But not stupid. If he would use his manifestation for violence, especially in front of me, then he was dared or ordered to do so. It looks like your group is not the only one who enjoys mischief."

"But that makes no sense. Why attack me in front of others so blatantly?"

Baltaszar responded, "He was moving so fast that he probably didn't even see me and Desmond. We didn't even notice him until you fell down."

Desmond chimed in. "He probably didn't think we'd help. Baltaszar's right; maybe he didn't even see us either."

Marshall shook his head. "And why the insults? Why insult my people like that? Does he have something against Taurani?"

"It makes sense, if you think about it," Max weighed in. "Reverron never wanted a fight. He wanted a reaction out of you, but it did not work in his favor."

Marshall understood. "He wanted me to fight back. He wanted me to be violent and attack him. But Desmond and Tasz stopped him. And you two did not even use violence. You just contained him. Violence would get me put in the dungeon or expelled from here. So what, does somebody want me to be dismissed from here?"

Max shrugged, "That seems the most logical explanation."

"But who? And why?"

"I do not have an answer for you, my friend. However, Reverron unwittingly gave you an opportunity to get into the dungeon."

Marshall looked at Max curiously, "How's that?"

"He works in the dungeon. Reverron is the one who brings food to his countryman down there." Marshall furrowed his brow in confusion. Max quietly uttered, "The Prince. Remember, he is Cerysian. Reverron is very proud of his people and his nation, despite how they treat Descendants. Find him. Think of a way to threaten him and have him do your bidding. One way or another, you must use this opportunity to get down there if you wish to see...the captive."

Marshall gritted his teeth. "Coward. Let us see how he runs away when I have him by the neck, pinned against a wall. Thank you for the advice, Max. I will extort him. My word is my bond."

CHAPTER 17
SOLITUDE

From *The Book of Orijin*, Verse Three Hundred
O Chosen Ones, We shall challenge you with crucibles more difficult than most can handle. Once you overcome, your faith shall be unbreakable.

"ONLY THE MAVENS and a few others know that you are even here. Most of them would have you hanged. In fact, they grow angrier with each day that you are still alive." Garrison's Uncle Roland sat outside the bars of the dungeon cell. Garrison had not known much of his uncle, and hardly had any recollection of him. Roland Edevane was his mother's older brother and had left Cerysia before Garrison had been born. While he enjoyed the security of having a family member to be concerned for him, Garrison wished that his uncle offered more sympathy and less bluntness.

Garrison had hardly the energy to speak with any gestures of animation. Since he'd been thrown into the bare cell, he'd been given only enough food and drink to keep him alive. Before he had left Cerysia, his physique had been quite full and muscular from rigorous combat training and scores of missions. He now resembled a beggar. "Perhaps you could do more to raise my spirits?"

Roland scoffed and ran his hand over the stubble of hair on his head. "Raise your spirits? Boy, look at your body. They do not treat you this way as some idle threat or as a lesson. The only reason you have any nourishment is because I am here. Did I not make myself clear? These people want to kill you. And rightfully so. How many of our kind did you kill? Torture? Hunt? If I was not your uncle, I would want the same justice. The only argument in your favor is that Orijin knows the hearts of all men. If he manifested his gifts in you, then perhaps you are worth saving. That is the only argument I can present to Zin Marlowe and the Mavens."

"They have to know that I have changed."

"And why is that? Why do they have to know that? Until, what, a year ago, you were hunting them down. Hunting *us* down. You were leading armies throughout Ashur to find them. You struck down so many of them for bearing the very mark that undeservingly stains your face. I want you to do something for me."

Garrison looked Roland in the eye, "What?"

Roland returned the stare. "Recount the last Descendant that you hunted down. Take a few moments to remember, and then tell me the details. I want to know how you felt. How many men you brought. How the killing was done. And how much satisfaction you got from doing it."

"Uncle, I…"

"No. If you are going to refuse, then do not call me that. Tell me what I ask or I shall no longer help you. My word is my bond." Roland stood and turned.

"Wait. I will do it. I will tell you." Garrison closed his eyes and breathed deeply for several moments. He rubbed his face with his hands and then clasped them on his lap. The stone floor felt even harder and colder beneath him. "We were at the Sanai, about to cross into Shivaana. We wanted to watch the animal fights in Sundari–my men had been teasing me about having never seen a vrschika. By then, I had already known that I no longer wanted to kill Descendants, so I thought that would be a nice, time-consuming diversion that would get their minds off of killing.

"Right after we crossed, some of our scouts were waiting for us on the other side with news of a nearly a dozen Descendants hiding in Rayan, a city in Fangh-Haan not far across the Sanai. We had sent those scouts out weeks before–they had taken so long that I did not expect any results. We shifted our course. I could not ignore the findings even if I had wanted. My men smelled blood. They were killers once more. Rayan was less than a day's ride, so there was no stalling. Thirty of us arrived in Rayan just after midday. The gatekeepers did not even protest; they let us right in. We essentially stormed the city. My men invaded a few houses and inns, grabbed random people and dragged them into the center of town. I will never forget the looks on people's faces as we rode through the streets. Nobody objected. They were like cattle accepting that lions had come to thin out their herd. They simply moved aside. If you are unfamiliar with Rayan, it thrives from its fishing industry. Every wide road in the town has large wooden platforms lining the middle of the street; a stranger would assume that Rayanese love to hang people, but the platforms are used to weigh their hauls.

"We brought our hostages to the center, climbed atop several platforms, and demanded that the Descendants be brought out of hiding. At first, nobody moved. Then one of my men, Trevor, sliced open a middle-aged man's throat. I remember fighting back tears at that. Within seconds, mobs of Rayanese ran through the streets, storming houses and buildings. Three Descendants were brought before us. Defiance marked their faces and they struggled until they saw that we had hostages. I commanded them to kneel before me with their arms behind their backs. They looked at one another and then back at me. They stood there for moments, simply scowling at me. Trevor killed another innocent bystander–walked around to face him and then planted a dagger through his gut. Trevor shoved the man down and let him squirm for minutes until the life drained out of him. The three Descendants just stood there watching.

"I was already sick to my stomach at what had transpired, but there was no saving any of these people. If I had tried to stop my men or commanded them any differently, they might have killed me as well." Garrison paused and rapped the back of his head against the stone wall of his cell a few times. He sighed and continued, "I raised my arm and signaled for my men to draw their bows. In another moment, all three Descendants had arrows through their skulls. Just as these three–all three of them were men likely not much over twenty years–just as their limp bodies fell, another five were being led toward us. They arrived just in time to see the others die. This group consisted of two boys and a girl near my age, a woman old enough to be my mother, and…" Garrison closed his eyes once more and paused for several moments.

Roland urged him on. "Go on. And?"

"And a little girl. Likely no older than seven years. She probably had not borne the Mark for very long. When I saw them, I knew I could not hide my emotions any longer. I donned my helmet to avoid having my tears seen. My men cheered at the site. They thought I was ready to take part and copied me, putting their helmets on. Willard, my second in command, came to me and said that they wanted me to kill the first of this new batch. I had already sworn to myself that I would no longer kill Descendants. I refused Willard. It took me several moments to think of a reason. Finally I told him that I had already killed so many that I wanted the rest of them to start catching up. I gave him my sword. Willard took it as an honor. He asked if he could kill all five. I left the decision to him.

"Willard was smart. He allowed four others to take part so there would be minimal chance of the Descendants fighting back. Willard killed the little girl first. I turned away, but it was obvious he'd beheaded her. It is a very distinct series of sounds, from start to finish. As for the others, I think seeing the little girl killed made them reckless. Made them feel like they had nothing to lose. The other girl, the one closer to my age, took one of my soldiers gently by the neck and kissed him deeply. In seconds he dropped to the ground, lifeless. One of the boys raised his hand toward our horses and beckoned. Every single one of our horses, save four, ran from the platforms toward the edges of the city. The other four ran to the Descendants. They mounted and raced off as my men shot arrows at them. We swore that we had shot all four of them down, but when we went to inspect the fallen bodies, nothing remained. It was an illusion.

"We demanded for the remaining Descendants to be brought to us. Two men came forward and informed us that they and their families had been housing the other three Descendants, but that the ones who stole our horses had taken them. I believed them. I nodded to Willard to indicate as such. He misinterpreted my signal. You see, there was a time when the same deliberate nod was a signal to kill them. Willard slit their throats. Once again, I nearly retched. Willard asked if we should kill both of their families and I stopped him. I told him that killing those two would be enough of an example. I told all of my men that I believed the two men and that we would have to accept that the Descendants escaped.

"We left Rayan immediately. Luckily, the nearest city in Cerysia was not far across the Sanai. It took us almost a week to walk to Killington and get new horses. That was the last time we ever killed a Descendant on a mission. I felt so relieved watching those four ride away, and even more joy when we realized that we had not killed them. That was the turning point. The whole mission confirmed my doubts."

Roland sounded skeptical. "How long ago was that?"

"Somewhere around two years ago."

"So for two years, your father and your soldiers have allowed you to simply stop hunting and killing Descendants? I find that hard to believe."

"It was not as difficult to fool my father as it was to get my soldiers to understand me. You have met my father. He is easily satisfied if you are telling him what he wants to hear. For almost two years I simply lied to him. We would depart on missions and I would make up stories of Descendants we killed."

"And your soldiers–how did they come to see the light?"

"I killed Willard."

Roland looked impressed, but only for a moment. "Do tell."

"On our next mission, a few weeks later, we rode out to Galicea. As soon as we crossed the border, I insisted that we set up camp for the night. As we ate, I commanded them that no Descendants would die on the mission. That we would no longer kill Descendants at all. They all laughed. They thought I was joking–understandably so.

"I had Willard stand up next to me. You see, my manifestation is the ability to invent and create things, and over the years, I have focused on creating weapons. I dabble most with elements like poisons to see how they will react with nature–things like water, blood, air, wood, and saliva. Once I find results that I like, I create pouches of the mixtures and assign different colors to them.

"The two greatest things about Willard are that he is eager and that he is an idiot. As everyone watched, I handed Willard a black pouch and instructed him to pour some of his water on it, then immediately empty the pouch into his mouth. I sat back down. He thought nothing of it. He likely thought I was giving him dessert. He followed my orders. In a few moments, Willard was writhing on the ground, coughing hysterically. His clothes decayed and his body turned black and then all of his blood oozed from his skin as he clawed at himself.

"The others stood and looked on in horror. I watched their reactions. I stood again, unsure of whether Willard had even died yet. I repeated my command. 'No more killing Descendants.' I told them that if they disobeyed or betrayed me, I had enough pouches to kill all of them. They would suffer the same fate if anyone outside of our company was notified. Future missions would include only the men present. If they failed to report, I would find them and kill them. When we returned to Alvadon, we would say that Willard was killed by a Descendant, and we quickly carried out vengeance on his murderer. Going forward, we would travel and upon return, I would give my father the report."

"And for how long did you fool King Edmund?"

"The entire time. We continued missions until I finally confronted him that I wanted to come to the House of Darian. You know him, he does not question it if he likes what he hears. I concocted dozens of fantastic stories of hunting and killing Descendants. He had no reason to doubt me. In retrospect, I was likely better off being honest with him much earlier. Maybe he would not have disowned me."

Roland stood and walked to the bars of the cell. "Do you…"

Garrison held up his hand to cut off Roland. "I know what you are going to say, Uncle. Save it. I understand the hypocrisy of my actions. Of my life. I also understand why everyone hates me and wants to see me dead. But they cannot be so stupid to think I would come here if I had not changed."

"Do you think changing, after all that you've done, excuses your past sins?"

"That is for the Orijin to decide, not men. If they would call themselves 'Descendants of Darian', then they should follow the word of the Orijin as well. Only minutes ago you said that the Orijin knows the hearts of men. If I was only meant for evil, then why would he bless me with a manifestation?"

Roland nodded. "That is true. But before I say anything to Zin Marlowe on your behalf, convince me of why I should defend you."

Garrison shook his head, then summoned his strength. He stood and walked to face Roland. "If I wanted to, I could have stayed in Alvadon. If I was truly as evil as everyone here thinks I am, I could have stayed put and lived out my glamourous princely life in which I would have anything I want at a simple request. My life in Cerysia consisted of traveling Ashur, returning home to feasts, merriment, commanding an army, and best of all, sleeping with a beautiful woman who only wanted to please me. On top of all of that, I was destined to become King of Ashur. Most men have nothing beyond a small home that they can call their own; from the time I could ride a horse, the Stones of Gideon were my personal place of serenity. If I truly wanted to destroy the Descendants, I could have simply waited for my turn as King and continued to hunt them down.

"I willingly sacrificed all of that. I have even killed my own men to stand up for what I realized too late in my life was right. I threw a helmet at my father while he sat in his throne. I abandoned my brother and my best friend and left them to form an army that would defy my father. I fought alongside Taurani to kill my own soldiers. I stayed in the Tower of the Blind and worked with Taurani and Augurs to deceive the King's men."

This time, Roland held up his palm. "All right, I see your point, boy. That is enough. More than enough. I may need some help from Vasher in convincing the others, but I think that you have a solid argument. I am curious though, you were in the Tower. Did they share any prophecies with you?"

"Only one. I did not really know what to make of it, as it seemed rather outlandish and cryptic. It was about Jahmash's return. Something about a night of fire and water. A man was being killed in the middle of a town called Haedon. It was a tremendous rainfall but a fire broke out. They told me that this occurrence would signal Jahmash's return."

A Descendant came running over from down the corridor, with two small balls of fire hovering in front of him the whole way. The boy grabbed the bars to Garrison's cell with one hand while the two fireballs hovered on each side at eye level, "What did you say about Haedon? About the man being killed in the middle of town?" He was of an age with Garrison; his complexion placed him as Shivaani, though his accent contradicted that.

Garrison eyed him suspiciously. He must have been listening to them the entire time. "Excuse me. Who are you?"

The brown-skinned Descendant's mouth worked faster than his words could come out. "My name is Baltaszar Kontez. I am from Haedon. Did you not just say that name?"

"Why are you listening to our conversation?"

"I apologize. This is my first day of dungeon responsibilities. I did not know how else to pass the time, aside from honing my manifestation." Baltaszar nodded to the fireballs.

Garrison had not expected an apology, and lightened his manner after a moment. "A Blind Man shared a prophecy with me that a night of fire and water in the town of Haedon would mark Jahmash's return. And now you claim that you are from Haedon. Where exactly is this place?" Roland turned to Baltaszar as well, waiting expectantly.

Baltaszar rubbed his temples with both of his hands. "Haedon is a mountain village a few days into the Never up north. Just north of Vandenar, across the river. You said a night of fire and water. That was just over three months ago. I remember it well because it was the night my father was hanged. It was the same night that I left Haedon to come here." Baltaszar took a deep breath and looked back and forth at Garrison and Roland incredulously. "The Blind Men's prophecies are always true, correct?" Garrison nodded at him. "Then all of this is real. It's all true. Jahmash is coming. Truthfully, according to your prophecy, his return started months ago.

"What do we do now? I mean, should we not do something? Tell Marlowe or someone else that this is the case? This...this is a huge bloody deal!" Baltaszar stepped back toward the corridor wall and leaned back, breathing heavily. Roland looked at Garrison; his right eye twitched rapidly, and hurried away. Baltaszar slid down the wall until he was sitting on the ground and continued to breathe loudly.

Garrison sat back down as well. "He is likely off to report this to Zin Marlowe."

Baltaszar half-smiled and then looked around suspiciously. "That doesn't necessarily mean anything. Marlowe has done nothing to prepare us for Jahmash. We cannot learn combat. We are not allowed to use our manifestations for violence. All we do is learn about history and the world. Sure, those things are interesting, but they are not practical when a Harbinger wants to kill you."

Garrison eyed him suspiciously once more. "Tell me something. Do you know who I am?"

Baltaszar twisted his mouth and shook his head. "No. Why? You are a Descendant, so you cannot be that bad, right? I figure you're in here because you refused to follow Marlowe's directives or maybe you broke one of his rules."

"Before that one night, had you ever left Haedon before?" Baltaszar shook his head to refute once more. "Now I understand. You lived in the middle of the forest for your entire life. You never learned about the rest of Ashur? Why did your people hide away in the forest then?"

"I never even knew there was a rest of Ashur until I left. Never really put much thought into it, to be honest with you. As to why? I am still trying to investigate all of the details about that myself. And should I know who you are? Marlowe instructed me to not interact with the prisoners and to ask no questions. But then you were talking about that prophecy and it was too important to simply stand over there and stay quiet."

"I am Garrison Brighton. Former Prince of Ashur and now prisoner of the House of Darian. My father, the King, raised me to hate Descendants, despite the Mark on my face, and so for many years, I led battalions to hunt down and kill Descendants. At a certain point, I started to wonder about why I was killing others with the same Mark that I bear, so I educated myself about the Orijin and the Harbingers. The more I learned, the more I realized that my actions were wrong, and over time, I stopped my hunts and finally renounced my future throne. My father made me a criminal in my own country, so I fled to here, where they also viewed me as a criminal for killing scores of Descendants. And that is why I am in here. You obviously knew none of that, which is why you did not judge me, nor did you hesitate to speak to me. Even my uncle thinly hides his disgust for me."

"I don't know you. I don't know anything about you, nor have I heard of you. It would be silly for me to judge you just because you are in that cell. Especially after having spoken to Marlowe a few times and having seen how he treats us. I am not saying that I completely trust you–you are a prisoner, after all. But there is no reason for me to disrespect you. Ashur is still new to me, as is the House. I think that if I was to go around making assumptions about everyone, it would be nearly impossible to fit in with this world."

"Do you plan to stay here or eventually return to Haedon?"

"There is not much for me in Haedon. I will return the first chance I get, but only to see a girl. She has likely forgotten about me by now, but I can't say the same for myself. I need to put my mind at ease about whether there is still hope for us."

"Aside from your father, you have no family there?"

"My mother…died…or was kidnapped–when I was a baby. My twin brother and I went separate ways when we left Haedon. He stubbornly wanted to return to Haedon, though I hope he was not so foolish. They would have killed him if he had. So when I do return, I hope that no one there has any news of him. That would give me the most hope that he is alive."

Garrison waited thoughtfully before responding; too many times in his life, he ignored the struggles that others lived with regularly. He realized more and more, each day that he sat in the cell, that on every one of his missions, he'd seen hundreds of people living as poorly as he currently was, except that they were free and could not afford any luxuries. Because of his father's taxes, none of those people would ever live comfortably. That was why so many of them would ignore him, spit at him, or turn their heads away whenever he and his company rode by. He had always ignored it, and until recently, thought he was being noble by restricting his men from killing them or apprehending them. In retrospect, many of those people would probably have welcomed death over the daily suffering they faced. He looked at Baltaszar once more. "Your father, why..." before Garrison could finish his sentence, Baltaszar tapped on the line intersecting his left eye.

"Haedonians do not know about Descendants or manifestations or the House of Darian. I never even knew about manifestations or that I had one until days after I left Haedon. Mine is that I can control fire. But nobody told me that throughout my whole childhood. So for years and years, accidents would happen every now and then like burning down a store or a house, and it was always blamed on my father. Not long ago, one of the fires killed a girl and my father took the fall. The whole town thought he was doing dark magic or something. He died for me and all we had to do the whole time was leave Headon. And since he was branded a criminal, Bo'az and I were ostracized as well. Our chancellor never came out and called us criminals, but the rest of Haedon didn't need him to. So we fled on our own. After our father was killed, there was no point in going back."

"Except for the girl?"

"Her name is Yasaman. You don't understand. I have seen and encountered many women on my journey down here and I have yet to see one that compares to her beauty. She turned me away, I think because after my father was sentenced to death, she was afraid to be associated with me. That, and her parents did not approve. But we had love. We had passion, humor, everything. I would have married her. Had children and grandchildren with her. And if there is a chance that she still feels the same, then I have to know. The only way I can move on from her is if she tells me that that is not possible."

"You sound rather matter-of-fact about moving on."

Baltaszar half-smiled. "I don't mean to. I just know that there is a possibility that I'll have to move on. Since leaving my home, I have come to realize that the easiest way to handle life is to mentally prepare for the worst, but hope for the best. And have no expectation of any person or situation. Expectations breed disappointment."

Garrison contemplated for a moment once more. Looking at Baltaszar, he saw an unassuming boy. But that 'boy' possessed a wealth more wisdom than he let on. Despite all his former wealth and luxury, Garrison realized he and Baltaszar were strikingly similar in spite of their vastly different backgrounds. Neither of them knew much of how the world worked. At least Baltaszar had had an excuse. Garrison had likely seen more of the world than anyone else in Ashur, but in the past several months, he realized that he barely knew anything about Ashur.

Just as Garrison raised his head to ask Baltaszar about Haedon, another Descendant rushed down the hallway.

***

Marshall grew suspicious at how empty the dungeon seemed. Maven Maximillian hadn't sounded as if he was exaggerating when he gave Marshall such a foreboding warning. No one guarded the entrance. No sentries at the top or bottom of the staircases. He'd run through three corridors and finally he found a single Descendant– Baltaszar of all people–slouched against the wall, sitting and talking to a prisoner, who he now realized was another Descendant.

"Tasz? What are you doing down here? And where is everyone?"

"Marlowe just appointed me to the dungeon today. I think he felt like it was a favor since I played peacekeeper between you and Reverron. He wasn't even angry about the burnt grass–then again, your friend Maven Maximillian was furious."

"Why are you the only one in the dungeon, though? And why are you so casually talking to a prisoner? Maven Max seemed quite adamant that things were run very strictly down here. I truthfully just walked right in here and had free rein."

"Both of your questions lead to the same answer. I was stationed toward that end of the corridor," Baltaszar nodded down the hallway. "I heard Garrison here talking about my village to another Descendant. It had to do with a prophecy about Jahmash's return. Turns out Jahmash has been active for a few months now and could likely strike at any time. That was what sent the other Descendant running. I imagine the others followed, then. So much for discretion."

Marshall froze for a few moments, then swiveled his head back and forth between Baltaszar and the prisoner. "Now I understand why your disposition is such." Marshall sat down next to Baltaszar and leaned back against the wall. He looked Garrison directly in the eye. "I presume you are *the* Garrison? As in the Prince of Ashur?"

Garrison closed his eyes and nodded his head. After a few more moments of silence, Garrison responded, his annoyed countenance clearly expecting more questions. "Is that all? Do you have any other questions or are you just going to sit there?"

"Sometimes I sit. Sometimes I like to sit down and think. This is one of those times where the latter is necessary. I have heard of your crimes. Even so deep in the forest, gossip reaches the Taurani village." Garrison trembled and attempted to speak, but Marshall cut him off. "You are not dead. Which means that they did not capture you. Your crimes are against more than just man. You have spit on the very foundations of everything the Orijin has created. Despite Marlowe's utter hatred for violence or aggression in any form, I have to believe that if anyone here encountered you outside of these walls, they would have killed you. So you came here on your own. I suppose wealth and royalty do not guarantee intelligence? And even Marlowe is not powerful enough to protect you from the masses here that would rightfully hate you. Scorn you. Despise you. So either your being here is a secret. Or you are being protected by others besides Marlowe. Or both."

Garrison stood up and crossed his arms in front of him. "I meant to employ diplomacy with you before you cut me off. But apparently you think you know everything about me and my situation. You claim that you are Taurani, but you look nothing like one. And no Taurani would step foot into the House of Darian, much less side with Descendants." This time, Marshall attempted a retort but was shut down as Garrison raised his voice. "Listen to what I am saying, Taurani. Because you have much to learn, despite what you think you know. I left my nation and family, renounced my throne, and killed my own people to come here. I am no prince now. You are right, my uncle protects me here because he knows that I am genuine in having changed from my old ways.

"I can help the House of Darian. I stopped hunting and killing Descendants years ago. You are right, my crimes are against the Orijin himself. But even the Orijin made clear that we will all be judged by man before we are judged by Him. So sit there and judge me. But I have repented. I have faced my sins and have vowed to change. The Orijin knows there is goodness in my heart, otherwise I would not have this Mark in the first place. And before you label me a hypocrite, perhaps you should look in the mirror." Marshall knew his annoyance was visible at that remark, but Garrison would have no way of knowing about his reflection. "Were you sitting here comfortably while your village was destroyed?"

Marshall could barely contain his anger. "No…"

"Let me finish. I am not done. During my journey down here, I met Taurani on the way. We fought alongside one another, despite our different views. Despite my crimes. They knew where I was headed. They vowed to help me get here before setting off on their own journey." Marshall's anger cooled and transformed into curiosity and intrigue. But Garrison spoke again before he could decide what question he wanted to ask first. "And despite all that, you were living here comfortably, were you not? Eating a nice hot meal while three of them risked their lives to get me here. You slept in a nice warm bed while we hid in trees, while Kavon accepted death in order to let me, Yorik, and Marika escape."

Marshall jumped up to meet Garrison's eyes. "What were the names you said? You said Yorik, Kavon, and what was the last one?"

"Marika?"

"And where is she? Where did she go? You said Kavon died, but you, Marika, and Yorik moved on and they helped you get here. Where did they go? Tell me now?"

"What is it to you, coward? You abandoned them."

"I am the only one of my people who was able to fight back, you damn imbecile! I fought one of Jahmash's generals with an arrow in my shoulder. Three of us engaged him with swords and I am the only one who survived to tell of it. I did not flee our village, Your Majesty. The Descendants found me there, left for dead, and brought me here. I woke a week later. I did not ask to be here. More importantly, where are Yorik and Marika? Marika is my mother. Yorik my uncle. Since waking here, I have vowed that I would find my mother. I have already buried my father and two sisters. I knew my mother would still be alive. But my uncle as well – that is incredible news.

"So please," Marshall did not bother to hold back the tear that formed in his right eye. "I apologize for judging you and for speaking to you so offensively. But please, where did my mother and uncle go after they helped you to get here? I need to find them."

Garrison dropped to his knees and looked at the ground. After a moment, he looked up at Marshall, his eye glistening. "You never told me your name, but I know that it is Marshall. I know it because Marika spoke of you. She assumed you were dead. That is why she fought so ardently to protect me. She knew we were of a similar age and she refused to let me die. It is my turn to apologize to you, Marshall. Yorik died fighting our attackers. It took four men to bring him down. And your mother–she sacrificed herself so that I could cross the Serpent and flee the remaining soldiers. She turned the river to ice, and they killed her right after." Marshall dropped to his hands and knees. He heard nothing else that Garrison said. He punched the stone ground for so long that he could no longer feel his hands, despite both of them being misshapen knobs of blood.

CHAPTER 18
THE SON OF A DAUGHTER

From *The Book of Orijin,* Verse Twenty-Eight
Envy not those around you. Each of you has a story. A hardship. A weakness. A secret.

VASHER JAI SLOWLY exhaled a puff of tambaku from his pipe. He always used the kind that was infused with mint when celebrating, and because his victory came in Fangh-Haan, he bought a bag that used Fangh-Haan mint. The flavor was stronger than the Shivaani mint, but also sweeter. "Sweeter flavor for a sweeter victory," he mumbled to himself.

"I'm sorry?"

He had temporarily forgotten that Maven Savaiyon sat beside him. "Nothing. I was merely appreciating my tambaku. Last offer. Are you sure you don't want to at least try it? It is not often I share tambaku this good."

Savaiyon smiled. "Once again, no thank you. My father smoked tambaku every day that I can remember. Anything that would make a man cough so much cannot be good for him."

Vasher knew that that was an indirect hint that he should stop. Back at the House, a few of the boys there would be more than happy to share. He actually looked forward to bringing back the Fangh-Haan mint. He normally met with Baltaszar, Lincan, and Desmond to share a pipe on Abraday evenings. Vasher looked forward to returning to his friends. He had been on this mission for a month, cut off from anyone he knew. "Why exactly are you here with me? You could have easily waited to come here once I was ready. And you don't seem like the type to watch beasts fight to the death."

Savaiyon looked around at the other people sitting in their vicinity, then lowered his voice. "Truthfully, I only want to take in Sundari. It is quite literally the only city in Ashur that I have not visited."

Vasher nearly scoffed, but kept it in. "But you are Shivaani. How is that possible? Not even once?"

"Well yes, I came once with my father when I was much younger, but I did not have the luxury of taking in the city. And since then, I have always felt insecure about coming here alone. News travels fast to Gansishoor and all Shivaani love to gossip. I would bring shame to my family if they heard I walked these streets. As far as anyone here knows, I am here so that my desperately curious nephew can place a few bets on a silberlow."

"I see. So I am your nephew, then?"

"Most of Ashur thinks all Shivaani look the same. No one here will question it. Besides, if someone questions us, all you have to do is persuade them otherwise. Is that not your specialty?"

Vasher waved off a man selling pastries. "That is why I am here celebrating. But you are not very creative. I have been to these pits dozens of times. People likely recognize me. Growing up, coming here was the only way to have my tambaku without my mother finding out." Vasher looked around him, now paranoid. Nobody else bothered to glance at him, even if they had heard him speak. They were too busy watching a vrschiika—a giant scorpion indigenous to the largest island of the Wolf's Paw—use one claw to clamp down a twenty-five foot long bhujanga, a venomous serpent known for hiding in the caves of the Shivaani Mountains. The bhujanga slithered and writhed to get free, which only deepened the gash from the vrschiika claw. The vrschiika used its other claw to pierce the giant snake's skull, driving it deep inside and then ripping the bhujanga's head in half with ease. Vasher shuddered. He peered at Maven Savaiyon from the corner of his eye; the man looked down at his hands, showing the smallest evidence of discomfort. "If you'd like to leave, I would not object. Give me a few minutes to finish my tambaku, though."

"I will wait for you outside the nearest gate. Then you will explain to me your upbringing and the Daughters of Tahlia." Without hesitation, Savaiyon arose and descended the arena steps.

Vasher did not mind the solitude. He preferred to focus on the tambaku and savor it as much as possible. Any companion would take away from that. He supposed that was why he had always come here to smoke. Nobody bothered him and so many others smoked as well. He blended right in, even at an early age. He remembered often resenting his mother for having to sneak off to the beast pits to smoke, but as he matured he understood why she did not approve. The more he analyzed and spoke about his upbringing, the more Vasher realized how different it had been from every other child of a Daughter of Tahlia.

"Daughters of Tahlia," he chuckled. His laugh was more at himself than anything else, though he looked around to see if anyone had taken notice. Vasher then remembered that Savaiyon was still waiting and arose to go meet him. He brought his pipe with him, certain that Savaiyon would not object. He easily eyed Savaiyon leaning against one of the arena's stone walls. Savaiyon was often the tallest man in sight. "You blend in quite well."

Savaiyon pushed off from the wall and initiated a walk down the busy main road. "Save the humor. These streets are too busy for anyone to care about us. Let us go watch the snake charming women."

Vasher felt compelled to correct him, "Daughters of Tahlia."

He'd grown up walking through the street markets, helping the adults take wagers on beasts, scampering after his mother and the other dancers. His mother was the only dancer that allowed her child to be involved with their preparation. Then again, she was likely the only Sundari woman ever that allowed her child to stay in contact with his father. But Vasher never shared that secret, so he had no idea if any other children were allowed the same leniency.

He had been at the House of Darian for just over a year, though Marlowe had sent him on this mission over a month ago. In his time at the House, Vasher paid close attention to the customs and ways of others, and often times inquired with others about habits in other nations. He found it intriguing, how others lived and the things they deemed important. Thus far, he had yet to find any culture, nation, or town that functioned even partially like Sundari.

Even aside from the chaos of the beast pits and men from all over Ashur flocking in to see the street dancers, family life alone resembled nothing from any other culture. Vasher inhaled another puff of tambaku very slowly. He held it in his mouth for a moment, and then softly released it through a thin opening in his lips. He was enjoying the Fangh-Haan mint more than the local variety.

They walked a few blocks in silence before Savaiyon finally spoke up. "You said that you are celebrating. Does that mean that Fangh-Haan has agreed to support the House?"

Vasher gave Savaiyon a sideways glance. "Yes."

"Yes is not good enough. You know that. What of this alliance?

Not supporting the king is one thing. But will the Anonymi fight for us?" Vasher looked at him and was about to say something, but then closed his mouth again. "The truth, boy. If you have this much trouble telling me the truth without your manifestation, then how do you plan to tell Zin Marlowe?"

Vasher rolled his eyes. "Fine. The Elders of Fangh-Haan have agreed to shift their allegiance from Cerysia to the House. But they do not speak for the Anonymi. The Elders made it perfectly clear that, while the Anonymi reside within the nation of Fangh-Haan, the Anonymi govern themselves. Fangh-Haan has no jurisdiction over them."

Savaiyon's eyes narrowed. "So why then do you consider this a victory? Clearly you did not succeed with the more difficult part of your mission."

Vasher smiled and spoke insistently. "It is a victory for every other Descendant except Zin Marlowe. Including yourself. Do you not see it, Maven Savaiyon? If Marlowe cannot rely on the Anonymi for protection and support, then sooner or later he will have to loosen his reigns and give us more allowances. We are all tired of not being able to train in combat. Look at the two of us! If we were to be attacked on these streets, what could we do to fight back? Even with our manifestations, our only options would be for me to persuade our attackers not to fight us while you create a doorway for us to run away. If Jahmash does return in our lifetime, how are we even close to being prepared to fight back? It's as though everyone takes the threat of Jahmash seriously except for Marlowe.

"Most Descendants who can use their manifestations for combat would love the opportunity to learn how to do just that. So while Marlowe's mission components were not fulfilled, I consider this a victory for us. And for all the others back home who are tired of being treated like children."

"We will have to meet with the Anonymi."

"Say that again?" Vasher could hardly believe what he'd heard. "Are you truly suggesting this? One does not simply walk into the Anonymi fortress and demand to meet with them."

"Marlowe entrusted you with a mission. You have not fulfilled his request. It is that simple."

Vasher stopped himself just short of glaring at Savaiyon. "Whose side are you on?" His tone was more accusing than he intended.

"Remember yourself, Master Jai. I am not some casual friend of yours. I am on the side of the entire House. And aside from that, I know Marlowe much better than you do. When you return and tell him exactly what happened, he will tell you to return and speak with the leaders of the Anonymi. He will not care how you arrange such a meeting, but he will expect that you do as he says. You stand here complaining about the horrors of your living conditions, and yet you have the luxury of relaxing in the city where you grew up, watching beasts fight and smoking your pipe. Do you know how many Descendants, how many of your friends, would sacrifice anything to be able to return home for even an hour?

"I am not telling you this because I am against you. I am saving you the trouble of returning to the House and losing Marlowe's trust. If you return now, it will be a waste of time for both of us. We will stay here tonight, and tomorrow we will develop a strategy for arranging this meeting. In two days, we will make our attempt to speak with the Anonymi. Understood?"

"Fine." It wasn't an argument Vasher could win. Sometimes he wondered what the point was of having a manifestation that could persuade people, if he lost most of the arguments that mattered, anyway.

"Good. Now I suppose we must hurry. The Daughters of Tahlia await and we no longer have a great deal of time for you to tell me about them."

Vasher chuckled as he scurried to catch up. "They await? What is your obsession with them? Are you in love with one of them or something?" A horrible thought popped in his head of Savaiyon fancying his mother. "Never mind. Seriously, though, what is your fixation with them? All they are, are a bunch of dancers–very good dancers–that do some crazy things with snakes."

"I am simply curious. I have heard many stories of them and have never had the opportunity to come here until now. You can call it a learning experience."

"*You* can call it a learning experience. I'll call it something else. Do you think that two days will be enough time to develop a sound plan for the Anonymi? Even if I use my manifestation to try and persuade them, would it even work on them? I have heard that they are not affected by certain manifestations. And how do we even know where to find them?"

Savaiyon put up a hand to stop him from talking. "Leave finding them to me. I have certain…correspondences. We will create several plans. Neither of us knows what to expect in this situation. Therefore, we must be prepared for everything. We will attempt to convince them in many ways, and will simply fall back on a new plan every time something does not work out."

Vasher stifled a protest. There was only so much planning they could do. The Anonymi would only sit and listen to them for so long. Instead of responding, he walked beside Savaiyon the rest of the way until they reached one of the squares where the Daughters of Tahlia performed. They could have stopped at other sections, but Vasher knew this to be the best location. *If Savaiyon wants to see the Daughters, he'll see the best performance.* From their side of the street, they could barely see the commotion. Several rows of men and women stood in front of them watching the Daughters of Tahlia dance and thrust and gyrate on a stage the length of the square. Vasher filed in behind Savaiyon as the statuesque man pushed his way to the front of the crowd. *It's always good to have a tall friend in situations like this.* It also helped that they bore the Descendants' Mark, as Sundari tended to celebrate unconventional people and things more so than the rest of the world.

They stopped when nothing or no one else stood in front of them except the platforms where the dancers performed. Vasher felt a tinge of guilt since Savaiyon was well taller than anyone else in the crowd. He'd grown close to Savaiyon in his time at the House, yet had never seen this side of the man. Savaiyon always maintained an even keel and, while the man was not dry or drab, barely ever displayed any elevated emotions, except for when he had to put some of the novices in their places.

Vasher was unsure of whether his manifestation was the reason, but over the years he had formed a penchant for being able to read people and the emotions that hid behind the things they said and did. *Curiosity isn't the only reason Savaiyon was here. There's definitely something more.* But even aside from Savaiyon being a Maven of the House, Vasher held too much respect for the man to question Savaiyon's motives. Not for something like this, anyway. If there was something that he wasn't telling Vasher, then it was for good reason. "So you know the history, right?" He shouted over the hooting and hollering crowd.

Savaiyon did not even turn his head away from the platform. "Darian's wife, Alaina, confined their daughter, Tahlia, to a single room in their house because of her beauty and permanently implanted into Tahlia's mind the notion that all men were dangerous. She refused to free Tahlia from confinement until the girl promised that she would avoid men and the dangers they posed. Tahlia agreed. And from the time she was barely a woman, Tahlia's beauty drove men mad, but she turned them all away. However, she grew lonely and desperately sought companionship, so she found other avenues. She fell in love with a woman and spent the rest of her years with her, though made arrangements for a man to impregnate her on a few occasions. Is that accurate?"

"Spot on."

Savaiyon nodded toward the dancers. "And all of these women still follow that example?"

"I am living proof. I technically have two mothers and a father. And I can say the same for every person I have met who was born of a Daughter of Tahlia."

"But how do the men take this lifestyle? As I understand it, they are merely used to conceive a child and then have no interaction whatsoever."

"It is an interesting dynamic. You have to realize, though, that nearly all men who enter this arrangement understand how it works. They do not have any romantic interest in the women and they are not looking to raise a child. If anything, for many of them it is an ideal situation; they get to lay with a sensual, beautiful woman and face none of the consequences or responsibilities after. Often times, the woman will call on the same man when she is ready to have another child."

"You said nearly all men understand. What happens when they do not?" Savaiyon still had not turned his gaze from the dancers.

"There can be...complications. I suppose it depends. Sundari protects the Daughters very well. So if the men get violent, they can be imprisoned or banished. That does not really happen very often though."

"What about emotionally? What if the men become attached?"

Vasher paused for a moment. "I am not sure." He did not want to have this conversation in the most crowded part of Sundari. He could tell Savaiyon about his father another time. "I have never really heard of a situation like that."

Savaiyon glanced at him and nodded briefly, then returned his gaze to the Daughters. Vasher was grateful for the gesture. He looked around at the platforms and the dancers. Despite having spent his whole childhood in the center of this town, he could understand why so many people were drawn to it. The dancers were captivating, and although it was common knowledge that they had no interest in men, men flocked to watch them every day and threw money at them without remorse.

The Daughters wore skimpy, shiny outfits and regularly performed with snakes on their stages. Sometimes the snakes would be in barrels and other times the snakes would be out in the open. People always doubted that the snakes were truly venomous, but a childhood friend of Vasher's had learned the truth the hard way.

It was something in the music and the way the Daughters danced that mesmerized the vipers and the men alike. Both were at the mercy of the Daughters and could not shake their hypnotizing appeal. Although Vasher had a different experience with the Daughters, he knew why men fell into the trap. The way these women looked at every man in the audience, each one of them likely believed that they had a chance with any of the women. Vasher obviously knew better, and even if he hadn't seen most of these women as family members, he was too afraid of them to ever consider fancying one. The Daughters were tough and usually quite crazy. Despite their sensual nature on the stage, they acted much differently outside of the public's gaze.

One Daughter, Vesta, who was not much older than Vasher, stepped down from her stage to tantalize the crowd. Her green and gold outfit, full of tassels and leaving barely anything to imagination, glistened in the sunlight and drew the men and women wild as she smiled at them. She moved along one side of the crowd, dancing with a thick snake draped across her shoulders and arms. A man from the other side grew brave and ran out to her. Most spectators would have assumed that Vesta hadn't noticed, but when the man got within ten feet of Vesta, she flung a thin dagger from a fold in her corset and struck the man in the throat. He writhed for a few moments until life and blood drained from him. The Daughters and audience continued on like nothing had happened as two large soldiers broke through the crowd and searched the dead man's pockets. They tossed a pouch of coins to toward Vesta's stage and dragged the body away.

"I haven't seen that happen in a while." Vasher said to Savaiyon. He had been so lost in thought that he'd forgotten Savaiyon was with him. He turned back toward the man only to see someone else standing there. *Where is he? How could I lose someone so big?*

Vasher turned to the man behind him, "Did you see where my fr...where my uncle went? The tall man that was standing next to me?"

The man gave him an almost blank stare. "Sorry mate, didn't even know there was anyone next to ya. Too busy lookin at what matters."

"Right." Vasher shook his head and bustled through the crowd, walking away from the stages. If Savaiyon could create doorways with his mind at will, it would be impossible to know where to even start looking for him.

***

"Stop feeling guilty. It is selfish for you to feel guilt. I understand our situation and I accept it. So have your brothers. So should you."

Vasher's father always seemed to know what was on his mind. He had barely even walked into the house and his father knew what he was thinking. He hadn't seen his father in nearly two years, by far the longest he'd gone without seeing him. "You just know, don't you?"

"You are my son. And if I was in your position, I would feel just like you do. Which is why I am telling you not to. You are lucky. We are lucky, Wassa. Most children of the Daughters never see their fathers' faces even once. I am blessed by the Orijin and by your mother that I can see you and bond with you. So please, for both of our sakes, do not feel any guilt. Feel appreciation that we even have this. I have never told anyone of our arrangement, but I see the faces of some of the men who were never able to let go. Many of them carry a great burden. You should thank the Orijin every day that He allows you this blessing. I certainly do."

Vasher shifted on his cushion. He had not missed having to sit on the floor all the time. "Very well. Tell me how you are doing then."

"I am restless. That is how I am doing. There is no longer any need for an old military man in Sundari...or in most of Shivaana. Now that this nation is at peace with everyone, many of us have no purpose."

"Become a sentry. Spit of a Janga, you could even protect Mother from the rooftop."

His father waved a hand dismissively. "Those jobs are for young men your age who take their lives too seriously. Not that I am too old, but I prefer to avoid that kind of stress."

Vasher grew impatient. His father was clearly trying to tell him something, but as usual, preferred to do so the long way. "So then what?"

"Fine, rob me of my fun." He continued to smile. "There is a ship leaving Gansishoor in a few weeks. A friend of mine has informed me that it is the largest, best equipped ship Shivaana has ever built. The captain and crew plan to set sail to find other nations beyond Ashur. They will accommodate capable guests with housing, food, and entertainment for the duration of the journey. Obviously the cost is a handsome amount, but I have been compensated well for my involvement in our military."

Vasher pressed his hands to his thighs. "Why this? Why now?"

"I know what you are thinking…"

"Stop empathizing with me and give me an answer."

His father knew him too well to be offended at Vasher's curtness. "You are correct. Wassa, all I do these days is sit home and let the time go by. On exciting days, I walk through the streets to take in the sights, but that quickly becomes old when you have lived here your whole life. Your brothers have gone off to live their lives, and now you have your life at the House of Darian. You know me, Wassa. I need to live. I need adventure. This is my opportunity to do so in a way that is not dangerous. I get to live at sea for who knows how long. I can finally live my life on my terms again."

Vasher paused for a moment. His first instinct would have been to argue, but his father was one of the most stubborn people he knew. He wasn't asking Vasher for his advice; his mind was already made up.

His second instinct would have been to grasp his manifestation and persuade his father otherwise. However, Vasher could not recall the last time he had sensed so much hope in his father's voice or even seen it in his eyes.

Vasher finally thought of something appropriate to say, that would show his father that he supported the decision, when a flash of yellow seared the air in the middle of the room and expanded into a giant square. Savaiyon stepped out of the empty space as the yellow lines closed in behind him. "We must go to Fangh-Haan now."

Vasher could feel the heat in his face. "That's it? You disappear without a word and then show up here a day later making demands? We are in the middle of an important conversation. You can wait. Fangh-Haan can wait. The Anonymi can drink Janga venom."

"You forget your place, Vasher."

"No. I know exactly what my place is. You have forgotten yours. The title 'Maven' does not mean you can treat me like some dust-ridden child pulling at your cloak for money. You begged me to take you through the city and then left me in an instant. Well I am talking to my father now, and we have matters to discuss."

Savaiyon maintained his calm demeanor. "Very well, I apologize for offending you. If you knew the nature of my business in this city, you might be more forgiving. That being said, your conversation with Albarran can wait. He is not leaving for another four weeks."

Vasher glared at Savaiyon, more from incredulity than anger. "Were you spying from outside? How would you even know about that?"

"Did your father not tell you he is leaving from Gansishoor? Do you not recall that my family lives in Gansishoor? Why do you think my family is so wealthy? They are the ship builders, fool. My own cousins will be manning the ship that your father plans to board. So you can rest assured that he will be in good hands. Now, we must go. I have gotten word that the Anonymi will see us, but our window is small. And we will have to ride to them from a certain distance."

Vasher looked to his father, who spoke before Vasher could get a word out. "He is right, Wassa. I will be here for some time. Go handle your responsibilities. Those are more important right now. You can always come back and see me before I go."

Vasher had been so fixated on his father that he didn't realize Savaiyon had already created a bridge in the middle of the room. Savaiyon waited on the other side, facing away and tapping his boot against the dusty ground. Vasher hugged his father tightly for a moment then walked through the opening. He looked back at his smiling father just in time before the bridge closed. "Why do you call them bridges when they act more like doorways?"

Savaiyon did not turn around. "A bridge connects two places that are far from one another. A doorway connects two rooms. Or separates the inside world from the outside."

"You step through a doorway; but you walk over a bridge."

"I suppose that we are both correct, then. So there is no need to change my terminology…Wassa?"

Vasher snickered. "My oldest brother, Seylaan, could not pronounce Vasher when I was a baby. He could only say 'Wassa'. Both of my parents call me that to this day." He looked ahead at the desolate flatland before them. "Where exactly are we going?"

A rider on a horse caught up to them from behind, leading two rider-less horses. Savaiyon raised a hand, inviting him to mount the chestnut horse. "We will follow him. Our destination is ahead, somewhere in that empty space of land."

"You were gone for less than a day. How did you manage to arrange this?"

"It took some serious pleading and convincing."

Vasher smirked. "And I thought persuasion was my manifestation. You have been busy."

"I have been *incredibly* busy."

"I thought we were supposed to hatch a plan. Several plans, in fact, because we need to be beyond prepared for this meeting."

"The plan changed."

"You mean the plan to make a plan changed. We never actually made a plan."

Savaiyon simply stared at Vasher, as if to see if he had more nonsense to say. "We had two choices. See them now or wait weeks. We do not have the luxury of waiting."

"All right, all right. No need to get sensitive about it." Vasher studied the rider next to him. The cloaked rider rode on his left while Savaiyon rode on his right. Aside from the billowing tan cloak, all Vasher could discern was a strangely colored helmet that extended further outward from the crown of the head to the bottom, toward the neck. The helmet was simultaneously several colors and no color. Only briefly did Vasher glimpse the face of the rider, which truthfully was no face at all. Beneath the helmet, the rider's face was covered by a shiny silver face plate with barely any features, save for eye and nostril holes. Because his nation had bordered Fangh-Haan, Vasher had heard dozens of outlandish stories about the Anonymi, but he had never seen one in person.

The rider never turned to face them. After they rode on for several minutes in silence, the rider extended his right arm vertically, clenching his gauntleted fist. For a few hundred yards, Vasher wondered why the gesture was necessary. However, they soon came to an opening in the ground–a ramp that descended into darkness, as if there had been a door in the desert sand that someone had opened from below. Vasher ogled Savaiyon from the corner of his eye. The Maven simply put a finger to his mouth and followed the cloaked rider down the ramp. It became clear that Savaiyon would do the talking for the two of them. *So much for manifestations.*

After descending several yards, the ramp led to a spacious chamber. Torches on the walls revealed a wide room with stone walls. Once they all reached a second chamber, the rider dismounted. Savaiyon and Vasher followed the lead as three figures identical to the rider entered and led the horses away. One figure led them forward through several more chambers. Some were dimly lit while others were bright; some were filled with weapons and armor, others had books stacked neatly from floor to ceiling. One or two were decorated with scriptures written in another language. Vasher knew it to be an ancient language, from the time of the Five, when the Anonymi were first formed.

If Vasher had counted correctly, it was the ninth chamber that had drawn a deep curiosity from him. The ninth chamber had been the largest one yet. Along one wall, nine suits of elaborate armor stood side by side. Each set was identical to the rest and they all bore the same strange color that the rider had on his helmet. Vasher stared at them in wonder until he realized that the décor on the rest of the walls consisted of meticulously illustrated tapestries. The tapestries depicted several scenes of nine Anonymi warriors in combat. Distantly, Vasher heard Savaiyon clear his throat harshly and he scuttled ahead to catch up. Vasher wished there was someone to ask about that ninth chamber.

They soon came to a stop in a dim chamber that led into darkness. The Anonymi that escorted him and Savaiyon gestured with his arm that they would walk straight ahead through the darkness, then turned and went forth. Vasher followed Savaiyon and dared to only walk in a straight line. He assumed that when it was time to stop, he would likely bump into Savaiyon. It seemed like a silly way to proceed.

He walked on in the darkness. His only comfort was hearing the soft footsteps ahead of him. Vasher could no longer tell if he'd walked for one minute or for ten, but he suddenly heard numerous footsteps around him. A few pairs of hands grabbed him and halted him, but not violently. He panicked for a split second, then resisted the urge to defend himself. *I am in the darkness of the Anonymi fortress. If they truly wanted to attack me, they could.* Vasher breathed deeply and calmed his nerves. Something had been placed around his shoulders and then over his head. His eyes didn't feel blindfolded, so it was likely a mask of some sort. The front felt cold while the sides and back felt soft and plush. Vasher did not attempt to touch his new attire, as the hands firmly held his arms and legs in place.

The hands on his legs and arms let go and one set nudged Vasher's back for him to move again. He walked forward for a few moments until he was led into a room with one small torch on the ground in the center, and it was now clear that he wore a mask, as he could see through small slits. Based on the shadows, it seemed that the room was circular and draped in black. The hands at his back belonged to a figure that stood directly behind him. Vasher did not bother to turn around or swivel his neck. He already had a hunch about the figure's appearance. Several other figures filtered into the room and stood around the perimeter along with Vasher, forming a circle. He wondered where they had taken Savaiyon.

Though the light was dim, Vasher could tell that the figures all wore black cloaks and the same masks as the rider he originally encountered. At once, the figures turned around and disappeared into the blackness of the walls. The hands on Vasher's back spun him around and led him into an enclave, then forcefully sat him down, facing away from the center of the room. *So that's where they all disappeared to.* The hands then let him go and Vasher heard the echoing footsteps walk away. He was too awestruck to get up. This was obviously some sort of ritual, so he would play along. He wished he knew where Savaiyon was, though. This was twice in two days that the man had disappeared on him.

Each person must have been situated in an enclave around the main room. Vasher sat on a bench in the tiny circular space and waited.

"Let us begin, Anonymi." A voice echoed deeply throughout the room and even more strongly into Vasher's enclave. Goosebumps sprung from his arms and shoulders. The voice continued. "Descendant, you have come with a request for us. State your business. If you use any manifestation in here, you will die." The echo made it impossible for Vasher to determine the speaker's tone or even accent, or from which enclave it came. He understood immediately that that was the point. Vasher waited a moment, still assuming that Savaiyon would somehow speak for both of them. After a few seconds, the voice spoke again. "Very well. It has been concluded that there is no business to discuss."

Vasher panicked, "No! There is business! Please! I thought my associate would speak for us! Please allow me to state my request!" Sweat rolled down his neck and back, despite the chill of the room. Silence controlled the room for agonizing moments.

"State your business now, Descendant."

The echo provided no comfort whatsoever. If anything, Vasher was awestruck. He was unsure of how loudly to speak, and raised his voice short of yelling. "My headmaster, Zin Marlowe, has requested your combat services in the event that Jahmash makes his return." He hoped he'd spoken eloquently enough.

"Why can you not defend yourselves? The very nature of your existence is that you can perform deeds that ordinary men cannot." The voice surrounded him.

"Zin Marlowe has put forth a decree that we are not allowed to practice violence, so that we may prove to Ashur that we are peaceful and trustworthy. It is his way of appeasing King Edmund."

"Zin Marlowe knows that the Anonymi do not take sides in the conflicts of men. We only care for the well-being of Ashur."

Vasher spoke up again, hoping that he wasn't cutting the speaker off. "The work of the Descendants and the House of Darian is for the well-being of Ashur. We do not ask you to oppose any Ashurians, only to help us in fighting our greatest threat. If and when Jahmash returns, he will be the gravest danger that Ashur has ever seen. What better reason is there to support us? We cannot defeat Jahmash without you." Vasher almost felt proud of himself. He hadn't even used his manifestation and he'd presented a sound argument.

"What you ask of us is revolutionary and falls outside of our responsibilities. We have no obligation to you. If we are to accept, then we ask that the House of Darian first meets a request of ours to maintain equilibrium on both sides."

Great, now they want favors. Marlowe didn't say anything about bargaining, but he and Savaiyon will both be satisfied with an alliance if it means meeting a simple request. "Very well. What is it that you need from us?" Vasher assumed they wanted money or services in return. There wasn't much else the House could offer.

"You will kill two men for us. Violence is not your way, just as alliances are not ours. If you prove that you are serious about this alliance, then we will defend you to no end."

Vasher's throat dried. He swallowed his spit several times just so he could respond. "It is not our way to kill innocent men. We are not murderers."

"Nor are we. Anonymi kill for justice. For balance. The two men you must kill are Ashur's biggest detriments in the fight against Jahmash. By killing them, you are not only doing the Anonymi a favor. You are helping all of Ashur and helping it prepare for Jahmash. Those are the terms. Do you accept or decline, Descendant?"

Vasher shook his head. *Of all times, Savaiyon picked now to be somewhere else. How is it that I am the one who has to make this decision for the entire House?* He sighed deeply. "Very well. I accept." He hoped a weight would fall from his shoulders. Instead, they grew tenser. "And these two men, where can we find them?"

"The first is in Alvadon of Cerysia. He sits on the throne."

Vasher's hands trembled. "K-king Edmund?"

"It is no secret that King Edmund is the greatest oppressor of Ashur. Kill him and Ashurian conflicts will end."

Thoughts and questions flooded Vasher's mind, almost carrying him away from the conversation. He shook his head vigorously. He would worry about how to tell Marlowe about this later. "Very well. Who is the second man?

"The second oppressor is your Headmaster, Zin Marlowe."

"What? You would have us kill our own leader?"

"There are many among your kind that would gladly bear that burden, given the opportunity. You must simply return home and give that opportunity a voice."

Vasher never cared for Marlowe, but that was a long way from wanting to see the man dead. "There has to be another way. Another person." He yearned for the sweet melody of his manifestation.

"None. If Marlowe dies by any other hand besides a Descendant's, there is no agreement between the Anonymi and the House of Darian. You came to us. If you require our assistance, then accommodate our terms. That is all. You may go now."

CHAPTER 19
A MOUSE ON A SHIP

From *The Book of Orijin*, Verse Thirty-Eight
Salvation shall come from your faith in Us. It is not enough to practice righteous deeds or to have pure intentions. When you wonder why the righteous suffer and the mischievous find happiness, remember that each of you has a place in the Three Rings.

DRAHKUNOV FINALLY STEPPED below deck once again and Adria smiled for the first time in as long as she could remember. The man was likely old enough to be her father and more persistent than any boy she'd encountered at the House. *Oh, how I miss that place, though.* She had forced herself to stop thinking about The House of Darian as much as she could. Adria had been gone for several months and she knew the Descendants had assumed she and Gunnar were dead. She would have made the same assumption.

The strange thing, however, was that she was not necessarily happy to see Drahkunov walk away. Despite her being tied up to a mast and hardly fed, Drahkunov was decent company. Adria would have obviously preferred Gunnar, but who knew which of the hundreds of galleys he was on. After Gunnar, though, Drahkunov was preferable to most of the others she'd spent time with. Even some of the captives tried her patience. After just one conversation with Aric, Adria knew she had no patience to speak with him. The boy only cared for combat and strategy. Adria didn't mind talking about those things, but Aric talked about nothing else. Just thinking about him made her bored.

Then there was Bo'az. Bo'az was a nice enough boy, but his greatest talent was feeling sorry for himself. Granted, they were prisoners and it was easy to be sad and depressed, but Bo'az's sadness hadn't even come from being a prisoner. He droned on and on about a girl he'd loved and how everything always happens to him. Adria had only encountered him a handful of times, but she was actually thankful that Jahmash kept his captives separated. She would have hated to have been kept in the same room as Bo'az day after day.

Jahmash. The Red Harbinger. It feels so strange to say the name. It's like he was never a real person until a few months ago. Adria had seen the man, spoken to him, even had him repeatedly attempt to infiltrate her mind. She did not miss that, though since they set out on the galleys, she felt a jab inside her head every now and then. If she died on this journey, the thing she would be proudest of in her life would be that she'd resisted Jahmash's power. It had been a scary feeling at first, like the edge of a dull knife trying to cut open her mind. She'd learned to harden herself and brace herself against the pain. Sometimes it was so severe that she would fall to the ground and writhe until he gave up.

In the end, it didn't matter anyway. Jahmash was smart. He threatened to kill her if Gunnar didn't direct the galleys to the House of Darian. Adria was sure it had been an easy decision for Gunnar, though Adria had tried to gesture to Gunnar to let her die. She knew that for Gunnar, there had never been a choice. He wouldn't let her die. From the time the galleys had departed, Jahmash had controlled Gunnar's mind, forcing him to use his eyesight manifestation to locate Ashur and then the island where the House of Darian resided. Adria had never known that Gunnar's eyesight was that good. She knew he could see miles away, even in dim light, but they had been sailing for roughly a week. Either they were going to kill Gunnar with his own manifestation, or they were keeping him very well-fed. She assumed the former. Adria only hoped that the Descendants could defend themselves well enough to make it all worthwhile.

For the first time since she'd initially arrived at the House, Adria felt guilty for not letting one of the boys influence her mind. Badalao had asked quite a few times to bond her mind, but she refused to trust him. She knew exactly what boys his age were capable of and had heard dozens of rumors about Badalao's forays with girls. She assumed he just wanted her to be his next accomplishment. But even if her instincts about him were right, that bond would change the complexion of this surprise attack. She would have easily been able to warn him of their coming. Adria knew she would feel guilty for every casualty and injury that resulted from this attack. She only hoped that there would be Descendants left after this that she might be able to atone for her shortcomings.

"Lost in thought?"

She didn't even realize Drahkunov had returned until he was sitting down next to her. Every time the man came close to her, he confused Adria even more. He didn't touch her or make any advances. He didn't outwardly flirt or make lewd remarks. He would simply smile and continue wherever the conversation had left off from the previous time. Adria almost swore that Drahkunov needed a friend more than anything else. "You could say that. So what exactly do you want with me?"

"So direct. No subtlety." He smiled again. "Careful, you might take away the fun of talking to you."

Adria rolled her eyes, but she wasn't truly annoyed. "You didn't answer my question. I am very confused about your intentions. And the books say you are from Galicea. Your accent should be much stronger, then."

"There are books about me? Oh, what an honor! I have been gone from Ashur too long and been to too many places for that accent to be helpful. Even people in Ashur have trouble understanding Galiceans. The accent only holds me back. But tell me, do these books treat me fairly? Or am I only judged for my treachery?"

"Concerning you, I've only read historical and military books about the war between Galicea and Fangh-Haan, as well as the construction of the wall. They only provide the military facts. And the facts certainly speak to your strengths. But answer me; I only want to know what to expect. What do you want with me?"

Drahkunov shook his head. "Right now, I want only to speak with you. You are quite literally the most interesting person that I have met in the past twenty years. Right now, I simply enjoy our conversations. I am making the most of my time with you. Who knows whether Jahmash will have me kill you once we destroy the House of Darian?"

"Is that a certainty for you? How can you be so sure of yourself?"

"I do not make assumptions when it comes to war, my dear. Jahmash has eyes on the inside of your precious House. He knows very well that most of you haven't the slightest clue how to use your manifestations. Why do you think we are sailing? He knows that the House of Darian cannot be attacked from land."

Adria was mad at herself for not having thought about that. She blamed it on the lack of food. Normally, that would have been a detail she would have noticed right away. "I understand why he wants to kill us all. But why you? What do *you* have against us?"

"Oh it is nothing personal. I hate all of Ashur. I even hate the word 'Ashur'. Ashur is a lie. Ashur is an illusion. It is an idea that men a long time ago contrived so they could fool everyone else into believing something that was never there."

"What?"

"Ashur is a name given to a collective of nations. But those nations hate one another. There is no brotherhood. No peace. There has never been peace and there never will be. That is why I left in the first place. Our war with Fangh-Haan disgusted me. I got so caught up believing that the Haans were the enemy that I never questioned why we were fighting in the first place. Do you know the reason? Do your books explain that objectively?"

"I read that it was because neither side could ever agree on a border. Your leaders were always at odds over whose land belonged to whom."

"What's the word you all love to use? Oh–gobshite! That's a lie. The Haan leaders are very meticulous people. The borders have been set for ages. The real reason is because the Haans wanted to set up a border post on the Serpent so they could regulate boats going back and forth between the nations. They were concerned about Haan smugglers in Zebulon–their own city! Our own Lords took offense, thinking the Haans wanted to inspect Galicean merchants, and destroyed the post. How stupid is that? Every nation should be able to regulate their borders, especially if it is doing so to maintain the integrity of its own people. And look at how many people died because of that. I have no problem with all of Ashur being wiped out so we can start over and live in peace."

"So you would kill everyone in the name of peace?"

"Is that not what mankind has done since the time of the Harbingers? At least if I had it my way, we could destroy everyone until the lesson is learned."

"That is stupid. And if you did kill everyone, who would be left to fill your 'peaceful' nations?"

"This is why I enjoy speaking with you. You ask meaningful questions. Every nation that I have visited outside of Ashur is more peaceful than Ashur. Even those that are founded on military ideals know how to maintain peace so that violence is not necessary."

Adria got stuck on one thought. "There are nations beyond Ashur?"

"I thought you were smarter than that, dear. Most of Ashur is too stupid to think that life exists beyond its waters. When Darian drowned the world, he did not kill all of it except for Ashur. He simply put oceans between the nations. However, it seems that only Ashur has not learned to live in peace. Our world is so much larger than just Ashur."

"So then why not just leave for one of these better places? Why be concerned with Ashur if you have better options?"

"I have seen too much violence to ignore the hearts of men. Sooner or later, Ashurians will find these other nations. And when they do, they will likely bring their violence and narrowmindedness with them, like a plague. Ashur is dangerous for the rest of the world. Better to destroy it now than allow it to fester and become a problem later on. Do not misinterpret the metaphor in my words. There are those in Ashur who would welcome peace. We would likely spare them. But once Ashur is clear of all the vermin, the rest of the world can come here in peace, as well."

"Jahmash will be satisfied then? Is that all he wants–for the Ashurians to be wiped out? And what, he'll live among you in peace?"

Drahkunov chuckled. "All Jahmash cared about is righting the wrongs that Darian committed. You all think that Darian was so righteous. So heroic. He had his flaws, just like the rest of them. And he allowed Abram and Lionel to die for him while he ran away."

"And he saved the lives of thousands by drowning the world and trapping Jahmash. Obviously his intent was not to kill, considering that he spared Jahmash's life."

"He treated women like whores. How many children did he father, from how many different women?"

"He loved every one of his wives. Why else would each of them willingly wed him, when they knew about the other women? If they were being used or only wanted to be attached to Darian's status, they wouldn't have bothered."

"And you would marry a man with twelve wives? Just because he told you that he loved you equally?"

Adria stumbled to find a retort. She desperately said the first thing that came to mind. "How many lives have been brought into this world because of him? Valuable lives?"

"Pointless lives. Weak, violent lives."

Adria's shoulders tensed even more. She hadn't thought that could be possible. "It is clear that no amount of logic will win with you. There is no point in arguing."

Drahkunov stared at her from the corner of his eye, then huffed and stood. "I had hoped for a better argument. You disappoint me. Perhaps your mind is too tired from resisting Jahmash. I shall bring you some food." He walked back below deck.

Adria looked forward to the meal. They did not feed her much, but the food was the same that Drahkunov ate. She felt somewhat disappointed that she'd let him down, but the man was right. She hadn't eaten a proper portion in months. Once or twice, they needed her manifestation, so they fed her well. She hadn't really thought clearly in a long time. Hunger always seemed to get in the way and she never knew when Jahmash would try to trespass her thoughts again.

Drahkunov had mentioned that Jahmash had someone on the inside. If true, then there was at least one traitor in the House. Maybe even more. But Drahkunov could easily have been lying to her. Regardless, it was a disturbing notion. She regretted not bonding with Lao even more.

Adria also regretted that no fight training was allowed at the House. When Gunnar had proposed the idea of sparring at night so that Marlowe wouldn't know, Adria had strictly opposed it. She had figured that if Marlowe had a rule against it, then it was likely a bad thing. Since then, especially now, she had regretted opposing Gunnar and those whom he'd recruited.

The only comfort was that physically fighting back would do no good right now. She was in the middle of hundreds of ships in the ocean, on a ship with dozens of men who likely did know how to fight. As angry as she was, Adria knew she had to maintain her composure and wait for a better time. She would have to save her energy and fight with her mind.

Before she left her parents in Taiju, Adria had visited the Blind Woman in the city to see if anything pertained to her. All that the woman, Katre, had told her was that she would return home to see her parents. At the time, Adria had been disappointed at the banality of the prophecy. It hadn't spoken of anything exciting or adventurous. At this point, however, Adria could not have asked for a more uplifting thought. She wondered if Katre had known more and simply held back some information. Luckily, Adria would have the option of finding out one day.

Despite the prophecy, she would not tempt fate. It would be

stupid to fight these men. The prophecy said she would return home. She didn't want to return home missing an arm or disfigured. She would fight back when it made the most sense.

Drahkunov resurfaced with a member of his crew. They each carried a plate, though Drahkunov also had a corked bottle in his hand. He set his plate and the bottle down on a barrel and instructed the sinewy crewman to set the other plate on another barrel. Together they pushed the barrel in front of Adria. "You may go now, Faadi. Unless you prefer to stay and feed her for me."

Faadi didn't seem to appreciate the sentiment. He scowled. "You feed her the same meal that you eat? While your crew eats barely seasoned fish soup every day?" Faadi threw the plate at the mast, smashing it into dozens of shards while chunks of food landed on Adria's head and shoulders. "She is a Darian-loving whore! My people would spit on me if they knew I was even on the same ship and let her live!" He then grabbed the dinner knife and cocked his arm to stab her. From behind, Drahkunov seized Faadi's hand and plunged the knife into Faadi's chest. A few other crew members on the deck turned to see the commotion, but went right back to their responsibilities and conversations.

Faadi convulsed for a moment, and Drahkunov took advantage of the opening by stabbing him a few more times in the chest and stomach. He then pulled Faadi to the the ship's rail and pushed him over the side. A splash shortly ensued.

Adria looked at him incredulously as Drahkunov walked back to her. She felt relieved and terrified all at once. "What was that?"

Drahkunov smiled. "What do you mean?"

"You are too intelligent for that to be an accident! The man obviously knew I was up here and more obviously hates me! Why would you bring him up here? Did…how could you not know he would try something like that?"

"I knew. You are correct. I knew he hated you. Knew he would want to kill you."

"So what, do you think that is supposed to impress me? Do you think I respect you because you killed him?"

"Perhaps you should not focus on honoring yourself so much." Drahkunov almost sounded bored to speak to her any longer.

"Excuse me?" Her cheeks warmed, filled with anger and embarrassment.

Drahkunov crouched beside her and spoke softly. "Though you

may think it does, Faadi's death has nothing to do with you. I simply needed a reason to kill him. You see, Faadi is…was a very angry and selfish man. He came because he hates Ashurians, especially ones like you who descend from Darian. However, he barely gets along with the rest of the crew, complains about everything, and throws the others out of sync when he is required to row. Unfortunately, those are not justifiable excuses for killing him. Trying to kill one of Jahmash's prized prisoners, on the other hand, is definitely a good excuse."

Adria continued to sulk. "You could have been more discreet. And then told Jahmash that he died during your attack on the House."

"Do you know how many eyes Jahmash has? Or where they are at any given time? Even the birds perched atop our sails could be watching from his eyes. That is why we whisper now."

Adria smirked. "So I could easily shout out the truth of what just happened, and he would be angry with you."

Drahkunov nodded and smiled back. "You could very well do that. And then you would watch your friend Gunnar lose his other arm, right in front of you." He continued to smile. "Do not test me, Adria. While I do like you, my obligation is to Jahmash, not you. I would not hesitate to sacrifice you if it meant my well-being."

"Fine. You win. At least you have a code. A sense of rules. Your traveler friend is much crazier than you are."

He glanced at her sideways. "My traveler friend?"

"You know, Maqdhuum. The one who disappears and reappears. I assumed he was a general, just like you. Jahmash treats him like one, anyway."

Drahkunov was definitely interested. He looked directly at her and maintained a soft voice. "I do know Maqdhuum and he is a general, but I do not know why you call him a traveler or about disappearing and reappearing. What exactly are you talking about?"

"You're telling me that you didn't know Maqdhuum could vanish into thin air and reappear somewhere else?" Maqdhuum had threatened her and Gunnar not to tell anyone about it, but if he was keeping secrets from his own people, Adria could use it to create discord.

"You lie. He bears no Descendant's Mark. I have been all over the world. Only Descendants have such an ability to do these things. Even beyond Ashur."

"I have lived for nearly twenty years and have never seen any nation beyond Ashur, but you just told me that there is, in fact, such a thing. Perhaps you should also entertain other possibilities. I have seen him do this with my own eyes. How do you think he captured me and Gunnar? One moment we were standing around, talking to other Descendants. In seconds, he appeared, cut off Gunnar's arm, and before I could process a thought, we were at the edge of a forest, boarding a galley just like this."

Drahkunov's brow furrowed, and then he looked down at the wooden deck. He spoke even more softly than before. "Could it...no there is no way..."

"What is it?"

He seemed surprised that she'd heard. "There have been stories in certain parts of the world...never mind. I forget myself."

Adria pushed on. "But what about being worthy of conversation. I thought that was why you enjoyed my company. Perhaps I could help with whatever it is that you do not understand."

Drahkunov seemed to have recovered from whatever troubled him. "A nice attempt. I'll give you that. But still a fairly novice tactic. I am not so easily influenced." He smiled once more.

In the distance, a red flame appeared from the crow's nest of another ship. A shout came from the crow's nest of their own ship and Drahkunov looked up. He then raised his arm straight up and made a fist. Adria tried to contort her neck to see what was happening up there, but could not. Drahkunov trotted back below deck. After several moments, the red flame on the other ship disappeared.

It was only after Drahkunov left that Adria realized neither of them had actually eaten. Food still littered her hair and Drahkunov's plate still sat atop the barrel. She tried for several minutes to reach it, but the exertion wore her out quickly. As her eyes got heavy, she thought she could feel the galley moving faster than before. However, she was too tired to question what was happening, and nodded off to sleep.

***

The shouts of many men startled Adria from her sleep. She didn't think she'd slept for very long, but vaguely remembered dreaming about Drahkunov. Her face flushed, hoping that no one around her could read her thoughts. *What if Jahmash can force his way into my head while I'm sleeping?* She panicked at the thought.

Adria lifted her head to see the galley alongside another one, which was slightly larger. Planks had been extended and Maqdhuum walked across to their ship, followed by a girl with a Descendant's Mark, and Gunnar, who looked incredibly skinny. Gunnar was being prodded on by two crewmen. Drahkunov greeted them as they stepped onto the deck and gestured toward Adria. His face looked serious, but she could not read it beyond that.

Maqdhuum walked to her, but did not crouch or kneel, as Drahkunov had done every time he'd spoken to her. "Look at me girl." She knew he would not have the same patience as Drahkunov. "Your friend here with the good eyes refuses to give us directions. All we know is that we are a day or two away from Ashur, but he will not tell us whether to navigate toward the east or west of Ashur to get to the House."

Gunnar spoke from behind Maqdhuum. "I do not refuse! I need energy to see! Zey are going to kill me, Mouse! I am starving. All I am asking for is some food! Ze manifestation requires energy, anz I have none. Look at me!"

Adria felt ashamed that he was going through this only so they would not kill her. The Gunnar she remembered was a stocky, muscular man. This skinny decrepit man standing behind Maqdhuum was a pitiable thing–something she never would have imagined of Gunnar. "He is right. He needs food. We cannot use our manifestations without energy. Without nourishment. You are going to kill him by trying to force him. Are you looking at him? Do you see his condition?" She was shouting now. "There is nothing you can do, aside from feeding him, that would enable him to use his manifestation for you. Even if Jahmash himself were in Gunnar's head, it would not work!"

Maqdhuum kicked her hard in the stomach. "Do not make assumptions about Jahmash. You know nothing of him. So you are saying he is useless to us if we do not feed him?" Adria was still gasping from the kick to be able to respond. "We have enough food for our crew, and that is it. If we have to keep worrying about him to eat enough, our whole ship will be starving!"

Adria wanted to tell Maqdhuum to disappear to somewhere else and bring back food for his ship, but she was still catching her wind. Maqdhuum continued over her heaves. "The arrangement was that you would die if he refused to help. Maybe watching you suffer and slowly die will inspire him to find the energy without food."

She was finally able to speak up. "If you kill me, then you have nothing. He will still refuse and you would have to kill him as well.

Then you will not have either of us." Adria realized she might have sounded too smug in saying that.

Maqdhuum did not looked pleased at what Adria thought was a victory. She missed the days when she was sure that she'd won arguments. Maqdhuum turned and pulled Gunnar next to him. They stood only a few feet from Adria. She could see the pain and exhaustion in her friend's face. She could only imagine how sick of his own manifestation he'd become, to be so drained. Maqdhuum then nodded his head for the female Descendant to come to them. The girl was beautiful and obviously taken care of on the ship. She wore a white dress and her blonde hair was braided neatly. Adria didn't understand. *Is she a captive? Why does she look so healthy? Why are there no crewmen guarding her?*

"Once we board our ship again, do you agree to use your sight to help us?" He asked Gunnar impatiently.

"I vill if you feed me. Zat is ze only vay." Even the defiance was fading from Gunnar's voice.

Maqdhuum mumbled something about a waste of time. He looked at the girl and extended his arm, palm up. "He is all yours, Farrah. Adria, you have not met Farrah, have you? She is a Descendant, just like you. However, unlike you, she sees the truth of this world."

"And what truth is that?"

"That the true power lies with Jahmash." He folded his arms behind his back and smiled. As he did, the girl, Farrah, took Gunnar in her arms and kissed him deeply on the mouth for several moments. Adria was dumbfounded as to what was happening before her, until Farrah released Gunnar and he fell to the floor in a thud. His unmoving face was turned to Adria, and it became immediately clear that there was no life in his eyes. Adria tried to scuttle back, forgetting that she was secured to the mast.

"No! What did you do? Why! Why would you kill one of your own! How could you! All he needed was food!" Tears streamed down her face. She pulled so hard against her shackles that her hands scraped against the mast. "You filthy bink! You should know! All he needed was to eat! How dare you bear the Mark and do this!" She continued shouting at Farrah until Maqdhuum kicked her in the stomach again.

Farrah finally spoke. "Do you know why I would do this? Because not too long ago, one of our own did the same to us. We stood in the middle of Rayan and watched as your bloody prince had his men kill Descendants publicly. The same prince who bears the Mark. He had my sister beheaded. She had barely reached eight years! Eight! Is that what Descendants do? I will help Jahmash kill every last one of you."

It was only once Farrah spoke that Adria realized she had a Markosi accent. Her skin tone, however, was too dark to be pure Markosi. Like Adria, her parents must have been from different nations. Regardless, Adria felt a sudden fear grip her. *For the love of Orijin, how many others are going to respond to Garrison's crimes the same way? That scoundrel will get us all killed by our own people!* Farrah stepped toward her and slapped her in the face sharply. "Was that from you or from Jahmash?" Farrah slapped her again.

"The first one was me. That one was from Jahmash. Or would you like a kiss as well?" She puffed her lips into a smile and glanced from Gunnar's body to Adria. "Speaking of Jahmash, he sends a message. If you do not direct us properly once Ashur is in sight, he will ensure that Badalao, Desmond, Horatio, Lincan, and Savaiyon are spared when the House is destroyed. They will all be brutally murdered in different ways for you to enjoy. He says that we can even behead one of them, as payback for my sister."

Adria surprised herself that she was able to control her anger. "Farrah, we are not like Prince Garrison. We hate him as well. He does not represent us. You and I feel exactly the same way about him."

"Then why is he at the House of Darian?" Adria had no idea what she was talking about. "Ohhh, you were not aware? Yes, he rode to the House of Darian and joined its ranks. He is just like you. And so you will all be killed." Farrah did not wait for a response. She turned and stepped onto the plank to return to her own ship. As they walked back, Drahkunov instructed two of his own men to toss Gunnar's body overboard. Adria felt a small protest inside, but the truth was that there would be no honorable ceremony for Gunnar. They would not even reach land for several days. Instead, she closed her eyes and cried into her knees.

Drahkunov stepped heavily toward her, she assumed so it wouldn't be a surprise when he sat next to her. Adria heard Maqdhuum shout "Drahkunov!" from the other ship. A few moments later, she understood why.

"Adria, Farrah's threat was real. Anyone you loved at the House of Darian will be spared only to be tortured and killed in front of you later on, if you do not lead us in the right direction. Jahmash has sent scouting ships in the past and none could find the island. We know you access it from the mainland of Ashur, but have not found where it is you go. Farrah informed us that if you do not allow Jahmash into your mind, the suffering will increase for your friends."

Adria lifted her head and let the tears drip from her chin. "Whether I do or don't you will kill them all anyway. At least if I refuse, it buys them more time."

Drahkunov nodded. "Think about it. You know time does not matter. Whether it is a month from now or a day from now, there is nothing that the House of Darian can do differently to prepare for us. Every ship has cannons. You Descendants cannot even fight with your abilities. Look at me." Adria hesitated, knowing that her stubbornness would disappear if she had to look at his face, but eventually gave in. "I have seen more war in my life than you can imagine. If you refuse, you will never forgive yourself. I know I would not, put in your situation. Look at your reaction to one friend's death. What will you do when it is ten of them? Twenty of them? One hundred? And all of their suffering will be because of you. I know Jahmash. He has over a thousand years' worth of vengeance and he is excited to see it carried out. He will make sure that you live a long, long life. And that every moment of that life is spent watching another Descendant suffer. This is not the time to be stubborn for the sake of being stubborn."

Adria stared at Drahkunov's eyes. There was genuine concern in them. He might have been saying what Jahmash wanted to hear, but there was emotion in them. Adria looked back down at the ground, closed her eyes, and took a deep breath. *I will return to Markos. I will see my parents again.* "Very well. I will not resist."

Drahkunov yelled "Farrah!" across to the other ship. Adria assumed he nodded or signaled to her. *She is the one communicating with Jahmash.* In a split second, a warm, gentle sensation wrapped her mind, as if covered by a blanket. It caught Adria off-guard, as she'd expected another painful invasion attempt. She supposed the difference was because she did not resist. Before she could finish forming her next thought, it evaporated and she had no control of the words and images that appeared in her mind. *If you do not resist, it will be this comfortable every time.* Adria did not know why, but she looked up and smiled widely.

CHAPTER 20
CLANDESTINE INTENTIONS

From *The Book of Orijin,* **Verse Four Hundred Seven**
Hold dearly to loyalty, for it shall be the salvation of Mankind.

VASHER SHIFTED IN HIS CHAIR. He was sure that Marlowe had made him sit there to keep him from feeling at ease. It was only the third time he'd been in Zin Marlowe's office. He glanced at Savaiyon and then looked at Marlowe once more.

"Do not look at Maven Savaiyon, he cannot help you. He informed me that you bear a piece of news that must be dealt with immediately. Maven Savaiyon would not lie to me. He would not waste my time."

Vasher glared at Savaiyon. "If it was so important to you, why didn't you just tell him yourself? I told you everything anyway." He felt slightly betrayed for having confided in Savaiyon.

Savaiyon did not look offended by Vasher's tone. "The Anonymi spoke to you. I was not in the room. It is your message to present, because the pact was made with you. The details would be corrupted if I were to relay them."

More than anything, Vasher wished he had another pipe at the moment. He stared at Savaiyon for another second, then turned to Marlowe. "The Anonymi want a fair deal for helping us. They are all about balance, and they are reluctant to help us without something in return."

"Yes, yes. I know all about their need for balance. But why would they be reluctant?"

Vasher no longer felt the need to mask his annoyance toward Marlowe. "They do not agree with your stance against violence. They believe that we should be able to help ourselves, considering we all have abilities that others do not. They basically said that if we are not willing to help ourselves, we have to help them bring balance to Ashur. Then they will agree to defend us."

Marlowe sat down. "For people like them, violence is always the answer. Ashur breeds violence and The House of Darian is the only society that preaches nonviolence. And look at us—still we are judged for it. If I had another option, I would choose it in a heartbeat. We need the protection of the Anonymi. The King's soldiers will not help us. What were their terms, Vasher?"

"They want us to kill King Edmund."

Marlowe choked and coughed for several moments before he could finally speak. Even then, his face was still red. "Kill King Edmund? They would have The House of Darian murder the very man that stands against it, just to form an alliance? What sense does that make? How does that help anyone? How does that bring the balance they so often preach?"

"The Anonymi explained their reasoning to me. They said that King Edmund is the greatest enemy to balance in Ashur. With all of his power, he is guilty of preventing Ashur from becoming a peaceful nation."

Marlowe stood and pointed at Vasher. "I do not believe that for an instant. No one man, even if he is the king, can hold so much influence that he would affect the balance of an entire continent. So what, if we kill King Edmund, the Anonymi vow that they would protect us?"

"It is a test to ensure that we are serious. They want to make us uncomfortable by requiring this, so that they know we are deserving of their help."

"You did not answer my question. For the sake of entertaining this request. If The House of Darian assassinated King Edmund, the Anonymi would fulfill their end of the bargain immediately?"

"Well." Vasher paused. "No." He looked back at Savaiyon and again at Marlowe.

"Again, Maven Savaiyon cannot answer for you. What else did they say? What more could they possibly ask, you fool, if killing King Edmund is not enough?"

Vasher reddened and his eyes narrowed. He'd been uncomfortable enough, but being spoken down to made him angry. Vasher stood from his seat. "They want us to kill the two men in Ashur who hold it back from being a great continent. A fair one. A balanced one. King Edmund is the greatest perpetrator against Ashur, despite having the ability to help it the most. And according to the Anonymi, you are the second biggest threat to the balance of Ashur."

Marlowe gasped and sat down. "The Anonymi want us to kill you and

King Edmund. And then they will help us."

Marlowe stared at the top of his desk and spoke softly. "This is…impossible. I have done nothing to hurt Ashur. Since I've been the Headmaster of the House of Darian, I have preached only peace and tolerance." He looked up at Vasher. "And what? The very alliance that I requested hinges upon my death? How does that make sense?"

Vasher felt a rush of anger and as he raised his arm to point right back at Marlowe, Savaiyon clasped his shoulder from behind. "Vasher is loyal to you and the House. He related this news to me exactly the same way. I have heard much of the Anonymi in my travels, my lord. This is how they work. I know that you sent Vasher because of his manifestation, but the Anonymi would have killed him if he had tried. They gave me the same threat." Savaiyon took a deep breath. "What would you have us do now? I would not recommend returning to the Anonymi with a counter offer. I have heard stories of pacts falling through because others have tried such things."

Marlowe suddenly looked very tired, as if he were straining to focus on Vasher and Savaiyon. "No one from The House of Darian is to go back there. I need answers first. You and Vasher must go to the Augurs. Surely the Tower of the Blind will have at least one prophecy related to this."

Savaiyon stepped forward, next to Vasher, and nodded. "If you want to be safe, that will not be enough. There are Blind Men and Women in many cities throughout Ashur. The answers you seek could be found right away, or they could be with the last Augur we meet. There is a chance that Vasher and I could take a while to bring you answers."

"You are suggesting that others join you?"

"It seems to be the most sensible solution."

"I need answers as soon as possible. I cannot wait weeks or months. But I also do not want news of the terms of this deal to leave this room. The more people who know of this, the more likely it is that I will be killed."

Vasher cut in. "There are ways of phrasing things. If the questions are asked a certain way, then no one need know how this connects to you or King Edmund."

"And what if you are wrong?"

"I have been getting my way with people for most of my life, Headmaster Marlowe. I do not always need my manifestation for that. Much of it is how you say things and the semantics of speech."

Savaiyon patted Vasher on the shoulder again. "I can vouch for him, my lord. Vasher is true to his word. He will not betray you. Let us assemble a team to spread through Ashur and find the prophecies you desire."

Marlowe rubbed his temples. "I apologize, Vasher Jai. I have been unfairly harsh with you. My anger is toward the Anonymi, not with you. I can only imagine how difficult it would be to relate this information to me. Maven Savaiyon, I will entrust you with selecting trustworthy Descendants to send on this mission. Time is of the essence, but this cannot be done sloppily. Use extreme caution in how you share information and ask questions. Assemble a mission team and leave immediately. Take what you need; anything is at your disposal. Do not return without answers for me."

Vasher took the cue to leave the room and Savaiyon followed him out. A doorway appeared in the middle of the next room as Blastevahn walked back into Marlowe's office. Vasher looked through into the evening sky to see one of the shores of the island outside the House. Obviously, Savaiyon wanted to speak privately. Vasher stepped through and turned to Savaiyon once the doorway closed. "What is it?"

"I am letting you choose. But this discussion must be for our ears only."

"Letting me choose? You mean who we bring?" Vasher blinked and stared at Savaiyon. "Why?"

"You have the potential to be a leader here. A strong one. Many men would have crumbled before the Anonymi. You made split second decisions in my absence. And for what it is worth, I would have agreed to their offer just as you did. You did well, so why not start now?"

"But Marlowe said for you to choose."

"You will tell me your selections. If you choose unwisely, I will counsel you. First choice?"

Vasher made no hesitation. "If we are going to be separating to cities all over Ashur, we will need to be able to communicate. Badalao. Which means you will have to bond with him as well."

"Smart. I agree. Who else?"

Vasher had thought it would be more difficult to convince Savaiyon about Lao. The truth was, he really only trusted his friends on this mission. They would do things exactly as he asked, especially once they understood the importance. "Lincan."

Vasher could not determine the nature of Savaiyon's countenance. "Why? His manifestation is arbitrary for something like this. If anyone is hurt I can transport them back here immediately."

"First of all, anything can happen on this mission. Who knows how people will respond all over Ashur at seeing us. Second, have you ever spoken to Lincan? He knows how to talk to people. He has the charisma and charm to work over just about anyone if he puts his mind to it."

Savaiyon simply nodded in approval. "Go on."

"We should start in Vandenar. Desmond is one of the few Descendants who has a friendly relationship with an Augur. We can start there, let the rest of the group see how Desmond interacts with the Augur, and then everyone can disperse while we go to the Tower." Vasher knew that Savaiyon would be impressed by that strategy.

"Not bad. Your thinking is quite sound. I am glad that you are proving me right. Continue."

Vasher knew he would have to include a wild card, someone that would keep Savaiyon from thinking this was an adventure for his friends. "It might sound far-fetched, but can we take Kadoog'han from his post for the sake of the mission?"

"Intriguing. But why?"

"Well-traveled. Great patience. Gets along with anyone. Can get anyone to do a favor for him. Besides, when was the last time he was even allowed to leave the House?"

"You assume he wants to leave his post."

"The man hides at the base of the mountain that hides the touch portal to this island. That is a lot of hiding. And how often do we get visitors there? I agree, Kadoog'han enjoys his post, but that does not mean he wouldn't enjoy a mission that involves travel."

"Very well. If he agrees to it, then he comes. Anyone else?"

"Galiceans don't trust most people in Ashur. I figure if we send the Taurani, they would leave him alone. Marshall is tough enough to handle himself in most Galicean cities. He doesn't camouflage like Kadoog'han, but Taurani are trained to know their surroundings."

"I am starting to sense a pattern here. Aside from Kadoog'han, is this not your circle of friends?"

"And there is very good reason for that. I trust them. We have a very sensitive mission ahead of us. We all know each other, know how to work with each other and communicate well with each other. Marshall is stubborn, but not stupid. You should know better than anyone how difficult it is to meet with a Galicean Augur. If I am unable to go there myself and use my manifestation to persuade them, then what? I would send Lincan there in a heartbeat, but he cannot defend himself the way Marshall can. No one in the House can."

Savaiyon nodded again, "I see your point. It makes sense. That makes seven of us. I do not think that will be enough to cover everything."

"Two more. Horatio." Savaiyon's eyes met Vasher's quickly. "Before you protest, think. Horatio is from the Wolf's Paw, just like Kadoog'han. Horatio has also traveled, just like Kadoog'han. I know he talks too much. *I know.* But we need Descendants who have seen Ashur's customs. Horatio traveled most of Ashur before coming here. I don't know how he did not get killed or beaten in those travels, because I'm sure there were many who wanted to, but that is another testament as to why he should come. There is obviously a certain charm to him that people see. We are about to send Descendants out into the world, and half of that world does not like us. We cannot fight back with our fists. Some of us can fight back with lightning. That is why we need Horatio."

"Fine. He can come. You said two more. Who is the last one?"

Vasher felt nervous. He knew Baltaszar would be a difficult sell. "Well, if lightning can defend us, then so can fire."

"No."

"What?"

"No Baltaszar. As it is, Marshall does not understand Ashur. We cannot afford to have two people who have no concept of this land. At least Marshall has fighting skill. Baltaszar controls fire. The last thing we need is for him to burn down a city because he panics at an angry mob."

"Have you sat down and ever spoken to him? Baltaszar isn't built that way. Besides, we have all studied and learned from you about the cultures of Ashur. If you are that good of a teacher, then Baltaszar should be fine."

"I still disagree. Look, Vasher, I like the boy. Baltaszar is polite and very low key, but he is new to Ashurian customs, untested with his manifestation, and therefore, dangerous. We do not have the time for unexpected complications on this mission."

Vasher pushed his frustration back and focused. He focused so hard on Savaiyon's response that a few moments passed before he realized the melody flowing through him. "I can vouch for him.

Baltaszar has already been to Vandenar, Khiry, and the City of the Fallen. That's more than many other Descendants who have been exposed to Ashur for their whole lives. Trust me, Savaiyon. Baltaszar works well with all of us. He is on the same page as the rest of our circle. He is the one you want defending you when things get out of hand."

Savaiyon seemed confused for a moment. "That makes sense. I see it now. It makes perfect sense." Vasher released his manifestation slowly, only to be filled with guilt. He regretted manipulating Savaiyon, but he knew Savaiyon was wrong, and this was the only way to get things right. Lately, none of his victories truly felt like victories. Vasher took it as a poor omen that so many situations were turning out to be bittersweet.

"When do we leave?" He asked Savaiyon hesitantly, unsure of whether the Maven was aware of what just happened.

"Two days. I have to speak to Kadoog'han. And everyone needs time to prepare and set their affairs in order. There is no telling how long this mission could take. Since you selected the team, I will give you the responsibility of telling them all, with the exception of Kadoog'han, of course. Do so tonight. It is still early enough that no one should be sleeping. Then again, tell Lincan first, if he is still awake. That boy takes naps at the strangest times." A yellow outline formed and spread into an opening, leading to one of the common rooms on the first floor of the House. Vasher followed Savaiyon through. The idea that he was shaping this mission was exciting, yet terrifying at the same time. If anything went wrong, it would be his fault.

***

Horatio still didn't understand why they needed to bring so much. The packs were one thing, but horses seemed excessive. Even if they were each going to different cities after Vandenar, it couldn't be too difficult to find a horse. He wasn't angry about it, though. If anything, he loved horses. But the only explanation was that it was winter now, so bringing horses would help if they needed to move quickly. It made no sense. He turned to Baltaszar, who brought up the rear behind Savaiyon, Vasher, Kadoog'han, Lincan, Desmond, Badalao, and Marshall. Horatio would have made a few different selections for the team. *You'd think they would have asked a girl or two. Man.* "You think this will be any fun? Vasher sold it to me as an opportunity to travel and see my home. Honestly, I don't really need a reason to get a break from that place."

"You don't like it at the House? You sure look like you've been enjoying it for the past seven months." Baltaszar walked while a fireball hovered ahead of him. It was rare to see Baltaszar without a fireball somewhere close to him anymore.

"No, I didn't mean that. I guess I could just use a break is all. It can feel a little tight on the island at times."

"Yeah, I can relate to that. And that's exactly why I'm here. I suppose I couldn't have said no to Vasher anyway, but Marlowe promised me that I could make a trip back to Haedon once I finished reading *The Book of Orijin*. I finished it a month ago and he's always got another excuse for why I can't go." Baltaszar nodded to him and lowered his voice. "As soon as Vash mentioned Vandenar, I was in. At some point while we're here, I'm going to sneak away to head home."

"Seriously? I don't think that's smart. They'll be angry about that. Maven Savaiyon is creating a doorway for each of us. How are you going to avoid that?"

"I will leave before we get to that point. Trust me, I have to do this."

Horatio didn't really understand Baltaszar's desperation, considering that he'd made it clear that there was nothing left for him in Haedon. "What is so important about going back? I thought you said your family was gone." They stepped through Savaiyon's doorway and onto the road leading to Vandenar's gates.

"Three things. The man in charge of Haedon is still there and I need to speak to him. I need to know about my father, and my mother if he knows anything about her. I want to see if my house is still there. I doubt it, but I still want to check. And...there is Yas."

Horatio shook his head. "You're still stuck on her? That girl must be worth a haul of fish for you to be still thinking about her. You do realize we're going to see Anahi in a matter of minutes, right?" Horatio sympathized with him. He'd never actually loved a girl, but having seen how tormented Baltaszar was, he knew that what his friend had with Yasaman was more than just love. "If ending a relationship means feeling how you do right now I think I'd rather do what Lao does. No chance of getting hurt when you're just having a go all the time."

"It's not all bad. What we had before things got bad was incredible. And that's why I have to go back. I owe her that much before I move on. Anyway, yeah, I have no idea what I am going to do about Anahi. You think she'll understand about my situation? I mean, it's not like I had time to go and get closure before."

Horatio looked at Baltaszar sideways, "Wait, are you planning on doing something with Anahi while you're here? Tasz, I didn't think you had it in you!"

"Shh. Calm down, fool. I'm not planning anything. At least not until I know definitively where I stand with Yas. I'm just saying that I have not ruled out pursuing Anahi in the future. What I meant was that I hope she doesn't think I'm ready for that right now, because I would feel bad."

"Oh, well that makes sense. And after you finish your business in Haedon and with the Augurs, you could always ask Maven Savaiyon to bring you back here to see Anahi again. Assuming Marlowe allows it. That's just like when my brother was in love with this girl in the next town...wait, was that Leonard?" He was no longer sure whether that situation involved his brother or someone else. Horatio hated that his memory could be such a confusing thing. He glanced sheepishly at Baltaszar, "I'm sorry. I really thought that was going somewhere."

"No big deal. I know how frustrating it must be for you."

"Thanks." Whenever this happened, most of his circle of friends would be short on patience with him. Lincan and Baltaszar tended to be better at hiding their frustrations.

Horatio hadn't realized they were walking down Vandenar's main avenue. Sunset neared and most vendors were packing up their wares for the night.

"I don't know about the rest of you, but I'm ready to get drunk as soon as we get there," Lincan shouted from the front.

Savaiyon promptly responded, "No. First is business. When we arrive at the inn, we get ourselves and our rooms situated, then we go to the Augur."

"The what?" Marshall apparently hadn't known their formal titles.

Horatio snickered, "The Blind Man."

"Oh."

Savaiyon continued, "As I was saying, once we talk to Master Keeramm, we can return to the inn and relax until tomorrow. Remember, our first priority is prophecy. Tonight, we will all go together so that everyone knows what questions to ask and understands the etiquette. Most Augurs are friendly and are open about their blindness, but if you happen to anger one, they have been known to refuse your company for life. So again, it is critical that you pay attention and understand the nature of this mission. Either Desmond or Baltaszar can do the introductions, or both. After that, Vasher and I will do the talking. Understood?"

The rest of them, even Kadoog'han nodded in agreement and mumbled some form of affirmation.

"What did you say his name was?" Lincan was always asking people's names. Then again, he was always remembering people's names. Horatio wondered if Lincan would make an attempt at talking to the Augur.

"Keeramm. Munn Keeramm."

"You mean like two animals? His name is Monkey Ram?"

All of them laughed, save Savaiyon. "Munn. Keeramm. First name, Munn. Last name, Keeramm. It is that simple. Understood?" Lincan nodded. Savaiyon turned to Vasher, "This is why you chose these people?"

Vasher shrugged as if to imply that it wasn't his fault. He replied, sarcastically, "I barely know them."

They finally arrived at The Happy Elephant as the sky had begun its transformation from blue to pink and orange. Horatio was surprised at how well he remembered the inn. It had been about seven months since he'd met Baltaszar for the first time. When the innkeeper, he'd forgotten his name, told Horatio that there was another Descendant staying there, he was beside himself. It had been the first time he'd actually met another one in his travels. They tied their horses out front and entered.

As they walked into the common room of the inn, everyone's eyes turned to them. "Maybe we should have told them we were coming," he mumbled to Savaiyon. Baltaszar shouldered his way in front of Horatio and stood in the middle of everyone. "Are you hiding? I don't even see her in the room. There's hardly anyone in here except a dozen people sitting at the counter. Calm down, man." The others all turned to glance at Baltaszar. Horatio mumbled, "Sorry."

Truthfully, he hadn't really scanned the whole room, but he didn't see Anahi anywhere at first glance. The innkeeper hurried to them from behind the counter. "Desmond! How ya doin', boy? Yer the last person I woulda expected ta see here! An' ya brought yer friends! Oh I recognize some o' ya! Let's see, uh…Horatio, right? An' is that Baltaszar back there? Sorry, I don't know the rest o' ya, but yer all welcome in the Elephant! Just tell me what ya need!"

Savaiyon stepped to the front. "Thank you, Cyrus. I am Maven Savaiyon. We appreciate your hospitality, especially in these tenuous times. If you have rooms that accommodate two each, we will require five, as there are nine of us."

"Ah, that'll be a tough push. We only have two rooms with two separate beds. I can give ya singles, but I dunno if I can afford ta give ya all fer free this time. Got an unusually high number o' people stayin' here. If there were less of ya, I …"

Savaiyon cut him off, "That is not a concern. We have plenty of coin to pay you and I will not allow you to give us anything free."

"Nonsense, I take care o' Descendants! I would be ashamed if I couldn't do somethin' fer ya! How 'bout ya pay fer half the rooms?"

"Seriously, friend. We do not want to stretch your profits thin. We have no trouble with paying our way. You obviously have many finances to manage."

Horatio could see this conversation going back and forth for a while. He wondered if Vasher would step in and use his manifestation to persuade Cyrus. Just as the thought passed through his mind, Lincan actually spoke up. "How about we pay for rooms and we drink for free? We will only be here for tonight and tomorrow, so that wouldn't make a significant difference."

Cyrus nodded, "Yes. That sounds fair. But don't feel guilty about enjoyin' yerselves. Drink as much as ye'd like!"

Savaiyon acquiesced. "Very well. I can agree to that." Lincan had a way of setting things at ease. Horatio sometimes thought of Lincan's manifestation as symbolic to his personality. Although he could physically heal people, Lincan had a way of healing situations as well. At the same time, he also knew how to talk people into getting his way or agreeing with him. Horatio wondered how powerful Lincan could be with Vasher's manifestation instead. *Maybe he would be too dangerous with it. Maybe the Orijin knew better.*

Cyrus turned to the girl behind the bar counter. "Wenda, can ya grab the other girls an' get some rooms prepared? The two doubles an' five regulars. An' anythin' these boys need, make sure ya get it fer 'em!" Wenda left and walked up the stairs on the other side of the room.

Savaiyon extended his hand, "Thank you Master Cyrus. We

know that you appreciate the Descendants and the House of Darian. But understand that we also appreciate you and anyone who goes out of their way to protect us. That is why I insisted on paying, to show you our appreciation in return."

Cyrus laughed, "Seems there's lotsa respect ta go around the room, huh. I'm proud ta have ya here. Can I have dinner ready fer ya once yer done settlin' down?"

"Perhaps later. We would like to see Master Keeramm as soon as we can. We will assuredly be hungry upon our return, though."

"No trouble at all. Ya can leave yer packs here. I'll tell the girls ta bring 'em ta yer rooms." Cyrus turned and scampered to the staircase where Wenda had ascended, yelling the whole way. "Anahi! Anahi! You an' the girls come down an' help these gentlemen with their things!"

Horatio nudged Baltaszar's arm and whispered, "She *is* here." He couldn't help but smile. While he felt bad for his friend, Baltaszar's awkwardness was too much to not enjoy. Though if Baltaszar knew Horatio was enjoying this, he'd likely punch him.

"There is no need for them to exert themselves. We can put our things away." Savaiyon turned to the rest of them, "Kadoog'han and I will share a room. Any volunteers to share the other double?"

"Lao an' I will take it. It'll keep Lao on his best behavior in my town anyway." Desmond flashed a mischievous grin at Badalao. "The last thing I want is Lao sleepin' with any girl I grew up with."

"Good. That was easy. We'll put our packs away and then meet back down here in within a few minutes." Cyrus attempted a protest but Savaiyon walked past him and up the stairs. Horatio and the rest of them followed.

On the second floor, Savaiyon, Kadoog'han, Desmond, and Badalao were led all the way to the end of the hall by Wenda and another young girl. As the six of them walked away, Horatio noticed Anahi walking toward them. She waved her hand in a circular motion at three doors on one side and two on the other. "These are yers, lads. Nice ta see ya again, Horatio. Choose which ever ones suit yer fancy, but they're all pretty much the same."

Horatio smiled back at her, "You, too." Anahi watched as they all sorted out their rooms. She had a certain glow to her that he hadn't noticed the last time he saw her. He was somewhat taken aback that she hadn't greeted Baltaszar. *Maybe the awkwardness is on both sides.* He walked into the room next to Baltaszar's. *This is going to be fun.* Horatio dropped his pack on the bed, not bothering to open it. *I can change when we get back. We're going to see a Blind Man, for Orijin's sake.*

He stepped back into the hallway to see Lincan doing the same. Before Lincan could walk away, Horatio stopped him. "Linc," he whispered and pointed to Baltaszar's door. Lincan looked at him curiously and scratched his head. Horatio put a finger to his mouth and then leaned against the door. Lincan did the same. Horatio could only hear muffled voices. *She's definitely in there. They're not talking very loud. At least no one is angry.*

The conversation went on for another minute or two before he heard Anahi raise her voice. He was almost certain she'd said, "Then when!" Baltaszar said something in response, but he was talking too low and too fast for Horatio to understand. Then there was silence. The door opened too quickly for Horatio and Lincan to be able to hide or pretend they were doing something else. Anahi saw the two of them and glowered before storming off. *Definitely no glow that time.*

Baltaszar exited the room as well, but seemed more relieved than angry to see the two of them. "You two were listening the whole time?"

"It was Raish's idea." Lincan pointed his finger at Horatio while looking at Baltaszar.

"I just wanted to make sure everything was going well. And I was kind of nosy, too."

Baltaszar shook his head, "It's fine, I'm not mad at you two." He continued walking and Horatio and Lincan followed. "I guess I should have expected it though. She was angry that I haven't spoken to Yasaman yet."

"Did you tell her that you want to, though? Does she at least know how you feel?"

"I told her, but who knows if she believes me. She got quiet when I told her that I would come back here as soon as I spoke with Yas. She was trying not to cry. She didn't look at me after that. That's when she rushed out."

Lincan spoke up as they descended the stairs. "I thought you were done with Yasaman."

"Well, I am and I'm not. I mean, I don't know. That's the problem. I haven't been back home in almost eight months. I don't really have a clue about what we are. I thought once my father died, I would continue being angry with her, but I'm not. I've kind of missed her this whole time."

Horatio was confused. "So you're saying that if you can salvage what you have with Yas, you'll stick with her?"

"Maybe. Probably. Who knows? I suppose I'll find out when I see her. I honestly won't know how I feel until I see her face to face. Until I know what she's thinking. And that's the biggest reason I need to see her again."

Lincan gave Baltaszar a little shove. "That's why she's pissed at you. She probably knows that she's your second option."

"It's not like that. Maybe it is. Anyway, can we save this conversation for later? I don't feel like explaining this to the whole group." All of the others were waiting by the main doorway.

Marshall shook his head, "You girls done getting pretty for the Blind Man?"

Baltaszar punched him in the arm. "Shut up. Let's go. We're here." With that, Desmond led them out and down the street.

Cyrus had given them a few torches to carry in case the side streets proved too dark. Before anyone could light a torch, though, Baltaszar flicked his wrists and two fireballs hovered about his open palms. They moved so that both were in front of the group. Baltaszar moved to the front, Horatio assumed for better control.

They walked on for a short while until Desmond stopped them in front of a porch with a rocking chair on it. "Here." Lights shone through the windows. Desmond waved for them to follow as he walked up the porch stairs and knocked on the door. Baltaszar's fireballs fell to the ground and disappeared. A shaggy-haired boy answered the door. Upon seeing Desmond, the boy grinned widely and flung his arms around Desmond's waist. "Farco! I'm so glad yer still here!" Desmond walked inside with Farco still draped around him. Once everyone crowded inside and Kadoog'han shut the door, Desmond hoisted up Farco with one arm so that Farco was at eye level with the rest of them. "Farco is my cousin. His parents were killed by the King's men, so I arranged fer him ta be Master Keeramm's apprentice an' servant. Munn Keeramm is a good man. No hesitation ta take him in. Once he's old enough, Farco'll go ta the Anonymi fer trainin'." Desmond set down the boy. "Is he asleep?"

"Nah, just restin'. I'll get him." Farco shuffled off to another room and returned a several moments later leading an elderly man. His appearance surprised Horatio. He'd been expecting someone less frail. Munn Keeramm was a short, bald, old man with spots dotting his skin. He walked slowly, and Horatio suspected that wasn't just because he was blind. Horatio wondered why he resided here, rather than at the Tower of the Blind. Farco led him to sit down at a table covered in books, varying between open and closed, but all dusty.

"Welcome, fellas. I don't normally get visitors after sundown, but I would never turn away a Descendant. Especially Desmond. Oh, an' nice ta see ya again, Baltaszar." Keeramm chuckled. Horatio had heard that most Augurs routinely made light of their lack of vision. He wondered if Keeramm actually knew on his own that Desmond and Baltaszar were there, or if Farco had told him. "Obviously ya seek a prophecy. About what?"

Savaiyon spoke up. "Good evening, Master Keeramm. I am Maven Savaiyon, of the House of Darian. Zin Marlowe has charged us with a mission to find out if there will be an attempt to assassinate him. He has reason to believe that his life is in danger." Savaiyon looked around at the rest of them sternly. Horatio understood that the details of this meeting would not be discussed beyond the people in this room. *So that's why Vasher was so awkward about the details.*

"I see. Nothin' comes directly ta mind, but that's why we've got the books, right? Farco, ya know which ones I need. Grab 'em fer me, dear boy." Farco walked to the bookshelf behind Keeramm and scanned the dozens of volumes on the shelves. "Fellas, think ya can help me clear this table? I'll have ta look through more than one volume ta see if anything fits what yer lookin' for. I don't usually care 'bout most people seein' the mess, but yer all Descendants. An' there's lotsa ya, so I can put ya ta work!"

Savaiyon spoke for all of them. "It would be our pleasure, Master Keeramm. Where would you have us put your books?" He waved for the whole group to gather at the table.

"There's another table in the corner back there. Ya can just put 'em on top o' it. Once I give Farco some free time, he'll find a good place fer 'em. Permanent place. Desmond, I thank ya an' the Orijin every day that ya brought that boy ta me. He is truly a blessin' an' I'll be helpless once he leaves fer his trainin'." Horatio and the others all started grabbing thick, heavy books from the table and moved them. As they worked, Farco set one volume in front of Keeramm and the man passed his fingers over wordless pages of the book. Horatio had never seen the Blind's system of words but found it to be remarkable. Farco sat on the floor next to him with another volume. "Don't be alarmed. I know Augurs don't allow anyone else ta read their prophecy books, but Farco is an exception. I trust him with my life. Way I see it, that means I can trust him ta read these books an' keep their secrets." None of them had an issue with Farco reading the other volume.

They continued to move the books for several minutes until Farco broke the silence. "Think I found somethin', Master Keeramm." The boy stood and placed his volume on the table, then directed Keeramm's hand to the left page.

"Hmm. Yes, this is from when I was still in the Tower. Give me a moment ta review it all." Keeramm slid his hand meticulously across the page. All of them had stopped what they were doing to stare at Keeramm. *This is serious. Someone wants to kill Marlowe?* "Yes. Oh dear. I apologize in advance. The prophecy itself doesn' specifically address yer question. But Farco is quite astute an' had a keen eye ta notice this one. It says, 'Zin Marlowe shall be betrayed within the House o' Darian durin' his ninetieth year.' Again I apologize. That's a vague statement, an' it doesn't give ya much ta work with."

Horatio was shocked. *What? Betrayed? Does that mean one of us will kill him? That's impossible! No one in the House is that crazy! How could someone kill him just because they don't like him?*

Lincan scratched his head. "I think 'betrayed' is a little vague, no? We train for fighting without his knowledge. Technically that is a betrayal."

Baltaszar chimed in as well, "And ninetieth year? That's not even any time soon! Marlowe has to be what, just around his fortieth year?"

Savaiyon looked as if he had something to say, but paused for a moment. "I agree that this prophecy does not give us much. However, it still tells us that there is, or will be, a traitor in the House of Darian. That in itself is unsettling. Because if someone among us has the potential to turn to evil, everything we know and understand about Descendants is wrong. It means that the Orijin's 'chosen ones' do not always have pure hearts. Master Keeramm, how much more of those volumes do you need to peruse? Is there a possibility that there is another prophecy pertaining to Marlowe?"

Horatio couldn't hold in his curiosity. "How? How could someone even make it to the House and not one of us realize he means any harm? We have to find out if this person is already there!"

"Oh I'm afraid I barely got through a quarter, Maven Savaiyon. It will take much time if I have ta read through the whole thing. Not that I mind. Farco here is quick with his readin' as well. Farco, how much o' yers ya got left?"

"About the same."

"No worries, Master Savaiyon. Ye should all should get comfortable. Farco, go put on tea fer everyone. We could be here fer a while."

Savaiyon rubbed his chin, looking back and forth between Keeramm and the group. "No. These boys do not need to stay. Kadoog'han, you and I will stay. The rest of you can return to the inn. However, remember that I am doing this as a favor to you. You will return to the Elephant and enjoy yourselves tonight. Once we separate tomorrow, your first priority is the mission. There will be no time for fun. Understood?"

They all agreed. Horatio always found it annoying how Savaiyon ended with 'understood' so often, as if they were his children. He and the others shook hands with Farco and Keeramm and thanked them for their hospitality. Desmond gave Farco a tight, prolonged hug and tousled his hair before leaving. Horatio could have sworn they all walked a little faster in exiting Keeramm's house.

***

Baltaszar was sure she was doing it on purpose. They'd returned to the "Elephant" less than a half an hour ago and Anahi had been next to Desmond the entire time. Cyrus had attempted to comfort him by explaining that Desmond and she had known each other for years and were simply catching up. *Yeah right. Nobody is that excited to see a person. He's your nephew, of course you'll defend him.* He gulped more ale and contorted his mouth in frustration. Horatio was no help. He made jokes to lighten the mood, but none of them were funny. Every so often, Anahi would glance over at him, pretending she was scanning the whole room.

Cyrus came over once more and sat down. "I know you an' her are havin' some trouble an' I'd like ta help ya, Baltaszar, I really would. But she isn' workin' right now so I can't even send her off ta do somethin'. Maybe ya should try talkin' ta her again. After the ale wears off, though."

"Yeah. Maybe." No matter how smart any advice was, Baltaszar didn't want to listen. He preferred to sit there and watch her, and feel sorry for himself. He wanted to be annoyed and angry, especially watching the rest of his friends drinking and laughing and telling stories. He wasn't angry that they were having fun. He was angry that he wasn't in the mood to. Baltaszar stared at Desmond and Anahi again. They continued swaying and laughing. *I bet they're laughing at me. I bet she's telling him how naïve I am. Or that I turned her away the first time we met and how stupid I am to have rejected her. Or that I'm still in love with another girl even though I haven't seen or spoken to her in almost a year, but I swear that there is still hope for us. Maybe I really am as stupid as they're saying.* "Cyrus, can you get me another?" He chugged and emptied his glass.

Horatio stood. "I'll get it. I'm getting another anyway. And my attempts to cheer you up so far have been poor, so it's the least I can do."

"Thanks, brother." Baltaszar felt guilty. Horatio meant well. Truthfully, nothing Horatio could have said would have been enough. "You don't have to sit here with me. I'm going to head upstairs anyway, so have some fun with the others."

"Fair enough. I'll bring you your drink first. You good on your own?"

"Yeah, I'll be fine. I just want to numb myself a little and then fall asleep without any trouble. Thanks." Horatio returned promptly with another mug. He gripped Baltaszar's shoulder and nodded, then walked away to the others at the counter. "You don't have to stay either, Cyrus. I appreciate your advice. But I'd rather just be angry right now. I won't do anything stupid, don't worry."

Cyrus hesitated, then stood. "I know ya got a good head, boy. Get some sleep an' in the mornin' ye'll be in a better mood. Ye two will work this out before ya leave. I know it. Feel better lad. An' I know yer not fond o' Desmond right now, but he's my nephew. I know him. He wouldn't do that ta ya." Cyrus' countenance looked like he felt just as bad as Baltaszar.

Baltaszar stared at his glass. Then gulped down half of it. He repeated the process and arose from the table. Anahi glanced over once more, mid-laugh. *She is definitely laughing at me. So is he. The hell with them. He took a few steps toward the stairs. No. Damn them. They don't even feel bad. They don't care about me.* Baltaszar walked to Desmond and Anahi at the end of the counter. He faced Desmond and shoved him off his stool. "This is a shitty thing you're doing. Friend. You knew I liked her! You knew how I felt! We're part of a bloody brotherhood! How could you flirt with her while I'm in the same room, you filthy prat!"

Desmond stood and gripped Baltaszar by the neck of his shirt.

"We haven't friggin even mentioned ya, ya spoiled little bitch! I haven't seen Anahi in a year! Neither of us've even thought about ya! Who the hell are ya ta come ta me like that?" Desmond lifted him and threw him toward the front door. Baltaszar hit a table and then crashed to the floor.

His back hurt in a few places, as well as his elbow, but the ale dulled most of the pain. He stood up and let the manifestation course through him. He flicked his wrists and two fireballs appeared, hovering just about his palms. Cyrus yelled from behind the counter, "Baltaszar, put those away! Put 'em out right now!"

Baltaszar barely heard him, his focus solely on Desmond. He flung his fireballs at Desmond, but something was holding them back. Desmond smiled at him. *Bastard. He's stopping them.* They stood like that for several moments. The fireballs shifted mere inches back and forth as Desmond returned Baltaszar's cold stare. As Baltaszar pushed and pushed, the anger slowly dissipated. *Damn it. If I don't extinguish them, I'll burn down the whole bloody Elephant.* He let go of his manifestation and the fireballs blinked out. "I'm...sorry," he said sheepishly. He put his hands on his hips and stared at the ground. Baltaszar truly felt badly at how reckless he'd acted. He walked to Desmond slowly and clapped his shoulder, "I'm sorry, man." Desmond just stared at him. He turned to Cyrus, "You too, Cyrus. I'm sorry," and walked upstairs without waiting for a response. He could feel the eyes of everyone in the room pressing into his back.

Baltaszar fell into his bed and stared at the ceiling for more than half an hour. He'd never let his anger influence him so severely, and he'd been angry plenty of times. *I don't even care if the rest of them are mad. I just hope Cyrus forgives me. Orijin, please let him forgive me. I've ruined any chance with Anahi, but please let Cyrus forgive me.* Someone knocked at his door. "Go away!"

The door opened, despite Baltaszar's command, and Anahi walked in, a nervous look on her face. She shut the door and laid next to Baltaszar on the bed. She stared up at the ceiling along with him. "Hey." The sight of her brought the final touches of sobering up. "Still fergettin' ta lock the door..."

Well she isn't yelling. She doesn't even look mad. "You're the last person I would have expected to come up here and not yell at me."

"I think I deserve more credit than yer givin me."

"I'm not complaining. It's just, I figured that if you did speak to me again, you wouldn't have nice things to say. I definitely would never have expected you to lay next to me and say 'Hey'." He smirked.

"I could be mad. I could very easily be mad. But I know where all that down there came from, an' so I figure it's better ta not focus on what ya probably already know ya did wrong." She turned her head toward Baltaszar. "Ya did apologize. An' we all saw ya realized yer mistake."

"Cyrus?"

"Cyrus isn't mad. He was more concerned about ya. Wanted ta make sure ya weren't takin' it out on yerself up here. Look, our conversation earlier. I coulda handled that better. I know. Ye've been busy at the House o' Darian an' I shoulda understood that ya wouldn't have time ta talk ta her yet. I guess I just got excited when I saw ya here an' got selfish. I care fer ya, Baltaszar. I'm still waitin' fer when yer ready. As long as ya promise that I'm not wastin' my time."

"I'll be completely honest with you." He paused and looked at her. "I have feelings for both of you. It's not that I want her over you, it's just that I have a history with her and I need to know whether that is definitely over with. We were both emotional when she broke things off and I need to know that that's how she really felt. I could easily just tell you that I'm done with her and that she doesn't matter, but that wouldn't be completely true. If I were to start something with you right now, I would still have Yasaman at the back of my mind, wondering about where we stand. I know that's not what you want to hear, but that is how it is with me."

"Yer right. That's not what I want ta hear. How long do you expect me ta keep waiting? The past seven months have felt like forever. I can't wait another seven."

"How about a week? Help me sneak out of here tonight and I'll go back to Haedon immediately."

"Are ya mad? Don't ya have a mission ta worry about?"

"The mission will still be there when I return. Trust me. I'll take care of that once I'm done in Haedon."

"Why not just tell yer friends what ya want ta do? Doesn't seem like ya have ta sneak around."

"If I get in trouble for this, I don't want any of them to be associated. It wouldn't be fair. And Marlowe, our Headmaster at the House, promised me a long time ago that he would allow me to go back home once I finished reading *The Book of Orijin*. I finished it a while ago and I'm still waiting. I need to go back there to tie up more than one loose end. There are at least two people that I need to talk to. Look, I can leave tonight and get there in two to three days. I can handle all of my responsibilities within a few hours, and then I'll come right back. Five to six days at most. I promise."

A tear flowed from her eye to the bed. Baltaszar wasn't sure if it was genuine or because of the position of her head. "Fine, I can handle that. But if yer not back here within a week, I'm not gonna wait fer ya any longer. Not that the boys are linin' up ta see me, but I'll make it a point ta forget ya."

"The boys are stupid to not be lining up. You saw how jealous I was down there. I don't know how anyone else wouldn't act that way."

"Yeah, yeah. So when do ya want my help?"

"Why not right now? I don't need much from you. I just need you to tell the others to leave me alone until the morning. That way I am long gone by the time they notice."

"How will ya leave?"

Baltaszar nodded his head, "Window. The jump isn't far. I'll grab my horse and ride away."

Anahi seemed reluctant. "An' when do ya want me ta go back downstairs?"

Baltaszar rose from the bed and pulled Anahi by the hand to do the same. He held her by the waist and once again looked intently at her as she put her arms on his shoulders. He wanted to kiss her. He'd wanted to since he returned to Vandenar, but he was nervous that she'd be mad. The hell with it. Baltaszar took that chance and kissed her deeply. Anahi immediately kissed back. They stood there for several moments before Baltaszar pulled away. "I know you were strict about us waiting to do that, but I think we both needed it."

Anahi laughed. "For once, ya did somethin' smart."

He grinned toothily. "Now you can go back. I'll pack up my things, wait a few minutes, and then I'll leave." She put her head against his shoulder. "And when I see you again, I'll be all yours." Baltaszar hugged her tightly and then kissed her hand as she walked away. She turned and smiled once she got to the door, then blew him a kiss before she walked away.

He shut the door and locked it, then gathered his things. *I guess I finally made a decision about Yas. Right? Does that mean that I'm finally over her now?* Baltaszar sighed. *What if the feelings return when I see her?* He mumbled to himself, "I suppose I'll find out when

I get there."

Baltaszar looked out the window. No one. He climbed out and dropped to the ground below. The impact was a little harder than he expected, but he was sure the pain in his ankle would go away. His back still ached a bit from his fight with Desmond. *Stop being a pansy.* Baltaszar crept to his horse, untied it and mounted quickly, then rode away into the night as fast as he could. He had a more important mission to worry about than Marlowe's.

CHAPTER 21
RAGE

From *The Book of Orijin,* **Verse Three Hundred Eighteen**
We have nourished you with emotions so that you may live fruitful lives. Only by mastering your emotions will your lives find success.

SEVEN MONTHS BEFORE Baltaszar would not have been able to make such a clandestine journey so easily. His second attempt to cross the river had been infinitely more successful, especially since he'd heated the water around him as he swam so that no poisonous snakes could bite him. All he had to do once across was to create a big enough fire to dry himself quickly, and it was as if he'd never stepped foot into the water. He'd traveled another two days since crossing and luckily the snow had only started a few hours ago. Baltaszar missed the wool cloak that he used to have, but at least Marlowe had provided him with a grey wool coat. No one at the House ever had to worry about clothes. Baltaszar always wondered where they came from, but always forgot to ask.

The edge of the Never lay a few minutes away, he could already see the clearing because of the fireball that floated in the air a few yards ahead of him, even in the steady snowfall. It had been what he'd practiced the most in his time at the House. He loved to flick his wrists and make fireballs appear. Most of the time, he would release them right away. The fireballs came in handy during his late night escapades with his friends. *I hope they forgive me for leaving them. I've already pissed them off once in a big way.*

He stepped out of the forest and into the calmness of a sleeping Haedon. Baltaszar had worked the plan over in his mind repeatedly since he left Vandenar. *Speak to Oran Von. See what is left of home. Speak to Yasaman. Now I just have to go through with the plan. Especially the last part.*

Baltaszar wanted most to see Yas again, yet it was the last thing he wanted. He needed answers from Von more than anything and he needed the element of surprise. Baltaszar released his manifestation and walked on in darkness. The midnight streets were just as familiar as they had been seven months ago, despite the accumulating snow. Oran Von lived on the northern end of the village, on the other side of Haedon Square. Baltaszar would avoid the Square at all costs. He'd been unsure of what emotions would arise if he went back there and he could not risk those emotions overwhelming his confidence. *Who knows when I'll have another opportunity to do this?* He drove all thoughts of his father, for the time being, to the furthest reaches of his mind.

Despite the snow, no lanterns were lit at this time of night. If the snow persisted so aggressively his footprints would be gone by the time his business in Haedon was finished. *Von. Home. Yas. Leave. And back to Anahi in plenty of time. It all sounds so easy. If I'm lucky, Bo will be hiding here, too. I can sneak him back with me and find a safe place for him. Maybe even in Vandenar.* Baltaszar chuckled at the thought of Bo'az eating an elephant steak.

He walked on through the calmness of the snowfall until the northern half of Haedon was in sight. He had seen Oran Von's house a handful of times, on those few occasions when he'd joined his father on an errand. He walked down the road leading to Von's house. He wondered if Von's guards would be outside at this time of night, and in this weather. After his father's death, Baltaszar couldn't imagine any other disturbances in Haedon that would cause a threat to Von.

"No guards," he mumbled to himself. Baltaszar had never actually been inside the house. He chose the closest window. Though Von had once been a tall man, the windows were not unusually high. He pried a pane open as quietly as he could. *Good thing I had so much practice with Yas' window!*

Baltaszar hoisted himself up and scaled the window. He hit the floor with a loud squeak and slipped onto his back. *Bloody snow!*

A deep voice boomed. "What! Who is there?" Its owner was unmistakable.

Baltaszar scrambled to get up. "Tell me this isn't his bedroom," he sighed. With a hushed voice, Baltaszar hurriedly pleaded, "Please don't be afraid. It is Baltaszar Kontez. I mean you no harm. I only want to speak with you. I have questions about my father and I know you have answers."

A heavy knock came at the door. Von answered in the dark, "I am fine! Just some unexpected company, but I am quite fine! Make a pot of tea for me, then bring it in when it is ready!" Von lit a lantern and Baltaszar could finally see. He hobbled over to a chair by the wall and invited Baltaszar to sit next to him. As old as Von was, he hadn't really aged since Baltaszar had last seen him. "You look different," Von said. "Filled out. Have you finally gone to the House of Darian?" He asked the question with a smile.

"Yes, sir."

"And since you made it all the way there you obviously had at least one stop into the City of the Fallen. Oh Orijin, I hate that name. That would be the only reason for you to have questions. You have figured out who I am."

"I have, Master Von. Or should I say, Vitticus Khou."

Von smiled genuinely. "Ha, nobody has called me that in a long, long time. I'd almost forgotten that name, myself."

"Why are you not afraid of me?" Baltaszar was almost offended that he had been able to sit down and talk with Von so easily.

"I stopped worrying about death the night your father died. The night I allowed him to die."

"What's that?" Baltaszar gulped. Von wasn't supposed to be this open about things.

"I never wanted your father to die, dear boy. It was his idea. I only agreed to go along with it because I grew so exhausted arguing with him. Surely you remember me coming to your farm over the years? Before his confinement?" Baltaszar nodded. "He always asked for you and Bo'az to leave us because he knew I wanted to argue about telling you."

"Telling me what?"

"The truth, boy! The truth! He lied to you about that black line! He knew what it was! He came to Haedon because of it! You had that line from the time you were a little boy, the same night your mother disappeared. It scared the shit out of him."

Baltaszar's focus did not waver as a hulking man came in with a teapot and two cups. He set them down on a table next to Von, filled both cups and handed one to each of them. "Look, Zin Marlowe told me as soon as I got to the House of Darian that my father was a liar. At least he sacrificed himself to save me. I love my father, more than anyone could ever know, but at the moment I have mixed feelings about how he handled my life. I know my mother was abducted. I know why he came here. What I don't know is, why was it so important to hide me here? Why didn't he go looking for my mother? Is there any chance that my mother is still alive? Marlowe teased me with information when I first met him and then barely spoke to me again."

"Shortly after your mother vanished your father went to the Tower of the Blind. He hoped to find out if he would ever see your mother again. Hoped for clues on how to find her. He received a different prophecy and I doubt it had anything to do with your mother."

"What was it?"

"I have no idea. He never shared it. But it scared him so much that he brought you and Bo'az here. I imagine he thought he could get the better of the prophecy by hiding you here for your whole life."

"So why could you not go to the Tower and ask for the same prophecy?"

"That is not how it works. The Augurs will never share a prophecy about another person, simply because you demand to hear it. Prophecies are private. Sacred."

"Fine. My mother, though. Is there any hope that she is alive?"

Von sighed. "I suppose I could not give you a definite answer. But realistically, I would say no, Baltaszar. She has been gone for almost your whole lifetime. If she was abducted, fourteen years is a long time to keep someone prisoner. I do not believe that Raya abandoned you, Bo'az, and Joakwin. Though I never actually met your mother, her family was well-known throughout Galicea and southern Mireya. They were upstanding people. Good character. Your mother and her brother, your uncle, were not known to be any different. In my opinion she was taken. I would imagine by an agent of Jahmash. It wasn't King Edmund's way to *kidnap* Descendants."

"Why didn't my father try to look for her? Or was he too afraid to do that, as well?" Baltaszar felt tense. For seventeen years his father had been the greatest man he knew. And it turned out that the man he knew was a lie.

"I can only imagine how you must feel about him, especially to find it all out from someone else. But hold your judgment for now. There was much good in Joakwin. Asarei searched for your mother because Joakwin refused to leave you and Bo'az for even a moment.

For years Asarei searched Ashur and beyond. Not a soul had heard of or seen your mother. It was as if she had vanished from existence. Given her manifestation, she might have had the ability to do just that. But even then, she would have returned to you at some point if she was alive."

Her manifestation? "What was it? Marlowe never got around to telling me."

"It was something rather remarkable. She was able to travel to the Three Rings and back. I imagine that was why she was abducted. It is an attractive thing to a great many people to be able to interact with the dead."

Baltaszar steeled himself for a moment. If he let himself go, the conversation would have made him more emotional than he wanted in front of Von. He changed the subject quickly. "Who is this 'Asarei' that you speak of? Marlowe mentioned him as well."

Von nodded. "Asarei was a Maven at the House a long time ago, though he was not much older than your parents. He was one of very few Taurani to leave his people for the House. Once Edmund took the throne in Cerysia and deemed Descendants criminals, Marlowe decided that the House would abandon all violent acts. That meant that Descendants could no longer learn combat, nor could they use their manifestations to attack. I am sure you know those rules well. However, Asarei vehemently opposed this decision. Once it became clear that Marlowe would not change his mind, Asarei left. Many rumors circulated that he left to start his own version of the House of Darian."

"We could use a man like that at the House. People are quite upset about that rule. We do certain things in secret, though."

"I do not blame you. I have my…connections…to the rest of Ashur. There is a growing fear that Jahmash's return is not far off. You would do well to learn how to attack. Discreetly, of course."

Baltaszar suddenly realized that they'd been talking for quite a while. He looked outside to see the sky was still black and dotted with white snowflakes. "I came here expecting more tension. I still have to decide how I feel about my father, but I don't think that will be sorted out for some time. I was hoping to see my house again before I leave Haedon. Will I have trouble if I go there?"

"Ah. That clears up that argument."

Baltaszar looked at him sideways. "What do you mean?"

"The night after your father died someone returned to your house. However, once the people of Haedon found out someone was in there, they stormed your farm and set everything on fire. In the darkness of the night nobody could be sure of whether it was you or Bo'az there. Now it is clear that it was Bo'az. However, he was with three men who took him into the forest. They killed and hurt many of our people who tried to follow. In fairness, our people were trying to do the same to them. From the descriptions I was given of these three strangers, I believe one of them was Rhadames Slade, an old friend of mine and your father's."

"I met him. The same night that my father died. He was the one who told me to go to the House of Darian."

"If Slade is with Bo'az then he is safe. But as I said, there is nothing left where your house and farm once were. Having put on the charade of wanting to sentence your father, I could not refuse those who insisted on destroying and clearing the property. I apologize, lad."

"I do not blame you. I just hoped to see it, for old time's sake I guess. I should be going. I should be far from Haedon by the time the sun is up."

"I wish only the best for you, Baltaszar. I hope you accomplish great things at the House. I would strongly suggest, if you have the time, go to the Tower and see if that prophecy had anything to do with you. It only makes sense that it was about you or Bo'az. At least ask about your father. If I catch wind of anything pertaining to Bo'az, I will have my connections contact you at the House." Baltaszar rose and shook Von's hand heartily. He was about to climb the window when Von stopped him. "Dear boy, why not just go out through the door? It would prove much easier." Baltaszar reddened and walked to the bedroom door.

"Thank you. This was more helpful than you know."

***

Baltaszar had been surprised at how easy it had been to get in and speak to Von, as well as get the answers he'd wanted. He was almost disappointed that Von hadn't argued or put up a fight. Darkness still prevailed, though Baltaszar speculated he had about two hours until dawn. Yasaman's farm was within sight. *It's been almost a year; she'll be so happy to see me again. Right?*

Baltaszar could see Yas' home clearly enough to discern a flicker of light through one window. He lifted his knees high as he stepped through the snow to the house and peeked in a window. Yas' house was only one level and he could see the door to her room. A portly woman exited Yas' door and Baltaszar stifled a gasp. *That can't be her. A new maid, maybe?* The woman walked toward the kitchen and Baltaszar turned to circle around to Yas' own window. If he could avoid confrontation with Yas' parents or anyone else, things would go smoothly. As he took a step, one of the floor boards of the porch groaned loudly, causing Baltaszar to freeze. Footsteps immediately bounded to the front door of the house as Baltaszar froze where he stood.

The door flung open and the rotund silhouette in the doorway proved much too large to be Yas or her mother. "Who's there? I can see you! Answer me now or there will be a knife in your belly!" There was no hesitation in the woman's voice. Baltaszar pulled his hood down and raised his hands high as he stepped cautiously toward her.

"I am Baltaszar Kontez. I used to live in Haedon and am…an acquaintance…of Yasaman's." He continued to step slowly toward the woman, arms still raised. "I have not seen her in nearly a year and simply wish to speak to her. I trust you are a maid or nurse here?"

The large woman nodded a confirmation. "Do you not realize that it is the middle of the night, fool?"

"I do. But I am not welcome in this town any longer. I am not welcome by Yasaman's parents, either. I only came so that I could see her again; I did not want to bother anyone else. Please let me speak to her and I promise that I will not cause any trouble." Baltaszar could have charred the woman in seconds. It was humorous how, several months ago, he too would have thought that holding a knife to a complete stranger meant power over him.

A taller woman, Yasaman's mother, stood behind the knife-wielding one and whispered something to her. "Very well. You may come in."

Baltaszar entered the house and Yasaman's mother grabbed him by his coat. "I am only allowing you in my house because I fear your family's black magic and do not want it to burn down. Have your words with my daughter and then leave. I do not want your magic anywhere near this place. Do you understand me?"

Baltaszar nodded. "Lady Adin, I understand. I know that you and Master Adin do not like me, but I…" Yasaman's mother broke into tears and ran off before Baltaszar could finish his attempt at a truce. Baltaszar turned to the other woman, "What did I say?"

"I would think you would know, fool. Master Adin died eight months ago chasing after you and Yasaman."

"What? I...I was not with Yas eight months ago. She stopped speaking to me about two months before I left."

"It was definitely you. She was at your home and you both ran off with your friends in the middle of the night into the forest. One of your friends cut his head off as Isaan tried to take Yasaman back."

"I promise you, I left without having seen Yasaman for at least two...oh. Oh no. Bo'az." *That's what Von was talking about.* "Bloody Bo'az. I need to see her. I need to speak to her now. NOW." Baltaszar didn't wait for the woman to agree. He walked to Yasaman's door, swung it open, and saw her lying in her bed with her back to the door. "Yas?" Baltaszar sat on the bed and touched her shoulder. "Yas, it's me. It's Tasz." Only after looking her over did Baltaszar realize that Yasaman lay under several blankets and that bandages encased her head. He turned to the other woman, "What's wrong with her? Is she sick?"

"Yes and no. Although, given your history, it is better that this conversation only involves the two of you. She is well enough to speak to you. Wake her gently and allow her to get her bearings. Be quick, though. She needs her rest." The portly woman exited the room and shut the door.

Baltaszar squeezed Yas' shoulder and shook her gently. He leaned to her ear and whispered, "Yas, wake up. It's Tasz." After a moment, Yasaman grunted and turned her head to Baltaszar, opening her eyes. She blinked a few times and looked at him incredulously.

"Tasz." Her voice was faint. "What...what are you doing here?"

"I needed to see you. Ever since I left this blasted town, I haven't stopped thinking about you. I needed to know about us. But forget that for now. Are you sick? What happened? Are you seriously hurt?"

"I will be well in time. It's...complicated." She remained turned away from Baltaszar and turned her face away from him.

"Tell me what happened."

Yas stared into the darkness for several seconds. "I went back to your house to see you the night after your father died. I felt guilty for shutting you out and I had been hoping to perhaps rekindle what we'd had." She choked as if holding down a sob. "I found Bo'az...but...he was pretending to be you. It was dark Tasz, I had no way of knowing the difference. I didn't even know why he would lie."

"Pretending to be me? Why? Why would he do that?"

"I realized the truth later on and confronted him. He apparently...had fancied me and...I don't really understand it to be honest."

Baltaszar closed his eyes and shook his head. He hadn't prepared for anything like this. "Fine. We can get back to that. What happened at my house?"

Yas' voice was stable now, but still soft. "We weren't there for very long. Three men came looking for you, and Bo'az continued to pretend to be you. They wanted to take you with them to see their master. Linas was the leader. He was very tall. The other two were Slade and Gibreel. Slade was quiet; Gibreel was a bloody chuff."

"Slade came to me the night my father died. He is the one who told me to leave Haedon. He would have known that Bo'az was not me. Light of Orijin, there's a bloody line down my face!"

"I didn't understand what was happening, Baltaszar. Slade told the others that Bo'az was you. So either he was fooled or he was lying. We agreed to go with them because we thought it was the safest thing. They promised to protect you...well, Bo'az. They barely cared about me."

Baltaszar grasped his jaw for a few moments. "Where were they taking you? How did you get back here? If you are here, then where is Bo? Is he safe?"

Yasaman sighed and again stared into nothingness. She pursed her lips and then spoke. "They never said exactly where. Bo'az mentioned a name, something with a D. Dari...Dorian..."

"Hold on. Do you mean Darian?"

"I think that's what he said to them. They told us Darian was their master. They were taking us...well Bo'az...to him."

Baltaszar pulled Yas' shoulder so she could face him. "Look at me. Is Bo'az still with these men?"

She nodded. "I...I don't know. It's been months since I left them."

"If Slade is with him, then there is hope. Slade wouldn't protect me only to...or would he?"

"What are you talking about? What's going on?"

"They were lying to you. They're not going to Darian. Darian has been dead for thousands of years. Light of Orijin, where could they be going?" Baltaszar closed his eyes for a moment. "Yas, tell me the rest. Maybe I can piece this together and make sense of all of it. Where did they take you and how did you manage to escape?"

"We were traveling north. We rode through the Never and into the mountains beyond. They were trying to reach their boat beyond the mountains. I never made it that far. Though, I did not actually escape."

"What do you mean? Sit up, won't you? I can help you up."

"I cannot. My legs and arms are still weak from being broken and also the...there are other things. Let me just lie here. Baltaszar, I made it back here because they tried to kill me." Baltaszar stared at her wide-eyed. "We were attacked by giant wildcats on the mountain. The cats killed our horses and my leg was broken in the process. Gibreel thought I would be a hindrance so he pushed me over the mountain."

"He what! From how high? How are you alive?"

"He pretended he was going to help me and then threw me over the edge. It was high up. I fell for what felt like minutes. Honestly, I don't know why I'm alive. I know I hit something at some point. I mean, I would've had to, to break so many bones. But I don't remember the actual impact. After falling I remember being in so much pain that I felt as if my whole body was on fire. But even then, I don't think I was awake. I just remember this constant intense heat. Every now and then I would be aware of the world around me and I knew that someone was moving me. I don't know how long that went on; I only remember seeing these blood-red eyes every so often. But who knows if that was even real?" Baltaszar perked up at that, but kept quiet. "Tasz, all I know is that I'm back here and I'm safe. The nurse said that my bones should heal just fine. She's staying here until I'm well. And once I heal and after everything else is over in a couple of months, maybe I can be completely healthy again."

Baltaszar's brow furrowed. "After what else is over? What's happening in a couple of months?" Yas put her hand to her mouth and tears poured from her eyes as she trembled. "Yas. What is it? You have to tell me." She closed her eyes and continued to lie motionless. Baltaszar arose and walked to the other side of the bed to face her. He was about to sit before her but changed his mind and forced the blankets away from Yasaman's body. "What? What...is...this?"

Her face contorted as she tried to force something out, her words as ugly and distorted as her countenance. "I don't know how to explain it."

"Yas. Who did this to you? Did one of those three men do this? Did they do this? Tell me. Tell me who and I will bloody kill the gobshite excuse for man!"

Yasaman cried even more than before. "No. It wasn't them Tasz. It wasn't them. I'm sorry Tasz, it wasn't them."

Baltaszar's face twitched and he gritted his teeth in order to get the words out. "Then who?"

Yas' face was slick with unending tears. "I'm sorry, Tasz. It was a mistake. We…we thought we were going to die. We only wanted to comfort each other. All we had left was each other. You…you have to understand. You left. It was only us."

Baltaszar could feel the blood smearing on his fingertips from clenching his fists so hard. He barely opened his mouth. "You will tell me his goddamned name." He already knew. He wanted her to say it. To admit to it. To feel the weight of the pain she'd caused him.

"Bo'az." Her voice cracked. "I'm sorry Tasz. It was Bo'az."

"You bloody whore. You were afraid of death? I've faced worse in the past eight months. There were other girls who fancied me. I refrained because of you. I drowned. I was poisoned. I was shot by an arrow. I kept going because of you. I came back to see you. I needed to see you so I could know how to get on with my shitty life. And this is what I return to? You're having the baby of my goddamned coward of a twin brother? I'm going to kill him. The Blind Man was right. I am going to bloody kill Bo'az."

"Tasz, no! It's my fault, not his! I started it! Please! He is innocent!"

Baltaszar walked to the door. "Good. Then I'll burn down all of Haedon and let you watch it. The agony you'll see in all those faces will be nothing compared to what you've done to me." He left the house, opened himself to his manifestation, and all around him snowflakes turned to drops of fire, falling from the sky on Haedon, with the exception of the Adin farm. Several minutes later, as Baltaszar reached the Never, the houses burned brightly while snow melted from the streets. *They were so afraid of the bloody fire before. Good. Now their fears are real.*

Baltaszar continued the fire drops as he walked through the forest for several minutes and let them grow into fireballs. The flames spread quickly once the firedrops landed on houses and trees. Trees groaned and collapsed around him. The air thickened. Smoke billowed from all sides. Baltaszar walked on, uncaring whether he even made it back to Vandenar. Flames emanated from his body, so close that they turned his clothes to ashes. His skin burned and charred but he continued to call forth more fire. His flesh flaked off of him like ash. He dropped to hands and knees, no longer able to feel anything but searing pain. Baltaszar's eyes watered so profusely that he could not be sure if the silhouettes in the distance were real or just his imagination.

CHAPTER 22
INDEFINITELY

From *The Book of Orijin*, Verse Twenty-Three
No experience is worthless if you are able to learn from and improve from it.

Baltaszar awoke frenetically twitching about in the bed. He tried to move, but his arms were tied down. He craned his neck to look at his body. He lay under a few blankets. His legs were restrained as well. Baltaszar attempted to summon his manifestation, but he didn't have the energy. Only then did he feel the severe pangs of hunger stabbing at his stomach. Aside from that, his body was mostly numb.

"Yeah, they didn't trust you to do as you wished once you woke up. I'm sure you can understand why." Baltaszar looked to his right to see Lincan in a chair at the wall. "Then again, do you even know what happened?"

Baltaszar took a moment to let the question register in his aching head. *That whore. That bastard.* "I remember walking into the Never, wanting to set the whole world on fire. I'm assuming I did my best to try? I know it got me—I was definitely burning. Are we back at the House?"

Lincan nodded and snorted. "You're incredibly lucky that we found you. And even luckier that Maven Savaiyon and I were there. I had to start healing you right there, while Maven Savaiyon made a gateway in the middle of the burning forest. We could hardly see clearly enough to get to the gateway. Desmond had to levitate you through because you were too charred to carry. You were black, crisp, and missing chunks of flesh all over the place."

Pangs of guilt replaced the hunger attacking his stomach. "I'm sorry Linc. Really, I am. You don't know what happened, though. I wasn't just throwing a tantrum."

"You'd better have a hell of a reason for what happened. You have a lot of people angry at you. Though I don't know that any reason will be enough to quench that. So what did happen in Haedon? Did Yas get married? Run away? Angry parents?"

A tear formed at the corner of Baltaszar's eye, but he steeled himself. "Worse. So much worse. I still can hardly believe it. She's...she's pregnant with Bo'az's baby." He cut himself off there. He could have said more, but it would only make him angrier. If Lincan didn't understand the severity from that, there was no point in continuing to talk anyway.

"Oh. Wow. Damn. I'm sorry, Tasz. I...I didn't expect that."

"Yeah. I can't believe this whole time I was so desperate to go back."

"You don't have to go back to Haedon ever again. Maybe you should start telling everyone you're Shivaani. Wipe Haedon from your memory."

"Oh trust me, I'm not going back. If I ever see Bo'az again, I'll kill him."

"At least you got your closure?"

Baltaszar's countenance softened slightly. "There's closure and then there's that. I guess it's safe to say that we're done."

"On the bright side, Anahi is basically sitting there waiting for you."

What! How could I have forgotten about her! "Oh no! How long have we been back here?"

"I'd say about four days?"

"Four? No. No! Dammit, I have to bloody go! I have to go back to Vandenar now!"

"Whoa, calm down. First, you have to get your strength back. Then you have to get back into the good graces of Marlowe and all of the Mavens. Even then, I doubt they'll let you leave this place any time soon. It's not just that you burned yourself and the forest. You set your village on fire, too! There's crossing the line and then there's harming innocent people, Tasz. What if people are dead now because of you?"

Baltaszar closed his eyes and let it all sink in. *He's right. There's no excuse for what I did. I have to learn to control myself. I have to prove to them that I can use my manifestation wisely. Prove that...no, wait. If they were willing to bloody teach me something here, then maybe this wouldn't have happened.* "You know what, the House is just as guilty as I am. I've been here over seven months and I've taught myself as much about my manifestation as they have. Maybe if Marlowe opened his eyes and saw us for what we are, things like this wouldn't happen because I'd know how to control myself. Yeah, I should have been more responsible with my fire, but Light of Orijin, Linc, I control fire! How stupid is Marlowe that he thinks I'm better off not learning how to use it and control it? Instead, I've been relegated to lighting torches and fireplaces."

"That's not what they're going to want to hear, Tasz. Like I said, they're angry. It would be stupid to yell at them the first chance you get."

Baltaszar turned his head, "What about you? You mad?"

Lincan smirked, "I was annoyed until last night. It took us three days and nights, almost nonstop, to heal you. I don't think I've done that much healing if I combined everyone I've ever healed."

"So what happened last night?"

"Oh yeah, that was the best part. Well for those three days and nights, it was pretty much me and Delilah working on you together. You know, since I've had infirmary duty ever since you framed me. And I tried my usual charm like always, just jokingly, figuring she's a Daughter of Tahlia, so I have no chance. But when we were finally finished and split up and I went back upstairs to relax, she knocked on the door half an hour later. She pushed me onto the bed and pretty much took control of everything. We went at it almost the whole night. I was so damn tired this morning you should've seen how much I ate for breakfast! That was almost as exhausting as healing you!"

Baltaszar was dumbfounded. Delilah was the Maven who ran the infirmary. She had the ability to pass through objects, walls, and basically any other substance she wanted. It was a manifestation that worked extremely well in healing people. "Strange. Are you sure she didn't just want you to give her a baby?"

"Trust me, I asked! There was no way I was making a baby, even if she wouldn't expect me to be a father. She made it clear that there were no intentions of the sort. For the love of everything in the sea, Tasz, what we did last night was worth more than the last three days! If this turns into a regular thing, I think I'll be in your debt instead."

"I can't believe it, Linc. You bloody turned a Daughter of Tahlia! Does Vasher know? He'll be angry on so many levels!" Baltaszar stopped as a thought entered his head. "Wait a minute, how the hell did you know where I was? How did you find me? Did Raish bloody tell you? I told him it was a damn secret! What a bloody traitor!"

"You have way too much anger in you for your own good, man. Raish had nothing to do with it. You apparently snuck out just as Maven Savaiyon and Maven Kadoog'han were walking in. Kadoog'han noticed and stayed outside. He followed you all the way to the river, but couldn't follow you across. He came back and told us immediately. Cyrus told us no boats would be there until the morning, so we went to sleep and waited until sunrise. We all knew by then where you were going. So don't worry, none of your friends are out to get you or hurt you, Tasz. And speaking of hurt, I think I might have made you impervious to your own fire in the process of healing you. Thought you'd like to know."

Baltaszar furrowed his brow. *What?* "What do you mean, 'impervious'? That's impossible."

"One of my talents with my manifestation is that I can sort of 'read' people's bodies. I can't really explain how I do it—it's just that I understand what's wrong in people and when things are different. With you, it was almost as if I activated something. I don't really know how to explain it. Something just changed in your system and I have a hunch that that's what it is. When you are well enough to use your manifestation again, try it on yourself. I'm almost positive you'll be fine. If not, well then I'll just heal you again, no hard feelings. Nothing to lose."

The door opened beside Lincan, and Maven Savaiyon stormed in. He barely acknowledged Lincan and glared at Baltaszar. "Good, you are awake. Finally we can get some answers." Savaiyon glanced at Lincan and Lincan scuttled out of the room. "Well?"

Baltaszar's throat was suddenly dry. He swallowed hard a few times. "I went back to Haedon. I needed to speak to a few people. It turns out that the girl I used to love is having a child with my twin brother. I was angry, I overreacted. I know I did. Can you just tell me what my punishment is so that I can get on with it and start redeeming myself?"

Savaiyon seemed to soften for a moment, but then it was gone. "The situation is not as simple as that. You burned down part of the forest. You put lives at risk. People in your village are injured, but we did not stay because we had to rush back here to save your life, and then explain to Zin Marlowe why the mission fell apart. You disregarded a mission. And you abandoned your brothers. They seem to have forgiven your actions. However, Zin Marlowe and the Mavens of the House are not as sympathetic. Your actions are almost comparable to Prince Garrison's. You have heard of him by now, correct?" Baltaszar nodded solemnly. "Good. Prince Garrison is a criminal to the House of Darian and, as a result, does not walk among our ranks."

Baltaszar interrupted him, "I get the idea. So then what are you saying will happen to me?"

Interrupting wasn't the wisest choice, as Savaiyon instantly seemed more perturbed. "Your punishment has not been decided yet. I am about to bring you to the Room of Judgment. There, Marlowe will decide your fate. No matter what he chooses, I do not see this going well for you, Baltaszar. Whatever expectations you have that things will simply work out in the end, get rid of them. You did not lie or steal. You tried to burn down a town. Out there in the rest of Ashur, that is grounds for execution."

Baltaszar exhaled deeply and turned away. There was nothing else to say. No one else really cared about the pain he felt. About the betrayal he was dealing with. His fear bordered on self-pity and despair, but he quickly filled himself with scorn instead. "Then take me there now." He turned his head back to Savaiyon. "Give me my judgment now. Why wait? Anyone who wishes to see me leave this place is a hypocrite and shares the guilt in this matter. Take me to Marlowe now and I'll bloody tell him myself."

Savaiyon looked taken aback. Baltaszar never relished the misery of others, but he knew that Savaiyon thought he'd had the upper hand in this conversation. Baltaszar continued to look him in the eyes and Savaiyon finally nodded. He left the room and returned in a few moments with a small, dark sack hefted over his shoulder. Savaiyon emptied the sack as the contents clanged against the floor, then placed it over Baltaszar's head and tied it loosely around his neck. "Very well," he said gravely.

Baltaszar heard the door open and shut and there was a terrible silence for several minutes. The door opened and closed once more, and Savaiyon said, "They are ready for you now." He untied Baltaszar's arms from the bed, only to secure them in manacles behind Baltaszar's back. Finally, he untied Baltaszar's legs and clamped chains to each ankle. "You are no longer trusted to navigate this House. You are not allowed to know the location of the Room of Judgment. You are not trusted to walk freely."

Savaiyon pulled Baltaszar from the bed and led him out of the room. They walked for a few minutes, making a few turns here and there, and then down a long set of stairs. For the first time, Baltaszar felt nervous. *Do they want me to prove myself again or are they kicking me out?* He was finally stopped and the sack removed. Baltaszar stood at a podium and faced Marlowe, who sat on a platform with nearly two dozen Mavens, save Savaiyon, sitting behind him. All of them stared directly at Baltaszar. He didn't have to look twice to see the contempt in their eyes.

Baltaszar saw his friends off to the side. Though there was no anger in any of their countenances, they looked remorseful, especially Vasher. *Dammit. This was his mission to lead and I let him down. Because of me, Marlowe will likely not trust him anymore.* Baltaszar looked down at his feet as he waited for someone to speak. He could handle being reprimanded or yelled at, but having everyone stare at him in disapproval was torture.

Finally, Marlowe said, "Baltaszar Kontez, do you understand why you are here?" He didn't wait for an answer. "You are charged with abandoning a mission ordered by me." *Charged?* "You are charged with abandoning your brothers in time of need. You are charged with using your manifestation to commit violence. You are charged with endangering the lives of innocent people. And you are charged with attempting to end your own life." *Am I a criminal now?* Baltaszar hoped his confusion was not so apparent. "Your friends have all claimed that they knew nothing of your plan to leave them. They have also expressed no vitriol toward you. Those are the only reasons why you stand in this room now. I have given you your charges. You now have the opportunity to speak on your behalf if you believe that these charges are unreasonable. Choose your words wisely."

Baltaszar looked down at the ground for a moment. He then glanced at the chains around his ankles. Anger filled him. *Nothing I say will change his mind. That's pretty clear.* He looked back up at Marlowe with resentment. "You charge me with these crimes, but what have you done to prepare me for anything? I came to this place because I was different. I was lost and I needed guidance. All you have given me is a handful of history lessons and minimal instruction about my manifestation. You are a hypocrite! A coward! From the very moment I arrived you promised I could visit my home once I finished the *Book of Orijin*. For the past two months you have stalled so I wouldn't return! You bloody liar! You never planned on letting me go back!

"And your bloody stance against violence? Of all the people on this island, I have seen the least of the world. And even *I* can see that it is a violent world! How blind can *you* be? Will we gain the respect of the King or of Ashur by sitting here, cut off from the world, only caring for ourselves? We do nothing for the people of Ashur! Yet many of them love us! For what? Because I can make a blasted fireball? What is the point of having us here if you are turning us into farm animals? My father was a coward just like you are! He hid me away just like you do with the Descendants! Too afraid to let us see the world for what it is and function properly in it!" He noticed the Mavens slightly shifting in their seats. "How much of our lives are you wasting here? Look at them! Look at my friends! When Jahmash comes they will be dead and so will I. And it will be your bloody fault! We are the greatest weapon the world has to stop him and you hide in your quarters every day, then you have the nerve to tell other people to teach us about things we will never need.

"I am *charged*? Light of Orijin, *charge* me, dammit! What difference does it make whether you kill me or put me in a dungeon like the Prince? You're wasting my bloody life away, just like you've been doing for the past eight months! My father lived as a coward but died a martyr! But you, you will hide away behind your door for your whole bloody existence! And I refuse to follow any man who would make decisions for my life while spending his whole life hidden in a room! So tell me, *Headmaster*, what you plan to do with your blasted charges and stop wasting my damn time!"

Marlowe's countenance had not changed. He sat there and took Baltaszar's entire tirade. "Are you finished, Baltaszar?"

"Oh trust me, I could go on and on, but I don't want to waste my voice on you any longer."

"Very well. Baltaszar Kontez, you are hereby banished from the House of Darian. Indefinitely. You are not allowed on these premises. If any Descendant should feel even the slightest concern for his or her safety in your presence elsewhere in Ashur, you will be captured and imprisoned in our dungeons. Indefinitely. Maven Savaiyon shall transport you to your new…home." Marlowe looked past Baltaszar to Savaiyon, "Remember Maven, only high enough to hurt him. Do not kill him." Baltaszar turned to Savaiyon, who nodded with understanding.

Baltaszar took a deep breath and glanced at Vasher. He shouted, "I'm sorry Vash, I know I messed everything up for you. I didn't mean for things to get so crazy."

Vasher smiled, "Don't worry about it, Tasz. I'm not angry. I probably would have done the same thing if I was you!" Vasher gave Baltaszar a nod and he understood immediately. All of his friends sitting there forgave him unconditionally. He suspected he'd changed the minds of some of the Mavens as well.

Baltaszar took another deep breath as Savaiyon pulled on his chain for him to follow. He led Baltaszar out of the room and into the corridor, where one of Savaiyon's yellow-framed gateways stood. Through it, Baltaszar could see endless treetops and mountains faintly peeking up at the horizon.

"Hey," Savaiyon uttered from behind him. Baltaszar turned to look at him with disdain. "Try to figure out how to use the chains to ease your fall. It's a long way down, so you will have plenty of time."

Baltaszar tilted his head in confusion, "Wh…"

Savaiyon shoved Baltaszar violently with both arms. Baltaszar fell backwards and saw the gateway blink out. As he fell, branches whacked him in the arms, legs, back, and head. The pain was accumulating until finally his head slammed into a huge branch and everything went black.

***

Vasher barely understood what happened to Baltaszar before Zin Marlowe called him to the same podium where Baltaszar had stood only moments before. He looked up at Marlowe, unable to wipe the bewildered expression from his face. "Am I to be banished as well, Master Marlowe?"

Marlowe simply stared at Vasher as if he hadn't said anything at all. After a moment, Marlowe spoke. "Vasher Jai, you are charged with assembling a team of Descendants unfit for the mission at hand. You are charged with using biased judgment to carry out an initiative directed by me. I have given you your charges. You now have the opportunity to speak on your behalf if you believe that these charges are unreasonable. Choose your words *wisely*." Marlowe hung onto the last word and Vasher understood that if he revealed anything of the Anonymi plot, his fate would likely be as bad as Baltaszar's.

"Headmaster, I chose people I believed I could trust the most for such a sensitive mission. The nature of our mission was secretive and I brought these individuals specifically because I knew they would do things exactly as I asked. I had no idea that Baltaszar had an additional agenda. But at the same time, I am not angry at him. His reasons for being angry were genuine. I agree that he did not handle the situation in the best manner. But, truthfully, I could not tell you how I would act if put into his situation. I would like to think that I would maintain a cool head and stay calm. I believe all of us in this room would like to think that. But I firmly believe all of us would also regret our actions if put in Baltaszar's situation, just as he does now. I am not questioning your decision about his fate, but I am standing by my decision and if given the same responsibility again, I would choose Baltaszar every time." Vasher took a deep breath and clutched his hands behind his back. He continued to look directly at Marlowe.

"It is an admirable thing to stand by your friends unconditionally. It is also a foolish thing. Maven Savaiyon informed me that he saw potential in you as a leader. However, I do not share this sentiment. It is clear that you are not suited to lead." Vasher clenched his teeth. *Funny, that's what everyone says about you*, he thought as Marlowe continued. "Looking at the grand scheme, your mission failed because of one person. I cannot say with any accuracy that it would have failed had Baltaszar not been with you. Therefore, as punishment, you are hereby confined to the House of Darian and its grounds. Indefinitely. You are no longer eligible for missions or leisure trips to other cities. You are restricted from leisure time within the House of Darian or on its grounds. At all times you will either be learning or working. When you are not doing either, you will be eating, sleeping, or confined to your room. Your new room. In solitude. Indefinitely."

Vasher looked at the floor to avoid glaring at Marlowe. He could handle confinement and being barred from missions. That made sense. But the rest was nonsense to him. All he could do was mutter, "I understand."

"Good. You may leave now. Maven Blastevahn awaits you outside this chamber. He will bring you to your new quarters." Marlowe turned to the rest of Vasher's company sitting off to the side. "The rest of you may leave now as well. Return to your quarters for the remainder of the day. Leave only for your meals.

***

The three men led Garrison on, though he had no idea where he was going. The only thing he knew for sure was that he was no longer in the dungeon. It was the first day since he'd come to the House that there was no chill in his bones. Through the sack on his head he heard a group of people walk by, bickering about something. Some of their comments might have been directed at him, but he couldn't be sure. Garrison wasn't even sure he cared anymore. The only saving grace of his situation was that Donovan and Vanna had no way of knowing his fate on arriving here. It wasn't that they would gloat at being right; Garrison hated being wrong. Embarrassment would be an understatemend if either of them knew his situation. There was too much wrong in his past to continue allowing more.

This is ridiculous. Chains? On my hands and feet? Since Garrison first arrived at the House, he hadn't had the energy to use his manifestation. His captors made sure that he'd stayed that way. Despite having no mirror to see, Garrison knew he wouldn't recognize his own reflection. He felt confident that if he returned home in his current state, no one else would recognize him either.

Thinking about home quickly reminded Garrison of why he was in his current situation. *Would I even trust myself? Would I have treated someone like me any better than they have? How would I respond if Descendants came to Cerysia and attacked my people? How would I react if some of those very Descendants were Cerysian?* Garrison was suddenly grateful for the talks he'd had with his Uncle Roland. He'd finally begun to rid himself of the sense of entitlement that his uncle constantly berated him about.

The blindfold was ripped from his face, disturbing his train of thought. Garrison found himself in a room walking toward a platform. On it sat several men and women, though one man sat in front of the others. *That must be the 'Marlowe' they all talk about. Complain about. And they call me the hypocrite.* Garrison was led to a podium. His three escorts, all much bigger than he, stood behind him and faced the platform. Garrison looked straight ahead. He found solace in focusing on the fact that he was finally warm.

The man in front spoke first. "Prince Garrison Brighton..."

Garrison cut him off, "I am NOT a prince. I renounced my title in order to come here and live among you."

The man stared at him, as if telling him to shut up. "Garrison Brighton, you are charged with the murder of scores of Descendants throughout Ashur. You are charged with the capture and torture of scores of Descendants throughout Ashur. You are charged with attempting to trespass upon the property of the House of Darian in order to commit more murder. I have given you your charges. You have the opportunity to speak on your behalf if you believe that these charges unreasonable. Choose your words wisely." The man sat down, his expression dismissive. Nothing Garrison could say would put him in a better situation. He would have to make sure he wasn't put into something worse.

"Headmaster Marlowe?" The man nodded in affirmation. Garrison hesitated for a moment. *Cite the Book of Orijin. Connect with him.* "Sir, if the actions of my past would define my whole character, then I should be dead. However, in *The Book of Orijin*, it clearly states that we will each have an opportunity to repent before mankind and correct our mistakes before being judged by the Orijin. I have made many mistakes in my life, but I am trying to correct them. You say that I came here to kill more Descendants. Ask your sentry at the mountain if that was true. He saw Cerysian soldiers chase me down as I ran toward him. I say Cerysian soldiers because they are no longer mine. I command them no longer.

"You say that I hunted and killed Descendants and that is true. I did that until I saw truth. What you did not see was that I killed my own soldier for defying me when I ordered my men to stop killing Descendants. What you did not see was that I defied my brother's advice in coming here. What you did not see was that my father threatened to kill me when I told him I was coming here. What you did not see was that I fought my father's Royal Guard in front of his throne, then threw my friend's helmet at him in front of his subjects. What you did not see was that the Blind Men granted me asylum as I fled my father's kingdom. What you did not see was that Taurani sacrificed their lives to get me here—the very people who oppose the existence of this place. And what you did not see is that I have prayed every day since I have been here that you people might grant me mercy. Starve me for as long as you like. Do what you believe is necessary to make yourselves feel safe, but please allow me to function in this place.

"My manifestation is powerful. One that my father fears. If you want revenge for the crimes against you, let me help you against him. I was barely an adult when he sent me to hunt down Descendants. That is how he raised me. I agree, I am guilty and responsible for my actions. But so is he. Jahmash is coming. And I can guarantee to you that if my father sits on the throne when that happens, then Ashur will be lost. My father only cares for himself. I am an asset that you can use. I have come to terms that you do not want to treat me well. I can live with that. Whatever you decide, please just do not kill me. I do not believe that the Orijin is done with me yet."

Marlowe responded immediately. "You have wisdom, Garrison Brighton, I give you that. If you could be trusted, you would be a great ally. And a strong member of this household. You have read *The Book of Orijin* and you can quote it. You understand its lessons. However, you have also committed great sin. No man is ever completely rid of sin. I do not believe in violence. We will not kill you. But you will go back to the dungeon and live as you have since you arrived here. Indefinitely. However, if you somehow prove to us that you have been rehabilitated while in confinement, I shall consider freeing you."

Garrison looked at Marlowe. Defeat weighed heavy on his eyes and cheeks. He turned and walked away from the podium, clenching his chained fists behind his back. His three escorts quickly stepped in line with him and blindfolded him again. As he walked away from Marlowe, Garrison turned his head back to the man. "Go ahead. Imprison me indefinitely. My will is stronger than your spite. I will wait for my revenge indefinitely. My father is a small man. I am ashamed to have come here only to find that you are exactly the same." Garrison turned and walked to the door.

CHAPTER 23
ABRADAY

From *The Book of Orijin,* **Verse Four Hundred Seventy-Nine**
When all other methods have been exhausted, it may be necessary to destroy everything you know, and begin anew.

"You seek Maven Savaiyon. He is the only one I know who would be capable of something like this." The words left Adria's mouth before she had even made the decision to answer. She found she wanted desperately to answer Maqdhuum's question.

"What does he look like? Would he be at the house? If not, where else can I find him? What is his full name?"

"He is very tall. Shivaani. Brown-skinned and short, short black hair. I do not know his full name. I have called him Maven Savaiyon ever since I met him. It is the same thing with his whereabouts. I do not have the privilege of knowing his comings and goings. Someone with his manifestation can come and go as he pleases."

"If he is in The House of Darian where would I find his quarters?"

Once again, Adria felt almost excited to answer. "The Mavens reside on the upper levels of the right side of the House. He is on the top floor. I believe there are four floors on that side."

"Good. Good. You may release her now, if you wish, Lord Jahmash. I have no further questions. I know exactly what must be done." Maqdhuum walked away and traversed the plank that led back to his ship.

Adria still felt the grip on her mind, though it loosened somewhat. It was warm, comfortable, especially in the chill of the late winter. Her galley was hundreds of yards away from the gateway. Luckily, Drahkunov had insisted days ago that they move near the front of the formation, along with Maqdhuum's galley. Aric had spotted the gateway in the night by its yellow fringes and Drahkunov had sent the signal for all galleys to stop immediately. Aric said that the gateways clearly curved as if forming a ring around something. Adria could not be sure if they had always been there or not. She had never seen the House of Darian from the sea.

Through the gateway all that could be seen was ocean that stretched out forever. It would be impossible to get to the House by ship as long as the gateway stood. She had no idea how Maqdhuum planned to stop Maven Savaiyon from keeping the gateways in place, but there was an anger growing inside of her aimed solely at the thought of Maqdhuum. Adria could not understand why. The anger pounded in her mind so strongly that her head began to ache. The anger turned to hatred. Her body tensed as the pain in her head neared unbearable. Blood flowed from her nose and her vision grew hazy.

The grip released and Adria felt her mind and body decompress. Tears streamed from her eyes and mixed with the blood dripping from her chin. She thought about Maqdhuum, whom she swore had stood before her only moments ago. Adria had no idea why, but she suddenly adored the man and wanted to do everything she could to help him.

***

Maqdhuum reached the top of his galley's crow's nest. It was too dangerous to attempt to Travel to the island if he could not see where he was going. Even from this height, he could not see over the gateway. He crossed his arms and stared out at the sea. *Of everything I have experienced, I've never had this challenge.* He stared up at the sky as snowflakes danced around him, almost cursing the Orijin, when a thought dawned on him. He looked back at the gateway to judge his height, then back at the sky. "Well this is going to be a first," he muttered to himself.

How difficult can it be? Travel as high up as I can. Get a good enough look. Find a destination. Fall. Travel again. Before hitting the water. Easy. He eyed the scout that sat up there with him. "You. How loyal are you to Jahmash?"

The scrawny man responded instantly, "I would give my life for Jahmash." Maqdhuum had hoped the man's loyalty wouldn't have been so strong.

Fool. All of you are fools. Giving your life for a Harbinger. For any Harbinger. He spat at the word. None of them were willing to do the same until they had to. Until there were no other options. "Good." He leaned to the man and grasped him by the arm. "You are about to." The man eyed him curiously as Maqdhuum pictured a place in the sky that would give him the best view. All it ever required to Travel was to concentrate hard enough on his destination. In a blink, Maqdhuum and his scout disappeared from the crow's nest and appeared in the sky, hundreds of feet above the ships. Their plummet began instantly. With as much force as he could, Maqdhuum shoved the other man away from him. Luckily, they were moving too fast for the man's scream to be heard. The man's loyalty to Jahmash would be his death, simply because Maqdhuum could not trust him to witness his Traveling.

Island. Focus on the island. He looked toward the gateways. There it is. Clever. They are smarter than Jahmash gave them credit for. Past the gateways the island was clear. A few hundred yards from the coast stood The House of Darian. *Impressive. Likely holds a couple hundred. We'll attack at night. Catch them in their sleep. If the girl is right, they won't know how to fight back. Stupid. Modern day Harbingers, my ass.* He knew exactly where he would land, but it would be unwise to start the attack in the daylight. Maqdhuum Traveled back to the crow's nest on his galley. He watched the scout fall from the sky far off in the distance. From this far away, no one would know who it was, or even that it was a person.

He climbed back down to the deck and his crew gathered around him immediately, expecting a directive of some sort. "We wait here until night fall. Ready the cannons when the sunlight has completely gone and the sky is black. Once you see the gateways disappear, advance the ships. It may take a while for them to go down, but be at the ready. The scout on the crow's nest is gone. Replace him. The rest of you must be vigilant. The coast is not far off. Fire the cannons first. Only when you have no more cannonballs do you leave the ship to attack. We may be able to destroy them without leaving our ships. We'll try that first. I am retreating below deck. Do not disturb me. I have given you your orders. Obey them or I will kill you." They all nodded or gave an affirmation and returned to their duties.

Maqdhuum returned to his cabin below deck. It was the only private area on the ship, but his crew feared him too much to disobey his orders. *How best to kill Savaiyon? Perhaps go to his quarters. If he is there, stab him. If not, hide until he returns. Then stab him. He must be very powerful to maintain the gateways for so long and still function. I wonder how long they have been there. Do they know we're coming? No matter. They cannot stop me. He cannot stop me.*

He sat there in thought for nearly two hours before looking outside again. The snow had stopped and the sun had begun its descent, but too much light remained. Maqdhuum waited another hour and assessed the light once more.

He finally appeared on the shores of the island in complete darkness. He hadn't bothered to bring his armor, just two of his swords on his back and a dagger belt around his waist. It helped that his breeches and shirt, as usual, were black as well. He didn't bother with a coat, despite the cold. Maqdhuum traversed the sand to the frost-laden grass and came upon The House of Darian within a few minutes. *Magnificent structure. Almost like a castle. Shame it has Darian's name. No Harbinger would want this. Maybe Jahmash. But he doesn't count.* He walked toward the right of what seemed to be the main entrance. The wing on the right extended farther back than he'd originally thought. *Maybe there are more here than we expected. The girl wouldn't lie though. She can't. Shame Jahmash has her. She's a nice kid. Probably kill her once he doesn't need her anymore. Even Farrah isn't so bad. Slade either. I'm sure they'll all die soon. Of course he'll keep around dimwits like Aric.*

The entrance to the right wing was locked. *Dammit. If only it had a window, then I could Travel inside.* Maqdhuum walked around to the side. Most of the windows were dark or covered in blinds. He assumed those were private quarters of Descendants. Through one or two windows he could see the main hallway. He looked up. Sure enough, the windows were four stories high. *I'll have to get close to the window to be able to see in.* As soon as he'd thought it, Maqdhuum was eye level with a window on the fourth floor, looking in. He'd chosen one with a light on. He clung to the frame and looked in. A short woman paced back and forth around the room, talking to herself. She walked around in her undergarments; she was not nearly the most attractive woman he'd ever seen. Maqdhuum waited until her back was to the window once more and Traveled inside.

He walked right up behind her and swiftly struck a dagger into her back while covering her mouth. *That's right. Lie down gently.* He pulled the dagger back out before resting her on the floor, then put a finger to his lips. He whispered, "If you scream, I will kill you. Tell me where Maven Savaiyon's quarters are or I will kill you." He pressed the dagger to her neck. "Do you understand?" She nodded as tears streamed from her eyes into her light brown hair.

"I will not tell you." She choked out the words, her eyes defiant.

"I do not have time to waste." He pressed the blade more firmly into her neck, gripping her throat more tightly. "If you refuse, I will do the same to every Descendant I find in this place until I find him. You have two choices. Tell me and live. Be stupid and cause many deaths.

She gasped out what she could. "You aren't here in peace. You will still kill them. Do what you must."

Bitch. This is getting nowhere. She isn't scared enough. "Very well." They reappeared hundreds of feet above the House, falling together. "We can go back to your quarters as soon as you tell me. Or you can fall and be a lovely bloodstain on the ground!" Maqdhuum was finally thankful for the cold, windy day.

The woman finally acquiesced once the details of the ground became distinct. "The third room after mine! Three rooms past mine! Please! Please!"

Maqdhuum promptly brought her back into the room, to the same position they'd been in. He slit her throat quickly. He stood up and wiped the blade on her bed. *I wanted to let you fall. Too much noise. Before we're done destroying this place, maybe I'll get to do it to someone else. These Descendants aren't so bad though. She had some fire. Shame we're killing them. They might've stood a chance.* He appeared outside of the building once more, in front of the window that should have been his destination. *Dark. Good. Maybe away. Hopefully sleeping.* Just as with the previous window, Maqdhuum positioned himself close enough to grasp the outside. He peeked in as well as he could to glimpse inside the room. All he needed was a fleeting image.

He let go and Traveled inside the room shortly after his fall began. He appeared less than an inch in front of a bed. *Too close. Have to be more careful.* He had never tested his theory, but he assumed that he could appear in the middle of something solid and be hurt by it. He'd never tried it with water either. The last thing Maqdhuum wanted was to drown in the process of testing a theory.

No one lay in the bed. *Dammit. He's out. Closet. Hopefully not for too long.* He opened a slatted door that led to a closet. There was barely enough room to stand inside, so he left the door ajar and hid behind it.

Maqdhuum stood there for nearly an hour. At times he stretched or squatted just to keep alert. Finally, he heard the door open. In the moonlight he saw the silhouette of the man. It was the dark, statuesque Shivaani that had been in the Taurani village when he'd taken Adria and Gunnar, just as Adria had described. *Good girl. Maybe I will inform Jahmash of how valuable you are.*

Savaiyon walked to a lantern beside the bed and leaned over to light it. Maqdhuum quickly crept to him, dagger in hand, and thrust the blade into Savaiyon's midsection. The tall man doubled over before Maqdhuum could pull the blade back. As he reached for another, Savaiyon seized him and threw him across the room, too fast for him to be able to Travel and avoid the impact. He crashed into a wooden dresser, breaking it in the process. He shook his head to regain his bearings. As he looked up, he saw Savaiyon fleeing through a gateway and hurled another dagger at the man's head. It struck Savaiyon beneath the shoulder blade as the gateway closed. Maqdhuum grunted. *Too dizzy.*

But before the gateway closed, Maqdhuum saw that Savaiyon had run to Sundari. Maqdhuum Traveled there immediately behind him. As he appeared on the street, he saw Savaiyon still running, head turned behind him. Another gateway had formed before Savaiyon. *I know that city, too, Savaiyon. Wolf's Paw. Damaszur.* He shook his head and Traveled once more as Savaiyon's gateway closed. *Dammit. Still dizzy.* He ran as soon as his feet touched the ground, though his balance was still somewhat off. Sure enough, Savaiyon ran ahead, gateway already formed. *Port of Granis. This is going to be extremely fun. I am going to be so proud to kill you.* He Traveled once more, another dagger in hand.

***

The booms had come from all over the House, shaking Lincan out of deep sleep. He blinked several times as the House trembled again with a thunderous boom, Lincan knew he would soon need more out of his manifestation than a few hours of sleep could provide. For the first time, he'd regretted that Delilah slept in his bed. An attack on the House meant that dying from overexertion was just as likely as dying in combat. He'd definitely overexerted himself with Delilah throughout the night.

Lincan looked across at the other bed. It had been less than a day since Baltaszar had been exiled. Though Tasz hadn't slept in the room for over four days, Lincan doubted he would ever grow accustomed to it. Delilah stirred as he nudged her a little too harshly. "Get up! We're being attacked!" He jumped out of bed, glanced at the beam of moonlight shining through the window, and cursed as he ran out of the room just ahead of Delilah. *Lao won't be able help us for a long time.* The other residing Descendants on the third floor scurried about, still half asleep. Most just leaving their rooms.

He looked back and forth from one end of the hallway to the other. *For the love of Orijin, the front of the House has been torn open!* Lincan could clearly see the night sky where the wall once stood. The floor had given way, a number of Descendants were running from the collapsing floor past Lincan and Delilah. He spotted Malikai, a tall Markosi boy, running past, and grasped his arm. "Kai! I need your help! We need to take the injured down to the infirmary!"

"Now, Linc? We should find shelter first!"

"There won't be any shelter soon if floors are already collapsing! Find anyone you can and have them help you! Any injured! Infirmary! The sooner we can heal people, the easier it will be to fight back! Your skin will protect you well enough. Just get them downstairs so Delilah and I can start working!"

Malikai nodded and ran back the other way, pulling his friends to help him. His skin could harden into an almost rock-like protective layer. It could withstand strikes from swords, clubs, maces, and numerous other weapons; they'd tested as many as they could find in the past several months, and perhaps had a little too much fun in the process.

"Come, Lincan! We do not have time to waste!" Delilah pulled him to the staircase, following the others who fled. He felt embarrassed getting lost in thought at a time like this.

As they reached the first floor, Lincan marveled that no one had been trampled. The booms were more frequent now and the House shook constantly. Anger filled him as he followed Delilah. *We all knew this day was coming and still Marlowe refused to prepare us. What are we supposed to do now? The infirmary will likely have collapsed by the time we get there.*

They wove their way into the main common room in the central section of the House. Delilah had a girl limping at her shoulder and Lincan scraped a boy from the floor and hefted him over his shoulder. The infirmary lay beneath the main floor. It was big enough to hold almost all of the Descendants currently in the House. *Hopefully it doesn't come to that*, Lincan thought as he and Delilah ran down the final flight of stairs at the back of the room and set their companions onto cots. Malikai stormed down shortly after with a following of helpers. They placed a dozen more injured Descendants onto surrounding cots.

"Good. Get us more! As many as you can find! They'll be safe down here for now! And if any of you think that you can't fight back or help up there, then come back to us! We could use your help!" The House shook again. "Go! We don't have much time down here!"

Malikai and the others ran off and Lincan looked at Delilah as the woman gave him an order. "We'll start with Sindha. It's just a broken leg. If we get her back up there, she can help to repel whatever they are hitting us with." Sindha was a wiry Shivaani who could repel nearly anything that was about to hit her. Hopefully she could prevent the walls and ceilings from falling in on people. The ceiling thundered again and dust fell on them.

"Let's start. I'm numbing her now. You set the bone." Lincan held Sindha's bloody knee firmly and submitted to his manifestation. The girl let out a sigh of relief as the numbing began. Delilah set her hand on Sindha's shin and closed her eyes. *I love when she does this.* Her hand disappeared into Sindha's leg and within moments she brought it up again. Lincan could only imagine how much trouble he would get into if he could make his body pass through objects. He smirked for a moment, then quickly refocused. As soon as Delilah pulled her hand out, Lincan focused on healing the bone and torn muscle and skin. After a few minutes, he stopped the numbing and looked at Sindha. "How does it feel?"

Sindha smiled, "Sore, but good as new. Thank you." She hopped off the cot and clasped his shoulder. She gave Delilah a tight hug and ran up the stairs. The ceiling boomed again. *We don't have much time.*

***

Desmond ran toward the rubble, Badalao in tow, and instantly the melody flowed through his veins. He flung the collapsed floors and walls out of the House so that the others could escape the ground floor corridor. Shortly after, the halls brightened drastically and he noticed Marshall running along with them. "How did ya get down here so quickly? Fall through the floor?"

"I was already down here. Couldn't sleep! Still angry about my mother! What do you think this is?"

"I'm puttin' my coin on Jahmash. We're definitely bein' attacked! Worst part is, Lao is useless 'til the mornin'!" As Desmond finished clearing the destruction at the end of the corridor, more of the ceiling caved in from where they had just come. "We're not goin' ta be able ta save this wing. Move ta the front o' the House! Maybe we can properly assess everythin' from there." Another chunk of the front wall exploded inward as they moved on. "Let's go!"

Desmond ran; Badalao and Marshall kept pace. *Most of us will be useless to fight back*, Desmond thought. *Those of us who can must do something.* Desmond looked around as dozens of Descendants ran by in every direction. The walls were exploding in the Mavens' wing as well. *They must know the layout of the House. They know exactly where to attack.* Another explosion hit the common room where scores of Descendants were finding shelter. Before Desmond even realized he'd summoned his manifestation again, the melody screamed to him. Hundreds of broken pieces of the wall and glass hung in the air above everyone in the room. Only then did he see the cause. A large iron ball hung in the midst. He'd heard rumors of weapons that could propel such things. Usually they were held on ships. *Cannons?* Another explosion came. He put all of his focus into the front wall. Several minutes, and as many explosions, passed. Where a solid wall and entryway once stood, hundreds of fragments and a dozen cast-iron balls hung in mid-air.

Desmond didn't care how long he would have to hold it all up. He knew he could handle more. He cleared his mind. Explosion after explosion came, breaking fragments into smaller fragments. He pulled deeper from his manifestation and willed everything to float in the air.

Badalao yelled as he ran away, pulling Marshall with him. "We're useless to you right now, Des! We are going to deliver the injured to the infirmary! We just heard that Linc and Delilah are down there healing people!"

Just as Badalao and Marshall turned away, Sindha came running to Desmond. "Let me help you! There's no way you will be able to maintain this!"

"No! There aren't enough o' us ta be doublin' up! Protect another area o' the House! Once everythin' falls down, we're all dead! Repel the attacks on another front!" She listened, nodded, and ran off.

Desmond was relieved.

All around him, Descendants lay injured or lifeless. Bloodied bodies were strewn throughout the room. Marshall, Badalao, and several others carried body after body down the stairs at the back of the room. *Where the hell is Marlowe in all this? Coward.* Anger spiked within Desmond, but he pushed it back down. *Focus. Save yer strength fer the wall. The whole House needs ya.* He closed his eyes, breathed several times, and then reopened them. Once he refocused, Desmond knew he hadn't nearly reached his manifestation's capacity.

Desmond maintained his position for over an hour and finally allowed himself to kneel down. If he had gotten a full sleep and had eaten breakfast, he knew he would still be standing. It didn't help that he also had to fight back his anger. He couldn't be sure if he were angrier at their attackers or at Marlowe for allowing the attack to happen and then not even showing his face. *Maybe he's dead. I guess we wouldn't be so lucky. Keeramm said he wouldn't die 'til he was much older. Shame.* A piece of the wall slammed to the ground at one end of the room. Desmond shook his head and refocused.

Marshall came running back. "Hey! You think you can hold for a little longer? I have an idea!"

His breathing was starting to labor. "I'll stay here 'til it kills me. Just get everyone ta safety an' figure out how ta fight back!"

"It doesn't have to be that difficult! They have Maximilian down there. The ceiling caved on him—broken back. But Linc and Delilah are sure they can heal him. If he has enough energy..."

Desmond saw Marshall's plan, "Then he can transfer his stored energy ta me! I could keep the whole damn House up with that kind o' energy!"

"I'll get him as soon as he's ready! Do not die before then!"

Desmond gritted his teeth and stood up once more. The amount of iron balls hovering had more than doubled. He could see portions of the night sky clearly through all of the wall fragments. It almost looked as if lightning was coming down from the sky. *But it's not rainin'. That Raish?*

***

Savaiyon ran through another alleyway, then through the yellow-fringed doorway and into a field of tall grass. Every time he looked back, his pursuer was right behind him. *His method is faster than mine. I cannot outrun him.* His back and side ached. Savaiyon wasn't even sure if the blade was still in his back, though it wouldn't have fallen out on its own. His back was at least starting to numb a little. He knew if he didn't outsmart Maqdhuum soon, he would die in the process of running.

He formed another gateway over the water outside the House of Darian, designed to fall from the sky. As he fell, he created another gateway that brought him further up. Savaiyon created gateway after yellow-framed gateway, each time fluctuating his altitude, hoping that Maqdhuum would be lost in the confusion. In the process, another dagger struck him in the back of his left arm, just below the shoulder. *I dazed him when I threw him. Is he missing my head because he is dizzy, or on purpose?* Every time Savaiyon turned around, Maqdhuum was right behind him. *Even in this darkness, he knows exactly where I am going. How?*

The gash in his abdomen hadn't stopped bleeding. *He could have just killed me. Why didn't he?* He ran on as he clutched his stomach. *Focus on what matters. No time for questions. First, hurt him or kill him. Second, find Lincan. Third, put the gateways back up to protect the island.* Savaiyon turned his head before stepping through another gateway. *Still there.* He ran across the wet sand along one of Gansishoor's beaches. *I need someone else who can hurt him. Quickly. Something like...fire. What a terrible, terrible time to not have Baltaszar. No time to find him; he might not even be in the same place by now. Who else? Reverron? No. Cannot risk hand to hand combat. Someone who can strike from afar.*

Savaiyon ran through another gateway that brought him back to the grounds of The House of Darian. Another dagger struck him in the calf. Savaiyon maintained his focus. Embracing his manifestation helped against the pain. He ran on through more gateways. Every time he created a new one, Savaiyon already knew where the next one would lead. *He can see through all of my bridges. He has traveled. He always knows exactly where I'm going.* Savaiyon had even led Maqdhuum into the Never a few times already, but could not shake him.

His muscles were tearing where the knives stuck in him. Despite his tolerance and focus, his body would give out soon. *Horatio. I need to find Horatio. Find him, then go back to him a few times. No time to stop and talk.* Savaiyon had no clue as to where Horatio would even be. He had seen lightning strikes, despite no evidence of rain clouds.

He knew Horatio must be alive. The novice wing was collapsing. Horatio's quarters were at the very end of the top floor.

Three outcomes. He made it to the first floor and is alive somewhere there. He is trapped in his room. He is on the roof. Start in the room. If he is trapped, I can save him. Another blade sliced into Savaiyon's back.

***

Maximilian lay face-down on the cot next to Reverron. Lincan and Delilah stood over him, discussing something. The only reason he knew that Lincan's hand was on his back was because he no longer felt pain anywhere in his body. *What if that is not Lincan? What if I have no feeling any longer?* As soon as the ceiling had crashed down on him and Reverron, Maximilian had immediately lost feeling in his body halfway down his back and through his legs. Reverron had been unresponsive ever since. He hoped that the boy was only unconscious.

Strangely enough, Maximilian still felt energized. He absorbed energy for a week at a time, then transferred it every Lionsday to the grounds to help the gardens and plants grow. If he remembered correctly, it was Abraday morning. *Two days away. Still a great deal of power. If they can heal me, I could aid in a great attack on our enemies.*

He felt the slightest tickle pass through his back. The sensation remained for several moments as Lincan and Delilah whispered to each other. Even his hearing felt numb. *Perhaps they were not even whispering.*

The numbness dissipated somewhat and the pain intensified. He could feel his face and head once more, though he hated the fuzzy stinging as his nerves returned to life. "Your head should be able to move and feel now. Nod if you can hear me." Maximilian did as he was told. "Good. You're probably feeling some pain now, Maven Maximilian. I still have you partially numbed, but that's mostly to make the pain bearable. Your spine is fixed and just as it used to be. I would suggest lying here for a short while until you get used to the pain." Lincan crouched down, his voice close to Maximilian's ear. "I would truly keep you numbed the entire time to ease your pain, but there are too many others down here to see to."

He had so many questions, but the only thing he could muster was, "Reverron?"

"We're almost certain that Rev will be fine. Delilah and I will heal him, then keep him a while to make sure his head and eyes feel normal. As long as there's no cause for concern, he'll join you back upstairs in a little while."

"Turn me over." Lincan and Delilah rolled him so that he lay on his back. His body felt sore, but Maximilian was glad to be feeling anything at all. The past hour or two had been hazy. He knew Reverron had saved his life and he knew that the ceiling had fallen on them both, but not as badly or directly as it could have. Maximilian had been lucky that Reverron happened to be nearby. The room shook. "Am I free to return upstairs? I can handle the pain."

Just as he asked the question, Marshall came rushing down the staircase. "Now?" Maximilian looked at him and back at Lincan. Lincan scratched his head and breathed deeply, "Yes you can take him now, Marsh." He turned to Maximilian, "This is the eighth time within the hour that Marsh has come to check on your status. He and Desmond apparently need you up above for some grand scheme. It's only a matter of time before this ceiling comes crashing down. Any extra minutes that you and Desmond can give us means more Descendants' lives are saved." Lincan reached his arm out for Maximilian to grasp.

He gladly clutched Lincan's and Delilah's hands and stood up. He was much more steady and balanced than he thought he might be. "Thank you. Both. From the bottom of my heart. When you've healed Rev, share my gratitude with him as well. Only the Orijin knows whether any of us will survive this to be able to give thanks or share endearing sentiments." He bowed deeply to Lincan and Delilah, with a grimace, then gestured for Marshall to lead the way to Desmond.

They rushed up the stairs to the back of the common room. Marshall waved his hand for Maximilian to follow. "Hurry! If the front wall falls, then all of this is pointless!"

As he reached the top, he saw Desmond on one knee, arms raised. Above, hundreds upon hundreds of wall fragments and cannonballs hung in the air like a new wall meant to deflect further blasts, exactly as cannonballs were always described. Maximilian had only ever heard of cannons and cannonballs; they were as mythical as the stories of people from other lands beyond Ashur. If cannons were real, the Descendants and perhaps even Ashur were in grave trouble.

He ran toward Desmond and knelt next to him. Desmond turned and nodded excitedly, but didn't say anything.

"What is the plan?"

"No plan, Maven. Just keep up the wall fer as long as possible. Marsh an' I had an idea that ya could help keep my energy up by transferrin' yers."

Maximilian placed his hand on Desmond's shoulder. "I will have to maintain contact with you the entire time. Keep doing what you are doing." He opened himself to his manifestation as he grasped Desmond's shoulder tightly. "I have a wealth of energy. I am going to transfer it to you gradually, so that you can handle the power without being overwhelmed. Be overly careful! It is incredibly easy to become lustful for such a wealth of power! What we are doing is extremely dangerous!"

He started to allow the energy to escape him and flow into Desmond, who turned to him and grinned widely. "We might just save the House."

***

Horatio held tightly to the wooden shingles with both hands. *What a stupid idea. Who goes on the roof of a building this high while it's falling down?* The only reason he had come up here in the first place was because his room was on the verge of collapsing. The only option had been to climb out of the window and up to the roof. Luckily, he had enough time to run to the front of the House before the back of it caved in.

He didn't see the ships until he ran to the front of the building. Row after row sat in the water surrounding their island, all firing projectiles toward the House—projectiles which now hung suspended in mid-air along with large blocks and chunks of building. Horatio had never seen or imagined anything like it before. The only logical explanation was that Desmond was holding up the fragments, otherwise most of the front of the building would also have caved in by now.

Horatio was doing his best to help Desmond and the others. The only issue was that he could not see all of the galleys in such darkness. Only the ones floating at the front of the formation were visible.

He summoned down lightning on as many galleys as he could see. If those caught fire he would have a better view of the ones behind them. The barrage on the front of the House had somewhat died down, but that no longer mattered. The front of the House was going to collapse soon unless Desmond or another Descendant could hold it up longer. Horatio knew he was likely the only one with this vantage point; he would have to destroy as many ships as possible, despite the darkness. *Where the hell is Marshall when you need him? I could really use some light right now*, he thought.

As he tried to think of how he might destroy the ships that were further away, Savaiyon appeared through a gateway, followed by a dark man with long, stringy hair. As quickly as they appeared, Savaiyon was through another gateway and the other man disappeared in an instant. A few seconds later, Savaiyon reappeared, gasping, "The next time I..." and disappeared through another doorway. The other man briefly glanced at him before disappearing. Horatio only then realized he had stopped attacking the ships and had released his manifestation.

Savaiyon appeared again, gasping once more, "Next time, come with me!" He disappeared once again, as did the shadowy man who followed him.

A few moments later, the gateway opened right next to Horatio and he immediately started running alongside Savaiyon. *He's littered with daggers! How is he still running? How is he still alive?* Another gateway appeared before them.

"When we go through, you stay there. Then when I come back, summon the lightning down everywhere you possibly can! Don't worry about hitting me! Lightning everywhere!" They appeared near the mountain containing the touch portal to the House of Darian. Normally Kadoog'han would be hiding within the boulders in front of the cave. He desperately hoped Kadoog'han wasn't still there.

Savaiyon formed another gateway as Horatio stopped to wait for his return. As he wiped the sweat from his forehead, something cold struck him right between his shoulder blades and knocked him face-first to the ground. The impact of the ground against his head left him in a daze. He lay there for several minutes. *Don't...black...out. Don't...black out...*

His head dropped again. Horatio summoned all of his strength and pulled himself up to his forearms and knees. He barely heard a shout in the distance, but was too dizzy to know where to turn. He blinked several times. A few moments later, he heard the shout again.

What the hell just happened? He looked around and realized where he was. *Why am I back here?* Once again, he heard shouting nearby, though this time he recognized his name was being yelled.

Horatio shook his head vigorously and turned to the source. *Savaiyon! What is he doing?* He saw Savaiyon, being chased by another man, leave through a gateway. *Lightning! He wanted me to summon the lightning!*

The next time Savaiyon appeared, Horatio was still in the process of standing up and getting his bearings. The world was still blurry and he swayed, but he was coherent enough to open up to his manifestation. However, by the time Horatio had fully grasped it, Savaiyon and his pursuer were gone again.

A few minutes later, Savaiyon appeared out of the gateway a few yards away from Horatio. As soon as the other man appeared, the man felled Savaiyon with a dagger to the hamstring. Horatio wasted no more time. He growled. Anger and hatred filled him. He called forth as much lightning as he could and filled nearly the entire landscape, looking at the mysterious man the entire time. Horatio thought, for the briefest moment, that he'd caught him. The man fell, but disappeared in the process and Horatio could not be sure if he had really been hit. Horatio continued the lightning for several minutes, just in case the man dared to return. He hated the man for attacking them, but deep down, something elusive fueled his hatred for the man.

The prolonged surge of energy left Horatio exhausted. He took a step toward Savaiyon, who lay on the ground, unmoving, and collapsed once more.

***

The common room had thankfully been cleared of people except for Marshall, who kept it lit. Maximilian was providing Desmond with enough energy to prevent further damage to the House. The power and energy that flowed through him were intoxicating. Desmond felt as if he could destroy every single one of his attackers.

The front of the House was completely reduced to dust. Desmond focused solely on the cannonballs, as Maximilian had called them, keeping them from crashing into anything. He yelled to Maximilian, "Why are they only firin' these at us? Why aren't they rushin' us and fightin'?"

"Because they do not have to! Look at all the destruction they have caused. If we hadn't reacted so quickly, they could have killed almost all of us by just firing from their ships!"

More cannonballs came and Desmond held them. Dozens upon dozens of the metal projectiles filled the air. With the force that they'd been fired, Desmond was surprised he was able to stop them, especially since the front of the building was no longer a barrier against them.

They had already been there for hours. Aside from some sleepiness, Desmond had a wealth of energy. "How ya feelin', Maven? We goin' ta have ta stop any time soon?"

Maximilian chuckled. It caught Desmond off guard that the man could find some levity in a time like this. He was almost annoyed, but there was definitely no time for fighting with their own. "I have at least half a day left at this pace! Hold as many as you can! Sooner or later, they will have to run out!"

This stupid place. If Marlowe'd been doin' his job, I woulda thought o' this hours ago. Maybe he'll banish me fer attackin' just like he did ta Tasz. "That's not what I had in mind! We've been here long enough! Let's turn the attack back on 'em! Raish is helpin' from somewhere with all that lightnin'! That's too much fer it ta be natural! I need a stronger output from ya, though! I'm gonna fire these things right back at 'em!"

"Are you sure? That much power, Desmond. I fear for what it might do to you!"

"We don't have a choice right now, Maven! There is no 'might'! We only have right now!"

Maximilian nodded. Desmond felt a surge in his energy. He stood up and extended his arms out at his sides. He felt connected to every single cannonball in the air. He closed his eyes to focus. With more power than he'd ever used before, Desmond launched every cannonball back out into the night toward the ships. Toward the ocean. Toward the fires. He could feel them breaking and cracking into things and people. The impact was terrific and terrible all at once. Finally, he could no longer feel them. He smiled and looked at Marshall and Maximilian.

"Take advantage o' the moment ta rest a little! Soon enough, more ships'll push through an' start firin' at us again! I've given us some respite. If there're as many ships as I think, then we still have lots more work ta do. Maybe half an hour at most 'til more o' 'em reach us. Both o' ya should go down ta the infirmary an' relax with the others. It'll be safe there fer now."

Marshall looked at him strangely. "You're coming down with us. You need a break just as much as we do. You have no idea how much energy you just used, but once Max lets you go, you will feel it."

Desmond bit his lip. He hadn't even considered that Maximilian would release him from the energy transfer. He looked at Maximilian reluctantly and nodded. "Go ahead."

The surge of energy within him slowed. "I will leave you with enough to keep you awake and alert, as if you have gotten a full-night's sleep." After several moments, he said, "There. You will be just fine on that." Maximilian turned and walked toward the back staircase without waiting for a response. Desmond followed quickly as Marshall joined him.

"Go down the stairs. One of us should stand at the top, as a lookout." Once again, Marshall eyed him suspiciously.

***

Savaiyon woke to the feeling of coldness ripping through his body. He lay face down and attempted to turn his head. "Stay still! You have almost a dozen blades sticking out of you! If you keep moving around, it'll only hurt more!"

"Do not worry about the pain, boy. Just get them out of me. Did you hit him?" Savaiyon gritted his teeth and girded himself for the process. He assumed that he'd awoken while the first dagger was being removed.

"I can't be sure. I thought I did, but he disappeared right after."

"Hopefully you did. And hopefully it was enough to keep him away for a while." *Focus.* It was too dark to focus on his surroundings, so he closed his eyes and pictured the ship-building docks at Gansishoor. Watching the workers build them always filled him with serenity and wonder. The process of building good ships, especially the large ones that were being made recently, was so intricate. The builders were able to fit so much below the deck; Savaiyon could not imagine how many people could live on the ship comfortably, even on a long voyage. He imagined what it might be like to live at sea, with no wars or conflicts or threats to interfere. The only thing that would matter would be to catch one's meals each day and then relax.

Savaiyon was suddenly shaking. "Wake up! Did you fall asleep again while I was pulling out the daggers? How does that even happen?" Horatio rolled Savaiyon onto his back and hoisted him to a sitting position. "I need you to do the same thing to me. You have no idea how painful it is to pull daggers out of someone while you have one in your own back!" Horatio turned around and sat on his knees, awaiting Savaiyon's help.

"I know how to control myself better than you, boy. And I know better than to whine about pain." If he had had the energy, Savaiyon would have pulled the blade out slowly, just to annoy Horatio even more. Instead, he removed it quickly and inspected the weapon. Horatio cursed loudly and lay down. The dagger's hilt was not ornate, laden with jewels or anything flashy, but the engravings were intricate and the symbols were nothing Savaiyon had seen before. He inspected the others on the ground beside him. Each was similar. "These are not Ashurian. This Maqdhuum is a confusing man. He works for Jahmash; that is obvious. But why did he not kill us? He certainly had the opportunity to kill me and many others inside the House. In fact, given his ability to Travel anywhere, even faster than I can, he could have been killing Descendants long ago. I am too tired to think clearly. Help me up, boy. I do not have the energy to create a bridge back to The House. You are going to have to be a crutch for me so we can walk over to the touch portal. Honestly, it would be better if you could carry me. I have lost too much blood."

Horatio's response was strained. "I can barely walk there myself, much less carry you. I used up most of my energy on that massive lightning strike, and even still I don't know if I hit him. He definitely hit me though. I'm still woozy from it. Is he a Descendant?"

"That was Maqdhuum. He has no Mark. We only became aware of his existence about eight months ago. For someone who can appear and disappear so easily, I would imagine one of two scenarios. Either many people know of him because of his ability without bearing the Mark. Or more likely, nobody knows of him because he has chosen to hide what he can do. My suspicion is that he is not from Ashur. But everything about him changes our understanding of the world." Savaiyon shifted to his hands and knees. "Come. We have to start moving. It will take some time to get to the touch portal. Let's stop wasting our energy talking."

Over half of an hour later they reached the touch portal within the cave and were transported to the main common room of the House. The process, along with the amount of blood he'd lost, made Savaiyon dizzy. Horatio vomited.

Savaiyon struggled to raise himself to hands and knees. He heard a voice. "Stay down, Maven. I'll get you!" It was Marshall. He hoisted him up and threw Savaiyon's arm over his shoulder, acting as a crutch. Savaiyon could barely coordinate as he drifted in and out of consciousness.

He opened his eyes to see Lincan and Delilah standing over him. Above them, the ceiling was severely cracked. "How long have I been out?"

Delilah held up a hand, as if sure that Savaiyon would attempt to get up. "Not long. Twenty minutes or so. Long enough for us to patch you up and for your heart to start replenishing your blood. You are almost healed. You might be tired for a while though, while your heart makes up for the blood loss and your body recovers."

"Horatio?" He looked around for the boy.

"Horatio is fine. His wounds were fewer than yours. More than anything, he needs to rest. Whatever it was that you two did, it drained him. How much lightning did he summon, Savaiyon?" She nodded toward a cot on Savaiyon's right.

He looked over to see Horatio sleeping. "I do not know. I was lying on the ground, face down, full of daggers, and without much sense of my surroundings."

"Please tell us as much as you can, Maven Savaiyon." The voice came from the wall, where Zin Marlowe walked through an opening escorted by Maven Blastevahn. Blastevahn was the only Maven in the House as tall as Savaiyon, although his stockier build made him look brutish. In truth, Blastevahn was one of the nicest people Savaiyon had ever met. Marlowe continued, "You were missing for hours, and the gateways that were protecting the island disappeared. Obviously you were in serious trouble."

Savaiyon assumed that Marlowe had been confined to his chamber, the sturdiest and most secure location in the House, and used a hidden passageway to access the infirmary. Now that Savaiyon assessed the surroundings, he realized that the infirmary was filled with two to three dozen Descendants. He was shocked, "This is all that is left? Thirty of us?"

Badalao stepped forth. "As far as we know. There was too much destruction. Both housing wings were decimated. Most of the deaths were caused by collapsing walls and floors. Desmond was the only one capable of stopping the whole House from crumbling. We were nearly crushed trying to keep the first floor ceiling up. He focused on the front. If there had been daylight I could have communicated with several Descendants to stay coordinated. Our enemies knew too much about us. The Augur in Vandenar had to have been right. There is a traitor within." They looked around at one another. "That being said, Desmond returned fire with their own weapons. Many of their ships have sunk. Marshall briefly cast a light over the ocean. There are still scores of galleys out there. It is likely only a matter of time before they engage us with more cannons or on foot. As you said Maven, there are only about thirty of us, but we have to make the best of our numbers." He looked at Marlowe and then back at Savaiyon. "Those who can fight should fight, with manifestations or hand-to-hand. There is no…"

Marlowe stepped to the center of the room. "Enough. Let us hear what Maven Savaiyon has to say. I have a feeling it might be crucial to the outcome of this battle. Savaiyon?"

Savaiyon stroked his short hair and looked at Badalao regretfully. "Very well. I was attacked in my room. By Maqdhuum, a man who can Travel faster than I can. He stabbed me and I managed to throw him against the wall and daze him. Every time I created a new doorway and escaped he was right behind me. Every time he knew exactly where I was going. Only he was not creating doors. He was simply disappearing and reappearing. All we know about this man is that he works for Jahmash. How is Maqdhuum capable of these abilities if he does not bear the Mark? Only a few of you in this room are aware that there are nations beyond Ashur. Even in those nations, while there is the possibility that Descendants of Darian are there, there have never been reports of others with such remarkable abilities without the Mark. Maqdhuum is something completely different. Unless…"

Marshall suddenly came running down the stairs with Maven Maximilian, "They are coming! Their soldiers are leaving the ships and coming ashore! A general leads them! Maven Maximilian has confirmed that it is Drahkunov! We need everyone up here now! Especially you, Max!"

Before anyone could react, Marlowe stopped them. "Wait! Everyone stay here for a moment! Maven Maximilian, go back upstairs and help Desmond. The rest of you, wait! I am going to tell you what must be done. We will not win this fight based on numbers. Especially if Drahkunov is their general. It is time you all saw the truth for what it is." In mere seconds, Marlowe's appearance changed drastically from his normal appearance to that of a withered and wrinkly old man. His skin tone remained the same Cerysian hue, but gone were the full head of hair, straight posture, and young face and skin. Gasps filled the room, almost as loud as the cannonballs earlier.

Marlowe continued, "For so long, I am sure that most of you assumed I simply did not age. However, the truth is that I can change my form to resemble anyone I wish. I am actually ninety years old, not the young man you assumed me to be. There is no time for an explanation now. It is time to fight. I will go to the shore and assume the appearance of Drahkunov. He will look like this." Marlowe changed appearances once more to a middle-aged, slightly overweight Galicean man with dark hair. "If I can fool his soldiers long enough, then I can buy time for the rest of you by giving them false orders and commanding them to retreat." Marlowe looked like an old, frail man once more. "Do not attack Drahkunov until you see me appear in this form again. Now let us go and defend our home!"

Everyone in the room hurried up stairs ahead of Marlowe. Savaiyon, still in disbelief, shook himself and hurtled out of the cot. It made so much sense now. He ran upstairs as Lincan roused Horatio. They reached the common room a few moments after Savaiyon. *Delilah was right,* he thought, *I am too tired for this. Oh no, did Horatio just sleep through all of that?*

* * *

The first few glimpses of dawn allowed Adria to watch every crew member abandon the galley and run ashore as she sat shivering and still tied to the mast. Something still gripped her mind, sometimes more strongly than others. She was angry at the whole world, but felt flashes of elation rise here and there. Sometimes she would cry for several minutes at a time.

As far as she could tell, the ship was now empty except for her. It had been hit with a few cannonballs and was sinking at a moderate pace. Adria guessed that within the hour, the ship would be completely underwater. She was unsure whether the thought was hers or not.

Did I think that? Or was it Jahmash? It took her a moment to realize that nothing gripped her mind any longer. As happy and relieved as she was, a sudden wave of shame came over her. *How am I going to escape? The prophecy said I would go back home! Was there some hidden meaning in the words? Did I not understand it correctly?*

From the time that Adria had been captured, and then again when she was secured to the ship mast, she swore that she would escape. Adria was many things at the moment: exhausted, starving, numb, and desperate, but the only notion that angered her was that she was a victim. All that fighting, all that energy expended trying to be respected and treated as an equal, and now she would have to be rescued by others in order to survive.

She sulked for a few more moments until she grew bored of feeling sorry for herself. "No. I am not a victim. Those who sit by and do nothing end up in Oblivion. Not me. Not. Me!" Her hands were bound by a metal chain around the mast. The chain wasn't long enough for her to turn around, so she would have to scrape it back and forth against the mast while facing away from it.

She closed her eyes, gritted her teeth, and furiously worked the chain against the thick wooden mast. She pivoted her arms back and forth relentlessly for several minutes. "Don't stop to check. Just keep working," she thought as she tightened her eyes and fought against exhaustion. She focused so hard on her escape that she had no idea of the man crouching down in front of her.

"I hate to have to tell you this," his voice was low, but Adria jumped as if she'd just been screamed at, "but what you're doing...you'll drown long before your chain saws through the mast."

She looked up, finally calm. *Maqdhuum.* "You? What do you want?"

"I was thinking about rescuing you. Doesn't seem like your friend Drahkunov plans to. Your Descendant friends don't even know you're here."

"Rescue me? If I wasn't dehydrated, I would spit on you! You only want to take me back to Jahmash! I would rather die than go with you! Especially back to him!"

Maqdhuum laughed. "I highly doubt Jahmash is willing to work with me any longer. I'm willing to bet that I've lost his trust. You're safer with me than with anyone else. Especially against him." Adria noticed Maqdhuum's left hand hanging limp. It was severely bloodied and discolored, and his sleeve was in tatters, with several holes.

"That arm of yours going to protect me?"

He looked down in annoyance. "This thing? Scratch. I've had worse. Listen. I will save you. Only problem is I can't remove your shackles. If I concentrate hard enough, we can Travel away without the shackles and when we reappear, your arms wouldn't be bound. Naturally you would agree to not attack me in the process."

The offer sounded tempting. Agreeing to his terms seemed like the only opportunity to escape death. "Fine. I will let you free me. But we appear right back on this deck. No tricks. I want to be sure I can trust you. Then, I'll consider going with you."

He nodded, "Fair. No moving while I Travel. It might not work correctly. Last thing we want is to mess up your pretty little self in any way."

"What are you planning to do with me?"

Maqdhuum looked at her suspiciously. "Do?" He looked her up and down for a moment. "Oh, I see. Don't worry. I have no ulterior motives. Might as well tell you the truth, if I'm to take you with me." He looked back at her. "We need to form an army. People who will actually fight against Jahmash. Not like your friends in that sorry House of Darian. Once he manages to get off that island of his, Ashur's in big trouble. I like you. You have passion. Conviction. Figure you're a good place to start. Any of your friends survive this attack, maybe I'll take them, too. That one he's looking for, Baltaszar; got to find him as well. He would be quite the asset against our Red Harbinger. Surprised we haven't been attacked by Baltaszar out here yet. Unless he doesn't know what is happening. Hopefully he's not dead already. Anyway, here. Take my hand."

Adria hesitated. *How do I keep getting into these situations?* "Don't know Baltaszar. One more question. Then…then I'll go with you." Adria put her hands down to the deck and leaned back against the mast. She took a deep breath, nervous about the answer to what she was about to ask. "What are you? You're not a Descendant. That's obvious. But no one else can do what we can. So why can you disappear and reappear if you aren't a Descendant?"

Maqdhuum grinned widely and then walked behind her. "Answer to that is easy. But I'm not going to tell you here. Take too long. Let's get out of here. Then you get the truth. Give me your hand." He held out his hand, palm up, to her.

Adria lifted her right hand somewhat reluctantly. She was simultaneously intrigued and afraid. She rested her hand in his palm. Adria instantly saw a split-second flash of hundreds of colors extending toward her, then she was sitting on the deck at the other end of the boat. Traveling like this was much preferable to the touch portal leading to the House. "Wow." Finally free of the shackles, she thanked Orijin.

"See. No reason to be afraid."

A shout came from where they'd just been. "Let her go! Right now!"

Marshall. He was with Maven Savaiyon, who also barked a command. "Mouse! Run!" Both of them ran to her instantly. Adria felt Maqdhuum grip her arm and she saw the same brilliant spectrum of colors once more. *No!*

***

Horatio stood on the shore, fighting exhaustion and fatigue just as much as he was fighting the soldiers attacking him and his brethren. Books had described stories of Descendants dying from using their manifestations for too long without rest or sustenance. He assumed that this day would bring the same for him.

He brought forth lightning bolt after bolt, striking soldiers down as they ran ashore. Most were not even aware of him, which made things easier. It was always easier to kill his enemies when he didn't have to look at their faces. If they were charging someone else, all the better. It had been easy to forget how tired he was because the waves of soldiers were unrelenting. *Marlowe said something about Drahkunov. Keep an eye out for him. What did he look like again?*

Many of the others had made it clear that they'd accepted the possibility of dying in this battle. Horatio had held his tongue. He didn't want to die. He wasn't sure if that meant he wouldn't sacrifice his life if the time came, but he might have second thoughts. Perhaps it might depend on the situation. *I guess it's probably bad to tell them I wish Tasz was here.* He, Tasz and Desmond could have wiped out the whole army within an hour.

He did appreciate the help that actually was on the shore with him, though. Reverron confused soldiers by dashing around and striking them before they could defend. Sindha created a sort of force field to prevent another front from advancing, which allowed other Descendants like Badalao and Malikai to engage them in combat. Behind them, Desmond and Maximilian returned any cannonballs still being fired. Horatio was very appreciative of his manifestation. It did not require much focus to execute simple attacks. Lightning was deadly even when it wasn't completely accurate. *What did they say Drahkunov looked like? Chubby? Overweight. Galicean feature. And loud. That's what Savaiyon said. Got to be aware of him.*

Suddenly, he felt the need to sit. Despite being healed in the infirmary when he and Savaiyon returned, the only remedy for exhaustion was sleep. Horatio dropped to a knee. More ships were arriving on their perimeter. Soldiers swam in from farther out. His lightning bolts were striking less frequently. And with less accuracy. Horatio put a hand to the ground. He was barely holding on to his manifestation. To let it go would mean certain unconsciousness.

For a moment, Horatio forgot where he was. He saw a different island shore before him. *Damaszur?* This place didn't look familiar. He shook his head and came back to his reality. In the distance, Horatio saw a chubby man barking orders to his soldiers. *That has to be him. Drahkunov.* The soldiers were following his commands. Horatio attempted to call forth more lightning. Three bolts struck down near Drahkunov, but they hit the soldiers near him instead of the man himself.

The soldiers scuttled away from the area in all directions. Horatio put both hands to the ground. He took several breaths. He shook his head vigorously. *Two. Three attacks left. At most.* His eyes were shutting on him. He dropped to his forearms and struggled to look up. His vision was blurry, but he could still distinguish Drahkunov from the soldiers.

Horatio summoned more lightning. Five or six bolts struck. One of them knocked Drahkunov down, but the others missed completely. Horatio heaved. He could see Drahkunov struggling on the ground, though he looked somewhat different. *Burnt. I must've burnt him. Severed body parts. Charred him.* It was the only explanation he could think of. He could barely form a thought. His head touched the ground. *C'mon. Finish...him.* Horatio looked at Drahkunov writhing once more. With all of his remaining energy, he brought forth several lightning bolts. He kept his head up long enough to see them directly strike the man. Drahkunov no longer moved. Horatio managed to form half of a smile before collapsing to the ground.

***

It amazed Desmond just how many ships there were. He would have guessed several hundred. As soon as Maximilian joined him, another brilliant idea formed in Desmond's mind. If he could get rid of the ships, the battle would end. It wasn't enough to just fire the cannonballs back at them anymore. "More energy, Maven. More power! We're gonna end this once an' fer all!'"

Desmond felt the surge right after he made the request. Unfortunately, it came with advice. "I am warning you, Desmond. What you are taking in is dangerous. Promise if we get out of this, you'll take a break from your manifestation. It would be stupid to do all this to survive, only to die from the very thing that saved your life."

"I promise, Maven. My word is my bond. Just trust me!" The entire front of the House of Darian was gone, so they could see all of the ships coming upon the shore several hundred feet before them. It helped that the sun was rising. *Hopefully this is over fast enough that we don't even need Lao for mental communication.*

He focused on a single galley. Desmond kept his eyes open and, slowly and unsteadily, raised it out of the water. He hovered it above the ship next to it, then let it fall. He repeated the same action over and over again. Desmond soon felt comfortable enough that he could raise two at a time and crash them into multiple galleys.

Desmond had hoped for more help from Horatio in destroying the ships, but he was likely busy engaging the soldiers. "Come ta think o' it, I haven't seen any lightnin' in a while. Where is he?" he wondered as he continued the barrage on the ships. Desmond relished the wealth of energy that flowed through him. He wished his manifestation was always so easy and powerful.

He could no longer see any ships intact and focused his attention on the shore. "Come, Maven! We should help with the soldiers on the shore!" Desmond ran ahead, not waiting for Maximilian to follow. He remembered quite quickly that he needed to maintain contact with Maximilian to enable the energy surge. Desmond slowed and let Maximilian catch up. They reached one of the shores where the soldiers had engaged the Descendants. With Maximilian's help, Desmond took soldiers nearly ten at a time and flung them high into the air over the ocean, far enough away that they wouldn't be able to swim back, even if the fall didn't hurt or kill them. Others were thrown into the wreckage of the ships. Desmond had no idea when he'd have this much power at his disposal again. He took full advantage. A group of soldiers was swimming in from a nearby sinking galley. Desmond raised the ship and dropped it on the men. Their screams were short-lived.

Desmond reveled in his accomplishment a moment too long. As he smiled at what he'd done, an arrow caught him in the side.

"Dammit!" He fell to his knees and Maximilian immediately dragged him back toward the House. They stopped behind a pile of debris. As Maximilian crouched next to Desmond, he realized that the Maven had also been struck through the arm and the chest. The pain that Desmond felt was nothing compared to the longing for the power he'd just been controlling.

Savaiyon suddenly appeared through a gateway next to them, with Marshall behind him. "Get out of here! Now!" He created another gateway that led to a dimly lit alley. "We are not going to win this battle! More soldiers are coming! Too many of us are down! Our only chance is to flee!" Savaiyon shoved Desmond and Maximilian through the gateway. "I will send Lincan to tend to you! Try not to stray too far!"

Desmond looked through the gateway, listening to Savaiyon's orders. He leaned back against a brick wall and slumped to the ground. His head pounded, craving the manifestation. "Hopefully Lincan gets here soon." He looked to Maximilian, who lay on the ground, heaving. Blood trickled from the Maven's mouth.

***

If his old friends could have seen the statues, they would have scoffed. *Pretentious. Overdone. Unnecessary. Contradictory to everything the Harbingers stood for.* Maqdhuum crouched atop the statue of Abram. *City of the Fallen. What a stupid name.* Adria sat next to him, clinging to his arm. The statue's head alone was big enough for at least two dozen people to stand on. He spit a few feet in front of him and watched as it streamed down the front of the statue's head. "These statues represent everything that's wrong with the world. Human beings are so caught up in dedications to others and paying homage to the past that, most of the time, they forget what it means to live a good life and take care of the people who should matter the most to them."

The girl responded with a witty retort, "Killing people. Cutting off their arms. Is that what it means to live a good life?"

"I do what is necessary. My fate has already been decided." Soon enough, he would see his life's purpose fulfilled and then he could be done with humanity. He would be satisfied. Even if it meant an eternity in Opprobrium. The way he saw it, the Orijin owned his soul anyway. If the Orijin wanted him to stay in solitude in Opprobrium forever, it was a fair exchange for his sins and for the undeserved gifts he'd received in his ridiculously long lifetime. Maqdhuum had had enough of people. He could spend the rest of existence never talking to anyone again. "Once we kill Jahmash, you will be rid of me. Tolerate me for that long and then you can have your peace."

"You still owe me an explanation. Tell me what you are."

"How about this? I'll tell you about what's weighing me down. If you can guess what I am, I promise that you will never feel like a prisoner with me."

"Do you expect me to say no?"

Maqdhuum smirked. "Enough sarcasm. Just listen. It revolves around a woman named Raya. I showed up at her house about fifteen years ago. I had a request. Raya came with me willingly. I didn't do anything to force her. She knew that her actions could ultimately lead to Jahmash's downfall. I didn't lie to her or deceive her in that regard. Her manifestation allowed her to travel back and forth to the Three Rings. She brought me there. To the Orijin. She knew what I wanted and did not hesitate to help me. Her actions and willingness to help allowed me to acquire a new body. A new face. In exchange for eternal suffering. And mortality. And once I made my deal with the Orijin, bringing Raya to Jahmash was the only way to ensure that Jahmash would trust me. She agreed to be a pawn in the whole endeavor. Maybe not in those exact words. But it's all semantics." Maqdhuum spat again. He would feel no guilt. "Abram had been a coward. Had run away in the face of opportunity. Maqdhuum would not. He would do what was necessary. Even if he must betray people. Even if he must betray Raya, who had left her husband and child at a whimsical but grave request. That was so long ago. She is dead now. If she truly wants revenge, she can exact it when I see her again in the Three Rings. For the rest of my existence."

"What?"

"Let me continue. Raya's life and death were tools. She was the first step to Jahmash's downfall." *And to humanity's downfall.* Though he hadn't told Raya about that part of it. He wouldn't tell this girl, either. He wanted to see humanity's destruction as much as Jahmash's. Mankind deserved to be obliterated. If not for mankind's devolution, the world would not be in this state to begin with. Even if he spent the rest of his existence in Opprobrium it was worth it to bring the world down with him. Mankind's arrogance had cost him Darian. Gideon. Lionel. "Mankind's stupidity turned Jahmash into a monster. Into the 'Red Harbinger.' The Orijin had told each Harbinger that, despite the miracles bestowed on each of them, there would be flaws. Weaknesses."

"You." Adria gripped his arm more tightly, but let go as her eyes widened. "You are...Abram. How...why?" Tears streamed from the girl's eyes.

"Jahmash's weakness is water. Abram's was loneliness. I have lived for centuries and no one in that time has managed to fill the void left by the loss of Darian, Gideon, and Lionel. Immortality means nothing if there is no one to share it with. Jahmash will soon realize it as well, if he has not already. Once you Descendants started surfacing, I knew the Orijin had something new in the works. I also knew that Jahmash must be working at something. I needed two things to stop him. First, try to gain his trust. No chance of that if I looked like Abram. Second, by killing people when he asked for them to be killed."

"Why can't you simply appear behind him and kill him?"

"Most people he meets are blindfolded, especially if he is unable to penetrate their minds. Whenever we met, it was either like that or in darkness. I would not even know where to Travel to sneak up on him. And he knows not to trust me by now. I realized too late that by accessing your mind, he could access your memories. You have seen me Travel numerous times. He would have made the connection. From now on, though, you must fight back when he tries to control you. I have been too careless. There is also the issue of him never being alone. He surrounds himself with guards at all times, and I would bet that they are all being controlled. Jahmash is smart. He doesn't trust anyone, though he pretends that he does. I am an exceptional swordsman, but he is even better. I would never get the best of him. That is where you Descendants come in. If used properly, your abilities could be weapons that he can not match. I believe that is why the Orijin has blessed you with them. You are the new Harbingers. As for me, I am no longer worthy of the title 'Harbinger.' Nor do I want to be. I am no longer responsible for humanity's salvation. I am no longer Abram. I am vengeance. I am the Master of Justice. I am Adl Maqdhuum."

"I love the irony of it all," Adria muttered next to him.

He turned to her. "What's that?"

"Today is Abraday."

***

Savaiyon was running out of energy. He would need to save his strength and use gateways just to help the Descendants escape. On the bright side, Marshall, Vasher, and Blastevahn were covering separate fronts of the battle to round up the wounded and keep them safe. Several Descendants still fought, though Savaiyon knew there would be more deaths. Those whom he could save he would send off for the time being, just as he'd done to Desmond and Maximilian. He hoped they'd find help soon. He was so tired he couldn't even remember where he'd sent them.

He searched the main battlefront. Sindha was still managing to keep many soldiers held back with a force field, but even that only stopped a portion of them. Savaiyon ran by a burnt and bloody body, still smoking. He almost disregarded it, except that he noticed the face staring straight up to the sky and recognized it immediately. *Orijin, no. Not like this. Not like this. Burnt? Charred? Horatio, please tell me this was not your doing.*

A few hours ago, Savaiyon wouldn't have known the man, but Zin Marlowe had revealed his truth to the surviving Descendants, and his old, withered face was imprinted in Savaiyon's mind. He formed a gateway next to the body. It led to another island where the graves of Lionel, Abram, and Darian were. His body would be safe there. Savaiyon pushed the frail body through and released the gateway. As he arose to move on, an arrow struck him through the forearm and brought him back to his knees. Savaiyon quickly broke the arrow's shaft and pulled out the rest. *No time for pain.*

He ducked down behind a low wooden fence and ran along it to search for more wounded. *Cursed height! Without Marlowe, we cannot stop them. We do not have the weapons to win a battle. We must retreat!*

As Savaiyon passed an opening in the fence, he saw another body lying on the ground, rocking ever so slightly. *Reverron. At least he is moving.* A few enemy soldiers were running toward Reverron. From where he stood, Savaiyon opened a gateway on the ground next to Reverron. He kept it small enough that Reverron could roll through, just as he'd done to Marlowe's body. *If I shout, I expose my location. You owe me, Rev.* "Reverron! Gateway! Roll to your right! Rev! Roll to your right!" The boy rolled more slowly than Savaiyon would have liked, but finally he made it through and Savaiyon sealed the gateway.

The oncoming soldiers altered their course and charged at Savaiyon. Their armor resembled that which he'd seen in the ruins of the Taurani village. *Not enough time.* Savaiyon formed a gateway right in front of them. He was sure it led into the ocean. It was too close for them to avoid. Once they were through, he sealed it and moved forward. *This is taking too much energy. I have to hurry. Where are the others?* He ran out from behind the fence to inspect the landscape. Horatio lay far to his left, where Savaiyon had seen him standing before.

Savaiyon hesitated a split second about going to him. *No, he can answer for his actions another time. It could have been a mistake.* Savaiyon ran to him after ensuring no enemies remained nearby. Just as with the others, he formed a gateway and pushed Horatio through. Exhaustion clouded his mind. Moments after closing the gateway, he forgot where he'd sent the boy. He'd actually forgotten where he'd sent most of them. Not far off, Badalao and Sindha fought nearly a dozen soldiers. Their backs were to each other and they were fending off attacks rather than fighting. Savaiyon knelt down to focus better. He started a gateway and wrapped it around Badalao and Sindha, creating a circle around them. Thankfully, his gateways were transparent from the other side, and he could see the two walk through. He closed it immediately and the stunned soldiers collapsed upon one another.

Another arrow grazed the side of his neck, taking a chunk of flesh with it. The glancing blow sent him to the ground. He heard another arrow land not far from his head. Multiple shouts ensued until he heard a voice coming near. "Come on Maven, we have to go!"

Savaiyon clasped his neck and stood gingerly, only to see Marshall and Kadoog'han standing by a lifeless soldier. Marshall had already taken the dead woman's bow and arrow. "Inside! We have to go back in and bring the rest to safety!"

Marshall took a step in the opposite direction. "Nonsense. We have to stop these attackers! We can finish this now!"

"Too many of us are dead and wounded already! We must save whom we can! Marshall, this is not a discussion, it is a command! Marlowe is dead! We must preserve those Descendants who are left! There is a bigger battle than this to fight!"

"I've already watched the Taurani die and let Adria get taken away. I will not sit back this time!" Marshall glared at him and continued toward the remaining enemy soldiers. Savaiyon created another gateway, not far in front of Marshall, and watched the boy run right through it. He was surprised at how astute the boy was, as Marshall turned around almost immediately. Savaiyon closed the gateway right away.

Savaiyon turned quickly to Kadoog'han, "Let's go! We are running out of people to save!" They ran back toward the House, searching every remaining hallway and room for survivors. Sweat poured from Savaiyon. His clothes were drenched and only helped the exhaustion weigh him down. He had to resort to gateways a few times throughout the House in order to avoid enemy soldiers. They'd almost been seen by Drahkunov himself. Savaiyon would have relished a fight with the man, but it was not one he would win at the moment.

Over the next hour they covered almost every inch of what was left of the House and Savaiyon had created several gateways to help others escape. Many of his fellow Mavens had perished in the initial attack, but he managed to save a few. They would be necessary if the Descendants were to regroup. He and Kadoog'han even managed to save Delilah and Lincan before the infirmary collapsed. The two were stubborn enough to refuse to come upstairs. Savaiyon eventually created tight circular gateways around them so they'd had no choice.

"There is one more place we must go, my friend. There is one last Descendant we will need, if we hope to stand a chance against Drahkunov, cannons, and Jahmash." He clasped Kadoog'han's shoulder more in need for support than because he felt amiable. "If I have anything left in me to create another bridge."

Kadoog'han shot him a knowing, but reluctant smile. "Dungeon." He nodded. "The Prince."

"We get him, then we leave."

They wasted no time in moving on to the dungeon, but Kadoog'han carried Savaiyon practically the whole way. He wasn't positive, but he might have blacked out once or twice along the way.

Savaiyon barely realized they'd arrived at Garrison's cell. Once he recognized Garrison, he shook his head and stroked his hair. He briefly pressed his neck and saw that he was still bleeding, though not quite as much as before. Savaiyon took a step toward the cell and looked down at Garrison. The Prince crouched against the wall at the back of the cell and stared down.

Savaiyon blinked several times. His vision was becoming hazy. He was about to say something when he and Kadoog'han heard a man sprinting loudly down the hall. The man was as tall, if not taller, than he was. His face bore a thick brownish beard.

"Baltaszar! Where is Baltaszar Kontez? I have searched this whole damn island for the boy! Where is he? And Zin Marlowe? I have no time to explain! I need to find them before it's too late!"

Savaiyon did not recognize the man's accent, but it surely was not from anywhere in Ashur he'd ever been. Regardless, the man would have already killed them if he was an enemy. "Who are you?"

"We do not have time for this!" The man glowered at him but Savaiyon stared at him blankly. "Fine. My name is Slade. Rhadames Slade. I was a friend of Baltaszar's father. And Asarei. I need Baltaszar now! If the wrong people get to him, he will be controlled by Jahmash! Do you not understand the urgency?"

In truth, Savaiyon sympathized with Slade's predicament, but he had no energy for urgency. Every movement was labor. He dropped to a knee and rested his jaw in his palm. "Baltaszar is no longer here."

"What? Then where is he?"

"Marlowe banished him yesterday. The boy is mad. He attempted to burn down his own village. He likely would have if we had not arrived when we did."

Slade sighed, "Light of Orijin. No. Where is he now? Where did Marlowe send him?"

Savaiyon glanced at Kadoog'han and then back at Slade. "Into the Never. He instructed me to drop the boy into the Never. From high enough that the fall would hurt him, but not kill him."

To Savaiyon's surprise, Slade flashed a brief smile. "Good. That's good."

Savaiyon had no idea what the man was talking about. He was about to ask Slade to clarify when he heard someone talking from Garrison's cell. It was a familiar voice, but not Garrison's. He turned and was startled by a second man in the cell. "You."

***

Maqdhuum grinned more widely and genuinely than he had in a long time. The look of shock on Savaiyon's face was worth being struck by lightning. Before any of them could move, he flung daggers through the cell bars at the two men beside Savaiyon, knocking them down. "I'm going to take this one." He nodded at Garrison "I like his past. Appreciate his work. I think I can use him better than you can."

Savaiyon labored to respond. "I know who you are, Abram. I am not afraid of you. I am disappointed to see what you have become."

"Boy, you cannot begin to fathom who I am, who I was, or who I've become. Abram is no more. All that is left is Maqdhuum." The other two men were starting to recover. "While we're on the subject, do your Descendant friends know who you are? Only a soldier of the Ancient Clan would be able to maintain such focus after being struck by a dozen daggers." Maqdhuum laughed at the shocked look on Savaiyon's face. "You didn't think I'd know? Idiot." The other two were standing once more. Maqdhuum fired another dagger at Savaiyon, striking him in the shin. *No sense killing him. He'll be needed soon.* He looked down at the prisoner, who'd crept to the corner. The scrawny boy cowered and hid his face from Maqdhuum. "See what you've done to him? He's broken. This is how you treat your own? Good. I need him. I'll take him off your hands. Doubt he'll trust you anyway." Maqdhuum knelt down and grabbed Garrison's arm. He smiled once again at the men outside the cell and disappeared.

***

Savaiyon forced himself to sit up and pulled the blade from his leg. "How many daggers does he *have*?" He shook his head, amazed and disappointed. Garrison would have been an incredible asset. Maqdhuum had been right, though. The House of Darian had ruined Garrison.

Kadoog'han bent down and helped him up. "What was he talking about? Did you say 'Abram?' And what Ancient Clan?"

"Never mind that now. We need to leave before anyone else finds us down here. We'll go to Gansishoor for now. Our wounds can be healed by regular doctors. I've forgotten where I sent Lincan and Delilah."

Slade nodded. "Very well. Then what? We need to recover quickly. Jahmash will strike fast now that the House of Darian has been destroyed. And we will eventually need to find Baltaszar again."

"Asarei. We find Asarei, if that's possible." Savaiyon was draped on the arms of Kadoog'han and Slade as they walked through the gateway. "He is the only one who can help us now." The yellow-fringed doorway disappeared behind them.

CHAPTER 24
RISE OF THE RED HARBINGER

From *The Book of Orijin*, **Verse Four Hundred Ninety-Four**
Have faith in Us, even when you are alone and in the darkness. For
We are the Darkness, surrounding you as a guardian. Protecting you
from what you do not comprehend. Hiding you from evil.

Baltaszar had wandered for the better part of a day. The forest seemed endless and he couldn't even be sure that he was still in Ashur. He'd landed on his arm after falling through several webs of branches, and he'd turned his ankle as well. In retrospect, the fall would likely have been much worse if not for the branches. A soft snow covered the ground. His left arm dangled as he limped on and the pain only grew more intense with time. The shackles on his wrists and ankles would be the death of him.

All he wanted was to find a safe and comfortable place to spend the night. Baltaszar was wary of creating a fire. The land was unfamiliar. Who knew what lurked here. Who knew what might be watching him.

The sun had begun its descent. As it got lower, he could hear more and more sounds around him. Along with some familiar buzzing, likely from insects, Baltaszar definitely heard low growls, though they didn't sound close. He also heard swishes, as if something else was brushing against the shrubs and leaves. And then there were the strange raspy sounds, as if something was scraping against the trees. Baltaszar continued on, walking gingerly and cautiously, and staying close to the trees. Strangely though, the falling snow melted before hitting the ground.

Even though he was tired, Baltaszar had no idea how he would sleep with the intense pain. His arm throbbed and burned. At times he was sure he saw stars if his arm swung too quickly.

He gritted his teeth and walked on for nearly an hour. The

sunlight had almost completely disappeared. *Is there no safe place around?* He looked ahead. In the distance, in the darkness, Baltaszar saw tiny, bright red dots piercing the blackness. They hovered in front of him, several yards away. He leaned in and squinted his eyes. One pair grew nearer, though never leaving the darkness. As he got closer, the air around him grew warmer and warmer. Intrigued, Baltaszar walked into the darkness toward the two bright red dots. They fascinated him and terrified him at the same time. After several moments, they hovered just before his face.

Suddenly, Baltaszar reluctantly smiled and a sense of shame came over him.

I don't know why I doubted you for so long. I'm sorry.

He felt dangerous, in a different way than ever before.

Because your faith wavered. In Orijin. In yourself. But once you saw me, you did not turn away. For that, your faith shall be rewarded. Your father instructed us to only appear to you once we were sure you were ready. You have much to learn. Your manifestation is one and the same with our very essence.

***

"What is your mission?"

Bo'az knew the answer before the question was even asked. "I am to visit every nation beyond Ashur, my Lord." He knelt before the man and, though the stone dug into his knee, enjoyed the pain of it.

"And?"

Over twenty soldiers surrounded Jahmash as he sat in his plain wooden chair, each man armed with a sword on his back, daggers at his belt, and a spear in his hand. Bo'az felt a certain admiration for them. "I am to tell them that you demand an army. A bigger army than before. More soldiers. More generals. More weapons. And even beasts that can be controlled."

"And how will you convince them?" Jahmash smiled at him. Bo'az felt happy once more. That smile made him know he was worthwhile.

"I will have Linas recount the story of how he became blind. I will ensure that they understand your warning not to defy them. Linas will then display your power and control on himself."

"Good. You are becoming a fine pet. And what if Linas cannot convince them?"

"Then I will present Aric to them as a token of your appreciation.

And your other "gifts", if need be. They will then understand that you are merciful and reasonable."

"If that is not enough? What will happen if you expend your resources before meeting with every nation?"

"You will use my eyes to find a specimen of theirs. To show them how easily you could destroy them."

"And if you fail?"

"Then I shall die. Either by their hand or by my own."

"Very good, Bo'az." It lifted Bo'az's spirits when Jahmash spoke his name. "And lastly, what is your message? What will you say to them?"

Bo'az was most excited about this part. "If you obey, you will be spared. You will be allowed vengeance on those devoted to Darian. You will also be allowed to claim a piece of The Drowned Realm for your own. A new era begins. The House of Darian has been destroyed. The Red Harbinger has risen."

***

Khurt Everitas dabbed the palette again with his index finger for another glob of black paint. With a slow, meticulous swipe, he outlined another patch on his son's arm.

"Khenzi, do you understand the significance of this? This is not merely another day of portraying our strength."

Khenzi sat next to his father on a bench just outside the orchard behind their home. It wasn't the first time Khurt had painted his son's body, but it was the first time he'd used the black on his son, signifying war, conquest, and invasion. "I know, father. We wear black today because we are leaving for war. But why black for war and not red? And am I truly allowed to come with you? Mother did not forbid it?"

Khurt rolled his eyes. The boy always thought his mother was trying to prevent him from doing things. "Your mother tells you that you cannot do a great many things because you have trouble controlling yourself. You must learn discipline. Which is why we both agree that you must make this journey."

"So you both do not think that I am just a child?"

Khurt rested a hand on his son's shouder. "Khenzi, you have seen six summers now. By my ninth, I had killed a man in battle. By the time our Greatmother Ashota, bless her soul, reached twelve summers, she had decided to turn this skin disease into something to be proud of. Always remember, it was she who first looked at this condition for what it is, and transformed it into something that the rest of this world fears. To many, Ashota was just a child then. And even beyond that, the Harbinger Gideon sacrificed his life for the good of humanity at only fifteen or sixteen summers. Do not let anyone tell you that you are just a child."

Khurt grasped his son's hand before continuing on with the paint. Khenzi would be considered frail by most, and Khurt firmly believed that any other general would find Khenzi to be an embarrassment of a son. But it was in Khenzi's mischievousness and constant insistence on doing what he wanted to do that Khurt saw potential. Khenzi's stature would never strike fear in others the way Khurt's did, but if anything, Khenzi's mind might prove to be even scarier, if given the right push. This invasion would provide Khurt the answers he needed.

Khenzi looked up at him and smiled. "Thank you, father. I will kill ten men for you in this invasion. No, twenty!"

Khurt chuckled so hard that he stopped painting his son's hand. "Boy, I am not bringing you because I need you to kill people. I am bringing you so that you can learn strategy and patience." He tapped on the side of his head. "Khenzi, if you put your mind to it, you might very well one day be a better general than I could ever be."

"Really, father? Do you really mean that?"

Khurt got up to start on Khenzi's other arm. "Of course I do. I pay attention to the things you do. The way your mind works, if you would only be productive with it, one day you could easily be more respected than any other general in our nation."

Khenzi nodded slowly and deeply, as if he was understanding who he was for the first time in his life. "I won't let you down, father. I promise."

"I know."

"And I'll do everything I can in this war to make sure you don't die."

Khurt stifled a laugh, realizing his son might be serious. "Thank you, Khenzi. With you coming along, I have no doubts that I shall return to Vitheligia very much alive."

Khenzi nodded excitedly once more. "But father, why black and not red?"

"Have we not had this conversation before? Surely you have seen me paint my skin patches black several times?"

"I have seen it, but I only started to wonder why in the past few months. Red would make us look much scarier because it would look like blood."

"It surely would. But the honor of wearing blood should belong to the man who kills his enemies and endures wounds in battle. There is no room in war for those who would only pretend to bleed. There is a reason for the black as well. Black represents the mourning for those whom we are about to lose. That is why Greatmother Ashota, bless her soul, outlined her patches in black. That is why we outline our own in black."

"I understand now."

Khurt stopped for a moment and looked at Khenzi's eyes. "I appreciate that you ask so many questions, you know." He paused for a moment. "I know that it can be…intimidating to talk to me at times. But beyond glory and pride, the one thing I want most in this life is for you to be a greater man than me. And the only way you will learn anything is by asking questions."

Khenzi looked Khurt right back in the eyes. He had his mother's light grey eyes. Khenzi simply stared for a moment and Khurt couldn't tell if Khenzi was afraid to ask the question or if Khenzi didn't know what he wanted to ask. Finally, Khenzi blurted out, "I do not understand why we go to war. Have we ever even met these…enemies, father?"

Khurt nodded tightly. He hadn't expected to be asked this question, much less by his son. He would have to be careful with his answer. He took a deep breath. "Tell me the story of the Harbingers. The Five, not The Three. Tell me of the downfall of The Five."

Khenzi responded without hesitation. "Gideon sacrificed himself first. After that, the other four lived peacefully and then Jahmash and Darian could not get along. Darian let Lionel and Abram fight Jahmash for him while he ran away, and Jahmash killed Lionel and Abram. Jahmash finally hunted down Darian and the two of them fought to the death."

"Good. Never forget that story. Recite it every day if you must. Our people descend from the children of Abram, who died for his friend Darian. We defend Abram's honor and his memory at all costs. That is the reason we go to war. That is the reason we leave tonight. My son, there have long been rumors of another continent, and only recently did we find out exactly where it is. You must not share that with anyone who is staying behind. Not even your sister. Understood?"

"Yes, father."

"Our destination is several weeks away. The continent calls itself Ashur. It is apparently a remnant from the time of The Five. It is the central point from where Darian drowned the world and we all believed that part of the world had been drowned as well. Now it turns out that civilization has thrived there even after the downfall of The Five. And it is apparently full of violent devotees of Darian. If they follow Darian, then they spit on Abram's death. That is why we go to war, Khenzi. That is why they are our enemies. That is why they all must die."

ACKNOWLEDGEMENTS

I would like to thank my parents and brother for their patience with me. It took a while for me to "find" myself, and they suffered through the process without disowning me. The one constant was that I was always creative, and that can be attributed to the first time I saw the comic book rack in Pathmark, when I was in sixth grade. Without my mother agreeing to buy that issue of *The Amazing Spider-Man*, this book wouldn't exist.

While so much of myself has been put into writing this book, so much time has been put into it because of my wife, Jen. Through too many late nights and countless hours spent writing and hanging out in my fictional world instead of with her, I was able to complete this book without a single complaint from her. It is a writer's dream to be married to her.

I would also like to thank Tam, Mike, Vishal, Dae, and Costa, from whom a number of the main characters are inspired. They have been there for me every step of the way and have always recognized the potential in me. Most importantly, they have always been honest with me, which has helped me to grow as a writer throughout the years.

If not for Dr. Susanna Rich, who knows how much longer it would have taken me to put that first scene into writing. After being her creative writing student, I asked to audit her class so I could model my own class after hers. She insisted that I actively take part instead. Because of her request, my story was first put to paper. I am forever grateful.

When I began writing, I thought this was a process I'd go through alone. I had the pleasure of knowing and working with fellow author, K.W. Penndorf, who gave me the confidence to see this endeavor through, who introduced me to an editor, and who still makes it a point to check on me and my progress.

I need to especially thank Karen Miller and Open Door Publications, for having so much patience with me, for honing my storytelling skills, and for giving me a chance. You have truly opened up a new path for me.

Two of my biggest fans through this process have been Amanda Riemenschneider and John Burkhart. It was surreal to have you both read my story and text me through the process with your reactions, as well as share your thoughts and theories. I am truly in your debt.

And lastly, this book and my sanity are not possible without Hannah, who showed me how strong a person I really am. Because of you, Hannah, I know that I can overcome any hardship or obstacle, and I know that I have it in me to achieve anything. I love you so much.

ABOUT THE AUTHOR

Khalid Uddin credits his creative beginnings to comic books, specifically *The Amazing Spider-Man* and *X-Men*. Throughout middle school and high school, his predominant hobby was drawing his favorite characters, original characters, and just about everything that was put in front of him. Once his college roommate introduced Khalid to Robert Jordan's *The Wheel of Time* book series, his imagination evolved and he saw the beginnings of his own fantasy world coming to life.

When his head is not stuck developing his fictional world, Khalid spends his free time with his wife, Jen, and adorable daughters, Emme and Ava, who bring boundless sunshine and laughter to his life. Except for when they're crying, because then laughing makes them angrier.

Khalid makes a living with literature as a high school English teacher in New Jersey. He regularly posts updates and news about his novel and the writing process on his website, www.khaliduddin.com. Feel free to connect with him there and leave your comments and feedback.

Made in the USA
Middletown, DE
15 May 2022

65643491R00246